The Editor

SHARON O'BRIEN is James Hope Caldwell Professor of American Cultures at Dickinson College. She is the author of *Willa Cather: The Emerging Voice, Willa Cather,* and *The Family Silver: A Memoir of Depression and Inheritance.* She is the editor of the Norton Critical Edition of *O Pioneers!* and of the Library of America *Willa Cather* (Volumes I–III) and *New Essays on* My Ántonia.

NORTON CRITICAL EDITIONS
MODERNIST & CONTEMPORARY ERAS

For a complete list of Norton Critical Editions, visit
wwnorton.com/nortoncriticals

A NORTON CRITICAL EDITION

Willa Cather

MY ÁNTONIA

AUTHORITATIVE TEXT

CONTEXTS AND BACKGROUNDS

CRITICISM

Edited by

SHARON O'BRIEN

DICKINSON COLLEGE

W · W · NORTON & COMPANY · *New York* · *London*

W. W. Norton & Company has been independent since its founding in 1923, when William Warder Norton and Mary D. Herter Norton first published lectures delivered at the People's Institute, the adult education division of New York City's Cooper Union. The firm soon expanded its program beyond the Institute, publishing books by celebrated academics from America and abroad. By midcentury, the two major pillars of Norton's publishing program—trade books and college texts—were firmly established. In the 1950s, the Norton family transferred control of the company to its employees, and today—with a staff of more than four hundred and a comparable number of trade, college, and professional titles published each year—W. W. Norton & Company stands as the largest and oldest publishing house owned wholly by its employees.

The text of this book is composed in Fairfield Medium
with the display set in Bernhard Modern.
Production manager: Vanessa Nuttry

Library of Congress Cataloging-in-Publication Data

Cather, Willa, 1873–1947.
   My Ántonia : Willa Cather ; authoritative text, contexts and backgrounds,
criticism, edited by Sharon O'Brien, Dickinson College.—First edition.
        pages cm—(A Norton critical edition)
   Includes bibliographical references.

   ISBN 978-0-393-96790-6 (pbk.)

   1. Cather, Willa, 1873–1947. My Ántonia. 2. Czechs—Nebraska—Fiction.
3. Americanization—Fiction. 4. Immigrants in literature. 5. Nebraska—
In literature. 6. Cather, Willa, 1873–1947. 7. Novelists, American—20th
century—Biography. I. O'Brien, Sharon, editor. II. Title.
   PS3505.A87M8 2015b
   813'.52—dc23

                                                                    2015010170

W. W. Norton & Company, Inc., 500 Fifth Avenue, New York, NY 10110-0017
wwnorton.com

W. W. Norton & Company Ltd., Castle House, 75/76 Wells Street, London
W1T 3QT

3   4   5   6   7   8   9   0

Contents

Criticism   329

Introduction

"Life began for me," Willa Cather once said, "when I ceased to admire and began to remember."[1] Her artistic power was also born when she moved from admiration to memory—but this was a long process. Cather began writing fiction as an undergraduate at the University of Nebraska in the early 1890s; in her first novel, *Alexander's Bridge* (1912), she was still writing as an admirer of the great writers who preceded her. Honoring in particular the fiction of Henry James, whom she once referred to as the "mighty master of language,"[2] Cather set her novel in the Jamesian drawing rooms of London and Boston. In *O Pioneers!* (1913) Cather began her literary breakthrough, returning to the Nebraska landscape and inventing a female character new to American fiction: a strong, creative woman who—unlike the heroines of Hawthorne and James—is able to exercise her power without punishment. Cather drew again on her Nebraska roots in *The Song of the Lark* (1915), her bildungsroman of a woman artist's emergence from a Western childhood very similar to her own.

It was in *My Ántonia* (1918), however, that Cather most fully transformed memory into art and created her most autobiographical novel. Many friends from her Red Cloud childhood inspired characters in her novel—most notably the Bohemian "hired girl," Annie Pavelka, who was the source for Ántonia Shimerda. The story of narrator Jim Burden's childhood uprooting from Virginia and transplanting to Nebraska was also Cather's own. Born in the small farming community of Back Creek, Virginia in 1873, Cather moved to Red Cloud in 1883 when her parents decided to join family members in Nebraska. She attended the University of Nebraska in Lincoln, graduating in 1895. She then began an eastward journey, working as a journalist and a teacher in Pittsburgh and moving to New York in 1906 to take up a staff position at *McClure's Magazine*, eventually becoming managing editor before plunging full-time into writing in 1912. Finding herself in a literary world dominated by East Coast values, Cather at first saw no way to link her regional past with her hopes for an

1. Elizabeth Shepley Sergeant, *Willa Cather: A Memoir* (Lincoln: U of Nebraska P, 1963), p. 107.
2. Cather, "Miss Jewett" in *Not Under Forty* (New York: Alfred A. Knopf), p. 91.

artistic future. During the early 1900s, she said later, Nebraska was considered "déclassé" as a literary background by snobbish Eastern critics. No one who was anyone "cared a damn" about Nebraska, no matter who wrote about it.

Willa Cather was shaped by nineteenth-century assumptions about gender as well as region. Confronted by an ideology of gender that linked femininity with domesticity, Cather for many years associated artistic greatness with masculinity. Central to Cather's evolution as woman and writer, and to her reconciliation of the seeming contradiction between gender and art, was the respected Maine writer Sarah Orne Jewett, whom Cather met in 1908. The two women formed a close friendship, with Jewett as Cather's literary mentor. The friendship she established with Jewett became a turning point in her life as an artist; the older woman believed in her and encouraged her talent and showed that a woman writer could create consummate art. Jewett urged Cather to return to her Nebraska roots for subject matter. Cather's dedication of *O Pioneers!* to Jewett connects her mentor's influence to her own literary emergence. Like *O Pioneers!*, *My Ántonia* reflects both Jewett's advice and her example. In this novel Cather returns to her own country for inspiration where she, like Jewett, finds creative power in the folk art of storytelling.

When Cather described her childhood uprooting from Virginia and transplanting to Nebraska, she spoke of being "thrown out" into a country "as bare as a piece of sheet-iron." She experienced an "erasure of personality" during her first months in Nebraska, almost dying, she later said, from homesickness.[3] In *My Ántonia*, Cather gives this wrenching experience of uprooting to her narrator Jim Burden, who shares her initial impression of Nebraska's bleak immensity:

> There seemed to be nothing to see; no fences, no creeks or trees, no hills or fields. If there was a road I could not make it out in the faint starlight. There was nothing but land: not a country at all, but the material out of which countries are made. No, there was nothing but land. . . .[4]

Eventually Cather came to love her new home. The wide expanse of prairie gave her a sense of freedom rather than annihilation, and her exhilaration with the West's open spaces lasted a lifetime. "When I strike the great open plains, I'm home," she would say. "That love of great spaces, of rolling open country like the sea—it's the grand passion of my life."[5]

3. L. Brent Bohlke, ed., *Willa Cather in Person: Interviews, Speeches, and Letters* (Lincoln: U of Nebraska P, 1986), p. 10.
4. Cather, *My Ántonia*, p. 12.
5. *Lincoln State Journal*, November 2, 1921, p. 7.

Helping Cather to feel at home on the prairies were the immigrant farmers who had come to the Midwest to start over; like the young Cather, they were surviving the trauma of uprooting and resettlement. Scandinavians, Russians, French, Germans, and Bohemians farmed alongside native-born Americans. Cather particularly loved to spend time with the immigrant pioneer women, who told her stories about their European homelands, just as Ántonia tells Jim stories about Bohemia.

Even after the Cather family moved into the small prairie town of Red Cloud in 1884, Cather kept up these attachments. She also found herself drawn to the daughters of these immigrant mothers, the "hired girls" like Annie Sadilek (later Annie Pavelka), who became the model for Ántonia Shimerda. In Red Cloud, Cather formed other new friendships with native-born Americans, in particular the daughters of the Miner family, Carrie and Irene—to whom she would dedicate *My Ántonia*. In the novel Carrie is transformed into Frances Harling, and Mrs. Miner, for whom Annie Sadilek worked, becomes Mrs. Harling. Cather also drew on her grandparents William and Caroline Cather for the portrait of Jim Burden's grandparents.

Transforming her own experiences into Jim Burden's narrative, reworking Nebraska friends and acquaintances into the fictional weave: in writing *My Ántonia*, Cather drew profoundly on her childhood memories—which may be the reason why, of all her fiction, *My Ántonia* was the novel about which she cared most deeply.

Yet *My Ántonia* is neither a childhood memoir nor a "young-adult" book (despite its popularity on high-school reading lists): instead, it is a midlife novel about childhood. Like Jim Burden, Cather needed emotional, aesthetic, and chronological distance from her Nebraska past in order to write about it. Cather's creative process was based on loss. To write, she needed to feel the desire to possess and re-create what was missing or absent. The creative process for her was joyous in that she could, in memory and imagination, bring to life what was gone, but it was also imbued with sadness. We can see this doubleness in Jim Burden's first-person narrative. During the act of writing—for we are asked to believe that he has written the text we read—the past comes alive for him. Phrases like "I can see them now" or "they are with me still" recur throughout the novel. "They were so much alive in me," Jim says of the Black Hawk friends he brings with him in memory to Lincoln, "that I scarcely stopped to wonder whether they were alive anywhere else, or how" (262). And yet there is a melancholy tone to *My Ántonia*, reflected in the epigraph from Virgil—"*Optima dies . . . prima fugit*," the best days are the first to flee.

Willa Cather was well aware of the reality of loss during the writing of *My Ántonia*. In 1916 Isabelle McClung, her closest friend,

creative inspiration, and romantic love of her life, announced that she
was going to marry the violinist Jan Hambourg. This was a terrible
blow to Cather. She had lived with Isabelle during her Pittsburgh
years, and after her move to New York had returned to Pittsburgh for
long visits. Isabelle had known how to nurture Cather's creativity, and
Cather wrote most of O Pioneers! and The Song of the Lark in the
McClung household. To lose Isabelle was like a divorce, or a death.
When she spoke to her friend Elizabeth Sergeant about the marriage,
her eyes were "vacant" and her face "bleak." "All her natural exuberance had been drained away," Sergeant remembers.[6]

But Cather was resilient in both her life and her art. In the summer
of 1916 she traveled west and spent several months in Red Cloud,
renewing attachments with family and friends, including Annie
Pavelka. When Cather returned to New York, My Ántonia was ready
to emerge. She spent several months writing happily in the city before
finding a summer retreat to replace Pittsburgh—the Shattuck Inn in
Jaffrey, New Hampshire. There she pitched a tent in a friend's meadow.
This became the morning retreat where she wrote My Ántonia—an
"ideal arrangement," observes her partner Edith Lewis:

> The tent was about a half a mile from the Inn, by an unused
> wood road, and across a pasture or two. Willa Cather loved this
> solitary half-mile walk through the woods, and found it the best
> possible prelude to a morning of work. She wrote for two or three
> hours every day, surrounded by complete silence and peace.[7]

We can see Cather's recent as well as remote experiences of loss
and change threading their way through My Ántonia—not just in
Jim's yearning for a golden past and Ántonia's transformation from a
"lovely girl" into a "battered woman" (170), but also in violent and disturbing episodes that may reflect Cather's anger at loss: the suicide of
Mr. Shimerda, Ántonia's seduction and betrayal, the brutal story of
Pavel and Peter, the villainy of Wick Cutter.

But Cather's own renewal of creative energy is also evident in the
novel. In My Ántonia, she affirms the power of people to weave the
sadness of loss—of homelands, of loved friends and family, of childhood, of the past—into the web of ongoing life by telling stories. Foremost is Cather's own story, the novel we read, but there is also Jim's
story, the manuscript we read after the Introduction; and within Jim's
story are many other stories, such as the Bohemian folk tales Ántonia tells, the story of Pavel and Peter (which she translates for him),
the story of Ántonia's seduction as told by the Widow Steavens, the
stories Ántonia and her children tell Jim while they look at old

---

6. Sergeant, p. 140.
7. Edith Lewis, Willa Cather Living: A Personal Record (New York: Knopf, 1953), p. 104.

photographs, and the stories of Jim that Ántonia has been telling her children during his twenty-year absence.

Just as the novel demonstrates the connection between loss and creativity, so it shows us the link between the oral and the written, the folk narrative and the novel. In *My Ántonia*, Cather honors the oral tradition of storytelling that nourished both the child and the writer. But oral narrative is more vulnerable to time and change than written narrative; after a while, stories may die out if there are no inheritors to keep telling them. And written narratives can also disappear if they do not find an audience through the act of publication.

Willa Cather was able to successfully transform the oral narrative into written form, thus giving one kind of permanence to the stories she heard, inherited, and created. By 1918, the year the novel was published, she was a well-known writer with literary authority. She was thus able to negotiate the transformation of her written manuscript into a published novel that embodied her own creative vision, guiding *My Ántonia* from the writer's desk into the world of contracts, book design, and advertising. The novel's fascinating publishing history reveals how Cather struggled to unite the role of writer with that of author and to integrate the private space of composition with the public space of commerce.

Publishing History

Willa Cather's first publisher was the Boston-based firm of Houghton Mifflin, inheritors of Ticknor and Fields, the nineteenth-century Boston publishers who brought Hawthorne, Emerson, Longfellow, and Jewett to the American reading public. So when Cather placed her first novel, *Alexander's Bridge* (1911), with the firm, she was joining distinguished company. During her Houghton Mifflin years, Cather at first played the deferential daughter to her editor Ferris Greenslet, welcoming his editorial suggestions and praising his advice. But as she began to accrue positive reviews for *O Pioneers!* (1913) and *The Song of the Lark* (1915), she became more assertive. When she began writing *My Ántonia* in 1916, Cather was becoming unhappy with Houghton Mifflin, feeling that the publisher did not pay sufficient attention to the aesthetic appeal of her books.

Cather was always concerned with her books' physical appearance, and her desire to influence the aesthetic shape of the book as a whole reached its height with *My Ántonia*. In addition to stating her preferences for the cover (darker blue than *The Song of the Lark*) and book jacket (bright yellow with heavy black lettering), Cather independently commissioned a series of line drawings from the Bohemian American artist W. T. Benda. Her correspondence with Greenslet and her production manager Roger Scaife reveals how strongly Cather wanted to shape her novel visually as well as verbally. She told the art department to print the illustrations low on the page, so the reader could sense the presence of air and space overhead. She also wanted the drawings on the right-hand pages, juxtaposed to the part of the text they illustrated, and printed in the same black ink. Even though Houghton Mifflin eventually followed her instructions (although paying for only eight illustrations, not the twelve she wanted), Cather felt her publisher never understood how aesthetically central the Benda illustrations were to her novel's design. After leaving Houghton Mifflin for Alfred Knopf, who became her permanent publisher, Cather had to fight to keep the Benda illustrations in later editions. In 1937, Ferris Greenslet wanted to replace Benda's sketches with fancier color plates by Grant Wood, finally backing down after Cather objected strenuously.[8]

Willa Cather's correspondence with Ferris Greenslet reveals that she had a complex, contradictory view of *My Ántonia* as a literary commodity. On one hand, Cather wanted to be a financially success- ful and well-reviewed novelist, and her letters to Greenslet feature many complaints about the publisher's failure to promote and dis- tribute her book adequately. On the other, she did not want *My Ánto- nia* to be distributed *too* widely and in forms she could not control. Even though she could have earned more money, after she left Houghton Mifflin Cather fought to keep the publisher (who had the copyright) from turning *My Ántonia* into a paperback edition, an annotated student edition, a movie, and a radio play—all forms of distortion that Cather though would cheapen and violate the integ- rity of her novel. In a 1946 letter Cather chided her editor for Hough- ton Mifflin's continuing desire to profit from her novel in ways that would violate its (and her) integrity:

> Really, my dear F.G. [Ferris Greenslet], you've never treated "Antonia" very gallantly. You are always trying to do her in and make her cheap. (That's exaggeration, of course, but I'm really very much annoyed.) And you know how you've suggested cheap editions, film possibilities, etc. Antonia has done well enough by her publishers <u>as she is</u>, not in the cut rate drugstores. . . . She made her way by being what she is, not by being the compromise her publishers have several times tried to make her. Even a cut in price would be a compromise in the case of that particular book, I think.[9]

Cather was not averse to gaining fame and making money: she just wanted to do so on her own terms, terms that defined herself as an

---

8. See Cather to Greenslet, January 29, 1937, p. 244. Houghton Mifflin Collection, Hough- ton Library, Harvard U.
9. Cather to Greenslet, n.d. (1946), p. 244. Houghton Mifflin Collection, Houghton Library, Harvard U.

artist and her novels as original, seamless expressions of an individual imagination. She was also quite willing to use the language of economics to bolster her arguments, as when she told Greenslet that it made no financial sense to sell *Ántonia* to a book club—that might boost sales temporarily, but diminish them in the long run. Better to keep the novel in hardback as a slow, steady, dignified seller. Author and publisher possessed a good property, Cather told Greenslet—they should keep *Ántonia* to themselves.

In one sense, Cather's efforts to limit access to *My Ántonia* (as by refusing a paperback edition) were a form of elitism: hardback editions could be purchased only by people of a certain class and income. From her perspective, she was trying both to prevent her novel's "cheapening"—paperbacks were then connected with best-selling, formulaic pulp fiction—and to preserve an author/reader bond based on sympathy rather than coercion. She did not want her work taught in high schools, for example, because she did not want students to grow up hating her. She thus resisted Houghton Mifflin's desire for an educational edition. Reading, Cather believed, should be like striking up a friendship—hence her suspicion of book clubs, which turned books into preselected, assigned friends. She did agree to an armed services paperback edition of *My Ántonia* in 1943—given the cause, she could hardly refuse.

Cather won nearly all her battles with her first publisher over *My Ántonia*. Years after the deaths of both Cather and Greenslet, Houghton Mifflin continued to agree to keep *Ántonia* out of the movies because of what a 1970 memo termed a "gentleman's agreement" with Willa Cather. So—as rebellious as she was in challenging gender roles in her life and art—Cather demanded that her publishers treat her novel as a lady. Now, of course, the copyright on *My Ántonia* has expired, along with Houghton Mifflin's control, and the novel has appeared in several paperback editions (some without the Benda illustrations) as well as a play and a made-for-TV movie.

Cather did not often make significant changes between the first and second editions of a novel, but *My Ántonia* is an exception. The text of the 1918 edition was printed unchanged until 1926, when Houghton Mifflin published a revised version from the first-edition plates. This edition included a few minor textual changes, but the major change was Cather's extensive revising and cutting of the Introduction, in which an unnamed narrator describes her train journey with Jim Burden and their reminiscences about Ántonia. Greenslet, who had never liked the Introduction, recommended that Cather eliminate it in the 1926 edition.[1] Cather had never been satisfied with

---

1. Greenslet to Cather, April 9, 1926, p. 243. Houghton Mifflin Collection, Houghton Library, Harvard U.

the Introduction herself (she termed it a "preface"). Writing to Greenslet in Febuary 1926, she told him that she did not want to eliminate the Introduction but to revise and condense it.

> Now, as to the preface. The preface is not very good; I had a kind of complex about it. I wrote and rewrote it, and it was the only thing about the story that was laborious. But I still think that a preface is necessary, even if it is not good in itself. Let me take a trial at shortening the preface. The later part of the book, I am sure, would be vague if the reader did not know something about the rather unsuccessful personal life of the narrator.[2]

Cather was evidently thinking about Jim's return to visit Ántonia after a twenty-year absence in "Cuzak's Boys," the last book of the novel, in which he gives a romanticized portrait of Ántonia as a fertile Earth Mother and reveals his desire to become almost a member of her family, returning often to share adventures with her sons. Cather evidently felt that the reader needed to know that Jim was childless and in an unhappy marriage to understand the powerful attraction that Ántonia and her family had for him.

The original 1918 version of the Introduction gives us more information about Jim Burden's wife, the narrator's dislike for Mrs. Burden's superficial enthusiasms, and Jim's unhappy marriage. We also learn much more about Jim's role as an entrepreneurial capitalist who has helped to develop the West, raising money "for new enterprises in Wyoming or Montana" and helping young men do "remarkable things with mines and timber and oil." The 1918 Introduction hints that Jim's passionate energies, unsatisfied in a childless marriage to a flashy, cause-driven woman, might have been channeled into a search for hidden riches in the land: he likes to go "hunting for lost parks or exploring new canyons" that might yield him new treasures.

The 1918 Introduction thus makes Jim a troubling narrator: to what extent might his urge to tell Ántonia's story betray a need to control feminine wealth and power, the same need he expresses when, in finding a sexualized landscape of "lost parks" and "new canyons," he turns these natural riches into capital? We see the connection between possession and storytelling in both versions when Jim changes the title of his story from "Ántonia" to "My Ántonia," the "My" suggesting both subjectivity and ownership, but this link is stronger in the 1918 edition.

In her revision of the Introduction for the 1926 edition, Cather also dramatically changes the relationship between the unnamed woman writer who narrates the Introduction and Jim Burden, her

---

2. Cather to Greenslet, February 16, 1926, p. 242. Houghton Mifflin Collection, Houghton Library, Harvard U.

old friend who writes the novel. In the 1926 edition, Cather gives us a genderless narrator who may or may not be a writer—all we know is that this person grew up in a small town in Nebraska, was friendly with Jim Burden, meets him on a train, shares his memories of Ántonia, and agrees to read his manuscript. Jim is the only author of *My Ántonia* in the 1926 edition.

In the 1918 version, by contrast, the narrator is a woman writer (assumed by most critics to be a version of the author, although I prefer the more abstract concept "narrator") who suggests that she and Jim *both* write down their memories of Ántonia. Thus the creative spark for the story comes from her. But Jim finishes a manuscript, while the narrator confesses that hers "had not gone beyond a few straggling notes." She then presents Jim's manuscript to the reader "substantially as he brought it to me." The word "substantially" (removed in the 1926 edition) changes our reading experience: the unnamed woman writer is also an editor, and we have no way of knowing what changes she may have made to Jim's manuscript. So the meaning of the 1918 *My Ántonia* is doubly indeterminate, because we have both an unreliable narrator/writer (Jim) and an unreliable editor/writer (the narrator of the Introduction).

When she revised the 1918 Introduction, Cather clearly gave over to Jim the novel's creative inspiration as well as its authorship. She may have decided that the double subjectivity of editor and writer was a needlessly complex narrative strategy and that her readers would find one unreliable narrator—Jim—enough to cope with. And by having Jim be already at work on Ántonia's story when he meets the narrator on the train, Cather gives him more of an inner need for creative expression.

Because Jim Burden shares so much of Cather's biography, many critics have assumed that he speaks for her. Such an assumption is problematic because it equates narrator and author. Jim is a character who has a story to tell, not a mask for the author, as Cather made clear in her letter to Ferris Greenslet. In both introductions, Cather underlines the subjectivity of his narrative by having Jim add the "My" to the title. Storytelling, as this addition suggests, is both possessive and subjective. In telling the story from his own angle of vision, Jim necessarily gives us "his" Ántonia. Cather's first readers were not disturbed by this, but in the last two decades literary critics concerned with the politics of representation have noted that we are never given Ántonia's story from her own perspective. Her stories, her conversation, even her memories are filtered through Jim Burden's imagination, memory, and desire.

Reception

When Willa Cather published *My Ántonia* in 1918, the time was ripe for her to be recognized as a major American novelist. Her first novel, *Alexander's Bridge*, had received polite but unenthusiastic reviews from critics, who noted her command of style along with her deference to Edith Wharton and Henry James. After Cather turned to her Nebraska past in *O Pioneers!* (1913) and *The Song of the Lark* (1915), she drew more favorable notices; reviewers saw emerging in her work an authentic American voice, freed from the formulaic structures of popular fiction.

Cather's literary emergence was aided by the fact that she was writing the kind of fiction influential reviewers wanted to see. During the 'teens, important critics such as H. L. Mencken and Randolph Bourne hoped for a revitalized and indigenous American literature. They wanted American writers who would challenge stifling middle-class pieties (as would Sinclair Lewis in *Babbitt*) and establish an American literary culture separate from that of England—and New England. After reading her first two novels, Mencken and Bourne had high hopes for Willa Cather; in *My Ántonia*, they found her promise fulfilled. Bourne praised Cather's breaking of "stiff moral molds" in the novel and congratulated her for leaving the ranks of "provincial" writers and entering the world of "modern literary art."[3] Delighted by the "extraordinary reality" and artistic command he found in the novel, Mencken became Cather's champion, giving *My Ántonia* two reviews in *Smart Set*, the influential cultural journal he edited. The novel was "not only the best done by Miss Cather herself, but also one of the best that any American has ever done, East or West, early or late."[4]

While not reaching the heights of Mencken's praise, other book reviewers found *My Ántonia* a remarkable novel for its realism—resulting from its shunning the usual fictional conventions and its dispensing with plot. The book "is a carefully detailed picture rather than a story," observed the *New York Times Book Review*;[5] the *New York Sun* concurred, noting that the novel had no "regulation plot" because Cather had surrendered "the usual methods of fiction in telling a story."[6] The result of Cather's originality was realism: the *Sun* thought that the novel read like "vivid autobiography." Praising *My Ántonia*'s "realness," the *Chicago Daily News* proclaimed that Cather "has given us three novels of the West that stand alone

3. Margaret Anne O'Conner, ed., *Willa Cather: The Contemporary Reviews* (Cambridge: Cambridge UP), p. 84.
4. Ibid., pp. 88–89.
5. Ibid., p. 79.
6. Ibid., p. 80.

in American literature" and were "above all, real."[7] Reviewers connected Cather's realism with her decision to tell, and tell accurately, the central American story of immigration and pioneer renewal.

Willa Cather's literary reputation, which began its ascent with her publication of *O Pioneers!* in 1913, was solidified by these glowing reviews of *My Ántonia.* Her next novel was the Pulitzer Prize–winning *One of Ours* (1922). In the following years, literary excellence kept pace with her literary production: *A Lost Lady* (1923), *The Professor's House* (1925), *My Mortal Enemy* (1926), *Death Comes for the Archbishop* (1928), *Shadows on the Rock* (1933), and *Sapphira and the Slave Girl* (1940), along with collections of short stories and essays. Considered one of American's foremost novelists during the 1920s, during the 1930s and 1940s Cather came under attack from left-wing critics such as Newton Arvin and Granville Hicks who found her work escapist and romantic, and her prominence began to fade. When Henry Seidel Canby described Cather's contribution to American literature in Robert Spiller's *Literary History of the United States,* he reflected this trend and seemed to find Cather's gender inconsistent with literary greatness. "Her art was not a big art," Canby concluded. "She is preservative, almost antiquarian, content with much space in little room—feminine in this, and in her passionate revelation of the values which conserve the life of the emotions."[8]

During the 1950s and 1960s, *My Ántonia* began to attract new critical voices—not reviewers or men of letters, but instead college and university professors who were creating the world of American literary scholarship by publishing articles in academic journals. The professional literary criticism of *My Ántonia,* which began during those decades, has been historically shaped by shifting cultural and academic schools of thought. When we read articles on *My Ántonia* in historical perspective, we see more than a range of different viewpoints: we see how the questions critics would ask and the interpretive strategies they employed changed over time. The scholars of the 1950s and 1960s drew on the critical discourse that dominated the academy during these years—the "New Criticism"—and as a result found Cather to be a conscious artist whose fiction reflected her aesthetic purposes.

Terence Martin's article "The Drama of Memory in *My Ántonia,*" published in the central journal of literary study, *Publications of the Modern Language Association,* reflects the principles of literary formalism that dominated the New Criticism: a focus on the literary

7. Ibid., pp. 89–90.
8. Canby, "Willa Cather," *Literary History of the United States,* vol. 2, ed. Robert Spiller et al. (New York: Macmillan, 1948), p. 1216.

text itself, with no exploration of historical or cultural contexts; a concentration on literary form and structure; and a concern with finding the unity of a work of art. "If structural coherence is to be found in *My Ántonia*," Martin writes (and finding this coherence will be his goal), "the character of Jim Burden seems necessarily to be involved."[9] Martin finds Cather's "principle of unity" in the novel by his analysis of what he terms a "drama of memory"—the retrospective ability of the adult narrator to give meaning to the figure of Ántonia. Through memory, Martin argues, Jim finds the value of his past and links it to the present. Thus, despite the episodic, plotless structure of the novel, in Martin's view Cather had attained the "structural coherence" valued by literary formalists.[1]

In "The Forgotten Reaping-Hook: Sex in *My Ántonia*," Blanche Gelfant uses the new critical techniques of close reading and analysis of narrative structure to challenge the formalist view that Cather's novel was unified.[2] She discovered a disturbing subtext: a discomfort with—even a fear of—sexuality, most evident in Jim Burden's fleeing from the sensuous Lena Lingard to the mythic safety of the maternal Ántonia. In developing this reading, Gelfant challenges earlier views of the novel, such as Martin's, which praised it as a "splendid celebration of American frontier life"; she argues that viewing Jim Burden as a reliable narrator, which preceding critics had done, was a "persistent misreading" (367). Viewing Burden as controlled by a "fear of sex" he cannot acknowledge, Gelfant finds a far more troubling and darker novel than preceding critics had (368). Although her reading techniques are based in formalism, in her willingness to destabilize the previous celebratory readings of the novel and deconstruct the narrator's sexual conflicts, she anticipates later feminist criticism of *My Ántonia* that would place gender and sexuality at the center of analysis. Jim Burden's fear of mature sexuality shaped his story, Gelfant contends, and the novel was marked by sexual disturbance, repression, and distortion. In her view, Cather had written neither an affirmative novel nor the unified one praised by formalist critics, but one "far more exciting—complex, subtle, aberrant" (367).

Beginning in the 1980s, some critics went beyond formalism by showing *My Ántonia*'s indebtedness to non-literary forms of art. In "The Benda Illustrations to *My Ántonia*: Cather's 'Silent' Supplement to Jim Burden's Narrative" (pp. 385–412 of this Norton Critical Edition), Jean Schwind shows how the Benda illustrations offer a counternarrative to Jim's voice, rescuing Ántonia from the mythic

9. Martin, *The Drama of Memory in "My Ántonia,"* PMLA 84.1 (1969), pp. 304–11.
1. "The elements of the novel cohere in Jim Burden's drama of memory" (311).
2. *American Literature* 43.1 (1971): 60–82. Reprinted on pp. 367–85 of this Norton Critical Edition.

significance he seeks to impose upon her. The first scholar to draw on Cather's correspondence with her editors at Houghton Mifflin, Schwind shows how central the Benda illustrations were to Cather's conception of the book. She had commissioned from the Bohemian artist W. T. Benda a series of eight illustrations that would appear to be old woodcuts, modestly juxtaposed to the written text they illuminated. Cather struggled with her publisher over the illustrations, insisting that they be kept in all future editions of the novel and resisting Houghton Mifflin's attempt in 1936 to reissue *My Ántonia* with color illustrations by Grant Wood. In her article, Schwind offers close readings of the pictorial art to show how the illustrations undercut Jim Burden's romanticized vision of Ántonia and the West, revealing the harsher realities of the immigrant farming experience that Burden glosses over in his narrative.

In his article "Willa Cather and 'The Storyteller': Hostility to the Novel in *My Ántonia*" (1994; pp. 412–38), Richard Millington enlarges our reading of *My Ántonia* by showing its indebtedness to the oral tradition. Placing the novel in conversation with Walter Benjamin's "The Storyteller," he argues not only that *My Ántonia* endorses the world of oral narrative but also that it challenges the middle-class values associated with the rise of the novel. Following Benjamin, Millington views the story as oral expression linking the storyteller with listeners; as communal rather than private; and as open-ended, waiting for completion by the listener rather than containing its own ending. By contrast, the novel—associated with the rise of the middle class and private readership—endorses narrative structures that convey and support dominant social structures and expectations. Millington sees *My Ántonia* as pitting the story against the novel and its middle-class aspirations. Consequently he reads the ending, when Jim returns to Ántonia and her oral storytelling culture, as the triumph of what he calls the counter-novel—the story with its accompanying values of community and memory.

The critical movement that had the most impact on Cather scholarship from the 1970s to the 1990s was feminist criticism. Scholars began paying attention to issues of gender and sexuality in *My Ántonia*, raising important questions about the novel's meanings and structure. Was Jim Burden necessary as a male narrator because Cather, as a lesbian writer, was prevented by her culture from having a female narrator express an enduring preoccupation with another woman? Was Jim a mask for a lesbian consciousness? Or did he signify a patriarchal gaze, imposing a reductive vision on Ántonia by ultimately viewing her as a fertile Earth Mother? Did the novel endorse a feminist vision in its portrayal of a strong woman, or did it reinforce conventional gender stereotypes? Did the novel rewrite traditional male narratives about women, or did it challenge them?

While not agreeing on the answers to these questions, feminist critics agreed on their centrality to an understanding of Cather's achievement in *My Ántonia*. My 1987 biography *Willa Cather: The Emerging
Voice* played a role in the feminist conversation because it viewed
Cather as a lesbian writer who managed to reconcile the supposedly
contradictory categories of "woman" and "artist."[3]

The chapter included here from Susan Rosowski's *Birthing a
Nation: Gender, Creativity, and the West in American Literature* (1999;
pp. 438–51)—"Pro/Creativity and a Kinship Aesthetic"—argues
the case for Cather as a feminist writer rewriting male-authored narratives about the West as a virgin landscape to be conquered, offering her readers instead a female landscape of authority and creativity.[4]
In transforming Annie Sadelik into Ántonia Shimerda, Cather was
"revising the idea of creativity that she had inherited" (438)—that
artistic creation was masculine, procreation feminine. By portraying Ántonia as an Earth Mother who gave birth to stories as well as
to children, Cather was, Rosowski contends, narrating a "birth myth
for the New World" (441) in her novel. Countering the conventional
division of male author and female subject, Cather was placing
Ántonia "at the center of storytelling" (441) in a communal, rather
than an individualistic, economy.

Marilee Lindemann disputes Rosowski's view that the novel celebrates feminine power in "'It Ain't My Prairie': Gender, Power, and
Narrative in *My Ántonia*."[5] Also reading as a feminist critic, she finds
that the novel shows Cather's concern that female power and authorship cannot combat effectively the masculine power of representation. When Jim adds the "My" to the title "Ántonia," he is claiming
Ántonia both rhetorically and ideologically. While Jim's romantic
views are shown as limited, Lindemann argues that his power over
language and representation is not strongly contested by any women's
voices in the text. Jim controls the process of meaning-making in
the case of Ántonia; only Lena Lingard, with her sleepy sexuality,
has the power to undermine Jim's view of the world, and she is erased
from the text after their sensual interlude in Lincoln. Jim thus dis-
penses with "the most serious challenge to his authority" (450). Lindemann argues that Cather's revision of the introduction for the 1926
edition of *My Ántonia* shows her desire to underline the masculine
power of representation. In the 1918 introduction, the unnamed narrator is a writer who gives us Jim's narrative "substantially" as he gave
it to her, implying room for some editorial correction or alteration.

---

3. Sharon O'Brien, *Willa Cather: The Emerging Voice* (New York: Oxford UP, 1987).
4. Susan J. Rosowski, *Birthing a Nation: Gender, Creativity, and the West in American Literature* (Lincoln: U of Nebraska P, 1999).
5. Marilee Lindemann, "'It Ain't My Prairie': Gender, Power, and Narrative in *My Ántonia*,"
   in Sharon O'Brien, ed., *New Essays on* My Ántonia (Cambridge: Cambridge UP, 1999).

By contrast, in the 1926 edition the narrator's role as writer and editor is removed, and we are introduced to the novel as created solely by Jim. This alteration, Lindemann suggests, is consistent with the text that follows in revealing Cather's "deep skepticism about women's ability to compete in the contest to figure themselves in a culturally powerful way" (489). The novel's feminism, in Lindemann's view, rest not in portrayals of strong pioneer women or storytelling earth mothers but in its bleak, unflinching recognition of women's lack of cultural and narrative authority.

Other critics of the novel—who might be termed "new historicist" in their location of the novel in historical and cultural contexts—agree that gender is an important variable, but have chosen to focus their analyses on issues of ethnicity and race. When the focus is on ethnicity and the debate over Americanization in the early twentieth century, the novel appears as liberatory and progressive; when the focus is on race, the novel becomes less emancipatory and more revealing of conservative, indeed racist, cultural attitudes.

In "*My Ántonia* and the Americanisation Debate" (1996), Guy Reynolds places the novel in the context of the early twentieth-century debates over immigration, assimilation, and Americanization.[6] Published in 1918, the novel would be followed, in 1924, by the Immigration Act, which limited the numbers of immigrants from Southern and Eastern Europe. The Act reflected the growth of anti-immigrant sentiment in response to the increased numbers from these regions. In contrast to this rise of nativism, in *My Ántonia* Cather was suggesting the possibility of what Reynolds terms "kaleidoscopic cultural variety" (73). To be sure, Cather did suggest in her novel a "circumscribed pluralism," since she does not tell the stories of the new immigrants who were causing such public dismay, but nevertheless she did write about "a greater variety of European peoples" than did her contemporaries. Reynolds places the novel in the context of the debate over assimilation, distinguishing between "hard-line" Americanizationists who stressed the necessity of learning English and adapting to dominant American values and "liberal" Americanizationists, such as Randolph Bourne, who argued that immigrants, while adapting to American culture, should preserve native cultural traditions. Reynolds argues that Cather joined with Bourne and other liberals in calling for a culturally pluralistic rather than a narrowly uniform America. *My Ántonia* is, he observes, a novel about "bilingual communities" (83) in which language and stories link the Old World and the New. The Cuzak family that Jim discovers at the end of the novel is Cather's vision of a "capacious and fluid" definition of American: Ántonia has forgotten much of her English

6. Reynolds, *Willa Cather in Context: Progress, Race, Empire* (New York: St. Martin's, 1996).

but her children are bilingual, navigating easily between the memories of Bohemia and the cultures of America. The family continues old-world traditions: Ántonia makes *kolaches* (Bohemian pastries), and her son Leo plays Bohemian airs on the flute. Reynolds finds that Cather's footnote on the pronunciation of "Ántonia" and the use of the accent mark epitomizes the novel's respectful representation of the world and voice of the immigrant, just as the novel shows the importance of European cultural transmission and inheritance.

In "Pastoralism and Its Discontents: Willa Cather and the Burden of Imperialism" (pp. 451–66) Mike Fischer finds a novel much more problematic in its representation of difference than Reynolds found.[7] Fischer points out that American and European settlement of Nebraska rested on the removal of Native Americans who were its original inhabitants. Because Cather ignores and erases Native history, he contends, in *My Ántonia* she is telling "a story of origin for whites only" (451). When Jim arrives in Nebraska, he sees what seems to be an empty prairie, devoid of human habitation: "not a country at all, but the material out of which countries are made." He does not see—and Cather seems not to see—the suppressed history of the Native presence in Nebraska, even though it was represented by the naming of Red Cloud and Black Hawk after defeated Sioux chiefs. But this suppressed history still leaves traces in the text that we can see if we look for them, and Fischer calls upon readers of *My Ántonia* to be attentive to the "real" history of the American West as a story of conquest rather than settlement, and to note where this history is repressed, silenced, or elided in *My Ántonia*.

In "Coming to America / Escaping to Europe" (pp. 467–79) Janice Stout, while acknowledging Cather's sympathetic portrayal of Nebraska's Scandinavians, Russians, and Bohemians, focuses on the racial and ethnic groups that are either excluded from the novel or given a position lower than that of native-born settlers like the Burdens.[8] Agreeing with Mike Fischer that it was a "major distortion" for Cather to ignore the history of Indian displacement from ancestral lands, she notes that the railroad—central in the novel as bringing the immigrant settlers to Nebraska—was the key factor in erasing the Native American presence (473). Cather echoes this erasure as her novel tells the story of Nebraska as solely a story of white (and immigrant) settlement. As Stout argues, Cather also excludes African Americans from her celebratory vision, evident in her demeaning portrayal of Blind d'Arnault, the black piano player represented through racial and racist tropes. In portraying the

7. *Mosaic* 23.1 (1990): 33–44.
8. Janis P. Stout, *Willa Cather: The Writer and Her World* (Charlottesville: UP of Virginia, 2000), pp. 151–62.

immigrant groups she does favor, Cather reveals a hierarchical vision that marks the immigrants as lower class. When Jim asserts to Ántonia that he'd "have liked to have [her] for a sweetheart, or a wife, or my mother or my sister—anything that a woman can be to a man," he is engaging in romantic self-deception (156); as a member of the native-born Anglo Saxon settlers, Jim is separated from Ántonia not just by ethnicity but also by class.

Looking at the span of literary criticism of *My Ántonia* ranging from the 1950s to the 2000s, we see a shift from a vision of the novel as a positive celebration of immigrant life to a vision of the novel as culturally problematic because Cather can achieve her celebration of the Bohemian Ántonia only by excluding or belittling racial Others. Far from reducing the novel's importance, this shift in critical attention shows how powerfully readings of *My Ántonia* connect to their social, historical, and institutional contexts. The novel's contradictions, distortions, and erasures make it an endlessly open text, always ready for new critical readings as our reading strategies change.

As we can see from the differing critical views, the novel's meaning can never be finally fixed. Jim seeks to limit the woman's and the novel's meaning when he affixes "*My*" to "*Ántonia*," but we, as readers, do justice to the novel only when we allow for multiple meanings both intended and unintended by its author. We must place both author and novel in historical and social context so that we can see not just the story *My Ántonia* affirms but also the stories that are repressed or displaced. This kind of reading gives us a less affirmative and more troubling novel and so leaves us, finally, with a more intriguing and provocative one.

Acknowledgments

I thank the archivists at the Archives and Special Collections of the University of Nebraska for helping me find original documents. Guy Reynolds and Melissa Homestead of the University of Nebraska English Department made my stay in Lincoln a pleasure. Dickinson College gave me financial support, and my colleagues and friends cheered me on and up. I owe a special note of thanks to Maggy Sears.

Note on the Text

My Ántonia was published by Houghton Mifflin in September 1918. The volume included eight illustrations by W. T. Benda; their conception, design, execution, and placement were closely overseen by Cather. The text of this edition was printed unchanged until 1926, when a revised version was published. The major changes were to the introduction, which Cather shortened by more than a third. This Norton Critical Edition incorporates the 1926 introduction into the 1918 text (the version that represents Cather's original conception of the work).

The Text of
MY ÁNTONIA

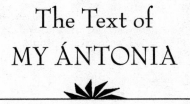

Optima dies . . . prima fugit[1]
VIRGIL

---

1. "The best days are the first to flee," from the Roman poet Virgil's *Georgics* (ca. 29 B.C.E.).

TO
CARRIE AND IRENE MINER
In memory of affections old and true

Contents

Introduction[†]

Last summer, in a season of intense heat, Jim Burden and I happened to be crossing Iowa on the same train. He and I are old friends, we grew up together in the same Nebraska town, and we had a great deal to say to each other. While the train flashed through never-ending miles of ripe wheat, by country towns and bright-flowered pastures and oak groves wilting in the sun, we sat in the observation car, where the woodwork was hot to the touch and red dust lay deep over everything. The dust and heat, the burning wind, reminded us of many things. We were talking about what it is like to spend one's childhood in little towns like these, buried in wheat and corn, under stimulating extremes of climate: burning summers when the world lies green and billowy beneath a brilliant sky, when one is fairly stifled in vegetation, in the colour and smell of strong weeds and heavy harvests; blustery winters with little snow, when the whole country is stripped bare and grey as sheet-iron. We agreed that no one who had not grown up in a little prairie town could know anything about it. It was a kind of freemasonry, we said.

Although Jim Burden and I both live in New York, I do not see much of him there. He is legal counsel for one of the great Western railways and is often away from his office for weeks together. That is one reason why we seldom meet. Another is that I do not like his wife. She is handsome, energetic, executive, but to me seems unimpressionable and temperamentally incapable of enthusiasm. Her husband's quiet tastes irritate her, I think, and she finds it worth while to play the patroness to a group of young poets and painters of advanced ideas and mediocre ability. She has her own fortune and lives her own life. For some reason, she wishes to remain Mrs. James Burden.

As for Jim, disappointments have not changed him. The romantic disposition which often made him seem very funny as a boy, has been one of the strongest elements of his success. He loves with a personal passion the great country through which his railway runs and branches. His faith in it and his knowledge of it have played an important part in its development.

During that burning day when we were crossing Iowa, our talk kept returning to a central figure, a Bohemian girl whom we had both known long ago. More than any other person we remembered, this girl seemed to mean to us the country, the conditions, the whole adventure of our childhood. I had lost sight of her altogether, but Jim had found her again after long years, and had renewed a friendship that meant a great deal to him. His mind was full of her that day. He made me see her again, feel her presence, revived all my old affection for her.

"From time to time I've been writing down what I remember about Ántonia," he told me. "On my long trips across the country, I amuse myself like that, in my stateroom."

When I told him that I would like to read his account of her, he said I should certainly see it—if it were ever finished.

Months afterward, Jim called at my apartment one stormy winter afternoon, carrying a legal portfolio. He brought it into the sitting-room with him, and said, as he stood warming his hands,

"Here is the thing about Ántonia. Do you still want to read it? I finished it last night. I didn't take time to arrange it; I simply wrote down pretty much all that her name recalls to me. I suppose it hasn't any form. It hasn't any title, either." He went into the next room, sat down at my desk and wrote across the face of the portfolio the word "Ántonia." He frowned at this a moment, then prefixed another word, making it "My Ántonia." That seemed to satisfy him.

Book I

The Shimerdas

I

I first heard of Ántonia[1] on what seemed to me an interminable journey across the great midland plain of North America. I was ten years old then; I had lost both my father and mother within a year, and my Virginia relatives were sending me out to my grandparents, who lived in Nebraska. I traveled in the care of a mountain boy, Jake Marpole, one of the "hands" on my father's old farm under the Blue Ridge, who was now going West to work for my grandfather. Jake's experience of the world was not much wider than mine. He had never been in a railway train until the morning when we set out together to try our fortunes in a new world.

We went all the way in day-coaches, becoming more sticky and grimy with each stage of the journey. Jake bought everything the newsboys offered him: candy, oranges, brass collar buttons, a watch-charm, and for me a "Life of Jesse James," which I remember as one of the most satisfactory books I have ever read. Beyond Chicago we were under the protection of a friendly passenger conductor, who knew all about the country to which we were going and gave us a great deal of advice in exchange for our confidence. He seemed to us an experienced and worldly man who had been almost everywhere; in his conversation he threw out lightly the names of distant States and cities. He wore the rings and pins and badges of different fraternal orders to which he belonged. Even his cuff-buttons were engraved with hieroglyphics, and he was more inscribed than an Egyptian obelisk. Once when he sat down to chat, he told us that in the immigrant car ahead there was a family from "across the water" whose destination was the same as ours.

"They can't any of them speak English, except one little girl, and all she can say is 'We go Black Hawk, Nebraska.' She's not much older than you, twelve or thirteen, maybe, and she's as bright as a new

---

1. The Bohemian name *Ántonia* is strongly accented on the first syllable, like the English name *Anthony*, and the *i* is, of course, given the sound of long *e*. The name is pronounced An'-ton-ee-ah. [*Author's note.*]

dollar. Don't you want to go ahead and see her, Jimmy? She's got the pretty brown eyes, too!"

This last remark made me bashful, and I shook my head and settled down to "Jesse James." Jake nodded at me approvingly and said you were likely to get diseases from foreigners.

I do not remember crossing the Missouri River, or anything about the long day's journey through Nebraska. Probably by that time I had crossed so many rivers that I was dull to them. The only thing very noticeable about Nebraska was that it was still, all day long, Nebraska.

I had been sleeping, curled up in a red plush seat, for a long while when we reached Black Hawk. Jake roused me and took me by the hand. We stumbled down from the train to a wooden siding, where men were running about with lanterns. I could n't² see any town, or even distant lights; we were surrounded by utter darkness. The engine was panting heavily after its long run. In the red glow from the fire-box, a group of people stood huddled together on the platform, encumbered by bundles and boxes. I knew this must be the immigrant family the conductor had told us about. The woman wore a fringed shawl tied over her head, and she carried a little tin trunk in her arms, hugging it as if it were a baby. There was an old man, tall and stooped. Two half-grown boys and a girl stood holding oil-cloth bundles, and a little girl clung to her mother's skirts. Presently a man with a lantern approached them and began to talk, shouting and exclaiming. I pricked up my ears, for it was positively the first time I had ever heard a foreign tongue.

Another lantern came along. A bantering voice called out: "Hello, are you Mr. Burden's folks? If you are, it's me you're looking for. I'm Otto Fuchs. I'm Mr. Burden's hired man, and I'm to drive you out. Hello, Jimmy, ain't you scared to come so far west?"

I looked up with interest at the new face in the lantern light. He might have stepped out of the pages of "Jesse James." He wore a sombrero hat, with a wide leather band and a bright buckle, and the ends of his mustache were twisted up stiffly, like little horns. He looked lively and ferocious, I thought, and as if he had a history. A long scar ran across one cheek and drew the corner of his mouth up in a sinister curl. The top of his left ear was gone, and his skin was brown as an Indian's. Surely this was the face of a desperado. As he walked about the platform in his high-heeled boots, looking for our trunks, I saw that he was a rather slight man, quick and wiry, and light on his feet. He told us we had a long night drive ahead of us, and had better be on the hike. He led us to a hitching-bar where two farm wagons were tied, and I saw the foreign family crowding into one of

---

2. This unusual spacing for contractions, which occurs throughout *My Ántonia*, was a typographical oddity favored by Houghton Mifflin for all its writers.

with me, and have a nice warm bath behind the stove. Bring your things; there's nobody about."

"Down to the kitchen" struck me as curious; it was always "out in the kitchen" at home. I picked up my shoes and stockings and followed her through the living-room and down a flight of stairs into a basement. This basement was divided into a dining-room at the right of the stairs and a kitchen at the left. Both rooms were plastered and whitewashed—the plaster laid directly upon the earth walls, as it used to be in dugouts. The floor was of hard cement. Up under the wooden ceiling there were little half-windows with white curtains, and pots of geraniums and wandering Jew in the deep sills. As I entered the kitchen I sniffed a pleasant smell of gingerbread baking. The stove was very large, with bright nickel trimmings, and behind it there was a long wooden bench against the wall, and a tin washtub, into which grandmother poured hot and cold water. When she brought the soap and towels, I told her that I was used to taking my bath without help.

"Can you do your ears, Jimmy? Are you sure? Well, now, I call you a right smart little boy."

It was pleasant there in the kitchen. The sun shone into my bath-water through the west half-window, and a big Maltese cat came up and rubbed himself against the tub, watching me curiously. While I scrubbed, my grandmother busied herself in the dining-room until I called anxiously, "Grandmother, I'm afraid the cakes are burning!" Then she came laughing, waving her apron before her as if she were shooing chickens.

She was a spare, tall woman, a little stooped, and she was apt to carry her head thrust forward in an attitude of attention, as if she were looking at something, or listening to something, far away. As I grew older, I came to believe that it was only because she was so often thinking of things that were far away. She was quick-footed and energetic in all her movements. Her voice was high and rather shrill, and she often spoke with an anxious inflection, for she was exceedingly desirous that everything should go with due order and decorum. Her laugh, too, was high, and perhaps a little strident, but there was a lively intelligence in it. She was then fifty-five years old, a strong woman, of unusual endurance.

After I was dressed I explored the long cellar next the kitchen. It was dug out under the wing of the house, was plastered and cemented, with a stairway and an outside door by which the men came and went. Under one of the windows there was a place for them to wash when they came in from work.

While my grandmother was busy about supper I settled myself on the wooden bench behind the stove and got acquainted with the cat—he caught not only rats and mice, but gophers, I was told.

The patch of yellow sunlight on the floor traveled back toward the stairway, and grandmother and I talked about my journey, and about the arrival of the new Bohemian family; she said they were to be our nearest neighbors. We did not talk about the farm in Virginia, which had been her home for so many years. But after the men came in from the fields, and we were all seated at the supper-table, then she asked Jake about the old place and about our friends and neighbors there.

My grandfather said little. When he first came in he kissed me and spoke kindly to me, but he was not demonstrative. I felt at once his deliberateness and personal dignity, and was a little in awe of him. The thing one immediately noticed about him was his beautiful, crinkly, snow-white beard. I once heard a missionary say it was like the beard of an Arabian sheik. His bald crown only made it more impressive.

Grandfather's eyes were not at all like those of an old man; they were bright blue, and had a fresh, frosty sparkle. His teeth were white and regular—so sound that he had never been to a dentist in his life. He had a delicate skin, easily roughened by sun and wind. When he was a young man his hair and beard were red; his eyebrows were still coppery.

As we sat at the table Otto Fuchs and I kept stealing covert glances at each other. Grandmother had told me while she was getting supper that he was an Austrian who came to this country a young boy and had led an adventurous life in the Far West among mining-camps and cow outfits. His iron constitution was somewhat broken by mountain pneumonia, and he had drifted back to live in a milder country for a while. He had relatives in Bismarck, a German settlement to the north of us, but for a year now he had been working for grandfather.

The minute supper was over, Otto took me into the kitchen to whisper to me about a pony down in the barn that had been bought for me at a sale; he had been riding him to find out whether he had any bad tricks, but he was a "perfect gentleman," and his name was Dude. Fuchs told me everything I wanted to know: how he had lost his ear in a Wyoming blizzard when he was a stage-driver, and how to throw a lasso. He promised to rope a steer for me before sundown next day. He got out his "chaps" and silver spurs to show them to Jake and me, and his best cowboy boots, with tops stitched in bold design—roses, and true-lover's knots, and undraped female figures. These, he solemnly explained, were angels.

Before we went to bed Jake and Otto were called up to the living-room for prayers. Grandfather put on silver-rimmed spectacles and read several Psalms. His voice was so sympathetic and he read so interestingly that I wished he had chosen one of my favorite chapters in the Book of Kings. I was awed by his intonation of the word "Selah." *"He shall choose our inheritance for us, the excellency of Jacob whom He loved. Selah.*"[3] I had no idea what the word meant; perhaps he had not. But, as he uttered it, it became oracular, the most sacred of words.

Early the next morning I ran out of doors to look about me. I had been told that ours was the only wooden house west of Black Hawk—until you came to the Norwegian settlement, where there were several. Our neighbors lived in sod houses and dugouts—comfortable, but not very roomy. Our white frame house, with a story and half-story above the basement, stood at the east end of what I might call the farmyard, with the windmill close by the kitchen door. From the windmill the ground sloped westward, down to the barns and granaries and pig-yards. This slope was trampled hard and bare, and washed out in winding gullies by the rain. Beyond the corncribs, at the bottom of the shallow draw, was a muddy little pond, with rusty willow bushes growing about it. The road from the post-office came directly by our door, crossed the farmyard, and curved round this little pond, beyond which it began to climb the gentle swell of unbroken prairie to the west. There, along the western sky-line, it skirted a great cornfield, much larger than any field I had ever seen. This cornfield, and the sorghum patch behind the barn, were the only broken land in sight. Everywhere, as far as the eye could reach, there was nothing but rough, shaggy, red grass, most of it as tall as I.

North of the house, inside the ploughed fire-breaks, grew a thick-set strip of box-elder trees, low and bushy, their leaves already turning yellow. This hedge was nearly a quarter of a mile long, but I had to look very hard to see it at all. The little trees were insignificant against the grass. It seemed as if the grass were about to run over them, and over the plum-patch behind the sod chicken-house.

As I looked about me I felt that the grass was the country, as the water is the sea. The red of the grass made all the great prairie the color of wine-stains, or of certain seaweeds when they are first washed up. And there was so much motion in it; the whole country seemed, somehow, to be running.

I had almost forgotten that I had a grandmother, when she came out, her sunbonnet on her head, a grain-sack in her hand, and asked me if I did not want to go to the garden with her to dig potatoes for dinner. The garden, curiously enough, was a quarter of a mile from the house, and the way to it led up a shallow draw past the cattle corral. Grandmother called my attention to a stout hickory cane, tipped with copper, which hung by a leather thong from her belt. This, she said, was her rattlesnake cane. I must never go to the garden without a heavy stick or a corn-knife; she had killed a good many rattlers on her way back and forth. A little girl who lived on the

3. Psalms 47.4.

Black Hawk road was bitten on the ankle and had been sick all summer.

I can remember exactly how the country looked to me as I walked beside my grandmother along the faint wagon-tracks on that early September morning. Perhaps the glide of long railway travel was still with me, for more than anything else I felt motion in the landscape; in the fresh, easy-blowing morning wind, and in the earth itself, as if the shaggy grass were a sort of loose hide, and underneath it herds of wild buffalo were galloping, galloping . . .

Alone, I should never have found the garden—except, perhaps, for the big yellow pumpkins that lay about unprotected by their withering vines—and I felt very little interest in it when I got there. I wanted to walk straight on through the red grass and over the edge of the world, which could not be very far away. The light air about me told me that the world ended here: only the ground and sun and sky were left, and if one went a little farther there would be only sun and sky, and one would float off into them, like the tawny hawks which sailed over our heads making slow shadows on the grass. While grandmother took the pitchfork we found standing in one of the rows and dug potatoes, while I picked them up out of the soft brown earth and put them into the bag, I kept looking up at the hawks that were doing what I might so easily do.

When grandmother was ready to go, I said I would like to stay up there in the garden awhile.

She peered down at me from under her sunbonnet. "Are n't you afraid of snakes?"

"A little," I admitted, "but I'd like to stay anyhow."

"Well, if you see one, don't have anything to do with him. The big yellow and brown ones won't hurt you; they're bull-snakes and help to keep the gophers down. Don't be scared if you see anything look out of that hole in the bank over there. That's a badger hole. He's about as big as a big 'possum, and his face is striped, black and white. He takes a chicken once in a while, but I won't let the men harm him. In a new country a body feels friendly to the animals. I like to have him come out and watch me when I'm at work."

Grandmother swung the bag of potatoes over her shoulder and went down the path, leaning forward a little. The road followed the windings of the draw; when she came to the first bend she waved at me and disappeared. I was left alone with this new feeling of lightness and content.

I sat down in the middle of the garden, where snakes could scarcely approach unseen, and leaned my back against a warm yellow pumpkin. There were some ground-cherry bushes growing along the furrows, full of fruit. I turned back the papery triangular sheaths that protected the berries and ate a few. All about me giant grasshoppers,

twice as big as any I had ever seen, were doing acroba.
among the dried vines. The gophers scurried up and down
ploughed ground. There in the sheltered draw-bottom the wind did
not blow very hard, but I could hear it singing its humming tune up
on the level, and I could see the tall grasses wave. The earth was
warm under me, and warm as I crumbled it through my fingers.
Queer little red bugs came out and moved in slow squadrons around
me. Their backs were polished vermilion, with black spots. I kept as
still as I could. Nothing happened. I did not expect anything to
happen. I was something that lay under the sun and felt it, like the
pumpkins, and I did not want to be anything more. I was entirely
happy. Perhaps we feel like that when we die and become a part of
something entire, whether it is sun and air, or goodness and knowledge. At any rate, that is happiness; to be dissolved into something
complete and great. When it comes to one, it comes as naturally as
sleep.

III

On Sunday morning Otto Fuchs was to drive us over to make the
acquaintance of our new Bohemian neighbors. We were taking them
some provisions, as they had come to live on a wild place where there
was no garden or chicken-house, and very little broken land. Fuchs
brought up a sack of potatoes and a piece of cured pork from the
cellar, and grandmother packed some loaves of Saturday's bread, a
jar of butter, and several pumpkin pies in the straw of the wagon-
box. We clambered up to the front seat and jolted off past the little
pond and along the road that climbed to the big cornfield.

I could hardly wait to see what lay beyond that cornfield; but there
was only red grass like ours, and nothing else, though from the high
wagon-seat one could look off a long way. The road ran about like
a wild thing, avoiding the deep draws, crossing them where they
were wide and shallow. And all along it, wherever it looped or ran,
the sunflowers grew; some of them were as big as little trees, with
great rough leaves and many branches which bore dozens of blossoms. They made a gold ribbon across the prairie. Occasionally one
of the horses would tear off with his teeth a plant full of blossoms,
and walk along munching it, the flowers nodding in time to his bites
as he ate down toward them.

The Bohemian family, grandmother told me as we drove along,
had bought the homestead of a fellow-countryman, Peter Krajiek,
and had paid him more than it was worth. Their agreement with him
was made before they left the old country, through a cousin of his,
who was also a relative of Mrs. Shimerda. The Shimerdas were the
first Bohemian family to come to this part of the county. Krajiek was

their only interpreter, and could tell them anything he chose. They could not speak enough English to ask for advice, or even to make their most pressing wants known. One son, Fuchs said, was well-grown, and strong enough to work the land; but the father was old and frail and knew nothing about farming. He was a weaver by trade; had been a skilled workman on tapestries and upholstery materials. He had brought his fiddle with him, which would n't be of much use here, though he used to pick up money by it at home.

"If they're nice people, I hate to think of them spending the winter in that cave of Krajiek's," said grandmother. "It's no better than a badger hole; no proper dugout at all. And I hear he's made them pay twenty dollars for his old cookstove that ain't worth ten."

"Yes'm," said Otto; "and he's sold 'em his oxen and his two bony old horses for the price of good work-teams. I'd have interfered about the horses—the old man can understand some German—if I'd 'a' thought it would do any good. But Bohemians has a natural distrust of Austrians."

Grandmother looked interested. "Now, why is that, Otto?"

Fuchs wrinkled his brow and nose. "Well, ma'm, it's politics. It would take me a long while to explain."[4]

The land was growing rougher; I was told that we were approaching Squaw Creek, which cut up the west half of the Shimerdas' place and made the land of little value for farming. Soon we could see the broken, grassy clay cliffs which indicated the windings of the stream, and the glittering tops of the cottonwoods and ash trees that grew down in the ravine. Some of the cottonwoods had already turned, and the yellow leaves and shining white bark made them look like the gold and silver trees in fairy tales.

As we approached the Shimerdas' dwelling, I could still see nothing but rough red hillocks, and draws with shelving banks and long roots hanging out where the earth had crumbled away. Presently, against one of those banks, I saw a sort of shed, thatched with the same wine-colored grass that grew everywhere. Near it tilted a shattered windmill-frame, that had no wheel. We drove up to this skeleton to tie our horses, and then I saw a door and window sunk deep in the draw-bank. The door stood open, and a woman and a girl of fourteen ran out and looked up at us hopefully. A little girl trailed along behind them. The woman had on her head the same embroidered shawl with silk fringes that she wore when she had alighted from the train at Black Hawk. She was not old, but she was certainly not young. Her face was alert and lively, with a sharp chin and shrewd little eyes. She shook grandmother's hand energetically.

---

4. Bohemia and Austria had a history of military, political, and religious conflict dating back to the seventeenth century.

"Very glad, very glad!" she ejaculated. Immediately she pointed to the bank out of which she had emerged and said, "House no good, house no good!"

Grandmother nodded consolingly. "You'll get fixed up comfortable after while, Mrs. Shimerda; make good house."

My grandmother always spoke in a very loud tone to foreigners, as if they were deaf. She made Mrs. Shimerda understand the friendly intention of our visit, and the Bohemian woman handled the loaves of bread and even smelled them, and examined the pies with lively curiosity, exclaiming, "Much good, much thank!"—and again she wrung grandmother's hand.

The oldest son, Ambrož,—they called it Ambrosch,—came out of the cave and stood beside his mother. He was nineteen years old, short and broad-backed, with a close-cropped, flat head, and a wide, flat face. His hazel eyes were little and shrewd, like his mother's, but more sly and suspicious; they fairly snapped at the food. The family had been living on corncakes and sorghum molasses for three days.

The little girl was pretty, but Án-tonia—they accented the name thus, strongly, when they spoke to her—was still prettier. I remembered what the conductor had said about her eyes. They were big and warm and full of light, like the sun shining on brown pools in the wood. Her skin was brown, too, and in her cheeks she had a glow of rich, dark color. Her brown hair was curly and wild-looking. The little sister, whom they called Yulka (Julka), was fair, and seemed mild and obedient. While I stood awkwardly confronting the two girls, Krajiek came up from the barn to see what was going on. With him was another Shimerda son. Even from a distance one could see that there was something strange about this boy. As he approached us, he began to make uncouth noises, and held up his hands to show us his fingers, which were webbed to the first knuckle, like a duck's foot. When he saw me draw back, he began to crow delightedly, "Hoo, hoo-hoo, hoo-hoo!" like a rooster. His mother scowled and said sternly, "Marek!" then spoke rapidly to Krajiek in Bohemian.

"She wants me to tell you he won't hurt nobody, Mrs. Burden. He was born like that. The others are smart. Ambrosch, he make good farmer." He struck Ambrosch on the back, and the boy smiled knowingly.

At that moment the father came out of the hole in the bank. He wore no hat, and his thick, iron-gray hair was brushed straight back from his forehead. It was so long that it bushed out behind his ears, and made him look like the old portraits I remembered in Virginia. He was tall and slender, and his thin shoulders stooped. He looked at us understandingly, then took grandmother's hand and bent over it. I noticed how white and well-shaped his own hands were. They

looked calm, somehow, and skilled. His eyes were melancholy, and
were set back deep under his brow. His face was ruggedly formed,
but it looked like ashes—like something from which all the warmth
and light had died out. Everything about this old man was in keeping with his dignified manner. He was neatly dressed. Under his coat
he wore a knitted gray vest, and, instead of a collar, a silk scarf of a
dark bronze-green, carefully crossed and held together by a red coral
pin. While Krajiek was translating for Mr. Shimerda, Ántonia came
up to me and held out her hand coaxingly. In a moment we were
running up the steep drawside together, Yulka trotting after us.

When we reached the level and could see the gold treetops, I
pointed toward them, and Ántonia laughed and squeezed my hand
as if to tell me how glad she was I had come. We raced off toward
Squaw Creek and did not stop until the ground itself stopped—fell
away before us so abruptly that the next step would have been out
into the treetops. We stood panting on the edge of the ravine, looking down at the trees and bushes that grew below us. The wind was
so strong that I had to hold my hat on, and the girls' skirts were blown
out before them. Ántonia seemed to like it; she held her little sister
by the hand and chattered away in that language which seemed to
me spoken so much more rapidly than mine. She looked at me, her
eyes fairly blazing with things she could not say.

"Name? What name?" she asked, touching me on the shoulder.
I told her my name, and she repeated it after me and made Yulka
say it. She pointed into the gold cottonwood tree behind whose top
we stood and said again, "What name?"

We sat down and made a nest in the long red grass. Yulka curled
up like a baby rabbit and played with a grasshopper. Ántonia pointed
up to the sky and questioned me with her glance. I gave her the word,
but she was not satisfied and pointed to my eyes. I told her, and she
repeated the word, making it sound like "ice." She pointed up to the
sky, then to my eyes, then back to the sky, with movements so quick
and impulsive that she distracted me, and I had no idea what she
wanted. She got up on her knees and wrung her hands. She pointed
to her own eyes and shook her head, then to mine and to the sky,
nodding violently.

"Oh," I exclaimed, "blue; blue sky."

She clapped her hands and murmured, "Blue sky, blue eyes," as if
it amused her. While we snuggled down there out of the wind she
learned a score of words. She was quick, and very eager. We were so
deep in the grass that we could see nothing but the blue sky over us
and the gold tree in front of us. It was wonderfully pleasant. After
Ántonia had said the new words over and over, she wanted to give
me a little chased silver ring she wore on her middle finger. When
she coaxed and insisted, I repulsed her quite sternly. I did n't want

her ring, and I felt there was something reckless and extravagant about her wishing to give it away to a boy she had never seen before. No wonder Krajiek got the better of these people, if this was how they behaved.

While we were disputing about the ring, I heard a mournful voice calling, "Án-tonia, Án-tonia!" She sprang up like a hare. *"Tatinek, Tatinek!"*[5] she shouted, and we ran to meet the old man who was coming toward us. Ántonia reached him first, took his hand and kissed it. When I came up, he touched my shoulder and looked searchingly down into my face for several seconds. I became somewhat embarrassed, for I was used to being taken for granted by my elders.

We went with Mr. Shimerda back to the dugout, where grandmother was waiting for me. Before I got into the wagon, he took a book out of his pocket, opened it, and showed me a page with two alphabets, one English and the other Bohemian. He placed this book in my grandmother's hands, looked at her entreatingly, and said with an earnestness which I shall never forget, "Te-e-ach, te-e-ach my Án-tonia!"

IV

On the afternoon of that same Sunday I took my first long ride on my pony, under Otto's direction. After that Dude and I went twice a week to the post-office, six miles east of us, and I saved the men a good deal of time by riding on errands to our neighbors. When we had to borrow anything, or to send about word that there would be preaching at the sod schoolhouse, I was always the messenger. Formerly Fuchs attended to such things after working hours.

All the years that have passed have not dimmed my memory of that first glorious autumn. The new country lay open before me: there were no fences in those days, and I could choose my own way over the grass uplands, trusting the pony to get me home again. Sometimes I followed the sunflower-bordered roads. Fuchs told me that the sunflowers were introduced into that country by the Mormons; that at the time of the persecution, when they left Missouri and struck out into the wilderness to find a place where they could worship God in their own way, the members of the first exploring party, crossing the plains to Utah, scattered sunflower seed as they went. The next summer, when the long trains of wagons came through with all the women and children, they had the sunflower trail to follow. I believe that botanists do not confirm Otto's story, but insist that the sunflower was native to those plains. Nevertheless, that legend has

5. "Daddy, Daddy!"

stuck in my mind, and sunflower-bordered roads always seem to me the roads to freedom.

I used to love to drift along the pale yellow cornfields, looking for the damp spots one sometimes found at their edges, where the smart-weed soon turned a rich copper color and the narrow brown leaves hung curled like cocoons about the swollen joints of the stem. Some-times I went south to visit our German neighbors and to admire their catalpa grove, or to see the big elm tree that grew up out of a deep crack in the earth and had a hawk's nest in its branches. Trees were so rare in that country, and they had to make such a hard fight to grow, that we used to feel anxious about them, and visit them as if they were persons. It must have been the scarcity of detail in that tawny landscape that made detail so precious.

Sometimes I rode north to the big prairie-dog town to watch the brown earth-owls fly home in the late afternoon and go down to their nests underground with the dogs. Ántonia Shimerda liked to go with me, and we used to wonder a great deal about these birds of sub-terranean habit. We had to be on our guard there, for rattlesnakes were always lurking about. They came to pick up an easy living among the dogs and owls, which were quite defenseless against them; took possession of their comfortable houses and ate the eggs and pup-pies. We felt sorry for the owls. It was always mournful to see them come flying home at sunset and disappear under the earth. But, after all, we felt, winged things who would live like that must be rather degraded creatures. The dog-town was a long way from any pond or creek. Otto Fuchs said he had seen populous dog-towns in the des-ert where there was no surface water for fifty miles; he insisted that some of the holes must go down to water—nearly two hundred feet, hereabouts. Ántonia said she did n't believe it; that the dogs proba-bly lapped up the dew in the early morning, like the rabbits.

Ántonia had opinions about everything, and she was soon able to make them known. Almost every day she came running across the prairie to have her reading lesson with me. Mrs. Shimerda grum-bled, but realized it was important that one member of the family should learn English. When the lesson was over, we used to go up to the watermelon patch behind the garden. I split the melons with an old corn-knife, and we lifted out the hearts and ate them with the juice trickling through our fingers. The white Christmas mel-ons we did not touch, but we watched them with curiosity. They were to be picked late, when the hard frosts had set in, and put away for winter use. After weeks on the ocean, the Shimerdas were famished for fruit. The two girls would wander for miles along the edge of the cornfields, hunting for ground-cherries.

Ántonia loved to help grandmother in the kitchen and to learn about cooking and housekeeping. She would stand beside her, watching her every movement. We were willing to believe that Mrs. Shimerda was a good housewife in her own country, but she managed poorly under new conditions: the conditions were bad enough, certainly!

I remember how horrified we were at the sour, ashy-gray bread she gave her family to eat. She mixed her dough, we discovered, in an old tin peck-measure that Krajiek had used about the barn. When she took the paste out to bake it, she left smears of dough sticking to the sides of the measure, put the measure on the shelf behind the stove, and let this residue ferment. The next time she made bread, she scraped this sour stuff down into the fresh dough to serve as yeast.

During those first months the Shimerdas never went to town. Krajiek encouraged them in the belief that in Black Hawk they would somehow be mysteriously separated from their money. They hated Krajiek, but they clung to him because he was the only human being with whom they could talk or from whom they could get information. He slept with the old man and the two boys in the dugout barn, along with the oxen. They kept him in their hole and fed him for the same reason that the prairie dogs and the brown owls housed the rattlesnakes—because they did not know how to get rid of him.

V

We knew that things were hard for our Bohemian neighbors, but the two girls were light-hearted and never complained. They were always ready to forget their troubles at home, and to run away with me over the prairie, scaring rabbits or starting up flocks of quail.

I remember Ántonia's excitement when she came into our kitchen one afternoon and announced: "My papa find friends up north, with Russian mans. Last night he take me for see, and I can understand very much talk. Nice mans, Mrs. Burden. One is fat and all the time laugh. Everybody laugh. The first time I see my papa laugh in this kawn-tree. Oh, very nice!"

I asked her if she meant the two Russians who lived up by the big dog-town. I had often been tempted to go to see them when I was riding in that direction, but one of them was a wild-looking fellow and I was a little afraid of him. Russia seemed to me more remote than any other country—farther away than China, almost as far as the North Pole. Of all the strange, uprooted people among the first settlers, those two men were the strangest and the most aloof. Their last names were unpronounceable, so they were called Pavel and Peter. They went about making signs to people, and until the Shimerdas came they had no friends. Krajiek could understand them a little, but he had cheated them in a trade, so they avoided him. Pavel, the tall one, was said to be an anarchist; since he had no means of

imparting his opinions, probably his wild gesticulations and his generally excited and rebellious manner gave rise to this supposition.
He must once have been a very strong man, but now his great frame,
with big, knotty joints, had a wasted look, and the skin was drawn
tight over his high cheek-bones. His breathing was hoarse, and he
always had a cough.

Peter, his companion, was a very different sort of fellow; short,
bow-legged, and as fat as butter. He always seemed pleased when
he met people on the road, smiled and took off his cap to every
one, men as well as women. At a distance, on his wagon, he looked
like an old man; his hair and beard were of such a pale flaxen color
that they seemed white in the sun. They were as thick and curly as
carded wool. His rosy face, with its snub nose, set in this fleece,
was like a melon among its leaves. He was usually called "Curly
Peter," or "Rooshian Peter."

The two Russians made good farmhands, and in summer they
worked out together. I had heard our neighbors laughing when they
told how Peter always had to go home at night to milk his cow. Other
bachelor homesteaders used canned milk, to save trouble. Sometimes
Peter came to church at the sod schoolhouse. It was there I first saw
him, sitting on a low bench by the door, his plush cap in his hands,
his bare feet tucked apologetically under the seat.

After Mr. Shimerda discovered the Russians, he went to see them
almost every evening, and sometimes took Ántonia with him. She
said they came from a part of Russia where the language was not
very different from Bohemian, and.if I wanted to go to their place,
she could talk to them for me. One afternoon, before the heavy frosts
began, we rode up there together on my pony.

The Russians had a neat log house built on a grassy slope, with a
windlass well beside the door. As we rode up the draw we skirted a
big melon patch, and a garden where squashes and yellow cucumbers lay about on the sod. We found Peter out behind his kitchen,
bending over a washtub. He was working so hard that he did not hear
us coming. His whole body moved up and down as he rubbed, and
he was a funny sight from the rear, with his shaggy head and bandy
legs. When he straightened himself up to greet us, drops of perspiration were rolling from his thick nose down on to his curly beard.
Peter dried his hands and seemed glad to leave his washing. He took
us down to see his chickens, and his cow that was grazing on the
hillside. He told Ántonia that in his country only rich people had
cows, but here any man could have one who would take care of her.
The milk was good for Pavel, who was often sick, and he could make
butter by beating sour cream with a wooden spoon. Peter was very
fond of his cow. He patted her flanks and talked to her in Russian
while he pulled up her lariat pin and set it in a new place.

After he had shown us his garden, Peter trundled a load of water-melons up the hill in his wheelbarrow. Pavel was not at home. He was off somewhere helping to dig a well. The house I thought very comfortable for two men who were "batching." Besides the kitchen, there was a living-room, with a wide double bed built against the wall, properly made up with blue gingham sheets and pillows. There was a little storeroom, too, with a window, where they kept guns and saddles and tools, and old coats and boots. That day the floor was covered with garden things, drying for winter; corn and beans and fat yellow cucumbers. There were no screens or window-blinds in the house, and all the doors and windows stood wide open, letting in flies and sunshine alike.

Peter put the melons in a row on the oilcloth-covered table and stood over them, brandishing a butcher knife. Before the blade got fairly into them, they split of their own ripeness, with a delicious sound. He gave us knives, but no plates, and the top of the table was soon swimming with juice and seeds. I had never seen any one eat so many melons as Peter ate. He assured us that they were good for one—better than medicine; in his country people lived on them at this time of year. He was very hospitable and jolly. Once, while he was looking at Ántonia, he sighed and told us that if he had stayed at home in Russia perhaps by this time he would have had a pretty daughter of his own to cook and keep house for him. He said he had left his country because of a "great trouble."

When we got up to go, Peter looked about in perplexity for some-thing that would entertain us. He ran into the store-room and brought out a gaudily painted harmonica, sat down on a bench, and spread-ing his fat legs apart began to play like a whole band. The tunes were either very lively or very doleful, and he sang words to some of them.

Before we left, Peter put ripe cucumbers into a sack for Mrs. Shi-merda and gave us a lard-pail full of milk to cook them in. I had never heard of cooking cucumbers, but Ántonia assured me they were very good. We had to walk the pony all the way home to keep from spilling the milk.

VI

One afternoon we were having our reading lesson on the warm, grassy bank where the badger lived. It was a day of amber sunlight, but there was a shiver of coming winter in the air. I had seen ice on the little horse-pond that morning, and as we went through the gar-den we found the tall asparagus, with its red berries, lying on the ground, a mass of slimy green.

Tony was barefooted, and she shivered in her cotton dress and was comfortable only when we were tucked down on the baked earth, in

the full blaze of the sun. She could talk to me about almost anything by this time. That afternoon she was telling me how highly
esteemed our friend the badger was in her part of the world, and
how men kept a special kind of dog, with very short legs, to hunt
him. Those dogs, she said, went down into the hole after the badger
and killed him there in a terrific struggle underground; you could
hear the barks and yelps outside. Then the dog dragged himself back,
covered with bites and scratches, to be rewarded and petted by his
master. She knew a dog who had a star on his collar for every badger he had killed.

The rabbits were unusually spry that afternoon. They kept starting up all about us, and dashing off down the draw as if they were
playing a game of some kind. But the little buzzing things that lived
in the grass were all dead—all but one. While we were lying there
against the warm bank, a little insect of the palest, frailest green
hopped painfully out of the buffalo grass and tried to leap into a
bunch of bluestem. He missed it, fell back, and sat with his head
sunk between his long legs, his antennæ quivering, as if he were waiting for something to come and finish him. Tony made a warm nest
for him in her hands; talked to him gayly and indulgently in Bohemian. Presently he began to sing for us—a thin, rusty little chirp.
She held him close to her ear and laughed, but a moment afterward I saw there were tears in her eyes. She told me that in her
village at home there was an old beggar woman who went about
selling herbs and roots she had dug up in the forest. If you took her
in and gave her a warm place by the fire, she sang old songs to the
children in a cracked voice, like this. Old Hata, she was called, and
the children loved to see her coming and saved their cakes and sweets
for her.

When the bank on the other side of the draw began to throw a
narrow shelf of shadow, we knew we ought to be starting homeward;
the chill came on quickly when the sun got low, and Ántonia's dress
was thin. What were we to do with the frail little creature we had
lured back to life by false pretenses? I offered my pockets, but Tony
shook her head and carefully put the green insect in her hair, tying
her big handkerchief down loosely over her curls. I said I would go
with her until we could see Squaw Creek, and then turn and run
home. We drifted along lazily, very happy, through the magical light
of the late afternoon.

All those fall afternoons were the same, but I never got used to
them. As far as we could see, the miles of copper-red grass were
drenched in sunlight that was stronger and fiercer than at any other
time of the day. The blond cornfields were red gold, the haystacks
turned rosy and threw long shadows. The whole prairie was like the

bush that burned with fire and was not consumed.[6] That hour always had the exultation of victory, of triumphant ending, like a hero's death—heroes who died young and gloriously. It was a sudden transfiguration, a lifting-up of day.

How many an afternoon Ántonia and I have trailed along the prairie under that magnificence! And always two long black shadows flitted before us or followed after, dark spots on the ruddy grass.

We had been silent a long time, and the edge of the sun sank nearer and nearer the prairie floor, when we saw a figure moving on the edge of the upland, a gun over his shoulder. He was walking slowly, dragging his feet along as if he had no purpose. We broke into a run to overtake him.

"My papa sick all the time," Tony panted as we flew. "He not look good, Jim."

As we neared Mr. Shimerda she shouted, and he lifted his head and peered about. Tony ran up to him, caught his hand and pressed it against her cheek. She was the only one of his family who could rouse the old man from the torpor in which he seemed to live. He took the bag from his belt and showed us three rabbits he had shot, looked at Ántonia with a wintry flicker of a smile and began to tell her something. She turned to me.

"My *tatinek* make me little hat with the skins, little hat for winter!" she exclaimed joyfully. "Meat for eat, skin for hat,"—she told off these benefits on her fingers.

Her father put his hand on her hair, but she caught his wrist and lifted it carefully away, talking to him rapidly. I heard the name of old Hata. He untied the handkerchief, separated her hair with his fingers, and stood looking down at the green insect. When it began to chirp faintly, he listened as if it were a beautiful sound.

I picked up the gun he had dropped; a queer piece from the old country, short and heavy, with a stag's head on the cock. When he saw me examining it, he turned to me with his far-away look that always made me feel as if I were down at the bottom of a well. He spoke kindly and gravely, and Ántonia translated:—

"My *tatinek* say when you are big boy, he give you his gun. Very fine, from Bohemie. It was belong to a great man, very rich, like what you not got here; many fields, many forests, many big house. My papa play for his wedding, and he give my papa fine gun, and my papa give you."

I was glad that this project was one of futurity. There never were such people as the Shimerdas for wanting to give away everything

---

6. Exodus 3.2: "And the angel of the Lord appeared unto [Moses] in a flame of fire out of the midst of a Bush; and he looked, and behold, the bush burned with fire, and the bush was not consumed."

they had. Even the mother was always offering me things, though I knew she expected substantial presents in return. We stood there in friendly silence, while the feeble minstrel sheltered in Ántonia's hair went on with its scratchy chirp. The old man's smile, as he listened, was so full of sadness, of pity for things, that I never afterward forgot it. As the sun sank there came a sudden coolness and the strong smell of earth and drying grass. Ántonia and her father went off hand in hand, and I buttoned up my jacket and raced my shadow home.

VII

Much as I liked Ántonia, I hated a superior tone that she sometimes took with me. She was four years older than I, to be sure, and had seen more of the world; but I was a boy and she was a girl, and I resented her protecting manner. Before the autumn was over she began to treat me more like an equal and to defer to me in other things than reading lessons. This change came about from an adventure we had together.

One day when I rode over to the Shimerdas' I found Ántonia starting off on foot for Russian Peter's house, to borrow a spade Ambrosch needed. I offered to take her on the pony, and she got up behind me. There had been another black frost the night before, and the air was clear and heady as wine. Within a week all the blooming roads had been despoiled—hundreds of miles of yellow sunflowers had been transformed into brown, rattling, burry stalks.

We found Russian Peter digging his potatoes. We were glad to go in and get warm by his kitchen stove and to see his squashes and Christmas melons, heaped in the storeroom for winter. As we rode away with the spade, Ántonia suggested that we stop at the prairie-dog town and dig into one of the holes. We could find out whether they ran straight down, or were horizontal, like mole-holes; whether they had underground connections; whether the owls had nests down there, lined with feathers. We might get some puppies, or owl eggs, or snake-skins.

The dog-town was spread out over perhaps ten acres. The grass had been nibbled short and even, so this stretch was not shaggy and red like the surrounding country, but gray and velvety. The holes were several yards apart, and were disposed with a good deal of regularity, almost as if the town had been laid out in streets and avenues. One always felt that an orderly and very sociable kind of life was going on there. I picketed Dude down in a draw, and we went wandering about, looking for a hole that would be easy to dig. The dogs were out, as usual, dozens of them, sitting up on their hind legs over the doors of their houses. As we approached, they barked, shook their tails at us, and scurried underground. Before the mouths of the holes were little patches of sand and gravel, scratched up, we supposed, from a long way below the surface. Here and there, in the town, we came on larger gravel patches, several yards away from any hole. If the dogs had scratched the sand up in excavating, how had they carried it so far? It was on one of these gravel beds that I met my adventure.

We were examining a big hole with two entrances. The burrow sloped into the ground at a gentle angle, so that we could see where the two corridors united, and the floor was dusty from use, like a little highway over which much travel went. I was walking backward, in a crouching position, when I heard Ántonia scream. She was standing opposite me, pointing behind me and shouting something in Bohemian. I whirled round, and there, on one of those dry gravel beds, was the biggest snake I had ever seen. He was sunning himself, after the cold night, and he must have been asleep when Ántonia screamed. When I turned he was lying in long loose waves, like a letter "W." He twitched and began to coil slowly. He was not merely a big snake, I thought—he was a circus monstrosity. His abominable muscularity, his loathsome, fluid motion, somehow made me sick. He was as thick as my leg, and looked as if millstones could n't crush the disgusting vitality out of him. He lifted his hideous little head, and rattled. I did n't run because I did n't think of it—if my back had been against a stone wall I could n't have felt more cornered. I saw his coils tighten—now he would spring, spring his length, I remembered. I ran up and drove at his head with my spade, struck him fairly across the neck, and in a minute he was all about my feet in wavy loops. I struck now from hate. Ántonia, barefooted as she was, ran up behind me. Even after I had pounded his ugly head flat, his body kept on coiling and winding, doubling and falling back on itself. I walked away and turned my back. I felt seasick. Ántonia came after me, crying, "O Jimmy, he not bite you? You sure? Why you not run when I say?"

"What did you jabber Bohunk for? You might have told me there was a snake behind me!" I said petulantly.

"I know I am just awful, Jim, I was so scared." She took my handkerchief from my pocket and tried to wipe my face with it, but I snatched it away from her. I suppose I looked as sick as I felt.

"I never know you was so brave, Jim," she went on comfortingly. "You is just like big mans; you wait for him lift his head and then you go for him. Ain't you feel scared a bit? Now we take that snake home and show everybody. Nobody ain't seen in this kawn-tree so big snake like you kill."

She went on in this strain until I began to think that I had longed for this opportunity, and had hailed it with joy. Cautiously we went back to the snake; he was still groping with his tail, turning up his ugly belly in the light. A faint, fetid smell came from him, and a thread of green liquid oozed from his crushed head.

"Look, Tony, that's his poison," I said.

I took a long piece of string from my pocket, and she lifted his head with the spade while I tied a noose around it. We pulled him out straight and measured him by my riding-quirt; he was about five and a half feet long. He had twelve rattles, but they were broken off before they began to taper, so I insisted that he must once have had twenty-four. I explained to Ántonia how this meant that he was twenty-four years old, that he must have been there when white men first came, left on from buffalo and Indian times. As I turned him over I began to feel proud of him, to have a kind of respect for his age and size. He seemed like the ancient, eldest Evil. Certainly his kind have left horrible unconscious memories in all warm-blooded life. When we dragged him down into the draw, Dude sprang off to the end of his tether and shivered all over—would n't let us come near him.

We decided that Ántonia should ride Dude home, and I would walk. As she rode along slowly, her bare legs swinging against the pony's sides, she kept shouting back to me about how astonished everybody would be. I followed with the spade over my shoulder, dragging my snake. Her exultation was contagious. The great land had never looked to me so big and free. If the red grass were full of rattlers, I was equal to them all. Nevertheless, I stole furtive glances behind me now and then to see that no avenging mate, older and bigger than my quarry, was racing up from the rear.

The sun had set when we reached our garden and went down the draw toward the house. Otto Fuchs was the first one we met. He was sitting on the edge of the cattle-pond, having a quiet pipe before supper. Ántonia called him to come quick and look. He did not say anything for a minute, but scratched his head and turned the snake over with his boot.

"Where did you run onto that beauty, Jim?"

"Up at the dog-town," I answered laconically.

"Kill him yourself? How come you to have a weepon?"

"We'd been up to Russian Peter's, to borrow a spade for Ambrosch."

Otto shook the ashes out of his pipe and squatted down to count the rattles. "It was just luck you had a tool," he said cautiously. "Gosh! I would n't want to do any business with that fellow myself, unless I had a fence-post along. Your grandmother's snake-cane would n't more than tickle him. He could stand right up and talk to you, he could. Did he fight hard?"

Ántonia broke in: "He fight something awful! He is all over Jimmy's boots. I scream for him to run, but he just hit and hit that snake like he was crazy."

Otto winked at me. After Ántonia rode on he said: "Got him in the head first crack, did n't you? That was just as well."

We hung him up to the windmill, and when I went down to the kitchen I found Ántonia standing in the middle of the floor, telling the story with a great deal of color.

Subsequent experiences with rattlesnakes taught me that my first encounter was fortunate in circumstance. My big rattler was old, and had led too easy a life; there was not much fight in him. He had probably lived there for years, with a fat prairie dog for breakfast whenever he felt like it, a sheltered home, even an owl-feather bed, perhaps, and he had forgot that the world does n't owe rattlers a living. A snake of his size, in fighting trim, would be more than any boy could handle. So in reality it was a mock adventure; the game was fixed for me by chance, as it probably was for many a dragon-slayer. I had been adequately armed by Russian Peter; the snake was old and lazy; and I had Ántonia beside me, to appreciate and admire.

That snake hung on our corral fence for several days; some of the neighbors came to see it and agreed that it was the biggest rattler ever killed in those parts. This was enough for Ántonia. She liked me better from that time on, and she never took a supercilious air with me again. I had killed a big snake—I was now a big fellow.

VIII

While the autumn color was growing pale on the grass and corn-fields, things went badly with our friends the Russians. Peter told his troubles to Mr. Shimerda: he was unable to meet a note which fell due on the first of November; had to pay an exorbitant bonus on renewing it, and to give a mortgage on his pigs and horses and even his milk cow. His creditor was Wick Cutter, the merciless Black Hawk money-lender, a man of evil name throughout the county, of whom I shall have more to say later. Peter could give no very clear account of his transactions with Cutter. He only knew that he had first borrowed two hundred dollars, then another hundred, then fifty—that each time a bonus was added to the principal, and the debt grew faster than any crop he planted. Now everything was plastered with mortgages.

Soon after Peter renewed his note, Pavel strained himself lifting timbers for a new barn, and fell over among the shavings with such a gush of blood from the lungs that his fellow-workmen thought he would die on the spot. They hauled him home and put him into his bed, and there he lay, very ill indeed. Misfortune seemed to settle like an evil bird on the roof of the log house, and to flap its wings there, warning human beings away. The Russians had such bad luck that people were afraid of them and liked to put them out of mind.

One afternoon Ántonia and her father came over to our house to get buttermilk, and lingered, as they usually did, until the sun was low. Just as they were leaving, Russian Peter drove up. Pavel was very bad, he said, and wanted to talk to Mr. Shimerda and his daughter; he had come to fetch them. When Ántonia and her father got into the wagon, I entreated grandmother to let me go with them: I would gladly go without my supper, I would sleep in the Shimerdas' barn and run home in the morning. My plan must have seemed very foolish to her, but she was often large-minded about humoring the desires of other people. She asked Peter to wait a moment, and when she came back from the kitchen she brought a bag of sandwiches and doughnuts for us.

Mr. Shimerda and Peter were on the front seat; Ántonia and I sat in the straw behind and ate our lunch as we bumped along. After the sun sank, a cold wind sprang up and moaned over the prairie. If this turn in the weather had come sooner, I should not have got away. We burrowed down in the straw and curled up close together, watching the angry red die out of the west and the stars begin to shine in the clear, windy sky. Peter kept sighing and groaning. Tony whispered to me that he was afraid Pavel would never get well. We lay still and did not talk. Up there the stars grew magnificently bright. Though we had come from such different parts of the world, in both of us there was some dusky superstition that those shining groups have their influence upon what is and what is not to be. Perhaps Russian Peter, come from farther away than any of us, had brought from his land, too, some such belief.

The little house on the hillside was so much the color of the night that we could not see it as we came up the draw. The ruddy windows guided us—the light from the kitchen stove, for there was no lamp burning.

We entered softly. The man in the wide bed seemed to be asleep. Tony and I sat down on the bench by the wall and leaned our arms on the table in front of us. The firelight flickered on the hewn logs that supported the thatch overhead. Pavel made a rasping sound when he breathed, and he kept moaning. We waited. The wind shook the doors and windows impatiently, then swept on again, singing through the big spaces. Each gust, as it bore down, rattled the panes, and swelled off like the others. They made me think of defeated armies, retreating; or of ghosts who were trying desperately to get in for shelter, and then went moaning on. Presently, in one of those sobbing intervals between the blasts, the coyotes tuned up with their whining howl; one, two, three, then all together—to tell us that winter was coming. This sound brought an answer from the bed,—a long complaining cry,—as if Pavel were having bad dreams or were waking to some old misery. Peter listened, but did not stir. He was sitting on the floor by the kitchen stove. The coyotes broke out again; yap, yap, yap—then the high whine. Pavel called for something and struggled up on his elbow.

"He is scared of the wolves," Ántonia whispered to me. "In his country there are very many, and they eat men and women." We slid closer together along the bench.

I could not take my eyes off the man in the bed. His shirt was hanging open, and his emaciated chest, covered with yellow bristle, rose and fell horribly. He began to cough. Peter shuffled to his feet, caught up the tea-kettle and mixed him some hot water and whiskey. The sharp smell of spirits went through the room.

Pavel snatched the cup and drank, then made Peter give him the bottle and slipped it under his pillow, grinning disagreeably, as if he had outwitted some one. His eyes followed Peter about the room with a contemptuous, unfriendly expression. It seemed to me that he despised him for being so simple and docile.

Presently Pavel began to talk to Mr. Shimerda, scarcely above a whisper. He was telling a long story, and as he went on, Ántonia took my hand under the table and held it tight. She leaned forward and strained her ears to hear him. He grew more and more excited, and kept pointing all around his bed, as if there were things there and he wanted Mr. Shimerda to see them.

"It's wolves, Jimmy," Ántonia whispered. "It's awful, what he says!"

The sick man raged and shook his fist. He seemed to be cursing people who had wronged him. Mr. Shimerda caught him by the shoulders, but could hardly hold him in bed. At last he was shut off by a coughing fit which fairly choked him. He pulled a cloth from under his pillow and held it to his mouth. Quickly it was covered with bright red spots—I thought I had never seen any blood so bright. When he lay down and turned his face to the wall, all the rage had gone out of him. He lay patiently fighting for breath, like a child with croup. Ántonia's father uncovered one of his long bony legs and rubbed it rhythmically. From our bench we could see what a hollow case his body was. His spine and shoulderblades stood out like the bones under the hide of a dead steer left in the fields. That sharp backbone must have hurt him when he lay on it.

Gradually, relief came to all of us. Whatever it was, the worst was over. Mr. Shimerda signed to us that Pavel was asleep. Without a word Peter got up and lit his lantern. He was going out to get his team to drive us home. Mr. Shimerda went with him. We sat and watched the long bowed back under the blue sheet, scarcely daring to breathe.

On the way home, when we were lying in the straw, under the jolting and rattling Ántonia told me as much of the story as she could. What she did not tell me then, she told later; we talked of nothing else for days afterward.

* * *

When Pavel and Peter were young men, living at home in Russia, they were asked to be groomsmen for a friend who was to marry the belle of another village. It was in the dead of winter and the groom's party went over to the wedding in sledges. Peter and Pavel drove in the groom's sledge, and six sledges followed with all his relatives and friends.

After the ceremony at the church, the party went to a dinner given by the parents of the bride. The dinner lasted all afternoon; then it became a supper and continued far into the night. There was much dancing and drinking. At midnight the parents of the bride said good-bye to her and blessed her. The groom took her up in his arms and carried her out to his sledge and tucked her under the blankets. He sprang in beside her, and Pavel and Peter (our Pavel and Peter!) took the front seat. Pavel drove. The party set out with singing and the jingle of sleigh-bells, the groom's sledge going first. All the drivers were more or less the worse for merry-making, and the groom was absorbed in his bride.

The wolves were bad that winter, and every one knew it, yet when they heard the first wolf-cry, the drivers were not much alarmed. They had too much good food and drink inside them. The first howls were taken up and echoed and with quickening repetitions. The wolves were coming together. There was no moon, but the starlight was clear on the snow. A black drove came up over the hill behind the wedding party. The wolves ran like streaks of shadow; they looked no bigger than dogs, but there were hundreds of them.

Something happened to the hindmost sledge: the driver lost control,—he was probably very drunk,—the horses left the road, the sledge was caught in a clump of trees, and overturned. The occupants rolled out over the snow, and the fleetest of the wolves sprang upon them. The shrieks that followed made everybody sober. The drivers stood up and lashed their horses. The groom had the best team and his sledge was lightest—all the others carried from six to a dozen people.

Another driver lost control. The screams of the horses were more terrible to hear than the cries of the men and women. Nothing seemed to check the wolves. It was hard to tell what was happening in the rear; the people who were falling behind shrieked as piteously as those who were already lost. The little bride hid her face on the groom's shoulder and sobbed. Pavel sat still and watched his horses. The road was clear and white, and the groom's three blacks went like the wind. It was only necessary to be calm and to guide them carefully.

At length, as they breasted a long hill, Peter rose cautiously and looked back. "There are only three sledges left," he whispered.

"And the wolves?" Pavel asked.

"Enough! Enough for all of us."

Pavel reached the brow of the hill, but only two sledges followed him down the other side. In that moment on the hilltop, they saw behind them a whirling black group on the snow. Presently the groom screamed. He saw his father's sledge overturned, with his mother and sisters. He sprang up as if he meant to jump, but the girl shrieked and held him back. It was even then too late. The black ground-shadows were already crowding over the heap in the road, and one horse ran out across the fields, his harness hanging to him, wolves at his heels. But the groom's movement had given Pavel an idea.

They were within a few miles of their village now. The only sledge left out of six was not very far behind them, and Pavel's middle horse was failing. Beside a frozen pond something happened to the other sledge; Peter saw it plainly. Three big wolves got abreast of the horses, and the horses went crazy. They tried to jump over each other, got tangled up in the harness, and overturned the sledge.

When the shrieking behind them died away, Pavel realized that he was alone upon the familiar road. "They still come?" he asked Peter.

"Yes."

"How many?"

"Twenty, thirty—enough."

Now his middle horse was being almost dragged by the other two. Pavel gave Peter the reins and stepped carefully into the back of the sledge. He called to the groom that they must lighten—and pointed to the bride. The young man cursed him and held her tighter. Pavel tried to drag her away. In the struggle, the groom rose. Pavel knocked him over the side of the sledge and threw the girl after him. He said he never remembered exactly how he did it, or what happened afterward. Peter, crouching in the front seat, saw nothing. The first thing either of them noticed was a new sound that broke into the clear air, louder than they had ever heard it before—the bell of the monastery of their own village, ringing for early prayers.

Pavel and Peter drove into the village alone, and they had been alone ever since. They were run out of their village. Pavel's own mother would not look at him. They went away to strange towns, but when people learned where they came from, they were always asked if they knew the two men who had fed the bride to the wolves. Wherever they went, the story followed them. It took them five years to save money enough to come to America. They worked in Chicago, Des Moines, Fort Wayne, but they were always unfortunate. When Pavel's health grew so bad, they decided to try farming.

Pavel died a few days after he unburdened his mind to Mr. Shimerda, and was buried in the Norwegian graveyard. Peter sold off everything, and left the country—went to be cook in a railway construction camp where gangs of Russians were employed.

At his sale we bought Peter's wheelbarrow and some of his harness. During the auction he went about with his head down, and never lifted his eyes. He seemed not to care about anything. The Black Hawk money-lender who held mortgages on Peter's livestock was there, and he bought in the sale notes at about fifty cents on the dollar. Every one said Peter kissed the cow before she was led away by her new owner. I did not see him do it, but this I know: after all his furniture and his cook-stove and pots and pans had been hauled off by the purchasers, when his house was stripped and bare, he sat down on the floor with his clasp-knife and ate all the melons that he had put away for winter. When Mr. Shimerda and Krajiek drove up in their wagon to take Peter to the train, they found him with a dripping beard, surrounded by heaps of melon rinds.

The loss of his two friends had a depressing effect upon old Mr. Shimerda. When he was out hunting, he used to go into the empty log house and sit there, brooding. This cabin was his hermitage until the winter snows penned him in his cave. For Ántonia and me, the story of the wedding party was never at an end. We did not tell Pavel's secret to any one, but guarded it jealously—as if the wolves of the Ukraine had gathered that night long ago, and the wedding party been sacrificed, to give us a painful and peculiar pleasure. At night, before I went to sleep, I often found myself in a sledge drawn by three horses, dashing through a country that looked something like Nebraska and something like Virginia.

IX

The first snowfall came early in December. I remember how the world looked from our sitting-room window as I dressed behind the stove that morning: the low sky was like a sheet of metal; the blond cornfields had faded out into ghostliness at last; the little pond was frozen under its stiff willow bushes. Big white flakes were whirling over everything and disappearing in the red grass.

Beyond the pond, on the slope that climbed to the cornfield, there was, faintly marked in the grass, a great circle where the Indians used to ride. Jake and Otto were sure that when they galloped round that ring the Indians tortured prisoners, bound to a stake in the center; but grandfather thought they merely ran races or trained horses there. Whenever one looked at this slope against the setting sun, the circle showed like a pattern in the grass; and this morning, when the first light spray of snow lay over it, it came out with wonderful distinctness, like strokes of Chinese white on canvas. The old figure stirred me as it had never done before and seemed a good omen for the winter.

As soon as the snow had packed hard I began to drive about the country in a clumsy sleigh that Otto Fuchs made for me by fastening a wooden goods-box on bobs. Fuchs had been apprenticed to a cabinet-maker in the old country and was very handy with tools. He would have done a better job if I had n't hurried him. My first trip was to the post-office, and the next day I went over to take Yulka and Ántonia for a sleigh-ride.

It was a bright, cold day. I piled straw and buffalo robes into the box, and took two hot bricks wrapped in old blankets. When I got to the Shimerdas' I did not go up to the house, but sat in my sleigh at the bottom of the draw and called. Ántonia and Yulka came running out, wearing little rabbit-skin hats their father had made for them. They had heard about my sledge from Ambrosch and knew why I had come. They tumbled in beside me and we set off toward the north, along a road that happened to be broken.

The sky was brilliantly blue, and the sunlight on the glittering white stretches of prairie was almost blinding. As Ántonia said, the whole world was changed by the snow; we kept looking in vain for familiar landmarks. The deep arroyo through which Squaw Creek wound was now only a cleft between snow-drifts—very blue when one looked down into it. The tree-tops that had been gold all the autumn were dwarfed and twisted, as if they would never have any life in them again. The few little cedars, which were so dull and dingy before, now stood out a strong, dusky green. The wind had the burning taste of fresh snow; my throat and nostrils smarted as if some one had opened a hartshorn bottle.[7] The cold stung, and at the same time delighted one. My horse's breath rose like steam, and whenever we stopped he smoked all over. The cornfields got back a little of their color under the dazzling light, and stood the palest possible gold in the sun and snow. All about us the snow was crusted in shallow terraces, with tracings like ripple-marks at the edges, curly waves that were the actual impression of the stinging lash in the wind.

The girls had on cotton dresses under their shawls; they kept shivering beneath the buffalo robes and hugging each other for warmth. But they were so glad to get away from their ugly cave and their mother's scolding that they begged me to go on and on, as far as Russian Peter's house. The great fresh open, after the stupefying warmth indoors, made them behave like wild things. They laughed and shouted, and said they never wanted to go home again. Could n't we settle down and live in Russian Peter's house, Yulka asked, and could n't I go to town and buy things for us to keep house with?

7. A bottle filled with smelling salts.

All the way to Russian Peter's we were extravagantly happy, but when we turned back,—it must have been about four o'clock,—the east wind grew stronger and began to howl; the sun lost its heartening power and the sky became gray and somber. I took off my long woolen comforter and wound it around Yulka's throat. She got so cold that we made her hide her head under the buffalo robe. Ántonia and I sat erect, but I held the reins clumsily, and my eyes were blinded by the wind a good deal of the time. It was growing dark when we got to their house, but I refused to go in with them and get warm. I knew my hands would ache terribly if I went near a fire. Yulka forgot to give me back my comforter, and I had to drive home directly against the wind. The next day I came down with an attack of quinsy, which kept me in the house for nearly two weeks.

The basement kitchen seemed heavenly safe and warm in those days—like a tight little boat in a winter sea. The men were out in the fields all day, husking corn, and when they came in at noon, with long caps pulled down over their ears and their feet in red-lined overshoes, I used to think they were like Arctic explorers.

In the afternoons, when grandmother sat upstairs darning, or making husking-gloves, I read "The Swiss Family Robinson" aloud to her, and I felt that the Swiss family had no advantages over us in the way of an adventurous life. I was convinced that man's strongest antagonist is the cold. I admired the cheerful zest with which grandmother went about keeping us warm and comfortable and well-fed. She often reminded me, when she was preparing for the return of the hungry men, that this country was not like Virginia; and that here a cook had, as she said, "very little to do with." On Sundays she gave us as much chicken as we could eat, and on other days we had ham or bacon or sausage meat. She baked either pies or cake for us every day, unless, for a change, she made my favorite pudding, striped with currants and boiled in a bag.

Next to getting warm and keeping warm, dinner and supper were the most interesting things we had to think about. Our lives centered around warmth and food and the return of the men at nightfall. I used to wonder, when they came in tired from the fields, their feet numb and their hands cracked and sore, how they could do all the chores so conscientiously: feed and water and bed the horses, milk the cows, and look after the pigs. When supper was over, it took them a long while to get the cold out of their bones. While grandmother and I washed the dishes and grandfather read his paper upstairs, Jake and Otto sat on the long bench behind the stove, "easing" their inside boots, or rubbing mutton tallow into their cracked hands.

Every Saturday night we popped corn or made taffy, and Otto Fuchs used to sing, "For I Am a Cowboy and Know I've Done Wrong,"

or, "Bury Me Not on the Lone Prairee." He had a good baritone voice
and always led the singing when we went to church services at the
sod schoolhouse.

I can still see those two men sitting on the bench; Otto's close-
clipped head and Jake's shaggy hair slicked flat in front by a wet comb.
I can see the sag of their tired shoulders against the whitewashed
wall. What good fellows they were, how much they knew, and how
many things they had kept faith with!

Fuchs had been a cowboy, a stage-driver, a bar-tender, a miner;
had wandered all over that great Western country and done hard
work everywhere, though, as grandmother said, he had nothing to
show for it. Jake was duller than Otto. He could scarcely read, wrote
even his name with difficulty, and he had a violent temper which
sometimes made him behave like a crazy man—tore him all to pieces
and actually made him ill. But he was so soft-hearted that any one
could impose upon him. If he, as he said, "forgot himself" and swore
before grandmother, he went about depressed and shamefaced all
day. They were both of them jovial about the cold in winter and the
heat in summer, always ready to work overtime and to meet emer-
gencies. It was a matter of pride with them not to spare themselves.
Yet they were the sort of men who never get on, somehow, or do anything but work hard for a dollar or two a day.

On those bitter, starlit nights, as we sat around the old stove that
fed us and warmed us and kept us cheerful, we could hear the coyotes howling down by the corrals, and their hungry, wintry cry used
to remind the boys of wonderful animal stories; about gray wolves
and bears in the Rockies, wildcats and panthers in the Virginia
mountains. Sometimes Fuchs could be persuaded to talk about the
outlaws and desperate characters he had known. I remember one
funny story about himself that made grandmother, who was working her bread on the bread-board, laugh until she wiped her eyes with
her bare arm, her hands being floury. It was like this:—

When Otto left Austria to come to America, he was asked by one
of his relatives to look after a woman who was crossing on the same
boat, to join her husband in Chicago. The woman started off with
two children, but it was clear that her family might grow larger on
the journey. Fuchs said he "got on fine with the kids," and liked the
mother, though she played a sorry trick on him. In mid-ocean she
proceeded to have not one baby, but three! This event made Fuchs
the object of undeserved notoriety, since he was traveling with her.
The steerage stewardess was indignant with him, the doctor regarded
him with suspicion. The first-cabin passengers, who made up a purse
for the woman, took an embarrassing interest in Otto, and often
inquired of him about his charge. When the triplets were taken
ashore at New York, he had, as he said, "to carry some of them." The

trip to Chicago was even worse than the ocean voyage. On the train it was very difficult to get milk for the babies and to keep their bottles clean. The mother did her best, but no woman, out of her natural resources, could feed three babies. The husband, in Chicago, was working in a furniture factory for modest wages, and when he met his family at the station he was rather crushed by the size of it. He, too, seemed to consider Fuchs in some fashion to blame. "I was sure glad," Otto concluded, "that he did n't take his hard feeling out on that poor woman; but he had a sullen eye for me, all right! Now, did you ever hear of a young feller's having such hard luck, Mrs. Burden?"

Grandmother told him she was sure the Lord had remembered these things to his credit, and had helped him out of many a scrape when he did n't realize that he was being protected by Providence.

X

For several weeks after my sleigh-ride, we heard nothing from the Shimerdas. My sore throat kept me indoors, and grandmother had a cold which made the housework heavy for her. When Sunday came she was glad to have a day of rest. One night at supper Fuchs told us he had seen Mr. Shimerda out hunting.

"He's made himself a rabbit-skin cap, Jim, and a rabbit-skin collar that he buttons on outside his coat. They ain't got but one overcoat among 'em over there, and they take turns wearing it. They seem awful scared of cold, and stick in that hole in the bank like badgers."

"All but the crazy boy," Jake put in. "He never wears the coat. Krajiek says he's turrible strong and can stand anything. I guess rabbits must be getting scarce in this locality. Ambrosch come along by the cornfield yesterday where I was at work and showed me three prairie dogs he'd shot. He asked me if they was good to eat. I spit and made a face and took on, to scare him, but he just looked like he was smarter'n me and put 'em back in his sack and walked off."

Grandmother looked up in alarm and spoke to grandfather. "Josiah, you don't suppose Krajiek would let them poor creatures eat prairie dogs, do you?"

"You had better go over and see our neighbors to-morrow, Emmaline," he replied gravely.

Fuchs put in a cheerful word and said prairie dogs were clean beasts and ought to be good for food, but their family connections were against them. I asked what he meant, and he grinned and said they belonged to the rat family.

When I went downstairs in the morning, I found grandmother and Jake packing a hamper basket in the kitchen.

"Now, Jake," grandmother was saying, "if you can find that old rooster that got his comb froze, just give his neck a twist, and we'll take him along. There's no good reason why Mrs. Shimerda could n't have got hens from her neighbors last fall and had a henhouse going by now. I reckon she was confused and did n't know where to begin. I've come strange to a new country myself, but I never forgot hens are a good thing to have, no matter what you don't have."

"Just as you say, mam," said Jake, "but I hate to think of Krajiek getting a leg of that old rooster." He tramped out through the long cellar and dropped the heavy door behind him.

After breakfast grandmother and Jake and I bundled ourselves up and climbed into the cold front wagon-seat. As we approached the Shimerdas' we heard the frosty whine of the pump and saw Ánto-nia, her head tied up and her cotton dress blown about her, throw-ing all her weight on the pump-handle as it went up and down. She heard our wagon, looked back over her shoulder, and catching up her pail of water, started at a run for the hole in the bank.

Jake helped grandmother to the ground, saying he would bring the provisions after he had blanketed his horses. We went slowly up the icy path toward the door sunk in the drawside. Blue puffs of smoke came from the stovepipe that stuck out through the grass and snow, but the wind whisked them roughly away.

Mrs. Shimerda opened the door before we knocked and seized grandmother's hand. She did not say "How do!" as usual, but at once began to cry, talking very fast in her own language, pointing to her feet which were tied up in rags, and looking about accusingly at every one.

The old man was sitting on a stump behind the stove, crouching over as if he were trying to hide from us. Yulka was on the floor at his feet, her kitten in her lap. She peeped out at me and smiled, but, glancing up at her mother, hid again. Ántonia was washing pans and dishes in a dark corner. The crazy boy lay under the only window, stretched on a gunnysack stuffed with straw. As soon as we entered he threw a grainsack over the crack at the bottom of the door. The air in the cave was stifling, and it was very dark, too. A lighted lan-tern, hung over the stove, threw out a feeble yellow glimmer.

Mrs. Shimerda snatched off the covers of two barrels behind the door, and made us look into them. In one there were some potatoes that had been frozen and were rotting, in the other was a little pile of flour. Grandmother murmured something in embarrassment, but the Bohemian woman laughed scornfully, a kind of whinny-laugh, and catching up an empty coffee-pot from the shelf, shook it at us with a look positively vindictive.

Grandmother went on talking in her polite Virginia way, not admitting their stark need or her own remissness, until Jake arrived with the hamper, as if in direct answer to Mrs. Shimerda's reproaches. Then the poor woman broke down. She dropped on the floor beside her crazy son, hid her face on her knees, and sat crying bitterly. Grandmother paid no heed to her, but called Ántonia to come and help empty the basket. Tony left her corner reluctantly. I had never seen her crushed like this before.

"You not mind my poor *mamenka*,[8] Mrs. Burden. She is so sad," she whispered, as she wiped her wet hands on her skirt and took the things grandmother handed her.

The crazy boy, seeing the food, began to make soft, gurgling noises and stroked his stomach. Jake came in again, this time with a sack of potatoes. Grandmother looked about in perplexity.

"Have n't you got any sort of cave or cellar outside, Ántonia? This is no place to keep vegetables. How did your potatoes get frozen?"

"We get from Mr. Bushy, at the post-office,—what he throw out. We got no potatoes, Mrs. Burden," Tony admitted mournfully.

When Jake went out, Marek crawled along the floor and stuffed up the door-crack again. Then, quietly as a shadow, Mr. Shimerda came out from behind the stove. He stood brushing his hand over his smooth gray hair, as if he were trying to clear away a fog about his head. He was clean and neat as usual, with his green neckcloth and his coral pin. He took grandmother's arm and led her behind the stove, to the back of the room. In the rear wall was another little cave; a round hole, not much bigger than an oil barrel, scooped out in the black earth. When I got up on one of the stools and peered into it, I saw some quilts and a pile of straw. The old man held the lantern. "Yulka," he said in a low, despairing voice, "Yulka; my Ántonia!"

Grandmother drew back. "You mean they sleep in there,—your girls?" He bowed his head.

Tony slipped under his arm. "It is very cold on the floor and this is warm like the badger hole. I like for sleep there," she insisted eagerly. "My *mamenka* have nice bed, with pillows from our own geese in Bohemie. See, Jim?" She pointed to the narrow bunk which Krajiek had built against the wall for himself before the Shimerdas came.

Grandmother sighed. "Sure enough, where *would* you sleep, dear! I don't doubt you're warm there. You'll have a better house after while, Ántonia, and then you'll forget these hard times."

Mr. Shimerda made grandmother sit down on the only chair and pointed his wife to a stool beside her. Standing before them with his hand on Ántonia's shoulder, he talked in a low tone, and his daughter translated. He wanted us to know that they were not beggars in the old country; he made good wages, and his family were respected there. He left Bohemia with more than a thousand dollars in savings, after their passage money was paid. He had in some

8. Mama.

way lost on exchange in New York, and the railway fare to Nebraska was more than they had expected. By the time they paid Krajiek for the land, and bought his horses and oxen and some old farm machinery, they had very little money left. He wished grandmother to know, however, that he still had some money. If they could get through until spring came, they would buy a cow and chickens and plant a garden, and would then do very well. Ambrosch and Ántonia were both old enough to work in the fields, and they were willing to work. But the snow and the bitter weather had disheartened them all.

Ántonia explained that her father meant to build a new house for them in the spring; he and Ambrosch had already split the logs for it, but the logs were all buried in the snow, along the creek where they had been felled.

While grandmother encouraged and gave them advice, I sat down on the floor with Yulka and let her show me her kitten. Marek slid cautiously toward us and began to exhibit his webbed fingers. I knew he wanted to make his queer noises for me—to bark like a dog or whinny like a horse,—but he did not dare in the presence of his elders. Marek was always trying to be agreeable, poor fellow, as if he had it on his mind that he must make up for his deficiencies.

Mrs. Shimerda grew more calm and reasonable before our visit was over, and, while Ántonia translated, put in a word now and then on her own account. The woman had a quick ear, and caught up phrases whenever she heard English spoken. As we rose to go, she opened her wooden chest and brought out a bag made of bed-ticking, about as long as a flour sack and half as wide, stuffed full of something. At sight of it, the crazy boy began to smack his lips. When Mrs. Shimerda opened the bag and stirred the contents with her hand, it gave out a salty, earthy smell, very pungent, even among the other odors of that cave. She measured a teacup full, tied it up in a bit of sacking, and presented it ceremoniously to grandmother.

"For cook," she announced. "Little now; be very much when cook," spreading out her hands as if to indicate that the pint would swell to a gallon. "Very good. You no have in this country. All things for eat better in my country."

"Maybe so, Mrs. Shimerda," grandmother said drily. "I can't say but I prefer our bread to yours, myself."

Ántonia undertook to explain. "This very good, Mrs. Burden,"— she clasped her hands as if she could not express how good,—"it make very much when you cook, like what my mama say. Cook with rabbit, cook with chicken, in the gravy,—oh, so good!"

All the way home grandmother and Jake talked about how easily good Christian people could forget they were their brothers' keepers.

"I will say, Jake, some of our brothers and sisters are hard to keep. Where's a body to begin, with these people? They're wanting in everything, and most of all in horse-sense. Nobody can give 'em that, I guess. Jimmy, here, is about as able to take over a homestead as they are. Do you reckon that boy Ambrosch has any real push in him?"

"He's a worker, all right, mam, and he's got some ketch-on about him; but he's a mean one. Folks can be mean enough to get on in this world; and then, ag'in, they can be too mean."

That night, while grandmother was getting supper, we opened the package Mrs. Shimerda had given her. It was full of little brown chips that looked like the shavings of some root. They were as light as feathers, and the most noticeable thing about them was their penetrating, earthy odor. We could not determine whether they were animal or vegetable.

"They might be dried meat from some queer beast, Jim. They ain't dried fish, and they never grew on stalk or vine. I'm afraid of 'em. Anyhow, I should n't want to eat anything that had been shut up for months with old clothes and goose pillows."

She threw the package into the stove, but I bit off a corner of one of the chips I held in my hand, and chewed it tentatively. I never forgot the strange taste; though it was many years before I knew that those little brown shavings, which the Shimerdas had brought so far and treasured so jealously, were dried mushrooms. They had been gathered, probably, in some deep Bohemian forest . . . .

XI

During the week before Christmas, Jake was the most important person of our household, for he was to go to town and do all our Christmas shopping. But on the 21st of December, the snow began to fall. The flakes came down so thickly that from the sitting-room windows I could not see beyond the windmill—its frame looked dim and gray, unsubstantial like a shadow. The snow did not stop falling all day, or during the night that followed. The cold was not severe, but the storm was quiet and resistless. The men could not go farther than the barns and corral. They sat about the house most of the day as if it were Sunday; greasing their boots, mending their suspenders, plaiting whiplashes.

On the morning of the 22d, grandfather announced at breakfast that it would be impossible to go to Black Hawk for Christmas purchases. Jake was sure he could get through on horseback, and bring home our things in saddle-bags; but grandfather told him the roads would be obliterated, and a newcomer in the country would be lost ten times over. Anyway, he would never allow one of his horses to be put to such a strain.

We decided to have a country Christmas, without any help from town. I had wanted to get some picture-books for Yulka and Ántonia;

even Yulka was able to read a little now. Grandmother took me into the ice-cold storeroom, where she had some bolts of gingham and sheeting. She cut squares of cotton cloth and we sewed them together into a book. We bound it between pasteboards, which I covered with brilliant calico, representing scenes from a circus. For two days I sat at the dining-room table, pasting this book full of pictures for Yulka. We had files of those good old family magazines which used to publish colored lithographs of popular paintings, and I was allowed to use some of these. I took "Napoleon Announcing the Divorce to Josephine" for my frontispiece.[9] On the white pages I grouped Sunday-School cards and advertising cards which I had brought from my "old country." Fuchs got out the old candle-moulds and made tallow candles. Grandmother hunted up her fancy cake-cutters and baked gingerbread men and roosters, which we decorated with burnt sugar and red cinnamon drops.

On the day before Christmas, Jake packed the things we were sending to the Shimerdas in his saddle-bags and set off on grandfather's gray gelding. When he mounted his horse at the door, I saw that he had a hatchet slung to his belt, and he gave grandmother a meaning look which told me he was planning a surprise for me. That afternoon I watched long and eagerly from the sitting-room window. At last saw a dark spot moving on the west hill, beside the half-buried cornfield, where the sky was taking on a coppery flush from the sun that did not quite break through. I put on my cap and ran out to meet Jake. When I got to the pond I could see that he was bringing in a little cedar tree across his pommel. He used to help my father cut Christmas trees for me in Virginia, and he had not forgotten how much I liked them.

By the time we had placed the cold, fresh-smelling little tree in a corner of the sitting-room, it was already Christmas Eve. After supper we all gathered there, and even grandfather, reading his paper by the table, looked up with friendly interest now and then. The cedar was about five feet high and very shapely. We hung it with the ginger-bread animals, strings of popcorn, and bits of candle which Fuchs had fitted into pasteboard sockets. Its real splendors, however, came from the most unlikely place in the world—from Otto's cowboy trunk. I had never seen anything in that trunk but old boots and spurs and pistols, and a fascinating mixture of yellow leather thongs, cartridges, and shoemaker's wax. From under the lining he now produced a collection of brilliantly colored paper figures, several inches high and stiff enough to stand alone. They had been sent to him year after year, by his old mother in Austria. There was a bleeding heart, in

9. The painting is by Émile-Antoine Bayard (1837–1891), a popular French portrait painter and illustrator.

tufts of paper lace; there were the three kings, gorgeously appareled, and the ox and the ass and the shepherds; there was the Baby in the manger, and a group of angels, singing; there were camels and leopards, held by the black slaves of the three kings. Our tree became the talking tree of the fairy tale; legends and stories nestled like birds in its branches. Grandmother said it reminded her of the Tree of Knowledge. We put sheets of cotton wool under it for a snow-field, and Jake's pocket-mirror for a frozen lake.

I can see them now, exactly as they looked, working about the table in the lamplight: Jake with his heavy features, so rudely moulded that his face seemed, somehow, unfinished, Otto with his half-ear and the savage scar that made his upper lip curl so ferociously under his twisted mustache. As I remember them, what unprotected faces they were; their very roughness and violence made them defenseless. These boys had no practiced manner behind which they could retreat and hold people at a distance. They had only their hard fists to batter at the world with. Otto was already one of those drifting, case-hardened laborers who never marry or have children of their own. Yet he was so fond of children!

XII

On Christmas morning, when I got down to the kitchen, the men were just coming in from their morning chores—the horses and pigs always had their breakfast before we did. Jake and Otto shouted "Merry Christmas"! to me, and winked at each other when they saw the waffle-irons on the stove. Grandfather came down, wearing a white shirt and his Sunday coat. Morning prayers were longer than usual. He read the chapters from St. Matthew about the birth of Christ, and as we listened it all seemed like something that had happened lately, and near at hand. In his prayer he thanked the Lord for the first Christmas, and for all that it had meant to the world ever since. He gave thanks for our food and comfort, and prayed for the poor and destitute in great cities, where the struggle for life was harder than it was here with us. Grandfather's prayers were often very interesting. He had the gift of simple and moving expression. Because he talked so little, his words had a peculiar force; they were not worn dull from constant use. His prayers reflected what he was thinking about at the time, and it was chiefly through them that we got to know his feelings and his views about things.

After we sat down to our waffles and sausage, Jake told us how pleased the Shimerdas had been with their presents; even Ambrosch was friendly and went to the creek with him to cut the Christmas tree. It was a soft gray day outside, with heavy clouds working across the sky, and occasional squalls of snow. There were always odd jobs to be done about the barn on holidays, and the men were busy until afternoon. Then Jake and I played dominoes, while Otto wrote a long letter home to his mother. He always wrote to her on Christmas Day, he said, no matter where he was, and no matter how long it had been since his last letter. All afternoon he sat in the dining-room. He would write for a while, then sit idle, his clenched fist lying on the table, his eyes following the pattern of the oilcloth. He spoke and wrote his own language so seldom that it came to him awkwardly. His effort to remember entirely absorbed him.

At about four o'clock a visitor appeared: Mr. Shimerda, wearing his rabbit-skin cap and collar, and new mittens his wife had knitted. He had come to thank us for the presents, and for all grandmother's kindness to his family. Jake and Otto joined us from the basement and we sat about the stove, enjoying the deepening gray of the winter afternoon and the atmosphere of comfort and security in my grandfather's house. This feeling seemed completely to take possession of Mr. Shimerda. I suppose, in the crowded clutter of their cave, the old man had come to believe that peace and order had vanished from the earth, or existed only in the old world he had left so far behind. He sat still and passive, his head resting against the back of the wooden rocking-chair, his hands relaxed upon the arms. His face had a look of weariness and pleasure, like that of sick people when they feel relief from pain. Grandmother insisted on his drinking a glass of Virginia apple-brandy after his long walk in the cold, and when a faint flush came up in his cheeks, his features might have been cut out of a shell, they were so transparent. He said almost nothing, and smiled rarely; but as he rested there we all had a sense of his utter content.

As it grew dark, I asked whether I might light the Christmas tree before the lamp was brought. When the candle ends sent up their conical yellow flames, all the colored figures from Austria stood out clear and full of meaning against the green boughs. Mr. Shimerda rose, crossed himself, and quietly knelt down before the tree, his head sunk forward. His long body formed a letter "S." I saw grandmother look apprehensively at grandfather. He was rather narrow in religious matters, and sometimes spoke out and hurt people's feelings. There had been nothing strange about the tree before, but now, with some one kneeling before it,—images, candles, . . . Grandfather merely put his finger-tips to his brow and bowed his venerable head, thus Protestantizing the atmosphere.

We persuaded our guest to stay for supper with us. He needed little urging. As we sat down to the table, it occurred to me that he liked to look at us, and that our faces were open books to him. When his deep-seeing eyes rested on me, I felt as if he were looking far ahead into the future for me, down the road I would have to travel.

At nine o'clock Mr. Shimerda lighted one of our lanterns and put on his overcoat and fur collar. He stood in the little entry hall, the lantern and his fur cap under his arm, shaking hands with us. When he took grandmother's hand, he bent over it as he always did, and said slowly, "Good wo-man!" He made the sign of the cross over me, put on his cap and went off in the dark. As we turned back to the sitting-room, grandfather looked at me searchingly. "The prayers of all good people are good," he said quietly.

XIII

The week following Christmas brought in a thaw, and by New Year's Day all the world about us was a broth of gray slush, and the guttered slope between the windmill and the barn was running black water. The soft black earth stood out in patches along the roadsides. I resumed all my chores, carried in the cobs and wood and water, and spent the afternoons at the barn, watching Jake shell corn with a hand-sheller.

One morning, during this interval of fine weather, Ántonia and her mother rode over on one of their shaggy old horses to pay us a visit. It was the first time Mrs. Shimerda had been to our house, and she ran about examining our carpets and curtains and furniture, all the while commenting upon them to her daughter in an envious, complaining tone. In the kitchen she caught up an iron pot that stood on the back of the stove and said: "You got many, Shimerdas no got." I thought it weak-minded of grandmother to give the pot to her.

After dinner, when she was helping to wash the dishes, she said, tossing her head: "You got many things for cook. If I got all things like you, I make much better."

She was a conceited, boastful old thing, and even misfortune could not humble her. I was so annoyed that I felt coldly even toward Ántonia and listened unsympathetically when she told me her father was not well.

"My papa sad for the old country. He not look good. He never make music any more. At home he play violin all the time; for weddings and for dance. Here never. When I beg him for play, he shake his head no. Some days he take his violin out of his box and make with his fingers on the strings, like this, but never he make the music. He don't like this kawn-tree."

"People who don't like this country ought to stay at home," I said severely. "We don't make them come here."

"He not want to come, nev-er!" she burst out. "My *mamenka* make him come. All the time she say: 'America big country; much money, much land for my boys, much husband for my girls.' My papa, he cry for leave his old friends what make music with him. He love very much the man what play the long horn like this"—she indicated a slide trombone. "They go to school together and are friends from boys. But my mama, she want Ambrosch for be rich, with many cattle."

"Your mama," I said angrily, "wants other people's things."

"Your grandfather is rich," she retorted fiercely. "Why he not help my papa? Ambrosch be rich, too, after while, and he pay back. He is very smart boy. For Ambrosch my mama come here."

Ambrosch was considered the important person in the family. Mrs. Shimerda and Ántonia always deferred to him, though he was often surly with them and contemptuous toward his father. Ambrosch and his mother had everything their own way. Though Ántonia loved her father more than she did any one else, she stood in awe of her elder brother.

After I watched Ántonia and her mother go over the hill on their miserable horse, carrying our iron pot with them, I turned to grandmother, who had taken up her darning, and said I hoped that snooping old woman would n't come to see us any more.

Grandmother chuckled and drove her bright needle across a hole in Otto's sock. "She's not old, Jim, though I expect she seems old to you. No, I would n't mourn if she never came again. But, you see, a body never knows what traits poverty might bring out in 'em. It makes a woman grasping to see her children want for things. Now read me a chapter in 'The Prince of the House of David.'[1] Let's forget the Bohemians."

We had three weeks of this mild, open weather. The cattle in the corral ate corn almost as fast as the men could shell it for them, and we hoped they would be ready for an early market. One morning the two big bulls, Gladstone and Brigham Young, thought spring had come, and they began to tease and butt at each other across the barbed wire that separated them. Soon they got angry. They bellowed and pawed up the soft earth with their hoofs, rolling their eyes and tossing their heads. Each withdrew to a far corner of his own corral, and then they made for each other at a gallop. Thud, thud, we could hear the impact of their great heads, and their bellowing shook the pans on the kitchen shelves. Had they not been dehorned, they would have torn each other to pieces. Pretty soon the fat steers took it up and began butting and horning each other. Clearly, the affair had to be stopped. We all stood by and watched admiringly while Fuchs rode into the corral with a pitchfork and prodded the bulls again and again, finally driving them apart.

The big storm of the winter began on my eleventh birthday, the 20th of January. When I went down to breakfast that morning, Jake and Otto came in white as snow-men, beating their hands and

---

1. Biblical romance (1855) by American clergyman and novelist Joseph Holt Ingraham.

stamping their feet. They began to laugh boisterously when they saw me, calling:—

"You've got a birthday present this time, Jim, and no mistake. They was a full-grown blizzard ordered for you."

All day the storm went on. The snow did not fall this time, it simply spilled out of heaven, like thousands of feather-beds being emptied. That afternoon the kitchen was a carpenter-shop; the men brought in their tools and made two great wooden shovels with long handles. Neither grandmother nor I could go out in the storm, so Jake fed the chickens and brought in a pitiful contribution of eggs.

Next day our men had to shovel until noon to reach the barn—and the snow was still falling! There had not been such a storm in the ten years my grandfather had lived in Nebraska. He said at dinner that we would not try to reach the cattle—they were fat enough to go without their corn for a day or two; but to-morrow we must feed them and thaw out their water-tap so that they could drink. We could not so much as see the corrals, but we knew the steers were over there, huddled together under the north bank. Our ferocious bulls, subdued enough by this time, were probably warming each other's backs. "This'll take the bile out of 'em!" Fuchs remarked gleefully.

At noon that day the hens had not been heard from. After dinner Jake and Otto, their damp clothes now dried on them, stretched their stiff arms and plunged again into the drifts. They made a tunnel under the snow to the henhouse, with walls so solid that grandmother and I could walk back and forth in it. We found the chickens asleep; perhaps they thought night had come to stay. One old rooster was stirring about, pecking at the solid lump of ice in their water-tin. When we flashed the lantern in their eyes, the hens set up a great cackling and flew about clumsily, scattering down-feathers. The mottled, pin-headed guinea-hens, always resentful of captivity, ran screeching out into the tunnel and tried to poke their ugly, painted faces through the snow walls. By five o'clock the chores were done—just when it was time to begin them all over again! That was a strange, unnatural sort of day.

XIV

On the morning of the 22d I wakened with a start. Before I opened my eyes, I seemed to know that something had happened. I heard excited voices in the kitchen—grandmother's was so shrill that I knew she must be almost beside herself. I looked forward to any new crisis with delight. What could it be, I wondered, as I hurried into my clothes. Perhaps the barn had burned; perhaps the cattle had frozen to death; perhaps a neighbor was lost in the storm.

Down in the kitchen grandfather was standing before the stove with his hands behind him. Jake and Otto had taken off their boots and were rubbing their woolen socks. Their clothes and boots were steaming, and they both looked exhausted. On the bench behind the stove lay a man, covered up with a blanket. Grandmother motioned me to the dining-room. I obeyed reluctantly. I watched her as she came and went, carrying dishes. Her lips were tightly compressed and she kept whispering to herself: "Oh, dear Saviour!" "Lord, Thou knowest!"

Presently grandfather came in and spoke to me: "Jimmy, we will not have prayers this morning, because we have a great deal to do. Old Mr. Shimerda is dead, and his family are in great distress. Ambrosch came over here in the middle of the night, and Jake and Otto went back with him. The boys have had a hard night, and you must not bother them with questions. That is Ambrosch, asleep on the bench. Come in to breakfast, boys."

After Jake and Otto had swallowed their first cup of coffee, they began to talk excitedly, disregarding grandmother's warning glances. I held my tongue, but I listened with all my ears.

"No, sir," Fuchs said in answer to a question from grandfather, "nobody heard the gun go off. Ambrosch was out with the ox team, trying to break a road, and the women folks was shut up tight in their cave. When Ambrosch come in it was dark and he did n't see nothing, but the oxen acted kind of queer. One of 'em ripped around and got away from him—bolted clean out of the stable. His hands is blistered where the rope run through. He got a lantern and went back and found the old man, just as we seen him."

"Poor soul, poor soul!" grandmother groaned. "I'd like to think he never done it. He was always considerate and unwishful to give trouble. How could he forget himself and bring this on us!"

"I don't think he was out of his head for a minute, Mrs. Burden," Fuchs declared. "He done everything natural. You know he was always sort of fixy, and fixy he was to the last. He shaved after dinner, and washed hisself all over after the girls was done the dishes. Ántonia heated the water for him. Then he put on a clean shirt and clean socks, and after he was dressed he kissed her and the little one and took his gun and said he was going out to hunt rabbits. He must have gone right down to the barn and done it then. He layed down on that bunk-bed, close to the ox stalls, where he always slept. When we found him, everything was decent except,"—Fuchs wrinkled his brow and hesitated,—"except what he could n't nowise foresee. His coat was hung on a peg, and his boots was under the bed. He'd took off that silk neckcloth he always wore, and folded it smooth and stuck his pin through it. He turned back his shirt at the neck and rolled up his sleeves."

"I don't see how he could do it!" grandmother kept saying.

Otto misunderstood her. "Why, mam, it was simple enough; he pulled the trigger with his big toe. He layed over on his side and put the end of the barrel in his mouth, then he drew up one foot and felt for the trigger. He found it all right!"

"Maybe he did," said Jake grimly. "There's something mighty queer about it."

"Now what do you mean, Jake?" grandmother asked sharply.

"Well, mam, I found Krajiek's axe under the manger, and I picks it up and carries it over to the corpse, and I take my oath it just fit the gash in the front of the old man's face. That there Krajiek had been sneakin' round, pale and quiet, and when he seen me examinin' the axe, he begun whimperin', 'My God, man, don't do that!' 'I reckon I'm a-goin' to look into this,' says I. Then he begun to squeal like a rat and run about wringin' his hands. 'They'll hang me!' says he. 'My God, they'll hang me sure!'"

Fuchs spoke up impatiently. "Krajiek's gone silly, Jake, and so have you. The old man would n't have made all them preparations for Krajiek to murder him, would he? It don't hang together. The gun was right beside him when Ambrosch found him."

"Krajiek could 'a' put it there, could n't he?" Jake demanded.

Grandmother broke in excitedly: "See here, Jake Marpole, don't you go trying to add murder to suicide. We're deep enough in trouble. Otto reads you too many of them detective stories."

"It will be easy to decide all that, Emmaline," said grandfather quietly. "If he shot himself in the way they think, the gash will be torn from the inside outward."

"Just so it is, Mr. Burden," Otto affirmed. "I seen bunches of hair and stuff sticking to the poles and straw along the roof. They was blown up there by gunshot, no question."

Grandmother told grandfather she meant to go over to the Shimerdas with him.

"There is nothing you can do," he said doubtfully. "The body can't be touched until we get the coroner here from Black Hawk, and that will be a matter of several days, this weather."

"Well, I can take them some victuals, anyway, and say a word of comfort to them poor little girls. The oldest one was his darling, and was like a right hand to him. He might have thought of her. He's left her alone in a hard world." She glanced distrustfully at Ambrosch, who was now eating his breakfast at the kitchen table.

Fuchs, although he had been up in the cold nearly all night, was going to make the long ride to Black Hawk to fetch the priest and the coroner. On the gray gelding, our best horse, he would try to pick his way across the country with no roads to guide him.

"Don't you worry about me, Mrs. Burden," he said cheerfully, as he put on a second pair of socks. "I've got a good nose for directions, and I never did need much sleep. It's the gray I'm worried about. I'll save him what I can, but it'll strain him, as sure as I'm telling you!"

"This is no time to be over-considerate of animals, Otto; do the best you can for yourself. Stop at the Widow Steavens's for dinner. She's a good woman, and she'll do well by you."

After Fuchs rode away, I was left with Ambrosch. I saw a side of him I had not seen before. He was deeply, even slavishly, devout. He did not say a word all morning, but sat with his rosary in his hands, praying, now silently, now aloud. He never looked away from his beads, nor lifted his hands except to cross himself. Several times the poor boy fell asleep where he sat, wakened with a start, and began to pray again.

No wagon could be got to the Shimerdas' until a road was broken, and that would be a day's job. Grandfather came from the barn on one of our big black horses, and Jake lifted grandmother up behind him. She wore her black hood and was bundled up in shawls. Grandfather tucked his bushy white beard inside his overcoat. They looked very Biblical as they set off, I thought. Jake and Ambrosch followed them, riding the other black and my pony, carrying bundles of clothes that we had got together for Mrs. Shimerda. I watched them go past the pond and over the hill by the drifted cornfield. Then, for the first time, I realized that I was alone in the house.

I felt a considerable extension of power and authority, and was anxious to acquit myself creditably. I carried in cobs and wood from the long cellar, and filled both the stoves. I remembered that in the hurry and excitement of the morning nobody had thought of the chickens, and the eggs had not been gathered. Going out through the tunnel, I gave the hens their corn, emptied the ice from their drinking-pan, and filled it with water. After the cat had had his milk, I could think of nothing else to do, and I sat down to get warm. The quiet was delightful, and the ticking clock was the most pleasant of companions. I got "Robinson Crusoe" and tried to read, but his life on the island seemed dull compared with ours. Presently, as I looked with satisfaction about our comfortable sitting-room, it flashed upon me that if Mr. Shimerda's soul were lingering about in this world at all, it would be here, in our house, which had been more to his liking than any other in the neighborhood. I remembered his contented face when he was with us on Christmas Day. If he could have lived with us, this terrible thing would never have happened.

I knew it was homesickness that had killed Mr. Shimerda, and I wondered whether his released spirit would not eventually find its way back to his own country. I thought of how far it was to Chicago, and then to Virginia, to Baltimore,—and then the great wintry ocean.

No, he would not at once set out upon that long journey. Surely, his exhausted spirit, so tired of cold and crowding and the struggle with the ever-falling snow, was resting now in this quiet house.

I was not frightened, but I made no noise. I did not wish to disturb him. I went softly down to the kitchen which, tucked away so snugly underground, always seemed to me the heart and center of the house. There, on the bench behind the stove, I thought and thought about Mr. Shimerda. Outside I could hear the wind singing over hundreds of miles of snow. It was as if I had let the old man in out of the tormenting winter, and were sitting there with him. I went over all that Ántonia had ever told me about his life before he came to this country; how he used to play the fiddle at weddings and dances. I thought about the friends he had mourned to leave, the trombone-player, the great forest full of game,—belonging, as Ántonia said, to the "nobles,"—from which she and her mother used to steal wood on moonlight nights. There was a white hart that lived in that forest, and if any one killed it, he would be hanged, she said. Such vivid pictures came to me that they might have been Mr. Shimerda's memories, not yet faded out from the air in which they had haunted him.

It had begun to grow dark when my household returned, and grandmother was so tired that she went at once to bed. Jake and I got supper, and while we were washing the dishes he told me in loud whispers about the state of things over at the Shimerdas'. Nobody could touch the body until the coroner came. If any one did, something terrible would happen, apparently. The dead man was frozen through, "just as stiff as a dressed turkey you hang out to freeze," Jake said. The horses and oxen would not go into the barn until he was frozen so hard that there was no longer any smell of blood. They were stabled there now, with the dead man, because there was no other place to keep them. A lighted lantern was kept hanging over Mr. Shimerda's head. Ántonia and Ambrosch and the mother took turns going down to pray beside him. The crazy boy went with them, because he did not feel the cold. I believed he felt cold as much as any one else, but he liked to be thought insensible to it. He was always coveting distinction, poor Marek!

Ambrosch, Jake said, showed more human feeling than he would have supposed him capable of; but he was chiefly concerned about getting a priest, and about his father's soul, which he believed was in a place of torment and would remain there until his family and the priest had prayed a great deal for him. "As I understand it," Jake concluded, "it will be a matter of years to pray his soul out of Purgatory, and right now he's in torment."

"I don't believe it," I said stoutly. "I almost know it is n't true." I did not, of course, say that I believed he had been in that very kitchen all afternoon, on his way back to his own country. Nevertheless, after I went to bed, this idea of punishment and Purgatory came back on me crushingly. I remembered the account of Dives in torment, and shuddered.[2] But Mr. Shimerda had not been rich and selfish; he had only been so unhappy that he could not live any longer.

XV

Otto Fuchs got back from Black Hawk at noon the next day. He reported that the coroner would reach the Shimerdas' sometime that afternoon, but the missionary priest was at the other end of his parish, a hundred miles away, and the trains were not running. Fuchs had got a few hours' sleep at the livery barn in town, but he was afraid the gray gelding had strained himself. Indeed, he was never the same horse afterward. That long trip through the deep snow had taken all the endurance out of him.

Fuchs brought home with him a stranger, a young Bohemian who had taken a homestead near Black Hawk, and who came on his only horse to help his fellow-countrymen in their trouble. That was the first time I ever saw Anton Jelinek. He was a strapping young fellow in the early twenties then, handsome, warm-hearted, and full of life, and he came to us like a miracle in the midst of that grim business. I remember exactly how he strode into our kitchen in his felt boots and long wolfskin coat, his eyes and cheeks bright with the cold. At sight of grandmother, he snatched off his fur cap, greeting her in a deep, rolling voice which seemed older than he.

"I want to thank you very much, Mrs. Burden, for that you are so kind to poor strangers from my kawn-tree."

He did not hesitate like a farmer boy, but looked one eagerly in the eye when he spoke. Everything about him was warm and spontaneous. He said he would have come to see the Shimerdas before, but he had hired out to husk corn all the fall, and since winter began he had been going to the school by the mill, to learn English, along with the little children. He told me he had a nice "lady-teacher" and that he liked to go to school.

At dinner grandfather talked to Jelinek more than he usually did to strangers.

"Will they be much disappointed because we cannot get a priest?" he asked.

Jelinek looked serious. "Yes, sir, that is very bad for them. Their father has done a great sin," he looked straight at grandfather. "Our Lord has said that."

Grandfather seemed to like his frankness. "We believe that, too, Jelinek. But we believe that Mr. Shimerda's soul will come to its

2. Dives is the haughty rich man who suffers in hell in Jesus' parable (Luke 16.19–31).

Creator as well off without a priest. We believe that Christ is our only intercessor."

The young man shook his head. "I know how you think. My teacher at the school has explain. But I have seen too much. I believe in prayer for the dead. I have seen too much."

We asked him what he meant.

He glanced around the table. "You want I shall tell you? When I was a little boy like this one, I begin to help the priest at the altar. I make my first communion very young; what the Church teach seem plain to me. By 'n' by war-times come, when the Austrians fight us. We have very many soldiers in camp near my village, and the cholera break out in that camp, and the men die like flies. All day long our priest go about there to give the Sacrament to dying men, and I go with him to carry the vessels with the Holy Sacrament. Everybody that go near that camp catch the sickness but me and the priest. But we have no sickness, we have no fear, because we carry that blood and that body of Christ, and it preserve us." He paused, looking at grandfather. "That I know, Mr. Burden, for it happened to myself. All the soldiers know, too. When we walk along the road, the old priest and me, we meet all the time soldiers marching and officers on horse. All those officers, when they see what I carry under the cloth, pull up their horses and kneel down on the ground in the road until we pass. So I feel very bad for my kawntree-man to die without the Sacrament, and to die in a bad way for his soul, and I feel sad for his family."

We had listened attentively. It was impossible not to admire his frank, manly faith.

"I am always glad to meet a young man who thinks seriously about these things," said grandfather, "and I would never be the one to say you were not in God's care when you were among the soldiers."

After dinner it was decided that young Jelinek should hook our two strong black farmhorses to the scraper and break a road through to the Shimerdas', so that a wagon could go when it was necessary. Fuchs, who was the only cabinet-maker in the neighborhood, was set to work on a coffin.

Jelinek put on his long wolfskin coat, and when we admired it, he told us that he had shot and skinned the coyotes, and the young man who "batched" with him, Jan Bouska, who had been a fur-worker in Vienna, made the coat. From the windmill I watched Jelinek come out of the barn with the blacks, and work his way up the hillside toward the cornfield. Sometimes he was completely hidden by the clouds of snow that rose about him; then he and the horses would emerge black and shining.

Our heavy carpenter's bench had to be brought from the barn and carried down into the kitchen. Fuchs selected boards from a pile of

planks grandfather had hauled out from town in the fall to make a
new floor for the oats bin. When at last the lumber and tools were
assembled, and the doors were closed again and the cold drafts shut
out, grandfather rode away to meet the coroner at the Shimerdas',
and Fuchs took off his coat and settled down to work. I sat on his
work-table and watched him. He did not touch his tools at first, but
figured for a long while on a piece of paper, and measured the planks
and made marks on them. While he was thus engaged, he whistled
softly to himself, or teasingly pulled at his half-ear. Grandmother
moved about quietly, so as not to disturb him. At last he folded his
ruler and turned a cheerful face to us.

"The hardest part of my job's done," he announced. "It's the head
end of it that comes hard with me, especially when I'm out of practice. The last time I made one of these, Mrs. Burden," he continued, as he sorted and tried his chisels, "was for a fellow in the Black
Tiger mine, up above Silverton, Colorado. The mouth of that mine
goes right into the face of the cliff, and they used to put us in a bucket
and run us over on a trolley and shoot us into the shaft. The bucket
traveled across a box cañon three hundred feet deep, and about a
third full of water. Two Swedes had fell out of that bucket once, and
hit the water, feet down. If you'll believe it, they went to work the
next day. You can't kill a Swede. But in my time a little Eyetalian
tried the high dive, and it turned out different with him. We was
snowed in then, like we are now, and I happened to be the only man
in camp that could make a coffin for him. It's a handy thing to know,
when you knock about like I've done."

"We'd be hard put to it now, if you did n't know, Otto," grandmother
said.

"Yes, 'm," Fuchs admitted with modest pride. "So few folks does
know how to make a good tight box that'll turn water. I sometimes
wonder if there'll be anybody about to do it for me. However, I'm
not at all particular that way."

All afternoon, wherever one went in the house, one could hear the
panting wheeze of the saw or the pleasant purring of the plane. They
were such cheerful noises, seeming to promise new things for living
people: it was a pity that those freshly planed pine boards were to be
put underground so soon. The lumber was hard to work because it
was full of frost, and the boards gave off a sweet smell of pine woods,
as the heap of yellow shavings grew higher and higher. I wondered
why Fuchs had not stuck to cabinet-work, he settled down to it with
such ease and content. He handled the tools as if he liked the feel
of them; and when he planed, his hands went back and forth over
the boards in an eager, beneficent way as if he were blessing them.
He broke out now and then into German hymns, as if this occupation brought back old times to him.

At four o'clock Mr. Bushy, the postmaster, with another neighbor who lived east of us, stopped in to get warm. They were on their way to the Shimerdas'. The news of what had happened over there had somehow got abroad through the snow-blocked country. Grandmother gave the visitors sugar-cakes and hot coffee. Before these callers were gone, the brother of the Widow Steavens, who lived on the Black Hawk road, drew up at our door, and after him came the father of the German family, our nearest neighbors on the south. They dismounted and joined us in the dining-room. They were all eager for any details about the suicide, and they were greatly concerned as to where Mr. Shimerda would be buried. The nearest Catholic cemetery was at Black Hawk, and it might be weeks before a wagon could get so far. Besides, Mr. Bushy and grandmother were sure that a man who had killed himself could not be buried in a Catholic graveyard. There was a burying-ground over by the Norwegian church, west of Squaw Creek; perhaps the Norwegians would take Mr. Shimerda in.

After our visitors rode away in single file over the hill, we returned to the kitchen. Grandmother began to make the icing for a chocolate cake, and Otto again filled the house with the exciting, expectant song of the plane. One pleasant thing about this time was that everybody talked more than usual. I had never heard the postmaster say anything but "Only papers, to-day," or, "I've got a sackful of mail for ye," until this afternoon. Grandmother always talked, dear woman; to herself or to the Lord, if there was no one else to listen; but grandfather was naturally taciturn, and Jake and Otto were often so tired after supper that I used to feel as if I were surrounded by a wall of silence. Now every one seemed eager to talk. That afternoon Fuchs told me story after story; about the Black Tiger mine, and about violent deaths and casual buryings, and the queer fancies of dying men. You never really knew a man, he said, until you saw him die. Most men were game, and went without a grudge.

The postmaster, going home, stopped to say that grandfather would bring the coroner back with him to spend the night. The officers of the Norwegian church, he told us, had held a meeting and decided that the Norwegian graveyard could not extend its hospitality to Mr. Shimerda.

Grandmother was indignant. "If these foreigners are so clannish, Mr. Bushy, we'll have to have an American graveyard that will be more liberal-minded. I'll get right after Josiah to start one in the spring. If anything was to happen to me, I don't want the Norwegians holding inquisitions over me to see whether I'm good enough to be laid amongst 'em."

Soon grandfather returned, bringing with him Anton Jelinek, and that important person, the coroner. He was a mild, flurried old man, a Civil War veteran, with one sleeve hanging empty. He seemed to

find this case very perplexing, and said if it had not been for grandfather he would have sworn out a warrant against Krajiek. "The way
he acted, and the way his axe fit the wound, was enough to convict
any man."

Although it was perfectly clear that Mr. Shimerda had killed himself, Jake and the coroner thought something ought to be done to
Krajiek because he behaved like a guilty man. He was badly frightened, certainly, and perhaps he even felt some stirrings of remorse
for his indifference to the old man's misery and loneliness.

At supper the men ate like vikings, and the chocolate cake, which
I had hoped would linger on until to-morrow in a mutilated condition, disappeared on the second round. They talked excitedly about
where they should bury Mr. Shimerda; I gathered that the neighbors were all disturbed and shocked about something. It developed
that Mrs. Shimerda and Ambrosch wanted the old man buried
on the southwest corner of their own land; indeed, under the very
stake that marked the corner. Grandfather had explained to Ambrosch
that some day, when the country was put under fence and the roads
were confined to section lines, two roads would cross exactly on that
corner. But Ambrosch only said, "It makes no matter."

Grandfather asked Jelinek whether in the old country there was
some superstition to the effect that a suicide must be buried at the
cross-roads.[3]

Jelinek said he did n't know; he seemed to remember hearing there
had once been such a custom in Bohemia. "Mrs. Shimerda is made
up her mind," he added. "I try to persuade her, and say it looks bad
for her to all the neighbors; but she say so it must be. 'There I will
bury him, if I dig the grave myself,' she say. I have to promise her I
help Ambrosch make the grave to-morrow."

Grandfather smoothed his beard and looked judicial. "I don't know
whose wish should decide the matter, if not hers. But if she thinks
she will live to see the people of this country ride over that old man's
head, she is mistaken."

XVI

Mr. Shimerda lay dead in the barn four days, and on the fifth they
buried him. All day Friday Jelinek was off with Ambrosch digging
the grave, chopping out the frozen earth with old axes. On Saturday we breakfasted before daylight and got into the wagon with the
coffin. Jake and Jelinek went ahead on horseback to cut the body
loose from the pool of blood in which it was frozen fast to the ground.

3. In the Middle Ages, crossroads were associated with witches and diabolism, and it
became customary to bury criminals and suicides in this unhallowed ground.

When grandmother and I went into the Shimerdas' house, we found the women-folk alone; Ambrosch and Marek were at the barn. Mrs. Shimerda sat crouching by the stove, Ántonia was washing dishes. When she saw me she ran out of her dark corner and threw her arms around me. "Oh, Jimmy," she sobbed, "what you tink for my lovely papa!" It seemed to me that I could feel her heart breaking as she clung to me.

Mrs. Shimerda, sitting on the stump by the stove, kept looking over her shoulder toward the door while the neighbors were arriving. They came on horseback, all except the post-master, who brought his family in a wagon over the only broken wagon-trail. The Widow Steavens rode up from her farm eight miles down the Black Hawk road. The cold drove the women into the cave-house, and it was soon crowded. A fine, sleety snow was beginning to fall, and every one was afraid of another storm and anxious to have the burial over with.

Grandfather and Jelinek came to tell Mrs. Shimerda that it was time to start. After bundling her mother up in clothes the neighbors had brought, Ántonia put on an old cape from our house and the rabbit-skin hat her father had made for her. Four men carried Mr. Shimerda's box up the hill; Krajiek slunk along behind them. The coffin was too wide for the door, so it was put down on the slope outside. I slipped out from the cave and looked at Mr. Shimerda. He was lying on his side, with his knees drawn up. His body was draped in a black shawl, and his head was bandaged in white muslin, like a mummy's; one of his long, shapely hands lay out on the black cloth; that was all one could see of him.

Mrs. Shimerda came out and placed an open prayer-book against the body, making the sign of the cross on the bandaged head with her fingers. Ambrosch knelt down and made the same gesture, and after him Ántonia and Marek. Yulka hung back. Her mother pushed her forward, and kept saying something to her over and over. Yulka knelt down, shut her eyes, and put out her hand a little way, but she drew it back and began to cry wildly. She was afraid to touch the bandage. Mrs. Shimerda caught her by the shoulders and pushed her toward the coffin, but grandmother interfered.

"No, Mrs. Shimerda," she said firmly, "I won't stand by and see that child frightened into spasms. She is too little to understand what you want of her. Let her alone."

At a look from grandfather, Fuchs and Jelinek placed the lid on the box, and began to nail it down over Mr. Shimerda. I was afraid to look at Ántonia. She put her arms round Yulka and held the little girl close to her.

The coffin was put into the wagon. We drove slowly away, against the fine, icy snow which cut our faces like a sand-blast. When we reached the grave, it looked a very little spot in that snow-covered

waste. The men took the coffin to the edge of the hole and lowered
it with ropes. We stood about watching them, and the powdery snow
lay without melting on the caps and shoulders of the men and the
shawls of the women. Jelinek spoke in a persuasive tone to Mrs. Shimerda, and then turned to grandfather.

"She says, Mr. Burden, she is very glad if you can make some prayer
for him here in English, for the neighbors to understand."

Grandmother looked anxiously at grandfather. He took off his hat,
and the other men did likewise. I thought his prayer remarkable. I
still remember it. He began, "Oh, great and just God, no man among
us knows what the sleeper knows, nor is it for us to judge what lies
between him and Thee." He prayed that if any man there had been
remiss toward the stranger come to a far country, God would forgive him and soften his heart. He recalled the promises to the widow
and the fatherless, and asked God to smooth the way before this
widow and her children, and to "incline the hearts of men to deal
justly with her." In closing, he said we were leaving Mr. Shimerda at
"Thy judgment seat, which is also Thy mercy seat."

All the time he was praying, grandmother watched him through
the black fingers of her glove, and when he said "Amen," I thought
she looked satisfied with him. She turned to Otto and whispered,
"Can't you start a hymn, Fuchs? It would seem less heathenish."

Fuchs glanced about to see if there was general approval of her
suggestion, then began, "Jesus, Lover of my Soul,"[4] and all the men
and women took it up after him. Whenever I have heard the hymn
since, it has made me remember that white waste and the little group
of people; and the bluish air, full of fine, eddying snow, like long veils
flying:—

> "While the nearer waters roll,
> While the tempest still is high."

                    .   .   .

Years afterward, when the open-grazing days were over, and the
red grass had been ploughed under and under until it had almost
disappeared from the prairie; when all the fields were under fence,
and the roads no longer ran about like wild things, but followed the
surveyed section-lines, Mr. Shimerda's grave was still there, with a
sagging wire fence around it, and an unpainted wooden cross. As
grandfather had predicted, Mr. Shimerda never saw the roads going
over his head. The road from the north curved a little to the east
just there, and the road from the west swung out a little to the south;
so that the grave, with its tall red grass that was never mowed, was

---

4. A popular hymn written by the English clergyman Charles Wesley (1707–1788) in
1740; it was set to music by the Welsh composer Joseph Parry in 1879.

like a little island; and at twilight, under a new moon or the clear evening star, the dusty roads used to look like soft gray rivers flowing past it. I never came upon the place without emotion, and in all that country it was the spot most dear to me. I loved the dim superstition, the propitiatory intent, that had put the grave there; and still more I loved the spirit that could not carry out the sentence—the error from the surveyed lines, the clemency of the soft earth roads along which the home-coming wagons rattled after sunset. Never a tired driver passed the wooden cross, I am sure, without wishing well to the sleeper.

XVII

When spring came, after that hard winter, one could not get enough of the nimble air. Every morning I wakened with a fresh consciousness that winter was over. There were none of the signs of spring for which I used to watch in Virginia, no budding woods or blooming gardens. There was only—spring itself; the throb of it, the light restlessness, the vital essence of it everywhere; in the sky, in the swift clouds, in the pale sunshine, and in the warm, high wind—rising suddenly, sinking suddenly, impulsive and playful like a big puppy that pawed you and then lay down to be petted. If I had been tossed down blindfold on that red prairie, I should have known that it was spring.

Everywhere now there was the smell of burning grass. Our neighbors burned off their pasture before the new grass made a start, so that the fresh growth would not be mixed with the dead stand of last year. Those light, swift fires, running about the country, seemed a part of the same kindling that was in the air.

The Shimerdas were in their new log house by then. The neighbors had helped them to build it in March. It stood directly in front of their old cave, which they used as a cellar. The family were now fairly equipped to begin their struggle with the soil. They had four comfortable rooms to live in, a new windmill,—bought on credit,—a chicken-house and poultry. Mrs. Shimerda had paid grandfather ten dollars for a milk cow, and was to give him fifteen more as soon as they harvested their first crop.

When I rode up to the Shimerdas' one bright windy afternoon in April, Yulka ran out to meet me. It was to her, now, that I gave reading lessons; Ántonia was busy with other things. I tied my pony and went into the kitchen where Mrs. Shimerda was baking bread, chewing poppy seeds as she worked. By this time she could speak enough English to ask me a great many questions about what our men were doing in the fields. She seemed to think that my elders withheld helpful information, and that from me she might get valuable secrets. On this occasion she asked me very craftily when grandfather expected to begin planting corn. I told her, adding that he thought we should have a dry spring and that the corn would not be held back by too much rain, as it had been last year.

She gave me a shrewd glance. "He not Jesus," she blustered; "he not know about the wet and the dry."

I did not answer her; what was the use? As I sat waiting for the hour when Ambrosch and Ántonia would return from the fields, I watched Mrs. Shimerda at her work. She took from the oven a coffee-cake which she wanted to keep warm for supper, and wrapped it in a quilt stuffed with feathers. I have seen her put even a roast goose in this quilt to keep it hot. When the neighbors were there building the new house they saw her do this, and the story got abroad that the Shimerdas kept their food in their feather beds.

When the sun was dropping low, Ántonia came up the big south draw with her team. How much older she had grown in eight months! She had come to us a child, and now she was a tall, strong young girl, although her fifteenth birthday had just slipped by. I ran out and met her as she brought her horses up to the windmill to water them. She wore the boots her father had so thoughtfully taken off before he shot himself, and his old fur cap. Her outgrown cotton dress switched about her calves, over the boot-tops. She kept her sleeves rolled up all day, and her arms and throat were burned as brown as a sailor's. Her neck came up strongly out of her shoulders, like the bole of a tree out of the turf. One sees that draft-horse neck among the peasant women in all old countries.

She greeted me gayly, and began at once to tell me how much ploughing she had done that day. Ambrosch, she said, was on the north quarter, breaking sod with the oxen.

"Jim, you ask Jake how much he ploughed to-day. I don't want that Jake get more done in one day than me. I want we have very much corn this fall."

While the horses drew in the water, and nosed each other, and then drank again, Ántonia sat down on the windmill step and rested her head on her hand. "You see the big prairie fire from your place last night? I hope your grandpa ain't lose no stacks?"

"No, we did n't. I came to ask you something, Tony. Grandmother wants to know if you can't go to the term of school that begins next week over at the sod schoolhouse. She says there's a good teacher, and you'd learn a lot."

Ántonia stood up, lifting and dropping her shoulders as if they were stiff. "I ain't got time to learn. I can work like mans now. My mother can't say no more how Ambrosch do all and nobody to help him. I can work as much as him. School is all right for little boys. I help make this land one good farm."

She clucked to her team and started for the barn. I walked beside her, feeling vexed. Was she going to grow up boastful like her mother, I wondered? Before we reached the stable, I felt something tense in her silence, and glancing up I saw that she was crying. She turned her face from me and looked off at the red streak of dying light, over the dark prairie.

I climbed up into the loft and threw down the hay for her, while she unharnessed her team. We walked slowly back toward the house. Ambrosch had come in from the north quarter, and was watering his oxen at the tank.

Ántonia took my hand. "Sometime you will tell me all those nice things you learn at the school, won't you, Jimmy?" she asked with a sudden rush of feeling in her voice. "My father, he went much to school. He know a great deal; how to make the fine cloth like what you not got here. He play horn and violin, and he read so many books that the priests in Bohemie come to talk to him. You won't forget my father, Jim?"

"No," I said, "I will never forget him."

Mrs. Shimerda asked me to stay for supper. After Ambrosch and Ántonia had washed the field dust from their hands and faces at the wash-basin by the kitchen door, we sat down at the oilcloth-covered table. Mrs. Shimerda ladled meal mush out of an iron pot and poured milk on it. After the mush we had fresh bread and sorghum molasses, and coffee with the cake that had been kept warm in the feathers. Ántonia and Ambrosch were talking in Bohemian; disputing about which of them had done more ploughing that day. Mrs. Shimerda egged them on, chuckling while she gobbled her food.

Presently Ambrosch said sullenly in English: "You take them ox to-morrow and try the sod plough. Then you not be so smart."

His sister laughed. "Don't be mad. I know it's awful hard work for break sod. I milk the cow for you to-morrow, if you want."

Mrs. Shimerda turned quickly to me. "That cow not give so much milk like what your grandpa say. If he make talk about fifteen dollars, I send him back the cow."

"He does n't talk about the fifteen dollars," I exclaimed indignantly. "He does n't find fault with people."

"He say I break his saw when we build, and I never," grumbled Ambrosch.

I knew he had broken the saw, and then hid it and lied about it. I began to wish I had not stayed for supper. Everything was disagreeable to me. Ántonia ate so noisily now, like a man, and she yawned often at the table and kept stretching her arms over her head, as if they ached. Grandmother had said, "Heavy field work'll spoil that girl. She'll lose all her nice ways and get rough ones." She had lost them already.

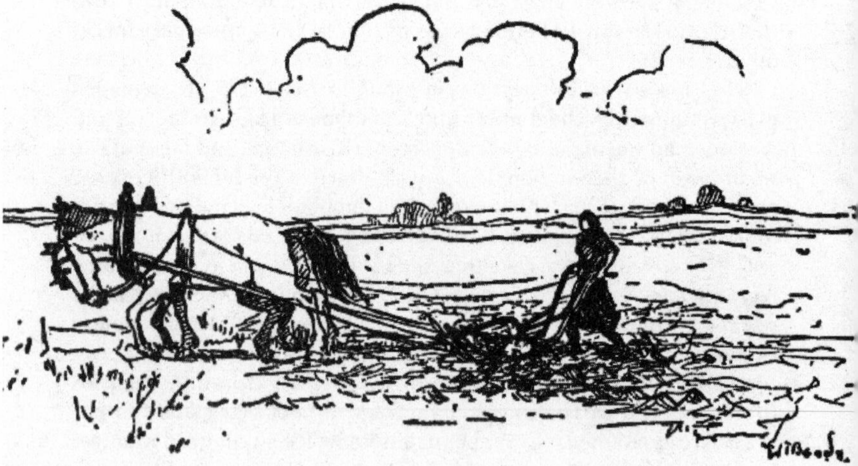

After supper I rode home through the sad, soft spring twilight. Since winter I had seen very little of Ántonia. She was out in the fields from sun-up until sun-down. If I rode over to see her where she was ploughing, she stopped at the end of a row to chat for a moment, then gripped her plough-handles, clucked to her team, and waded on down the furrow, making me feel that she was now grown up and had no time for me. On Sundays she helped her mother make garden or sewed all day. Grandfather was pleased with Ántonia. When we complained of her, he only smiled and said, "She will help some fellow get ahead in the world."

Nowadays Tony could talk of nothing but the prices of things, or how much she could lift and endure. She was too proud of her strength. I knew, too, that Ambrosch put upon her some chores a girl ought not to do, and that the farmhands around the country joked in a nasty way about it. Whenever I saw her come up the furrow, shouting to her beasts, sunburned, sweaty, her dress open at the neck, and her throat and chest dust-plastered, I used to think of the tone in which poor Mr. Shimerda, who could say so little, yet managed to say so much when he exclaimed, "My Án-tonia!"

XVIII

After I began to go to the country school, I saw less of the Bohemians. We were sixteen pupils at the sod schoolhouse, and we all came on horseback and brought our dinner. My schoolmates were none of them very interesting, but I somehow felt that by making comrades of them I was getting even with Ántonia for her indifference. Since the father's death, Ambrosch was more than ever the head of the house and he seemed to direct the feelings as well as the fortunes of his women-folk. Ántonia often quoted his opinions to me, and she let me see that she admired him, while she thought of me only as a little boy. Before the spring was over, there was a distinct coldness between us and the Shimerdas. It came about in this way.

One Sunday I rode over there with Jake to get a horse-collar which Ambrosch had borrowed from him and had not returned. It was a beautiful blue morning. The buffalo-peas were blooming in pink and purple masses along the roadside, and the larks, perched on last year's dried sunflower stalks, were singing straight at the sun, their heads thrown back and their yellow breasts a-quiver. The wind blew about us in warm, sweet gusts. We rode slowly, with a pleasant sense of Sunday indolence.

We found the Shimerdas working just as if it were a weekday. Marek was cleaning out the stable, and Ántonia and her mother were making garden, off across the pond in the drawhead. Ambrosch was up on the windmill tower, oiling the wheel. He came down, not very cordially. When Jake asked for the collar, he grunted and scratched his head. The collar belonged to grandfather, of course, and Jake, feeling responsible for it, flared up.

"Now, don't you say you have n't got it, Ambrosch, because I know you have, and if you ain't a-going to look for it, I will."

Ambrosch shrugged his shoulders and sauntered down the hill toward the stable. I could see that it was one of his mean days. Presently he returned, carrying a collar that had been badly used—trampled in the dirt and gnawed by rats until the hair was sticking out of it.

"This what you want?" he asked surlily.

Jake jumped off his horse. I saw a wave of red come up under the rough stubble on his face. "That ain't the piece of harness I loaned you, Ambrosch; or if it is, you've used it shameful. I ain't a-going to carry such a looking thing back to Mr. Burden."

Ambrosch dropped the collar on the ground. "All right," he said coolly, took up his oil-can, and began to climb the mill. Jake caught him by the belt of his trousers and yanked him back. Ambrosch's feet had scarcely touched the ground when he lunged out with a vicious kick at Jake's stomach. Fortunately Jake was in such a position that he could dodge it. This was not the sort of thing country boys did when they played at fisticuffs, and Jake was furious. He landed Ambrosch a blow on the head—it sounded like the crack of an axe on a cow-pumpkin. Ambrosch dropped over, stunned.

We heard squeals, and looking up saw Ántonia and her mother coming on the run. They did not take the path around the pond, but plunged through the muddy water, without even lifting their skirts. They came on, screaming and clawing the air. By this time Ambrosch had come to his senses and was sputtering with nose-bleed. Jake sprang into his saddle. "Let's get out of this, Jim," he called.

Mrs. Shimerda threw her hands over her head and clutched as if she were going to pull down lightning. "Law, law!" she shrieked after us. "Law for knock my Ambrosch down!"

"I never like you no more, Jake and Jim Burden," Ántonia panted. "No friends any more!"

Jake stopped and turned his horse for a second. "Well, you're a damned ungrateful lot, the whole pack of you," he shouted back. "I guess the Burdens can get along without you. You've been a sight of trouble to them, anyhow!"

We rode away, feeling so outraged that the fine morning was spoiled for us. I had n't a word to say, and poor Jake was white as paper and trembling all over. It made him sick to get so angry. "They ain't the same, Jimmy," he kept saying in a hurt tone. "These foreigners ain't the same. You can't trust 'em to be fair. It's dirty to kick a feller. You heard how the women turned on you—and after all we went through on account of 'em last winter! They ain't to be trusted. I don't want to see you get too thick with any of 'em."

"I'll never be friends with them again, Jake," I declared hotly. "I believe they are all like Krajiek and Ambrosch underneath."

Grandfather heard our story with a twinkle in his eye. He advised Jake to ride to town to-morrow, go to a justice of the peace, tell him he had knocked young Shimerda down, and pay his fine. Then if Mrs. Shimerda was inclined to make trouble—her son was still under age—she would be forestalled. Jake said he might as well take the wagon and haul to market the pig he had been fattening. On Monday, about an hour after Jake had started, we saw Mrs. Shimerda and her Ambrosch proudly driving by, looking neither to the right nor left. As they rattled out of sight down the Black Hawk road, grandfather chuckled, saying he had rather expected she would follow the matter up.

Jake paid his fine with a ten-dollar bill grandfather had given him for that purpose. But when the Shimerdas found that Jake sold his pig in town that day, Ambrosch worked it out in his shrewd head that Jake had to sell his pig to pay his fine. This theory afforded the Shimerdas great satisfaction, apparently. For weeks afterward, whenever Jake and I met Ántonia on her way to the post-office, or going along the road with her work-team, she would clap her hands and call to us in a spiteful, crowing voice:—

"Jake-y, Jake-y, sell the pig and pay the slap!"

Otto pretended not to be surprised at Ántonia's behavior. He only lifted his brows and said, "You can't tell me anything new about a Czech; I'm an Austrian."

Grandfather was never a party to what Jake called our feud with the Shimerdas. Ambrosch and Ántonia always greeted him respectfully, and he asked them about their affairs and gave them advice as usual. He thought the future looked hopeful for them. Ambrosch was a far-seeing fellow; he soon realized that his oxen were too heavy for any work except breaking sod, and he succeeded in selling them to a newly arrived German. With the money he bought another team of horses, which grandfather selected for him. Marek was strong, and Ambrosch worked him hard; but he could never teach him to cultivate corn, I remember. The one idea that had ever got through poor Marek's thick head was that all exertion was meritorious. He always bore down on the handles of the cultivator and drove the blades so deep into the earth that the horses were soon exhausted.

In June Ambrosch went to work at Mr. Bushy's for a week, and took Marek with him at full wages. Mrs. Shimerda then drove the second cultivator; she and Ántonia worked in the fields all day and did the chores at night. While the two women were running the place alone, one of the new horses got colic and gave them a terrible fright.

Ántonia had gone down to the barn one night to see that all was well before she went to bed, and she noticed that one of the roans was swollen about the middle and stood with its head hanging. She mounted another horse, without waiting to saddle him, and hammered on our door just as we were going to bed. Grandfather answered her knock. He did not send one of his men, but rode back with her himself, taking a syringe and an old piece of carpet he kept for hot applications when our horses were sick. He found Mrs. Shimerda sitting by the horse with her lantern, groaning and wringing her hands. It took but a few moments to release the gases pent up in the poor beast, and the two women heard the rush of wind and saw the roan visibly diminish in girth.

"If I lose that horse, Mr. Burden," Ántonia exclaimed, "I never stay here till Ambrosch come home! I go drown myself in the pond before morning."

When Ambrosch came back from Mr. Bushy's, we learned that he had given Marek's wages to the priest at Black Hawk, for masses for their father's soul. Grandmother thought Ántonia needed shoes more than Mr. Shimerda needed prayers, but grandfather said tolerantly, "If he can spare six dollars, pinched as he is, it shows he believes what he professes."

It was grandfather who brought about a reconciliation with the Shimerdas. One morning he told us that the small grain was coming on so well, he thought he would begin to cut his wheat on the first of July. He would need more men, and if it were agreeable to every one he would engage Ambrosch for the reaping and thrashing, as the Shimerdas had no small grain of their own.

"I think, Emmaline," he concluded, "I will ask Ántonia to come over and help you in the kitchen. She will be glad to earn something, and it will be a good time to end misunderstandings. I may as well ride over this morning and make arrangements. Do you want to go with me, Jim?" His tone told me that he had already decided for me.

After breakfast we set off together. When Mrs. Shimerda saw us coming, she ran from her door down into the draw behind the stable, as if she did not want to meet us. Grandfather smiled to himself while he tied his horse, and we followed her.

Behind the barn we came upon a funny sight. The cow had evidently been grazing somewhere in the draw. Mrs. Shimerda had run to the animal, pulled up the lariat pin, and, when we came upon her, she was trying to hide the cow in an old cave in the bank. As the hole was narrow and dark, the cow held back, and the old woman was slapping and pushing at her hind quarters, trying to spank her into the draw-side.

Grandfather ignored her singular occupation and greeted her politely. "Good-morning, Mrs. Shimerda. Can you tell me where I will find Ambrosch? Which field?"

"He with the sod corn." She pointed toward the north, still standing in front of the cow as if she hoped to conceal it.

"His sod corn will be good for fodder this winter," said grandfather encouragingly. "And where is Ántonia?"

"She go with." Mrs. Shimerda kept wiggling her bare feet about nervously in the dust.

"Very well. I will ride up there. I want them to come over and help me cut my oats and wheat next month. I will pay them wages. Goodmorning. By the way, Mrs. Shimerda," he said as he turned up the path, "I think we may as well call it square about the cow."

She started and clutched the rope tighter. Seeing that she did not understand, grandfather turned back. "You need not pay me anything more; no more money. The cow is yours."

"Pay no more, keep cow?" she asked in a bewildered tone, her narrow eyes snapping at us in the sunlight.

"Exactly. Pay no more, keep cow." He nodded.

Mrs. Shimerda dropped the rope, ran after us, and crouching down beside grandfather, she took his hand and kissed it. I doubt if he had ever been so much embarrassed before. I was a little startled, too. Somehow, that seemed to bring the Old World very close.

We rode away laughing, and grandfather said: "I expect she thought we had come to take the cow away for certain, Jim. I wonder if she would n't have scratched a little if we'd laid hold of that lariat rope!"

Our neighbors seemed glad to make peace with us. The next Sunday Mrs. Shimerda came over and brought Jake a pair of socks she had knitted. She presented them with an air of great magnanimity, saying, "Now you not come any more for knock my Ambrosch down?"

Jake laughed sheepishly. "I don't want to have no trouble with Ambrosch. If he'll let me alone, I'll let him alone."

"If he slap you, we ain't got no pig for pay the fine," she said insinuatingly.

Jake was not at all disconcerted. "Have the last word, mam," he said cheerfully. "It's a lady's privilege."

XIX

July came on with that breathless, brilliant heat which makes the plains of Kansas and Nebraska the best corn country in the world. It seemed as if we could hear the corn growing in the night; under the stars one caught a faint crackling in the dewy, heavy-odored cornfields where the feathered stalks stood so juicy and green. If all the

great plain from the Missouri to the Rocky Mountains had been
under glass, and the heat regulated by a thermometer, it could not
have been better for the yellow tassels that were ripening and fertil-
izing each other day by day. The cornfields were far apart in those
times, with miles of wild grazing land between. It took a clear, meditative eye like my grandfather's to foresee that they would enlarge
and multiply until they would be, not the Shimerdas' cornfields, or
Mr. Bushy's, but the world's cornfields; that their yield would be one
of the great economic facts, like the wheat crop of Russia, which
underlie all the activities of men, in peace or war.

The burning sun of those few weeks, with occasional rains at night,
secured the corn. After the milky ears were once formed, we had
little to fear from dry weather. The men were working so hard in
the wheatfields that they did not notice the heat,—though I was kept
busy carrying water for them,—and grandmother and Ántonia had
so much to do in the kitchen that they could not have told whether
one day was hotter than another. Each morning, while the dew was
still on the grass, Ántonia went with me up to the garden to get early
vegetables for dinner. Grandmother made her wear a sunbonnet, but
as soon as we reached the garden she threw it on the grass and let
her hair fly in the breeze. I remember how, as we bent over the pea-
vines, beads of perspiration used to gather on her upper lip like a
little mustache.

"Oh, better I like to work out of doors than in a house!" she used
to sing joyfully. "I not care that your grandmother say it makes me
like a man. I like to be like a man." She would toss her head and ask
me to feel the muscles swell in her brown arm.

We were glad to have her in the house. She was so gay and responsive that one did not mind her heavy, running step, or her clattery
way with pans. Grandmother was in high spirits during the weeks
that Ántonia worked for us.

All the nights were close and hot during that harvest season. The
harvesters slept in the hayloft because it was cooler there than in
the house. I used to lie in my bed by the open window, watching the
heat lightning play softly along the horizon, or looking up at the gaunt
frame of the windmill against the blue night sky. One night there was
a beautiful electric storm, though not enough rain fell to damage the
cut grain. The men went down to the barn immediately after supper,
and when the dishes were washed Ántonia and I climbed up on the
slanting roof of the chicken-house to watch the clouds. The thunder
was loud and metallic, like the rattle of sheet iron, and the lightning
broke in great zigzags across the heavens, making everything stand
out and come close to us for a moment. Half the sky was checkered
with black thunderheads, but all the west was luminous and clear: in
the lightning-flashes it looked like deep blue water, with the sheen of

moonlight on it; and the mottled part of the sky was like marble pavement, like the quay of some splendid seacoast city, doomed to destruction. Great warm splashes of rain fell on our upturned faces. One black cloud, no bigger than a little boat, drifted out into the clear space unattended, and kept moving westward. All about us we could hear the felty beat of the raindrops on the soft dust of the farmyard. Grandmother came to the door and said it was late, and we would get wet out there.

"In a minute we come," Ántonia called back to her. "I like your grandmother, and all things here," she sighed. "I wish my papa live to see this summer. I wish no winter ever come again."

"It will be summer a long while yet," I reassured her. "Why are n't you always nice like this, Tony?"

"How nice?"

"Why, just like this; like yourself. Why do you all the time try to be like Ambrosch?"

She put her arms under her head and lay back, looking up at the sky. "If I live here, like you, that is different. Things will be easy for you. But they will be hard for us."

Book II

The Hired Girls

I

I had been living with my grandfather for nearly three years when he decided to move to Black Hawk. He and grandmother were getting old for the heavy work of a farm, and as I was now thirteen they thought I ought to be going to school. Accordingly our homestead was rented to "that good woman, the Widow Steavens," and her bachelor brother, and we bought Preacher White's house, at the north end of Black Hawk. This was the first town house one passed driving in from the farm, a landmark which told country people their long ride was over.

We were to move to Black Hawk in March, and as soon as grandfather had fixed the date he let Jake and Otto know of his intention. Otto said he would not be likely to find another place that suited him so well; that he was tired of farming and thought he would go back to what he called the "wild West." Jake Marpole, lured by Otto's stories of adventure, decided to go with him. We did our best to dissuade Jake. He was so handicapped by illiteracy and by his trusting disposition that he would be an easy prey to sharpers. Grandmother begged him to stay among kindly, Christian people, where he was known; but there was no reasoning with him. He wanted to be a prospector. He thought a silver mine was waiting for him in Colorado.

Jake and Otto served us to the last. They moved us into town, put down the carpets in our new house, made shelves and cupboards for grandmother's kitchen, and seemed loath to leave us. But at last they went, without warning. Those two fellows had been faithful to us through sun and storm, had given us things that cannot be bought in any market in the world. With me they had been like older brothers; had restrained their speech and manners out of care for me, and given me so much good comradeship. Now they got on the westbound train one morning, in their Sunday clothes, with their oilcloth valises—and I never saw them again. Months afterward we got a card from Otto, saying that Jake had been down with mountain fever, but now they were both working in the Yankee Girl mine, and were doing

well. I wrote to them at that address, but my letter was returned to
me, "unclaimed." After that we never heard from them.

Black Hawk, the new world in which we had come to live, was a
clean, well-planted little prairie town, with white fences and good
green yards about the dwellings, wide, dusty streets, and shapely little trees growing along the wooden sidewalks. In the center of the
town there were two rows of new brick "store" buildings, a brick
schoolhouse, the courthouse, and four white churches. Our own
house looked down over the town, and from our upstairs windows
we could see the winding line of the river bluffs, two miles south of
us. That river was to be my compensation for the lost freedom
of the farming country.

We came to Black Hawk in March, and by the end of April we felt
like town people. Grandfather was a deacon in the new Baptist
Church, grandmother was busy with church suppers and missionary
societies, and I was quite another boy, or thought I was. Suddenly put
down among boys of my own age, I found I had a great deal to learn.
Before the spring term of school was over I could fight, play "keeps,"
tease the little girls, and use forbidden words as well as any boy in
my class. I was restrained from utter savagery only by the fact that
Mrs. Harling, our nearest neighbor, kept an eye on me, and if my
behavior went beyond certain bounds I was not permitted to come
into her yard or to play with her jolly children.

We saw more of our country neighbors now than when we lived
on the farm. Our house was a convenient stopping-place for them.
We had a big barn where the farmers could put up their teams, and
their women-folk more often accompanied them, now that they could
stay with us for dinner, and rest and set their bonnets right before
they went shopping. The more our house was like a country hotel,
the better I liked it. I was glad, when I came home from school at
noon, to see a farm wagon standing in the back yard, and I was always
ready to run downtown to get beefsteak or baker's bread for unexpected company. All through that first spring and summer I kept
hoping that Ambrosch would bring Ántonia and Yulka to see our
new house. I wanted to show them our red plush furniture, and the
trumpet-blowing cherubs the German paper-hanger had put on our
parlor ceiling.

When Ambrosch came to town, however, he came alone, and
though he put his horses in our barn, he would never stay for dinner,
or tell us anything about his mother and sisters. If we ran out and
questioned him as he was slipping through the yard, he would merely
work his shoulders about in his coat and say, "They all right, I guess."

Mrs. Steavens, who now lived on our farm, grew as fond of Ántonia as we had been, and always brought us news of her. All through
the wheat season, she told us, Ambrosch hired his sister out like a

man, and she went from farm to farm, binding sheaves or working with the thrashers. The farmers liked her and were kind to her; said they would rather have her for a hand than Ambrosch. When fall came she was to husk corn for the neighbors until Christmas, as she had done the year before; but grandmother saved her from this by getting her a place to work with our neighbors, the Harlings.

II

Grandmother often said that if she had to live in town, she thanked God she lived next the Harlings. They had been farming people, like ourselves, and their place was like a little farm, with a big barn and a garden, and an orchard and grazing lots,—even a windmill. The Harlings were Norwegians, and Mrs. Harling had lived in Christiania until she was ten ten years old. Her husband was born in Minnesota. He was a grain merchant and cattle buyer, and was generally considered the most enterprising business man in our county. He controlled a line of grain elevators in the little towns along the railroad to the west of us, and was away from home a great deal. In his absence his wife was the head of the household.

Mrs. Harling was short and square and sturdy-looking, like her house. Every inch of her was charged with an energy that made itself felt the moment she entered a room. Her face was rosy and solid, with bright, twinkling eyes and a stubborn little chin. She was quick to anger, quick to laughter, and jolly from the depths of her soul. How well I remember her laugh; it had in it the same sudden recognition that flashed into her eyes, was a burst of humor, short and intelligent. Her rapid footsteps shook her own floors, and she routed lassitude and indifference wherever she came. She could not be negative or perfunctory about anything. Her enthusiasm, and her violent likes and dislikes, asserted themselves in all the every-day occupations of life. Wash-day was interesting, never dreary, at the Harlings'. Preserving-time was a prolonged festival, and house-cleaning was like a revolution. When Mrs. Harling made garden that spring, we could feel the stir of her undertaking through the willow hedge that separated our place from hers.

Three of the Harling children were near me in age. Charley, the only son,—they had lost an older boy,—was sixteen; Julia, who was known as the musical one, was fourteen when I was; and Sally, the tomboy with short hair, was a year younger. She was nearly as strong as I, and uncannily clever at all boys' sports. Sally was a wild thing, with sunburned yellow hair, bobbed about her ears, and a brown skin, for she never wore a hat. She raced all over town on one roller skate, often cheated at "keeps," but was such a quick shot one could n't catch her at it.

The grown-up daughter, Frances, was a very important person in our world. She was her father's chief clerk, and virtually managed his Black Hawk office during his frequent absences. Because of her unusual business ability, he was stern and exacting with her. He paid her a good salary, but she had few holidays and never got away from her responsibilities. Even on Sundays she went to the office to open the mail and read the markets. With Charley, who was not interested in business, but was already preparing for Annapolis, Mr. Harling was very indulgent; bought him guns and tools and electric batteries, and never asked what he did with them.

Frances was dark, like her father, and quite as tall. In winter she wore a sealskin coat and cap, and she and Mr. Harling used to walk home together in the evening, talking about grain-cars and cattle, like two men. Sometimes she came over to see grandfather after supper, and her visits flattered him. More than once they put their wits together to rescue some unfortunate farmer from the clutches of Wick Cutter, the Black Hawk money-lender. Grandfather said Frances Harling was as good a judge of credits as any banker in the county. The two or three men who had tried to take advantage of her in a deal acquired celebrity by their defeat. She knew every farmer for miles about; how much land he had under cultivation, how many cattle he was feeding, what his liabilities were. Her interest in these people was more than a business interest. She carried them all in her mind as if they were characters in a book or a play.

When Frances drove out into the country on business, she would go miles out of her way to call on some of the old people, or to see the women who seldom got to town. She was quick at understanding the grandmothers who spoke no English, and the most reticent and distrustful of them would tell her their story without realizing they were doing so. She went to country funerals and weddings in all weathers. A farmer's daughter who was to be married could count on a wedding present from Frances Harling.

In August the Harlings' Danish cook had to leave them. Grandmother entreated them to try Ántonia. She cornered Ambrosch the next time he came to town, and pointed out to him that any connection with Christian Harling would strengthen his credit and be of advantage to him. One Sunday Mrs. Harling took the long ride out to the Shimerdas' with Frances. She said she wanted to see "what the girl came from" and to have a clear understanding with her mother. I was in our yard when they came driving home, just before sunset. They laughed and waved to me as they passed, and I could see they were in great good humor. After supper, when grandfather set off to church, grandmother and I took my short cut through the willow hedge and went over to hear about the visit to the Shimerdas.

We found Mrs. Harling with Charley and Sally on the front porch, resting after her hard drive. Julia was in the hammock—she was fond of repose—and Frances was at the piano, playing without a light and talking to her mother through the open window.

Mrs. Harling laughed when she saw us coming. "I expect you left your dishes on the table to-night, Mrs. Burden," she called. Frances shut the piano and came out to join us.

They had liked Ántonia from their first glimpse of her; felt they knew exactly what kind of girl she was. As for Mrs. Shimerda, they found her very amusing. Mrs. Harling chuckled whenever she spoke of her. "I expect I am more at home with that sort of bird than you are, Mrs. Burden. They're a pair, Ambrosch and that old woman!"

They had had a long argument with Ambrosch about Ántonia's allowance for clothes and pocket-money. It was his plan that every cent of his sister's wages should be paid over to him each month, and he would provide her with such clothing as he thought neces- sary. When Mrs. Harling told him firmly that she would keep fifty dollars a year for Ántonia's own use, he declared they wanted to take his sister to town and dress her up and make a fool of her. Mrs. Har- ling gave us a lively account of Ambrosch's behavior throughout the interview; how he kept jumping up and putting on his cap as if he were through with the whole business, and how his mother tweaked his coat-tail and prompted him in Bohemian. Mrs. Harling finally agreed to pay three dollars a week for Ántonia's services—good wages in those days—and to keep her in shoes. There had been hot dis- pute about the shoes, Mrs. Shimerda finally saying persuasively that she would send Mrs. Harling three fat geese every year to "make even." Ambrosch was to bring his sister to town next Saturday.

"She'll be awkward and rough at first, like enough," grandmother said anxiously, "but unless she's been spoiled by the hard life she's led, she has it in her to be a real helpful girl."

Mrs. Harling laughed her quick, decided laugh. "Oh, I'm not wor- rying, Mrs. Burden! I can bring something out of that girl. She's barely seventeen, not too old to learn new ways. She's good-looking, too!" she added warmly.

Frances turned to grandmother. "Oh, yes, Mrs. Burden, you did n't tell us that! She was working in the garden when we got there, barefoot and ragged. But she has such fine brown legs and arms, and splendid color in her cheeks—like those big dark red plums."

We were pleased at this praise. Grandmother spoke feelingly. "When she first came to this country, Frances, and had that genteel old man to watch over her, she was as pretty a girl as ever I saw. But, dear me, what a life she's led, out in the fields with those rough thrashers! Things would have been very different with poor Ánto- nia if her father had lived."

The Harlings begged us to tell them about Mr. Shimerda's death and the big snowstorm. By the time we saw grandfather coming home from church we had told them pretty much all we knew of the Shimerdas.

"The girl will be happy here, and she'll forget those things," said Mrs. Harling confidently, as we rose to take our leave.

III

On Saturday Ambrosch drove up to the back gate, and Ántonia jumped down from the wagon and ran into our kitchen just as she used to do. She was wearing shoes and stockings, and was breathless and excited. She gave me a playful shake by the shoulders. "You ain't forget about me, Jim?"

Grandmother kissed her. "God bless you, child! Now you've come, you must try to do right and be a credit to us."

Ántonia looked eagerly about the house and admired everything. "Maybe I be the kind of girl you like better, now I come to town," she suggested hopefully.

How good it was to have Ántonia near us again; to see her every day and almost every night! Her greatest fault, Mrs. Harling found, was that she so often stopped her work and fell to playing with the children. She would race about the orchard with us, or take sides in our hay-fights in the barn, or be the old bear that came down from the mountain and carried off Nina. Tony learned English so quickly that by the time school began she could speak as well as any of us.

I was jealous of Tony's admiration for Charley Harling. Because he was always first in his classes at school, and could mend the water-pipes or the door-bell and take the clock to pieces, she seemed to think him a sort of prince. Nothing that Charley wanted was too much trouble for her. She loved to put up lunches for him when he went hunting, to mend his ball-gloves and sew buttons on his shooting-coat, baked the kind of nut-cake he liked, and fed his setter dog when he was away on trips with his father. Ántonia had made herself cloth working-slippers out of Mr. Harling's old coats, and in these she went padding about after Charley, fairly panting with eagerness to please him.

Next to Charley, I think she loved Nina best. Nina was only six, and she was rather more complex than the other children. She was fanciful, had all sorts of unspoken preferences, and was easily offended. At the slightest disappointment or displeasure her velvety brown eyes filled with tears, and she would lift her chin and walk silently away. If we ran after her and tried to appease her, it did no good. She walked on unmollified. I used to think that no eyes in the world could grow so large or hold so many tears as Nina's.

Mrs. Harling and Ántonia invariably took her part. We were never given a chance to explain. The charge was simply: "You have made Nina cry. Now, Jimmy can go home, and Sally must get her arithmetic." I liked Nina, too; she was so quaint and unexpected, and her eyes were lovely; but I often wanted to shake her.

We had jolly evenings at the Harlings when the father was away. If he was at home, the children had to go to bed early, or they came over to my house to play. Mr. Harling not only demanded a quiet house, he demanded all his wife's attention. He used to take her away to their room in the west ell, and talk over his business with her all evening. Though we did not realize it then, Mrs. Harling was our audience when we played, and we always looked to her for suggestions. Nothing flattered one like her quick laugh.

Mr. Harling had a desk in his bedroom, and his own easy-chair by the window, in which no one else ever sat. On the nights when he was at home, I could see his shadow on the blind, and it seemed to me an arrogant shadow. Mrs. Harling paid no heed to any one else if he was there. Before he went to bed she always got him a lunch of smoked salmon or anchovies and beer. He kept an alcohol lamp in his room, and a French coffee-pot, and his wife made coffee for him at any hour of the night he happened to want it.

Most Black Hawk fathers had no personal habits outside their domestic ones; they paid the bills, pushed the baby carriage after office hours, moved the sprinkler about over the lawn, and took the family driving on Sunday. Mr. Harling, therefore, seemed to me autocratic and imperial in his ways. He walked, talked, put on his gloves, shook hands, like a man who felt that he had power. He was not tall, but he carried his head so haughtily that he looked a commanding figure, and there was something daring and challenging in his eyes. I used to imagine that the "nobles" of whom Ántonia was always talking probably looked very much like Christian Harling, wore caped overcoats like his, and just such a glittering diamond upon the little finger.

Except when the father was at home, the Harling house was never quiet. Mrs. Harling and Nina and Ántonia made as much noise as a houseful of children, and there was usually somebody at the piano. Julia was the only one who was held down to regular hours of practicing, but they all played. When Frances came home at noon, she played until dinner was ready. When Sally got back from school, she sat down in her hat and coat and drummed the plantation melodies that negro minstrel troupes brought to town. Even Nina played the Swedish Wedding March.

Mrs. Harling had studied the piano under a good teacher, and somehow she managed to practice every day. I soon learned that if I were sent over on an errand and found Mrs. Harling at the piano,

I must sit down and wait quietly until she turned to me. I can see her at this moment; her short, square person planted firmly on the stool, her little fat hands moving quickly and neatly over the keys, her eyes fixed on the music with intelligent concentration.

IV

> "I won't have none of your weevily wheat, and I won't have none
>   of your barley,
> But I'll take a measure of fine white flour, to make a cake for
>   Charley."[1]

We were singing rhymes to tease Ántonia while she was beating up one of Charley's favorite cakes in her big mixing-bowl. It was a crisp autumn evening, just cold enough to make one glad to quit playing tag in the yard, and retreat into the kitchen. We had begun to roll popcorn balls with syrup when we heard a knock at the back door, and Tony dropped her spoon and went to open it. A plump, fair-skinned girl was standing in the doorway. She looked demure and pretty, and made a graceful picture in her blue cashmere dress and little blue hat, with a plaid shawl drawn neatly about her shoulders and a clumsy pocketbook in her hand.

"Hello, Tony. Don't you know me?" she asked in a smooth, low voice, looking in at us archly.

Ántonia gasped and stepped back. "Why, it's Lena! Of course I did n't know you, so dressed up!"

Lena Lingard laughed, as if this pleased her. I had not recognized her for a moment, either. I had never seen her before with a hat on her head—or with shoes and stockings on her feet, for that matter. And here she was, brushed and smoothed and dressed like a town girl, smiling at us with perfect composure.

"Hello, Jim," she said carelessly as she walked into the kitchen and looked about her. "I've come to town to work, too, Tony."

"Have you, now? Well, ain't that funny!" Ántonia stood ill at ease, and did n't seem to know just what to do with her visitor.

The door was open into the dining-room, where Mrs. Harling sat crocheting and Frances was reading. Frances asked Lena to come in and join them.

"You are Lena Lingard, are n't you? I've been to see your mother, but you were off herding cattle that day. Mama, this is Chris Lingard's oldest girl."

Mrs. Harling dropped her worsted and examined the visitor with quick, keen eyes. Lena was not at all disconcerted. She sat down in the chair Frances pointed out, carefully arranging her pocketbook

---

1. Lines from the popular American folk song "Weevily Wheat."

and gray cotton gloves on her lap. We followed with our popcorn, but Ántonia hung back—said she had to get her cake into the oven.

"So you have come to town," said Mrs. Harling, her eyes still fixed on Lena. "Where are you working?"

"For Mrs. Thomas, the dressmaker. She is going to teach me to sew. She says I have quite a knack. I'm through with the farm. There ain't any end to the work on a farm, and always so much trouble happens. I'm going to be a dress-maker."

"Well, there have to be dressmakers. It's a good trade. But I would n't run down the farm, if I were you," said Mrs. Harling rather severely. "How is your mother?"

"Oh, mother's never very well; she has too much to do. She'd get away from the farm, too, if she could. She was willing for me to come. After I learn to do sewing, I can make money and help her."

"See that you don't forget to," said Mrs. Harling skeptically, as she took up her crocheting again and sent the hook in and out with nimble fingers.

"No, 'm, I won't," said Lena blandly. She took a few grains of the popcorn we pressed upon her, eating them discreetly and taking care not to get her fingers sticky.

Frances drew her chair up nearer to the visitor. "I thought you were going to be married, Lena," she said teasingly. "Did n't I hear that Nick Svendsen was rushing you pretty hard?"

Lena looked up with her curiously innocent smile. "He did go with me quite a while. But his father made a fuss about it and said he would n't give Nick any land if he married me, so he's going to marry Annie Iverson. I would n't like to be her; Nick's awful sullen, and he'll take it out on her. He ain't spoke to his father since he promised."

Frances laughed. "And how do you feel about it?"

"I don't want to marry Nick, or any other man," Lena murmured. "I've seen a good deal of married life, and I don't care for it. I want to be so I can help my mother and the children at home, and not have to ask lief of anybody."

"That's right," said Frances. "And Mrs. Thomas thinks you can learn dressmaking?"

"Yes, 'm. I've always liked to sew, but I never had much to do with. Mrs. Thomas makes lovely things for all the town ladies. Did you know Mrs. Gardener is having a purple velvet made? The velvet came from Omaha. My, but it's lovely!" Lena sighed softly and stroked her cashmere folds. "Tony knows I never did like out-of-door work," she added.

Mrs. Harling glanced at her. "I expect you'll learn to sew all right, Lena, if you'll only keep your head and not go gadding about to dances all the time and neglect your work, the way some country girls do."

"Yes, 'm. Tiny Soderball is coming to town, too. She's going to work at the Boys' Home Hotel. She'll see lots of strangers," Lena added wistfully.

"Too many, like enough," said Mrs. Harling. "I don't think a hotel is a good place for a girl; though I guess Mrs. Gardener keeps an eye on her waitresses."

Lena's candid eyes, that always looked a little sleepy under their long lashes, kept straying about the cheerful rooms with naïve admiration. Presently she drew on her cotton gloves. "I guess I must be leaving," she said irresolutely.

Frances told her to come again, whenever she was lonesome or wanted advice about anything. Lena replied that she did n't believe she would ever get lonesome in Black Hawk.

She lingered at the kitchen door and begged Ántonia to come and see her often. "I've got a room of my own at Mrs. Thomas's, with a carpet."

Tony shuffled uneasily in her cloth slippers. "I'll come sometime, but Mrs. Harling don't like to have me run much," she said evasively.

"You can do what you please when you go out, can't you?" Lena asked in a guarded whisper. "Ain't you crazy about town, Tony? I don't care what anybody says, I'm done with the farm!" She glanced back over her shoulder toward the dining-room, where Mrs. Harling sat.

When Lena was gone, Frances asked Ántonia why she had n't been a little more cordial to her.

"I did n't know if your mother would like her coming here," said Ántonia, looking troubled. "She was kind of talked about, out there."

"Yes, I know. But mother won't hold it against her if she behaves well here. You needn't say anything about that to the children. I guess Jim has heard all that gossip?"

When I nodded, she pulled my hair and told me I knew too much, anyhow. We were good friends, Frances and I.

I ran home to tell grandmother that Lena Lingard had come to town. We were glad of it, for she had a hard life on the farm.

Lena lived in the Norwegian settlement west of Squaw Creek, and she used to herd her father's cattle in the open country between his place and the Shimerdas'. Whenever we rode over in that direction we saw her out among her cattle, bareheaded and barefooted, scantily dressed in tattered clothing, always knitting as she watched her herd. Before I knew Lena, I thought of her as something wild, that always lived on the prairie, because I had never seen her under a roof. Her yellow hair was burned to a ruddy thatch on her head; but her legs and arms, curiously enough, in spite of constant exposure to the sun, kept a miraculous whiteness which somehow made her seem more undressed than other girls who went scantily clad. The first time I stopped to talk to her, I was astonished at her soft voice and easy, gentle ways. The girls out there usually got rough and man-nish after they went to herding. But Lena asked Jake and me to get off our horses and stay awhile, and behaved exactly as if she were in a house and were accustomed to having visitors. She was not embar-rassed by her ragged clothes, and treated us as if we were old acquain-tances. Even then I noticed the unusual color of her eyes—a shade of deep violet—and their soft, confiding expression.

Chris Lingard was not a very successful farmer, and he had a large family. Lena was always knitting stockings for little brothers and sis-ters, and even the Norwegian women, who disapproved of her, admit-ted that she was a good daughter to her mother. As Tony said, she had been talked about. She was accused of making Ole Benson lose the little sense he had—and that at an age when she should still have been in pinafores.

Ole lived in a leaky dugout somewhere at the edge of the settle-ment. He was fat and lazy and discouraged, and bad luck had become a habit with him. After he had had every other kind of misfortune, his wife, "Crazy Mary," tried to set a neighbor's barn on fire, and was sent to the asylum at Lincoln. She was kept there for a few months, then escaped and walked all the way home, nearly two hun-dred miles, traveling by night and hiding in barns and haystacks by day. When she got back to the Norwegian settlement, her poor feet were as hard as hoofs. She promised to be good, and was allowed to stay at home—though every one realized she was as crazy as ever, and she still ran about barefooted through the snow, telling her domestic troubles to her neighbors.

Not long after Mary came back from the asylum, I heard a young Dane, who was helping us to thrash, tell Jake and Otto that Chris Lingard's oldest girl had put Ole Benson out of his head, until he had no more sense than his crazy wife. When Ole was cultivating his corn that summer, he used to get discouraged in the field, tie up his team, and wander off to wherever Lena Lingard was herding. There he would sit down on the draw-side and help her watch her cattle. All the settlement was talking about it. The Norwegian preacher's wife went to Lena and told her she ought not to allow this; she begged Lena to come to church on Sundays. Lena said she had n't a dress in the world any less ragged than the one on her back. Then the minister's wife went through her old trunks and found some things she had worn before her marriage.

The next Sunday Lena appeared at church, a little late, with her hair done up neatly on her head, like a young woman, wearing shoes and stockings, and the new dress, which she had made over for her-self very becomingly. The congregation stared at her. Until that morn-ing no one—unless it were Ole—had realized how pretty she was, or that she was growing up. The swelling lines of her figure had been

hidden under the shapeless rags she wore in the fields. After the last hymn had been sung, and the congregation was dismissed, Ole slipped out to the hitch-bar and lifted Lena on her horse. That, in itself, was shocking; a married man was not expected to do such things. But it was nothing to the scene that followed. Crazy Mary darted out from the group of women at the church door, and ran down the road after Lena, shouting horrible threats.

"Look out, you Lena Lingard, look out! I'll come over with a corn-knife one day and trim some of that shape off you. Then you won't sail round so fine, making eyes at the men! . . ."

The Norwegian women did n't know where to look. They were formal housewives, most of them, with a severe sense of decorum. But Lena Lingard only laughed her lazy, good-natured laugh and rode on, gazing back over her shoulder at Ole's infuriated wife.

The time came, however, when Lena did n't laugh. More than once Crazy Mary chased her across the prairie and round and round the Shimerdas' cornfield. Lena never told her father; perhaps she was ashamed; perhaps she was more afraid of his anger than of the corn-knife. I was at the Shimerdas' one afternoon when Lena came bounding through the red grass as fast as her white legs could carry her. She ran straight into the house and hid in Ántonia's feather-bed. Mary was not far behind; she came right up to the door and made us feel how sharp her blade was, showing us very graphically just what she meant to do to Lena. Mrs. Shimerda, leaning out of the window, enjoyed the situation keenly, and was sorry when Ántonia sent Mary away, mollified by an apronful of bottle-tomatoes. Lena came out from Tony's room behind the kitchen, very pink from the heat of the feathers, but otherwise calm. She begged Ántonia and me to go with her, and help get her cattle together; they were scattered and might be gorging themselves in somebody's cornfield.

"Maybe you lose a steer and learn not to make somethings with your eyes at married men," Mrs. Shimerda told her hectoringly.

Lena only smiled her sleepy smile. "I never made anything to him with my eyes. I can't help it if he hangs around, and I can't order him off. It ain't my prairie."

V

After Lena came to Black Hawk I often met her downtown, where she would be matching sewing silk or buying "findings" for Mrs. Thomas. If I happened to walk home with her, she told me all about the dresses she was helping to make, or about what she saw and heard when she was with Tiny Soderball at the hotel on Saturday nights.

The Boys' Home was the best hotel on our branch of the Burlington, and all the commercial travelers in that territory tried to get

into Black Hawk for Sunday. They used to assemble in the parlor
after supper on Saturday nights. Marshall Field's man, Anson Kirkpatrick, played the piano and sang all the latest sentimental songs.
After Tiny had helped the cook wash the dishes, she and Lena sat
on the other side of the double doors between the parlor and the
dining-room, listening to the music and giggling at the jokes and stories. Lena often said she hoped I would be a traveling man when I
grew up. They had a gay life of it; nothing to do but ride about on
trains all day and go to theaters when they were in big cities. Behind
the hotel there was an old store building, where the salesmen opened
their big trunks and spread out their samples on the counters. The
Black Hawk merchants went to look at these things and order goods,
and Mrs. Thomas, though she was "retail trade," was permitted to
see them and to "get ideas." They were all generous, these traveling
men; they gave Tiny Soderball handkerchiefs and gloves and ribbons
and striped stockings, and so many bottles of perfume and cakes of
scented soap that she bestowed some of them on Lena.

One afternoon in the week before Christmas I came upon Lena
and her funny, square-headed little brother Chris, standing before
the drug-store, gazing in at the wax dolls and blocks and Noah's arks
arranged in the frosty show window. The boy had come to town with
a neighbor to do his Christmas shopping, for he had money of his
own this year. He was only twelve, but that winter he had got the
job of sweeping out the Norwegian church and making the fire in it
every Sunday morning. A cold job it must have been, too!

We went into Duckford's dry-goods store, and Chris unwrapped
all his presents and showed them to me—something for each of the
six younger than himself, even a rubber pig for the baby. Lena had
given him one of Tiny Soderball's bottles of perfume for his mother,
and he thought he would get some handkerchiefs to go with it. They
were cheap, and he had n't much money left. We found a tableful of
handkerchiefs spread out for view at Duckford's. Chris wanted those
with initial letters in the corner, because he had never seen any
before. He studied them seriously, while Lena looked over his shoulder, telling him she thought the red letters would hold their color
best. He seemed so perplexed that I thought perhaps he had n't
enough money, after all. Presently he said gravely,—

"Sister, you know mother's name is Berthe. I don't know if I ought
to get B for Berthe, or M for Mother."

Lena patted his bristly head. "I'd get the B, Chrissy. It will please
her for you to think about her name. Nobody ever calls her by it now."

That satisfied him. His face cleared at once, and he took three reds
and three blues. When the neighbor came in to say that it was time
to start, Lena wound Chris's comforter about his neck and turned up
his jacket collar—he had no overcoat—and we watched him climb

into the wagon and start on his long, cold drive. As we
together up the windy street, Lena wiped her eyes with th
her woolen glove. "I get awful homesick for them, all the same, ...
murmured, as if she were answering some remembered reproach.

VI

Winter comes down savagely over a little town on the prairie. The
wind that sweeps in from the open country strips away all the leafy
screens that hide one yard from another in summer, and the houses
seem to draw closer together. The roofs, that looked so far away across
the green treetops, now stare you in the face, and they are so much
uglier than when their angles were softened by vines and shrubs.

In the morning, when I was fighting my way to school against the
wind, I couldn't see anything but the road in front of me; but in the
late afternoon, when I was coming home, the town looked bleak
and desolate to me. The pale, cold light of the winter sunset did not
beautify—it was like the light of truth itself. When the smoky clouds
hung low in the west and the red sun went down behind them, leaving a pink flush on the snowy roofs and the blue drifts, then the
wind sprang up afresh, with a kind of bitter song, as if it said: "This
is reality, whether you like it or not. All those frivolities of summer,
the light and shadow, the living mask of green that trembled over
everything, they were lies, and this is what was underneath. This is the
truth." It was as if we were being punished for loving the loveliness of
summer.

If I loitered on the playground after school, or went to the post-
office for the mail and lingered to hear the gossip about the cigar-
stand, it would be growing dark by the time I came home. The sun
was gone; the frozen streets stretched long and blue before me; the
lights were shining pale in kitchen windows, and I could smell the
suppers cooking as I passed. Few people were abroad, and each one of
them was hurrying toward a fire. The glowing stoves in the houses
were like magnets. When one passed an old man, one could see nothing of his face but a red nose sticking out between a frosted beard
and a long plush cap. The young men capered along with their hands
in their pockets, and sometimes tried a slide on the icy sidewalk. The
children, in their bright hoods and comforters, never walked, but
always ran from the moment they left their door, beating their mittens against their sides. When I got as far as the Methodist Church,
I was about halfway home. I can remember how glad I was when
there happened to be a light in the church, and the painted glass
window shone out at us as we came along the frozen street. In the
winter bleakness a hunger for color came over people, like the Lap-
lander's craving for fats and sugar. Without knowing why, we used

to linger on the sidewalk outside the church when the lamps were lighted early for choir practice or prayer-meeting, shivering and talking until our feet were like lumps of ice. The crude reds and greens and blues of that colored glass held us there.

On winter nights, the lights in the Harlings' windows drew me like the painted glass. Inside that warm, roomy house there was color, too. After supper I used to catch up my cap, stick my hands in my pockets, and dive through the willow hedge as if witches were after me. Of course, if Mr. Harling was at home, if his shadow stood out on the blind of the west room, I did not go in, but turned and walked home by the long way, through the street, wondering what book I should read as I sat down with the two old people.

Such disappointments only gave greater zest to the nights when we acted charades, or had a costume ball in the back parlor, with Sally always dressed like a boy. Frances taught us to dance that winter, and she said, from the first lesson, that Ántonia would make the best dancer among us. On Saturday nights, Mrs. Harling used to play the old operas for us,—"Martha," "Norma," "Rigoletto,"—telling us the story while she played. Every Saturday night was like a party. The parlor, the back parlor, and the dining-room were warm and brightly lighted, with comfortable chairs and sofas, and gay pictures on the walls. One always felt at ease there. Ántonia brought her sewing and sat with us—she was already beginning to make pretty clothes for herself. After the long winter evenings on the prairie, with Ambrosch's sullen silences and her mother's complaints, the Harlings' house seemed, as she said, "like Heaven" to her. She was never too tired to make taffy or chocolate cookies for us. If Sally whispered in her ear, or Charley gave her three winks, Tony would rush into the kitchen and build a fire in the range on which she had already cooked three meals that day.

While we sat in the kitchen waiting for the cookies to bake or the taffy to cool, Nina used to coax Ántonia to tell her stories—about the calf that broke its leg, or how Yulka saved her little turkeys from drowning in the freshet, or about old Christmases and weddings in Bohemia. Nina interpreted the stories about the crêche fancifully, and in spite of our derision she cherished a belief that Christ was born in Bohemia a short time before the Shimerdas left that country. We all liked Tony's stories. Her voice had a peculiarly engaging quality; it was deep, a little husky, and one always heard the breath vibrating behind it. Everything she said seemed to come right out of her heart.

One evening when we were picking out kernels for walnut taffy, Tony told us a new story.

"Mrs. Harling, did you ever hear about what happened up in the Norwegian settlement last summer, when I was thrashing there? We were at Iversons', and I was driving one of the grain wagons."

Mrs. Harling came out and sat down among us. "Could you throw the wheat into the bin yourself, Tony?" She knew what heavy work it was.

"Yes, mam, I did. I could shovel just as fast as that fat Andern boy that drove the other wagon. One day it was just awful hot. When we got back to the field from dinner, we took things kind of easy. The men put in the horses and got the machine going, and Ole Iverson was up on the deck, cutting bands. I was sitting against a straw stack, trying to get some shade. My wagon was n't going out first, and somehow I felt the heat awful that day. The sun was so hot like it was going to burn the world up. After a while I see a man coming across the stubble, and when he got close I see it was a tramp. His toes stuck out of his shoes, and he had n't shaved for a long while, and his eyes was awful red and wild, like he had some sickness. He comes right up and begins to talk like he knows me already. He says: 'The ponds in this country is done got so low a man could n't drownd himself in one of 'em.'

"I told him nobody wanted to drownd themselves, but if we did n't have rain soon we'd have to pump water for the cattle.

"'Oh, cattle,' he says, 'you'll all take care of your cattle! Ain't you got no beer here?' I told him he'd have to go to the Bohemians for beer; the Norwegians did n't have none when they thrashed. 'My God!' he says, 'so it's Norwegians now, is it? I thought this was Americy.'

"Then he goes up to the machine and yells out to Ole Iverson, 'Hello, partner, let me up there. I can cut bands, and I'm tired of trampin'. I won't go no farther.'

"I tried to make signs to Ole, 'cause I thought that man was crazy and might get the machine stopped up. But Ole, he was glad to get down out of the sun and chaff—it gets down your neck and sticks to you something awful when it's hot like that. So Ole jumped down and crawled under one of the wagons for shade, and the tramp got on the machine. He cut bands all right for a few minutes, and then, Mrs. Harling, he waved his hand to me and jumped head-first right into the thrashing machine after the wheat.

"I begun to scream, and the men run to stop the horses, but the belt had sucked him down, and by the time they got her stopped he was all beat and cut to pieces. He was wedged in so tight it was a hard job to get him out, and the machine ain't never worked right since."

"Was he clear dead, Tony?" we cried.

"Was he dead? Well, I guess so! There, now, Nina's all upset. We won't talk about it. Don't you cry, Nina. No old tramp won't get you while Tony's here."

Mrs. Harling spoke up sternly. "Stop crying, Nina, or I'll always send you upstairs when Ántonia tells us about the country. Did they never find out where he came from, Ántonia?"

"Never, mam. He had n't been seen nowhere except in a little town they call Conway. He tried to get beer there, but there was n't any saloon. Maybe he came in on a freight, but the brakeman had n't seen him. They could n't find no letters nor nothing on him; nothing but an old penknife in his pocket and the wishbone of a chicken wrapped up in a piece of paper, and some poetry."

"Some poetry?" we exclaimed.

"I remember," said Frances. "It was 'The Old Oaken Bucket,'[2] cut out of a newspaper and nearly worn out. Ole Iverson brought it into the office and showed it to me."

"Now, wasn't that strange, Miss Frances?" Tony asked thoughtfully. "What would anybody want to kill themselves in summer for? In thrashing time, too! It's nice everywhere then."

"So it is, Ántonia," said Mrs. Harling heartily. "Maybe I'll go home and help you thrash next summer. Is n't that taffy nearly ready to eat? I've been smelling it a long while."

There was a basic harmony between Ántonia and her mistress. They had strong, independent natures, both of them. They knew what they liked, and were not always trying to imitate other people. They loved children and animals and music, and rough play and digging in the earth. They liked to prepare rich, hearty food and to see people eat it; to make up soft white beds and to see youngsters asleep in them. They ridiculed conceited people and were quick to help unfortunate ones. Deep down in each of them there was a kind of hearty joviality, a relish of life, not over-delicate, but very invigorating. I never tried to define it, but I was distinctly conscious of it. I could not imagine Ántonia's living for a week in any other house in Black Hawk than the Harlings'.

VII

Winter lies too long in country towns; hangs on until it is stale and shabby, old and sullen. On the farm the weather was the great fact, and men's affairs went on underneath it, as the streams creep under the ice. But in Black Hawk the scene of human life was spread out shrunken and pinched, frozen down to the bare stalk.

Through January and February I went to the river with the Harlings on clear nights, and we skated up to the big island and made bonfires on the frozen sand. But by March the ice was rough and choppy, and the snow on the river bluffs was gray and mournful-looking. I was tired of school, tired of winter clothes, of the rutted streets, of the dirty drifts and the piles of cinders that had lain in the yards so long. There was only one break in the dreary monotony of that month; when Blind d'Arnault, the negro pianist, came to town.

2. Popular nineteenth-century verse by Samuel Woodworth (1785–1842).

He gave a concert at the Opera House on Monday night, and he and his manager spent Saturday and Sunday at our comfortable hotel. Mrs. Harling had known d'Arnault for years. She told Ántonia she had better go to see Tiny that Saturday evening, as there would certainly be music at the Boys' Home.

Saturday night after supper I ran downtown to the hotel and slipped quietly into the parlor. The chairs and sofas were already occupied, and the air smelled pleasantly of cigar smoke. The parlor had once been two rooms, and the floor was sway-backed where the partition had been cut away. The wind from without made waves in the long carpet. A coal stove glowed at either end of the room, and the grand piano in the middle stood open.

There was an atmosphere of unusual freedom about the house that night, for Mrs. Gardener had gone to Omaha for a week. Johnnie had been having drinks with the guests until he was rather absent-minded. It was Mrs. Gardener who ran the business and looked after everything. Her husband stood at the desk and welcomed incoming travelers. He was a popular fellow, but no manager.

Mrs. Gardener was admittedly the best-dressed woman in Black Hawk, drove the best horse, and had a smart trap and a little white-and-gold sleigh. She seemed indifferent to her possessions, was not half so solicitous about them as her friends were. She was tall, dark, severe, with something Indian-like in the rigid immobility of her face. Her manner was cold, and she talked little. Guests felt that they were receiving, not conferring, a favor when they stayed at her house. Even the smartest traveling men were flattered when Mrs. Gardener stopped to chat with them for a moment. The patrons of the hotel were divided into two classes; those who had seen Mrs. Gardener's diamonds, and those who had not.

When I stole into the parlor Anson Kirkpatrick, Marshall Field's man, was at the piano, playing airs from a musical comedy then running in Chicago. He was a dapper little Irishman, very vain, homely as a monkey, with friends everywhere, and a sweetheart in every port, like a sailor. I did not know all the men who were sitting about, but I recognized a furniture salesman from Kansas City, a drug man, and Willy O'Reilly, who traveled for a jewelry house and sold musical instruments. The talk was all about good and bad hotels, actors and actresses and musical prodigies. I learned that Mrs. Gardener had gone to Omaha to hear Booth and Barrett, who were to play there next week, and that Mary Anderson was having a great success in "A Winter's Tale," in London.[3]

3. Edwin Thomas Booth (1833–1893), a member of the Booth family of actors, and Lawrence Barrett (1838–1891), an American tragedian, formed a partnership and acted in several revivals of plays by Shakespeare. Mary Anderson (1859–1940), a well-known American stage actress in the late nineteenth-century, starred in several Shakespearian roles.

The door from the office opened, and Johnnie Gardener came in, directing Blind d'Arnault,—he would never consent to be led. He was a heavy, bulky mulatto, on short legs, and he came tapping the floor in front of him with his gold-headed cane. His yellow face was lifted in the light, with a show of white teeth, all grinning, and his shrunken, papery eyelids lay motionless over his blind eyes.

"Good evening, gentlemen. No ladies here? Good-evening, gentlemen. We going to have a little music? Some of you gentlemen going to play for me this evening?" It was the soft, amiable negro voice, like those I remembered from early childhood, with the note of docile subservience in it. He had the negro head, too; almost no head at all; nothing behind the ears but folds of neck under close-clipped wool. He would have been repulsive if his face had not been so kindly and happy. It was the happiest face I had seen since I left Virginia.

He felt his way directly to the piano. The moment he sat down, I noticed the nervous infirmity of which Mrs. Harling had told me. When he was sitting, or standing still, he swayed back and forth incessantly, like a rocking toy. At the piano, he swayed in time to the music, and when he was not playing, his body kept up this motion, like an empty mill grinding on. He found the pedals and tried them, ran his yellow hands up and down the keys a few times, tinkling off scales, then turned to the company.

"She seems all right, gentlemen. Nothing happened to her since the last time I was here. Mrs. Gardener, she always has this piano tuned up before I come. Now, gentlemen, I expect you've all got grand voices. Seems like we might have some good old plantation songs to-night."

The men gathered round him, as he began to play "My Old Kentucky Home." They sang one negro melody after another, while the mulatto sat rocking himself, his head thrown back, his yellow face lifted, its shriveled eyelids never fluttering.

He was born in the Far South, on the d'Arnault plantation, where the spirit if not the fact of slavery persisted. When he was three weeks old he had an illness which left him totally blind. As soon as he was old enough to sit up alone and toddle about, another affliction, the nervous motion of his body, became apparent. His mother, a buxom young negro wench who was laundress for the d'Arnaults, concluded that her blind baby was "not right" in his head, and she was ashamed of him. She loved him devotedly, but he was so ugly, with his sunken eyes and his "fidgets," that she hid him away from people. All the dainties she brought down from the "Big House" were for the blind child, and she beat and cuffed her other children whenever she found them teasing him or trying to get his chicken-bone away from him. He began to talk early, remembered everything he heard, and his mammy said he "was n't all wrong." She named him Samson, because he was blind, but on the plantation he was known as "yellow Martha's simple child." He was docile and obedient, but when he was six years old he began to run away from home, always taking the same direction. He felt his way through the lilacs, along the boxwood hedge, up to the south wing of the "Big House," where Miss Nellie d'Arnault practiced the piano every morning. This angered his mother more than anything else he could have done; she was so ashamed of his ugliness that she could n't bear to have white folks see him. Whenever she caught him slipping away from the cabin, she whipped him unmercifully, and told him what dreadful things old Mr. d'Arnault would do to him if he ever found him near the "Big House." But the next time Samson had a chance, he ran away again. If Miss d'Arnault stopped practicing for a moment and went toward the window, she saw this hideous little pickaninny, dressed in an old piece of sacking, standing in the open space between the hollyhock rows, his body rocking automatically, his blind face lifted to the sun and wearing an expression of idiotic rapture. Often she was tempted to tell Martha that the child must be kept at home, but somehow the memory of his foolish, happy face deterred her. She remembered that his sense of hearing was nearly all he had,—though it did not occur to her that he might have more of it than other children.

One day Samson was standing thus while Miss Nellie was playing her lesson to her music-master. The windows were open. He heard them get up from the piano, talk a little while, and then leave the room. He heard the door close after them. He crept up to the front windows and stuck his head in: there was no one there. He could always detect the presence of any one in a room. He put one foot over the window sill and straddled it. His mother had told him over and over how his master would give him to the big mastiff if he ever found him "meddling." Samson had got too near the mastiff's kennel once, and had felt his terrible breath in his face. He thought about that, but he pulled in his other foot.

Through the dark he found his way to the Thing, to its mouth. He touched it softly, and it answered softly, kindly. He shivered and stood still. Then he began to feel it all over, ran his finger tips along the slippery sides, embraced the carved legs, tried to get some conception of its shape and size, of the space it occupied in primeval night. It was cold and hard, and like nothing else in his black universe. He went back to its mouth, began at one end of the keyboard and felt his way down into the mellow thunder, as far as he could go. He seemed to know that it must be done with the fingers, not with the fists or the feet. He approached this highly artificial instrument through a mere instinct, and coupled himself to it, as if he knew it was to piece him out and make a whole creature of him.

After he had tried over all the sounds, he began to finger out passages from things Miss Nellie had been practicing, passages that were already his, that lay under the bones of his pinched, conical little skull, definite as animal desires. The door opened; Miss Nellie and her music-master stood behind it, but blind Samson, who was so sensitive to presences, did not know they were there. He was feeling out the pattern that lay all ready-made on the big and little keys. When he paused for a moment, because the sound was wrong and he wanted another, Miss Nellie spoke softly. He whirled about in a spasm of terror, leaped forward in the dark, struck his head on the open window, and fell screaming and bleeding to the floor. He had what his mother called a fit. The doctor came and gave him opium.

When Samson was well again, his young mistress led him back to the piano. Several teachers experimented with him. They found he had absolute pitch, and a remarkable memory. As a very young child he could repeat, after a fashion, any composition that was played for him. No matter how many wrong notes he struck, he never lost the intention of a passage, he brought the substance of it across by irregular and astonishing means. He wore his teachers out. He could never learn like other people, never acquired any finish. He was always a negro prodigy who played barbarously and wonderfully. As piano playing, it was perhaps abominable, but as music it was something real, vitalized by a sense of rhythm that was stronger than his other physical senses,—that not only filled his dark mind, but worried his body incessantly. To hear him, to watch him, was to see a negro enjoying himself as only a negro can. It was as if all the agreeable sensations possible to creatures of flesh and blood were heaped up on those black and white keys, and he were gloating over them and trickling them through his yellow fingers.

In the middle of a crashing waltz d'Arnault suddenly began to play softly, and, turning to one of the men who stood behind him, whispered, "Somebody dancing in there." He jerked his bullet head toward the dining-room. "I hear little feet,—girls, I 'spect."

Anson Kirkpatrick mounted a chair and peeped over the transom. Springing down, he wrenched open the doors and ran out into the dining-room. Tiny and Lena, Ántonia and Mary Dusak, were waltzing in the middle of the floor. They separated and fled toward the kitchen, giggling.

Kirkpatrick caught Tiny by the elbows. "What's the matter with you girls? Dancing out here by yourselves, when there's a roomful of lonesome men on the other side of the partition! Introduce me to your friends, Tiny."

The girls, still laughing, were trying to escape. Tiny looked alarmed. "Mrs. Gardener would n't like it," she protested. "She'd be awful mad if you was to come out here and dance with us."

"Mrs. Gardener's in Omaha, girl. Now, you're Lena, are you?—
and you're Tony and you're Mary. Have I got you all straight?"

O'Reilly and the others began to pile the chairs on the tables. Johnnie Gardener ran in from the office.

"Easy, boys, easy!" he entreated them. "You'll wake the cook, and
there'll be the devil to pay for me. She won't hear the music, but she'll
be down the minute anything's moved in the dining-room."

"Oh, what do you care, Johnnie? Fire the cook and wire Molly to
bring another. Come along, nobody'll tell tales."

Johnnie shook his head. " 'S a fact, boys," he said confidentially.
"If I take a drink in Black Hawk, Molly knows it in Omaha!"

His guests laughed and slapped him on the shoulder. "Oh, we'll
make it all right with Molly. Get your back up, Johnnie."

Molly was Mrs. Gardener's name, of course. "Molly Bawn" was
painted in large blue letters on the glossy white side of the hotel bus,
and "Molly" was engraved inside Johnnie's ring and on his watch-
case—doubtless on his heart, too. He was an affectionate little man,
and he thought his wife a wonderful woman; he knew that without
her he would hardly be more than a clerk in some other man's hotel.

At a word from Kirkpatrick, d'Arnault spread himself out over the
piano, and began to draw the dance music out of it, while the perspiration shone on his short wool and on his uplifted face. He looked
like some glistening African god of pleasure, full of strong, savage
blood. Whenever the dancers paused to change partners or to catch
breath, he would boom out softly, "Who's that goin' back on me? One
of these city gentlemen, I bet! Now, you girls, you ain't goin' to let
that floor get cold?"

Ántonia seemed frightened at first, and kept looking questioningly
at Lena and Tiny over Willy O'Reilly's shoulder. Tiny Soderball was
trim and slender, with lively little feet and pretty ankles—she wore
her dresses very short. She was quicker in speech, lighter in movement and manner than the other girls. Mary Dusak was broad and
brown of countenance, slightly marked by smallpox, but handsome
for all that. She had beautiful chestnut hair, coils of it; her forehead
was low and smooth, and her commanding dark eyes regarded the
world indifferently and fearlessly. She looked bold and resourceful
and unscrupulous, and she was all of these. They were handsome
girls, had the fresh color of their country upbringing, and in their
eyes that brilliancy which is called,—by no metaphor, alas!—"the
light of youth."

D'Arnault played until his manager came and shut the piano.
Before he left us, he showed us his gold watch which struck the hours,
and a topaz ring, given him by some Russian nobleman who delighted
in negro melodies, and had heard d'Arnault play in New Orleans.
At last he tapped his way upstairs, after bowing to everybody, docile

and happy. I walked home with Ántonia. We were so excited that
we dreaded to go to bed. We lingered a long while at the Harlings'
gate, whispering in the cold until the restlessness was slowly chilled
out of us.

                                   VIII

The Harling children and I were never happier, never felt more
contented and secure, than in the weeks of spring which broke that
long winter. We were out all day in the thin sunshine, helping
Mrs. Harling and Tony break the ground and plant the garden, dig
around the orchard trees, tie up vines and clip the hedges. Every
morning, before I was up, I could hear Tony singing in the garden
rows. After the apple and cherry trees broke into bloom, we ran
about under them, hunting for the new nests the birds were building, throwing clods at each other, and playing hide-and-seek with
Nina. Yet the summer which was to change everything was coming
nearer every day. When boys and girls are growing up, life can't
stand still, not even in the quietest of country towns; and they
have to grow up, whether they will or no. That is what their elders
are always forgetting.

   It must have been in June, for Mrs. Harling and Ántonia were preserving cherries, when I stopped one morning to tell them that a
dancing pavilion had come to town. I had seen two drays hauling
the canvas and painted poles up from the depot.

   That afternoon three cheerful-looking Italians strolled about Black
Hawk, looking at everything, and with them was a dark, stout woman
who wore a long gold watch chain about her neck and carried a black
lace parasol. They seemed especially interested in children and
vacant lots. When I overtook them and stopped to say a word, I found
them affable and confiding. They told me they worked in Kansas City
in the winter, and in summer they went out among the farming towns
with their tent and taught dancing. When business fell off in one
place, they moved on to another.

   The dancing pavilion was put up near the Danish laundry, on a
vacant lot surrounded by tall, arched cottonwood trees. It was very
much like a merry-go-round tent, with open sides and gay flags flying from the poles. Before the week was over, all the ambitious mothers
were sending their children to the afternoon dancing class. At three
o'clock one met little girls in white dresses and little boys in the
round-collared shirts of the time, hurrying along the sidewalk on
their way to the tent. Mrs. Vanni received them at the entrance,
always dressed in lavender with a great deal of black lace, her important watch chain lying on her bosom. She wore her hair on the top
of her head, built up in a black tower, with red coral combs. When

she smiled, she showed two rows of strong, crooked yellow teeth. She taught the little children herself, and her husband, the harpist, taught the older ones.

Often the mothers brought their fancy-work and sat on the shady side of the tent during the lesson. The popcorn man wheeled his glass wagon under the big cottonwood by the door, and lounged in the sun, sure of a good trade when the dancing was over. Mr. Jensen, the Danish laundryman, used to bring a chair from his porch and sit out in the grass plot. Some ragged little boys from the depot sold pop and iced lemonade under a white umbrella at the corner, and made faces at the spruce youngsters who came to dance. That vacant lot soon became the most cheerful place in town. Even on the hottest after-noons the cottonwoods made a rustling shade, and the air smelled of popcorn and melted butter, and Bouncing Bets wilting in the sun. Those hardy flowers had run away from the laundryman's garden, and the grass in the middle of the lot was pink with them.

The Vannis kept exemplary order, and closed every evening at the hour suggested by the City Council. When Mrs. Vanni gave the sig-nal, and the harp struck up "Home, Sweet Home," all Black Hawk knew it was ten o'clock. You could set your watch by that tune as confidently as by the Round House whistle.

At last there was something to do in those long, empty summer evenings, when the married people sat like images on their front porches, and the boys and girls tramped and tramped the board sidewalks—northward to the edge of the open prairie, south to the depot, then back again to the post-office, the ice-cream parlor, the butcher shop. Now there was a place where the girls could wear their new dresses, and where one could laugh aloud without being reproved by the ensuing silence. That silence seemed to ooze out of the ground, to hang under the foliage of the black maple trees with the bats and shadows. Now it was broken by light-hearted sounds. First the deep purring of Mr. Vanni's harp came in silvery ripples through the black-ness of the dusty-smelling night; then the violins fell in—one of them was almost like a flute. They called so archly, so seductively, that our feet hurried toward the tent of themselves. Why had n't we had a tent before?

Dancing became popular now, just as roller skating had been the summer before. The Progressive Euchre Club arranged with the Van-nis for the exclusive use of the floor on Tuesday and Friday nights. At other times any one could dance who paid his money and was orderly; the railroad men, the Round House mechanics, the delivery boys, the iceman, the farmhands who lived near enough to ride into town after their day's work was over.

I never missed a Saturday night dance. The tent was open until midnight then. The country boys came in from farms eight and ten miles away, and all the country girls were on the floor,—Ántonia and Lena and Tiny, and the Danish laundry girls and their friends. I was not the only boy who found these dances gayer than the others. The young men who belonged to the Progressive Euchre Club used to drop in late and risk a tiff with their sweethearts and general con-demnation for a waltz with "the hired girls."

IX

There was a curious social situation in Black Hawk. All the young men felt the attraction of the fine, well-set-up country girls who had come to town to earn a living, and, in nearly every case, to help the father struggle out of debt, or to make it possible for the younger children of the family to go to school.

Those girls had grown up in the first bitter-hard times, and had got little schooling themselves. But the younger brothers and sisters, for whom they made such sacrifices and who have had "advantages," never seem to me, when I meet them now, half as interesting or as well educated. The older girls, who helped to break up the wild sod, learned so much from life, from poverty, from their mothers and grandmothers; they had all, like Ántonia, been early awakened and made observant by coming at a tender age from an old country to a new. I can remember a score of these country girls who were in ser-vice in Black Hawk during the few years I lived there, and I can remember something unusual and engaging about each of them. Physically they were almost a race apart, and out-of-door work had given them a vigor which, when they got over their first shyness on coming to town, developed into a positive carriage and freedom of movement, and made them conspicuous among Black Hawk women.

That was before the day of High-School athletics. Girls who had to walk more than half a mile to school were pitied. There was not a tennis court in the town; physical exercise was thought rather in-elegant for the daughters of well-to-do families. Some of the High-School girls were jolly and pretty, but they stayed indoors in winter because of the cold, and in summer because of the heat. When one danced with them their bodies never moved inside their clothes; their muscles seemed to ask but one thing—not to be disturbed. I remem-ber those girls merely as faces in the schoolroom, gay and rosy, or listless and dull, cut off below the shoulders, like cherubs, by the ink-smeared tops of the high desks that were surely put there to make us round-shouldered and hollow-chested.

The daughters of Black Hawk merchants had a confident, un-inquiring belief that they were "refined," and that the country girls, who "worked out," were not. The American farmers in our country were quite as hard-pressed as their neighbors from other countries.

All alike had come to Nebraska with little capital and no knowledge of the soil they must subdue. All had borrowed money on their land. But no matter in what straits the Pennsylvanian or Virginian found himself, he would not let his daughters go out into service. Unless his girls could teach a country school, they sat at home in poverty. The Bohemian and Scandinavian girls could not get positions as teachers, because they had had no opportunity to learn the language. Determined to help in the struggle to clear the homestead from debt, they had no alternative but to go into service. Some of them, after they came to town, remained as serious and as discreet in behavior as they had been when they ploughed and herded on their father's farm. Others, like the three Bohemian Marys, tried to make up for the years of youth they had lost. But every one of them did what she had set out to do, and sent home those hard-earned dollars. The girls I knew were always helping to pay for ploughs and reapers, brood-sows, or steers to fatten.

One result of this family solidarity was that the foreign farmers in our county were the first to become prosperous. After the fathers were out of debt, the daughters married the sons of neighbors,— usually of like nationality,—and the girls who once worked in Black Hawk kitchens are to-day managing big farms and fine families of their own; their children are better off than the children of the town women they used to serve.

I thought the attitude of the town people toward these girls very stupid. If I told my schoolmates that Lena Lingard's grandfather was a clergyman, and much respected in Norway, they looked at me blankly. What did it matter? All foreigners were ignorant people who could n't speak English. There was not a man in Black Hawk who had the intelligence or cultivation, much less the personal distinc-tion, of Ántonia's father. Yet people saw no difference between her and the three Marys; they were all Bohemians, all "hired girls."

I always knew I should live long enough to see my country girls come into their own, and I have. To-day the best that a harassed Black Hawk merchant can hope for is to sell provisions and farm machin-ery and automobiles to the rich farms where that first crop of stal-wart Bohemian and Scandinavian girls are now the mistresses.

The Black Hawk boys looked forward to marrying Black Hawk girls, and living in a brand-new little house with best chairs that must not be sat upon, and hand-painted china that must not be used. But sometimes a young fellow would look up from his ledger, or out through the grating of his father's bank, and let his eyes follow Lena Lingard, as she passed the window with her slow, undulating walk, or Tiny Soderball, tripping by in her short skirt and striped stockings.

The country girls were considered a menace to the social order. Their beauty shone out too boldly against a conventional background.

But anxious mothers need have felt no alarm. They mistook the mettle of their sons. The respect for respectability was stronger than any desire in Black Hawk youth.

Our young man of position was like the son of a royal house; the boy who swept out his office or drove his delivery wagon might frolic with the jolly country girls, but he himself must sit all evening in a plush parlor where conversation dragged so perceptibly that the father often came in and made blundering efforts to warm up the atmosphere. On his way home from his dull call, he would perhaps meet Tony and Lena, coming along the sidewalk whispering to each other, or the three Bohemian Marys in their long plush coats and caps, comporting themselves with a dignity that only made their eventful histories the more piquant. If he went to the hotel to see a traveling man on business, there was Tiny, arching her shoulders at him like a kitten. If he went into the laundry to get his collars, there were the four Danish girls, smiling up from their ironing-boards, with their white throats and their pink cheeks.

The three Marys were the heroines of a cycle of scandalous stories, which the old men were fond of relating as they sat about the cigar-stand in the drug-store. Mary Dusak had been housekeeper for a bachelor rancher from Boston, and after several years in his service she was forced to retire from the world for a short time. Later she came back to town to take the place of her friend, Mary Svoboda, who was similarly embarrassed. The three Marys were considered as dangerous as high explosives to have about the kitchen, yet they were such good cooks and such admirable housekeepers that they never had to look for a place.

The Vannis' tent brought the town boys and the country girls together on neutral ground. Sylvester Lovett, who was cashier in his father's bank, always found his way to the tent on Saturday night. He took all the dances Lena Lingard would give him, and even grew bold enough to walk home with her. If his sisters or their friends happened to be among the onlookers on "popular nights," Sylvester stood back in the shadow under the cottonwood trees, smoking and watching Lena with a harassed expression. Several times I stumbled upon him there in the dark, and I felt rather sorry for him. He reminded me of Ole Benson, who used to sit on the drawside and watch Lena herd her cattle. Later in the summer, when Lena went home for a week to visit her mother, I heard from Ántonia that young Lovett drove all the way out there to see her, and took her buggyriding. In my ingenuousness I hoped that Sylvester would marry Lena, and thus give all the country girls a better position in the town.

Sylvester dallied about Lena until he began to make mistakes in his work; had to stay at the bank until after dark to make his books balance. He was daft about her, and every one knew it. To escape from his predicament he ran away with a widow six years older than himself, who owned a half-section. This remedy worked, apparently. He never looked at Lena again, nor lifted his eyes as he ceremoniously tipped his hat when he happened to meet her on the sidewalk.

So that was what they were like, I thought, these white-handed, high-collared clerks and bookkeepers! I used to glare at young Lovett from a distance and only wished I had some way of showing my contempt for him.

X

It was at the Vannis' tent that Ántonia was discovered. Hitherto she had been looked upon more as a ward of the Harlings than as one of the "hired girls." She had lived in their house and yard and garden; her thoughts never seemed to stray outside that little kingdom. But after the tent came to town she began to go about with Tiny and Lena and their friends. The Vannis often said that Ántonia was the best dancer of them all. I sometimes heard murmurs in the crowd outside the pavilion that Mrs. Harling would soon have her hands full with that girl. The young men began to joke with each other about "the Harlings' Tony" as they did about "the Marshalls' Anna" or "the Gardeners' Tiny."

Ántonia talked and thought of nothing but the tent. She hummed the dance tunes all day. When supper was late, she hurried with her dishes, dropped and smashed them in her excitement. At the first call of the music, she became irresponsible. If she had n't time to dress, she merely flung off her apron and shot out of the kitchen door. Sometimes I went with her; the moment the lighted tent came into view she would break into a run, like a boy. There were always partners waiting for her; she began to dance before she got her breath.

Ántonia's success at the tent had its consequences. The iceman lingered too long now, when he came into the covered porch to fill the refrigerator. The delivery boys hung about the kitchen when they brought the groceries. Young farmers who were in town for Saturday came tramping through the yard to the back door to engage dances, or to invite Tony to parties and picnics. Lena and Norwegian Anna dropped in to help her with her work, so that she could get away early. The boys who brought her home after the dances sometimes laughed at the back gate and wakened Mr. Harling from his first sleep. A crisis was inevitable.

One Saturday night Mr. Harling had gone down to the cellar for beer. As he came up the stairs in the dark, he heard scuffling on the back porch, and then the sound of a vigorous slap. He looked out through the side door in time to see a pair of long legs vaulting

over the picket fence. Ántonia was standing there, angry and excited.
Young Harry Paine, who was to marry his employer's daughter on
Monday, had come to the tent with a crowd of friends and danced
all evening. Afterward, he begged Ántonia to let him walk home with
her. She said she supposed he was a nice young man, as he was one
of Miss Frances's friends, and she did n't mind. On the back porch
he tried to kiss her, and when she protested,—because he was going
to be married on Monday,—he caught her and kissed her until she
got one hand free and slapped him.

Mr. Harling put his beer bottles down on the table. "This is what
I've been expecting, Ántonia. You've been going with girls who have a
reputation for being free and easy, and now you've got the same reputation. I won't have this and that fellow tramping about my back yard
all the time. This is the end of it, to-night. It stops, short. You can quit
going to these dances, or you can hunt another place. Think it over."

The next morning when Mrs. Harling and Frances tried to reason with Ántonia, they found her agitated but determined. "Stop
going to the tent?" she panted. "I would n't think of it for a minute!
My own father could n't make me stop! Mr. Harling ain't my boss
outside my work. I won't give up my friends, either. The boys I go
with are nice fellows. I thought Mr. Paine was all right, too, because
he used to come here. I guess I gave him a red face for his wedding,
all right!" she blazed out indignantly.

"You'll have to do one thing or the other, Ántonia," Mrs. Harling
told her decidedly. "I can't go back on what Mr. Harling has said.
This is his house."

"Then I'll just leave, Mrs. Harling. Lena's been wanting me to get
a place closer to her for a long while. Mary Svoboda's going away
from the Cutters' to work at the hotel, and I can have her place."

Mrs. Harling rose from her chair. "Ántonia, if you go to the Cutters to work, you cannot come back to this house again. You know
what that man is. It will be the ruin of you."

Tony snatched up the tea-kettle and began to pour boiling water
over the glasses, laughing excitedly. "Oh, I can take care of myself!
I'm a lot stronger than Cutter is. They pay four dollars there, and
there's no children. The work's nothing; I can have every evening,
and be out a lot in the afternoons."

"I thought you liked children. Tony, what's come over you?"

"I don't know, something has." Ántonia tossed her head and set
her jaw. "A girl like me has got to take her good times when she can.
Maybe there won't be any tent next year. I guess I want to have my
fling, like the other girls."

Mrs. Harling gave a short, harsh laugh. "If you go to work for the
Cutters, you're likely to have a fling that you won't get up from in a
hurry."

Frances said, when she told grandmother and me about this scene, that every pan and plate and cup on the shelves trembled when her mother walked out of the kitchen. Mrs. Harling declared bitterly that she wished she had never let herself get fond of Ántonia.

XI

Wick Cutter was the money-lender who had fleeced poor Russian Peter. When a farmer once got into the habit of going to Cutter, it was like gambling or the lottery; in an hour of discouragement he went back.

Cutter's first name was Wycliffe, and he liked to talk about his pious bringing-up. He contributed regularly to the Protestant churches, "for sentiment's sake," as he said with a flourish of the hand. He came from a town in Iowa where there were a great many Swedes, and could speak a little Swedish, which gave him a great advantage with the early Scandinavian settlers.

In every frontier settlement there are men who have come there to escape restraint. Cutter was one of the "fast set" of Black Hawk business men. He was an inveterate gambler, though a poor loser. When we saw a light burning in his office late at night, we knew that a game of poker was going on. Cutter boasted that he never drank anything stronger than sherry, and he said he got his start in life by saving the money that other young men spent for cigars. He was full of moral maxims for boys. When he came to our house on business, he quoted "Poor Richard's Almanack" to me, and told me he was delighted to find a town boy who could milk a cow. He was particularly affable to grandmother, and whenever they met he would begin at once to talk about "the good old times" and simple living. I detested his pink, bald head, and his yellow whiskers, always soft and glistening. It was said he brushed them every night, as a woman does her hair. His white teeth looked factory-made. His skin was red and rough, as if from perpetual sunburn; he often went away to hot springs to take mud baths. He was notoriously dissolute with women. Two Swedish girls who had lived in his house were the worse for the experience. One of them he had taken to Omaha and established in the business for which he had fitted her. He still visited her.

Cutter lived in a state of perpetual warfare with his wife, and yet, apparently, they never thought of separating. They dwelt in a fussy, scroll-work house, painted white and buried in thick evergreens, with a fussy white fence and barn. Cutter thought he knew a great deal about horses, and usually had a colt which he was training for the track. On Sunday mornings one could see him out at the fair grounds, speeding around the race-course in his trotting-buggy, wearing yellow gloves and a black-and-white-check traveling cap, his whiskers blowing back in the breeze. If there were any boys about, Cutter would offer one of them a quarter to hold the stop-watch, and then drive off, saying he had no change and would "fix it up next time." No one could cut his lawn or wash his buggy to suit him. He was so fastidious and prim about his place that a boy would go to a good deal of trouble to throw a dead cat into his back yard, or to dump a sackful of tin cans in his alley. It was a peculiar combination of old-maidishness and licentiousness that made Cutter seem so despicable.

He had certainly met his match when he married Mrs. Cutter. She was a terrifying-looking person; almost a giantess in height, raw-boned, with iron-gray hair, a face always flushed, and prominent, hysterical eyes. When she meant to be entertaining and agreeable, she nodded her head incessantly and snapped her eyes at one. Her teeth were long and curved, like a horse's; people said babies always cried if she smiled at them. Her face had a kind of fascination for me; it was the very color and shape of anger. There was a gleam of something akin to insanity in her full, intense eyes. She was formal in manner, and made calls in rustling, steel-gray brocades and a tall bonnet with bristling aigrettes.

Mrs. Cutter painted china so assiduously that even her wash-bowls and pitchers, and her husband's shaving-mug, were covered with violets and lilies. Once when Cutter was exhibiting some of his wife's china to a caller, he dropped a piece. Mrs. Cutter put her handkerchief to her lips as if she were going to faint and said grandly: "Mr. Cutter, you have broken all the Commandments—spare the finger-bowls!"

They quarreled from the moment Cutter came into the house until they went to bed at night, and their hired girls reported these scenes to the town at large. Mrs. Cutter had several times cut paragraphs about unfaithful husbands out of the newspapers and mailed them to Cutter in a disguised handwriting. Cutter would come home at noon, find the mutilated journal in the paper-rack, and triumphantly fit the clipping into the space from which it had been cut. Those two could quarrel all morning about whether he ought to put on his heavy or his light underwear, and all evening about whether he had taken cold or not.

The Cutters had major as well as minor subjects for dispute. The chief of these was the question of inheritance: Mrs. Cutter told her husband it was plainly his fault they had no children. He insisted that Mrs. Cutter had purposely remained childless, with the determination to outlive him and to share his property with her "people," whom he detested. To this she would reply that unless he changed his mode of life, she would certainly outlive him. After listening to her insinuations about his physical soundness, Cutter would resume his dumb-bell practice for a month, or rise daily at the hour when his wife most liked to sleep, dress noisily, and drive out to the track with his trotting-horse.

Once when they had quarreled about household expenses, Mrs. Cutter put on her brocade and went among their friends soliciting orders for painted china, saying that Mr. Cutter had compelled her "to live by her brush." Cutter was n't shamed as she had expected; he was delighted!

Cutter often threatened to chop down the cedar trees which half-buried the house. His wife declared she would leave him if she were stripped of the "privacy" which she felt these trees afforded her. That was his opportunity, surely; but he never cut down the trees. The Cutters seemed to find their relations to each other interesting and stimulating, and certainly the rest of us found them so. Wick Cutter was different from any other rascal I have ever known, but I have found Mrs. Cutters all over the world; sometimes founding new religions, sometimes being forcibly fed—easily recognizable, even when superficially tamed.

XII

After Ántonia went to live with the Cutters, she seemed to care about nothing but picnics and parties and having a good time. When she was not going to a dance, she sewed until midnight. Her new clothes were the subject of caustic comment. Under Lena's direction she copied Mrs. Gardener's new party dress and Mrs. Smith's street costume so ingeniously in cheap materials that those ladies were greatly annoyed, and Mrs. Cutter, who was jealous of them, was secretly pleased.

Tony wore gloves now, and high-heeled shoes and feathered bonnets, and she went downtown nearly every afternoon with Tiny and Lena and the Marshalls' Norwegian Anna. We High-School boys used to linger on the playground at the afternoon recess to watch them as they came tripping down the hill along the board sidewalk, two and two. They were growing prettier every day, but as they passed us, I used to think with pride that Ántonia, like Snow-White in the fairy tale, was still "fairest of them all."

Being a Senior now, I got away from school early. Sometimes I overtook the girls downtown and coaxed them into the ice-cream parlor, where they would sit chattering and laughing, telling me all the news from the country. I remember how angry Tiny Soderball made me one afternoon. She declared she had heard grandmother was going to make a Baptist preacher of me. "I guess you'll have to stop dancing and wear a white necktie then. Won't he look funny, girls?"

Lena laughed. "You'll have to hurry up, Jim. If you're going to be a preacher, I want you to marry me. You must promise to marry us all, and then baptize the babies."

Norwegian Anna, always dignified, looked at her reprovingly.

"Baptists don't believe in christening babies, do they, Jim?"

I told her I did n't know what they believed, and did n't care, and that I certainly was n't going to be a preacher.

"That's too bad," Tiny simpered. She was in a teasing mood. "You'd make such a good one. You're so studious. Maybe you'd like to be a professor. You used to teach Tony, did n't you?"

Ántonia broke in. "I've set my heart on Jim being a doctor. You'd be good with sick people, Jim. Your grandmother's trained you up so nice. My papa always said you were an awful smart boy."

I said I was going to be whatever I pleased. "Won't you be surprised, Miss Tiny, if I turn out to be a regular devil of a fellow?"

They laughed until a glance from Norwegian Anna checked them; the High-School Principal had just come into the front part of the shop to buy bread for supper. Anna knew the whisper was going about that I was a sly one. People said there must be something queer about a boy who showed no interest in girls of his own age, but who could be lively enough when he was with Tony and Lena or the three Marys.

The enthusiasm for the dance, which the Vannis had kindled, did not at once die out. After the tent left town, the Euchre Club became the Owl Club, and gave dances in the Masonic Hall once a week. I was invited to join, but declined. I was moody and restless that winter, and tired of the people I saw every day. Charley Harling was already at Annapolis, while I was still sitting in Black Hawk, answering to my name at roll-call every morning, rising from my desk at the sound of a bell and marching out like the grammar-school children. Mrs. Harling was a little cool toward me, because I continued to champion Ántonia. What was there for me to do after supper? Usually I had learned next day's lessons by the time I left the school building, and I could n't sit still and read forever.

In the evening I used to prowl about, hunting for diversion. There lay the familiar streets, frozen with snow or liquid with mud. They led to the houses of good people who were putting the babies to bed, or simply sitting still before the parlor stove, digesting their supper. Black Hawk had two saloons. One of them was admitted, even by the church people, to be as respectable as a saloon could be. Handsome Anton Jelinek, who had rented his homestead and come to town, was the proprietor. In his saloon there were long tables where the Bohemian and German farmers could eat the lunches they brought from home while they drank their beer. Jelinek kept rye bread on hand, and smoked fish and strong imported cheeses to please the foreign palate.

I liked to drop into his bar-room and listen to the talk. But one day he overtook me on the street and clapped me on the shoulder.

"Jim," he said, "I am good friends with you and I always like to see you. But you know how the church people think about saloons. Your grandpa has always treated me fine, and I don't like to have you come into my place, because I know he don't like it, and it puts me in bad with him."

So I was shut out of that.

One could hang about the drug-store, and listen to the old men who sat there every evening, talking politics and telling raw stories. One could go to the cigar factory and chat with the old German who raised canaries for sale, and look at his stuffed birds. But whatever you began with him, the talk went back to taxidermy. There was the depot, of course; I often went down to see the night train come in, and afterward sat awhile with the disconsolate telegrapher who was always hoping to be transferred to Omaha or Denver, "where there was some life." He was sure to bring out his pictures of actresses and dancers. He got them with cigarette coupons, and nearly smoked himself to death to possess these desired forms and faces. For a change, one could talk to the station agent; but he was another malcontent; spent all his spare time writing letters to officials requesting a transfer. He wanted to get back to Wyoming where he could go trout-fishing on Sundays. He used to say "there was nothing in life for him but trout streams, ever since he'd lost his twins."

These were the distractions I had to choose from. There were no other lights burning downtown after nine o'clock. On starlight nights I used to pace up and down those long, cold streets, scowling at the little, sleeping houses on either side, with their storm-windows and covered back porches. They were flimsy shelters, most of them poorly built of light wood, with spindle porch-posts horribly mutilated by the turning-lathe. Yet for all their frailness, how much jealousy and envy and unhappiness some of them managed to contain! The life that went on in them seemed to me made up of evasions and negations; shifts to save cooking, to save washing and cleaning, devices to propitiate the tongue of gossip. This guarded mode of existence was like living under a tyranny. People's speech, their voices, their very glances, became furtive and repressed. Every individual taste, every natural appetite, was bridled by caution. The people asleep in those houses, I thought, tried to live like the mice in their own kitchens; to make no noise, to leave no trace, to slip over the surface of things in the dark. The growing piles of ashes and cinders in the back yards were the only evidence that the wasteful, consuming process of life went on at all. On Tuesday nights the Owl Club danced; then there was a little stir in the streets, and here and there one could see a lighted window until midnight. But the next night all was dark again.

After I refused to join "the Owls," as they were called, I made a bold resolve to go to the Saturday night dances at Firemen's Hall. I knew it would be useless to acquaint my elders with any such plan. Grandfather did n't approve of dancing anyway; he would only say that if I wanted to dance I could go to the Masonic Hall, among "the people we knew." It was just my point that I saw altogether too much of the people we knew.

My bedroom was on the ground floor, and as I studied there, I had a stove in it. I used to retire to my room early on Saturday night, change my shirt and collar and put on my Sunday coat. I waited until all was quiet and the old people were asleep, then raised my window, climbed out, and went softly through the yard. The first time I deceived my grandparents I felt rather shabby, perhaps even the second time, but I soon ceased to think about it.

The dance at the Firemen's Hall was the one thing I looked forward to all the week. There I met the same people I used to see at the Vannis' tent. Sometimes there were Bohemians from Wilber, or German boys who came down on the afternoon freight from Bismarck. Tony and Lena and Tiny were always there, and the three Bohemian Marys, and the Danish laundry girls.

The four Danish girls lived with the laundryman and his wife in their house behind the laundry, with a big garden where the clothes were hung out to dry. The laundryman was a kind, wise old fellow, who paid his girls well, looked out for them, and gave them a good home. He told me once that his own daughter died just as she was getting old enough to help her mother, and that he had been "trying to make up for it ever since." On summer afternoons he used to sit for hours on the sidewalk in front of his laundry, his newspaper lying on his knee, watching his girls through the big open window while they ironed and talked in Danish. The clouds of white dust that blew up the street, the gusts of hot wind that withered his vegetable garden, never disturbed his calm. His droll expression seemed to say that he had found the secret of contentment. Morning and evening he drove about in his spring wagon, distributing freshly ironed clothes, and collecting bags of linen that cried out for his suds and sunny drying-lines. His girls never looked so pretty at the dances as they did standing by the ironing-board, or over the tubs, washing the fine pieces, their white arms and throats bare, their cheeks bright as the brightest wild roses, their gold hair moist with the steam or the heat and curling in little damp spirals about their ears. They had not learned much English, and were not so ambitious as Tony or Lena; but they were kind, simple girls and they were always happy. When one danced with them, one smelled their clean, freshly ironed clothes that had been put away with rosemary leaves from Mr. Jensen's garden.

There were never girls enough to go round at those dances, but every one wanted a turn with Tony and Lena. Lena moved without exertion, rather indolently, and her hand often accented the rhythm softly on her partner's shoulder. She smiled if one spoke to her, but seldom answered: The music seemed to put her into a soft, waking dream, and her violet-colored eyes looked sleepily and confidingly at one from under her long lashes. When she sighed she exhaled a heavy perfume of sachet powder. To dance "Home, Sweet Home," with Lena was like coming in with the tide. She danced every dance like a waltz, and it was always the same waltz—the waltz of coming home to something, of inevitable, fated return. After a while one got restless under it, as one does under the heat of a soft, sultry summer day.

When you spun out into the floor with Tony, you did n't return to anything. You set out every time upon a new adventure. I liked to schottische with her; she had so much spring and variety, and was always putting in new steps and slides. She taught me to dance against and around the hard-and-fast beat of the music. If, instead of going to the end of the railroad, old Mr. Shimerda had stayed in New York and picked up a living with his fiddle, how different Ántonia's life might have been!

Ántonia often went to the dances with Larry Donovan, a passenger conductor who was a kind of professional ladies' man, as we said. I remember how admiringly all the boys looked at her the night she first wore her velveteen dress, made like Mrs. Gardener's black velvet. She was lovely to see, with her eyes shining, and her lips always a little parted when she danced. That constant, dark color in her cheeks never changed.

One evening when Donovan was out on his run, Ántonia came to the hall with Norwegian Anna and her young man, and that night I took her home. When we were in the Cutters' yard, sheltered by the evergreens, I told her she must kiss me good-night.

"Why, sure, Jim." A moment later she drew her face away and whispered indignantly, "Why, Jim! You know you ain't right to kiss me like that. I'll tell your grandmother on you!"

"Lena Lingard lets me kiss her," I retorted, "and I'm not half as fond of her as I am of you."

"Lena does?" Tony gasped. "If she's up to any of her nonsense with you, I'll scratch her eyes out!" She took my arm again and we walked out of the gate and up and down the sidewalk. "Now, don't you go and be a fool like some of these town boys. You're not going to sit around here and whittle store-boxes and tell stories all your life. You are going away to school and make something of yourself. I'm just awful proud of you. You won't go and get mixed up with the Swedes, will you?"

"I don't care anything about any of them but you," I said. "And you'll always treat me like a kid, I suppose."

She laughed and threw her arms around me. "I expect I will, but you're a kid I'm awful fond of, anyhow! You can like me all you want to, but if I see you hanging round with Lena much, I'll go to your grandmother, as sure as your name's Jim Burden! Lena's all right, only—well, you know yourself she's soft that way. She can't help it. It's natural to her."

If she was proud of me, I was so proud of her that I carried my head high as I emerged from the dark cedars and shut the Cutters' gate softly behind me. Her warm, sweet face, her kind arms, and the true heart in her; she was, oh, she was still my Ántonia! I looked with contempt at the dark, silent little houses about me as I walked home, and thought of the stupid young men who were asleep in some of them. I knew where the real women were, though I was only a boy; and I would not be afraid of them, either!

I hated to enter the still house when I went home from the dances, and it was long before I could get to sleep. Toward morning I used to have pleasant dreams: sometimes Tony and I were out in the country, sliding down straw-stacks as we used to do; climbing up the yellow mountains over and over, and slipping down the smooth sides into soft piles of chaff.

One dream I dreamed a great many times, and it was always the same. I was in a harvest-field full of shocks, and I was lying against one of them. Lena Lingard came across the stubble barefoot, in a short skirt, with a curved reaping-hook in her hand, and she was flushed like the dawn, with a kind of luminous rosiness all about her. She sat down beside me, turned to me with a soft sigh and said, "Now they are all gone, and I can kiss you as much as I like."

I used to wish I could have this flattering dream about Ántonia, but I never did.

XIII

I noticed one afternoon that grandmother had been crying. Her feet seemed to drag as she moved about the house, and I got up from the table where I was studying and went to her, asking if she did n't feel well, and if I could n't help her with her work.

"No, thank you, Jim. I'm troubled, but I guess I'm well enough. Getting a little rusty in the bones, maybe," she added bitterly.

I stood hesitating. "What are you fretting about, grandmother? Has grandfather lost any money?"

"No, it ain't money. I wish it was. But I've heard things. You must 'a' known it would come back to me sometime." She dropped into a chair, and covering her face with her apron, began to cry. "Jim," she said, "I was never one that claimed old folks could bring up their grandchildren. But it came about so; there was n't any other way for you, it seemed like."

I put my arms around her. I could n't bear to see her cry.

"What is it, grandmother? Is it the Firemen's dances?"

She nodded.

"I'm sorry I sneaked off like that. But there's nothing wrong about the dances, and I have n't done anything wrong. I like all those country girls, and I like to dance with them. That's all there is to it."

"But it ain't right to deceive us, son, and it brings blame on us. People say you are growing up to be a bad boy, and that ain't just to us."

"I don't care what they say about me, but if it hurts you, that settles it. I won't go to the Firemen's Hall again."

I kept my promise, of course, but I found the spring months dull enough. I sat at home with the old people in the evenings now, reading Latin that was not in our High-School course. I had made up my mind to do a lot of college requirement work in the summer, and to enter the freshman class at the University without conditions in the fall. I wanted to get away as soon as possible.

Disapprobation hurt me, I found,—even that of people whom I did not admire. As the spring came on, I grew more and more lonely, and fell back on the telegrapher and the cigar-maker and his canaries for companionship. I remember I took a melancholy pleasure in hanging a May-basket for Nina Harling that spring. I bought the flowers from an old German woman who always had more window plants than any one else, and spent an afternoon trimming a little work-basket. When dusk came on, and the new moon hung in the sky, I went quietly to the Harlings' front door with my offering, rang the bell, and then ran away as was the custom. Through the willow hedge I could hear Nina's cries of delight, and I felt comforted.

On those warm, soft spring evenings I often lingered downtown to walk home with Frances, and talked to her about my plans and about the reading I was doing. One evening she said she thought Mrs. Harling was not seriously offended with me.

"Mama is as broad-minded as mothers ever are, I guess. But you know she was hurt about Ántonia, and she can't understand why you like to be with Tiny and Lena better than with the girls of your own set."

"Can you?" I asked bluntly.

Frances laughed. "Yes, I think I can. You knew them in the country, and you like to take sides. In some ways you're older than boys of your age. It will be all right with mama after you pass your college examinations and she sees you're in earnest."

"If you were a boy," I persisted, "you would n't belong to the Owl Club, either. You'd be just like me."

She shook her head. "I would and I would n't. I expect I know the country girls better than you do. You always put a kind of glamour over them. The trouble with you, Jim, is that you're romantic. Mama's going to your Commencement. She asked me the other day if I knew what your oration is to be about. She wants you to do well."

I thought my oration very good. It stated with fervor a great many things I had lately discovered. Mrs. Harling came to the Opera House to hear the Commencement exercises, and I looked at her most of the time while I made my speech. Her keen, intelligent eyes never left my face. Afterward she came back to the dressing-room where we stood, with our diplomas in our hands, walked up to me, and said heartily: "You surprised me, Jim. I did n't believe you could do as well as that. You did n't get that speech out of books." Among my graduation presents there was a silk umbrella from Mrs. Harling, with my name on the handle.

I walked home from the Opera House alone. As I passed the Methodist Church, I saw three white figures ahead of me, pacing up and down under the arching maple trees, where the moonlight filtered through the lush June foliage. They hurried toward me; they were waiting for me—Lena and Tony and Anna Hansen.

"Oh, Jim, it was splendid!" Tony was breathing hard, as she always did when her feelings outran her language. "There ain't a lawyer in Black Hawk could make a speech like that. I just stopped your grandpa and said so to him. He won't tell you, but he told us he was awful surprised himself, did n't he, girls?"

Lena sidled up to me and said teasingly: "What made you so solemn? I thought you were scared. I was sure you'd forget."

Anna spoke wistfully. "It must make you happy, Jim, to have fine thoughts like that in your mind all the time, and to have words to put them in. I always wanted to go to school, you know."

"Oh, I just sat there and wished my papa could hear you! Jim,"— Ántonia took hold of my coat lapels,—"there was something in your speech that made me think so about my papa!"

"I thought about your papa when I wrote my speech, Tony," I said. "I dedicated it to him."

She threw her arms around me, and her dear face was all wet with tears.

I stood watching their white dresses glimmer smaller and smaller down the sidewalk as they went away. I have had no other success that pulled at my heartstrings like that one.

XIV

The day after Commencement I moved my books and desk upstairs, to an empty room where I should be undisturbed, and I fell to studying in earnest. I worked off a year's trigonometry that summer, and began Virgil alone. Morning after morning I used to pace up and down my sunny little room, looking off at the distant river bluffs and the roll of the blond pastures between, scanning the Æneid aloud and committing long passages to memory. Sometimes in the evening Mrs. Harling called to me as I passed her gate, and asked me to come in and let her play for me. She was lonely for Charley, she said, and liked to have a boy about. Whenever my grandparents had misgivings, and began to wonder whether I was not too young to go off to college alone, Mrs. Harling took up my cause vigorously. Grandfather had such respect for her judgment that I knew he would not go against her.

I had only one holiday that summer. It was in July. I met Ántonia downtown on Saturday afternoon, and learned that she and Tiny and Lena were going to the river next day with Anna Hansen—the elder was all in bloom now, and Anna wanted to make elder-blow wine.

"Anna's to drive us down in the Marshalls' delivery wagon, and we'll take a nice lunch and have a picnic. Just us; nobody else. Could n't you happen along, Jim? It would be like old times."

I considered a moment. "Maybe I can, if I won't be in the way."

On Sunday morning I rose early and got out of Black Hawk while the dew was still heavy on the long meadow grasses. It was the high season for summer flowers. The pink bee-bush stood tall along the sandy roadsides, and the cone-flowers and rose mallow grew everywhere. Across the wire fence, in the long grass, I saw a clump of flaming orange-colored milkweed, rare in that part of the State. I left the road and went around through a stretch of pasture that was always cropped short in summer, where the gaillardia came up year after year and matted over the ground with the deep, velvety red that is in Bokhara carpets. The country was empty and solitary except for the larks that Sunday morning, and it seemed to lift itself up to me and to come very close.

The river was running strong for midsummer; heavy rains to the west of us had kept it full. I crossed the bridge and went upstream along the wooded shore to a pleasant dressing-room I knew among the dogwood bushes, all overgrown with wild grapevines. I began to undress for a swim. The girls would not be along yet. For the first time it occurred to me that I would be homesick for that river after I left it. The sandbars, with their clean white beaches and their little groves of willows and cottonwood seedlings, were a sort of No Man's Land, little newly-created worlds that belonged to the Black Hawk boys. Charley Harling and I had hunted through these woods, fished from the fallen logs, until I knew every inch of the river shores and had a friendly feeling for every bar and shallow.

After my swim, while I was playing about indolently in the water, I heard the sound of hoofs and wheels on the bridge. I struck downstream and shouted, as the open spring wagon came into view on the middle span. They stopped the horse, and the two girls in the bottom of the cart stood up, steadying themselves by the shoulders of the two in front, so that they could see me better. They were charming up there, huddled together in the cart and peering down at me like curious deer when they come out of the thicket to drink. I found bottom near the bridge and stood up, waving to them.

"How pretty you look!" I called.

"So do you!" they shouted altogether, and broke into peals of laughter. Anna Hansen shook the reins and they drove on, while I zigzagged back to my inlet and clambered up behind an overhanging elm. I dried myself in the sun, and dressed slowly, reluctant to leave that green enclosure where the sunlight flickered so bright through the grapevine leaves and the woodpecker hammered away in the crooked elm that trailed out over the water. As I went along the road back to the bridge I kept picking off little pieces of scaly chalk from the dried water gullies, and breaking them up in my hands.

When I came upon the Marshalls' delivery horse, tied in the shade, the girls had already taken their baskets and gone down the east road which wound through the sand and scrub. I could hear them calling to each other. The elder bushes did not grow back in the shady ravines between the bluffs, but in the hot, sandy bottoms along the stream, where their roots were always in moisture and their tops in the sun. The blossoms were unusually luxuriant and beautiful that summer.

I followed a cattle path through the thick underbrush until I came to a slope that fell away abruptly to the water's edge. A great chunk of the shore had been bitten out by some spring freshet, and the scar was masked by elder bushes, growing down to the water in flowery terraces. I did not touch them. I was overcome by content and drowsiness and by the warm silence about me. There was no sound but the high, sing-song buzz of wild bees and the sunny gurgle of the water underneath. I peeped over the edge of the bank to see the little stream that made the noise; it flowed along perfectly clear over the sand and gravel, cut off from the muddy main current by a long sandbar. Down there, on the lower shelf of the bank, I saw Ántonia, seated alone under the pagoda-like elders. She looked up when she heard me, and smiled, but I saw that she had been crying. I slid down into the soft sand beside her and asked her what was the matter.

"It makes me homesick, Jimmy, this flower, this smell," she said softly. "We have this flower very much at home, in the old country. It always grew in our yard and my papa had a green bench and a table under the bushes. In summer, when they were in bloom, he used to sit there with his friend that played the trombone. When I was little I used to go down there to hear them talk—beautiful talk, like what I never hear in this country."

"What did they talk about?" I asked her.

She sighed and shook her head. "Oh, I don't know! About music, and the woods, and about God, and when they were young." She turned to me suddenly and looked into my eyes. "You think, Jimmy, that maybe my father's spirit can go back to those old places?"

I told her about the feeling of her father's presence I had on that winter day when my grandparents had gone over to see his dead body and I was left alone in the house. I said I felt sure then that he was on his way back to his own country, and that even now, when I passed his grave, I always thought of him as being among the woods and fields that were so dear to him.

Ántonia had the most trusting, responsive eyes in the world; love and credulousness seemed to look out of them with open faces. "Why did n't you ever tell me that before? It makes me feel more sure for him." After a while she said: "You know, Jim, my father was different from my mother. He did not have to marry my mother, and all his brothers quarreled with him because he did. I used to hear the old people at home whisper about it. They said he could have paid my mother money, and not married her. But he was older than she was, and he was too kind to treat her like that. He lived in his mother's house, and she was a poor girl come in to do the work. After my father married her, my grandmother never let my mother come into her house again. When I went to my grandmother's funeral was the only time I was ever in my grandmother's house. Don't that seem strange?"

While she talked, I lay back in the hot sand and looked up at the blue sky between the flat bouquets of elder. I could hear the bees humming and singing, but they stayed up in the sun above the flowers and did not come down into the shadow of the leaves. Ántonia seemed to me that day exactly like the little girl who used to come to our house with Mr. Shimerda.

"Some day, Tony, I am going over to your country, and I am going to the little town where you lived. Do you remember all about it?"

"Jim," she said earnestly, "if I was put down there in the middle of the night, I could find my way all over that little town; and along the river to the next town, where my grandmother lived. My feet remember all the little paths through the woods, and where the big roots stick out to trip you. I ain't never forgot my own country."

There was a crackling in the branches above us, and Lena Lingard peered down over the edge of the bank.

"You lazy things!" she cried. "All this elder, and you two lying there! Did n't you hear us calling you?" Almost as flushed as she had been in my dream, she leaned over the edge of the bank and began to demolish our flowery pagoda. I had never seen her so energetic; she was panting with zeal, and the perspiration stood in drops on her short, yielding upper lip. I sprang to my feet and ran up the bank.

It was noon now, and so hot that the dogwoods and scrub-oaks began to turn up the silvery under-side of their leaves, and all the foliage looked soft and wilted. I carried the lunch-basket to the top of one of the chalk bluffs, where even on the calmest days there was always a breeze. The flat-topped, twisted little oaks threw light shadows on the grass. Below us we could see the windings of the river, and Black Hawk, grouped among its trees, and, beyond, the rolling country, swelling gently until it met the sky. We could recognize familiar farmhouses and windmills. Each of the girls pointed out to me the direction in which her father's farm lay, and told me how many acres were in wheat that year and how many in corn.

"My old folks," said Tiny Soderball, "have put in twenty acres of rye. They get it ground at the mill, and it makes nice bread. It seems like my mother ain't been so homesick, ever since father's raised rye flour for her."

"It must have been a trial for our mothers," said Lena, "coming out here and having to do everything different. My mother had always lived in town. She says she started behind in farm-work, and never has caught up."

"Yes, a new country's hard on the old ones, sometimes," said Anna thoughtfully. "My grandmother's getting feeble now, and her mind wanders. She's forgot about this country, and thinks she's at home in Norway. She keeps asking mother to take her down to the water-side and the fish market. She craves fish all the time. Whenever I go home I take her canned salmon and mackerel."

"Mercy, it's hot!" Lena yawned. She was supine under a little oak, resting after the fury of her elder-hunting, and had taken off the high-heeled slippers she had been silly enough to wear. "Come here, Jim. You never got the sand out of your hair." She began to draw her fingers slowly through my hair.

Ántonia pushed her away. "You'll never get it out like that," she said sharply. She gave my head a rough touzling and finished me off with something like a box on the ear. "Lena, you ought n't to try to wear those slippers any more. They're too small for your feet. You'd better give them to me for Yulka."

"All right," said Lena good-naturedly, tucking her white stockings under her skirt. "You get all Yulka's things, don't you? I wish father did n't have such bad luck with his farm machinery; then I could buy more things for my sisters. I'm going to get Mary a new coat this fall, if the sulky plough's never paid for!"

Tiny asked her why she did n't wait until after Christmas, when coats would be cheaper. "What do you think of poor me?" she added; "with six at home, younger than I am? And they all think I'm rich, because when I go back to the country I'm dressed so fine!" She shrugged her shoulders. "But, you know, my weakness is playthings. I like to buy them playthings better than what they need."

"I know how that is," said Anna. "When we first came here, and I was little, we were too poor to buy toys. I never got over the loss of a doll somebody gave me before we left Norway. A boy on the boat broke her, and I still hate him for it."

"I guess after you got here you had plenty of live dolls to nurse, like me!" Lena remarked cynically.

"Yes, the babies came along pretty fast, to be sure. But I never minded. I was fond of them all. The youngest one, that we did n't any of us want, is the one we love best now."

Lena sighed. "Oh, the babies are all right; if only they don't come in winter. Ours nearly always did. I don't see how mother stood it. I tell you what, girls," she sat up with sudden energy; "I'm going to get my mother out of that old sod house where she's lived so many years. The men will never do it. Johnnie, that's my oldest brother, he's wanting to get married now, and build a house for his girl instead of his mother. Mrs. Thomas says she thinks I can move to some other town pretty soon, and go into business for myself. If I don't get into business, I'll maybe marry a rich gambler."

"That would be a poor way to get on," said Anna sarcastically. "I wish I could teach school, like Selma Kronn. Just think! She'll be the first Scandinavian girl to get a position in the High School. We ought to be proud of her."

Selma was a studious girl, who had not much tolerance for giddy things like Tiny and Lena; but they always spoke of her with admiration.

Tiny moved about restlessly, fanning herself with her straw hat. "If I was smart like her, I'd be at my books day and night. But she was born smart—and look how her father's trained her! He was something high up in the old country."

"So was my mother's father," murmured Lena, "but that's all the good it does us! My father's father was smart, too, but he was wild. He married a Lapp. I guess that's what's the matter with me; they say Lapp blood will out."

"A real Lapp, Lena?" I exclaimed. "The kind that wear skins?"

"I don't know if she wore skins, but she was a Lapp all right, and his folks felt dreadful about it. He was sent up north on some Government job he had, and fell in with her. He would marry her."

"But I thought Lapland women were fat and ugly, and had squint eyes, like Chinese?" I objected.

"I don't know, maybe. There must be something mighty taking about the Lapp girls, though; mother says the Norwegians up north are always afraid their boys will run after them."

In the afternoon, when the heat was less oppressive, we had a lively game of "Pussy Wants a Corner," on the flat bluff-top, with the little trees for bases. Lena was Pussy so often that she finally said she would n't play any more. We threw ourselves down on the grass, out of breath.

"Jim," Ántonia said dreamily, "I want you to tell the girls about how the Spanish first came here, like you and Charley Harling used to talk about. I've tried to tell them, but I leave out so much."

They sat under a little oak, Tony resting against the trunk and the other girls leaning against her and each other, and listened to the little I was able to tell them about Coronado and his search for the Seven Golden Cities. At school we were taught that he had not got so far north as Nebraska, but had given up his quest and turned back somewhere in Kansas. But Charley Harling and I had a strong belief that he had been along this very river. A farmer in the county north of ours, when he was breaking sod, had turned up a metal stirrup of fine workmanship, and a sword with a Spanish inscription on the blade. He lent these relics to Mr. Harling, who brought them home with him. Charley and I scoured them, and they were on exhibition in the Harling office all summer. Father Kelly, the priest, had found the name of the Spanish maker on the sword, and an abbreviation that stood for the city of Cordova.

"And that I saw with my own eyes," Ántonia put in triumphantly. "So Jim and Charley were right, and the teachers were wrong!"

The girls began to wonder among themselves. Why had the Spaniards come so far? What must this country have been like, then? Why had Coronado never gone back to Spain, to his riches and his castles and his king? I could n't tell them. I only knew the school books said he "died in the wilderness, of a broken heart."

"More than him has done that," said Ántonia sadly, and the girls murmured assent.

We sat looking off across the country, watching the sun go down. The curly grass about us was on fire now. The bark of the oaks turned red as copper. There was a shimmer of gold on the brown river. Out in the stream the sandbars glittered like glass, and the light trembled in the willow thickets as if little flames were leaping among them. The breeze sank to stillness. In the ravine a ringdove mourned plaintively, and somewhere off in the bushes an owl hooted. The girls sat listless, leaning against each other. The long fingers of the sun touched their foreheads.

Presently we saw a curious thing: There were no clouds, the sun was going down in a limpid, gold-washed sky. Just as the lower edge of the red disc rested on the high fields against the horizon, a great black figure suddenly appeared on the face of the sun. We sprang to our feet, straining our eyes toward it. In a moment we realized what it was. On some upland farm, a plough had been left standing in the field. The sun was sinking just behind it. Magnified across the distance by the horizontal light, it stood out against the sun, was exactly contained within the circle of the disc; the handles, the tongue, the share—black against the molten red. There it was, heroic in size, a picture writing on the sun.

Even while we whispered about it, our vision disappeared; the ball dropped and dropped until the red tip went beneath the earth. The fields below us were dark, the sky was growing pale, and that forgotten plough had sunk back to its own littleness somewhere on the prairie.

XV

Late in August the Cutters went to Omaha for a few days, leaving Ántonia in charge of the house. Since the scandal about the Swedish girl, Wick Cutter could never get his wife to stir out of Black Hawk without him.

The day after the Cutters left, Ántonia came over to see us. Grandmother noticed that she seemed troubled and distracted. "You've got something on your mind, Ántonia," she said anxiously.

"Yes, Mrs. Burden. I could n't sleep much last night." She hesitated, and then told us how strangely Mr. Cutter had behaved before he went away. He put all the silver in a basket and placed it under her bed, and with it a box of papers which he told her were valuable. He made her promise that she would not sleep away from the house, or be out late in the evening, while he was gone. He strictly forbade her to ask any of the girls she knew to stay with her at night. She would be perfectly safe, he said, as he had just put a new Yale lock on the front door.

Cutter had been so insistent in regard to these details that now she felt uncomfortable about staying there alone. She had n't liked the way he kept coming into the kitchen to instruct her, or the way he looked at her. "I feel as if he is up to some of his tricks again, and is going to try to scare me, somehow."

Grandmother was apprehensive at once. "I don't think it's right for you to stay there, feeling that way. I suppose it would n't be right for you to leave the place alone, either, after giving your word. Maybe Jim would be willing to go over there and sleep, and you could come here nights. I'd feel safer, knowing you were under my own roof. I guess Jim could take care of their silver and old usury notes as well as you could."

Ántonia turned to me eagerly. "Oh, would you, Jim? I'd make up my bed nice and fresh for you. It's a real cool room, and the bed's right next the window. I was afraid to leave the window open last night."

I liked my own room, and I did n't like the Cutters' house under any circumstances; but Tony looked so troubled that I consented to try this arrangement. I found that I slept there as well as anywhere, and when I got home in the morning, Tony had a good breakfast waiting for me. After prayers she sat down at the table with us, and it was like old times in the country.

The third night I spent at the Cutters', I awoke suddenly with the impression that I had heard a door open and shut. Everything was still, however, and I must have gone to sleep again immediately.

The next thing I knew, I felt some one sit down on the edge of the bed. I was only half awake, but I decided that he might take the Cutters' silver, whoever he was. Perhaps if I did not move, he would find it and get out without troubling me. I held my breath and lay absolutely still. A hand closed softly on my shoulder, and at the same moment I felt something hairy and cologne-scented brushing my face. If the room had suddenly been flooded with electric light, I could n't have seen more clearly the detestable bearded countenance that I knew was bending over me. I caught a handful of whiskers and pulled, shouting something. The hand that held my shoulder was instantly at my throat. The man became insane; he stood over me, choking me with one fist and beating me in the face with the other, hissing and chuckling and letting out a flood of abuse.

"So this is what she's up to when I'm away, is it? Where is she, you nasty whelp, where is she? Under the bed, are you, hussy? I know your tricks! Wait till I get at you! I'll fix this rat you've got in here. He's caught, all right!"

So long as Cutter had me by the throat, there was no chance for me at all. I got hold of his thumb and bent it back, until he let go with a yell. In a bound, I was on my feet, and easily sent him sprawling to the floor. Then I made a dive for the open window, struck the wire screen, knocked it out, and tumbled after it into the yard.

Suddenly I found myself running across the north end of Black Hawk in my nightshirt, just as one sometimes finds one's self behaving in bad dreams. When I got home I climbed in at the kitchen window. I was covered with blood from my nose and lip, but I was too sick to do anything about it. I found a shawl and an overcoat on the hatrack, lay down on the parlor sofa, and in spite of my hurts, went to sleep.

Grandmother found me there in the morning. Her cry of fright awakened me. Truly, I was a battered object. As she helped me to my room, I caught a glimpse of myself in the mirror. My lip was cut and stood out like a snout. My nose looked like a big blue plum, and one eye was swollen shut and hideously discolored. Grandmother said we must have the doctor at once, but I implored her, as I had never begged for anything before, not to send for him. I could stand anything, I told her, so long as nobody saw me or knew what had happened to me. I entreated her not to let grandfather, even, come into my room. She seemed to understand, though I was too faint and miserable to go into explanations. When she took off my nightshirt, she found such bruises on my chest and shoulders that she began to cry. She spent the whole morning bathing and poulticing me, and rubbing me with arnica. I heard Ántonia sobbing outside my door, but I asked grandmother to send her away. I felt that I never wanted to see her again. I hated her almost as much as I hated Cutter. She had let me in for all this disgustingness. Grandmother kept saying how thankful we ought to be that I had been there instead of Ántonia. But I lay with my disfigured face to the wall and felt no particular gratitude. My one concern was that grandmother should keep every one away from me. If the story once got abroad, I would never hear the last of it. I could well imagine what the old men down at the drug-store would do with such a theme.

While grandmother was trying to make me comfortable, grandfather went to the depot and learned that Wick Cutter had come home on the night express from the east, and had left again on the six o'clock train for Denver that morning. The agent said his face was striped with court-plaster, and he carried his left hand in a sling. He looked so used up, that the agent asked him what had happened to him since ten o'clock the night before; whereat Cutter began to swear at him and said he would have him discharged for incivility.

That afternoon, while I was asleep, Ántonia took grandmother with her, and went over to the Cutters' to pack her trunk. They found the place locked up, and they had to break the window to get into Ántonia's bedroom. There everything was in shocking disorder. Her clothes had been taken out of her closet, thrown into the middle of the room, and trampled and torn. My own garments had been treated so badly that I never saw them again; grandmother burned them in the Cutters' kitchen range.

While Ántonia was packing her trunk and putting her room in order, to leave it, the front-door bell rang violently. There stood Mrs. Cutter,—locked out, for she had no key to the new lock—her head trembling with rage. "I advised her to control herself, or she would have a stroke," grandmother said afterwards.

Grandmother would not let her see Ántonia at all, but made her sit down in the parlor while she related to her just what had occurred the night before. Ántonia was frightened, and was going home to stay for a while, she told Mrs. Cutter; it would be useless to interrogate the girl, for she knew nothing of what had happened.

Then Mrs. Cutter told her story. She and her husband had started home from Omaha together the morning before. They had to stop over several hours at Waymore Junction to catch the Black Hawk train. During the wait, Cutter left her at the depot and went to the Waymore bank to attend to some business. When he returned, he told her that he would have to stay overnight there, but she could go on home. He bought her ticket and put her on the train. She saw him slip a twenty-dollar bill into her handbag with her ticket. That bill, she said, should have aroused her suspicions at once—but did not.

The trains are never called at little junction towns; everybody knows when they come in. Mr. Cutter showed his wife's ticket to the conductor, and settled her in her seat before the train moved off. It was not until nearly nightfall that she discovered she was on the express bound for Kansas City, that her ticket was made out to that point, and that Cutter must have planned it so. The conductor told her the Black Hawk train was due at Waymore twelve minutes after the Kansas City train left. She saw at once that her husband had played this trick in order to get back to Black Hawk without her. She had no choice but to go on to Kansas City and take the first fast train for home.

Cutter could have got home a day earlier than his wife by any one of a dozen simpler devices; he could have left her in the Omaha hotel, and said he was going on to Chicago for a few days. But apparently it was part of his fun to outrage her feelings as much as possible.

"Mr. Cutter will pay for this, Mrs. Burden. He will pay!" Mrs. Cutter avouched, nodding her horselike head and rolling her eyes.

Grandmother said she had n't a doubt of it.

Certainly Cutter liked to have his wife think him a devil. In some way he depended upon the excitement he could arouse in her hysterical nature. Perhaps he got the feeling of being a rake more from his wife's rage and amazement than from any experiences of his own. His zest in debauchery might wane, but never Mrs. Cutter's belief in it. The reckoning with his wife at the end of an escapade was something he counted on—like the last powerful liqueur after a long dinner. The one excitement he really could n't do without was quarreling with Mrs. Cutter!

Book III

Lena Lingard

I

At the university I had the good fortune to come immediately under the influence of a brilliant and inspiring young scholar. Gaston Cleric had arrived in Lincoln only a few weeks earlier than I, to begin his work as head of the Latin Department. He came West at the suggestion of his physicians, his health having been enfeebled by a long illness in Italy. When I took my entrance examinations he was my examiner, and my course was arranged under his supervision.

I did not go home for my first summer vacation, but stayed in Lincoln, working off a year's Greek, which had been my only condition on entering the Freshman class. Cleric's doctor advised against his going back to New England, and except for a few weeks in Colorado, he, too, was in Lincoln all that summer. We played tennis, read, and took long walks together. I shall always look back on that time of mental awakening as one of the happiest in my life. Gaston Cleric introduced me to the world of ideas; when one first enters that world everything else fades for a time, and all that went before is as if it had not been. Yet I found curious survivals; some of the figures of my old life seemed to be waiting for me in the new.

In those days there were many serious young men among the students who had come up to the University from the farms and the little towns scattered over the thinly settled State. Some of those boys came straight from the cornfields with only a summer's wages in their pockets, hung on through the four years, shabby and underfed, and completed the course by really heroic self-sacrifice. Our instructors were oddly assorted; wandering pioneer school-teachers, stranded ministers of the Gospel, a few enthusiastic young men just out of graduate schools. There was an atmosphere of endeavor, of expectancy and bright hopefulness about the young college that had lifted its head from the prairie only a few years before.

Our personal life was as free as that of our instructors. There were no college dormitories; we lived where we could and as we could. I took rooms with an old couple, early settlers in Lincoln, who had married off their children and now lived quietly in their house at the edge of town, near the open country. The house was inconveniently situated for students, and on that account I got two rooms for the price of one. My bedroom, originally a linen closet, was unheated and was barely large enough to contain my cot bed, but it enabled me to call the other room my study. The dresser, and the great walnut wardrobe which held all my clothes, even my hats and shoes, I had pushed out of the way, and I considered them nonexistent, as children eliminate incongruous objects when they are playing house. I worked at a commodious green-topped table placed directly in front of the west window which looked out over the prairie. In the corner at my right were all my books, in shelves I had made and painted myself. On the blank wall at my left the dark, old-fashioned wallpaper was covered by a large map of ancient Rome, the work of some German scholar. Cleric had ordered it for me when he was sending for books from abroad. Over the bookcase hung a photograph of the Tragic Theater at Pompeii, which he had given me from his collection.

When I sat at work I half faced a deep, upholstered chair which stood at the end of my table, its high back against the wall. I had bought it with great care. My instructor sometimes looked in upon me when he was out for an evening tramp, and I noticed that he was more likely to linger and become talkative if I had a comfortable chair for him to sit in, and if he found a bottle of Bénédictine and plenty of the kind of cigarettes he liked, at his elbow. He was, I had discovered, parsimonious about small expenditures—a trait absolutely inconsistent with his general character. Sometimes when he came he was silent and moody, and after a few sarcastic remarks went away again, to tramp the streets of Lincoln, which were almost as quiet and oppressively domestic as those of Black Hawk. Again, he would sit until nearly midnight, talking about Latin and English poetry, or telling me about his long stay in Italy.

I can give no idea of the peculiar charm and vividness of his talk. In a crowd he was nearly always silent. Even for his classroom he had no platitudes, no stock of professorial anecdotes. When he was tired his lectures were clouded, obscure, elliptical; but when he was interested they were wonderful. I believe that Gaston Cleric narrowly missed being a great poet, and I have sometimes thought that his bursts of imaginative talk were fatal to his poetic gift. He squandered too much in the heat of personal communication. How often I have seen him draw his dark brows together, fix his eyes upon some object on the wall or a figure in the carpet, and then flash into the lamplight the very image that was in his brain. He could bring the drama of antique life before one out of the shadows—white figures against blue backgrounds. I shall never forget his face as it looked one night when he told me about the solitary day he spent among the sea temples at Paestum.[1] the soft wind blowing through the roofless columns, the birds flying low over the flowering marsh grasses, the changing lights on the silver, cloud-hung mountains. He had willfully stayed the short summer night there, wrapped in his coat and rug, watching the constellations on their path down the sky until "the bride of old Tithonus"[2] rose out of the sea, and the mountains stood sharp in the dawn. It was there he caught the fever which held him back on the eve of his departure for Greece and of which he lay ill so long in Naples. He was still, indeed, doing penance for it.

I remember vividly another evening, when something led us to talk of Dante's veneration for Virgil. Cleric went through canto after canto of the "Commedia," repeating the discourse between Dante and his "sweet teacher," while his cigarette burned itself out unheeded between his long fingers. I can hear him now, speaking the lines of the poet Statius, who spoke for Dante: *"I was famous on earth with the name which endures longest and honors most. The seeds of my ardor were the sparks from that divine flame whereby more than a thousand have kindled; I speak of the Æneid, mother to me and nurse to me in poetry."*[3]

Although I admired scholarship so much in Cleric, I was not deceived about myself; I knew that I should never be a scholar. I could never lose myself for long among impersonal things. Mental excitement was apt to send me with a rush back to my own naked land and the figures scattered upon it. While I was in the very act of yearning toward the new forms that Cleric brought up before me, my mind plunged away from me, and I suddenly found myself thinking of the places and people of my own infinitesimal past. They stood out strengthened and simplified now, like the image of the plough against the sun. They were all I had for an answer to the new appeal. I begrudged the room that Jake and Otto and Russian Peter took up in my memory, which I wanted to crowd with other things. But whenever my consciousness was quickened, all those early friends were quickened within it, and in some strange way they accompanied me through all my new experiences. They were so much alive in me that I scarcely stopped to wonder whether they were alive anywhere else, or how.

II

One March evening in my Sophomore year I was sitting alone in my room after supper. There had been a warm thaw all day, with mushy

---

1. Paestum, a coastal town in southern Italy, had Roman temples dedicated to Neptune and Ceres dating from the sixth and fifth centuries B.C.E.
2. Eos, or Aurora, goddess of the dawn.
3. Publius Pabinius Statius, Roman poet of the first century B.C.E. who appears as a character in Dante's epic poem *The Divine Comedy*.

yards and little streams of dark water gurgling cheerfully into the streets out of old snow-banks. My window was open, and the earthy wind blowing through made me indolent. On the edge of the prairie, where the sun had gone down, the sky was turquoise blue, like a lake, with gold light throbbing in it. Higher up, in the utter clarity of the western slope, the evening star hung like a lamp suspended by silver chains—like the lamp engraved upon the title-page of old Latin texts, which is always appearing in new heavens, and waking new desires in men. It reminded me, at any rate, to shut my window and light my wick in answer. I did so regretfully, and the dim objects in the room emerged from the shadows and took their place about me with the helpfulness which custom breeds.

I propped my book open and stared listlessly at the page of the Georgics[4] where to-morrow's lesson began. It opened with the melancholy reflection that, in the lives of mortals, the best days are the first to flee. "*Optima dies . . . prima fugit.*" I turned back to the beginning of the third book, which we had read in class that morning. "*Primus ego in patriam mecum . . . deducam Musas*"; "for I shall be the first, if I live, to bring the Muse into my country." Cleric had explained to us that "patria" here meant, not a nation or even a province, but the little rural neighborhood on the Mincio where the poet was born. This was not a boast, but a hope, at once bold and devoutly humble, that he might bring the Muse (but lately come to Italy from her cloudy Grecian mountains), not to the capital, the *palatia Romana*, but to his own little "country"; to his father's fields, "sloping down to the river and to the old beech trees with broken tops."

Cleric said he thought Virgil, when he was dying at Brindisi, must have remembered that passage. After he had faced the bitter fact that he was to leave the Æneid unfinished, and had decreed that the great canvas, crowded with figures of gods and men, should be burned rather than survive him unperfected, then his mind must have gone back to the perfect utterance of the Georgics, where the pen was fitted to the matter as the plough is to the furrow; and he must have said to himself with the thankfulness of a good man, "I was the first to bring the Muse into my country."

We left the classroom quietly, conscious that we had been brushed by the wing of a great feeling, though perhaps I alone knew Cleric intimately enough to guess what that feeling was. In the evening, as I sat staring at my book, the fervor of his voice stirred through the quantities on the page before me. I was wondering whether that particular rocky strip of New England coast about which he had so often told me was Cleric's *patria*. Before I had got far with my reading

4. A poem in four books by Virgil that takes agriculture as its central subject.

I was disturbed by a knock. I hurried to the door and when I opened it saw a woman standing in the dark hall.

"I expect you hardly know me, Jim."

The voice seemed familiar, but I did not recognize her until she stepped into the light of my doorway and I beheld—Lena Lingard! She was so quietly conventionalized by city clothes that I might have passed her on the street without seeing her. Her black suit fitted her figure smoothly, and a black lace hat, with pale-blue forget-me-nots, sat demurely on her yellow hair.

I led her toward Cleric's chair, the only comfortable one I had, questioning her confusedly.

She was not disconcerted by my embarrassment. She looked about her with the naïve curiosity I remembered so well. "You are quite comfortable here, aren't you? I live in Lincoln now, too, Jim. I'm in business for myself. I have a dressmaking shop in the Raleigh Block, out on O Street. I've made a real good start."

"But, Lena, when did you come?"

"Oh, I've been here all winter. Didn't your grandmother ever write you? I've thought about looking you up lots of times. But we've all heard what a studious young man you've got to be, and I felt bashful. I did n't know whether you'd be glad to see me." She laughed her mellow, easy laugh, that was either very artless or very comprehending, one never quite knew which. "You seem the same, though,—except you're a young man, now, of course. Do you think I've changed?"

"Maybe you're prettier—though you were always pretty enough. Perhaps it's your clothes that make a difference."

"You like my new suit? I have to dress pretty well in my business." She took off her jacket and sat more at ease in her blouse, of some soft, flimsy silk. She was already at home in my place, had slipped quietly into it, as she did into everything. She told me her business was going well, and she had saved a little money.

"This summer I'm going to build the house for mother I've talked about so long. I won't be able to pay up on it at first, but I want her to have it before she is too old to enjoy it. Next summer I'll take her down new furniture and carpets, so she'll have something to look forward to all winter."

I watched Lena sitting there so smooth and sunny and well cared-for, and thought of how she used to run barefoot over the prairie until after the snow began to fly, and how Crazy Mary chased her round and round the cornfields. It seemed to me wonderful that she should have got on so well in the world. Certainly she had no one but herself to thank for it.

"You must feel proud of yourself, Lena," I said heartily. "Look at me; I've never earned a dollar, and I don't know that I'll ever be able to."

"Tony says you're going to be richer than Mr. Harling some day. She's always bragging about you, you know."

"Tell me, how *is* Tony?"

"She's fine. She works for Mrs. Gardener at the hotel now. She's housekeeper. Mrs. Gardener's health is n't what it was, and she can't see after everything like she used to. She has great confidence in Tony, Tony's made it up with the Harlings, too. Little Nina is so fond of her that Mrs. Harling kind of overlooked things."

"Is she still going with Larry Donovan?"

"Oh, that's on, worse than ever! I guess they're engaged. Tony talks about him like he was president of the railroad. Everybody laughs about it, because she was never a girl to be soft. She won't hear a word against him. She's so sort of innocent."

I said I did n't like Larry, and never would.

Lena's face dimpled. "Some of us could tell her things, but it wouldn't do any good. She'd always believe him. That's Ántonia's failing, you know; if she once likes people, she won't hear anything against them."

"I think I'd better go home and look after Ántonia," I said.

"I think you had." Lena looked up at me in frank amusement. "It's a good thing the Harlings are friendly with her again. Larry's afraid of them. They ship so much grain, they have influence with the railroad people. What are you studying?" She leaned her elbows on the table and drew my book toward her. I caught a faint odor of violet sachet. "So that's Latin, is it? It looks hard. You do go to the theater sometimes, though, for I've seen you there. Don't you just love a good play, Jim? I can't stay at home in the evening if there's one in town. I'd be willing to work like a slave, it seems to me, to live in a place where there are theaters."

"Let's go to a show together sometime. You are going to let me come to see you, are n't you?"

"Would you like to? I'd be ever so pleased. I'm never busy after six o'clock, and I let my sewing girls go at half-past five. I board, to save time, but sometimes I cook a chop for myself, and I'd be glad to cook one for you. Well,"—she began to put on her white gloves,—"it's been awful good to see you, Jim."

"You need n't hurry, need you? You've hardly told me anything yet."

"We can talk when you come to see me. I expect you don't often have lady visitors. The old woman downstairs did n't want to let me come up very much. I told her I was from your home town, and had promised your grandmother to come and see you. How surprised Mrs. Burden would be!" Lena laughed softly as she rose.

When I caught up my hat she shook her head. "No, I don't want you to go with me. I'm to meet some Swedes at the drug-store. You would n't care for them. I wanted to see your room so I could write

Tony all about it, but I must tell her how I left you right here with
your books. She's always so afraid some one will run off with you!"
Lena slipped her silk sleeves into the jacket I held for her, smoothed
it over her person, and buttoned it slowly. I walked with her to the
door. "Come and see me sometimes when you're lonesome. But maybe
you have all the friends you want. Have you?" She turned her soft
cheek to me. "Have you?" she whispered teasingly in my ear. In a
moment I watched her fade down the dusky stairway.

When I turned back to my room the place seemed much pleasanter
than before. Lena had left something warm and friendly in the lamplight. How I loved to hear her laugh again! It was so soft and un-
excited and appreciative—gave a favorable interpretation to everything.
When I closed my eyes I could hear them all laughing—the Danish
laundry girls and the three Bohemian Marys. Lena had brought them
all back to me. It came over me, as it had never done before, the
relation between girls like those and the poetry of Virgil. If there
were no girls like them in the world, there would be no poetry.
I understood that clearly, for the first time. This revelation seemed to
me inestimably precious. I clung to it as if it might suddenly vanish.

As I sat down to my book at last, my old dream about Lena coming across the harvest field in her short skirt seemed to me like the
memory of an actual experience. It floated before me on the page
like a picture, and underneath it stood the mournful line: *Optima
dies . . . prima fugit.*

III

In Lincoln the best part of the theatrical season came late, when
the good companies stopped off there for one-night stands, after their
long runs in New York and Chicago. That spring Lena went with
me to see Joseph Jefferson[5] in "Rip Van Winkle," and to a war play
called "Shenandoah." She was inflexible about paying for her own
seat; said she was in business now, and she would n't have a schoolboy spending his money on her. I liked to watch a play with Lena;
everything was wonderful to her, and everything was true. It was
like going to revival meetings with some one who was always being
converted. She handed her feelings over to the actors with a kind of
fatalistic resignation. Accessories of costume and scene meant much
more to her than to me. She sat entranced through "Robin Hood"
and hung upon the lips of the contralto who sang, "Oh, Promise Me!"

Toward the end of April, the billboards, which I watched anxiously
in those days, bloomed out one morning with gleaming white

5. American actor and comedian (1829–1905).

posters on which two names were impressively printed in blue
Gothic letters: the name of an actress of whom I had often heard,
and the name "Camille."[6]

I called at the Raleigh Block for Lena on Saturday evening, and we
walked down to the theater. The weather was warm and sultry and
put us both in a holiday humor. We arrived early, because Lena liked
to watch the people come in. There was a note on the programme,
saying that the "incidental music" would be from the opera "Traviata," which was made from the same story as the play.[7] We had neither of us read the play, and we did not know what it was about—though
I seemed to remember having heard it was a piece in which great
actresses shone. "The Count of Monte Cristo," which I had seen
James O'Neill play that winter, was by the only Alexandre Dumas I
knew.[8] This play, I saw, was by his son, and I expected a family resem-
blance. A couple of jack-rabbits, run in off the prairie, could not have
been more innocent of what awaited them than were Lena and I.

Our excitement began with the rise of the curtain, when the moody
Varville, seated before the fire, interrogated Nanine. Decidedly, there
was a new tang about this dialogue. I had never heard in the theater lines that were alive, that presupposed and took for granted,
like those which passed between Varville and Marguerite in the
brief encounter before her friends entered. This introduced the most
brilliant, worldly, the most enchantingly gay scene I had ever looked
upon. I had never seen champagne bottles opened on the stage
before—indeed, I had never seen them opened anywhere. The memory of that supper makes me hungry now; the sight of it then, when
I had only a students' boarding-house dinner behind me, was delicate torment. I seem to remember gilded chairs and tables (arranged
hurriedly by footmen in white gloves and stockings), linen of dazzling whiteness, glittering glass, silver dishes, a great bowl of fruit,
and the reddest of roses. The room was invaded by beautiful women
and dashing young men, laughing and talking together. The men
were dressed more or less after the period in which the play was written; the women were not. I saw no inconsistency. Their talk seemed
to open to one the brilliant world in which they lived; every sentence
made one older and wiser, every pleasantry enlarged one's horizon.
One could experience excess and satiety without the inconvenience
of learning what to do with one's hands in a drawing-room! When
the characters all spoke at once and I missed some of the phrases

6. *Camille*, by Alexandre Dumas the younger, a romantic play popular in nineteenth-century
   America, based on his novel *La Dame aux camélias* (1848).
7. *La traviata*, Italian opera by Giuseppe Verdi, based on *La Dame aux camélias*, first per-
   formed in 1853.
8. Alexandre Dumas the elder, author of the novel *The Count of Monte Cristo*, source of
   the stage play of the same title. The Irish-born actor James O'Neill (1847–1920) was
   known for his frequent performances in the role of the count.

they flashed at each other, I was in misery. I strained my ears and eyes to catch every exclamation.

The actress who played Marguerite[9] was even then old-fashioned, though historic. She had been a member of Daly's famous New York company, and afterward a "star" under his direction.[1] She was a woman who could not be taught, it is said, though she had a crude natural force which carried with people whose feelings were accessible and whose taste was not squeamish. She was already old, with a ravaged countenance and a physique curiously hard and stiff. She moved with difficulty—I think she was lame—I seem to remember some story about a malady of the spine. Her Armand was disproportionately young and slight, a handsome youth, perplexed in the extreme. But what did it matter? I believed devoutly in her power to fascinate him, in her dazzling loveliness. I believed her young, ardent, reckless, disillusioned, under sentence, feverish, avid of pleasure. I wanted to cross the footlights and help the slim-waisted Armand in the frilled shirt to convince her that there was still loyalty and devotion in the world. Her sudden illness, when the gayety was at its height, her pallor, the handkerchief she crushed against her lips, the cough she smothered under the laughter while Gaston kept playing the piano lightly—it all wrung my heart. But not so much as her cynicism in the long dialogue with her lover which followed. How far was I from questioning her unbelief! While the charmingly sincere young man pleaded with her—accompanied by the orchestra in the old "Traviata" duet, *"misterioso, misterioso!"*—she maintained her bitter skepticism, and the curtain fell on her dancing recklessly with the others, after Armand had been sent away with his flower.

Between the acts we had no time to forget. The orchestra kept sawing away at the "Traviata" music, so joyous and sad, so thin and far-away, so clap-trap and yet so heart-breaking. After the second act I left Lena in tearful contemplation of the ceiling, and went out into the lobby to smoke. As I walked about there I congratulated myself that I had not brought some Lincoln girl who would talk during the waits about the Junior dances, or whether the cadets would camp at Plattsmouth. Lena was at least a woman, and I was a man.

Through the scene between Marguerite and the elder Duval, Lena wept unceasingly, and I sat helpless to prevent the closing of that chapter of idyllic love, dreading the return of the young man whose ineffable happiness was only to be the measure of his fall.

I suppose no woman could have been further in person, voice, and temperament from Dumas' appealing heroine than the veteran

9. Marguerite Gautier, the doomed consumptive heroine who sacrifices herself for her lover Armand.
1. John Augustin Daly (1838–1899), American producer, director, and playwright. The actress is probably Clara Morris (1848–1925), who starred in his production of *Camille*.

actress who first acquainted me with her. Her conception of the character was as heavy and uncompromising as her diction; she bore hard on the idea and on the consonants. At all times she was highly tragic, devoured by remorse. Lightness of stress or behavior was far from her. Her voice was heavy and deep: "Ar-r-r-mond!" she would begin, as if she were summoning him to the bar of Judgment. But the lines were enough. She had only to utter them. They created the character in spite of her.

The heartless world which Marguerite re-entered with Varville had never been so glittering and reckless as on the night when it gathered in Olympe's salon for the fourth act. There were chandeliers hung from the ceiling, I remember, many servants in livery, gaming-tables where the men played with piles of gold, and a staircase down which the guests made their entrance. After all the others had gathered round the card tables, and young Duval had been warned by Prudence, Marguerite descended the staircase with Varville; such a cloak, such a fan, such jewels—and her face! One knew at a glance how it was with her. When Armand, with the terrible words, "Look, all of you, I owe this woman nothing!" flung the gold and bank-notes at the half-swooning Marguerite, Lena cowered beside me and covered her face with her hands.

The curtain rose on the bedroom scene. By this time there was n't a nerve in me that had n't been twisted. Nanine alone could have made me cry. I loved Nanine tenderly; and Gaston, how one clung to that good fellow! The New Year's presents were not too much; nothing could be too much now. I wept unrestrainedly. Even the handkerchief in my breast-pocket, worn for elegance and not at all for use, was wet through by the time that moribund woman sank for the last time into the arms of her lover.

When we reached the door of the theater, the streets were shining with rain. I had prudently brought along Mrs. Harling's useful Commencement present, and I took Lena home under its shelter. After leaving her, I walked slowly out into the country part of the town where I lived. The lilacs were all blooming in the yards, and the smell of them after the rain, of the new leaves and the blossoms together, blew into my face with a sort of bitter sweetness. I tramped through the puddles and under the showery trees, mourning for Marguerite Gauthier as if she had died only yesterday, sighing with the spirit of 1840, which had sighed so much, and which had reached me only that night, across long years and several languages, through the person of an infirm old actress. The idea is one that no circumstances can frustrate. Wherever and whenever that piece is put on, it is April.

IV

How well I remember the stiff little parlor where I used to wait for
Lena: the hard horse-hair furniture, bought at some auction sale,
the long mirror, the fashion-plates on the wall. If I sat down even
for a moment I was sure to find threads and bits of colored silk clinging to my clothes after I went away. Lena's success puzzled me. She
was so easy-going; had none of the push and self-assertiveness that
get people ahead in business. She had come to Lincoln, a country
girl, with no introductions except to some cousins of Mrs. Thomas
who lived there, and she was already making clothes for the women
of "the young married set." She evidently had great natural aptitude
for her work. She knew, as she said, "what people looked well in."
She never tired of poring over fashion books. Sometimes in the evening I would find her alone in her work-room, draping folds of satin
on a wire figure, with a quite blissful expression of countenance.
I could n't help thinking that the years when Lena literally had n't
enough clothes to cover herself might have something to do with her
untiring interest in dressing the human figure. Her clients said that
Lena "had style," and overlooked her habitual inaccuracies. She
never, I discovered, finished anything by the time she had promised,
and she frequently spent more money on materials than her customer
had authorized. Once, when I arrived at six o'clock, Lena was usher-
ing out a fidgety mother and her awkward, overgrown daughter. The
woman detained Lena at the door to say apologetically:—

"You'll try to keep it under fifty for me, won't you, Miss Lingard?
You see, she's really too young to come to an expensive dressmaker,
but I knew you could do more with her than anybody else."

"Oh, that will be all right, Mrs. Herron. I think we'll manage to
get a good effect," Lena replied blandly.

I thought her manner with her customers very good, and wondered
where she had learned such self-possession.

Sometimes after my morning classes were over, I used to encounter
Lena downtown, in her velvet suit and a little black hat, with a veil
tied smoothly over her face, looking as fresh as the spring morning.
Maybe she would be carrying home a bunch of jonquils or a hyacinth
plant. When we passed a candy store her footsteps would hesitate and
linger. "Don't let me go in," she would murmur. "Get me by if you can."
She was very fond of sweets, and was afraid of growing too plump.

We had delightful Sunday breakfasts together at Lena's. At the
back of her long work-room was a bay-window, large enough to hold
a box-couch and a reading-table. We breakfasted in this recess, after
drawing the curtains that shut out the long room, with cutting-tables
and wire women and sheet-draped garments on the walls. The sunlight poured in, making everything on the table shine and glitter and

the flame of the alcohol lamp disappear altogether. Lena's curly black water-spaniel, Prince, breakfasted with us. He sat beside her on the couch and behaved very well until the Polish violin-teacher across the hall began to practice, when Prince would growl and sniff the air with disgust. Lena's landlord, old Colonel Raleigh, had given her the dog, and at first she was not at all pleased. She had spent too much of her life taking care of animals to have much sentiment about them. But Prince was a knowing little beast, and she grew fond of him. After breakfast I made him do his lessons; play dead dog, shake hands, stand up like a soldier. We used to put my cadet cap on his head—I had to take military drill at the University—and give him a yard-measure to hold with his front leg. His gravity made us laugh immoderately.

Lena's talk always amused me. Ántonia had never talked like the people about her. Even after she learned to speak English readily there was always something impulsive and foreign in her speech. But Lena had picked up all the conventional expressions she heard at Mrs. Thomas's dressmaking shop. Those formal phrases, the very flower of small-town proprieties, and the flat commonplaces, nearly all hypocritical in their origin, became very funny, very engaging, when they were uttered in Lena's soft voice, with her caressing intonation and arch naïveté. Nothing could be more diverting than to hear Lena, who was almost as candid as Nature, call a leg a "limb" or a house a "home."

We used to linger a long while over our coffee in that sunny corner. Lena was never so pretty as in the morning; she wakened fresh with the world every day, and her eyes had a deeper color then, like the blue flowers that are never so blue as when they first open. I could sit idle all through a Sunday morning and look at her. Ole Benson's behavior was now no mystery to me.

"There was never any harm in Ole," she said once. "People need n't have troubled themselves. He just liked to come over and sit on the draw-side and forget about his bad luck. I liked to have him. Any company's welcome when you're off with cattle all the time."

"But was n't he always glum?" I asked. "People said he never talked at all."

"Sure he talked, in Norwegian. He'd been a sailor on an English boat and had seen lots of queer places. He had wonderful tattoos. We used to sit and look at them for hours; there was n't much to look at out there. He was like a picture book. He had a ship and a strawberry girl on one arm, and on the other a girl standing before a little house, with a fence and gate and all, waiting for her sweetheart. Farther up his arm, her sailor had come back and was kissing her. 'The Sailor's Return,'[2] he called it."

2. Title of a traditional Irish air.

I admitted it was no wonder Ole liked to look at a pretty girl once in a while, with such a fright at home.

"You know," Lena said confidentially, "he married Mary because he thought she was strong-minded and would keep him straight. He never could keep straight on shore. The last time he landed in Liverpool he'd been out on a two years' voyage. He was paid off one morning, and by the next he had n't a cent left, and his watch and compass were gone. He'd got with some women, and they'd taken everything. He worked his way to this country on a little passenger boat. Mary was a stewardess, and she tried to convert him on the way over. He thought she was just the one to keep him steady. Poor Ole! He used to bring me candy from town, hidden in his feed-bag. He could n't refuse anything to a girl. He'd have given away his tattoos long ago, if he could. He's one of the people I'm sorriest for."

If I happened to spend an evening with Lena and stayed late, the Polish violin-teacher across the hall used to come out and watch me descend the stairs, muttering so threateningly that it would have been easy to fall into a quarrel with him. Lena had told him once that she liked to hear him practice, so he always left his door open, and watched who came and went.

There was a coolness between the Pole and Lena's landlord on her account. Old Colonel Raleigh had come to Lincoln from Kentucky and invested an inherited fortune in real estate, at the time of inflated prices. Now he sat day after day in his office in the Raleigh Block, trying to discover where his money had gone and how he could get some of it back. He was a widower, and found very little congenial companionship in this casual Western city. Lena's good looks and gentle manners appealed to him. He said her voice reminded him of Southern voices, and he found as many opportunities of hearing it as possible. He painted and papered her rooms for her that spring, and put in a porcelain bathtub in place of the tin one that had satisfied the former tenant. While these repairs were being made, the old gentleman often dropped in to consult Lena's preferences. She told me with amusement how Ordinsky, the Pole, had presented himself at her door one evening, and said that if the landlord was annoying her by his attentions, he would promptly put a stop to it.

"I don't exactly know what to do about him," she said, shaking her head, "he's so sort of wild all the time. I would n't like to have him say anything rough to that nice old man. The Colonel is long-winded, but then I expect he's lonesome. I don't think he cares much for Ordinsky, either. He said once that if I had any complaints to make of my neighbors, I must n't hesitate."

One Saturday evening when I was having supper with Lena we heard a knock at her parlor door, and there stood the Pole, coatless, in a dress shirt and collar. Prince dropped on his paws and began to growl like a mastiff, while the visitor apologized, saying that he could not possibly come in thus attired, but he begged Lena to lend him some safety pins.

"Oh, you'll have to come in, Mr. Ordinsky, and let me see what's the matter." She closed the door behind him. "Jim, won't you make Prince behave?"

I rapped Prince on the nose, while Ordinsky explained that he had not had his dress clothes on for a long time, and tonight, when he was going to play for a concert, his waistcoat had split down the back. He thought he could pin it together until he got it to a tailor.

Lena took him by the elbow and turned him round. She laughed when she saw the long gap in the satin. "You could never pin that, Mr. Ordinsky. You've kept it folded too long, and the goods is all gone along the crease. Take it off. I can put a new piece of lining-silk in there for you in ten minutes." She disappeared into her work-room with the vest, leaving me to confront the Pole, who stood against the door like a wooden figure. He folded his arms and glared at me with his excitable, slanting brown eyes. His head was the shape of a chocolate drop, and was covered with dry, straw-colored hair that fuzzed up about his pointed crown. He had never done more than mutter at me as I passed him, and I was surprised when he now addressed me.

"Miss Lingard," he said haughtily, "is a young woman for whom I have the utmost, the utmost respect."

"So have I," I said coldly.

He paid no heed to my remark, but began to do rapid finger-exercises on his shirt-sleeves, as he stood with tightly folded arms.

"Kindness of heart," he went on, staring at the ceiling, "senti-ment, are not understood in a place like this. The noblest qualities are ridiculed. Grinning college boys, ignorant and conceited, what do they know of delicacy!"

I controlled my features and tried to speak seriously.

"If you mean me, Mr. Ordinsky, I have known Miss Lingard a long time, and I think I appreciate her kindness. We come from the same town, and we grew up together."

His gaze traveled slowly down from the ceiling and rested on me. "Am I to understand that you have this young woman's interests at heart? That you do not wish to compromise her?"

"That's a word we don't use much here, Mr. Ordinsky. A girl who makes her own living can ask a college boy to supper without being talked about. We take some things for granted."

"Then I have misjudged you, and I ask your pardon,"—he bowed gravely. "Miss Lingard," he went on, "is an absolutely trustful heart. She has not learned the hard lessons of life. As for you and me, *noblesse oblige*,"—he watched me narrowly.

Lena returned with the vest. "Come in and let us look at you as you go out, Mr. Ordinsky. I've never seen you in your dress suit," she said as she opened the door for him.

A few moments later he reappeared with his violin case—a heavy muffler about his neck and thick woolen gloves on his bony hands. Lena spoke encouragingly to him, and he went off with such an important, professional air, that we fell to laughing as soon as we had shut the door. "Poor fellow," Lena said indulgently, "he takes everything so hard."

After that Ordinsky was friendly to me, and behaved as if there were some deep understanding between us. He wrote a furious article, attacking the musical taste of the town, and asked me to do him a great service by taking it to the editor of the morning paper. If the editor refused to print it, I was to tell him that he would be answerable to Ordinsky "in person." He declared that he would never retract one word, and that he was quite prepared to lose all his pupils. In spite of the fact that nobody ever mentioned his article to him after it appeared—full of typographical errors which he thought intentional—he got a certain satisfaction from believing that the citizens of Lincoln had meekly accepted the epithet "coarse barbarians." "You see how it is," he said to me, "where there is no chivalry, there is no *amour propre*." When I met him on his rounds now, I thought he carried his head more disdainfully than ever, and strode up the steps of front porches and rang doorbells with more assurance. He told Lena he would never forget how I had stood by him when he was "under fire."

All this time, of course, I was drifting. Lena had broken up my serious mood. I was n't interested in my classes. I played with Lena and Prince, I played with the Pole, I went buggy-riding with the old Colonel, who had taken a fancy to me and used to talk to me about Lena and the "great beauties" he had known in his youth. We were all three in love with Lena.

Before the first of June, Gaston Cleric was offered an instructorship at Harvard College, and accepted it. He suggested that I should follow him in the fall, and complete my course at Harvard. He had found out about Lena—not from me—and he talked to me seriously.

"You won't do anything here now. You should either quit school and go to work, or change your college and begin again in earnest. You won't recover yourself while you are playing about with this handsome Norwegian. Yes, I've seen her with you at the theater. She's very pretty, and perfectly irresponsible, I should judge."

Cleric wrote my grandfather that he would like to take me East with him. To my astonishment, grandfather replied that I might go if I wished. I was both glad and sorry on the day when the letter came. I stayed in my room all evening and thought things over; I even tried to persuade myself that I was standing in Lena's way—it is so necessary to be a little noble!—and that if she had not me to play with, she would probably marry and secure her future.

The next evening I went to call on Lena. I found her propped up on the couch in her bay window, with her foot in a big slipper. An awkward little Russian girl whom she had taken into her work-room had dropped a flat-iron on Lena's toe. On the table beside her there was a basket of early summer flowers which the Pole had left after he heard of the accident. He always managed to know what went on in Lena's apartment.

Lena was telling me some amusing piece of gossip about one of her clients, when I interrupted her and picked up the flower basket.

"This old chap will be proposing to you some day, Lena."

"Oh, he has—often!" she murmured.

"What! After you've refused him?"

"He does n't mind that. It seems to cheer him to mention the subject. Old men are like that, you know. It makes them feel important to think they're in love with somebody."

"The Colonel would marry you in a minute. I hope you won't marry some old fellow; not even a rich one."

Lena shifted her pillows and looked up at me in surprise. "Why, I'm not going to marry anybody. Did n't you know that?"

"Nonsense, Lena. That's what girls say, but you know better. Every handsome girl like you marries, of course."

She shook her head. "Not me."

"But why not? What makes you say that?" I persisted.

Lena laughed. "Well, it's mainly because I don't want a husband. Men are all right for friends, but as soon as you marry them they turn into cranky old fathers, even the wild ones. They begin to tell you what's sensible and what's foolish, and want you to stick at home all the time. I prefer to be foolish when I feel like it, and be accountable to nobody."

"But you'll be lonesome. You'll get tired of this sort of life, and you'll want a family."

"Not me. I like to be lonesome. When I went to work for Mrs. Thomas I was nineteen years old, and I had never slept a night in my life when there were n't three in the bed. I never had a minute to myself except when I was off with the cattle."

Usually, when Lena referred to her life in the country at all, she dismissed it with a single remark, humorous or mildly cynical. But to-night her mind seemed to dwell on those early years. She told me she could n't remember a time when she was so little that she was n't lugging a heavy baby about, helping to wash for babies, trying to keep their little chapped hands and faces clean. She remembered home as a place where there were always too many children, a cross man, and work piling up around a sick woman.

"It was n't mother's fault. She would have made us comfortable if she could. But that was no life for a girl! After I began to herd and milk I could never get the smell of the cattle off me. The few under-clothes I had I kept in a cracker box. On Saturday nights, after every-body was in bed, then I could take a bath if I was n't too tired. I could make two trips to the windmill to carry water, and heat it in the wash-boiler on the stove. While the water was heating, I could bring in a washtub out of the cave, and take my bath in the kitchen. Then I could put on a clean nightgown and get into bed with two others, who likely had n't had a bath unless I'd given it to them. You can't tell me anything about family life. I've had plenty to last me."

"But it's not all like that," I objected.

"Near enough. It's all being under somebody's thumb. What's on your mind, Jim? Are you afraid I'll want you to marry me some day?"

Then I told her I was going away.

"What makes you want to go away, Jim? Have n't I been nice to you?"

"You've been just awfully good to me, Lena," I blurted. "I don't think about much else. I never shall think about much else while I'm with you. I'll never settle down and grind if I stay here. You know that." I dropped down beside her and sat looking at the floor. I seemed to have forgotten all my reasonable explanations.

Lena drew close to me, and the little hesitation in her voice that had hurt me was not there when she spoke again.

"I ought n't to have begun it, ought I?" she murmured. "I ought n't to have gone to see you that first time. But I did want to. I guess I've always been a little foolish about you. I don't know what first put it into my head, unless it was Ántonia, always telling me I must n't be up to any of my nonsense with you. I let you alone for a long while, though, did n't I?"

She was a sweet creature to those she loved, that Lena Lingard!

At last she sent me away with her soft, slow, renunciatory kiss. "You aren't sorry I came to see you that time?" she whispered. "It seemed so natural. I used to think I'd like to be your first sweetheart. You were such a funny kid!" She always kissed one as if she were sadly and wisely sending one away forever.

We said many good-byes before I left Lincoln, but she never tried to hinder me or hold me back. "You are going, but you have n't gone yet, have you?" she used to say.

My Lincoln chapter closed abruptly. I went home to my grand-parents for a few weeks, and afterward visited my relatives in Vir-ginia until I joined Cleric in Boston. I was then nineteen years old.

Book IV

The Pioneer Woman's Story

I

Two years after I left Lincoln I completed my academic course at Harvard. Before I entered the Law School I went home for the summer vacation. On the night of my arrival Mrs. Harling and Frances and Sally came over to greet me. Everything seemed just as it used to be. My grandparents looked very little older. Frances Harling was married now, and she and her husband managed the Harling interests in Black Hawk. When we gathered in grandmother's parlor, I could hardly believe that I had been away at all. One subject, however, we avoided all evening.

When I was walking home with Frances, after we had left Mrs. Harling at her gate, she said simply, "You know, of course, about poor Ántonia."

Poor Ántonia! Every one would be saying that now, I thought bitterly. I replied that grandmother had written me how Ántonia went away to marry Larry Donovan at some place where he was working; that he had deserted her, and that there was now a baby. This was all I knew.

"He never married her," Frances said. "I have n't seen her since she came back. She lives at home, on the farm, and almost never comes to town. She brought the baby in to show it to mama once. I'm afraid she's settled down to be Ambrosch's drudge for good."

I tried to shut Ántonia out of my mind. I was bitterly disappointed in her. I could not forgive her for becoming an object of pity, while Lena Lingard, for whom people had always foretold trouble, was now the leading dressmaker of Lincoln, much respected in Black Hawk. Lena gave her heart away when she felt like it, but she kept her head for her business and had got on in the world.

Just then it was the fashion to speak indulgently of Lena and severely of Tiny Soderball, who had quietly gone West to try her fortune the year before. A Black Hawk boy, just back from Seattle, brought the news that Tiny had not gone to the coast on a venture, as she had allowed people to think, but with very definite plans.

One of the roving promoters that used to stop at Mrs. Gardener's hotel owned idle property along the water-front in Seattle, and he had offered to set Tiny up in business in one of his empty buildings. She was now conducting a sailors' lodging-house. This, every one said, would be the end of Tiny. Even if she had begun by running a decent place, she could n't keep it up; all sailors' boarding-houses were alike.

When I thought about it, I discovered that I had never known Tiny as well as I knew the other girls. I remembered her tripping briskly about the dining-room on her high heels, carrying a big tray full of dishes, glancing rather pertly at the spruce traveling men, and contemptuously at the scrubby ones—who were so afraid of her that they did n't dare to ask for two kinds of pie. Now it occurred to me that perhaps the sailors, too, might be afraid of Tiny. How astonished we would have been, as we sat talking about her on Frances Harling's front porch, if we could have known what her future was really to be! Of all the girls and boys who grew up together in Black Hawk, Tiny Soderball was to lead the most adventurous life and to achieve the most solid worldly success.

This is what actually happened to Tiny: While she was running her lodging-house in Seattle, gold was discovered in Alaska. Miners and sailors came back from the North with wonderful stories and pouches of gold. Tiny saw it and weighed it in her hands. That daring which nobody had ever suspected in her, awoke. She sold her business and set out for Circle City, in company with a carpenter and his wife whom she had persuaded to go along with her. They reached Skaguay in a snowstorm, went in dog sledges over the Chilkoot Pass, and shot the Yukon in flat-boats. They reached Circle City on the very day when some Siwash Indians came into the settlement with the report that there had been a rich gold strike farther up the river, on a certain Klondike Creek. Two days later Tiny and her friends, and nearly every one else in Circle City, started for the Klondike fields on the last steamer that went up the Yukon before it froze for the winter. That boatload of people founded Dawson City. Within a few weeks there were fifteen hundred homeless men in camp. Tiny and the carpenter's wife began to cook for them, in a tent. The miners gave her a lot, and the carpenter put up a log hotel for her. There she sometimes fed a hundred and fifty men a day. Miners came in on snowshoes from their placer claims twenty miles away to buy fresh bread from her, and paid for it in gold.

That winter Tiny kept in her hotel a Swede whose legs had been frozen one night in a storm when he was trying to find his way back to his cabin. The poor fellow thought it great good fortune to be cared for by a woman, and a woman who spoke his own tongue. When he was told that his feet must be amputated, he said he hoped he would not get well; what could a working-man do in this hard world without feet? He did, in fact, die from the operation, but not before he had deeded Tiny Soderball his claim on Hunker Creek. Tiny sold her hotel, invested half her money in Dawson building lots, and with the rest she developed her claim. She went off into the wilds and lived on it. She bought other claims from discouraged miners, traded or sold them on percentages.

After nearly ten years in the Klondike, Tiny returned, with a considerable fortune, to live in San Francisco. I met her in Salt Lake City in 1908. She was a thin, hard-faced woman, very well-dressed, very reserved in manner. Curiously enough, she reminded me of Mrs. Gardener, for whom she had worked in Black Hawk so long ago. She told me about some of the desperate chances she had taken in the gold country, but the thrill of them was quite gone. She said frankly that nothing interested her much now but making money. The only two human beings of whom she spoke with any feeling were the Swede, Johnson, who had given her his claim, and Lena Lingard. She had persuaded Lena to come to San Francisco and go into business there.

"Lincoln was never any place for her," Tiny remarked. "In a town of that size Lena would always be gossiped about. Frisco's the right field for her. She has a fine class of trade. Oh, she's just the same as she always was! She's careless, but she's level-headed. She's the only person I know who never gets any older. It's fine for me to have her there; somebody who enjoys things like that. She keeps an eye on me and won't let me be shabby. When she thinks I need a new dress, she makes it and sends it home—with a bill that's long enough, I can tell you!"

Tiny limped slightly when she walked. The claim on Hunker Greek took toll from its possessors. Tiny had been caught in a sudden turn of weather, like poor Johnson. She lost three toes from one of those pretty little feet that used to trip about Black Hawk in pointed slippers and striped stockings. Tiny mentioned this mutilation quite casually—did n't seem sensitive about it. She was satisfied with her success, but not elated. She was like some one in whom the faculty of becoming interested is worn out.

II

Soon after I got home that summer I persuaded my grandparents to have their photographs taken, and one morning I went into the photographer's shop to arrange for sittings. While I was waiting for him to come out of his developing-room, I walked about trying to recognize the likenesses on his walls: girls in Commencement dresses, country brides and grooms holding hands, family groups of three generations. I noticed, in a heavy frame, one of those depressing "crayon enlargements" often seen in farmhouse parlors, the subject being a round-eyed baby in short dresses. The photographer came out and gave a constrained, apologetic laugh.

"That's Tony Shimerda's baby. You remember her; she used to be the Harlings' Tony. Too bad! She seems proud of the baby, though; would n't hear to a cheap frame for the picture. I expect her brother will be in for it Saturday."

I went away feeling that I must see Ántonia again. Another girl would have kept her baby out of sight, but Tony, of course, must have its picture on exhibition at the town photographer's, in a great gilt frame. How like her! I could forgive her, I told myself, if she had n't thrown herself away on such a cheap sort of fellow.

Larry Donovan was a passenger conductor, one of those train-crew aristocrats who are always afraid that some one may ask them to put up a car-window, and who, if requested to perform such a menial service, silently point to the button that calls the porter. Larry wore this air of official aloofness even on the street, where there were no car-windows to compromise his dignity. At the end of his run he stepped indifferently from the train along with the passengers, his street hat on his head and his conductor's cap in an alligator-skin bag, went directly into the station and changed his clothes. It was a matter of the utmost importance to him never to be seen in his blue trousers away from his train. He was usually cold and distant with men, but with all women he had a silent, grave familiarity, a special handshake, accompanied by a significant, deliberate look. He took women, married or single, into his confidence; walked them up and down in the moonlight, telling them what a mistake he had made by not entering the office branch of the service, and how much better fitted he was to fill the post of General Passenger Agent in Denver than the roughshod man who then bore that title. His unappreciated worth was the tender secret Larry shared with his sweethearts, and he was always able to make some foolish heart ache over it.

As I drew near home that morning, I saw Mrs. Harling out in her yard, digging round her mountain-ash tree. It was a dry summer, and she had now no boy to help her. Charley was off in his battleship, cruising somewhere on the Caribbean sea. I turned in at the gate—it was with a feeling of pleasure that I opened and shut that gate in those days; I liked the feel of it under my hand. I took the spade away from Mrs. Harling, and while I loosened the earth around the tree, she sat down on the steps and talked about the oriole family that had a nest in its branches.

"Mrs. Harling," I said presently, "I wish I could find out exactly how Ántonia's marriage fell through."

"Why don't you go out and see your grandfather's tenant, the Widow Steavens? She knows more about it than anybody else. She helped Ántonia get ready to be married, and she was there when Ántonia came back. She took care of her when the baby was born. She could tell you everything. Besides, the Widow Steavens is a good talker, and she has a remarkable memory."

III

On the first or second day of August I got a horse and cart and set out for the high country, to visit the Widow Steavens. The wheat harvest was over, and here and there along the horizon I could see black puffs of smoke from the steam thrashing-machines. The old pasture land was now being broken up into wheatfields and corn-fields, the red grass was disappearing, and the whole face of the country was changing. There were wooden houses where the old sod dwellings used to be, and little orchards, and big red barns; all this meant happy children, contented women, and men who saw their lives coming to a fortunate issue. The windy springs and the blazing summers, one after another, had enriched and mellowed that flat tableland; all the human effort that had gone into it was coming back in long, sweeping lines of fertility. The changes seemed beautiful and harmonious to me; it was like watching the growth of a great man or of a great idea. I recognized every tree and sandbank and rugged draw. I found that I remembered the conformation of the land as one remembers the modeling of human faces.

When I drew up to our old windmill, the Widow Steavens came out to meet me. She was brown as an Indian woman, tall, and very strong. When I was little, her massive head had always seemed to me like a Roman senator's. I told her at once why I had come.

"You'll stay the night with us, Jimmy? I'll talk to you after supper. I can take more interest when my work is off my mind. You've no prejudice against hot biscuit for supper? Some have, these days."

While I was putting my horse away I heard a rooster squawking. I looked at my watch and sighed; it was three o'clock, and I knew that I must eat him at six.

After supper Mrs. Steavens and I went upstairs to the old sitting-room, while her grave, silent brother remained in the basement to read his farm papers. All the windows were open. The white summer moon was shining outside, the windmill was pumping lazily in the light breeze. My hostess put the lamp on a stand in the corner, and turned it low because of the heat. She sat down in her favorite rocking-chair and settled a little stool comfortably under her tired feet. "I'm troubled with callouses, Jim; getting old," she sighed cheerfully. She

crossed her hands in her lap and sat as if she were at a meeting of
some kind.

"Now, it's about that dear Ántonia you want to know? Well, you've
come to the right person. I've watched her like she'd been my own
daughter.

"When she came home to do her sewing that summer before she
was to be married, she was over here about every day. They've never
had a sewing machine at the Shimerdas', and she made all her things
here. I taught her hemstitching, and I helped her to cut and fit. She
used to sit there at that machine by the window, pedaling the life
out of it—she was so strong—and always singing them queer Bohemian songs, like she was the happiest thing in the world.

"'Ántonia,' I used to say, 'don't run that machine so fast. You won't
hasten the day none that way.'

"Then she'd laugh and slow down for a little, but she'd soon forget and begin to pedal and sing again. I never saw a girl work harder
to go to housekeeping right and well-prepared. Lovely table linen the
Harlings had given her, and Lena Lingard had sent her nice things
from Lincoln. We hemstitched all the tablecloths and pillow-cases,
and some of the sheets. Old Mrs. Shimerda knit yards and yards of
lace for her underclothes. Tony told me just how she meant to have
everything in her house. She'd even bought silver spoons and forks,
and kept them in her trunk. She was always coaxing brother to go
to the post-office. Her young man did write her real often, from the
different towns along his run.

"The first thing that troubled her was when he wrote that his run
had been changed, and they would likely have to live in Denver. 'I'm
a country girl,' she said, 'and I doubt if I'll be able to manage so well
for him in a city. I was counting on keeping chickens, and maybe a
cow.' She soon cheered up, though.

"At last she got the letter telling her when to come. She was shaken
by it; she broke the seal and read it in this room. I suspected then
that she'd begun to get faint-hearted, waiting; though she'd never
let me see it.

"Then there was a great time of packing. It was in March, if
I remember rightly, and a terrible muddy, raw spell, with the roads
bad for hauling her things to town. And here let me say, Ambrosch
did the right thing. He went to Black Hawk and bought her a set of
plated silver in a purple velvet box, good enough for her station. He
gave her three hundred dollars in money; I saw the check. He'd collected her wages all those first years she worked out, and it was but
right. I shook him by the hand in this room. 'You're behaving like a
man, Ambrosch,' I said, 'and I'm glad to see it, son.'

"'T was a cold, raw day he drove her and her three trunks into
Black Hawk to take the night train for Denver—the boxes had been

shipped before. He stopped the wagon here, and she ran in to tell me good-bye. She threw her arms around me and kissed me, and thanked me for all I'd done for her. She was so happy she was crying and laughing at the same time, and her red cheeks was all wet with rain.

"'You're surely handsome enough for any man,' I said, looking her over.

"She laughed kind of flighty like, and whispered, 'Good-bye, dear house!' and then ran out to the wagon. I expect she meant that for you and your grandmother, as much as for me, so I'm particular to tell you. This house had always been a refuge to her.

"Well, in a few days we had a letter saying she got to Denver safe, and he was there to meet her. They were to be married in a few days. He was trying to get his promotion before he married, she said. I did n't like that, but I said nothing. The next week Yulka got a postal card, saying she was 'well and happy.' After that we heard nothing. A month went by, and old Mrs. Shimerda began to get fretful. Ambrosch was as sulky with me as if I'd picked out the man and arranged the match.

"One night brother William came in and said that on his way back from the fields he had passed a livery team from town, driving fast out the west road. There was a trunk on the front seat with the driver, and another behind. In the back seat there was a woman all bundled up; but for all her veils, he thought 't was Ántonia Shimerda, or Ántonia Donovan, as her name ought now to be.

"The next morning I got brother to drive me over. I can walk still, but my feet ain't what they used to be, and I try to save myself. The lines outside the Shimerdas' house was full of washing, though it was the middle of the week. As we got nearer I saw a sight that made my heart sink—all those underclothes we'd put so much work on, out there swinging in the wind. Yulka came bringing a dishpanful of wrung clothes, but she darted back into the house like she was loath to see us. When I went in, Ántonia was standing over the tubs, just finishing up a big washing. Mrs. Shimerda was going about her work, talking and scolding to herself. She did n't so much as raise her eyes. Tony wiped her hand on her apron and held it out to me, looking at me steady but mournful. When I took her in my arms she drew away. 'Don't, Mrs. Steavens,' she says, 'you'll make me cry, and I don't want to.'

"I whispered and asked her to come out of doors with me. I knew she could n't talk free before her mother. She went out with me, bare-headed, and we walked up toward the garden.

"'I'm not married, Mrs. Steavens,' she says to me very quiet and natural-like, 'and I ought to be.'

"'Oh, my child,' says I, 'what's happened to you? Don't be afraid to tell me!'

"She sat down on the draw-side, out of sight of the house. 'He's run away from me,' she said. 'I don't know if he ever meant to marry me.'

"'You mean he's thrown up his job and quit the country?' says I.

"'He did n't have any job. He'd been fired; blacklisted for knocking down fares. I didn't know. I thought he had n't been treated right. He was sick when I got there. He'd just come out of the hospital. He lived with me till my money gave out, and afterwards I found he had n't really been hunting work at all. Then he just did n't come back. One nice fellow at the station told me, when I kept going to look for him, to give it up. He said he was afraid Larry'd gone bad and would n't come back any more. I guess he's gone to Old Mexico. The conductors get rich down there, collecting half-fares off the natives and robbing the company. He was always talking about fellows who had got ahead that way.'

"I asked her, of course, why she did n't insist on a civil marriage at once—that would have given her some hold on him. She leaned her head on her hands, poor child, and said, 'I just don't know, Mrs. Steavens. I guess my patience was wore out, waiting so long. I thought if he saw how well I could do for him, he'd want to stay with me.'

"Jimmy, I sat right down on that bank beside her and made lament. I cried like a young thing. I could n't help it. I was just about heartbroke. It was one of them lovely warm May days, and the wind was blowing and the colts jumping around in the pastures; but I felt bowed with despair. My Ántonia, that had so much good in her, had come home disgraced. And that Lena Lingard, that was always a bad one, say what you will, had turned out so well, and was coming home here every summer in her silks and her satins, and doing so much for her mother. I give credit where credit is due, but you know well enough, Jim Burden, there is a great difference in the principles of those two girls. And here it was the good one that had come to grief! I was poor comfort to her. I marveled at her calm. As we went back to the house, she stopped to feel of her clothes to see if they was drying well, and seemed to take pride in their whiteness—she said she'd been living in a brick block, where she did n't have proper conveniences to wash them.

"The next time I saw Ántonia, she was out in the fields ploughing corn. All that spring and summer she did the work of a man on the farm; it seemed to be an understood thing. Ambrosch did n't get any other hand to help him. Poor Marek had got violent and been sent away to an institution a good while back. We never even saw any of Tony's pretty dresses. She did n't take them out of her trunks. She was quiet and steady. Folks respected her industry and tried to treat her as if nothing had happened. They talked, to be sure; but not like they would if she'd put on airs. She was so crushed and quiet that nobody seemed to want to humble her. She never went anywhere. All that summer she never once came to see me. At first I was hurt, but I got to feel that it was because this house reminded her of too much. I went over there when I could, but the times when she was in from the fields were the times when I was busiest here. She talked about the grain and the weather as if she'd never had another interest, and if I went over at night she always looked dead weary. She was afflicted with toothache; one tooth after another ulcerated, and she went about with her face swollen half the time. She would n't go to Black Hawk to a dentist for fear of meeting people she knew. Ambrosch had got over his good spell long ago, and was always surly. Once I told him he ought not to let Ántonia work so hard and pull herself down. He said, 'If you put that in her head, you better stay home.' And after that I did.

"Ántonia worked on through harvest and thrashing, though she was too modest to go out thrashing for the neighbors, like when she was young and free. I did n't see much of her until late that fall when she begun to herd Ambrosch's cattle in the open ground north of here, up toward the big dog town. Sometimes she used to bring them over the west hill, there, and I would run to meet her and walk north a piece with her. She had thirty cattle in her bunch; it had been dry, and the pasture was short, or she would n't have brought them so far.

"It was a fine open fall, and she liked to be alone. While the steers grazed, she used to sit on them grassy banks along the draws and sun herself for hours. Sometimes I slipped up to visit with her, when she had n't gone too far.

"'It does seem like I ought to make lace, or knit like Lena used to,' she said one day, 'but if I start to work, I look around and forget to go on. It seems such a little while ago when Jim Burden and I was playing all over this country. Up here I can pick out the very places where my father used to stand. Sometimes I feel like I'm not going to live very long, so I'm just enjoying every day of this fall.'

"After the winter begun she wore a man's long overcoat and boots, and a man's felt hat with a wide brim. I used to watch her coming and going, and I could see that her steps were getting heavier. One day in December, the snow began to fall. Late in the afternoon I saw Ántonia driving her cattle homeward across the hill. The snow was flying round her and she bent to face it, looking more lonesome-like to me than usual. 'Deary me,' I says to, myself, 'the girl's stayed out too late. It'll be dark before she gets them cattle put into the corral.' I seemed to sense she'd been feeling too miserable to get up and drive them.

"That very night, it happened. She got her cattle home, turned them into the corral, and went into the house, into her room behind

the kitchen, and shut the door. There, without calling to a , without a groan, she lay down on the bed and bore her child.

"I was lifting supper when old Mrs. Shimerda came running dow the basement stairs, out of breath and screeching:—

"'Baby come, baby come!' she says. 'Ambrosch much like devil!'

"Brother William is surely a patient man. He was just ready to sit down to a hot supper after a long day in the fields. Without a word he rose and went down to the barn and hooked up his team. He got us over there as quick as it was humanly possible. I went right in, and began to do for Ántonia; but she laid there with her eyes shut and took no account of me. The old woman got a tubful of warm water to wash the baby. I overlooked what she was doing and I said out loud:—

"'Mrs. Shimerda, don't you put that strong yellow soap near that baby. You'll blister its little skin.' I was indignant.

"'Mrs. Steavens,' Ántonia said from the bed, 'if you'll look in the top tray of my trunk, you'll see some fine soap.' That was the first word she spoke.

"After I'd dressed the baby, I took it out to show it to Ambrosch. He was muttering behind the stove and would n't look at it.

"'You'd better put it out in the rain barrel,' he says.

"'Now, see here, Ambrosch,' says I, 'there's a law in this land, don't forget that. I stand here a witness that this baby has come into the world sound and strong, and I intend to keep an eye on what befalls it.' I pride myself I cowed him.

"Well, I expect you're not much interested in babies, but Ántonia's got on fine. She loved it from the first as dearly as if she'd had a ring on her finger, and was never ashamed of it. It's a year and eight months old now, and no baby was ever better cared-for. Ántonia is a natural-born mother. I wish she could marry and raise a family, but I don't know as there's much chance now."

I slept that night in the room I used to have when I was a little boy, with the summer wind blowing in at the windows, bringing the smell of the ripe fields. I lay awake and watched the moonlight shining over the barn and the stacks and the pond, and the windmill making its old dark shadow against the blue sky.

IV

The next afternoon I walked over to the Shimerdas'. Yulka showed me the baby and told me that Ántonia was shocking wheat on the southwest quarter. I went down across the fields, and Tony saw me from a long way off. She stood still by her shocks, leaning on her pitchfork, watching me as I came. We met like the people in the old song, in silence, if not in tears. Her warm hand clasped mine.

come, Jim. I heard you were at Mrs. Steavens's
looking for you all day."

er than I had ever seen her, and looked, as
d, "worked down," but there was a new kind of
avity of her face, and her color still gave her that
ed health and ardor. Still? Why, it flashed across
so much had happened in her life and in mine, she
was barely twenty-four years old.

Ántonia stuck her fork in the ground, and instinctively we walked
toward that unploughed patch at the crossing of the roads as the fit-
test place to talk to each other. We sat down outside the sagging wire
fence that shut Mr. Shimerda's plot off from the rest of the world.
The tall red grass had never been cut there. It had died down in winter and come up again in the spring until it was as thick and shrubby
as some tropical garden-grass. I found myself telling her everything:
why I had decided to study law and to go into the law office of one
of my mother's relatives in New York City; about Gaston Cleric's
death from pneumonia last winter, and the difference it had made
in my life. She wanted to know about my friends and my way of living, and my dearest hopes.

"Of course it means you are going away from us for good," she said
with a sigh. "But that don't mean I'll lose you. Look at my papa here;
he's been dead all these years, and yet he is more real to me than
almost anybody else. He never goes out of my life. I talk to him and
consult him all the time. The older I grow, the better I know him
and the more I understand him."

She asked me whether I had learned to like big cities. "I'd always
be miserable in a city. I'd die of lonesomeness. I like to be where I
know every stack and tree, and where all the ground is friendly. I
want to live and die here. Father Kelly says everybody's put into this
world for something, and I know what I've got to do. I'm going to
see that my little girl has a better chance than ever I had. I'm going
to take care of that girl, Jim."

I told her I knew she would. "Do you know, Ántonia, since I've
been away, I think of you more often than of any one else in this
part of the world. I'd have liked to have you for a sweetheart, or a
wife, or my mother or my sister—anything that a woman can be to
a man. The idea of you is a part of my mind; you influence my likes
and dislikes, all my tastes, hundreds of times when I don't realize it.
You really are a part of me."

She turned her bright, believing eyes to me, and the tears came
up in them slowly. "How can it be like that, when you know so many
people, and when I've disappointed you so? Ain't it wonderful, Jim,
how much people can mean to each other? I'm so glad we had each
other when we were little. I can't wait till my little girl's old enough

to tell her about all the things we used to do. You'll always remember me when you think about old times, won't you? And I guess everybody thinks about old times, even the happiest people."

As we walked homeward across the fields, the sun dropped and lay like a great golden globe in the low west. While it hung there, the moon rose in the east, as big as a cart-wheel, pale silver and streaked with rose color, thin as a bubble or a ghost-moon. For five, perhaps ten minutes, the two luminaries confronted each other across the level land, resting on opposite edges of the world. In that singular light every little tree and shock of wheat, every sunflower stalk and clump of snow-on-the-mountain, drew itself up high and pointed; the very clods and furrows in the fields seemed to stand up sharply. I felt the old pull of the earth, the solemn magic that comes out of those fields at nightfall. I wished I could be a little boy again, and that my way could end there.

We reached the edge of the field, where our ways parted. I took her hands and held them against my breast, feeling once more how strong and warm and good they were, those brown hands, and remembering how many kind things they had done for me. I held them now a long while, over my heart. About us it was growing darker and darker, and I had to look hard to see her face, which I meant always to carry with me; the closest, realest face, under all the shadows of women's faces, at the very bottom of my memory.

"I'll come back," I said earnestly, through the soft, intrusive darkness.

"Perhaps you will"—I felt rather than saw her smile. "But even if you don't, you're here, like my father. So I won't be lonesome."

As I went back alone over that familiar road, I could almost believe that a boy and girl ran along beside me, as our shadows used to do, laughing and whispering to each other in the grass.

Book V

Cuzak's Boys

I

I told Ántonia I would come back, but life intervened, and it was twenty years before I kept my promise. I heard of her from time to time; that she married, very soon after I last saw her, a young Bohemian, a cousin of Anton Jelinek; that they were poor, and had a large family. Once when I was abroad I went into Bohemia, and from Prague I sent Ántonia some photographs of her native village. Months afterward came a letter from her, telling me the names and ages of her many children, but little else; signed, "Your old friend, Ántonia Cuzak." When I met Tiny Soderball in Salt Lake, she told me that Ántonia had not "done very well"; that her husband was not a man of much force, and she had had a hard life. Perhaps it was cowardice that kept me away so long. My business took me West several times every year, and it was always in the back of my mind that I would stop in Nebraska some day and go to see Ántonia. But I kept putting it off until the next trip. I did not want to find her aged and broken; I really dreaded it. In the course of twenty crowded years one parts with many illusions. I did not wish to lose the early ones. Some memories are realities, and are better than anything that can ever happen to one again.

I owe it to Lena Lingard that I went to see Ántonia at last. I was in San Francisco two summers ago when both Lena and Tiny Soderball were in town. Tiny lives in a house of her own, and Lena's shop is in an apartment house just around the corner. It interested me, after so many years, to see the two women together. Tiny audits Lena's accounts occasionally, and invests her money for her; and Lena, apparently, takes care that Tiny does n't grow too miserly. "If there's anything I can't stand," she said to me in Tiny's presence, "it's a shabby rich woman." Tiny smiled grimly and assured me that Lena would never be either shabby or rich. "And I don't want to be," the other agreed complacently.

Lena gave me a cheerful account of Ántonia and urged me to make her a visit.

159

"You really ought to go, Jim. It would be such a satisfaction to her. Never mind what Tiny says. There's nothing the matter with Cuzak. You'd like him. He is n't a hustler, but a rough man would never have suited Tony. Tony has nice children—ten or eleven of them by this time, I guess. I should n't care for a family of that size myself, but somehow it's just right for Tony. She'd love to show them to you."

On my way East I broke my journey at Hastings, in Nebraska, and set off with an open buggy and a fairly good livery team to find the Cuzak farm. At a little past midday, I knew I must be nearing my destination. Set back on a swell of land at my right, I saw a wide farmhouse, with a red barn and an ash grove, and cattle yards in front that sloped down to the high road. I drew up my horses and was wondering whether I should drive in here, when I heard low voices. Ahead of me, in a plum thicket beside the road, I saw two boys bending over a dead dog. The little one, not more than four or five, was on his knees, his hands folded, and his close-clipped, bare head drooping forward in deep dejection. The other stood beside him, a hand on his shoulder, and was comforting him in a language I had not heard for a long while. When I stopped my horses opposite them, the older boy took his brother by the hand and came toward me. He, too, looked grave. This was evidently a sad afternoon for them.

"Are you Mrs. Cuzak's boys?" I asked.

The younger one did not look up; he was submerged in his own feelings, but his brother met me with intelligent gray eyes. "Yes, sir."

"Does she live up there on the hill? I am going to see her. Get in and ride up with me."

He glanced at his reluctant little brother. "I guess we'd better walk. But we'll open the gate for you."

I drove along the side-road and they followed slowly behind. When I pulled up at the windmill, another boy, bare-footed and curly-headed, ran out of the barn to tie my team for me. He was a handsome one, this chap, fair-skinned and freckled, with red cheeks and a ruddy pelt as thick as a lamb's wool, growing down on his neck in little tufts. He tied my team with two flourishes of his hands, and nodded when I asked him if his mother was at home. As he glanced at me, his face dimpled with a seizure of irrelevant merriment, and he shot up the windmill tower with a lightness that struck me as disdainful. I knew he was peering down at me as I walked toward the house.

Ducks and geese ran quacking across my path. White cats were sunning themselves among yellow pumpkins on the porch steps. I looked through the wire screen into a big, light kitchen with a white floor. I saw a long table, rows of wooden chairs against the wall, and a shining range in one corner. Two girls were washing dishes at the sink, laughing and chattering, and a little one, in a short pinafore, sat on a stool playing with a rag baby. When I asked for their mother, one of the girls dropped her towel, ran across the floor with noiseless bare feet, and disappeared. The older one, who wore shoes and stockings, came to the door to admit me. She was a buxom girl with dark hair and eyes, calm and self-possessed.

"Won't you come in? Mother will be here in a minute."

Before I could sit down in the chair she offered me, the miracle happened; one of those quiet moments that clutch the heart, and take more courage than the noisy, excited passages in life. Ántonia came in and stood before me; a stalwart, brown woman, flat-chested, her curly brown hair a little grizzled. It was a shock, of course. It always is, to meet people after long years, especially if they have lived as much and as hard as this woman had. We stood looking at each other. The eyes that peered anxiously at me were—simply Ántonia's eyes. I had seen no others like them since I looked into them last, though I had looked at so many thousands of human faces. As I confronted her, the changes grew less apparent to me, her identity stronger. She was there, in the full vigor of her personality, battered but not diminished, looking at me, speaking to me in the husky, breathy voice I remembered so well.

"My husband's not at home, sir. Can I do anything?"

"Don't you remember me, Ántonia? Have I changed so much?"

She frowned into the slanting sunlight that made her brown hair look redder than it was. Suddenly her eyes widened, her whole face seemed to grow broader. She caught her breath and put out two hard-worked hands.

"Why, it's Jim! Anna, Yulka, it's Jim Burden!" She had no sooner caught my hands than she looked alarmed. "What's happened? Is anybody dead?"

I patted her arm. "No. I did n't come to a funeral this time. I got off the train at Hastings and drove down to see you and your family."

She dropped my hand and began rushing about. "Anton, Yulka, Nina, where are you all? Run, Anna, and hunt for the boys. They're off looking for that dog, somewhere. And call Leo. Where is that Leo!" She pulled them out of corners and came bringing them like a mother cat bringing in her kittens. "You don't have to go right off, Jim? My oldest boy's not here. He's gone with papa to the street fair at Wilber. I won't let you go! You've got to stay and see Rudolph and our papa." She looked at me imploringly, panting with excitement.

While I reassured her and told her there would be plenty of time, the barefooted boys from outside were slipping into the kitchen and gathering about her.

"Now, tell me their names, and how old they are."

As she told them off in turn, she made several mistakes about ages, and they roared with laughter. When she came to my light-footed friend of the windmill, she said, "This is Leo, and he's old enough to be better than he is."

He ran up to her and butted her playfully with his curly head, like a little ram, but his voice was quite desperate. "You've forgot! You always forget mine. It's mean! Please tell him, mother!" He clenched his fists in vexation and looked up at her impetuously.

She wound her forefinger in his yellow fleece and pulled it, watching him. "Well, how old are you?"

"I'm twelve," he panted, looking not at me but at her; "I'm twelve years old, and I was born on Easter day!"

She nodded to me. "It's true. He was an Easter baby."

The children all looked at me, as if they expected me to exhibit astonishment or delight at this information. Clearly, they were proud of each other, and of being so many. When they had all been introduced, Anna, the eldest daughter, who had met me at the door, scattered them gently, and came bringing a white apron which she tied round her mother's waist.

"Now, mother, sit down and talk to Mr. Burden. We'll finish the dishes quietly and not disturb you."

Ántonia looked about, quite distracted. "Yes, child, but why don't we take him into the parlor, now that we've got a nice parlor for company?"

The daughter laughed indulgently, and took my hat from me. "Well, you're here, now, mother, and if you talk here, Yulka and I can listen, too. You can show him the parlor after while." She smiled at me, and went back to the dishes, with her sister. The little girl with the rag doll found a place on the bottom step of an enclosed back stairway, and sat with her toes curled up, looking out at us expectantly.

"She's Nina, after Nina Harling," Ántonia explained. "Ain't her eyes like Nina's? I declare, Jim, I loved you children almost as much as I love my own. These children know all about you and Charley and Sally, like as if they'd grown up with you. I can't think of what I want to say, you've got me so stirred up. And then, I've forgot my English so. I don't often talk it any more. I tell the children I used to speak real well." She said they always spoke Bohemian at home. The little ones could not speak English at all—did n't learn it until they went to school.

"I can't believe it's you, sitting here, in my own kitchen. You would n't have known me, would you, Jim? You've kept so young, yourself. But it's easier for a man. I can't see how my Anton looks any older than the day I married him. His teeth have kept so nice. I have n't got many left. But I feel just as young as I used to, and I can do as much work. Oh, we don't have to work so hard now! We've got plenty to help us, papa and me. And how many have you got, Jim?"

When I told her I had no children she seemed embarrassed. "Oh, ain't that too bad! Maybe you could take one of my bad ones, now? That Leo; he's the worst of all." She leaned toward me with a smile. "And I love him the best," she whispered.

"Mother!" the two girls murmured reproachfully from the dishes.

Ántonia threw up her head and laughed. "I can't help it. You know I do. Maybe it's because he came on Easter day, I don't know. And he's never out of mischief one minute!"

I was thinking, as I watched her, how little it mattered—about her teeth, for instance. I know so many women who have kept all the things that she had lost, but whose inner glow has faded. Whatever else was gone, Ántonia had not lost the fire of life. Her skin, so brown and hardened, had not that look of flabbiness, as if the sap beneath it had been secretly drawn away.

While we were talking, the little boy whom they called Jan came in and sat down on the step beside Nina, under the hood of the stairway. He wore a funny long gingham apron, like a smock, over his trousers, and his hair was clipped so short that his head looked white and naked. He watched us out of his big, sorrowful gray eyes.

"He wants to tell you about the dog, mother. They found it dead," Anna said, as she passed us on her way to the cupboard.

Ántonia beckoned the boy to her. He stood by her chair, leaning his elbows on her knees and twisting her apron strings in his slender fingers, while he told her his story softly in Bohemian, and the tears brimmed over and hung on his long lashes. His mother listened, spoke soothingly to him, and in a whisper promised him something that made him give her a quick, teary smile. He slipped away and whispered his secret to Nina, sitting close to her and talking behind his hand.

When Anna finished her work and had washed her hands, she came and stood behind her mother's chair. "Why don't we show Mr. Burden our new fruit cave?" she asked.

We started off across the yard with the children at our heels. The boys were standing by the windmill, talking about the dog; some of them ran ahead to open the cellar door. When we descended, they all came down after us, and seemed quite as proud of the cave as the girls were. Ambrosch, the thoughtful-looking one who had directed me down by the plum bushes, called my attention to the stout brick walls and the cement floor. "Yes, it is a good way from the house," he admitted. "But, you see, in winter there are nearly always some of us around to come out and get things."

Anna and Yulka showed me three small barrels; one full of dill pickles, one full of chopped pickles, and one full of pickled watermelon rinds.

"You would n't believe, Jim, what it takes to feed them all!" their mother exclaimed. "You ought to see the bread we bake on Wednesdays and Saturdays! It's no wonder their poor papa can't get rich, he has to buy so much sugar for us to preserve with. We have our own wheat ground for flour,—but then there's that much less to sell."

Nina and Jan, and a little girl named Lucie, kept shyly pointing out to me the shelves of glass jars. They said nothing, but glancing at me, traced on the glass with their fingertips the outline of the cherries and strawberries and crab-apples within, trying by a blissful expression of countenance to give me some idea of their deliciousness.

"Show him the spiced plums, mother. Americans don't have those," said one of the older boys. "Mother uses them to make *kolaches*,"[1] he added.

Leo, in a low voice, tossed off some scornful remark in Bohemian.

I turned to him. "You think I don't know what *kolaches* are, eh? You're mistaken, young man. I've eaten your mother's *kolaches* long before that Easter day when you were born."

"Always too fresh, Leo," Ambrosch remarked with a shrug.

Leo dived behind his mother and grinned out at me.

We turned to leave the cave; Ántonia and I went up the stairs first, and the children waited. We were standing outside talking, when they all came running up the steps together, big and little, tow heads and gold heads and brown, and flashing little naked legs; a veritable explosion of life out of the dark cave into the sunlight. It made me dizzy for a moment.

The boys escorted us to the front of the house, which I hadn't yet seen; in farmhouses, somehow, life comes and goes by the back door. The roof was so steep that the eaves were not much above the forest of tall hollyhocks, now brown and in seed. Through July, Ántonia said, the house was buried in them; the Bohemians, I remembered, always planted hollyhocks. The front yard was enclosed by a thorny locust hedge, and at the gate grew two silvery, moth-like trees of the mimosa family. From here one looked down over the cattle yards, with their two long ponds, and over a wide stretch of stubble which they told me was a rye-field in summer.

At some distance behind the house were an ash grove and two orchards; a cherry orchard, with gooseberry and currant bushes between the rows, and an apple orchard, sheltered by a high hedge from the hot winds. The older children turned back when we reached the hedge, but Jan and Nina and Lucie crept through it by a hole known only to themselves and hid under the low-branching mulberry bushes.

1. Tea cakes.

As we walked through the apple orchard, grown up in tall blue-grass, Ántonia kept stopping to tell me about one tree and another. "I love them as if they were people," she said, rubbing her hand over the bark. "There was n't a tree here when we first came. We planted every one, and used to carry water for them, too—after we'd been working in the fields all day. Anton, he was a city man, and he used to get discouraged. But I could n't feel so tired that I would n't fret about these trees when there was a dry time. They were on my mind like children. Many a night after he was asleep I've got up and come out and carried water to the poor things. And now, you see, we have the good of them. My man worked in the orange groves in Florida, and he knows all about grafting. There ain't one of our neighbors has an orchard that bears like ours."

In the middle of the orchard we came upon a grape-arbor, with seats built along the sides and a warped plank table. The three children were waiting for us there. They looked up at me bashfully and made some request of their mother.

"They want me to tell you how the teacher has the school picnic here every year. These don't go to school yet, so they think it's all like the picnic."

After I had admired the arbor sufficiently, the youngsters ran away to an open place where there was a rough jungle of French pinks, and squatted down among them, crawling about and measuring with a string. "Jan wants to bury his dog there," Ántonia explained. "I had to tell him he could. He's kind of like Nina Harling; you remember how hard she used to take little things? He has funny notions, like her."

We sat down and watched them. Ántonia leaned her elbows on the table. There was the deepest peace in that orchard. It was surrounded by a triple enclosure; the wire fence, then the hedge of thorny locusts, then the mulberry hedge which kept out the hot winds of summer and held fast to the protecting snows of winter. The hedges were so tall that we could see nothing but the blue sky above them, neither the barn roof nor the windmill. The afternoon sun poured down on us through the drying grape leaves. The orchard seemed full of sun, like a cup, and we could smell the ripe apples on the trees. The crabs hung on the branches as thick as beads on a string, purple-red, with a thin silvery glaze over them. Some hens and ducks had crept through the hedge and were pecking at the fallen apples. The drakes were handsome fellows, with pinkish gray bodies, their heads and necks covered with iridescent green feathers which grew close and full, changing to blue like a peacock's neck. Ántonia said they always reminded her of soldiers—some uniform she had seen in the old country, when she was a child.

"Are there any quail left now?" I asked. I reminded her how she used to go hunting with me the last summer before we moved to town. "You were n't a bad shot, Tony. Do you remember how you used to want to run away and go for ducks with Charley Harling and me?"

"I know, but I'm afraid to look at a gun now." She picked up one of the drakes and ruffled his green capote with her fingers. "Ever since I've had children, I don't like to kill anything. It makes me kind of faint to wring an old goose's neck. Ain't that strange, Jim?"

"I don't know. The young Queen of Italy said the same thing once, to a friend of mine. She used to be a great hunts-woman, but now she feels as you do, and only shoots clay pigeons."

"Then I'm sure she's a good mother," Ántonia said warmly.

She told me how she and her husband had come out to this new country when the farm land was cheap and could be had on easy payments. The first ten years were a hard struggle. Her husband knew very little about farming and often grew discouraged. "We'd never have got through if I had n't been so strong. I've always had good health, thank God, and I was able to help him in the fields until right up to the time before my babies came. Our children were good about taking care of each other. Martha, the one you saw when she was a baby, was such a help to me, and she trained Anna to be just like her. My Martha's married now, and has a baby of her own. Think of that, Jim!

"No, I never got down-hearted. Anton's a good man, and I loved my children and always believed they would turn out well. I belong on a farm. I'm never lonesome here like I used to be in town. You remember what sad spells I used to have, when I did n't know what was the matter with me? I've never had them out here. And I don't mind work a bit, if I don't have to put up with sadness." She leaned her chin on her hand and looked down through the orchard, where the sunlight was growing more and more golden.

"You ought never to have gone to town, Tony," I said, wondering at her.

She turned to me eagerly. "Oh, I'm glad I went! I'd never have known anything about cooking or housekeeping if I had n't. I learned nice ways at the Harlings', and I've been able to bring my children up so much better. Don't you think they are pretty well-behaved for country children? If it had n't been for what Mrs. Harling taught me, I expect I'd have brought them up like wild rabbits. No, I'm glad I had a chance to learn; but I'm thankful none of my daughters will ever have to work out. The trouble with me was, Jim, I never could believe harm of anybody I loved."

While we were talking, Ántonia assured me that she could keep me for the night. "We've plenty of room. Two of the boys sleep in the hay-mow till cold weather comes, but there's no need for it. Leo always begs to sleep there, and Ambrosch goes along to look after him."

I told her I would like to sleep in the haymow, with the boys.

"You can do just as you want to. The chest is full of clean blankets, put away for winter. Now I must go, or my girls will be doing all the work, and I want to cook your supper myself."

As we went toward the house, we met Ambrosch and Anton, starting off with their milking-pails to hunt the cows. I joined them, and Leo accompanied us at some distance, running ahead and starting up at us out of clumps of ironweed, calling, "I'm a jack rabbit," or, "I'm a big bull-snake."

I walked between the two older boys—straight, well-made fellows, with good heads and clear eyes. They talked about their school and the new teacher, told me about the crops and the harvest, and how many steers they would feed that winter. They were easy and confidential with me, as if I were an old friend of the family—and not too old. I felt like a boy in their company, and all manner of forgotten interests revived in me. It seemed, after all, so natural to be walking along a barbed-wire fence beside the sunset, toward a red pond, and to see my shadow moving along at my right, over the close-cropped grass.

"Has mother shown you the pictures you sent her from the old country?" Ambrosch asked. "We've had them framed and they're hung up in the parlor. She was so glad to get them. I don't believe I ever saw her so pleased about anything." There was a note of simple gratitude in his voice that made me wish I had given more occasion for it.

I put my hand on his shoulder. "Your mother, you know, was very much loved by all of us. She was a beautiful girl."

"Oh, we know!" They both spoke together; seemed a little surprised that I should think it necessary to mention this. "Everybody liked her, did n't they? The Harlings and your grandmother, and all the town people."

"Sometimes," I ventured, "it does n't occur to boys that their mother was ever young and pretty."

"Oh, we know!" they said again, warmly. "She's not very old now," Ambrosch added. "Not much older than you."

"Well," I said, "if you were n't nice to her, I think I'd take a club and go for the whole lot of you. I could n't stand it if you boys were inconsiderate, or thought of her as if she were just somebody who looked after you. You see I was very much in love with your mother once, and I know there's nobody like her."

The boys laughed and seemed pleased and embarrassed. "She never told us that," said Anton. "But she's always talked lots about you, and about what good times you used to have. She has a picture of you that she cut out of the Chicago paper once, and Leo says he recognized you when you drove up to the windmill. You can't tell about Leo, though; sometimes he likes to be smart."

We brought the cows home to the corner nearest the barn, and the boys milked them while night came on. Everything was as it should be: the strong smell of sunflowers and ironweed in the dew, the clear blue and gold of the sky, the evening star, the purr of the milk into the pails, the grunts and squeals of the pigs fighting over their supper. I began to feel the loneliness of the farm-boy at evening, when the chores seem everlastingly the same, and the world so far away.

What a tableful we were at supper; two long rows of restless heads in the lamplight, and so many eyes fastened excitedly upon Ántonia as she sat at the head of the table, filling the plates and starting the dishes on their way. The children were seated according to a system; a little one next an older one, who was to watch over his behavior and to see that he got his food. Anna and Yulka left their chairs from time to time to bring fresh plates of *kolaches* and pitchers of milk.

After supper we went into the parlor, so that Yulka and Leo could play for me. Ántonia went first, carrying the lamp. There were not nearly chairs enough to go round, so the younger children sat down on the bare floor. Little Lucie whispered to me that they were going to have a parlor carpet if they got ninety cents for their wheat. Leo, with a good deal of fussing, got out his violin. It was old Mr. Shimerda's instrument, which Ántonia had always kept, and it was too big for him. But he played very well for a self-taught boy. Poor Yulka's efforts were not so successful. While they were playing, little Nina got up from her corner, came out into the middle of the floor, and began to do a pretty little dance on the boards with her bare feet. No one paid the least attention to her, and when she was through she stole back and sat down by her brother.

Ántonia spoke to Leo in Bohemian. He frowned and wrinkled up his face. He seemed to be trying to pout, but his attempt only brought out dimples in unusual places. After twisting and screwing the keys, he played some Bohemian airs, without the organ to hold him back, and that went better. The boy was so restless that I had not had a chance to look at his face before. My first impression was right; he really was faun-like. He had n't much head behind his ears, and his tawny fleece grew down thick to the back of his neck. His eyes were not frank and wide apart like those of the other boys, but were deep-set, gold-green in color, and seemed sensitive to the light. His mother said he got hurt oftener than all the others put together. He was always trying to ride the colts before they were broken, teasing the turkey gobbler, seeing just how much red the bull would stand for, or how sharp the new axe was.

After the concert was over Ántonia brought out a big boxful of photographs; she and Anton in their wedding clothes, holding hands; her brother Ambrosch and his very fat wife, who had a farm of her own, and who bossed her husband, I was delighted to hear; the three Bohemian Marys and their large families.

"You would n't believe how steady those girls have turned out," Ántonia remarked. "Mary Svoboda's the best butter-maker in all this country, and a fine manager. Her children will have a grand chance."

As Ántonia turned over the pictures the young Cuzaks stood behind her chair, looking over her shoulder with interested faces. Nina and Jan, after trying to see round the taller ones, quietly brought a chair, climbed up on it, and stood close together, looking. The little boy forgot his shyness and grinned delightedly when familiar faces came into view. In the group about Ántonia I was conscious of a kind of physical harmony. They leaned this way and that, and were not afraid to touch each other. They contemplated the photographs with pleased recognition; looked at some admiringly, as if these characters in their mother's girlhood had been remarkable people. The little children, who could not speak English, murmured comments to each other in their rich old language.

Ántonia held out a photograph of Lena that had come from San Francisco last Christmas. "Does she still look like that? She has n't been home for six years now." Yes, it was exactly like Lena, I told her; a comely woman, a trifle too plump, in a hat a trifle too large, but with the old lazy eyes, and the old dimpled ingenuousness still lurking at the corners of her mouth.

There was a picture of Frances Harling in a be-frogged riding costume that I remembered well. "Is n't she fine!" the girls murmured. They all assented. One could see that Frances had come down as a heroine in the family legend. Only Leo was unmoved.

"And there's Mr. Harling, in his grand fur coat. He was awfully rich, was n't he, mother?"

"He was n't any Rockefeller," put in Master Leo, in a very low tone, which reminded me of the way in which Mrs. Shimerda had once said that my grandfather "was n't Jesus." His habitual skepticism was like a direct inheritance from that old woman.

"None of your smart speeches," said Ambrosch severely.

Leo poked out a supple red tongue at him, but a moment later broke into a giggle at a tintype of two men, uncomfortably seated, with an awkward-looking boy in baggy clothes standing between them; Jake and Otto and I! We had it taken, I remembered, when we went to Black Hawk on the first Fourth of July I spent in Nebraska. I was glad to see Jake's grin again, and Otto's ferocious mustaches. The young Cuzaks knew all about them.

"He made grandfather's coffin, did n't he?" Anton asked.

"Was n't they good fellows, Jim?" Ántonia's eyes filled. "To this day I'm ashamed because I quarreled with Jake that way. I was saucy

ent to him, Leo, like you are with people sometimes,
nebody had made me behave."

.. through with you, yet," they warned me. They produced
photograph taken just before I went away to college; a tall youth in
striped trousers and a straw hat, trying to look easy and jaunty.

"Tell us, Mr. Burden," said Charley, "about the rattler you killed
at the dog town. How long was he? Sometimes mother says six feet
and sometimes she says five."

These children seemed to be upon very much the same terms with
Ántonia as the Harling children had been so many years before. They
seemed to feel the same pride in her, and to look to her for stories
and entertainment as we used to do.

It was eleven o'clock when I at last took my bag and some blankets and started for the barn with the boys. Their mother came to
the door with us, and we tarried for a moment to look out at the white
slope of the corral and the two ponds asleep in the moonlight, and
the long sweep of the pasture under the star-sprinkled sky.

The boys told me to choose my own place in the haymow, and I
lay down before a big window, left open in warm weather, that looked
out into the stars. Ambrosch and Leo cuddled up in a hay-cave, back
under the eaves, and lay giggling and whispering. They tickled each
other and tossed and tumbled in the hay; and then, all at once, as
if they had been shot, they were still. There was hardly a minute
between giggles and bland slumber.

I lay awake for a long while, until the slow-moving moon passed
my window on its way up the heavens. I was thinking about Ántonia and her children; about Anna's solicitude for her, Ambrosch's
grave affection, Leo's jealous, animal little love. That moment, when
they all came tumbling out of the cave into the light, was a sight
any man might have come far to see. Ántonia had always been one
to leave images in the mind that did not fade—that grew stronger
with time. In my memory there was a succession of such pictures,
fixed there like the old woodcuts of one's first primer: Ántonia kick-
ing her bare legs against the sides of my pony when we came home
in triumph with our snake; Ántonia in her black shawl and fur cap,
as she stood by her father's grave in the snowstorm; Ántonia coming in with her work-team along the evening sky-line. She lent herself to immemorial human attitudes which we recognize by instinct
as universal and true. I had not been mistaken. She was a battered
woman now, not a lovely girl; but she still had that something which
fires the imagination, could still stop one's breath for a moment by
a look or gesture that somehow revealed the meaning in common
things. She had only to stand in the orchard, to put her hand on a
little crab tree and look up at the apples, to make you feel the goodness of planting and tending and harvesting at last. All the strong

things of her heart came out in her body, that had been so tireless in serving generous emotions.

It was no wonder that her sons stood tall and straight. She was a rich mine of life, like the founders of early races.

II

When I awoke in the morning long bands of sunshine were coming in at the window and reaching back under the eaves where the two boys lay. Leo was wide awake and was tickling his brother's leg with a dried cone-flower he had pulled out of the hay. Ambrosch kicked at him and turned over. I closed my eyes and pretended to be asleep. Leo lay on his back, elevated one foot, and began exercising his toes. He picked up dried flowers with his toes and brandished them in the belt of sunlight. After he had amused himself thus for some time, he rose on one elbow and began to look at me, cautiously, then critically, blinking his eyes in the light. His expression was droll; it dismissed me lightly. "This old fellow is no different from other people. He does n't know my secret." He seemed conscious of possessing a keener power of enjoyment than other people; his quick recognitions made him frantically impatient of deliberate judgments. He always knew what he wanted without thinking.

After dressing in the hay, I washed my face in cold water at the windmill. Breakfast was ready when I entered the kitchen, and Yulka was baking griddle-cakes. The three older boys set off for the fields early. Leo and Yulka were to drive to town to meet their father, who would return from Wilber on the noon train.

"We'll only have a lunch at noon," Ántonia said, "and cook the geese for supper, when our papa will be here. I wish my Martha could come down to see you. They have a Ford car now, and she don't seem so far away from me as she used to. But her husband's crazy about his farm and about having everything just right, and they almost never get away except on Sundays. He's a handsome boy, and he'll be rich some day. Everything he takes hold of turns out well. When they bring that baby in here, and unwrap him, he looks like a little prince; Martha takes care of him so beautiful. I'm reconciled to her being away from me now, but at first I cried like I was putting her into her coffin."

We were alone in the kitchen, except for Anna, who was pouring cream into the churn. She looked up at me. "Yes, she did. We were just ashamed of mother. She went round crying, when Martha was so happy, and the rest of us were all glad. Joe certainly was patient with you, mother."

Ántonia nodded and smiled at herself. "I know it was silly, but I could n't help it. I wanted her right here. She'd never been away from me a night since she was born. If Anton had made trouble about her when she was a baby, or wanted me to leave her with my mother, I would n't have married him. I could n't. But he always loved her like she was his own."

"I did n't even know Martha was n't my full sister until after she was engaged to Joe," Anna told me.

Toward the middle of the afternoon the wagon drove in, with the father and the eldest son. I was smoking in the orchard, and as I went out to meet them, Ántonia came running down from the house and hugged the two men as if they had been away for months.

"Papa" interested me, from my first glimpse of him. He was shorter than his older sons; a crumpled little man, with runover boot heels, and he carried one shoulder higher than the other. But he moved very quickly, and there was an air of jaunty liveliness about him. He had a strong, ruddy color, thick black hair, a little grizzled, a curly mustache, and red lips. His smile showed the strong teeth of which his wife was so proud, and as he saw me his lively, quizzical eyes told me that he knew all about me. He looked like a humorous philosopher who had hitched up one shoulder under the burdens of life, and gone on his way having a good time when he could. He advanced to meet me and gave me a hard hand, burned red on the back and heavily coated with hair. He wore his Sunday clothes, very thick and hot for the weather, an unstarched white shirt, and a blue necktie with big white dots, like a little boy's, tied in a flowing bow. Cuzak began at once to talk about his holiday—from politeness he spoke in English.

"Mama, I wish you had see the lady dance on the slack-wire in the street at night. They throw a bright light on her and she float through the air something beautiful, like a bird! They have a dancing bear, like in the old country, and two three merry-go-around, and people in balloons, and what you call the big wheel, Rudolph?"

"A Ferris wheel," Rudolph entered the conversation in a deep baritone voice. He was six foot two, and had a chest like a young blacksmith. "We went to the big dance in the hall behind the saloon last night, mother, and I danced with all the girls, and so did father. I never saw so many pretty girls. It was a Bohunk crowd, for sure. We did n't hear a word of English on the street, except from the show people, did we, papa?"

Cuzak nodded. "And very many send word to you, Ántonia. You will excuse"—turning to me—"if I tell her." While we walked toward the house he related incidents and delivered messages in the tongue he spoke fluently, and I dropped a little behind, curious to know what their relations had become—or remained. The two seemed to be on terms of easy friendliness, touched with humor. Clearly, she was the impulse, and he the corrective. As they went up the hill he kept glancing at her sidewise, to see whether she got his point, or how

she received it. I noticed later that he always looked at people sidewise, as a work-horse does at its yoke-mate. Even when he sat opposite me in the kitchen, talking, he would turn his head a little toward
the clock or the stove and look at me from the side, but with frankness and good-nature. This trick did not suggest duplicity or secre-
tiveness, but merely long habit, as with the horse.

He had brought a tintype of himself and Rudolph for Ántonia's
collection, and several paper bags of candy for the children. He looked
a little disappointed when his wife showed him a big box of candy
I had got in Denver—she had n't let the children touch it the night
before. He put his candy away in the cupboard, "for when she rains,"
and glanced at the box, chuckling. "I guess you must have hear about
how my family ain't so small," he said.

Cuzak sat down behind the stove and watched his womenfolk and
the little children with equal amusement. He thought they were nice,
and he thought they were funny, evidently. He had been off dancing with the girls and forgetting that he was an old fellow, and now
his family rather surprised him; he seemed to think it a joke that all
these children should belong to him. As the younger ones slipped
up to him in his retreat, he kept taking things out of his pockets;
penny dolls, a wooden clown, a balloon pig that was inflated by a
whistle. He beckoned to the little boy they called Jan, whispered to
him, and presented him with a paper snake, gently, so as not to startle him. Looking over the boy's head he said to me, "This one is bashful. He gets left."

Cuzak had brought home with him a roll of illustrated Bohemian
papers. He opened them and began to tell his wife the news, much
of which seemed to relate to one person. I heard the name Vasakova,
Vasakova, repeated several times with lively interest, and presently
I asked him whether he were talking about the singer, Maria Vasak.

"You know? You have heard, maybe?" he asked incredulously. When
I assured him that I had heard her, he pointed out her picture and
told me that Vasak had broken her leg, climbing in the Austrian Alps,
and would not be able to fill her engagements. He seemed delighted
to find that I had heard her sing in London and in Vienna; got out
his pipe and lit it to enjoy our talk the better. She came from his
part of Prague. His father used to mend her shoes for her when she
was a student. Cuzak questioned me about her looks, her popularity, her voice; but he particularly wanted to know whether I had
noticed her tiny feet, and whether I thought she had saved much
money. She was extravagant, of course, but he hoped she would n't
squander everything, and have nothing left when she was old. As a
young man, working in Wienn, he had seen a good many artists who
were old and poor, making one glass of beer last all evening, and "it
was not very nice, that."

When the boys came in from milking and feeding, the long table was laid, and two brown geese, stuffed with apples, were put down sizzling before Ántonia. She began to carve, and Rudolph, who sat next his mother, started the plates on their way. When everybody was served, he looked across the table at me.

"Have you been to Black Hawk lately, Mr. Burden? Then I wonder if you've heard about the Cutters?"

No, I had heard nothing at all about them.

"Then you must tell him, son, though it's a terrible thing to talk about at supper. Now, all you children be quiet, Rudolph is going to tell about the murder."

"Hurrah! The murder!" the children murmured, looking pleased and interested.

Rudolph told his story in great detail, with occasional promptings from his mother or father.

Wick Cutter and his wife had gone on living in the house that Ántonia and I knew so well, and in the way we knew so well. They grew to be very old people. He shriveled up, Ántonia said, until he looked like a little old yellow monkey, for his beard and his fringe of hair never changed color. Mrs. Cutter remained flushed and wild-eyed as we had known her, but as the years passed she became afflicted with a shaking palsy which made her nervous nod continuous instead of occasional. Her hands were so uncertain that she could no longer disfigure china, poor woman! As the couple grew older, they quarreled more and more about the ultimate disposition of their "property." A new law was passed in the State, securing the surviving wife a third of her husband's estate under all conditions. Cutter was tormented by the fear that Mrs. Cutter would live longer than he, and that eventually her "people," whom he had always hated so violently, would inherit. Their quarrels on this subject passed the boundary of the close-growing cedars, and were heard in the street by whoever wished to loiter and listen.

One morning, two years ago, Cutter went into the hardware store and bought a pistol, saying he was going to shoot a dog, and adding that he "thought he would take a shot at an old cat while he was about it." (Here the children interrupted Rudolph's narrative by smothered giggles.)

Cutter went out behind the hardware store, put up a target, practiced for an hour or so, and then went home. At six o'clock that evening, when several men were passing the Cutter house on their way home to supper, they heard a pistol shot. They paused and were looking doubtfully at one another, when another shot came crashing through an upstairs window. They ran into the house and found Wick Cutter lying on a sofa in his upstairs bedroom, with his throat torn open, bleeding on a roll of sheets he had placed beside his head.

"Walk in, gentlemen," he said weakly. "I am alive, you see, and competent. You are witnesses that I have survived my wife. You will find her in her own room. Please make your examination at once, so that there will be no mistake."

One of the neighbors telephoned for a doctor, while the others went into Mrs. Cutter's room. She was lying on her bed, in her night-gown and wrapper, shot through the heart. Her husband must have come in while she was taking her afternoon nap and shot her, hold-ing the revolver near her breast. Her nightgown was burned from the powder.

The horrified neighbors rushed back to Cutter. He opened his eyes and said distinctly, "Mrs. Cutter is quite dead, gentlemen, and I am conscious. My affairs are in order." Then, Rudolph said, "he let go and died."

On his desk the coroner found a letter, dated at five o'clock that afternoon. It stated that he had just shot his wife; that any will she might secretly have made would be invalid, as he survived her. He meant to shoot himself at six o'clock and would, if he had strength, fire a shot through the window in the hope that passers-by might come in and see him "before life was extinct," as he wrote.

"Now, would you have thought that man had such a cruel heart?" Ántonia turned to me after the story was told. "To go and do that poor woman out of any comfort she might have from his money after he was gone!"

"Did you ever hear of anybody else that killed himself for spite, Mr. Burden?" asked Rudolph.

I admitted that I had n't. Every lawyer learns over and over how strong a motive hate can be, but in my collection of legal anecdotes I had nothing to match this one. When I asked how much the estate amounted to, Rudolph said it was a little over a hundred thousand dollars.

Cuzak gave me a twinkling, sidelong glance. "The lawyers, they got a good deal of it, sure," he said merrily.

A hundred thousand dollars; so that was the fortune that had been scraped together by such hard dealing, and that Cutter himself had died for in the end!

After supper Cuzak and I took a stroll in the orchard and sat down by the windmill to smoke. He told me his story as if it were my busi-ness to know it.

His father was a shoemaker, his uncle a furrier, and he, being a younger son, was apprenticed to the latter's trade. You never got any-where working for your relatives, he said, so when he was a journey-man he went to Vienna and worked in a big fur shop, earning good money. But a young fellow who liked a good time did n't save any-thing in Vienna; there were too many pleasant ways of spending every night what he'd made in the day. After three years there, he came to New York. He was badly advised and went to work on furs during a strike, when the factories were offering big wages. The strikers won, and Cuzak was blacklisted. As he had a few hundred dollars ahead, he decided to go to Florida and raise oranges. He had always thought he would like to raise oranges! The second year a hard frost killed his young grove, and he fell ill with malaria. He came to Nebraska to visit his cousin, Anton Jelinek, and to look about. When he began to look about, he saw Ántonia, and she was exactly the kind of girl he had always been hunting for. They were married at once, though he had to borrow money from his cousin to buy the wedding-ring.

"It was a pretty hard job, breaking up this place and making the first crops grow," he said, pushing back his hat and scratching his grizzled hair. "Sometimes I git awful sore on this place and want to quit, but my wife she always say we better stick it out. The babies come along pretty fast, so it look like it be hard to move, anyhow. I guess she was right, all right. We got this place clear now. We pay only twenty dollars an acre then, and I been offered a hundred. We bought another quarter ten years ago, and we got it most paid for. We got plenty boys; we can work a lot of land. Yes, she is a good wife for a poor man. She ain't always so strict with me, neither. Sometimes maybe I drink a little too much beer in town, and when I come home she don't say nothing. She don't ask me no questions. We always get along fine, her and me, like at first. The children don't make trouble between us, like sometimes happens." He lit another pipe and pulled on it contentedly.

I found Cuzak a most companionable fellow. He asked me a great many questions about my trip through Bohemia, about Vienna and the Ringstrasse and the theaters.

"Gee! I like to go back there once, when the boys is big enough to farm the place. Sometimes when I read the papers from the old country, I pretty near run away," he confessed with a little laugh. "I never did think how I would be a settled man like this."

He was still, as Ántonia said, a city man. He liked theaters and lighted streets and music and a game of dominoes after the day's work was over. His sociability was stronger than his acquisitive instinct. He liked to live day by day and night by night, sharing in the excitement of the crowd.—Yet his wife had managed to hold him here on a farm, in one of the loneliest countries in the world.

I could see the little chap, sitting here every evening by the wind-mill, nursing his pipe and listening to the silence; the wheeze of the pump, the grunting of the pigs, an occasional squawking when the hens were disturbed by a rat. It did rather seem to me that Cuzak had been made the instrument of Ántonia's special mission. This was a fine life, certainly, but it wasn't the kind of life he had wanted to

live. I wondered whether the life that was right for one was ever right
for two!

I asked Cuzak if he did n't find it hard to do without the gay company he had always been used to. He knocked out his pipe against
an upright, sighed, and dropped it into his pocket.

"At first I near go crazy with lonesomeness," he said frankly, "but
my woman is got such a warm heart. She always make it as good for
me as she could. Now it ain't so bad; I can begin to have some fun
with my boys, already!"

As we walked toward the house, Cuzak cocked his hat jauntily over
one ear and looked up at the moon. "Gee!" he said in a hushed voice,
as if he had just wakened up, "it don't seem like I am away from there
twenty-six year!"

III

After dinner the next day I said good-bye and drove back to Hastings
to take the train for Black Hawk. Ántonia and her children gathered
round my buggy before I started, and even the little ones looked up at
me with friendly faces. Leo and Ambrosch ran ahead to open the
lane gate. When I reached the bottom of the hill, I glanced back. The
group was still there by the windmill. Ántonia was waving her apron.

At the gate Ambrosch lingered beside my buggy, resting his arm
on the wheel-rim. Leo slipped through the fence and ran off into
the pasture.

"That's like him," his brother said with a shrug. "He's a crazy kid.
Maybe he's sorry to have you go, and maybe he's jealous. He's jealous of anybody mother makes a fuss over, even the priest."

I found I hated to leave this boy, with his pleasant voice and his
fine head and eyes. He looked very manly as he stood there without a hat, the wind rippling his shirt about his brown neck and
shoulders.

"Don't forget that you and Rudolph are going hunting with me up
on the Niobrara next summer," I said. "Your father's agreed to let
you off after harvest."

He smiled. "I won't likely forget. I've never had such a nice thing
offered to me before. I don't know what makes you so nice to us boys,"
he added, blushing.

"Oh, yes you do!" I said, gathering up my reins.

He made no answer to this, except to smile at me with unabashed
pleasure and affection as I drove away.

My day in Black Hawk was disappointing. Most of my old friends
were dead or had moved away. Strange children, who meant nothing to me, were playing in the Harlings' big yard when I passed; the

mountain ash had been cut down, and only a sprouting stump was left of the tall Lombardy poplar that used to guard the gate. I hurried on. The rest of the morning I spent with Anton Jelinek, under a shady cottonwood tree in the yard behind his saloon. While I was having my mid-day dinner at the hotel, I met one of the old lawyers who was still in practice, and he took me up to his office and talked over the Cutter case with me. After that, I scarcely knew how to put in the time until the night express was due.

I took a long walk north of the town, out into the pastures where the land was so rough that it had never been ploughed up, and the long red grass of early times still grew shaggy over the draws and hillocks. Out there I felt at home again. Overhead the sky was that indescribable blue of autumn; bright and shadowless, hard as enamel. To the south I could see the dun-shaded river bluffs that used to look so big to me, and all about stretched drying cornfields, of the pale-gold color I remembered so well. Russian thistles were blowing across the uplands and piling against the wire fences like barricades. Along the cattle paths the plumes of golden-rod were already fading into sun-warmed velvet, gray with gold threads in it. I had escaped from the curious depression that hangs over little towns, and my mind was full of pleasant things; trips I meant to take with the Cuzak boys, in the Bad Lands and up on the Stinking Water. There were enough Cuzaks to play with for a long while yet. Even after the boys grew up, there would always be Cuzak himself! I meant to tramp along a few miles of lighted streets with Cuzak.

As I wandered over those rough pastures, I had the good luck to stumble upon a bit of the first road that went from Black Hawk out to the north country; to my grandfather's farm, then on to the Shimerdas' and to the Norwegian settlement. Everywhere else it had been ploughed under when the highways were surveyed; this half-mile or so within the pasture fence was all that was left of that old road which used to run like a wild thing across the open prairie, clinging to the high places and circling and doubling like a rabbit before the hounds. On the level land the tracks had almost disappeared—were mere shadings in the grass, and a stranger would not have noticed them. But wherever the road had crossed a draw, it was easy to find. The rains had made channels of the wheel-ruts and washed them so deep that the sod had never healed over them. They looked like gashes torn by a grizzly's claws, on the slopes where the farm wagons used to lurch up out of the hollows with a pull that brought curling muscles on the smooth hips of the horses. I sat down and watched the haystacks turn rosy in the slanting sunlight.

This was the road over which Ántonia and I came on that night when we got off the train at Black Hawk and were bedded down in the straw, wondering children, being taken we knew not whither.

I had only to close my eyes to hear the rumbling of the wagons in the dark, and to be again overcome by that obliterating strangeness. The feelings of that night were so near that I could reach out and touch them with my hand. I had the sense of coming home to myself, and of having found out what a little circle man's experience is. For Ántonia and for me, this had been the road of Destiny; had taken us to those early accidents of fortune which predetermined for us all that we can ever be. Now I understood that the same road was to bring us together again. Whatever we had missed, we possessed together the precious, the incommunicable past.

THE END

CONTEXTS
AND BACKGROUNDS

Biographical and Autobiographical Writings

EDITH LEWIS

My Ántonia[†]

That winter [1916] and the following spring [1917], Willa Cather worked without interruption on *My Ántonia*. Her friend Isabelle McClung, in the meantime, had married the violinist, Jan Hambourg; and in the early summer of 1917 the Hambourgs spent a few weeks at the Shattuck Inn, in Jaffrey, New Hampshire. They wrote to Willa Cather, urging her to join them there.

Aside from a few short excursions on Cape Ann, while she was living in Boston, this was Willa Cather's first experience of New England country. She took two small rooms on the top floor of the Shattuck Inn, and these rooms she always occupied when she went back to Jaffrey in later years. They had sloping ceilings, like her attic room in the old days in Red Cloud, and on the roof directly overhead she could hear the rain in wet weather. Her windows looked out over woods and juniper pastures toward Mount Monadnock, with its very individual outline. A bellboy occupied the room next hers, and he was told by the management that he must be very quiet.

Indeed, few guests, probably, were ever more cherished and protected than was Willa Cather, both by the Shattucks, and later by their daughter and her husband, the Austermanns, who afterward ran the Shattuck Inn. The fact that she was a celebrity meant, I think, little to them; they were too much New Englanders for that. They had a great admiration and liking for her character.

That first summer the Inn was crowded with guests, and to give her greater quiet and seclusion two Pittsburgh friends, Miss Lucy

† From *Willa Cather Living: A Personal Record* (New York: Knopf, 1953), pp. 103–08. Copyright 1953 by Edith Lewis. Used by permission of Alfred A. Knopf, an imprint of the Knopf Doubleday Publishing Group, a division of Random House LLC. All rights reserved. Edith Lewis (1881–1927), who shared an apartment and a life with Cather for almost forty years, worked as a magazine editor and a copywriter at an advertising agency. She also edited Cather's works in typescript, and the two women together read the page proofs of Cather's books.

Hine and Miss Acheson, who rented a place called *High Mowing* not far from the Shattuck Inn, had the idea of putting up a tent in their meadow-land for Willa Cather to work in.

This turned out an ideal arrangement. The tent was about half a mile from the Inn, by an unused wood road, and across a pasture or two. Willa Cather loved this solitary half-mile walk through the woods, and found it the best possible prelude to a morning of work. She wrote for two or three hours every day, surrounded by complete silence and peace. In the afternoons she took long walks about the countryside and up Monadnock mountain, often carrying with her Mathews' *Field Book of American Flowers*, her favourite botany.

Of all the places Willa Cather knew and enjoyed during her life— and places, different kinds of country, were rather a dominant note in her scale of enjoyment—Jaffrey became the one she found best to work in. The fresh, pine-scented woods and pastures, with their multitudinous wild flowers, the gentle skies, the little enclosed fields, had in them nothing of the disturbing, exalting, impelling memories and associations of the past—her own past. Each day there was like an empty canvas, a clean sheet of paper to be filled. She lived with a simple sense of physical well-being, of weather, and of country solitude.

For many years after that first summer Willa Cather spent her autumns in Jaffrey—going there about the middle of September and staying often late into November. Autumn was the most propitious season—the heat and the mosquitoes were gone then, the summer crowds had left, and there is nothing lovelier in the world than the New England Fall. When we later built a cottage on the island of Grand Manan in the Bay of Fundy, and went there for many of our summers, Willa Cather generally stopped for a month or so in Jaffrey on her way back, before returning to New York.

We read the proofs of *My Ántonia* together in Jaffrey early the following summer. Willa Cather liked to read proofs out of doors whenever it was possible; and one could always find convenient rocks to sit against in the woods near the Shattuck Inn. Those were wonderful mornings, full of beauty and pleasure. I remember how the chipmunks used to flash up and down along the trunks of the trees as we worked, and a mole would steal out of its hole near us and slide like a dark shadow along the ground. The air seemed full of the future—a future of bright prospects, limitless horizons.

It was very interesting to read proofs with Willa Cather. After a thing was written, she had an extremely impersonal attitude toward it. If there was "too much" of anything, she was not only ready, she was eager to cut it. She did not cherish her words and phrases. Sometimes she would have a sudden illumination and would make some radical change—always, I think, for the better. She had to pay nearly $150 for extra proof corrections on *My Ántonia*. Afterwards she was more provident, and made most of her changes in the typewritten copies of her manuscripts.

Houghton Mifflin published the book that Fall. Although Ferris Greenslet[1] wrote a highly favourable report on it to the publishers, Willa Cather was disappointed, and I think rather disheartened, by their reception of the story. She herself felt that it was the best thing she had done—that she had succeeded, more nearly than ever before, in writing the way she wanted to write.

It is hard, now, to realize how revolutionary in form *My Ántonia* was at that time in America. It seemed to many people to have no form. It had no love story—though the whole book was a sort of love story of the country. *The Virginian* was the popular type of Western novel. Even Mrs. Fields, so personally devoted to Willa Cather, rather deplored the book—because it was about "hired girls".[2] She preferred reading about the sort of people she found in Henry James' and Mrs. Humphrey Ward's[3] novels. Her "dear Mr. Dickens", although he wrote of low life, always had gentlefolk for his heroes and heroines.

Most of the press notices praised the book highly—though a critic writing for the *New York Herald* of October 6, 1918 said:—

> "I regret to see a writer of such fine literary quality as Miss Willa S. Cather seek expression through those dreary channels that traverse life on the Western prairies like so many irrigation ditches . . . As a novel, it will prove a disappointment to everyone who has read Miss Cather's earlier work."

On the other hand H. L. Mencken—from the beginning one of Willa Cather's warmest champions—wrote:—

> "*My Ántonia* is not only the best novel done by Miss Cather, but also one of the best any American has ever done."

The initial sale of *My Ántonia* was small—in the first year it brought Willa Cather about $1,300, and not quite $400 the second year. She had begun to feel that she could never write the kind of book that would be wholly satisfactory to Houghton Mifflin as publishers. Yet she had confidence in what she was doing, and the

1. Willa Cather's editor at Houghton Mifflin Company, which published her first four novels.
2. Annie Adams Fields (1834–1915) was married to James T. Fields of the Boston publishing house Ticknor and Fields and, after Fields's death, became the companion of the writer Sarah Orne Jewett. An important figure in the New England literary landscape, Mrs. Fields was venerated by Willa Cather, whom she befriended. However, Edith Lewis misremembers here. Mrs. Fields died three years before the publication of *My Ántonia*.
3. Mary Augusta Ward (1851–1920), British writer who published novels under the name of Mrs. Humphrey Ward.

reception of her books among people whose opinion she respected had increased that confidence.

*   *   *

ELIZABETH SHEPLEY SERGEANT

From Willa Cather: A Memoir[†]

My Ántonia
1916–1919

In the spring of 1916, I had the first inkling that Willa had a new story in mind. I never asked questions—she was the initiator of any communication about an unborn or unfinished work.

She had not been able to forget that, in these war days, the youth of Europe, its finest flower, was dying. Perhaps our American youth had also been designed for sacrifice—by now we feared so. But a growing vital work, with Willa, usually took precedence, even in her thoughts, over the life around her.

She had come in for tea at a small apartment facing south on a garden, in the East Sixties where I was living. As it was not far from Central Park, she arrived flushed and alert from one of her swift wintry walks. I think of her as always wearing red-brown fur in winter in those years; it made her hair shine, and she had the warmth, charm, assurance, and fullness of being that allied her, despite her individual direction, with *the* American woman in her forties. She said more than once to me that nobody under forty could ever really believe in either death or degeneration. She herself carried that physical nonchalance right on through her fifties.

While I boiled the kettle Willa sat down with Henry James's *Notes on Novelists* which lay on my writing table; turned to the passage where he says that the originator has one law and the reporter, however philosophic, another. "So that the two laws can with no sort of harmony and congruity make one household."

Willa was amused by James's elaborate, subtle phrases—a bit impatiently amused by now. But with this comment she fully agreed: she had not altogether banished the reporter in her last book.[1] Now she aimed at a more frugal, parsimonious form and technique.

† From *Willa Cather: A Memoir* (Philadelphia: Lippincott, 1953), pp. 138–53. Copyright 1953 by Elizabeth Shepley Sergeant. Reprinted by permission of HarperCollins Publishers. Sergeant (1881–1965), writer and journalist, was a close friend of Willa Cather, particularly during the early years of Cather's writing career.
1. *The Song of the Lark* (1915).

She then suddenly leaned over—and this is something I remembered clearly when *My Ántonia* came into my hands, at last, in 1918—and set an old Sicilian apothecary jar of mine, filled with orange-brown flowers of scented stock, in the middle of a bare, round, antique table.

"I want my new heroine to be like this—like a rare object in the middle of a table, which one may examine from all sides."

She moved the lamp so that light streamed brightly down on my Taormina jar, with its glazed orange and blue design.

"I want her to stand out—like this—like this—because she *is* the story."

Saying this her fervent, enthusiastic voice faltered and her eyes filled with tears.

Someone you knew in your childhood, I ventured.

She nodded, but did not say more.

So I sometimes wondered, later, whether she was thinking of Ántonia or Mrs. Forrester.[2] Often she thought about her heroines for years before they appeared in a book.

Another day, of the same period, when we were walking in the Park together, past skaters on the icy pond, under brilliant blue skies, she told me of a major change in her personal life—this rather drily, rather bluntly.

Her friend, Isabelle McClung, whom I knew to be an animating force, was getting married.[3] This, after first youth, one did not expect or foresee. But it had happened. Judge McClung, by then an old man, had died in the fall; 1180 Murray Hill Avenue would cease to be—and of course I knew that, even since she'd had a home in Bank Street, she had spent some months of every year writing in Pittsburgh, where Isabelle had always protected and quickened her work in her perfect way.

Isabelle was a musical amateur, and she had married music too: Jan Hambourg was a gifted and scholarly violinist, known on two continents for his concerts with two musician brothers, a violinist and a cellist. The three brothers had an old Russian father who was also a musical scholar, and a family home in Toronto. Isabelle and Jan would not desert American shores during the war. But Willa felt they might end up in Europe.

Her face—I saw how bleak it was, how vacant her eyes. All her natural exuberance had drained away.

"So you will have to find a new remote place to work," I said, grasping at the aspect of the situation most easy to talk about. It could not be South Berwick: Miss Mary Jewett[4] sat on at the front

2. Central character in *A Lost Lady* (1923).
3. Beloved friend of Willa Cather who nourished both her life and her work.
4. Sister of Sarah Orne Jewett.

window, but now it was her nephew, Dr. Eastman, whom she really watched for.

Red Cloud? She said no to that. Her father was always fancying she might write there but she never did or could. No, she would have to be quite on her own.

*　*　*

Our American declaration of war came in April, 1917. Of course, not unexpectedly, for President Wilson's speeches had been preparing the country gradually for what lay ahead. Willa had no patience with this aloof, stiff, intellectual leader of ours, who did not hesitate to borrow his phrases from *The New Republic*:[5] for instance, that one about Making the World Safe for Democracy; and that other which in our time sounds still more deluded, about Fighting the War to End War. But, in truth, that is what we the American people thought we were doing at the time. Our quest in Europe was one of ideal mercy and helpfulness.

By September, the underground currents that had been almost compulsively pulling at me since 1914 had swept me across the Atlantic to wartime Paris, which became my base for correspondence for *The New Republic*. In due course I was summoned to American General Headquarters by the Commander-in-Chief.

Then it was, when eating at the G-2 mess; or with that more worldly mess, reputed for its French cook, where one found Colonel Frank McCoy and Colonel Douglas MacArthur and others later known to fame and generalship, that I was able to compare the bluff, full-fashioned "C.-in-C.," as his staff called him, and as I saw him, with an earlier image Willa had left with me when I decided to go to France.

She had known General Pershing as young cadet, with a slim waist and yellow moustaches, stationed at the University of Nebraska when she was there. He was very gay, reputed a crack shot; had founded an organization called The Pershing Rifles which took prizes everywhere it went. You will find a passage in *One of Ours* to the same effect.

Randolph Bourne had reproached me sharply for not retiring to write a novel in some Western or New England retreat where war could be forgotten. Willa clearly realized that I had to go. She was herself, however, in no wise drawn to do anything but get on with her new story.[6] Before I sailed, I had the comfort of knowing that she had made her first connection with Jaffrey, New Hampshire, which was to prove, in a final sense, a new writing centre; a replacement of her Pittsburgh refuge.

5. American magazine of politics and culture that began publishing in 1914.
6. The manuscript that became *My Ántonia*.

Two women friends of Pittsburgh days had a hand in it. They had rented from Mrs. James Harvey Robinson, for the summer of 1917 and again in 1918, a charming house called High Mowing which has a sweeping view of Mount Monadnock.

Below High Mowing to the west, on the thickly wooded fern-green road from Jaffrey to Dublin, stood the quiet Shattuck Inn, a hostelry of good repute known to Bostonians. There, Willa found bed and board for the first time in 1917. Her newly married friends, the Hambourgs, were with her. But her engrossing work claimed her mornings and the kind ladies of High Mowing offered to pitch her a tent on their lower slopes of field and meadow, backed by a thick fringe of woods.

The tent was pegged to Mother Earth, furnished with table and camp chair. Willa, ever an early riser, found a path near the inn through this wood where lady's-slippers and Hooker's orchids grew.

Over a stone wall next: she was carrying her pens and paper, and the manuscript of *My Ántonia*—and to her tent for two good hours of work. Most of Book Two, "The Hired Girls," was written in this hideout.

This information came to me through the kindness of the present owner of High Mowing, whose son, a young Marine, fell in the Pacific in the Second World War. He had written Willa Cather a letter (now lost) about his joy in *My Ántonia*. He had read the book in his North Carolina camp, and wrote from there. Willa replied to many outpourings of young American hearts about her books.

Her intimate letter to the young Marine, which he sent to his parents for safekeeping before going overseas, had the ring of memory. It derived, she told him, from their mutual love of High Mowing, and from the fact that *My Ántonia* had a real connection with the place where it was—in part—written. Jaffrey people, by the way, have noted a number of their local proper names applied to Black Hawk characters.

Willa made the point that in general she never talked of her writing as she was doing it; her young correspondent was, then, the *"first"* to know what pages were written in the tent.

Was *My Ántonia* then (I asked myself in 1950 when I read this comment) a real turning point of literary maturity, when encouragement or criticism from without became irrelevant? Certainly I had received many disclosures about the writing of her first three novels. I was separated geographically from her during the writing of *My Ántonia*, which she completed in New York in the winter of 1917–1918, my first winter in beleagured Paris (air raids driving us into the wine cellar of the Hôtel de France et Choiseul; the American Army on the Boulevards, making the cocottes cry and throw red roses; the Big Bertha dropping pot shots into streets and a famous sanctuary).

Certainly I was to know much less, as time passed, of what Willa had "in the works." But she did when I saw her, sometimes suddenly, unburden herself.

In the following as it were, suspended, summer of 1918, the Boches swept over the Marne again and dug in fifty miles from Paris, where I continued to live and write: during the uncertain and bloody fortunes of the Meuse-Argonne battle, when our A.E.F.[7] gave all for victory, Willa was engrossed at last in her new story, *One of Ours*. The proof sheets of *My Ántonia* were hardly dry but she was working again.

In Paris I was waiting longingly for a copy of *My Ántonia*. Ferris Greenslet, my editor at Houghton Mifflin, sent me an early one to the American Hospital of Paris, where I found myself bedded down for seven months of care, infection and recuperation after a critical war accident that brought my correspondence for *The New Republic* to an abrupt conclusion.

With what eagerness I held this incomparable book in my hands, as Dakin's solution[8] dripped into my war fractures! Just to skim a page or two, to get the American measure and flow, the candor and newness, was better than a sedative to calm my pain.

When I was able to *read* rather than just *apprehend*, I was absorbed in the autobiographical elements of the book. Willa would never write a novel of her early life in the first person and, in talk, did not say much about her childhood and youth. As I read *My Ántonia*, I learned far more than she had ever recounted; from the point where, for her, Virginia ended, with an interminable railroad journey "across the great midland plain of North America." The platform where a boy alighted in the dark of night, was obviously the same on which the embalmed corpse of the sculptor was set down, in that early story. The Bohemian Shimerdas with their four children were huddled there too, ready to fare forth to the sod hut in which they were destined to suffer severe hardships and such sorrows as the suicide of a father. Jim (or Willie, his symbolic twin-sister) riding in his Grandfather Burden's wagon box in the cold dark night looked for creeks, rivers, fences, a mountain ridge against the sky. All he made out was "land not a country at all but the material out of which countries are made . . . the dome of heaven all there was of it. . . ."

I looked sharply to find Ántonia, (the "My" in the title indicated that she belonged to somebody) as I felt Willa had forecast her to

---

7. American Expeditionary Force.
8. Antiseptic solution used to combat infections in wounds, first used during World War I.

me; as a beautiful object in the middle of a table, which could be viewed from all sides and in varying lights. At first the story did not seem at all like that. The background was full and rich. There were other farm girls who became hired girls in Black Hawk besides Ántonia, the oldest Shimerda. All were described in terms of character and individual experience, through interweaving themes and detailed scenes in genre painting.

Willa had told me that the story "wrote itself" and that it had no plot. But if it had no plot it had a framework and—in itself a contrivance—a narrator. Jim Burden was presented informally to the reader in this rôle, in an introduction where he is seen to be intellectual and urban, a railroad lawyer with an unhappy personal life. (This story was wisely cut short in a later edition.) The memories of a pioneering experience at his grandmother's homestead, that came to him by an accident of fate at an age of acute sensibility, and lasted until he went East to study law, are the stuff of the story. Like Ántonia, Jim Burden's observations and perceptions had been sharpened and pointed by his migration from a more mellow region to the vast, inchoate land of Nebraska.

Jim would not have fallen in love with a woman like Alexandra Bergson, with her masculine vision and her power to "dominise," as the South Carolinians say, the land of her inheriting and increasing. Alexandra was as strong as the Virginian pioneers: could rival or surpass them. But Ántonia was simply and lustily contained in the country of her Bohemian parents' choosing. Her rôle was so primeval, and so much woman's, whether she plowed for her brother or cooked for Mrs. Harling in Black Hawk, that a detached lonely boy could think of her in the confused terms of a youthful projection of love and nature blended.

The first time Jim returned to the prairie after he went East he found Ántonia, slaving on her brother's farm, with a baby by a railroad conductor who had betrayed her. She was thin from farm work and still but twenty-four.

> "Do you know, Ántonia, since I've been away, I think of you more often than of anyone else in this part of the world. I'd have liked to have you for a sweetheart, or a wife, or my mother or my sister—anything that a woman can be to a man. The idea of you is part of my mind; you influence my likes and dislikes, all my tastes, hundreds of times when I don't realize it. You really are a part of me."

Anything a woman can be to a man? That the reader doubts. If so why had not Jim and Ántonia loved and married, why did not this happen now? Both were young and free. No, Ántonia was a big sister, or a kind of great earth mother, a symbol so central to Jim's

heart that he cherished her within himself, and surrounded her figure with a gentle clarity like the early morning or sunset light on
prairie and cornfields.

Twenty years later he came back to discover that "his" Ántonia
had married a kind negligible husband who had given her a nestful
of happy children.

> She was a battered woman now, not a lovely girl; but she still
> had that something which fires the imagination, could still stop
> one's breath for a moment by a look or a gesture that somehow
> revealed the meaning in common things.

Ántonia's passionate involvement with her surroundings is here
contrasted with the tender compassionate and semi-detached mood
of the observer, the oblique reflector of the *femme éternelle*.[9]

The story, I saw, was dedicated to Carrie and Irene Miner, childhood friends of Willa's in Red Cloud: "In memory of affections old
and true." The Miners were neighbors of the Cathers. It was no secret
that she had in "Mrs. Harling" drawn an exact portrait—her only
exact fictional portrait she said later—of Mrs. Miner, the musical wife
of the local grain merchant and storekeeper, who was born in Christiania, and had taken Ántonia as a hired girl. Mrs. Miner had died during the writing of the novel and Willa resolved to keep her in life:

> Mrs. Harling was short and square and sturdy-looking, like her
> house. Every inch of her was charged with an energy that made
> itself felt the moment she entered a room. Her face was rosy
> and solid, with bright, twinkling eyes and a stubborn little chin.
> She was quick to anger, quick to laughter, and jolly from the
> depths of her soul. . . . Her rapid footsteps shook her own floors,
> and she routed lassitude and indifference wherever she came. . . .

The "recurrences" in this story are striking and rendered in final
terms. Old Mr. Shimerda, with his homesickness for the musical life
and the cafés of the old world, his subjection by his hard son, Anton,
his burial at the barren crossroads, is a piercing portrait of an American immigrant in whom the will to live did not persist against intol-
erable odds. I was happy when I found the substance of that delicate
sketch of boyhood, "The Enchanted Bluff" distilled into the finer
essence of the hired girls' picnic on the river bluff—a noonday dream
full of fascination.

Later Willa would say delightedly after a trip to Red Cloud: "I saw
Ántonia—she . . ." A story had not detracted from a friendship—
rather added to it.

*   *   *

9. Eternal woman (French).

F. H.

Willa Cather Talks of Work[†]

* * *

"How did you come to write about that flat part of the prairie west, Miss Cather, which not many people find interesting?"

"I happen to be interested in the Scandinavian and Bohemian pioneers of Nebraska," said the young novelist, "because I lived among them when I was a child. When I was eight years old, my father moved from the Shenandoah Valley in Virginia to that Western country. My grandfather and grandmother had moved to Nebraska eight years before we left Virginia; they were among the real pioneers.

"But it was still wild enough and bleak enough when we got there. My grandfather's homestead was about eighteen miles from Red Cloud—a little town on the Burlington, named after the old Indian chief[1] who used to come hunting in that country, and who buried his daughter on the top of one of the river bluffs south of the town. Her grave had been looted for her rich furs and beadwork long before my family went West, but we children used to find arrowheads there and some of the bones of her pony that had been strangled above her grave."

"What was the country like when you got there?"

"I shall never forget my introduction to it. We drove out from Red Cloud to my grandfather's homestead one day in April. I was sitting on the hay in the bottom of a Studebaker wagon, holding on to the side of the wagon box to steady myself—the roads were mostly faint trails over the bunch grass in those days. The land was open range and there was almost no fencing. As we drove further and further out into the country, I felt a good deal as if we had come to the end of everything—it was a kind of erasure of personality.

"I would not know how much a child's life is bound up in the woods and hills and meadows around it, if I had not been jerked away from all these and thrown out into a country as bare as a piece of sheet iron. I had heard my father say you had to show grit in a new country, and I would have got on pretty well during that ride if it had not been for the larks. Every now and then one flew up and sang a few splendid notes and dropped down into the grass again. That reminded me of something—I don't know what, but my one purpose in life just then was not to cry, and every time they did it, I thought I should go under.

† F. H., Special Correspondence of the *Philadelphia Record*, August 10, 1913.
1. Makhpiya-Lúta, or Red Cloud (1822–1909), was one of the most important Lakota warriors in nineteenth-century America, a leader in the fight to preserve Indian autonomy and rights.

193

"For the first week or two on the homestead I had that kind of contraction of the stomach which comes from homesickness. I didn't like canned things anyhow, and I made an agreement with myself that I would not eat much until I got back to Virginia and could get some fresh mutton. I think the first thing that interested me after I got to the homestead was a heavy hickory cane with a steel tip which my grandmother always carried with her when she went to the garden to kill rattlesnakes. She had killed a good many snakes with it, and that seemed to argue that life might not be so flat as it looked there.

"We had very few American neighbors—they were mostly Swedes and Danes, Norwegians and Bohemians. I liked them from the first and they made up for what I missed in the country. I particularly liked the old women, they understood my homesickness and were kind to me. I had met 'traveled' people in Virginia and in Washington, but these old women on the farms were the first people who ever gave me the real feeling of an older world across the sea. Even when they spoke very little English, the old women somehow managed to tell me a great many stories about the old country. They talk more freely to a child than to grown people, and I always felt as if every word they said to me counted for twenty.

"I have never found any intellectual excitement any more intense than I used to feel when I spent a morning with one of those old women at her baking or butter making. I used to ride home in the most unreasonable state of excitement; I always felt as if they told me so much more than they said—as if I had actually got inside another person's skin. If one begins that early, it is the story of the maneating tiger over again—no other adventure ever carries one quite so far."

"Some of your early short stories were about these people, were they not?"

"Yes, but most of them were poor. It is always hard to write about the things that are near to your heart, from a kind of instinct of self-protection you distort them and disguise them. Those stories were so poor that they discouraged me. I decided that I wouldn't write any more about the country and people for which I had such personal feeling.

"Then I had the good fortune to meet Sarah Orne Jewett, who had read all of my early stories and had very clear and definite opinions about them and about where my work fell short. She said, 'Write it as it is, don't try to make it like this or that. You can't do it in anybody else's way—you will have to make a way of your own. If the way happens to be new, don't let that frighten you. Don't try to write the kind of short story that this or that magazine wants— write the truth, and let them take it or leave it.'

"I was not at all sure, however, that my feeling about the Western country and my Scandinavian friends was the truth—I thought perhaps that going among them so young I had a romantic personal feeling about them. I thought that Americans in general must see only the humorous side of the Scandinavian—the side often presented in vaudeville dialect sketches—because nobody had ever tried to write about the Swedish settlers seriously.

"What has pleased me most in the cordial reception the West has given this new book of mine, is that the reviewers in all those Western States say the thing seems to them true to the country and the people. That is a great satisfaction. The reviews have concerned themselves a good deal more with the subject matter of the story than with my way of telling it, and I am glad of that. I care a lot more about the country and the people than I care about my own way of writing or anybody else's way of writing."

LATROBE CARROLL
Willa Sibert Cather[†]

On the Nebraska prairie some years ago, a little girl rode about on her pony, among settlements of Scandinavians and Bohemians, listening to their conversation, fascinated by their personalities. She was Willa Sibert Cather, who, as a woman, was to give in her novels the story of their struggle with the soil. Ever since those early years, she has been studying people, until she is today one of that small group of American writers who tell of life with beauty and entire earnestness. She has won the praise of those critics whose standards are highest, whose condemnation of insincerity and distortion is severest. Listen to Randolph Bourne:[1] "She has outgrown provincialism and can now be reckoned among those who are richly interpreting youth all over the world." And to H. L. Mencken:[2] "There is no other American author of her sex, now in view, whose future promises so much."

Miss Cather's reputation is of recent growth. Though her first novel, "Alexander's Bridge", was published in 1912, she remained comparatively unknown until about five years ago. Then critics realized that every successive book of hers had shown an advance, and

† *The Bookman*, May 3, 1921.
1. Prominent writer and public intellectual of the early twentieth century (1886–1918). An admirer of Willa Cather's writing, he believed that immigrants should retain their own cultural heritage rather than assimilate in a "melting pot" America.
2. One of the most influential editors, critics, and men of letters in early twentieth-century America, H. L. Mencken (1880–1956) championed Willa Cather's early novels and contributed to her growing literary reputation.

began to look forward with interest to her future work. She is, however, still unknown to large sections of the American reading public.

Not long ago, she sat in her New York apartment in Greenwich
Village, and talked to me about her books. She seems just the one
to have written them. She is sincere, vigorous, self-controlled. There
is no flippancy about her. She has not made herself the heroine of
any of her novels, but she is akin to her own heroines. In "The Song
of the Lark", one of the characters remarks that Thea Kronborg, the
central figure, "doesn't sigh every time the wind blows". Miss Cather
herself is that sort. She has a mental sturdiness.

She spoke of the beginnings of her impulse to write.

"When I was about nine," she said, "father took me from our
place near Winchester, Virginia, to a ranch in Nebraska. Few of our
neighbors were Americans—most of them were Danes, Swedes,
Norwegians, and Bohemians. I grew fond of some of these
immigrants—particularly the old women, who used to tell me of
their home country. I used to think them underrated, and wanted
to explain them to their neighbors. Their stories used to go round
and round in my head at night. This was, with me, the initial
impulse. I didn't know any writing people. I had an enthusiasm for
a kind of country and a kind of people, rather than ambition.

"I've always had a habit of remembering mannerisms, turns of
speech," she explained. "The phraseology of those people stuck in
my mind. If I had made notes, or should make them now, the material collected would be dead. No, it's memory—the memory that goes
with the vocation. When I sit down to write, turns of phrase I've forgotten for years come back like white ink before fire. I think that
most of the basic material a writer works with is acquired before the
age of fifteen. That's the important period: when one's not writing.
Those years determine whether one's work will be poor and thin or
rich and fine."

After a high school preparation, Miss Cather entered the University of Nebraska. She said, of this time:

"Back in the files of the college magazine, there were once several of my perfectly honest but very clumsy attempts to give the story
of some of the Scandinavian and Bohemian settlers who lived not
far from my father's farm. In these sketches, I simply tried to tell
about the people, without much regard for style. These early stories
were bald, clumsy, and emotional.[3] As I got toward my senior year,
I began to admire, for the first time, writing for writing's sake. In
those days, no one seemed so wonderful as Henry James; for me, he
was the perfect writer."

---

3. One of these stories, "Peter," anticipated the description of Mr. Shimerda's suicide in
   My Ántonia.

When Willa Cather graduated at nineteen, her instructors and friends expected her to become a "writer" in a few months, and achieve popular success. But they were disappointed. For almost nine years she wrote little besides a volume of verse, the experimental "April Twilights", and a dozen stories for magazines. Most of these stories she now dismisses as "affected" and "bad".

"It wasn't that I didn't want to write," she said of this period. "But I was too interested in trying to find out something about the world and about people. I worked on the Pittsburg 'Leader', taught English in the Allegheny High School, went abroad for long periods, and traveled in the west. I couldn't have got as much out of those nine years if I'd been writing."

In 1905 there was published a collection of her stories, "The Troll Garden". Largely by reason of these, she was offered a position on "McClure's Magazine",[4] of which she was managing editor from 1908 until 1912.

"I took a salaried position," she said, "because I didn't want to write directly to sell. I didn't want to compromise. Not that the magazine demands were wrong. But they were definite. I had a delightful sense of freedom when I'd saved up enough to take a house in Cherry Valley, New York, and could begin work on my first novel, 'Alexander's Bridge'.

"In 'Alexander's Bridge' I was still more preoccupied with trying to write well than with anything else. It takes a great deal of experience to become natural. People grow in honesty as they grow in anything else. A painter or writer must learn to distinguish what is his *own* from that which he admires. I never abandoned trying to make a compromise between the kind of matter that my experience had given me and the manner of writing which I admired, until I began my second novel, 'O Pioneers!' And from the first chapter, I decided not to 'write' at all—simply to give myself up to the pleasure of recapturing in memory people and places I had believed forgotten. This was what my friend Sarah Orne Jewett[5] had advised me to do. She said to me that if my life had lain in a part of the world that was without a literature, and I couldn't tell about it truthfully in the form I most admired, I'd have to make a kind of writing that would tell it, no matter what I lost in the process."

"O Pioneers!" placed Miss Cather definitely among the writers who count. It is an epic of the early struggles of Swedish and Bohemian settlers in Nebraska—a book of beauty and power. In taking for a

4. Founded by S. S. McClure (1857–1949), *McClure's Magazine* was a popular periodical of the late-nineteenth and early-twentieth centuries, focusing on politics, social commentary, and the arts.
5. Novelist and short-story writer (1849–1909) whose work was inspired by her love of the Maine seacoast and its people; she was Willa Cather's most important literary guide and mentor.

title the name of one of Walt Whitman's poems, the author drew attention to his influence upon the mood of her narrative.

In "The Song of the Lark", Willa Cather chose a less impressionistic method. It is longer than "O Pioneers!", less concentrated, resembling more closely the conventional psychological novel. It is the story of Thea Kronborg, a Swedish-American singer, who wrenches herself away from an environment antagonistic to art, and becomes an opera "star". Critics took widely divergent attitudes toward the book. To many, it has not the same *aliveness* as "O Pioneers!" Randolph Bourne found it a digression into a field for which Miss Cather was not really fitted, either by her style, or her enthusiasm. But Edward Everett Hale discovered in it "a sense of something less common than life: namely, art as it exists in life—a very curious and elusive thing, but so beautiful, when one gets it, that one forgets all else."

Miss Cather's most recent novel, "My Antonia", is a fuller evocation of the "old, old west" than was "O Pioneers!" The descriptions of the western prairie, brief, poignant, lift us from our easy chairs and set us down on those high plains. The book is ruthless, poetical, tremendously alive. It is the finest thing Miss Cather has written. H. L. Mencken laid it down with the conviction that it is the best piece of fiction done by any woman in America. The portrayal of Antonia is masterly.

"She was a Bohemian girl," Miss Cather said, "who was good to me when I was a child. I saw a great deal of her from the time I was eight until I was twelve. She was big-hearted and essentially romantic."

Willa Cather's foreigners are true to type. August Brunius,[6] after noting that the Swede, as presented by writers outside his own country, usually seems absurd to a Swedish reader, goes on to say that in "O Pioneers!" and "The Song of the Lark", Swedes are presented with true insight and art. Small wonder that all Miss Cather's books have been translated into the Scandinavian and are to be translated into French.

Her latest volume, "Youth and the Bright Medusa", is a collection of eight short stories. Simply and vividly told, they are studies of the artistic temperament. In them, there is none of the usual sentimentalizing about the artist. They are widely recognized as work of distinction. An anonymous critic in "The Nation"[7] slyly remarks that the collection "represents the triumph of mind over Nebraska".

Willa Cather's best work is satisfying because it is sincere. In her books, there is none of the sweet reek that pervades the pages of so many "lady novelists". Love, to her, is "not a simple state, like

6. Swedish writer and critic (1879–1926).
7. Weekly magazine, founded in 1865, that focused on politics and culture.

measles". Her treatment of sex is without either squeamishness or sensuality. She loves the west, and the arts, particularly music, and she has sought to express feelings and convictions on these subjects. She tried, failed, and kept on trying until she succeeded. For example, we have her word for it that at college she attempted to tell about immigrants in rough sketches. She drew them more skillfully in "The Bohemian Girl", a short story which appeared in "McClure's Magazine" in 1912. Then came "O Pioneers!", a work of art. In "My Antonia", she reached what she had been advancing toward for many years. Similarly in her exploration of the minds and emotions of artists, she has striven to tell the truth—the truth stripped of sentimentality. She experimented in "The Troll Garden", succeeded partially in "Youth and the Bright Medusa", grasped fully what she had sought in "The Song of the Lark". It would, of course, be unfair to speak of the books and stories that led up to this novel and to "My Antonia" as preliminary studies, for there is too much in them not touched upon in the two later novels. But there is a certain summing up, in these books, of two subjects which have interested Miss Cather profoundly: the life of foreigners in the west, and the mind and heart of the artist. Of the books, the author herself said: "I think 'My Antonia' is the most successfully done. 'The Song of the Lark' was the most interesting to write."

"I work from two and a half to three hours a day," Miss Cather went on to say. "I don't hold myself to longer hours; if I did, I wouldn't gain by it. The only reason I write is because it interests me more than any other activity I've ever found. I like riding, going to operas and concerts, travel in the west; but on the whole writing interests me more than anything else. If I made a chore of it, my enthusiasm would die. I make it an adventure every day. I get more entertainment from it than any I could buy, except the privilege of hearing a few great musicians and singers. To listen to them interests me as much as a good morning's work.

"For me, the morning is the best time to write. During the other hours of the day I attend to my housekeeping, take walks in Central Park, go to concerts, and see something of my friends. I try to keep myself fit, fresh: one has to be in as good form to write as to sing. When not working, I shut work from my mind."

At present Miss Cather is writing a new novel—she says of it:

"What I always want to do is to make the 'writing' count for less and less and the people for more. In this new novel I'm trying to cut out all analysis, observation, description, even the picture-making quality, in order to make things and people tell their own story simply by juxtaposition, without any persuasion or explanation on my part.

"Just as if I put here on the table a green vase, and beside it a yellow orange. Now, those two things affect each other. Side by side, they produce a reaction which neither of them will produce alone. Why should I try to say anything clever, or by any colorful rhetoric detract attention from those two objects, the relation they have to each other and the effect they have upon each other? I want the reader to see the orange and the vase—beyond that, *I* am out of it. Mere cleverness must go. I'd like the writing to be so lost in the object, that it doesn't exist for the reader—except for the reader who knows how difficult it is to lose writing in the object. One must choose one's audience, and the audience I try to write for is the one interested in the effect the green vase brings out in the orange, and the orange in the green vase."

Miss Cather has never sought publicity, or quick success. It took her three years to write "The Song of the Lark", and three to write "My Antonia". Of the two paths of art—give the public what it wants, or make your work so fine that the public will want it—she has consistently chosen the path of fine work. She is moving unhurriedly toward a richer self-expression.

W. D. EDSON

A Talk with Miss Cather[†]

It always gives us much pleasure when some reader of the *Argus* here on a visit calls at the office for a friendly chat because of the feeling that those who read the paper and those who are charged with its preparation belong to one big family. Naturally we were especially pleased when last Friday Miss Willa Cather, whose address is New York City, but who is at home in Red Cloud, New York, London, Paris, or any other city on earth in which she happens to be, called at this office for that reason. Miss Cather is enjoying a several weeks' visit with her parents, Mr. and Mrs. C. F. Cather.

While her work has called her to other scenes Miss Cather told us that there is not any place in this world that is more interesting to her than Red Cloud. She came here from Virginia with her parents when a child, and here grew to womanhood, graduating from the local high school. During part of her course she wrote school items for the *Argus*, which may have been her first contributions to the public press. In those days she was often called upon to stay in her father's office while he was at the court house making abstracts or was out of the city on other business. She had her own desk in the office, and here she did much studying and writing. But the matter which she deems of greatest importance in this connection was

† *Webster County Argus*, September 29, 1921.

the acquaintances formed with the leaders in the life of the community who, calling to transact business with her father, remained to visit with her, telling her of personal affairs in the way that grownups will disclose to a child matters which they would not discuss with a mature person. Often she accompanied Dr. Damerall or Dr. McKeeby on their long trips into the country, and listened with childish admiration as they talked on a variety of subjects from their personal experiences. There were no trained nurses here in those days, so sometimes she was called upon to assist them with surgical operations. In the best homes of the city she was always a welcome visitor. Red Cloud had many men and women of exceptional ability. Miss Cather looks back to her association with these as one of the brightest and most helpful periods of her life.

But the time came when it was necessary that she leave her home and friends. Greater opportunities in other places called her. Times were hard in Nebraska. Her father had acquired large holdings of land, but these were not producing enough revenue to pay the taxes. She could not be contented to stay here and depend upon her parents for support. But the thought of leaving her family and friends who meant so much to her was almost too much, and she confessed during her visit the other day that at one time she was actually on the point of giving up, when some words of timely counsel from Mr. and Mrs. O. C. Case gave her new courage and led her to go on with her plans for self improvement.

The interest which has been felt by Red Cloud people in *My Ántonia*, many of the scenes of which are laid in this city, led us to turn the conversation to that subject. Three characters of the story, Miss Cather said, were intended as comparatively faithful pictures of citizens of Red Cloud about 1888 or 1889. These were the author's grandparents, whose characteristics made a deep impression upon her youthful mind when she first came here from Virginia, and Mrs. J. L. Miner—the Mrs. Harling of the book, in whose home she was a frequent guest. In the first draft of the story the picture of Mrs. Harling was of a very different character. While the manuscript was being revised by the author, news came to her of Mrs. Miner's death. So profound an impression did this make upon her, and so active were the memories of old times brought to mind by the news that she made changes in some parts of the book in honor of her friend of early days.

Another character in the book, she informed us, was in part a picture of a former Red Cloud man, and in part of a man she had known in the east. For some reason, she said, this treatment of a character is a very natural one for an author to give. We inquired if these were not because the life of the average person is so commonplace that a faithful delineation of him alone would not make interesting reading. Miss Cather wholly disagreed with this view. She contended that the average person has just as interesting emotions and experiences as public personages. She knew Red Cloud people whose experiences were no less intense and thrilling than those of the public personages with whom she was well acquainted. She found people here just as interesting as those she met in London and Paris, although in a different way. She summed up the matter by saying that if a person is wide awake and not self-centered he can see those interesting things in the life of those about him.

My Ántonia has been translated into a number of different languages, and has had a very large sale. Miss Cather is very familiar with the French tongue, and was able to revise the manuscript after the translator had completed his work in that language. This gentleman was a very scholarly man and in the main did excellent work, but he was a little handicapped by never having lived in the prairie states. Miss Cather found that when he came to the word "gopher" at various places in the book he had used the French word meaning "mole." This might have passed among the French readers had it not been for a passage where the gophers were spoken of as playing about in the sun.

Miss Cather writes of Nebraska, not from any sense of duty, but because her early life was so bound up with this commonwealth that this part of the world is of greatest interest to her. She has just completed a new book, some of the scenes of which are laid in this part of the state. That it is bound to be one of her greatest successes is indicated by a telegram received from her publisher, after reading the last installment of the manuscript.

> Just finished the book. Congratulations. It is masterly, a perfectly gorgeous novel, far ahead of anything you have ever yet done, and far ahead of anything I have read in a very long while. With it your position should be secure forever. I shall be proud to have my name associated with it.

ELEANOR HINMAN

Interview with Willa Cather[†]

"The old-fashioned farmer's wife is nearer to the type of the true artist and the prima donna than is the culture enthusiast," declared Miss Willa Cather, author of *The Song of the Lark, O Pioneers!, My Ántonia, Youth and the Bright Medusa*," who has earned the title of one of the foremost American novelists by her stories of prima

[†] *Lincoln Sunday Star*, November 6, 1921.

donnas and pioneers. She was emphasizing that the two are not so far apart in type as most people seem to imagine.

Miss Cather had elected to take her interview out-of-doors in the autumnal sunshine, walking. The fact is characteristic. She is an out-door person, not far different in type from the pioneers and prima donnas whom she exalts.

She walks with the gait of one who has been used to the saddle. Her complexion is firm with an outdoor wholesomeness. The red in her cheeks is the red that comes from the bite of the wind. Her voice is deep, rich, and full of color; she speaks with her whole body, like a singer.

"Downright" is the word that comes most often to the mind in thinking of her. Whatever she does is done with every fibre. There is no pretense in her, and no conventionality. In conversation she is more stimulating than captivating. She has ideas and is not afraid to express them. Her mind scintillates and sends rays of light down many avenues of thought.

When the interviewer was admitted to her, she was pasting press clippings on a huge sheet of brown wrapping paper, as whole-heartedly as though it were the most important action of her life.

"This way you get them all together," she explained, "and you can see who it is that really likes you, who that really hates you, and who that actually hates you but pretends to like you. I don't mind the ones that hate me; I don't doubt they have good reasons; but I despise the ones that pretend."

When she had finished, she went to her room and almost imme-diately came out of it again, putting on her hat and coat as she came down the stairs, and going out without a glance at the mir-ror. She dresses well, yet she is clearly one of the women to whom the chief requirement of clothes is that they should be clean and comfortable.

Although she is very fond of walking, it is evidently strictly subor-dinate in her mind to conversation. The stroll was perpetually slow-ing down to a crawl and stopping short at some point which required emphasis. She has a characteristic gesture to bring out a cardinal point; it commences as though it would be a hearty clap upon the shoulder of the person whom she is addressing, but it checks itself and ends without even a touch.

I had intended to interview her on how she gathers the material for her writings; but walking leads to discursiveness and it would be hard to assemble the whole interview under any more definite topic than that bugbear of authors, "an author's views on art." But the lon-ger Miss Cather talks, the more one is filled with the conviction that life is a fascinating business and one's own experience more fasci-nating than one had ever suspected it of being. Some persons have this gift of infusing their own abundant vitality into the speaker, as Roosevelt is said to have done.

"I don't gather the material for my stories," declared Miss Cather. "All my stories have been written with material that was gathered— no, God save us! not gathered but absorbed—before I was fifteen years old. Other authors tell me it is the same way with them. Sarah Orne Jewett insisted to me that she has used nothing in all her short stories which she did not remember before she was eight years old.

"People will tell you that I come west to get ideas for a new novel, or material for a new novel, as though a novel could be conceived by running around with a pencil and [paper] and jotting down phrases and suggestions. I don't even come west for local color.

"I could not say, however, that I don't come west for Inspiration. I do get freshened up by coming out here. I like to go back to my home town, Red Cloud, and get out among the folk who like me for myself, who don't know and don't care a thing about my books, and who treat me just as they did before I published any of them. It makes me feel just like a kid!" cried Willa Cather, writer of finely polished prose.

"The ideas for all my novels have come from things that happened around Red Cloud when I was a child. I was all over the country then, on foot, on horseback and in our farm wagons. My nose went poking into nearly everything. It happened that my mind was constructed for the particular purpose of absorbing impressions and retaining them. I always intended to write, and there were certain persons I studied. I seldom had much idea of the plot or the other characters, but I used my eyes and my ears."

Miss Cather described in detail the way in which the book *My Ántonia* took form in her mind. This is the most recent of her novels; its scene is laid in Nebraska, and it is evidently a favorite of hers.

"One of the people who interested me most as a child was the Bohemian hired girl of one of our neighbors, who was so good to me. She was one of the truest artists I ever knew in the keenness and sensitiveness of her enjoyment, in her love of people and in her willingness to take pains. I did not realize all this as a child, but Annie fascinated me, and I always had it in mind to write a story about her.

"But from what point of view should I write it up? I might give her a lover and write from his standpoint. However, I thought my Ántonia deserved something better than the *Saturday Evening Post* sort of stuff in her book. Finally I concluded that I would write from the point of a detached observer, because that was what I had always been.

"Then, I noticed that much of what I knew about Annie came from the talks I had with young men. She had a fascination for them, and they used to be with her whenever they could. They had to manage it on the sly, because she was only a hired girl. But they respected and admired her, and she meant a good deal to some of them. So I decided to make my observer a young man.

"There was the material in that book for a lurid melodrama. But I decided that in writing it I would dwell very lightly upon those things that a novelist would ordinarily emphasize and make up my story of the little, every-day happenings and occurrences that form the greatest part of everyone's life and happiness.

"After all, it is the little things that really matter most, the unfinished things, the things that never quite come to birth. Sometimes a man's wedding day is the happiest day in his life; but usually he likes most of all to look back upon some quite simple, quite uneventful day when nothing in particular happened but all the world seemed touched with gold. Sometimes it is a man's wife who sums up to him his ideal of all a woman can be; but how often it is some girl whom he scarcely knows, whose beauty and kindliness have caught at his imagination without cloying it!"

It was many years after the conception of the story that it was written. This story of Nebraska was finally brought to birth in the White Mountains.[1] And Miss Cather's latest novel, which will be published next fall, and which alone of all her prairie stories deals with the Nebraska of the present, was written largely on the Mediterranean coast in southern France, where its author has been during the past spring and summer.

It is often related that Miss Cather draws the greater part of her characters from the life, that they are actual portraits of individual people. This statement she absolutely denies.

"I have never drawn but one portrait of an actual person. That was the mother of the neighbor family, in *My Ántonia*. She was the mother of my childhood chums in Red Cloud. I used her so for this reason: While I was getting under way with the book in the White Mountains, I received the word of her death. One clings to one's friends so—I don't know why it was—but the resolve came over me that I would put her into that book as nearly drawn from the life as I could do it. I had not seen her for years.

"I have always been so glad that I did so, because her daughters were so deeply touched. When the book was published it recalled to them little traits of hers that they had not remembered of themselves— as, for example, that when she was vexed she used to dig her heels into the floor as she walked and go clump! clump! clump! across the floor. They cannot speak of the book without weeping.

1. Willa Cather wrote most of *My Ántonia* while staying in the Shattuck Inn in Jaffrey, near the White Mountains of New Hampshire.

"All my other characters are drawn from life, but they are all composites of three or four persons. I do not quite understand it, but certain persons seem to coalesce naturally when one is working up a story. I believe most authors shrink from actual portrait painting. It seems so cold-blooded, so heartless, so indecent almost, to present an actual person in that intimate fashion, stripping his very soul."

Although Miss Cather's greatest novels all deal with Nebraska, and although it has been her work which has first put Nebraska upon the literary map, this seems to have been more a matter of necessity with her than of choice. For when she was asked to give her reflections about Nebraska as a storehouse of literary or artistic material, her answer was not altogether conciliatory.

"Of course Nebraska is a storehouse of literary material. Everywhere is a storehouse of literary material. If a true artist was born in a pigpen and raised in a sty, he would still find plenty of inspiration for his work. The only need is the eye to see.

"Generally speaking, the older and more established the civilization, the better a subject it is for art. In an old community there has been time for associations to gather and for interesting types to develop. People do not feel that they all must be exactly alike.

"At present in the west there seems to be an idea that we all must be like somebody else, as much as if we had all been cast in the same mold. We wear exactly similar clothes, drive the same make of car, live in the same part of town, in the same style of house. It's deadly! Not long ago one of my dear friends said to me that she was about to move.

"'Oh,' I cried, 'how can you leave this beautiful old house!'

"'Well,' she said, 'I don't really want to go, but all our friends have moved to the other end of town, and we have lived in this house for forty years.'

"What better reason can you want for staying in a house than that you have lived there for forty years?

"New things are always ugly. New clothes are always ugly. A prima donna will never wear a new gown upon the stage. She wears it first around her apartment until it shapes itself to her figure; or if she hasn't time to do that, she hires an understudy to wear it. A house can never be beautiful until it has been lived in for a long time. An old house built and furnished in miserable taste is more beautiful than a new house built and furnished in correct taste. The beauty lies in the associations that cluster around it, the way in which the house has fitted itself to the people.

"This rage for newness and conventionality is one of the things which I deplore in the present-day Nebraska. The second is the prevalence of a superficial culture. These women who run about from one culture club to another studying Italian art out of a textbook and an encyclopedia and believing that they are learning something about it by memorizing a string of facts, are fatal to the spirit of art. The nigger boy who plays by ear on his fiddle airs from *Traviata* without knowing what he is playing, or why he likes it, has more real understanding of Italian art than these esthetic creatures with a head and a larynx, and no organs that they get any use of, who reel you off the life of Leonardo da Vinci.

"Art is a matter of enjoyment through the five senses. Unless you can see the beauty all around you everywhere, and enjoy it, you can never comprehend art. Take the cottonwood, for example, the most beautiful tree on the plains. The people of Paris go crazy about them. They have planted long boulevards with them. They hold one of their fetes when the cotton begins to fly; they call it 'summer snow.' But people of Red Cloud and Hastings chop them down.

"Take our Nebraska wild flowers. There is no place in the world that has more beautiful ones: But they have no common names. In England, in any European country, they would all have beautiful names like eglantine, primrose, and celandine. As a child I gave them all names of my own. I used to gather great armfuls of them and sit and cry over them. They were so lovely, and no one seemed to care for them at all! There is one book that I would rather have produced than all my novels. That is the Clements botany[2] dealing with the wild flowers of the west.

"But why am I taking so many examples from one sense? Esthetic appreciation begins with the enjoyment of the morning bath. It should include all the activities of life. There is real art in cooking a roast just right, so that it is brown and dripping and odorous and 'saignant.'[3]

"The farmer's wife who raises a large family and cooks for them and makes their clothes and keeps house and on the side runs a truck garden and a chicken farm and a canning establishment, and thoroughly enjoys doing it all, and doing it well, contributes more to art than all the culture clubs. Often you find such a woman with all the appreciation of the beautiful bodies of her children, of the order and harmony of her kitchen, of the real creative joy of all her activities, which marks the great artist.

"Most of the women artists I have known—the prima donnas, novelists, poets, sculptors—have been women of this same type. The very best cooks I have ever known have been prima donnas. When I visited them the way to their hearts was the same as to the hearts of the pioneer rancher's wife in my childhood—I must eat a great deal, and enjoy it.

2. Frederic E. Clements, *Rocky Mountain Flowers: An Illustrated Guide for Plant-lovers and Plant-users* (New York: Wilson, 1914).
3. "Rare."

"Many people seem to think that art is a luxury to be imported and tacked on to life. Art springs out of the very stuff that life is made of. Most of our young authors start to write a story and make a few observations from nature to add local color. The results are invariably false and hollow. Art must spring out of the fullness and the richness of life."

This glorification of the old-fashioned housewife came very naturally from Willa Cather, chronicler of women with careers. What does Miss Cather think of the present movement of women into business and the arts?

"It cannot help but be good," was her reply. "It at least keeps the woman interested in something real.

"As for the choice between a woman's home and her career, is there any reason why she cannot have both? In France the business is regarded as a family affair. It is taken for granted that Madame will be the business partner of her husband; his bookkeeper, cashier or whatever she fits best. Yet the French women are famous housekeepers and their children do not suffer for lack of care.

"The situation is similar if the woman's business is art. Her family life will be a help rather than a hinderance to her; and if she has a quarter of the vitality of her prototype on the farm she will be able to fulfill the claims of both."

Miss Cather, however, deplores heartily the drift of the present generation away from the land.

"All the farmer's sons and daughters seem to want to get into the professions where they think they may find a soft place. 'I'm sure not going to work the way the old man did,' seems to be the slogan of today. Soon only the Swedes and Germans will be left to uphold the prosperity of the country."

She contrasts the university of the present with that in the lean days of the nineties, "when," as she says, "the ghosts walked in this country." She came to Lincoln, a child barely in her teens, with her own way to make absolutely. She lived on thirty dollars a month, worked until 1 or 2 o'clock every night, ate no breakfast in the morning by way of saving time and money, never really had enough to eat, and carried full college work. "And many of the girls I was with were much worse off than I." Yet the large majority of the famous alumni of the university date from precisely this period of hard work and little cash.

In making her way into the literary world she never had, she declares, half the hardships that she endured in this battle for an education. Her first book of short stories, to be sure, was a bitter disappointment. Few people bought it, and her Nebraska friends could find no words bad enough for it. "They wanted me to write propaganda for the commercial club," she explained.

"An author is seldom sensitive except about his first volume. Any criticism of that hurts. Not criticism of its style—that only spurs one on to improve it. But the root-and-branch kind of attack is hard to forget. Nearly all very young authors write sad stories and very many of them write their first stories in revolt against everything. Humor, kindliness, tolerance come later."

Some of the stories from this unsuccessful volume, *The Troll Garden*, were reprinted in *Youth and the Bright Medusa*, the recent volume which has had a wide success.

Miss Cather spent Monday, Tuesday, and Wednesday with Mrs. Max Westerman, going from here to Omaha to deliver a lecture before the fine arts club.

OMAHA WORLD-HERALD

Willa Cather Raps Language Law and Antles' Boxing Regulations[†]

"No nation has ever produced great art that has not made a high art of cookery, because art appeals primarily to the senses," declared Miss Willa Sibert Cather, who spoke Saturday afternoon before the Omaha Society of Fine Arts at the Fontenelle on the subject, "Standardization and Art."

Miss Cather told her audience that one of the things which retarded art in America was the indiscriminate Americanization work of overzealous patriots who implant into the foreign minds a distaste for all they have brought of value from their own country.

"The Americanization committee worker who persuades an old Bohemian housewife that it is better for her to feed her family out of tin cans instead of cooking them a steaming goose for dinner is committing a crime against art," declared Miss Cather, who kept her audience laughing and gasping at the daring but simple exposition she gave the meaning of art.

Laws which stifle personal liberty are forever a bar to the real development of art, Miss Cather insists.

"No Nebraska child now growing up will ever have a mastery of a foreign language," said Miss Cather, "because your legislature has made it a crime to teach a foreign language to a child in its formative years—the only period when it can really lay a foundation for a thorough understanding of a foreign tongue.

"Why," she added, "your laws are so rigid in Nebraska that a Nebraska farm boy can't stage a wrestling match in his barn unless

† October 30, 1921.

he gives the state a minute description of himself and pays five dollars. One may receive a permit to travel all over France for $1.50, for a year, but a Nebraska farmboy has to pay five dollars to wrestle in his barn."

LINCOLN EVENING STAR JOURNAL

State Laws Are Cramping†

Miss Willa Cather is expected to come to Lincoln Monday afternoon from Omaha where she has given several addresses. She will be a guest at the home of Mr. and Mrs. Max Westermann for a couple of days, leaving for New York, Wednesday. Miss Cather had much to say of Nebraska's "cramping laws" in her lecture at the Fontenelle hotel.

"Nebraska is particularly blessed with laws calculated to regulate the personal life of her citizens," said Miss Cather according to an Omaha report. "They are not laws that trample you underfoot and crush you but laws that just sort of cramp one. Laws that put the state on a plane between despotism and personal liberty.

"Why, it costs two farm boys five dollars and the filling out of a questionnaire as long as your arm if they want to go out in the barn loft and hold a wrestling match for the neighbors after the day's work is done. It costs them five dollars, and you can get a passport good for a year in France for $1.50."

Miss Cather denounced the language law vehemently, declaring that no child born in Nebraska can hope to gain a fluent speaking knowledge of a foreign language because the languages are barred from the schools under the eighth grade.

"Will it make a boy or a girl any less American to know one or two other languages?" she asked. "According to that sort of argument, your one hundred percent American would be a deaf mute."

"Art can find no place in such an atmosphere as these laws create," declared Miss Cather. "Art must have freedom. Some people seem afraid to say or do anything that is the least bit different from the things everyone else says and does. They think anything irregular is naughty. It was an irregular thing that Father Damien did when he went to the South Sea islands to devote his life to helping the poor lepers. That was just as irregular as any of the reported antics of James A. Stillman—more irregular, indeed, because it was so much rarer! Yet we don't censure Father Damien for his noble work."

Miss Cather added that "cookery is one of the fundamentals of true art," and declared that "any American housewife who teaches

† October 31, 1921.

her good Bohemian or other foreign neighbor that it is as well for her to feed her family off a can of salmon as a roast goose is committing a crime against Americanism and art.

"Too many women are trying to take short cuts to everything," she said. "They take short cuts in their housework, short cuts in their reading—short cuts, short cuts. We have music by machines, we travel by machines—soon we will be having machines to do our thinking. There are no short cuts in art. Art has nothing to do with smartness. Times may change, inventions may alter a world, but birth, love, maternity, and death cannot be changed."

MYRTLE MASON

Nebraska Scored for Its Many Laws
by Willa Cather[†]

Miss Willa Cather, noted authoress, spoke before the Omaha Society of Fine Arts Saturday afternoon at the Fontenelle hotel. The subject doesn't matter.

"I am not a public speaker," said Miss Cather, and perhaps she is not. That, too, does not matter.

What does matter very much is that she is a great woman, and one feels it when she speaks as one knows it when she writes.

She sounded all her "r's" speaking in a rich, incisive voice. She was gowned with the good taste any woman in a small Nebraska town might show, but with no suggestion of Fifth Avenue shops. Utter absence of superficiality was there in Willa Cather. As a true perceiver of the true art, did she impress her audience. Miss Cather calls Red Cloud, Nebraska, where her parents are, home, despite years of residence in New York and abroad.

"Nebraska is not as propitious" a place for an artist as it was twenty years ago, she declared, adding that the same is true of the entire country. Among the things she named as having "helped retard art" are: standardization, indiscriminate Americanism, false conventions of thought and expression, aversion to taking pains, and superficial culture.

Speaking of standardization, she said: "Nebraska is particularly blessed with legislation that restricts personal liberty." The law forbidding instruction in foreign languages below the eighth grade and the anti-wrestling law were cited. "Everybody is afraid of not being standard. There is no snobbishness so cowardly as that which thinks the only way to be correct is to be like everyone else.

† *Omaha Bee*, October 30 and 31, 1921.

"Art is made out of the love of old and intimate things. We always underestimate the common things."

One common thing for which she made a plea was the cottonwood tree, against which she charged there is social prejudice. "They are not smart," she said.

"Art cannot live in an atmosphere of manufactured cheer, much less can it be born," Miss Cather declared in a brief discussion of the "Sunny Jim" and "Pollyanna schools" of "grape nuts" optimism.[1]

"Life is a struggle or a torpor. All art must be serious, and comedy is the most serious of all. Art and religion express the same thing in us,—that hunger for beauty that we, of all animals, have.

"It has been said, 'Genius is the capacity for taking pains,'" she quoted. "Art is taking the pains for the love of it; art is just taking pains. A man must be made for his art; he must work for it, and he must work intelligently. Art thrives best where the personal life is richest, fullest, and warmest, from the kitchen up."

Letters are a "dead form of love," she stated, in referring to the warm details of life we are omitting to save time. "Time for what?" she asked.

"The poorest approach to art yet discovered is by way of the encyclopedia," Miss Cather told her audience.

"The greatest love of art we have is among simple, earnest people who love the natural things."

Amid the "money madness, the movies, and machine-made music" we have today, Miss Cather has a hope born on Armistice day. "The war developed a new look in the faces of people," she concluded, "a look like the pioneers used to have when they were conquering the soil. A new color was over the land. I cannot name it," she said. "But it was the color of glory."

ROSE C. FELD

Restlessness Such as Ours Does Not Make for Beauty[†]

Tea with Willa Sibert Cather is a rank failure. The fault is entirely hers. You get so highly interested in what she had to say and how she says it that you ask for cream when you prefer lemon and let the butter on your hot toast grow cold and smeary. It is vastly more important to you to watch her eyes and lips which betray her when she seems to

1. Sunny Jim was a happy character invented for advertising purposes by Force Cereal in 1902. Polyanna—the name taken from the eponymous heroine of Eleanor H. Porter's best-selling novel *Polyanna* (1913)—signified a person with consistent, perhaps simplistic, optimism.

† *New York Times Book Review*, December 21, 1924, p. 11, cols. 1–5.

be giving voice to a serious concept, but is really poking fun at the world—or at your own foolish question. For Willa Sibert Cather has a rare good sense, homespun sense, if you will—and that is rare enough—which she drives home with a well-wrought mallet of humor.

It started with the question of books and the overwhelming quantities which the American public of today is buying. What exactly was the explanation of that? Did it mean that we were becoming a more cultured people, a more artistic people? Miss Cather was suffering from neuritis that day. It was difficult to understand, therefore, whether the twinge that crossed her face was caused by the pain we gave her or that of her temporary illness.

"Don't confuse reading with culture or art," she said, when her face cleared. There was laughter in her blue eyes. "Not in this country, at any rate. So many books are sold today because of the economic condition of this country, not the cultural. We have a great prosperous middle class, in cities, in suburbs, in small towns, on farms, to whom the expediture of $2 for a book imposes no suffering. What's more, they have to read it. They want a book which will fill up commuting boredom every morning and evening; they want a book to read mornings after breakfast when the maid takes care of the apartment housework; they want a book to keep in the automobile while they're waiting for tardy friends or relatives; they want fillers-in, in a word, something to take off the edge of boredom and empty leisure. Publishers, who are, after all, business men, recognize the demand and pour forth their supply. It's good sense; it's good psychology. It's the same thing that is responsible for the success of the cinema. It is, as a matter of fact, the cinema public for whom this reading material is published. But it has no more to do with culture than with anarchy or philosophy. You might with equal reason ask whether we are becoming a more cultured people because so many more of us are buying chiffoniers and bureaus and mirrors and toilet sets. Forty or fifty years ago these things were not to be found in the average home. Forty or fifty years ago we couldn't afford them, and today we can. As a result, every home has an increased modicum of comfort and luxury. But, carrying the thought a step further, every home has not increased in beauty.

"Not so long ago I was speaking to William Dean Howells[1] about this subject of book reading and book publication. He said something which was of interest to me and which may be of interest to you. Forty years ago, he maintained, we were in the midst of a great literary period. Then, only good books were published, only cultivated people read. The others didn't read at all, or if they did it was the newspapers, the almanac, and the Bible on Sundays. This public doesn't exist today any more than the cinema public existed then.

1. Howells (1837–1920) was a prominent American writer, critic, and man of letters.

Fine books were written for fine people. Fine books are still written for fine people. Sometimes the others read them, too, and if they can stand it, it doesn't hurt them."

Her lips twitched in a smile she tried to suppress. She shook her head at a wayward thought.

"That discrimination is not a snobbish one," she went on. "Don't think that. By the fine reader I don't necessarily mean the man or woman with a cultivated background, an academic, or a wealthy background. I mean the person with quickness and richness of mentality, fineness of spirituality. You found it often in a carpenter or a blacksmith who went to his few books for recreation and inspiration. The son of a long line of college presidents may be nothing but a dolt and idiot in spite of the fact that he knows how to enter a room properly or to take off a lady's wraps. It's the shape of the head that's of importance; it's the something that's in it that can bring an ardor and an honesty to a masterpiece and make it over until it becomes a personal possession.

"I am not making generalities, I hope. I hate generalities. There's no sense to them. They're superficial; they're easy. People in talking of art and art appreciation make the generality, for instance, that all singers come out of the mud. Mud has nothing to do with it, just as being a carpenter has nothing to do with the accident of a good mind. Art requires a vast amount of character. It's a whole lot more than talent. It demonstrates itself in relationships the artist thinks important. I am not speaking of morality. It means great, good sense, as well as the gift of expression. The singer who is born in the mud doesn't arrive unless he's very good; there are so many obstacles which he must surmount. It requires a very little effort for a person with a mediocre voice and a deep, lined purse to get a hearing; it requires unusual ability for the poor man. When the latter arrives, it is because he has proved his genius. Mud had nothing to do with it; it only made his progress more difficult.

"Because of this vast amount of writing and reading, there are many among us who make the mistake of thinking we are an artistic people. Talking about it won't make us that. We can build excellent bridges; we can put up beautiful office buildings, factories; in time, it may be, we shall be known for the architecture which our peculiar industrial progress has fostered here, but literary art, painting, sculpture, no. We haven't yet acquired the good sense of discrimination possessed by the French, for instance. They have a great purity of tradition; they all but murder originality, and yet they worship it. The taste of the nation is represented by the Academy;[2] it is

---

2. Founded in 1635, L'Académie française, or French Academy, is the official authority on the French language.

a corrective rod which the young artist ever dreads. He revolts against it, but he cannot free himself from it. He cannot pull the wool over the eyes of the academy by saying his is a new movement, an original movement, a breaking away from the old. His work is judged on its merits, and if it isn't good, he gets spanked. Here in America, on the other hand, every little glimmer of color calls itself art; every youth that misuses a brush calls himself an artist, and an adoring group of admirers flatter and gush over him. It's rather pathetic.

"Read the life of Manet and Monet;[3] both great artists, great masters. The French people had to be sure of their genius before it would acclaim them. Death almost took them before acknowledgment of their power was given them. It is good sense, deliberation, and an eagerness for the beautiful that keeps up the fine front of French art. That is true of her literature as well as of her painting.

"France is sensitive; we are not. It may be that our youth has something to do with it, and yet I don't know whether that is it. It's our prosperity, our judging success in terms of dollars. Life not only gives us wages for our toil but a bonus besides. It makes for nice, easy family life but not for art. The French people, on the other hand, have had no bonus. Their minds have been formed by rubbing up cruelly with the inescapable realities of life; they've played a close game, wresting their wages from a miserly master. Mrs. Wharton[4] expressed it very well in a recent article when she said that the Frenchman elected to live at home and use his wits to make his condition happy. He don't want an easier land. He chose France, above all, as the home of his family and his children after them. There you are.

"The Frenchman doesn't talk nonsense about art, about self-expression; he is too greatly occupied with building the things that make his home. His house, his garden, his vineyards, these are the things that fill his mind. He creates something beautiful, something lasting. And what happens? When a French painter wants to paint a picture he makes a copy of a garden, a home, a village. The art in them inspires his brush. And twenty, thirty, forty years later you'll come to see the original of that picture, and you'll find it, changed only by the mellowness of time.

"Restlessness such as ours, success such as ours, striving such as ours, do not make for beauty. Other things must come first: good cookery; cottages that are homes, not playthings; gardens; repose. These are first-rate things, and out of first-rate stuff is art made. It is possible that machinery has finished us as far as this is concerned. Nobody stays at home any more; nobody makes anything beautiful

---

3. Édouard Manet (1832–1883) and Claude Monet (1840–1926), prominent French impressionist painters.
4. A contemporary of Willa Cather, the novelist and short story writer Edith Wharton (1862–1937) maintained a residence in Paris for several years.

any more. Quick transportation is the death of art. We can't keep still because it is so easy to move about.

"Yet it isn't always a question of one country being artistic and another not. The world goes through periods or waves of art. Between these periods come great resting places. We may be resting right now. Older countries have their wealth of former years to fall back upon. We haven't. But, like older countries, we have a few individuals who have caught the flame of former years and are carrying the torch into the next period. Whistler was one of these; Whitman was another."[5]

Miss Cather poured some tea into a cup and diluted it with the cream we asked for but didn't want. We let it stand on the arm of the chair and proceeded with a question that her words had awakened.

"If we have no tradition of years behind us, the people who come to live here have. Are they contributing anything to the artistic expression of the country?"

Again that twinge crossed her face. This time it was plain that the question had started it.

"Contribute? What shall they contribute? They are not peddlers with something to sell; they are not gypsies. They have come here to live in the sense that they lived in the Old World, and if they were let alone their lives might turn into the beautiful ways of their homeland. But they are not let alone. Social workers, missionaries—call them what you will—go after them, hound them pursue them and devote their days and nights toward the great task of turning them into stupid replicas of smug American citizens. This passion for Americanizing everything and everybody is a deadly disease with us. We do it the way we build houses. Speed, uniformity, dispatch, nothing else matters.

"It wasn't so years ago. When I was a child, all our neighbors were foreigners. Nobody paid any attention to them outside of the attention they wanted. We let them alone. Work was assigned them, and they made good houseworkers and splendid craftsmen. They furnished their houses as they had in the countries from which they came. Beauty was there and charm. Nobody investigated them; nobody regarded them as laboratory specimens. Everybody had a sort of protective air toward them, but nobody interfered with them. A 'foreigner' was a person foreign to our manners or custom of living, not possible prey for reform. Nobody ever cheated a foreigner. A man lost everything in the esteem of the community when he was discovered in a crime of false barter. It was very much better that way. I hate this poking into personal affairs by social workers, and I

5. American painter James Whistler (1834–1903) and American poet Walt Whitman (1819–1892).

know the people hate it, too. Yet settlement work is a mark of progress, our progress. That's that. I know there's much to be said for it, but nevertheless, I hate it."

We spoke about *My Ántonia*, Miss Cather's story about the immigrant family of Czechs.

"Is *My Ántonia* a good book because it is the story of the soil?" we asked. She shook her head.

"No, no, decidedly no. There is no formula; there is no reason. It was a story of people I knew. I expressed a mood, the core of which was like a folksong, a thing Grieg[6] could have written. That it was powerfully tied to the soil had nothing to do with it. Ántonia was tied to the soil. But I might have written the tale of a Czech baker in Chicago, and it would have been the same. It was nice to have her in the country; it was more simple to handle, but Chicago could have told the same story. It would have been smearier, joltier, noisier, less sugar and more sand, but still a story that had as its purpose the desire to express the quality of these people. No, the country has nothing to do with it; the city has nothing to do with it; nothing contributes consciously. The thing worth while is always unplanned. Any art that is a result of preconcerted plans is a dead baby."

Miss Cather is now writing a new novel which will come out next Autumn.[7] "There will be no theories, no panaceas, no generalizations. It will be a story about people in a prosperous provincial city in the Middle West. Nothing new or strange, you see."

6. Norwegian composer and pianist Edvard Grieg (1843–1907).
7. *The Professor's House* (1925).

Letters

TO FAMILY AND FRIENDS[†]

To Roscoe Cather, July 8, 1916[1]

* * *

I have a new idea for a novel which I'd like to talk over with you—not very new, none of my ideas ever are. I don't seem to have acquired a single new idea since Sandy Point.[2] The trouble about this story is that the central figure must be a man, and that is where all women writers fall down. I get a great many bouquets about my men, but if they are good it is because I'm careful to have a woman for the central figure and to commit myself only through her. I give as much of the men as she sees and has to do with—and I can do that much with absolute authority. But I hate to try more than that. And yet, in this new-old idea, the chief figure must be a boy and a man. I'd like to talk it over with you. You might help me a good deal. I wish you'd keep a diary on your Yellowstone trip of long ago—it's a little that kind of story.

* * *

To Douglass, July 10, 1916[3]

* * * I've had a very hard winter and have got no work done except two short stories—one very poor. Judge McClung's death and Isabelle's marriage have made a tremendous difference in my life.[4] The loss of a home like that leaves one pretty lonely and miserable. I can

---

† All letters from Cather reprinted with the permission of the Willa Cather Literary Trust.
1. Roscoe and Meta Cather Collection, Archives and Special Collections, U of Nebraska, Lincoln. Roscoe was one of Willa's younger brothers.
2. The new novel is most likely *My Ántonia*, although she was also working on a short story, "The Blue Mesa," at this time. Sandy Point was a sandbar in a river near Cather's Red Cloud home where she and her siblings and friends told stories and created dramas.
3. Philip L. and Helen Cather Southwick Collection, Archives and Special Collections, U of Nebraska, Lincoln. Douglass was one of Willa's younger brothers.
4. Isabelle McClung, Cather's beloved friend, married violinist Jan Hambourg in 1916. Her father, Judge McClung, died the same year, and the house—where Isabelle had created a writing sanctuary for Cather—was sold.

fight it out, but I've not as much heart for anything as I had a year ago. . . . I am quiet a meek proposition now, I can tell you. I think I've had my belting, and it has taken the fizz out of me all right—and I'll tell you this, it's positively ship-wreck for work. I doubt whether I'll ever write anything worthwhile again. To write well you have to be all wrapped up in your game and think it completely worthwhile. I only hope I'm not so spiritless I won't be able to make a living. I had two stories turned down this winter because they had no "pep" in them. The editor said they hadn't and I knew they hadn't.

To Elsie Cather, May 4, 1917 [5]

My Dear Bobbie;
   * * * I am fairly stuck on the novel I wrote you about, and will either have to give it up or try it over again a new way.[6] Two Houghton Mifflin men were here last night and I had to make the sad admission to them that I couldn't get a new book out this fall. They are disappointed, and so am I. There is a great deal that's good in the new story, but I have not gone at it right, somehow, and I'm going to quit it for awhile and do some short stories to build up my bank account.
   * * * [The] magazine business is cramped and made harder by the war. High cost of ink and paper take all the profits and shut down advertising.

*   *   *

Now I must stop for this time, dear girl. I'll try to do better hereafter, if you forgive me.

With heaps of love to you
Willie

To Roscoe Cather, July 14, 1918
(written on Shattuck Inn stationery)[7]

My Dear Brother:
   * * * I am here in this quiet hotel in the woods and reading the proofs of my new book, and hope to finish things by the 6th of August.[8] It's a queer sort of book. It's at least not like either of the others. Did you know that both the others are studied in a good many colleges now, for "style"?

*   *   *

5. Roscoe and Meta Cather Collection, Archives and Special Collections, U of Nebraska, Lincoln. Elsie was one of Willa's younger sisters.
6. The reference is to *My Ántonia*.
7. Charles Cather Collection, Archives and Special Collections, U of Nebraska, Lincoln.
8. Cather was reading proofs of *My Ántonia* while staying at the Shattuck Inn in Jaffrey, New Hampshire.

To Roscoe Cather, November 28, 1918
[Thanksgiving Day][9]

My Dear Roscoe:

Your nice letter demand a speedy answer. I am so glad that you and father and mother liked this book. Most of the critics, too, seem to find this the best book I have done. I got quite a wonderful letter about it from France today, and it will be published in France very soon. Personally, I like the book before this one better, because there is more warmth and struggle in it. All the critics find "Ántonia" more artistic. A man in the Nation writes that "it exists in an atmosphere of its own—an atmosphere of pure beauty."[1] Nonsense, it's the atmosphere of my grandmother's kitchen, and nothing else. Booth Tarkington[2] writes that it is as "simple as a country prayer meeting or a Greek temple—and as beautiful." There [are] lots of these people who can't write anything true themselves who yet recognize it when they see it. And whatever is really true is true for all people. As long as one says "will people stand this, or that?" one gets nowhere. You either have to be utterly common place or else do the thing people don't want, because it has not yet been invented. No really new and original thing is wanted: people have to learn to like new things.

To Roscoe Cather, December 8, 1918[3]

My Dear Roscoe;

It has been a long time since I began this letter to you. The town is full of newly returned soldiers now; I have been seeing as much of them as I can. They like to talk to almost anyone who will talk to them about France.

I am sending you a copy of one of the best reviews, from the Sunday "Sun," a full page with a large photograph of me.[4] I had some copies made because in these paperless days one can't get extra copies of Sunday papers. This man surely had a good time with the book. It amazes me how many people feel that way. I thought nearly everybody in this country had to have a story. I never did like stories much, and the older I grow the less they interest me. I see and feel only the carpenter work in them. In this book the pitch of life as it was lived isn't raised half a tone, and yet, you see, how many people do like it. Professor Goeghegan writes me that it is certainly the best novel that has come out of America. "We know," he says, "that

9. Charles Cather Collection, Archives and Special Collections, U of Nebraska, Lincoln.
1. *The Nation*, November 2, 1918.
2. American novelist and dramatist (1869–1946). A prolific writer, he is best known for *The Magnificent Ambersons* (1918), which won the Pulitzer Prize in 1919.
3. Charles Cather Collection, Archives and Special Collections, U of Nebraska, Lincoln.
4. *The Sun* (NY), October 6, 1918.

perfect art returns to nature, [but] only a very great artist can so return, or can make the nakedness of nature beautiful in art." Yet Father likes it "as well as any book he ever read." I feel well content to have touched two extremes. If only I can do as well with the next!

*   *   *

Now goodbye, my boy, forgive this scrappy letter and write me when you have time. I am always glad to hear about everything that goes on in your pretty little house. * * * I am wrestling with the Blue Mesa story a little; but the commonplace way to do it is so utterly manufactured, and the only way worth while is so alarmingly difficult. Wish me luck!

Lovingly
Willie

To Roscoe Cather, January 5, 1919[5]

Dear Roscoe;

The other day I sent you an important notice of Ántonia by a critic who has since died of influenza.[6] He was the ablest of our critics, and I had rather dreaded his review. He gave me some sharp knocks on the Song of the Lark, though he liked the first part of it very much. I like his comparison of the book with White's.[7] Long before I began to write anything worth while, I hated White and Grahame Phillips[8] for the way they wrote about the West. I knew that there was a common way of presenting common life, which is worthless, and a finer way of presenting it which would be much more true. Of course Ántonia's story could be told in exactly the same jocular, familiar, grapenutsy way that Mr. White thinks is so American. He thinks he is presenting things as they are, but what he really presents is his own essentially vulgar personality. I don't deny that Mr. White sells a thousand to my hundred, but nobody can really reach both audiences, so I don't bother about that, so long as I have some of the savings of my old McClure salary left to live on.

Weeks ago I got such a heart-warming letter from a former president of the Missouri Pacific, Edwin Winter, who as a young man helped to carry the U.P.[9] across Nebraska, and who built the bridge over Dale Creek canyon—the first bridge, which was of timber![1] He

5. Roscoe and Meta Cather Collection, Archives and Special Collections, U of Nebraska, Lincoln.
6. Randolph Bourne.
7. William Allen White. See n. 1, p. 338.
8. American novelist and journalist (1867–1911).
9. Union Pacific Railroad.
1. The longest bridge on the Union Pacific Railroad.

asked if he could come to see me, and on Friday he came. Such a man! all that one's proudest of in one's country. He picked the book up in his club and sat right down and wrote me the most beautiful of letters. I'd rather have the admiration of one man like that than sell a thousand books. He said that reading the story was a stirring adventure to him, that he felt he must get at me at once somehow, and he wondered if I were a Swede, because, he said, "the book looked to me too much like literature to be American." I feel that I've made a new friend who is going to teach me a lot and give me a great deal of pleasure. He has the most brilliant mind I've come up with in a long while, and such a vast and varied experience. I think I must copy his letter for you, sometime.

Please send a copy of the Dial and the notice about poor Bourne back to me when you've done with it. Tell Meta I am still eating that delicious jam on my toast at tea every afternoon when I have tea at home. I have finished the <u>scuppernong</u> jam,[2] and am now on the pineapple. I wish I could have been with you for the Holidays.

To Carrie Miner Sherwood, February 11, 1919[3]

Dear Carrie:

I am sending you today a bunch of the most important notices of our book. You need not return them to me, but you must let Irene see them. The one in the "Dial" is the one I like best, because it was written by the most intelligent man. He died a few months after this article was printed, of influenza, and his death is a great loss to American letters. I enclose a notice about him along with the review. I have had more than a hundred letters about the book, from all sorts of people, and answering them has really been a serious drain on my time. Mr. Edwin W. Winter, for many years president of the Missouri Pacific Railroad, after writing me two letters, came to see me to tell me how much he liked the book, and now he often drops in on Friday and seems like an old friend. From first to last this book has been a great pleasure and satisfaction to me, and nothing pleases me quite so much as that you and father like it so much.

Affectionately,
Willie

2. A kind of grape jam.
3. Willa Sibert Cather Collection, Nebraska State Historical Society, Lincoln. Sherwood, who lived in Red Cloud, was Willa Cather's closest childhood friend.

To Elsie Cather, November 11, 1919[4]

My Dear Sister:

I meant long ago to answer your nice letter about "Ántonia." You must ask mother to let you see one wonderful review of it I sent home, and then send it back to me for I have no other copy. People seem to love the book in a more personal way than they did any of the others. It's funny, but the less you "make up" in a work the harder it is to write. It takes so much more experience and skill and maturity to interpret life in it than it does to spin yarns. And the longer I live the more I want to write "nothing but the truth." One grows to have a kind of scorn for the other thing This is so purely a literary treatment in "Ántonia," and yet so many un-literary people seem not to like but to love it. I went into a bookstore to buy blotting paper the other night, and I actually saw two women buy the book. * * * "Send the others, I'll take this" and went out and got into her motor with the book under her arm, unwrapped. I longed to ask her name, but I was afraid my manner might betray me.

To Mary Virginia Boak Cather and Elsie Cather, December 6, 1919[5]

My Dearest Mother;

I know I've not written for a long time, but I did not mean to be neglectful. I thought Daddy would tell you about me and about how torn up my apartment was. It has taken so much work to get it even a little in order and the way I want it. You know I have no maid this year, and as Edith is away from eight-thirty in the morning until six-thirty at night, most of the housekeeping falls on me. Father will tell you how we are boarding out for our dinners, and you know I don't like that. Josephine[6] now gets $80 a month; any good maid would now cost us $60 a month, and we would have to send the washing out! With eggs at $1.00 a dozen, and butter $1.04 a pound, we simply can't afford to entertain any more, and what a servant would eat would be a very considerable item. Mrs. Winn, that noble widow, of whom father will tell you, comes three half-days a week and keeps us clean, but there are so many, many other things to do, and I have been far from well.

* * *

In addition to painting the bathroom and doing the house work and trying to write a novel, I have been becoming rather "famous" lately,

4. Charles Cather Collection, Archives and Special Collections, U of Nebraska, Lincoln.
5. Andrew Jewell and Janis Stout, eds., *The Selected Letters of Willa Cather* (New York: Knopf, 2013), pp. 281–85.
6. Willa Cather's French cook.

and that is an added care. In other years, when I was living like a lady, with an impressive French maid, I could have been famous quite conveniently, but then I had only to receive a few high-brows. Now the man in the street seems to have "got onto" me, and it's very inconvenient. The enclosed, on the editorial page of the Tribune, is only one of a dozen articles that have come out in all the New York papers in the last two weeks. People write furious letters to the Sun to ask why their editor has not stated that I am the "greatest living American author"; the Sun editor replies, give him time, maybe he will say that. I have had nothing to do with this little whirlwind of publicity, God knows! My publishers have had nothing to do with it.[7] They are the most astonished people you ever saw. One of them came racing down from Boston to see me, and he kept holding his head and saying, "but why should this book, this one catch on? Anybody would have said it could never be a popular book." You see they advertised it hardly at all, and I didn't urge them. I thought it was a book for the very few. And now they are quite stunned.

I'm like Roscoe when he said, if only his twins had waited till next year to come. This is such an awkward time to be famous; the stage is not set for it. Reporters come running to the house all the time and finding me doing housework. They demand new photographs, and I have no new clothes and no time to get any. Yesterday, when I was washing dishes at the sink with one of Mother's long gingham aprons tied round my neck—I've never had time to shorten it— I heard a knock at the front door and didn't stir. Then a knock at the kitchen door; such a very dapper young man asked if Miss Cather the Author lived here that I hesitated. He said, "Tell her I'm from the N.Y. Sun, and want to see her on very important business." I told him that Miss Cather had gone to Atlantic City for a rest! I simply couldn't live up to the part, do you see? He left saying there was to be a big article about her on Sunday.

Now, at least, Elsie, you don't have to wash dishes and be famous at the same time. Now, in other years, Josephine and I with our haughty French, thrown lightly back and forth when a visitor was brought in, could have made a great impression on reporters. We made a great impression last winter on the editor of the Chicago News, who has been my passionate press agent ever since.

By the way, Elsie, you must write the Chicago News for translations of the Swedish review. They are fine. The new Swedish edition of "O Pioneers" is one of the handsomest books I have ever seen. I have ordered several from Stockholm, and when they come I will send Mother one. The Swedish looks so funny to me, Mother; like the

---

7. Cather frequently complained that Houghton Mifflin did not adequately advertise her books.

Petersons' newspapers I used to bring home from Mr. Cowley's in a flour sack, on horseback. You remember? A very fine French translation is being made of Ántonia, some of the chapters have been sent over to me for suggestions, and it is simply beautiful French, clear as Latin. Miss Herbek was here for dinner last week—I got the dinner—to see about getting the rights for translation into Bohemian. You see the tide seems to be coming in for me pretty strong. It won't make me any richer, but it makes me a great deal happier, dear Mother.

We have not been able to have our dear Fridays at home yet, but will begin next week, and on our cards we have written that it is only December and January that we will be at home. That is because I want to go West later,—I mean home, of course. The reason I could not go home for Christmas was that my Publisher came up to Jaffrey to see me and begged me to get as far along with the novel as I could before I broke off, for he is going to England in March, and if he can take about one-half or two thirds of the story in its final shape, he hopes to be able to make good terms for it there. You see Hugh Walpole,[8] author of "The Dark Forest", is lecturing in this country now, and he talks about my books everywhere he goes, even at dinner parties, "raves" about them the newspaper men tell me, and he says the younger men in England are getting very much stirred up about me. So my publishers think this is the time to try for good contracts in England. I have got about two-thirds of my book written through for the first time; next week I begin to write it through from the first again. Some of it will have to be done over four or five, or even six times, but there is good life and movement through it. I hope I will be at home when it comes out, for it was almost the greatest pleasure I ever had to be at home when Ántonia came out, and you and Father were reading it, both of you at once, and I could see how much you really did enjoy it. Yes, I think that was about the most satisfactory experience I ever had. It made me happy the way I used to be when I was a little girl and felt that you were both pleased with me.

* * *

Dear Mother, I send you such heaps of love. I think daughters understand and love their mothers so much more as they grow older themselves. I find myself loving to do things with you now, just as I did when I was a little girl, and I used to ride up to Aunt Rhuie's on the horse behind you and feel so proud that I had such a handsome young mother. Oh, I don't forget those things! They are all there, deep down in my mind, and the older I grow, the more they come to light. Of course, there was a time when I was "All for books" as Mrs. Grice

---

8. A British novelist who published *The Dark Forest* in 1916.

says, and didn't think much about people. I suppose that had to be; but, thank God, I got over it!

* * *

To Carrie Miner Sherwood, January 27, 1934[9]

My dear Carrie:

Mr. Cyril Clemens, son of Mark Twain,[1] is President of the International Mark Twain Society, to which men of letters in all countries belong. The Society recently held a contest to decide what is the most memorable and representative American novel in the last thirty-five years, the writer of this novel to be awarded a silver medal by the Mark Twain Society. The majority votes were for Ántonia, and the medal is waiting for me in St. Louis whenever I have time to go and get it.

Out of a number of reports on Ántonia which were sent to the Society, there is one which I think you might like to have (chiefly because it is so well written) to keep in your copy of Ántonia. Now, don't show it to the town cats or put it in the paper, or do anything to make [blacked out] and [blacked out] want to scratch my eyes out any worse than they do. Of course, I want you to show it to Mary, and you might show it to Helen Mac. some time, because I know neither of them wants to murder me. I want you to have it because it particularly takes notice of the fact that, though there have been many imitations of Ántonia and some of them good, I really was the one who first broke the ground.

Oh yes, there is another reason why I don't want you to show this article about; a lot of our fellow townsmen would go chasing out to look poor Annie[2] over and would agree as to what a liar I am. You never can get it through peoples heads that a story is made out of an emotion or an excitement, and is not made out of the legs and arms and faces of one's friends or acquaintances. Two Friends, for instance, was not really made out of your father [James L. Miner] and Mr. [William Newman] Richardson; it was made out of an effect they produced on a little girl who used to hang about them. The story, as I told you, is a picture; but it is not the picture of two men, but of a memory. Many things about both men are left out of this sketch because they made no impression on me as a child; other things are exaggerated because they seemed just like that to me then.

As for Ántonia, she is really just a figure upon which other things hang. She is the embodiment of all my feeling about those early

9. Jewell and Stout, pp. 492–93.
1. Actually a distant cousin.
2. Annie (or Anna) Pavelka, whom Willa Cather knew growing up in Red Cloud, was the model for Ántonia Shimerda.

emigrants in the prairie country. The first thing I heard of when I
got to Nebraska at the age of eight was old Mr. Sadalaak's suicide,[3]
which had happened some years before. It made a great impression
on me. People never stopped telling the details. I suppose from that
time I was destined to write Ántonia if I ever wrote anything at all.

Now I don't often write, even to my dearest friends, about my own
work, but you just tuck this away where you can read it and when
people puzzle you, or come at you and say that I idealize everything
and exaggerate everything, you can turn to this letter and comfort
yourself. The one and sole reason that my "exaggerations" get across,
get across a long way (Ántonia has now been translated into eight
languages), is that these things were not exaggerations to me. I felt
just like that about all those early people. If I had exaggerated my
real feeling or stretched it one inch, the whole book would have fallen
as flat as a pancake, and would have been a little ridiculous. There
is just one thing you cannot fake or counterfeit in this world, my
dear Carrie, and that is real feeling, feeling in people who try to govern their hearts with their heads.

I did not start out to write you a long lecture, but some day I might
get bumped off by an automobile, and then you'd be glad to have a
statement which is just as true as I have the power to make it.

My heart to you always,
Willie

P.S. I had a wonderful afternoon with Irene[4] when she was here, and
I am so happy that she and Mr. Weisz are going to escape from this
troubled part of the world. Isn't he a good sport?

FROM ANNA PAVELKA[†]

October 31, 1934[1]

Dear Friend Willa

I received both checks for 25 dollars each although I didn't cash
them right away I was keeping them to buy feed for us and the
stock. . . . Well Willa I have the feathers already for you and I was
waiting for the ticking I could send for could get nothing so good
here   I will keep them nice for you you sure deserve more than I can
do for you   Well Im thanking you ever so much and if ever you want

---

3. Francis Sadilek was the father of Annie Pavelka and the model for Mr. Shimerda in *My
   Ántonia.*
4. Irene Miner Weisz was the sister of Carrie Miner Sherwood and a childhood friend of
   Willa Cather.
† All letters from Pavelka are reprinted with the permission of the Willa Cather Literary
   Trust.
1. Kurth Collection, Nebraska State Historical Society, Lincoln.

any favor be sure and mention it with best love from Anna and her family   I didn't mention these checks to nobody because I couldn't help any of them for Im in need of money myself very bad

February 15, 1935[2]

Dear friend Willa
    * * * I don't know the wheat will turn out this year it has been rather dry now since Christmas time, we haven't had any snow since fall and a very little rain this week and today its snowing and the wind is blowing   the snow melts right away because its not very cold   if it snows lots it will drift they say the wheat looks better little farther east as they had more rain in the fall then we did here
    Well Willa we have moved in our new kitchen after New Years   its nicer and lighter I have everything handier. Clement built me a nice cabinet, its built so it can be moved and I have a nice work shelf on it. . . . I have the stove right close and the table to so I don't   have to walk far back and forth.
    Dear Willa I was hoping that you would come out there this winter as I didn't here from you so long but you are like a magnet when I least expect anything then you generally appear in some wonderfful way   I either read something nice about you or hear people phrasing your books—and to think you are one of my best friends. . . .
I remain as ever
Anna Pavelka

April 5, 1936[3]

Dear friend Willa
    Well what a surprise   Emil came home Friday with a mail and said he had a surprise for me and sure enough he handed me a letter from you and when I opened it there was a check for five dollars and Im writing and thanking you for the same   I sure will use it for most important things.
    And I will tell you what I used my Chrismus money from you   we got a gasoline power washing machine with a good wringer that we needed very bad and I will have lots of use out of it   I have been washing on the washboard since last summer when my old wash machine wore out . . . The children didn't like to see me washing on the washboard they think Iv worked hard enough   we always have big washings and ironing   Im working all the time fromm early morn till late at nite but still it seems we cant get nowhere   if we could only raise some crops and again it seems that we wont have a

---

2. Charles Cather Collection, Archives and Special Collections, U of Nebraska, Lincoln.
3. Kurth Collection, Nebraska State Historical Society, Lincoln.

good crop   the wind is blowing cold nearly every day, and we don't
get no rain only some blizzards   we also had very little snow and
January and Febuary was 2 awful cold months   it was freezing so
hard that even things froze in peoples cellars   even some of our
potatoes froze in our cellar but I fed them to the checken so they
didn't go to waste

* * *

Well Willa Im thanking you once more for everything you have
done for us an I hope you will have a very joyous Easter and that
God will send his blessing upon you and I hope you will write and
tell us how you are. . . . I remain as ever

Anna Pavelka

February 24, 1955[4]

Dear Frantiska
* * * My father wanted to bring us to this country so we would
have it better here as he used to hear how good it was hear as he
had letters from here how wonderfull it was out here that there
were beautiful houses lots of trees and so on   but how disappointed
he was when he saw them pretty houses dugout in the banks of the
deep draws   you couldn't see them until you came rite to the door
just steel chimney in the roof   there were no roads just tracks from
wagon wheels people cut across land to get anywhere at all. . . .
    our first meal there was corn meal mush and molasses that was
what the people lived on and wild fowls and rabbits   well my father
bought [a] farm there was nothing on it except sod shack it had just
a board bed and 4 lid stove no well just 5 aikers of land . . . we had
to sleep on the dirt floor with hay for mattress   that was hard on
father in the old country in the evenings he would sit and make lin-
ens and any kind of weaving material always and was always joking
and happy . . . he never swore or used dirty words like other men
nor he never drank or play cards he was a clean man in every way . . .
    then one afternoon it was 15 of Feb he told mother he was going to
hunt rabbits he brought a shot gun from the old country . . . when he
didn't return by five o'clock mothers older brother and the man we
lived with went to look for him   it was dark when they found him
half sitting in that old house . . . shot in the head and already cold
nearly frozen   the sheriff said it was a suicide there was no cemetery
or nothing   one of the near neighbors had to make a wooden box and
they had to make his grave in the corner of our farm but my brother
him moved and him and my mother and brother are sleeping in Red

---

4. Willa Sibert Cather Collection, Nebraska State Historical Society, Lincoln. Frantiska
    was a friend of Pavelka's.

Cloud cemetery and they have a tombstone. I hope they are resting sweetly   most all is true that you read in the. Book though most of the names are changed, our name was Sadilek, Lena Lingard was Mary . . . I will close for this time I hope this will help you in anyway

Your friend
Mrs Pavelka

April 3[5]

Dear friend Willa

Went to the mailbox this morning and was surprised to have a letter there from you and when I got home and opened it found money order for 25 dollars for which I thank you very much   it will be a fine Easter for me   Yes Willa I did cash the check from you at Christmas time as soon as I received it . . . I know you always want me to cash it as soon as I get it, as you have to pay just so much for having it in the bank. . . . I was thinking if you were writing another book, there was a lady in California wrote to Roxine and asked her if she ever read the book my Antonia written by Willa Cather, that she was just reading it and that it's the best book she ever read, so that was a swell phrase wasn't [it], they were reading that book in all schools around here 2 years ago they all seemed to like it. . . . I wish you a very happy Easter and many thanks for the fine gift, and I hope you will come to Nebraska soon   we would all like to see you

With best love and luck
Anna Pavelka

TO AND FROM
CATHER'S PUBLISHER[†]

From Ferris Greenslet,[1] *January 2, 1917*

Dear Miss Cather,

The fifty further pages of "My Antonia" reached me several days ago, but it is only this morning that it has become possible for me to write to you.

I think the story is going very soundly. Your method, I take it, is not to aim so much at the continuous increase of attention that the romantic writers aim at as to proceed steadily and convincingly on the level

---

5. No year known. Kurth Collection, Nebraska State Historical Society, Lincoln.
† All letters to and from the publisher are from MS Am 1925 (341) in the Houghton Mifflin Collection, reprinted by permission of Houghton Library, Harvard U, Cambridge, MA. Although Cather insisted on the accented *Á* for the title and throughout *My Ántonia*, in her letters to Greenslet she most often used an unaccented *A*.
1. Willa Cather's editor and director of Houghton Mifflin Company, Greenslet (1875–1959) was also a writer of biographies and an autobiography.

of life with an occasional "big punch" increasing in force as the story develops. This, I think you are doing very successfully. The rattle-snake fight is one of the snakiest snake stories I ever remember to have read. Antonia's character is developing steadily and vividly. I don't get anywhere within these first ninety pages any very strong dramatic thrill, but I suppose that is scheduled to arrive before very long.

In short, as far as I can judge the story now, it promises, I should think, to please both critics and public more than any of your other books to date. When do we get some more of them?

Cather to Roger L. Scaife,[2] March 13, 1917

Dear Mr. Scaife;
Since you can give me good lee-way, I think I ought to be able to get the story done in time for fall publication. . . . Unless I can find just the right person to do some head and tailpieces, I had rather not have illustrations. As for the cover design, I rather wish you could reproduce the "Song of the Lark" cover in a darker blue, a strong navy blue, with, of course, quite a different jacket. I wish you could have a bright yellow jacket, with very heavy black type, if that paper would not be too expensive. * * *

Cather to Scaife, April 7, 1917

Dear Mr. Scaife;
* * * With regard to the decoration of my book, I think Benda[3] might be able to do it. His half-tone illustrations are rather too mannered, but he used to do good head and tailpieces,[4] and he knows the material. I will try to have a talk with him and let you know about it later. The samples of binding I will return soon, naming a first and second choice. Within the next four weeks I shall know whether this story is going to come together in time for fall publication or not. I think it will.

* * *

Cather to Greenslet, October 18, 1917

Dear Mr. Greenslet:

* * *

Do let me know when you come to New York. I want very much to talk to you about the physical make-up of the next book. I want to

2. Production manager at Houghton Mifflin Company.
3. Władysław T. Benda (1873–1948), well-known Polish-born graphic designer and artist. He became a naturalized American citizen in 1911.
4. Illustrations.

try something a trifle new in color of the binding and jacket. I am
going to ask Benda to dinner and talk to him about head and tail-
pieces. If he doesn't get the idea, no one else would, and I'd rather
go un-illustrated.

The truth is, I've tried to make my own head and tail-pieces in
the text itself, and unless the artist can echo this, I'd rather not.

Cather to Greenslet, November 24, 1917

Dear Mr. Greenslet;

Mr. Scaife put me in an awkward position when he was here, and
as I have not been able to get any work done since, and the first of
December approaches, I think I had better write and tell you my
troubles.

You will remember that illustration was not my idea at all. When
Mr. Scaife was here last spring, he urged it very strongly. I told him
then I didn't want a mere conventional frontispiece; unless I could
get a set of decorations done that would have some character and
interpret and embellish the text, I didn't want anything. He distinctly
said that I could go ahead and see what I could do.

I selected Benda as a man who knew both Bohemia and the west;
and because he has imagination. He has already given me a great
deal of time, making preliminary sketches and trying to get exactly
what I want. Our plan was for twelve line drawings, which would
print on text paper, to be scattered through the book where there
were blank half-pages at the ends of chapters. Three of the completed
drawings are already in; they are admirable and give the tone of the
text better than I could have hoped for.

For the price Mr. Scaife named when he was here, I can't let
Benda do more than these three. * * * These three were meant to
be part of a developing scheme of decoration. One can't ask a man
to do twelve difficult compositions in an exacting medium, for
$150.

* * *

Of course, it would be much easier for Benda to do one conventional wash drawing, which is his usual medium, than to work out
sympathetic compositions in pen and ink which require a careful
study of the text and some work from models. I am clearly the one
who is making the trouble.

I know, now, that I should have got a definite figure of expenditure from your office before I proceeded at all. But I know Benda
would do the work more cheaply than anyone else for me—for one
thing I knew he would like the story—and a figure like $150 did not
occur to me. * * *

The misunderstanding, apparently, has come on the meaning of the word "illustration." But I told Mr. Scaife last spring that if I had any pictures at all, I wanted real illustrations, not a conventional frontispiece. He also said that illustrations "enriched" a book, which I think, since he had only a frontispiece in mind, was misleading. * * *

* * *

It's a misunderstanding, and I am willing to admit that I am to blame for it. I absolutely misunderstood Mr. Scaife's language and his meaning.

If you can see your wait to write Benda a polite letter, offering him $200 and telling him you know it is very little for his work, I will try to get him to do eight, or perhaps even ten of the decorations as originally planned.—These decorations, you understand, are pictures, like the old woodcuts in effect, and evolved out of close study of the text and western photographs which I have been at great pains to get.—That, it seems to me, would only be evidence of good will on the part of the publishers. It wouldn't by any means pay for the work Benda began at my solicitation, but it would somewhat cover my retreat.

If this is impossible, then we will have to pay Benda for three drawings and not use them. I don't see anything else to do, unless Mr. Scaife wishes to withdraw entirely from the responsibility of this book, for which I am now, as always, perfectly ready. In any case, please do not go ahead with the dummy until you have told me what you can do. I don't think it was quite fair play of Mr. Scaife to repudiate, without examination, a scheme of decoration which I had worked out with so much pains, or to destroy the zeal of the artist. He said something to me over the telephone about "little pictures" not being worth as much as big ones! * * *

Scaife to Cather, November 26, 1917

Dear Miss Cather,

I am greatly concerned at the misunderstanding which seems to have arisen over Benda's illustrations.

Mr. Greenslet has let me see your letter, and I have never had any other thought than of cooperating with you, and I thought you understood this.

When we talked last year about Benda's little head and tail pieces, it seemed to me a delightful suggestion and one which would provide the book with a charm and appearance in harmony with your own work.

After talking with you last week, I called up Mr. Benda and he was good enough to come in and show me his drawings, and we had quite a chat on all sorts of topics. In the course of the conversation, I explained to him that $150 was an outside price for this work, and the misunderstanding may have arisen from the fact that I explained to him that while these drawings were admirably suited for illustrations, they were not as adaptable for advertising and publicity purposes, and that, as a general rule, a full page drawing in color which could be used on the jacket was of more commercial value to the publisher because of this added factor. I never, however, suggested for a moment his changing over from this series of pen and inks to a colored picture.

Now as to the price. * * * A perfectly reasonable rate for book work is $15.00 per drawing. This would give you ten drawings on this basis. I know from what you said over the telephone that this price seems quite inadequate, but I think if you could peek into the cost books of publishing houses, you would find that these figures are very reasonable. * * * With the increasing cost of paper, printing, ink, cloths for binding, and labor, the cost of making books has risen to an alarming extent. It is for these reasons that I am not tempted, as I should otherwise be, to fall into line with your suggestion and increase our figure to Mr. Benda. * * *

Cather to Scaife, December 1, 1917

My Dear Mr. Scaife;

The series of pen-and-ink drawings I had in mind, and Mr. Benda's fitness to do them, was suggested by a similar set of pen drawings he made to illustrate Jacob Riis' book "The Old Town."[5]

* * * Mr. Benda telephoned me after your conversation with him. He was very polite and considerate, as he always is, but he said that Doubleday had paid him $150 and $200 for one or two wash drawings to illustrate novels, and that had he known how little he was to receive for these pen pictures he would not have felt that he could undertake them. He also said he could not do the drawings we had blocked out, as they would require a great deal of work and some of them would have to be done from models. On the other hand, he had already spent a good deal of time in studying the manuscript, collecting material, and making preliminary sketches, and he thought perhaps we might be able to substitute a set of drawings more conventional and less exciting.

These drawings, however, would have to be done at odd moments of his time, and he could not promise to deliver them before the first of March, as he could not afford to put more remunerative work aside for them. On this point he was very firm.

---

5. Danish-born muckraking journalist and photographer Jacob Riis (1849–1914) is best known for *How the Other Half Lives: Studies among the Tenements of New York* (1890). *The Old Town* (1909) chronicles his boyhood in the town of Ribe, Denmark.

* * *

I am cutting the story a good deal in revision, and I can now say positively that it will run very little, if at all, longer than "O Pioneers!" I hope you can use the same type as in that book, and give the text pages the same look. I have broken it up into chapters as much as I can, and liberal page-margins and spaces at chapter-ends will make the decorations look better. * * *

* * *

Scaife to Cather, December 3, 1917

Dear Miss Cather,

Perhaps Mr. Benda's courtesy concealed from me any sense of disappointment he may have felt when I made an offer of the price which I named for the little head pieces for your book. I hope you will not feel that we are niggardly in this matter nor do I want you to form the idea that we are not enthusiastic over the book. I had pictured an attractive little book with illustrations that would appeal to the dilettante, rather than to the average novel reader, and the price we had settled upon was governed by the figure which we had spent on other volumes, where the illustrations are not advertising assets.

Under separate cover, you will receive a copy of "Susanna and Sue" by Kate Douglas Wiggin,[6] with a number of pen and ink drawings by Wyeth,[7] a well known artist, whose work is of distinct value. These are about the size of the drawings which were to go in your book, and as I recollect our arrangement, the price would be about the same. * * * Of course, the difference of a few dollars, one way or another, is of small moment. I beg you, therefore, to do what you can with Mr. Benda to bring about results which will be satisfactory to you, for we are anxious to have the book as you wish it. * * *

Cather to Greenslet, December 26, 1917

Dear Mr. Greenslet

This morning I sent you fifty pages of ms by registered mail. I will be ever so grateful if you will read the story through now, as far as you have copy, and let me know how it strikes you. Any personal impressions gratefully received. * * *

6. Author of several children's books, Wiggin (1856–1923) is best known for *Rebecca of Sunnybrook Farm* (1903).
7. N. C. Wyeth (1882–1945), prominent artist and illustrator (and father of painter Andrew Wyeth).

Greenslet to Cather, January 30, 1918

Dear Miss Cather,

I enclose herewith contracts in duplicate for the publication of "My Antonia", drawn up upon the same basis as those for "The Song of the Lark."

Peculiarly difficult and expensive conditions of manufacture and distribution are forcing us, like most other publishers, to propose lower rates of royalty to many popular authors than they have been receiving in the past. We have not, however, felt justified in making this suggestion in your case and for "My Antonia". We believe in the book, and we are going to do our best to see that it proves a sound property for both author and publisher. * * *

Cather to Greenslet, February 28, 1918

Dear Mr. Greenslet:

Did you get some copy and two drawings from me this week? I sent them by express on Saturday.

I detest to have to tell you that I've been ill for two weeks; and my good French girl has been ill for a month now. Unexpected difficulties in housekeeping and getting a temporary knock-out in health have put me terribly behind in my work. I've just been going over the notes of the last third of the work. They are better than I remembered—I think they are much the best part of it. They seem rather too good to be hurried over and spoiled by haste.

Now what about it? Tell me honestly what you think. I feel sure that I can get a considerable wad of copy to you by March 15th, and I feel <u>almost</u> sure that I can get it all to you by April 1st. But it will be a crowd; and isn't that too late for spring publication anyhow?

Would it be better now to let the book go over until the autumn? I hate to suggest it, but I think that would be better than crowding it along. It's the kind of story that has to be pretty carefully written, after all. The proofs might not take much work, but there are some things that only type decides for one. I've been fairly industrious, and I've pushed the thing along as fast as I could. But writing is a slow business, and that's all there is to it. There's no sufficient reason why this story should take two winters; I feel as humble as possible about it, but there is no getting around the fact that it has.

Please let me know if you think it would be better to wait until fall now, or if you still want me to try to get through by the end of March. I know I couldn't finish before that. Even if you agree with me and decide to defer publication, I will get the copy along to you as fast as I can and even at a relaxed pace I would probably finish early in April. Let me know your wisest thoughts on this. I'm fairly perplexed myself.

Greenslet to Cather, February 28, 1918

Dear Miss Cather,

I read the new batch of chapters last night with much pleasure. It is quite remarkable how you manage continually to tighten the interest without dramatic entanglement. * * * When do we get the last of the manuscript?

Greenslet to Cather, March 1, 1918

Dear Miss Cather,

I think we would better give up the idea of spring publication definitely. You can then go ahead and finish the book at your leisure, completely to your mind, and we will publish it when we get it. * * * I am not sure, anyway, but that conditions for fiction will be better in the summer and fall than they are now. At the moment, we are having a pretty tough time of it.

In short, go as you please, and good luck to you!

Cather to Greenslet, March 7, 1918

Dear Mr. Greenslet;

* * *

Will you please ask your printing house to save enough of the cream-tinted, rough-finished paper used in the dummy to print the full edition in the summer?

I will send you three Benda drawings tomorrow; the two full figure ones, of Antonia and Lena Lingard—the latter fairly busting out of her clothes—I think extremely good. I wouldn't ask for better. That will make eight drawings I have sent you. I have still two more which do not quite suit me. Unless I can get Benda to re-draw them for me someday, I won't use them. But will you please ask Mr. Scaife to send Benda his check as soon as you receive the three drawings I am sending to you by express? His work is all done. If there is any business office formality which prevents your paying an artist in the middle of the month or the dark of the moon, won't you please send him the check and charge it to me. * * *

* * *

Greenslet to Cather, June 24, 1918

Dear Miss Cather,
  The manuscript of the balance of "My Antonia" came the middle
of last week. I did not get around to read it until Saturday afternoon, when I perused it on the train en route to New Hampshire for
a day's fishing, and found it all most enormously interesting.
  The introduction is very skillfully slanted, and the final upshot of
the book, I think, very impressive and memorable. * * *

Greenslet to Cather, September 23, 1918

Dear Miss Cather,
  I have your letter of September 19 and note your request in
regard to complimentary copies of "My Antonia."
  I don't know whether I have ever written you just how fine I think
that book is. I ran through it yesterday in its manufactured form,
and was more than ever impressed both by its human appeal and
its cleanly drawn structure. Unless I am much mistaken, it will hit
the critics in the eye, and take its place as one of the outstanding
American novels. * * *

Greenslet to Cather, October 22, 1918

Dear Miss Cather,
  * * * [Our publicity department] say they are waiting until they
get one [review] with really quotable nuggets in it, before turning
loose the publicity they have planned. You may be very sure that we
are thoroughly alive to the importance of the book, and shall not
hide its light under a bushel.
  Within the past five minutes our sales manager has just been in
to report the conversation that he had with a certain Miss Mahoney
of the Women's Industrial Union of Boston,[8] who is very active in
organizing children's departments of libraries. She is very enthusiastic of "My Antonia," both as an outstanding piece of American literature and as a book for children.
  I hadn't seen it before myself in just that light but I think the point
is well taken.

---

8. Founded in Boston in 1877, the Women's Education and Industrial Union provided education, training, and support for women and children, particularly immigrants and children of immigrants.

Cather to Scaife, December 9, 1918

Dear Mr. Scaife:

The dummy will reach you Tuesday morning, also two Benda drawings, with the size marked on the margins. Mr. Greenslet and I agreed when he was here that it would be better to give each of these drawings a full page, with plenty of margin about it, than to use them as tail-pieces. They are illustrations, in reality, not tail-pieces, but should be printed small on a liberal page, to give the effect of old woodcuts, and without captions.

The drawings will be more effective if they all occur on right-hand pages. That, I think, is rather important.

They should be printed in the same black ink as the text.

Please use the accent mark over the initial A in Antonia in the running title. Even if many of the accents break, the majority will remain and give character to the title.

Cather to Greenslet, date unknown, 1918

Dear Mr. Greenslet:

My French girl[9] has been ill for weeks, and I have been so busy carrying Antonia with one hand and serving the kitchen-gods with the other that I have delayed sending you the contract. I return it herewith, however, and thank you for not trimming my royalties.

Cather to Greenslet, date unknown, 1918

Dear Mr. Greenslet:

I am afraid the Introduction will be almost the last thing I write. I shall have to wait to see how far the story tells itself before I know how much to put in the Introduction. But I will do it as soon as I can.

Greenslet to Cather, January 14, 1919

Dear Miss Cather:

What do you say if I enter you for the Pulitzer prize for 1918—submitting "My Antonia" for the running. The terms of the competition are stated in these words: "For the American novel published during the year which shall best present the wholesome atmosphere of American life, and the highest standard of American manners and manhood, One Thousand dollars ($1,000)."

In "My Antonia", of course one has to construe manners and manhood somewhat broadly. The book, nevertheless, seems to fall

9. Willa Cather's cook, Josephine Bourda.

distinctly within the spirit of the competition. The "melting-pot" aspect of it, is, of course, timely. What do you say?

Cather to Greenslet, January 15, 1919

Dear Mr. Greenslet:

I would be very much pleased if you saw fit to enter "Antonia" for the Pulitzer prize. I suppose its chances would depend on how the judges define manners, as you say, and also what they consider "American life." But if they turned the work down, we would be no worse off for the attempt, would we?

Cather to Greenslet, February 5, 1920

Dear Mr. Greenslet:

* * * Miss Roseboro',[1] former reader on McClure's and Collier's, has been in several times to groan to me about a copy of "Antonia" that she has been trying to get for Mr. W. C. Brownell, who is ill. She has been going to Brentano's[2] for over two weeks for it now, and they say they ordered some when Heywood Broun's comments were running in the Tribune, but they cannot get the book. Have Brentano's still an order in, or are they merely talking? It is absolutely true that there was not a copy of the book in Chicago for two weeks before Christmas or immediately after Christmas. It is hard enough, in a way, to get purchasers for a book; and when you get the purchasers, then you can't get the manufactured article. So it goes!

Greenslet to Cather, February 12, 1920

Dear Miss Cather:

* * * A memorandum about Brentano's and Chicago has come to my attention. Yesterday, Mr. Bruce, who has charge of our New York sales, was present at our stockholders meeting and stated that the book was in stock at all of the principal stores in New York. I have checked this up and find that orders received from Brentano's for your books have been filled by us. We did have several orders some little time ago, which were delayed, but this was all attended to later.

Would you mind following this up? And will you let me hear from you? Because Mr. Bruce has given us to understand that, not only were your titles in stock at Brentano's, but they were represented on the front counters; and if, for any reason they have been placed elsewhere, I should like to know it. If, of course, the books have been sold, as I hope they have, they should have re-orders. * * *

---

1. Willa Cather began her friendship with journalist Viola Roseboro' when the two were working together at *McClure's Magazine*. Roseboro', initially a manuscript reader, went on to become fiction editor.
2. One of a chain of bookstores.

Scaife to Cather, February 19, 1920

Dear Miss Cather:

* * * On receiving word from you of the difficulties in securing books in Chicago we wired our representative to see what on earth the trouble was. * * * Here is Mr. Geer's reply: "Your wire about the Cather books hurt my feelings. It is true that her books do not sell as well as they deserve but it is also true that I am not at fault as far as the shortages are concerned, at least in Chicago. For example, of the last McClurg order for 75 copies of "My Antonia" in October they have on hand now 48 copies. . . ."

I hope that this letter will not in any way discourage you from writing us when you have information such as this. On the other hand, I hope also that these complaints, which I think you would find quite common throughout all the publishing houses, will not bear too heavily upon Houghton Mifflin Company.

Cather to Scaife, February 21, 1920

Dear Mr. Scaife:

Your letter about the supply of "Antonia" in Chicago is a distinct shock. The three people who wrote to me before Christmas were not "investigators", but bone fide buyers who wanted the book, were unable to get it, and two of them sent me checks, begging me to send a copy if I had one. I am convinced that they had made an honest effort to get the book at home before they took that trouble. It must be, as you say, that they applied to a green salesman, or to several green salesmen. Could the fact that the buyers called my name rightly, and that clerks in book stores usually call it "Kay-thur" have anything to do with it. It is all nonsense that an unusual name in authorship is an advantage in authorship. One had much better be named Jones. Salesmen in New York and Chicago always correct me when I pronounce my own name. Mr. Sell published a paragraph telling people that the name rhymed with 'rather', but if it convinced others, it did not convince the bookstores.

*   *   *

Scaife to Cather, February 26, 1920

Dear Miss Cather:

* * * It seems that when you called the Brentano people were under the impression that the books were ordered but that they were in a shipment from Boston which was held up on account of the storm and had not arrived. As a matter of fact copies of each one of the titles were in the store at the time you were there and were discovered a few minutes after your left. * * * I am told that if you go to Brentanos you will find "My Antonia" and "The Song of the Lark" somewhere on the front shelf of the fiction section. * * * Frankly, I cannot quite understand the situation, for we have talked Cather to the bookstores all over the country, and not only that but we have had a good reaction. The men in charge of the bookstores appreciate your work and want it to succeed as we do. * * *

Greenslet to Cather, January 6, 1926

Dear Miss Cather:

A little before the Christmas holidays, during the course of a correspondence with—as the lawyers say—my learned brother, Knopf, on another matter, he asked me whether the next time I came to New York I could not get together with him to discuss the matter which you had raised last autumn. I replied that I supposed that the matter referred to was the question of the transfer to him of ALEXANDER'S BRIDGE, O PIONEERS, THE SONG OF THE LARK, and MY ANTONIA. I said further that we * * * were unanimous in feeling very decidedly that we valued the presence of your books on our list very highly, that they were valuable publishing property, and that any price at which we could afford to sell them would be more than he could afford to pay. * * *

It seems to us, however, that in our common interest, steps might well be taken to increase still further the present sales of your books on our list. It has been suggested that you might now feel disposed to make some change in the Introduction and opening machinery of MY ANTONIA (I believe we discussed this several years ago) with a view to its reissue as a definite new edition. * * * With its established position as one of the classic American novels and, in the opinion of a large number of your readers, perhaps the best of your books, I think that a very great increase—both in the immediate and in the continuing sales—would result from such a step. * * *

Cather to Greenslet, February 16, 1926

My dear Mr. Greenslet:

Mr. Knopf told me of your decision with regard to the question of transferring my books to him. If the company is not willing to sell the books to him, then I think it ought to be willing to make some effort to sell them as if they were live property—and not merely 'creditable' books on the list, by Charles Egbert Craddock[3] or Celia Thaxter,[4] or somebody long deceased.

3. The pen name for American novelist and short-story writer Mary Noailles Murfree (1850–1922.)
4. American poet and woman of letters (1835–1894).

Now, I come to the question of "Antonia." Of course, I do not think that in pushing "Antonia" or "O Pioneers", it is quite fair for you to disparage a book I published last year or the book I will publish next year. As I told you, I do not like the attitude that "A Lost Lady" was in any sense a repetition of "Antonia", though Mrs. Forrester was one of the women who employed the "hired girls" to whom Antonia belonged. (Confidentially, let me tell you that the real Antonia actually did work for the real Mrs. Forrester.) * * *

Now, as to the preface. The preface is not very good; I had a kind of complex about it. I wrote and rewrote it, and it was the only thing about the story that was laborious. But I still think that a preface is necessary, even if it is not good in itself. Let me take a trial at shortening the preface. The later part of the book, I am sure, would be vague if the reader did not know something about the rather unsuccessful personal life of the narrator.

I am terribly busy just now and shrink from breaking in at all on the story I have in hand. When do you want to bring out this new edition and when would you need the copy of the revised preface?

Regarding the Benda illustrations; you would, of course, retain those. It is one of the few cases where I think the pictures really help the story, and I would not be willing to leave them out.

Greenslet to Cather, February 17, 1926

Dear Miss Cather:

I am delighted to learn from your letter of February 15th that you are agreeable to the reissue of MY ANTONIA with a new prologue. To sell your books as if they were "live property" is precisely what we want to do. * * * We have, of course, retained the Benda illustrations, and shall be careful not to exalt ANTONIA by disparaging your other books.

Greenslet to Cather, April 9, 1926

Dear Miss Cather:

* * * I have just been re-reading the book (with very fresh and deep pleasure) and still feel that the story would be stronger without any introduction whatever. The atmosphere of the narrator's later life is implicit throughout the last section and is, I think, more impressive to the reader's imagination that way. The introduction, with its narration of the social activities of Mrs. Burden and its sophisticated background, is like a prelude to a symphony that doesn't pre-lude. The reader has to change his base entirely when he starts on the actual story, and doesn't get into the spirit of the thing for a good many pages. Personally, therefore, I should vote for the complete omission of the introduction, and think the classic outline of the story would be clearer and brighter without it. If, however, this seems to

you impossible, I wonder whether it wouldn't be feasible to omit all of the paragraph that begins on page x with the words "When Jim" and of almost all of the paragraph on the following page which begins "As for him." As for the first paragraph mentioned, I think your own statement "I do not like his wife" sufficiently does for that lady, while Jim's characters and temperament—his persistent romanticism—are sufficiently exhibited in what follows. Three strokes of the blue-pencil—at least it seems to me—do all that is really necessary. Won't you think it over? * * *

Cather to Greenslet, January 29, 1937[5]

My dear Ferris Greenslet:

* * *

* * * I have thought your proposition over carefully and I am still, as I was when I first read your letter, strongly against any plan to make an illustrated edition of <u>Antonia</u> for next year, or for any other year.

Certainly, I like Grant Wood's[6] work, but his whole view of the West, and his experience of it, is very different from my own. * * *

Why can't we let <u>Antonia</u> alone? She has gone her own way quietly and with some dignity, and neither you nor I have any reason to complain of her behavior. She wasn't played up in the first place, and surely a coming-out party, after twenty years, would be a little funny. I think it would be all wrong to dress her up and push her. We have saved her from text books, from dismemberment, from omnibuses, and now let us save her from colored illustrations. I like her just as she is.

I would, of course, be pleased if I could feel sure that the Benda illustrations will never be ripped out again, and I would be greatly gratified if one of the excellent proof-readers at the Riverside Press[7] would run through the book and mark the broken letters and illegible words which should be replaced. In case you should ever decide to reset the book, I beg you to use just the same type and the same slightly tinted paper now used.

* * *

Cather to Greenslet, date unknown, 1946

Dear Mr. Greenslet,

This morning I received from a Miss Hahn, with no sort of letter or apology, a barbarously reconstructed version of "Antonia." You

5. Possibly December rather than January.
6. Best known for his painting *American Gothic*, Grant Wood (1891–1942) was a prominent artist associated with the landscapes and people of the Midwest.
7. The printing press associated with Houghton Mifflin.

spoke to me of using a portion of the book, some twenty pages; you did not mention such a horror as a skeletonized version of the whole novel. The lady has tried to make it a story of action; now it was never meant to be a story of action.

I had decided, after your talk with me, to allow your educational department to use the first thirty pages of the book, minus the introduction. If it would be an accommodation to you, personally, I would still be willing to allow that, on condition that there shall be no cuts at all in the text, and that this lady shall not write the introduction.

Can't we just drop the whole matter, anyway? You tell me they want something of 'mine.' Then your educators go and make this text as much like Zane Grey[8] as possible. The reconstruction by Miss Hahn has neither Zane Grey's merits nor mine.

Really, my dear F.G., you've never treated "Antonia" very gallantly. You are always trying to do her in and make her cheap. (That's exaggeration, of course, but I'm really very much annoyed.) And you know how you've suggested cheap editions, film possibilities, etc. Antonia has done well enough by her publishers <u>as she is</u>, not in the cut rate drugstores or re-written by Miss Hahn. She made her way by being what she is, not by being the compromise her publishers have several times tried to make her. Even a cut in price would be a compromise in the case of that particular book, I think. And as to a cut in <u>text</u> reducing the whole book to some few thousand words: Those horrible boil-downs of "Notre Dame de Paris"[9] and "Adam Bede"[1] which are handed out to children are poison, as you well know. . . .

You see I don't want to go into a book that is made up of reconstructions of this kind, where the text is boiled down. It doesn't give youngsters even a chance to come in contact with the writing personality of a single one of the writers presented to them in this packing-house form. I think it's the lowest trick ever put over on young people.

* * *

Enraged though I am, I'm still your very good friend, and I send you good New Year wishes from my heart. Only let me hear no more of Miss Hahn and her stupid, brutal trade.

---

8. Popular and prolific author (1872–1939) whose adventure novels created a romantic portrayal of the American West.
9. Also known as *The Hunchback of Notre Dame*, the novel was published by Victor Hugo in 1831.
1. First novel by George Eliot, published in 1859.

FROM READERS[†]

September 17 [1919]

My Dear Miss Cather:

With great pleasure I have been reading your book, "My Antonia," the story of Bohemians in Nebraska. I do not think I have ever read any book pertaining to my people with so much interest. You certainly have given to the reading world a wonderful word picture of their life.

Miss Cather would there be any possibility of making a translation in the Bohemian—I feel it should be given to the people, that they might know that their actions are being closely observed by others. I think it would tend for better citizenship among them and then also I feel that the older people, those who can no read any but the Bohemian Language are being withheld a genuine treat.

I would like to have the pleasure of making this translation if you would be willing to have your work translated. Hoping to hear from you at your convenience, regarding the above request, I remain,

Yours truly,
Francis E. Kroulik

October 18 [1919]

Dear Miss Cather:

May one who has spent the best years of his life west of the Mississippi * * * and loved the frontier of which only undying memories are left, speak a world of appreciation of your elemental, wholesome, loveable <u>Antonia</u>. A splendid type of the rare commonplace, so seldom discovered, less often understood, and still less often given the breath of life in her native atmosphere with such deftness and understanding of value. The whole book is a joy and brings back the aroma of newly turned sod, burning grass and corn in the field. And just now I've reread the last two pages of the first chapter of "Cuzak's Boys" and if I could write at all, which I cannot, I should like to have written the lines beginning with "I lay awake for a long while."

Very truly,
Edwin Whirter

[†] All letters from readers are from the Charles Cather Collection, Archives and Special Collections, University of Nebraska, Lincoln. Reprinted with the permission of the Willa Cather Literary Trust. Many reviews of *My Ántonia* make use of an unaccented A, perhaps because American reviewers, unfamiliar with the spelling of immigrants' names, failed to notice the importance of the accent.

November 18, 1919

Dear Miss Cather:

Mrs. White and I have just finished reading "My Antonia"—a wonderful book. How strong it is, how splendidly repressed, how beautifully tragic it is in its quiet understatement. You are a wonder. I take off my hat to you. I want to use your book for a Christmas present. I want to send it out to the friends whose names I have written below. Will you kindly ask Mr. Greenslet of Houghton Mifflin Company to furnish you with copies and send the bill to me, and then will you autograph these copies as coming from me with your Christmas greetings. * * *

Truly and sincerely yours,
W. A. White[1]

[March 6, 1923]

For the second time I read "My Antonia" and I'm so in love with the book, its sincerity and realness that I feel you ought to know. * * * Now I feel that you know me, for really, Miss Cather, Antonia's thoughts, emotions, both good and bad—they were mine. I just lived her life while I read it. And now I finish it for second time, I keep thinking about her, knowing her. She is so real to me, because I am she.

You, indeed, are a great master, for you paint pictures in words of my very soul without even knowing me—or seeing me. I love you for your understand. Some day I meet you, maybe, and I tell you story of a little Russian girl—a little girl who worships you because you understand that girl, she is,

Your faithful
Nadya Olyanova

February 20, 1924

Dear Willa Cather,

I suppose you get thousands of these but I can't keep [from] writing, a treat I've denied myself for three years. When I first read <u>My Antonia</u>, I had never heard of you. It was up at our camp in Minnesota, and the book so impressed me that I lay awake long into the night listening to the lapping water and the mourning loon far down the beach, and thought about what you must be like—to write so. <u>My Antonia</u> is so beautifully written—as an artist should paint. (You <u>must</u> paint!)

Of course, since, I've heard about you and always felt a sort of personal triumph in the fact I recognized your genius all by myself. You must be a comfortable genius, though. Your feeling of beauty is

---

1. William Allen White. See n. 1, p. 338.

tremendously lovely. I cannot write as I feel, but anyway thank you for much.

I am twenty two, teaching my first year, in North Dakota (no-man's land, but the sunsets are God's.) * * * [I want to] one day see you— but for the present am teacher of Latin verbs to a set of wriggling little Norwegians.

Thank you for your beauty and life and light.

Mary Jean Forbes

May 12, 1924

Dear Miss Cather,

* * * [In] the last few days I have read <u>My</u> <u>Antonia</u> and <u>O</u> <u>Pioneers!</u>, and I am sitting down this evening to tell you about it, in my laboratory. I am an Iowa farm boy of a long line of pioneers and you recall to me so much of what I have seen, and known and felt, in the days of struggle on the soil, and in the University. You have done something fine and real, and have made real books about our country. * * * You speak of the real America, as you know it, and it is a great joy to me to read what you have written.

* * * I am no critic, but I feel I know what is real, when I find it, and I know whereof you speak and know you speak the truth. Please accept my heartfelt thanks in the spirit in which they are given by one who loves his own land, and loves those who portray it truly. May you long continue such work.

Yours very sincerely,
Carl D. La Rue

July 4, 1925

My dear Miss Cather:

Such an aura of delicious enchantment has surrounded me upon laying down My Antonia that I've not even thought seriously of curbing the impulse to tell you how much I liked it and what an enormous admiration I have for all your work.

Yours sincerely,
Wilton Ratcliffe-Graff

October 6, 1926

My dear Miss Cather:

I have decided to write you, for it has been in the back of my head ever since I read My Antonia. I was born in Crete, Nebraska, in 1875, and my parents moved to Omaha the following spring, where I have lived since. * * * [My father] established, in 1890, a Bohemian farm paper the Hospodar (The Husbandman) and my brother and I are continuing the business since my father's death in 1910. I explain thus fully to show you that all my recollections of youth are bound up in the very things you describe in My Antonia. * * * reading your book brings back the old times as nothing else has done that has been written in English.

When I heard that you had written a book about Bohemians, my first thought was that, in this day of much writing, you took for a theme something you thought would be novel, but when I read the book I found you had written about them not only with sympathy, but what is rarer still, with complete understanding. It is seldom that an American can have that understanding and insight. * * * when I came to where Antonia was deceived by Larry, it seemed an almost uncanny touch, for I too remember a number of girls like that. I think those girls felt complimented by the attentions of an American and that, with their great truthfulness and natural emotion, completed the work. * * *

It may interest you to know that I have just finished, for our State Historical Society, a history of Bohemians in Nebraska. In this I have taken the liberty to say, in describing Webster County, that the Bohemian pioneers there have gained fame in Nebraska literature through your book, and in the chapter on cemeteries * * * I have quoted your description of Shimerda's grave.

Yours very truly,
Rose Rosicky[2]

May 8 [1928]

My dear Miss Cather—

Perhaps you do not remember my writing you from college a year or so ago telling you how I loved, with all my heart, your "Antonia." Now, after having spent the year in Czechoslovakia, I realize even more how wonderfully you have created her, how you have grasped the full spirit of the people—of the Slavic race. * * * I, too, am a Nebraska girl—my grandparents are some of the first Czech pioneers to that state. * * * I was encouraged in college with the acceptance of my short stories * * * I wrote of Nebraska—and Nebraska! I wrote about it because I love it and understand it, because I have learned to see more of its immense beauty through the eyes of people like you, because, I may, perhaps, still have some of that Slavic blood in my veins. * * *

Most sincerely and devotedly yours,
Olga Folda

August 12, 1941

Dear Miss Cather:

I have just finished reading My Antonia. It is one of the most enjoyable experiences I have ever had. * * * I was a boy of ten about

---

2. Author of *History of Czechs of Nebraska* (1929).

the time Jimmy Burden and Antonia were crossing Iowa and a part of Nebraska to make their homes near Black Hawk. * * * Your vivid description of the prairie country around Black Hawk would nicely fit the country around our old homestead home. I still recall the reddish grass always billowing under the winds, the wagon roads and the badgers.

Yours very sincerely,
Charles Chester

[date unknown]

My dear Miss Cather—
   For two years I have been tempted to write to you. I can resist no longer. You must receive so many letters from people you do not know that one more can mean very little to you; but to me every one of your books has been such a joy that merely the thought of there existing in the world such a person as you must be to have written them, is a real inspiration. I think My Antonia is one of the most beautiful things I have ever read. * * *

Yours most sincerely,
Hester Walrath Hunter

Americanization and Immigration

WILLA CATHER

Peter[†]

[handwritten annotation: Peter like man / playing violin, / even he is not / good with that. / He doesn't want to sell / it until he dies.]

"No, Antone, I have told thee many times, no, thou shalt not sell it until I am gone."

"But I need money; what good is that old fiddle to thee? The very crows laugh at thee when thou art trying to play. Thy hand trembles so thou canst scarce hold the bow. Thou shalt go with me to the Blue to cut wood tomorrow. See to it thou art up early."

"What, on the Sabbath, Antone, when it is so cold? I get so very cold, my son, let us not go tomorrow."

"Yes, tomorrow, thou lazy old man. Do not I cut wood upon the Sabbath? Care I how cold it is? Wood thou shalt cut, and haul it too, and as for the fiddle, I tell thee I will sell it yet." Antone pulled his ragged cap down over his low heavy brow, and went out. The old man drew his stool up nearer the fire, and sat stroking his violin with trembling fingers and muttering, "Not while I live, not while I live."

Five years ago they had come here, Peter Sadelack, and his wife, and oldest son Antone, and countless smaller Sadelacks, here to the dreariest part of southwestern Nebraska, and had taken up a homestead. Antone was the acknowledged master of the premises, and people said he was a likely youth, and would do well. That he was mean and untrustworthy every one knew, but that made little difference. His corn was better tended than any in the county, and his wheat always yielded more than other men's.

Of Peter no one knew much, nor had any one a good word to say for him. He drank whenever he could get out of Antone's sight long enough to pawn his hat or coat for whisky. Indeed there were but two things he would not pawn, his pipe and his violin. He was a lazy, absent-minded old fellow, who liked to fiddle better than to plow,

† "Peter" (1892), written while Willa Cather was a student at the University of Nebraska, was her first published work of fiction, in *The Mahogany Tree* (May 31, 1892), pp. 323–24. She later said she had based the story on an actual event—the suicide of Annie Pavelka's father—and drew on it for her description of the suicide of Mr. Shimerda in *My Ántonia*.

251

[handwritten annotation: Presbyteenism → hardworking, extremely practical, focused making money.]

though Antone surely got work enough out of them all, for that matter. In the house of which Antone was master there was no one, from the little boy three years old, to the old man of sixty, who did not earn his bread. Still people said that Peter was worthless, and was a great drag on Antone, his son, who never drank, and was a much better man than his father had ever been. Peter did not care what people said. He did not like the country, nor the people, least of all he liked the plowing. He was very homesick for Bohemia. Long ago, only eight years ago by the calendar, but it seemed eight centuries to Peter, he had been a second violinist in the great theatre at Prague. He had gone into the theatre very young, and had been there all his life, until he had a stroke of paralysis, which made his arm so weak that his bowing was uncertain. Then they told him he could go. Those were great days at the theatre. He had plenty to drink then, and wore a dress coat every evening, and there were always parties after the play. He could play in those days, ay, that he could! He could never read the notes well, so he did not play first; but his touch, he had a touch indeed, so Herr Mikilsdoff, who led the orchestra, had said. Sometimes now Peter thought he could plow better if he could only bow as he used to. He had seen all the lovely women in the world there, all the great singers and the great players. He was in the orchestra when Rachel played, and he heard Liszt play when the Countess d'Agoult sat in the stage box and threw the master white lilies. Once, a French woman came and played for weeks, he did not remember her name now.[1] He did not remember her face very well either, for it changed so, it was never twice the same. But the beauty of it, and the great hunger men felt at the sight of it, that he remembered. Most of all he remembered her voice. He did not know French, and could not understand a word she said, but it seemed to him that she must be talking the music of Chopin. And her voice, he thought he should know that in the other world. The last night she played a play in which a man touched her arm, and she stabbed him. As Peter sat among the smoking gas jets down below the footlights with his fiddle on his knee, and looked up at her, he thought he would like to die too, if he could touch her arm once, and have her stab him so. Peter went home to his wife very drunk that night. Even in those days he was a foolish fellow, who cared for nothing but music and pretty faces.

It was all different now. He had nothing to drink and little to eat, and here, there was nothing but sun, and grass, and sky. He had forgotten almost everything, but some things he remembered well enough. He loved his violin and the holy Mary, and above all else he feared the Evil One, and his son Antone.

---

1. Sarah Bernhardt (1845–1923) in Victorien Sardou's *La Tosca* (1887).

Bohemian → geografical place. It were a
using as a caracter meas louing ont.

The fire was low, and it grew cold. Still Peter sat by the fire remembering. He dared not throw more cobs on the fire; Antone would be angry. He did not want to cut wood tomorrow, it would be Sunday, and he wanted to go to mass. Antone might let him do that. He held his violin under his wrinkled chin, his white hair fell over it, and he began to play "Ave Maria." His hand shook more than ever before, and at last refused to work the bow at all. He sat stupefied for a while, then arose, and taking his violin with him, stole out into the old sod stable. He took Antone's shotgun down from its peg, and loaded it by the moonlight which streamed in through the door. He sat down on the dirt floor, and leaned back against the dirt wall. He heard the wolves howling in the distance, and the night wind screaming as it swept over the snow. Near him he heard the regular breathing of the horses in the dark. He put his crucifix above his heart, and folding his hands said brokenly all the Latin he had ever known, *"Pater noster, qui in coelum est."*[2] Then he raised his head and sighed, "Not one kreutzer will Antone pay them to pray for my soul, not one kreutzer, he is so careful of his money, is Antone, he does not waste it in drink, he is a better man than I, but hard sometimes. He works the girls too hard, women were not made to work so. But he shall not sell thee, my fiddle, I can play thee no more, but they shall not part us. We have seen it all together, and we will forget it together, the French woman and all." He held his fiddle under his chin a moment, where it had lain so often, then put it across his knee and broke it through the middle. He pulled off his old boot, held the gun between his knees with the muzzle against his forehead, and pressed the trigger with his toe.

In the morning Antone found him stiff, frozen fast in a pool of blood. They could not straighten him out enough to fit a coffin, so they buried him in a pine box. Before the funeral Antone carried to town the fiddle-bow which Peter had forgotten to break. Antone was very thrifty, and a better man than his father had been.

GUY REYNOLDS

My Ántonia and the Americanisation Debate[†]

Theories of Americanisation

'This passion for Americanizing everything and everybody is a deadly disease with us', announced Willa Cather during an interview in

---

2. "Our Father, who art in heaven."
† From Guy Reynolds, *Willa Cather in Context: Progress, Race, Empire* (New York: St. Martin's, 1996), pp. 73–98. © Guy Reynolds 1996. Reproduced with permission of Palgrave Macmillan. Bracketed page references are to this Norton Critical Edition.

1924. What did she mean by 'Americanizing'? This chapter examines Cather's changing responses to what I will call the Americanisation debate; the aim is to read her novel *My Ántonia* (1918) in the context of the political, sociological and educational arguments which had developed early this century around the issues of immigration and assimilation. Cather made her own distinctive contribution to that debate: letters, journalism and fiction continually testify to her fascination with immigrant culture. Drawing on this material we can read Cather's novel within its historical context. We will then be able to understand the subtleties and shifts in her commentary on one of the United States's most urgent cultural problems. Writing *My Ántonia* during the First World War, Cather suggested that a liberal form of Americanisation could encompass a kaleidoscopic cultural variety. Between 1916 and 1918, when the Americanisation debate began to form, but before the issue was usurped by nativism, it was possible to imagine a multinational America in which different cultures co-existed. The war, the upsurge in patriotism, and the concomitant legislation to regulate immigration and foreign languages put an end to the idea that the America coming into being would be a multicultural Utopia. *My Ántonia* was written during this apparent new dawn; she crystallised in fiction the hopes for a pluralist community. From the hopefulness of 1916–18 Cather retreated to her denunciations of modern America made in the early 1920s. This essay follows the development of Cather's ideas about multiculturalism during the period, placing them within their cultural context and teasing out the paradoxes in her position.

I am particularly concerned with the issue of biculturalism, a topic which has recently and brilliantly been explored by Werner Sollors. Sollors describes a pattern of 'consent and descent' in American culture, as citizens identify themselves ancestrally with their ethnic community (descent) and culturally with their new families, new culture and political system (consent):

> Descent relations are those defined by anthropologists as relations of 'substance' (by blood or nature); consent relations describe those of 'law' or 'marriage.' Descent language emphasizes our positions as heirs, our hereditary qualities, liabilities, and entitlements; consent language stresses our abilities as mature free agents and 'architects of our fates' to choose our spouses, our destinies, and our political systems.[1]

I return at several points to the distinction made by Sollors, and use the concepts of 'consent' and 'descent' to examine the dilemmas facing Cather's heroine, Ántonia.

1. Werner Sollors, *Beyond Ethnicity: Consent and Descent in American Culture* (New York and Oxford, 1986), p. 6.

In *Americanization* (1916) Royal Dixon discussed 'hyphenates', the term he used for recent immigrants into the United States. Dixon felt that waves of immigration meant that America had lost the sense of itself as a nation; he urged his countrymen to 'Americanize America'. This could be achieved through the teaching of English: 'and we need only add that the wonder of it is that a step so simple as approaching the foreigner and teaching him English has not long before this been recognized and put in practice by law and by grace, since it is the logical and all-powerful key to the situation of converting the foreigner from an alien to an American'. 'Americanization' was the term used to describe this process: through the acquisition of English the immigrant would be acculturated and lose his or her foreignness. The immigrant was then an American rather than, say, a German-American. Contending his thesis on pragmatic grounds, Dixon stated that 'it is in the Babel of tongues that the alien is debased and defrauded'. But his underlying principles—indeed, the principles of Americanisation in general—were ideological: American English was the means to transmit the ideals of the United States, to inculcate citizenship and the 'American way'.[2]

Dixon, editor of *The Immigrant in America Review*, was one of a number of Americanisation pundits who debated this issue during and after the First World War. The theorists of Americanisation— educationalists, social scientists, politicians—responded to the social upheaval brought about by wave upon wave of immigration. Rates of European immigration had at last begun to slow down in the post-war period: from 3,687,564 (1891–1900), to 8,795,386 (1901–10) and 5,735,811 (1911–20), the huge influxes of migrants had now passed their peak.[3] Legislative controls were brought in to regulate immigration. The 1924 Immigration Act, also known as the National Origins Act, controlled entry according to the origin of the prospective American citizen; quotas were set as a percentage of the number of each national group resident in the United States in 1890 (thus favouring immigrants from northern and western Europe, who were more numerous than immigrants from southern and eastern Europe at that time). The debate now shifted to the question of assimilation: how was America to deal with the foreigners it had already received?

Assimilation raised a central question, to which the Americanisation theorists provided a range of answers: should the immigrants adjust themselves to American culture, or should American national identity redefine itself in the face of a multicultural population? The English language is the hook on which this question is hung; and

2. Royal Dixon, *Americanization* (New York, 1916), pp. 4, 31, 17.
3. Maldwyn A. Jones, *The Limits of Liberty: American History, 1607–1980* (Oxford, 1983), p. 648.

the English language becomes the symbolic centre of the Americanisation debate. One reason for the heightening of interest in Americanisation was the sharpened awareness that American English
constituted an autonomous language, a language that could be used
as the index of national identity. In 1919 H. L. Mencken published
his first edition of *The American Language*; and in 1925 the magazine *American Speech* was founded. Using such works Americans
could isolate their language from its European mother tongue; and
this helped to weld American English onto a strengthened sense of
purely American identity.

For Peter Roberts, in *The Problem of Americanization* (1920), the
argument could be stated simply: 'the alien who does not know the
English language will never understand America'.[4] Several years later,
George Stephenson, one of the first historians of immigration, also
emphasised the centrality of English teaching: 'Speaking in sweeping generalizations, the Americanisation movement involves the
teaching of English, cultivating a friendly feeling between natives
and immigrants and between the various racial groups, giving
instruction in the fundamentals of citizenship, preventing undesir-
able segregation in cities, and meeting the demand for immigrants
in desirable locations and occupations.'[5]

But this was where the problems began. How, for instance, was
Americanisation to be administered? Should the teaching of English
be a matter for government, for the local state, or for the individual
employer who took on the tongue-tied immigrant? And what happened to the immigrant's former language and, by extension, former
culture: how desirable were old world customs in the new world? It
was obviously impossible to prohibit a bilingual American/European
culture in the home, church or temple; but was a dualistic culture
practical in society as a whole?[6]

Broadly speaking, we can distiguish between hard-line and liberal Americanisationists. The hard-liners rejected 'alien' values and
sanctioned a violent rupture between the immigrant and the old
world. The melting pot idea had, of course, been canvassed somewhat earlier (Israel Zangwill's play, *The Melting Pot*, was published
in 1909); but the war helped to stir the pot. Americanisation, in this
view, was a homogenising process that would meld a nation out of
disparate stock. Thus Roberts and Dixon allow for a degree of linguistic and cultural pluralism, but these traces become part of what
Dixon termed the 'American epic consciousness': 'let us say that the

---

4. Peter Roberts, *The Problem of Americanization* (New York, 1920), p. 68.
5. George M. Stephenson, *A History of American Immigration, 1820–1924* (Boston and New
   York, 1926), p. 235.
6. Surveys of Americanisation include *Americanization* ed. Winthrop Talbot (New York,
   1917), a handbook of articles and speeches, and Robert A. Carlson, *The Americanization Syndrome: A Quest for Conformity* (London, 1987), especially pp. 92–100.

ideal towards which Americanism must press is that in which epic consciousness of each nationality shall contribute to and find expression in the American epic consciousness'.[7] At the extreme wing of the hard-liners were those sceptical commentators who doubted the efficacy of Americanisation. Gino Speranza, despite a name which suggests a not entirely WASPish ancestry, gave a pessimistic account of assimilation in his article of 1920, 'Does Americanization Americanize?':

> To feel that the powers of attraction and assimilation of America are tremendous, is both true and patriotic; but to practise the belief that such powers can work miracles—such as the rapid conversion of the mixed and unstable immigrants of Europe into *real* American citizens—is sheer superstition and, as such, the child of ignorance . . . There cannot be two nationalisms even if one is major and one minor, even if one claims to be American first and German second . . . Yet the more 'raw' citizens (if I may use the term) you take in, helping the process by a veneer of Americanization, the more you threaten our characteristically American form of democracy.[8]

In the same issue, demonstrating that Americanisation stirred up a highly partisan debate, John Kulamer responded more sympathetically than Speranza (though he refused to support the legislative encouragement of assimilation): 'Liberal and generous treatment, in accord with the principles of Americanism, on the part of individuals in their daily contact with the foreigners will do more than volumes of laws.'[9]

On the other hand, liberal Americanisationists advocated a transfer or migration of old world culture from Europe; American life would benefit from the resulting pluralism. In this view America encompasses a variety of cultures rather than subordinates them to its own 'epic consciousness'. An example of this position was *Old World Traits Transplanted* (1921), a study produced by sociologists at the University of Chicago as one in a series of *Americanization Studies*. Robert Park and his colleagues pointed out that 'all emigration represents some crisis in the life of the emigrants' and proceeded to develop a psycho-pathology of immigrant life. They maintained that settled, assimilated Americans must respect the recent immigrants, and they showed how immigrant organisations aided Americanisation. Liberal thinkers defined America through the diveristy of its peoples, claiming that immigration made the United States unique:

7. Dixon, p. 176.
8. Gino Speranza, 'Does Americanization Americanize?,' *Atlantic Monthly*, 125 (1920), 263–9.
9. John Kulamer, 'Americanization: the other side of the case,' *Atlantic Monthly*, 125 (1920), 416–23.

Immigration in the form it has taken in America differs from
all previous movements of population. Populous countries have
planted colonies, states have been conquered and occupied,
slaves have been imported. But when a single country is peacefully invaded by millions of men from scores of other countries,
when there are added to one American city as many Jews as
there are Danes in Denmark, and to the same city more Italians than there are Italians in Rome, we have something new
in history.

Liberal Americanisation recognised that the new world could only
be created with due appreciation of the European heritage. This leads
the Chicago writers to esteem memory. The immigrant, they say,
comes to understand America through similarities with the world
that was left behind. Patriotism is cited as a devotion that is shared
by American and immigrant: the immigrant understands patriotic
allegiance because he has felt this emotion for his homeland; such
a feeling could be regenerated in the new world. 'If we wish to help
the immigrant to get a grip on American life, to understand its conditions, and find his own role in it, we must seize on everything in
his old life which will serve either to interpret the new or to hold
him steady while he is getting adjusted.' Memory, then, is politicised
by the Americanisation debate; it is enmeshed in arguments about
citizenship and patriotism.[1]

Interest in the European heritage also led Americanisation pundits to draw parallels between the United States and great European
civilisations. The sociologist Carol Aronovici asserted in 1919 that
'Drawing from the example of Spain we might almost say that where
race amalgamation and race assimilation stop, advancement stops'.
Aronovici hoped that the European assimilative process would be
accelerated in America: 'A synthetic process of social and national
integration brought about by an intensified democratic state will
merge the present heterogeneous masses of racial and national groups
into one great people'.[2]

Sociologists and educationalists surveyed the overall picture, trying to evaluate America's progress towards 'one great people'; but
Americanisation was not only a subject discussed by academics.
Within the popular culture there were accounts of what it meant to
be 'Americanized'—immigrant testimonies and autobiographies form
a major genre in early twentieth-century America. The most famous
of these were Jacob Riis's *The Making of an American* (1901) and
The Americanization of Edward Bok (1920). The latter, a Pulitzer

1. William I. Thomas with Robert E. Park and Herbert A. Miller, *Old World Traits Transplanted* (1921. New Jersey, 1971), pp. 83, 259, 295.
2. Carol Aronovici, 'Americanization: Its Meaning and Function,' *American Journal of Sociology*, 25 (1919–20), 695–730.

prize–winner, was a bestseller from 1922 to 1924.[3] Bok's success is entirely founded on his facility in English. An immigrant Dutch boy, Bok learns English, works for newspapers and becomes an important editor. The book celebrates in a reassuringly eulogistic manner the opportunities that America has given him, but the one moment of critical asperity occurs when Bok attacks his early education: 'if there is one thing that I, as a foreign-born child, should have been carefully taught, it is the English language'.[4]

Willa Cather and Americanisation

The burst of writing on Americanisation coincides with Willa Cather's interest in the subject. In 1918, two years after Royal Dixon's *Americanization*, Cather published *My Ántonia*, a novel which explores the same areas as the texts I have just adduced: immigration, settlement, memory, language-acquisition. And in the 1920s, when Americanisation continued to arouse controversy, Cather gave some of her rare public speeches on this topic. In 1921, during speeches in the Nebraskan towns of Hastings and Omaha, she attacked hard-line Americanisation. The *Omaha World-Herald* reported that 'Miss Cather told her audience that one of the things which retarded art in America was the indiscriminate Americanization work of overzealous patriots who implant into the foreign minds a distaste for all they have brought of value from their own country.' She reiterated her case in a 1924 interview with Rose Feld for the *New York Times Book Review*: 'Social workers, missionaries—call them what you will—go after them, pursue them and devote their days and nights toward the great task of turning them into stupid replicas of smug American citizens. This passion for Americanizing everything and everybody is a deadly disease with us'.[5]

Americanisation brought out this urgent, impassioned and homiletic tone in Cather for several reasons. First, it was a major issue in her home state, Nebraska. As she herself pointed out, Nebraska had a large foreign population—the 1910 census recorded 900,000 foreigners to 300,000 native stock.[6] Many of these immigrants were from a Germanic background. During the First World War, which led to an upsurge in patriotism after America entered on the allied side, German-Americans became objects of suspicion, as did the German language: there was a campaign to drop German from school

3. James D. Hart, *The Popular Book: A History of America's Literary Taste* (New York, 1950), p. 242.
4. Edward Bok, *The Americanization of Edward Bok*, 29th edition (New York, 1924), p. 438.
5. Newspaper reports of Cather's speeches and the *NYTBR* interview in Brent L. Bohlke, *Willa Cather in Person: Interviews, Speeches, and Letters* (Lincoln and London: University of Nebraska Press, 1986), pp. 71–2, 146–7.
6. Willa Cather, 'Nebraska,' 236–8.

curricula. The teaching of languages became a much-debated point.
Edward A. Ross, a prominent sociologist and political scientist, lec-
tured an audience in 1924 that

> It is a burning shame that at present American-born children
> are leaving church elementary foreign-language schools not only
> unable to read and write English, but scarcely able to under-
> stand or speak it. That we should permit native Americans to
> receive all the schooling they will ever get in a foreign language
> is the pinnacle of imbecile amiability.[7]

Nebraska had already extirpated 'imbecile amiability'. Responding to this xenophobic *Zeitgeist* the state passed measures to prohibit
the teaching of languages before the eighth grade. This in turn led
to the Meyer v. Nebraska case of 1923: a teacher was convicted for
giving German lessons, and although the Supreme Court overturned
the conviction (citing the Fourteenth Amendment) it affirmed its
resistance to foreign languages:

> The legislature had seen the baneful effects of permitting for-
> eigners, who had taken residence in this country, to rear and
> educate their children in the language of their native land. The
> result of that condition was found to be inimical to our own
> safety. To allow the children of foreigners, who had emigrated
> here, to be taught from early childhood the language of the
> country of their parents was to rear them with that language as
> the mother tongue.[8]

The Meyer case marked the culmination of a patriotic upsurge
that began with the First World War. Nebraska had prohibited
foreign-language teaching in 1919. The years 1919–20 saw a flowering of anti-Bolshevik agitation, a distrust of radicalism and 'Reds'.
Cather's speeches on language and immigration (1921) are therefore
placed in a period and a place dominated by Americanisation. A provincial state such as Nebraska, recently created (1867) and flooded
with immigrants, was paradoxically at the centre of American politics with regard to this issue.

The other reasons for Cather's impassioned tone stem from her
trenchantly-held view of an ideal American culture. The desire to
proscribe foreign languages was a manifestation of what she termed
'standardization'; it smacked of the uniformity that seemed to be over-
taking modern society. Americanisation undermined the European

---

7. Edward A. Ross, *Roads to Social Peace—the Weil Lectures, 1924, On American Citizenship* (Chapel Hill, 1924), p. 60.
8. Cited by Shirley Brice Heath, 'English in Our Language Heritage,' in Charles A. Ferguson
   and S. B. Heath (eds). *Language in the USA* (Cambridge, 1981), p. 18. The adjudication
   reference was 262 US390 (1923). See Kenneth B. O'Brien Jr, 'Education, Americanization and the Supreme Court: The 1920s,' *American Quarterly*, 13 (1961), 161–71.

cultural legacy which Cather cherished. She believed, in fact, that a heterogeneous, Europeanised Midwestern society could nurture a cosmopolitan culture: 'it is in that great cosmopolitan country known as the Middle West that we may hope to see the hard molds of American provincialism broken up'.[9]

It needs to be admitted that Cather's heterogeneous, pluralist immigrant culture is, nonetheless, essentially white and of North European descent. The culture described in the letters, the speeches and the novels overlooks the immigration from Southern and Eastern Europe; it also omits the Chinese and the Jews who made up so much of the immigrant population. As I noted in the 'Introduction', there is extensive evidence in Cather's work of indifference to, if not hostility towards certain ethnic groups—notably, America's Jews. But I also noted a certain developing self-consciousness about this issue, as evident in Cather's revisions to her texts so as to remove anti-Semitic references. Cather, then, tends to display an attentive sympathy within the context of a circumscribed pluralism. That is, she does not write about such ethnic groups as the Chinese-Americans, but she does write about a greater variety of European peoples than many of her contemporaries. And within the framework of this localised ethnic spectrum, her fictions of race and multi-culturalism can often seem strikingly receptive to difference. *My Ántonia*, as I will now show, is a major instance of this attentive sympathy.

My Ántonia, written at the end of the war, is noticeably reticent about a conflict which as Hermione Lee comments, 'makes the loudest silence in the book'; but the book has much to say about one of the effects of the war, namely the intensified Americanisation programme.[1] The military draft had revealed that of 10 million registrants, 700,000 were so illiterate that they could not even sign their names. Government agencies accordingly increased their work: the Bureau of Education published its *Americanization Bulletin* for the first time; Independence Day was especially directed towards the immigrant and a mobilisation of patriotism.[2] Against this background, Cather wrote a novel that reads as if it were a rebuff to the hard-line Americanisationists and a prescient commentary on Nebraska's rejection of foreign languages in 1919.

In *My Ántonia*, Cather describes lives that are shaped by the need to learn a new language and a new culture. The novel's heroine, Ántonia Shimerda, comes from an immigrant Bohemian family which at

9. Interview with John Chapin Mosher in *The Writer* (November, 1926), rept. Bohlke, p. 94.
1. Hermione Lee, *Willa Cather: Double Lives* (New York: Pantheon, 1990), p. 136.
2. Edward G. Hartmann, *The Movement to Americanize the Immigrant* (New York, 1948), pp. 187, 200, 207.

first knows no English: 'they could not speak enough English to ask for advice, or even to make their most pressing wants known' [18]. Ántonia's friendship with Jim Burden is initiated by her desire to learn English (the oblique tentativeness of this romance might have more to do with cultural factors—learning a language—than with Cather's famous difficulties in representing successful heterosexual relationships). While she learns words and phrases, the Nebraskan landscape takes shape before us, described as if for the first time. The fresh and almost naive immediacy of Cather's descriptive passages is, in part, the result of the defamiliarisation of language that occurs when we are shown how English is learned:

> Ántonia pointed up to the sky and questioned me with her glance. I gave her the word, but she was not satisfied and pointed to my eyes. I told her, and she repeated the word, making it sound like 'ice'. She pointed up to the sky, then to my eyes, then back to the sky, with movements so quick and impulsive that she distracted me, and I had no idea what she wanted. She got up on her knees and wrung her hands. She pointed to her own eyes and shook her head, then to mine and to the sky, nodding violently.
>   'Oh,' I exclaimed, 'blue; blue sky!' [20]

We have here the 'reign of wonder' that Tony Tanner has located as a central motif in American literature.[3] Words are used with novelty and wonder to describe the world. The most clichéd elements of our environment ('blue sky') are imbued with mystery when they are named afresh. Edenic analogues move within the comedy of this scene, suggested by the paradisiacal resonance of the act of naming. Some Americanisationists felt that the nation had lost its selfhood beneath a tide of immigration. Cather, however, demonstrates that immigration renews America's myths about its own identity. With each wave of immigration, America is once again perceived as paradise, as Eden; and through the Americanisation process the land is literally named for the first time.

To write at all about the English language and language acquisition was to enter into a highly charged discourse about American nationalism and immigration—indeed, a discourse about American culture itself. My Ántonia signals, from its very title, an engagement with the Americanisation debate. My Ántonia: a footnote guides us to the correct pronunciation of Ántonia, 'the Bohemian name' [9]. Cather does not aim for a veneer of exoticism, the patina that could be achieved simply through the deployment of foreign names and strange words. Instead, she gives due respect to the alien name

3. Tony Tanner, *The Reign of Wonder* (Cambridge, 1977), pp. 1–15.

that her metic carries, and so carefully underlines her heroine's foreignness.[4]

This sympathy recurs throughout the novel; Cather's American characters are responsive to foreign cultures and languages. Jim Burden is intrigued when he hears Bohemian: 'I pricked up my ears, for it was positively the first time I had ever heard a foreign tongue' [10]. There are moments when characters use foreign words without being aware of their meaning, but the power of a strange language nonetheless communicates itself. Jim's grandfather at one point reads from the psalms and says the word 'Selah': 'I had no idea what the word meant; perhaps he had not. But, as he uttered it, it became oracular, the most sacred of words' [15]. The epiphany exemplifies Cather's ecumenical generosity: her characters find spiritual value even in experiences that are foreign to them and therefore baffling or opaque. Moreover, Cather shows how a commonplace devotion, a cornerstone of Protestant daily life, turns on a word that is unknown. Domestic religious life is made strange and made sacred by the admission of the foreign. Cather elliptically reminds us that American Protestantism inevitably incorporated elements of that 'alien' culture which hard-line Americanisation rejected. There is nothing melodramatic or confrontational in Cather's prose; one can easily read over these sentences without heeding their low-key subversiveness. But in her own distinctively oblique fashion Cather rewrites Americanisation rhetoric.[5]

My Ántonia is, above all, a novel about bilingual communities. Cather shows how the immigrant, accustomed to two or more cultures, uses different languages for different purposes. Otto Fuchs uses his first language when he writes to his mother: 'he spoke and wrote his own language so seldom that it came to him awkwardly. His effort to remember entirely absorbed him' [49]. Fuchs has practically lost his European language; other characters absorb American English so readily that a similar slippage might occur. Ántonia herself is rapidly attuned to English: 'Tony learned English so quickly that by the time school began she could speak as well as any of us' [82]. Cather observes that children do adapt linguistically much more readily and completely than adults. Fuchs and Ántonia are quickly 'Americanized', in the narrow sense of learning English. Yet, in Cather's liberal definition of Americanisation, this does not mean that the immigrant's earlier language and

4. Immigrant names were often anglicised. See J. B. Dudek, 'The Americanization of Czech given names,' *American Speech*, I (1926), 18–22. Cather's interest in the names of immigrants anticipates recent work on ethnicity and naming. 'From such a perspective, contrastive strategies—naming and name-calling among them—become the most important thing about ethnicity' writes Sollors, *Beyond Ethnicity*, p. 28.
5. On the Protestant hegemony see John Higham, *Strangers in the Land: Patterns of American Nativism 1860–1925*, revised edition (New York, 1971), pp. 234–99.

culture are forsaken. When Jim returns to look for Ántonia after 20 years he finds she is married to her fellow Bohemian, Cuzak. Their children speak Bohemian; the family have a domestic culture that is solidly European. We hear again the language-switching that prevailed at the beginning of the novel; 'Cuzak began at once to talk about his holiday—from politeness he spoke English' [172]. The novel has turned full circle: the immigrant leaves her European homeland, becomes an American, but preserves European culture at home and in her language. Finally, Cather shows, there can be an amalgamation of Europe and America; the Cuzak children are at ease in both worlds. Ántonia's family stands as a repudiation of those Americanisation pundits who advocated the severance of ties with the old world. The Cuzaks are the culmination of many subtle and unexpected reversals in this novel: 'native' Americans are receptive to foreign cultures; the foreigners learn English; Ántonia fulfils the American dream of pioneer settlement even as she revivifies a European way of life.

Within the context of the Americanisation debate, these details add up to a radical commentary on what it is to be 'American'. Whereas Americanisation ideology sought to fix the meaning of 'American' (making it synonymous with 'Protestant', 'English-speaking', 'North European'), Cather's sense of the word is far more capacious and fluid. To return to the terminology I mentioned at the start of this chapter: Cather is interested in an American culture based on both 'consent' and 'descent'. The domestic culture of the Cuzaks, for instance its use of the Bohemian language, exemplifies descent. Ántonia preserves the language of her ancestors, and by marrying one of her countrymen the continuities of descent are further emphasised. However, in her pioneering endeavours and her settlement of the land Ántonia has lived out the principles of consent—hers is a thoroughly American life of autonomy and self-making. Indeed, in one memorable phrase Jim Burden explicitly sees Ántonia as the *originator*, and not the descendant, of a race: 'She was a rich mine of life, like the founders of early races' [171].

Readings of the novel, nevertheless, sometimes ignore the political intricacy of Cather's writing, particularly in the final Book, 'Cuzak's Boys'. James E. Miller in 'My Ántonia and the American Dream' reads My Ántonia as a novel about disillusion: 'by and large, the dreams of the pioneers lie shattered, their lives broken by the hardness of wilderness life'.[6] He is correct to say that something has been broken. Cather describes the physical 'breaking' of her heroine, who now has hair 'a little grizzled' [161] and many teeth missing [162, 163]. But because he neglects the theme of Americanisation, Miller reads the latter section of the novel as bleaker than it really is. In

6. James E. Miller, 'My Ántonia and the American Dream,' *Prairie Schooner* 48 (1974), 112–23.

counterpoint to disillusion, Cather writes of a creativity and renewal
that is the result of her idiosyncratically pluralist version of Americanisation. Jim and Ántonia are in a nostalgic mood, and they spend
their time with old photographs or in reminiscence; but they are surrounded by children, many speaking Bohemian, who offset the mel-
ancholia with their vitality and joy. One of the most memorable
scenes in the book—a scene that demonstrates Cather's sensitivity to
physical energy, to light and to food—occurs when the children
burst from the fruit cave, 'a veritable explosion of life out of the dark
cave into the sunlight' [164]. The fruit cave, where food is preserved
during the winter months, cyclically returns us to the sod houses in
which characters at the start of the novel lived—it is another domestic space hollowed out of the earth itself. But it is also an apt symbol
of conserved energy; Cather shows immigrant life—a conserved
European heritage—erupting from the American soil:

> We turned to leave the cave; Ántonia and I went up the stairs
> first, and the children waited. We were standing outside talk-
> ing, when they all came running up the steps together, big and
> little, tow heads and gold heads and brown, and flashing little
> naked legs; a veritable explosion of life out of the dark cave into
> the sunlight. It made me dizzy for a moment. [164]

Cather's first full-length interview was for the *Philadelphia Record*
in 1913; in it she discussed the immigrant communities of Red Cloud
and mentioned the narrative skills of the old women:

> Even when they spoke very little English, the old women some-
> how managed to tell me a great many stories about the old coun-
> try. They talk more freely to a child than to grown people, and
> I always felt as if every word they said to me counted for twenty.[7]

It is likely that the origins of *My Ántonia* lay in such a tale. Cather
recalled that when she arrived in Nebraska as a girl the first thing
she heard about was the suicide of a Mr. Sadalaak, even though he
had died several years earlier. This story made a great impression
on her, and she remembered that people never stopped retelling it.
Cather claimed that having heard this repeatedly-told story she was
destined to write *My Ántonia*. The novel is, then, the latest formu-
lation in a series of tellings of the same tale.[8]

Immigrant life is oral and narrative, in spite of the old women's
faltering knowledge of English. The immigrants are habitual story-
tellers, preserving memories of Europe through anecdotes and
tales. *My Ántonia*, faithful to the immigrant experience, has an

---

7. Bohlke, p. 10.
8. Letter to Carrie Sherwood, 27 January 1934, WCPM [Willa Cather Pioneer Memorial,
   Red Cloud, Nebraska].

extraordinary multiplicity of voices. Cather deploys a series of discrete stories and anecdotes, many of which deal with the immigrants' lives in Europe, with language acquisition, with the making of new lives in America. The novel is a tissue of recollections of European domestic life, simple anecdotes about lost people and places, stray memories. Ántonia, for instance, tells Jim about her home country, about hunting badgers and 'Old Hata' who sang to the children [26].

Cather's perception of immigrant folk-culture affects the form of *My Ántonia*, a novel which she said seemed to lack typical novelistic features:

> *My Ántonia*, for instance, is just the other side of the rug, the pattern that is supposed not to count in a story. In it there is no love affair, no courtship, no marriage, no broken heart, no struggle for success. I knew I'd ruin my material if I put it in the usual fictional pattern. I just used it the way I thought absolutely true.[9]

Cather's image for *My Ántonia*—the 'other side of the rug, the pattern that is supposed not to count'—hints at a Jamesian notion of the story as the woven pattern of a carpet; yet it also suggests parallels with popular women's crafts such as weaving or quilt-making. This conflation of Jamesian theorising and folk-art is analogous to the method of *My Ántonia*; the novel's loose, barely plotted structure is an experiment in form *and* an embodiment of the Midwest's oral folk-culture. We find a similar synthesis of 'art' and 'folk-art' in Cather's comment that, when she listened to the immigrant women, 'I always felt as if every word they said to me counted for twenty'. The inability of the immigrants to express themselves fully means that the listener has to imagine a fuller, richer account behind their faltering, spartan English narratives. Words, Cather implies, can suggest or stand for many other words. Apparently limited or depleted accounts can paradoxically adumbrate a denser shadow-narrative. Her theory of composition was based on an analogous paradox: through selection and excision the writer can produce a prose of greater suggestive power than writing that is, superficially, more dense or rich. Compare the comment on the immigrant women (1913) to her dicta on writing (1922):

> If the novel is a form of imaginative art, it cannot be at the same time a vivid and brilliant form of journalism. Out of the teeming, gleaming stream of the present it must select the eternal material of art . . . Whatever is felt upon the page without being specifically named there—that, one might say, is created. It is

9. Interview with Flora Merrill for the *New York World*, 19 April 1925, in Bohlke, p. 77. This interview develops points Cather made in a letter, where she highlighted the lack of action in *My Ántonia* and suggested that this novel omitted almost everything deemed necessary to a story. To Mrs. Seibel, 2 February 1919, WCPM.

sented the living, diverse culture she promulgated in her Americanisation speeches.

Cather's theories of art and her practice of fiction were conditioned by her upbringing in Nebraska; she seems to have understood the composition of fiction as a creative act analogous to the
telling and retelling of folk-tales. Her approach to the actual business of writing turned on the different material incarnations of the
same story. Her diligent revision of manuscripts and typescripts
involved changing the physical appearance of drafts; the draft would
be written, typed, retyped in a different colour—the aim was to
facilitate the revision of material, since the eye can discern sole-
cisms more easily when the form of the text is altered. Writing, as
Cather worked at her desk day after day, was essentially redrafting
(she told Sinclair Lewis that she was unconcerned with preserving
the first drafts of her work). And this technique, the keystone of her
craft, evoked the tellings, retellings and repetitions-with-variation of
the folk-tales she heard as a girl. As Cather wrote, her own work
became, as it were, translated; the original, primary draft was lost
within an accreting series of later versions. The drafts are rather like
the later tellings and retellings of the Peter and Pavel story; they have
an autonomous existence of their own, and come to replace the original tale.[4]

In translation, too, the basic story serves as a template for re-
formulations which are at once the same and different. For Cather,
a much translated writer, the spread of her work into different languages provided another opportunity to see transmission and retelling at work. She was, for instance, pleased with the foreign
reception of *Death Comes for the Archbishop*, and she boasted that *My
Ántonia* had been translated into eight languages. Gratified by the
French thesis on her work by René Rapin, Cather wanted to have it
translated for her American friends. The last example concludes a
chain of transmissions: from America to France; from the novelist
to the critic; and then the reversal of this process as Cather plans to
have translated a French critical study for an American readership.
It is also worth noting how, as with the wolf-story, we have different
kinds of audience receiving the work (the author herself, the French
scholarly community, the American circle of friends)—one story
holds together different communities of listeners and readers.[5]

Cather understood from her Nebraskan youth that disparate
aspects of her experience (translating Latin texts, listening to immigrant women, writing fiction) were underpinned by the shared

4. Cather detailed her working methods in a letter to Sinclair Lewis, 22 March 1944,
   WCPM. The basic process consisted of drafts in manuscript and typescript by Cather
   herself, followed by a professional typist's copy in a different colour of ink.
5. Letters to Carrie Sherwood, 9 June 1943, 27 January 1934, 28 June 1939, WCPM.

foundation of transmission. She interpreted a range of apparently
unrelated cultural phenomena in this way, finding a common structure of transmission. The beginning of *My Ántonia* demonstrates this
cultural anthropology in action. Jim Burden meets the unnamed narrator of the 'Introduction'. They talk about Ántonia Shimerda; Jim
has written an account of her, which he later delivers to the narrator,
scribbling on the front of his manuscript *My Ántonia*. Remembering,
telling stories, writing, handing over the manuscript: the 'Introduction' is a glancing vignette, but it embraces a gamut of transmissions—it
can be read almost as an overture, a prefiguring of the motifs developed in the main text. The similarities with the gossipy, folky intima-
cies of the immigrant women are striking, but Cather neatly updates
the context, placing this moment of transmission in a railway
carriage—the train compartment unobtrusively becoming the typical modern setting for recollection, gossip:

> Last summer, in a season of intense heat, Jim Burden and I
> happened to be crossing Iowa on the same train. He and I are
> old friends, we grew up together in the same Nebraska town,
> and we had a great deal to say to each other. While the train
> flashed through never-ending miles of ripe wheat, by country
> towns and bright-flowered pastures and oak groves wilting in
> the sun, we sat in the observation car, where the woodwork
> was hot to the touch and red dust lay deep over everything.
> The dust and heat, the burning wind, reminded us of many
> things. We were talking about what it is like to spend one's
> childhood in little towns like these, buried in wheat and corn,
> under stimulating extremes of climate: burning summers when
> the world lies green and billowy beneath a brilliant sky, when
> one is fairly stifled in vegetation, in the colour and smell
> of strong weeds and heavy harvests; blustery winters with
> little snow, when the whole country is stripped bare and grey
> as sheet-iron. ('Introduction')

The land takes shape as a memory, becoming focused before us.
What happens here is a typically Catheresque moment of memory
and repetitive recall. In a phrase that is picked up and echoed many
pages later in the wolf-story, the narrator says, 'During that burning day when we were crossing Iowa, our talk kept returning to a
central figure, a Bohemian girl whom we had both known long ago'.
Talk keeps returning: Cather is intrigued by these moments when
the loose web of chat and memory begins to tighten and centre
around a figure, an episode. The major theme adumbrated here is,
simply, transmission: Jim and the narrator share their memories of
Ántonia, exchanging collections. We know that Cather had at first
tried to write the novel as a third-person narrative before opting for
the first-person story with a male narrator. Cather discussed the

implications of this gender shift (female author and male narrator) in her letters, and commentators have been quick to fit this compositional history into discussions of gender and sexual role-playing in the life and the fiction. But the effect of having a narrator in the novel is also to foreground the processes of writing and transmission. We see, quite literally, the text being created, named and handed over. Thus the effect of an overture, a pre-capitulation of the novel's fascination with all kinds of translation and transmission.[6]

At the end of the Pavel and Peter episode Jim dreams of a composite landscape through which he travels: 'At night, before I went to sleep, I often found myself in a sledge drawn by three horses, dashing through a country that looked something like Nebraska and something like Virginia' [37]. Jim's memory transfers and fuses various terrains. The Ukraine becomes America; that America is, in turn, a composite of Nebraska and Virginia (Jim's home states and Cather's too). The landscape undergoes a process of amalgamation that is similar to the experiences of Cather's characters, who are also European *and* American, Southern *and* Western. Cather's American soil is here a shifting and various land, as much a patchwork terrain as her Americans are a patchwork people. Cather thereby fends off the American myth of a native soil on which a 'native' (that is, white, north European and Protestant) population lives.

To gauge the subtlety of Cather's method in *My Ántonia* we need to turn back to the Americanisation debate. Theorists of liberal Americanisation went beyond the question of language learning and used the basic idea of Americanisation as a vehicle to carry their speculations about other cultural matters. As we saw earlier, the Chicago sociologists were led to meditate about memory and its role in helping the migrant to adapt to a new land. *My Ántonia* works in a similar way. Cather deploys the fundamental stuff of Americanisation ('blue sky!'), but she then goes further and reflects on memory, on folk-art, on the very foundations of culture. Cather's descriptions of how a story is transmitted and how a novel of American life can be constructed further the insights of liberal Americanisation. It is to these broader cultural matters that I now want to turn.

An Americanised Culture: Idealism and Disillusion

Two years before *My Ántonia* was published Randolph Bourne wrote his remarkably prescient article, 'Trans-National America' (1916).

---

6. James Leslie Woodress, *Willa Cather: A Literary Life* (Lincoln: University of Nebraska Press, 1987), pp. 289–90. For a bleaker account of memory in the novel see Blanche H. Gelfant, 'The Forgotten Reaping-Hook: Sex in *My Ántonia*,' *American Literature*, 43 (1971), 60–82. On the male narrator see Susan J. Rosowski, *The Voyage Perilous: Willa Cather's Romanticism* (Lincoln, 1986), p. 88, and Deborah G. Lambert, 'The Defeat of a Hero: Autonomy and Sexuality in *My Ántonia*,' *American Literature*, 53 (1982), 676–90.

Bourne, a progressive, an opponent of America's entry into the War and a radical educationalist was also a sympathetic reviewer of *My Ántonia*.[7] He described a cosmopolitan America where what he termed, in typically progressive fashion, the 'Beloved Community' would grow out of multiculturalism. 'Trans-National America' was an attack on the authoritarianism of Americanisation ('We act as if we wanted Americanization to take place only on our own terms, and not by the consent of the governed') and an outline of a cosmopolitan Utopia, an America capaciously receptive to a variety of peoples. This piece, published before the First World War had precipitated an upswing in patriotic fervour and hardened attitudes against foreigners, opposed the conservatism of the Anglo-American establishment to an exciting racial heterogeneity. For Bourne, as for Cather, the recognition of America's failings is set against the potential cultural successes of a pluralist society ('America is a unique sociological fabric, and it bespeaks poverty of imagination not to be thrilled at the incalculable potentialities of so novel a union of men').[8] Again like Cather, Bourne despised the encroaching uniformity of America and sought a revitalisation through ethnic and cultural diversity:

> We have needed the new peoples—the order of the German and Scandinavian, the turbulence of the Slav and Hun—to save us from our own stagnation . . . What we emphatically do not want is that these distinctive qualities should be washed out into a tasteless, colorless fluid of uniformity.[9]

In Bourne's article the question of assimilation is used as a lever to prise open the extant American culture. Bourne wants to know what kind of a country America is, what its culture is like; 'Americanization' is used to interpret 'American'. His conclusion is that America needs to find a means to integrate its diverse constituent cultures while preserving their idiosyncratic differences:

> This is the cultural wreckage of our time, and it is from the fringes of the Anglo-Saxon as well as the other stocks that it falls. America has as yet no impelling integrating force. It makes too easily for this detritus of cultures. In our loose, free country, no constraining national purpose, no tenacious folk-tradition and folk-style hold the people to a line . . . America is transplanted Europe, but a Europe that has not been disintegrated and scattered in the transplanting as in some Dispersion. Its

7. Randolph Bourne, review of *My Ántonia*, *The Dial*, 65 (1918), 557.
8. Bourne, 'Trans-National America,' *Atlantic Monthly*, 118 (1916), 86–97. A recent account of Bourne's work is Lesley J. Vaugnan, 'Cosmopolitanism, Ethnicity and American Identity: Randolph Bourne's "Trans-National America,"' *Journal of American Studies*, 25 (1991), 443–59.
9. Bourne, 87, 90.

colonies live here inextricably mingled, yet not homogeneous. They merge but they do not fuse.[1]

Bourne alighted in 1916 on a problem Cather had begun to explore in O Pioneers! and pursued in My Ántonia: how was this heterogeneously centrifugal society to find cultural coherence? Bourne understood that America risked fragmentation socially and culturally. The language he used sought to redeem a vocabulary of dispersal ('The influences at the fringe, however, are centrifugal, anarchical') with a diction of coherence ('impelling integrating force'). What was needed was a 'folk-tradition and folk-style'. When Bourne tried to imagine the cosmopolitan culture that would result he used images from the folk-arts of weaving and quilt-making:

> America is coming to be, not a nationality but a trans-nationality, a weaving back and forth, with the other lands, of many threads of all sizes and colors. Any movement which attempts to thwart this weaving, or to dye the fabric any one color, or disentangle the threads of the strands, is false to this cosmopolitan vision.[2]

We can note here the congruences between Cather and Bourne. They used similar images of weaving: Bourne to envisage what a cosmopolitan America would be like; Cather, to describe the form her novel of cosmopolitan America took. For these writers images of weaving were suggested by the recognition that the culture of the new 'Trans-National America' would be a folk-art. It needs to be stressed that for Bourne and Cather a national folk-art was not already, as it were, out there, latent within the national life. Cather had glimpsed the shards of a now-disintegrated folk-culture in the tales told by the old immigrant women; but there is no suggestion that this oral tradition had a wider currency. America, though, required a folk-culture. Bourne suggested that America needed a folk-tradition by which to integrate itself; Cather's art attempted to work out how that American folk-art might develop. In the wolf-story she showed how community might be created by stories.

The wolf-story also demonstrates that Americanisation was complexly related to the status of artistry in America. The story, as it is told and retold, shifts from the communal to the individual and then back to the communal; it is inherited from European folklore, refashioned by the individual storyteller and returned to the burgeoning American popular culture. There is an interplay between individual and folk forms of art. Cather here displays a broader awareness of Americanisation than the professed Americanisation experts, for whom the transplanting of Europeans into the US was largely a

1. Bourne, 91.
2. Bourne, 96.

matter of language acquisition and the sociology of settlement. In
Cather's hands Americanisation pans out into wider reflections on
culture itself. How do cultures evolve? Can they be transferred from
one part of the globe to another? Is it possible to belong to two cultures? Does the novelist inherit a storytelling form with its origins
in communal arts, or is the novelist's craft inevitably severed from
folk-culture?

These questions were discussed in Cather's intellectual milieu.
Louise Pound, one of Cather's oldest friends from her student days
at the University of Nebraska, went on to become an eminent literary critic and folklorist; her work was often concerned with the
survival of European oral culture in its new American home. The
friendship between Cather and Pound is usually discussed in biographical terms: their meeting as students, a possible lesbian relationship, and the resentment and estrangement that disrupted
their intimacy.[3] Such biographical investigation has its own validity, but it can lead to the occlusion of Pound's intellectual output,
a body of work that was prolific and important (and eventually
made her the first woman president of the Modern Language Association). Louise Pound's work on American folklore provides us with
analogues to Cather's fictionalisation of this subject. And furthermore, in reading Pound's scholarship on folklore and cultural
transmission we become aware of the contradictions and complexities of Cather's fiction. The scholar articulates a series of striking,
assertive propositions; the novelist, in contrast, explores the ambi-
valences of the Americanisation debate.

Pound was a specialist in ballads and oral literature. She became
an editor of *American Speech*, a journal that was started in 1926 and
examined American etymology, dialect and folklore; it published
pieces on the American transformations of transplanted European
culture, for instance Herbert H. Vaughan's 'Italian and Its Dialects
as Spoken in the United States'. Pound's own research traced the
importation of European culture into America. In the first volume
of *American Speech* she wrote a scholarly note on 'An American Text
of "Sir James the Rose"' in which she discussed an eighteenth-
century Scottish ballad that had made its way by oral transmission
to Lincoln, Nebraska. And she argued that Walt Whitman, rather
than being a demotically American poet, was a polyglot user of
Romance languages in his verse. Pound wrote the entry on 'Oral
Literature' for the Cambridge *History of American Literature* (1921),
a piece that declared 'the main interest of oral literature is historical. From it may be seen how songs and verse tales develop, how

3. Woodress, *Willa Cather*, pp. 84–8, and O'Brien, *Willa Cather*, pp. 129–31.

themes and styles are transmitted from generation to generation, and from one region or land to another.[4]

Pound speculates about cultural transmission: how are ballads communicated? Do they change as they filter down through the ages? Her hypothesis is that transmission—through time and across countries—produces artistic degeneration. In *Poetic Origins and the Ballad* (1921) Pound traced the American versions of ballads that had been collected by F. J. Child in his famous nineteenth-century anthology:

> Contrast, where dates are available, early pieces with late, or American versions with their Old World parents, and make inference from the mass. The crudity and the unliterary quality increase with the lapse of time, and by popular presentation. The epic completeness and effectiveness of the Child piece is likely to sink downward to simplicity or fragmentariness.[5]

Although Pound collected and wrote on American ballads, and was a contributor to the *Journal of American Folklore*, she often took a hard line on that material. 'Simplicity' and 'fragmentariness' are the fate of American oral literature, and the main reason for this is that the ballad in America exists 'by popular preservation'—that is, it is the product of *communal* artistic effort. Pound argues that the lack of individual creativity in the American ballads means that they are 'crude, structureless, incoherent, and lacking in striking and memorable qualities'. Earlier in *Poetic Origins* Pound had advanced the contentious theory that the ballad was, in its origin, the product of autonomous and solitary artistic endeavour rather than, as one might expect, a manifestation of collective creativity. Thus:

> That it is an absurd chronology which assumes that individuals have choral utterance before they are lyrically articulate as individuals, seems—extraordinarily enough—to have little weight with theorists of this school. Did primitive man sing, dance, and compose in a throng, while he was yet unable to do so as an individual?[6]

And she concludes her first chapter with a trenchant rejection of communal artistic creativity: 'the assumption that group power to sing, to compose songs, and to dance, precedes individual power to do these things, is fatuously speculative.'[7]

4. Herbert H. Vaughan, 'Italian and its Dialects,' *American Speech*, I (1926), 431–5. Louise Pound, 'An American Text' and 'Walt Whitman and the French language,' *American Speech*, I, 481–3 and 421–30. 'Oral Literature' in *A History of American Literature* ed. W. P. Trent, John Erskine *et al.*, 4 vols (Cambridge and New York, 1918–21), IV, 502–16.
5. Louise Pound, *Poetic Origins and the Ballad* (New York, 1921), p. 116.
6. *Poetic Origins*, p. 9.
7. *Poetic Origins*, p. 35.

Pound, then, revises the literary history of the ballad, undermining it as a group art and vaunting it as the expression of individuals. The ballad becomes a quasi-romantic form of self-expression. Poetic degeneration occurs in the shift from individual to wholly collective creativity; and this also happens in the cultural transmission from the old world to the new. The degeneration of the ballad presages further cultural disintegration, since communal art cannot survive for long: 'in general, real communalistic or people's poetry, composed in the collaborating manner sketched out by Professor Gunmere and Professor Kittredge, is too crude, too structureless, too unoriginal, too lacking in coherence and in striking or memorable qualities, to have much chance at survival'.[8] Working around the same issues that Cather had dealt with in *My Ántonia*—cultural transmission, individual as opposed to collective creativity—Pound reached pessimistic conclusions. To the central question of whether transmission inevitably entailed degeneration Pound could only answer that this was indeed the case. This makes her the overseer of the death of European folk-culture as it fades and disintegrates in its new home.

Comparing Pound's work on cultural transmission to Cather's, we can see the ambiguities and contradictions in the novelist's position. *My Ántonia*, published three years before the Americanisation speeches (and before nativism had a legislative impact in Nebraska), reads as a remarkably optimistic text about cultural transmission and continues to be relevant to America's ongoing controversies about assimilation and bilingualism. As we saw in the wolf-story—a tale that seems folkloric in its portrayal of lurid melodrama emerging from a humdrum, domestic context—in Cather's fiction the oral narratives of Europe continue to retain their power. Whereas Pound sees cultural transmission as a two-stage process of decline (individual creativity falling towards the communal; the old world becoming the new) Cather repositions these stages as a regenerative dialectic: folk-culture is renewed by being shunted to and fro between Europe and America, the individual and the community. The 'crisis in the life of the emigrants' diagnosed by the Chicago sociologists (1921) is, of course, present in the novel, but the crisis is also seen as a means to renewal: of folktales, of America, of the storyteller's art and, by implication, of the novelist's own creativity. She 'poeticized' the politics of Americanisation, taking the raw material (language learning, immigration, a multinational society) and showing how this all came down to the question of stories; and in so doing Cather showed that simply to *tell* a story can become a political act.

But at the same time there are foreshadowings of the failure of Americanisation. Intriguingly, while the wolf-story celebrates the

8. *Poetic Origins*, pp. 218–19.

gets the leftovers of America from her progressive family; she does not become Americanized; she does not absorb new ideals and ideas; she learns little about American foods and about ways for caring for her children in the new and very different climate. It is not unusual after fifteen years in this country to find English spoken by every member of the family but mother, and American clothes worn by all but mother. Even this superficial distinction closes many doors to her. Her grown-up daughter in a highly Americanized hat does not want to go shopping with her mother who still wears a black shawl over her head. It is not that the mother looks so ugly, but that the clinging to the old black shawl typifies to the daughter her mother's whole lack of understanding of the new world and the new ideas in which the daughter is living. The mother, far from being an aid in Americanizing her family, becomes a reactionary force. Sadly or obstinately as it may be, but always ignorantly, she combats every bit of Americanism that her husband and children try to force into the Southern European home. Yet when the husband passes tests entitling him to citizenship she becomes a full-fledged citizen also, as do her children—all prepared but the mother.

The United States Bureau of Education, the National Americanization Committee,[1] the Bureau of Naturalization and other organizations interested in the immigrant—in the elimination of illiteracy and in the conversion of the immigrant into the fairly educated citizen—turn to the club women of, the country for practical help.

What good those club women can do in the way of definite work to promote this real Americanization, especially among the immigrant women, can be placed somewhat in this wise: Find out how many immigrant women there are in the community. Do they speak English? Do their husbands? Are their husbands naturalized? Is the home a Southern European or an American home? Is the family American in its loyalty? Does it know enough of America to be loyal to it? Undoubtedly the children speak English; but what is the real nature of their Americanism? Did they learn it chiefly at school and at home—or on the corner and in the pool room? Reach the immigrant woman. It is the only way to produce American homes. See that she learns English. Through it she gets her first American contacts. But immigrant women can rarely attend night school. Organize for them, as has been done in a number of places, classes from two to three in the afternoon.

Just as immigrant men are taught English successfully only when the instruction deals with the subject matter of their daily life and work, so the method of teaching English to women can best be

1. The most important private organization promoting Americanization—the adaptation of immigrants to American social and political culture—during World War I and the 1920s [Ed.].

associated with methods of housekeeping, cooking, sewing, etc. Moreover, many American standards and customs can be brought to the immigrant woman in this way. She can really be initiated into Americanism and the language at once.

Especially at first it will be very difficult to get immigrant women to attend classes in the public schools—and so at first, and perhaps later also—there must be friendly visitors and teachers, "domestic educators" as they have been called, to carry the English language and American ways of caring for babies, ventilating the house, preparing American vegetables, instead of the inevitable cabbage, right into the new homes. The State of California has through its department of public education provided for these friendly visitors. Until other places with heavy immigrant population act with similar enlightenment, may not women's clubs step in and blaze the trail for a public education policy? Can they not pay domestic educators, or meet local boards of education half way in so doing? They can organize mothers' classes, cooking classes, sewing classes, classes for entertainment. Remember that immigrant women, if of different races, often know one another even less than they know Americans.

Make immigrant women good citizens. Help them make the homes they care for into American homes. Give their children American ideals at home, as well as in school. Make American standards of living prevail *throughout* the community, not merely in the "American sections." Above all show the rest of the community that this work of Americanizing immigrant mothers and immigrant homes is in the highest sense a work of citizenship, a part of a *national* patriotic ideal.

The relationship of Americanizing the foreign-born women in their homes to all the aspects of the development of our industries is tremendous, and will become more and more clear to us as being the work to which we should set our hands.

* * *

It is the privilege and it is the duty of club women to give their time, their powers of instruction and their enthusiasm to the work of getting our language and understanding of the principles of our common life into the hearts and minds of the foreign-born women. Once start these foreign women in the paths of learning and your task is not difficult; they believe in you, and after a little while will break away from their hidebound traditions and will become plastic for your moulding.

* * *

WOODROW WILSON

The Meaning of Citizenship[†]

This is the only country in the world which experiences constant and repeated rebirth. Other countries depend upon the multiplication of their own native people. This country is constantly drinking strength out of new sources by the voluntary association with it of great bodies of strong men and forward-looking women of other lands. And so by the gift of the free will of independent people it is being constantly renewed from generation to generation by the same process by which it was originally created. It is as if humanity had determined to see to it that this great Nation, founded for the benefit of humanity, should not lack for the allegiance of the people of the world.

You have just taken an oath of allegiance to the United States. Of allegiance to whom? Of allegiance to no one, unless it be to God— certainly not of allegiance to those who temporarily represent this great Government. You have taken an oath of allegiance to a great ideal, to a great body of principles, to a great hope of the human race. You have said, "We are going to America not only to earn a living, not only to seek the things which it was more difficult to obtain where we were born, but to help forward the great enterprises of the human spirit—to let men know that everywhere in the world there are men who will cross strange oceans and go where a speech is spoken which is alien to them if they can but satisfy their quest for what their spirits crave; knowing that whatever the speech there is but one longing and utterance of the human heart, and that is for liberty and justice." And while you bring all countries with you, you come with a purpose of leaving all other countries behind you—bringing what is best of their spirit, but not looking over your shoulders and seeking to perpetuate what you intended to leave behind in them. I certainly would not be one even to suggest that a man cease to love the home of his birth and the nation of his origin. These things are very sacred and ought not to be put out of our hearts, but it is one thing to love the place where you were born and it is another thing to dedicate yourself to the place to which you go. You can not dedicate yourself to America unless you become in every respect and with every purpose of your will thorough Americans. You can not become thorough Americans if you think of yourselves in groups. America does not consist of groups. A man who thinks of himself as belonging to a particular national group in America has not yet become an

† Reprinted in Talbot, ed., *Americanization* (1917). Wilson (1856–1924), twenty-eighth President of the United States, gave this address to newly naturalized citizens in Philadelphia on May 10, 1915.

American, and the man who goes among you to trade upon your nationality is no worthy son to live under the Stars and Stripes.

My urgent advice to you would be not only always to think first of America, but always also to think first of humanity. You do not love humanity if you seek to divide humanity into jealous camps. Humanity can be welded together only by love, by sympathy, by justice, not by jealousy and hatred. I am sorry for the man who seeks to make personal capital out of the passions of his fellow-men. He has lost the touch and ideal of America, for America was created to unite mankind by those passions which lift and not by the passions which separate and debase. We came to America, either ourselves or in the persons of our ancestors, to better the ideals of men, to make them see finer things than they had seen before, to get rid of the things that divide and to make sure of the things that unite. It was but an historical accident no doubt that this great country was called the "United States"; yet I am very thankful that it has that word "United" in its title, and the man who seeks to divide man from man, group from group, interest from interest in this great Union is striking at its very heart.

It is a very interesting circumstance to me, in thinking of those of you who have just sworn allegiance to this great Government, that you were drawn across the ocean by some beckoning finger of hope, by some belief, by some vision of a new kind of justice, by some expectation of a better kind of life. No doubt you have been disappointed in some of us. Some of us are very disappointing. No doubt you have found that justice in the United States goes only with a pure heart and a right purpose as it does everywhere else in the world. No doubt what you found here did not seem touched for you, after all, with the complete beauty of the ideal which you had conceived beforehand. But remember this: If we had grown at all poor in the ideal, you brought some of it with you. A man does not go out to seek the thing that is not in him. A man does not hope for the thing that he does not believe in, and if some of us have forgotten what America believed in, you, at any rate, imported in your own hearts a renewal of the belief. That is the reason that I, for one, make you welcome. If I have in any degree forgotten what America was intended for, I will thank God if you will remind me. I was born in America. You dreamed dreams of what America was to be, and I hope you brought the dreams with you. No man that does not see visions will ever realize any high hope or undertake any high enterprise. Just because you brought dreams with you, America is more likely to realize dreams such as you brought. You are enriching us if you came expecting us to be better than we are.

See, my friends, what that means. It means that Americans must have a consciousness different from the consciousness of every other nation in the world. I am not saying this with even the slighest thought of criticism of other nations. You know how it is with a family. A family gets centered on itself if it is not careful and is less interested in the neighbors than it is in its own members. So a nation that is not constantly renewed out of new sources is apt to have the narrowness and prejudice of a family; whereas, America must have this consciousness, that on all sides it touches elbows and touches hearts with all the nations of mankind. The example of America must be a special example. The example of America must be the example not merely of peace because it will not fight, but of peace because peace is the healing and elevating influence of the world and strife is not. There is such a thing as a man being too proud to fight. There is such a thing as a nation being so right that it does not need to convince others by force that it is right.

You have come into this great Nation voluntarily seeking something that we have to give, and all that we have to give is this: We can not exempt you from work; no man is exempt from work anywhere in the world. We can not exempt you from the strife and the heartbreaking burden of the struggle of the day; that is common to mankind everywhere. We can not exempt you from the loads that you must carry; we can only make them light by the spirit in which they are carried. That is the spirit of hope, it is the spirit of liberty, it is the spirit of justice.

When I was asked, therefore, by the Mayor and the committee that accompanied him to come up from Washington to meet this great company of newly admitted citizens I could not decline the invitation. I ought not to be away from Washington, and yet I feel that it has renewed my spirit as an American to be here. In Washington men tell you so many things every day that are not so, and I like to come and stand in the presence of a great body of my fellow citizens, whether they have been my fellow citizens a long time or a short time, and drink, as it were, out of the common fountains with them and go back feeling what you have so generously given me—the sense of your support and of the living vitality in your hearts of the great ideals which have made America the hope of the world.

PETER ROBERTS

From The Problem of Americanization[†]

* * * The alien who does not know the English language will never understand America. Of course, many men who know the language

† From The Problem of Americanization (New York: Macmillan, 1920), pp. 68–70.

in every particular are as far from the spirit of America as imperialism is from democracy, but speaking generally of the immigrants coming from foreign-speaking countries to America, we affirm that they will never understand the spirit of this country unless they understand the language of the court and the press, the pulpit and the forum. They may learn much about American history, they may be versed in the form of American government, but they will never understand Americans unless they can converse in English, read the American newspaper and magazine, and freely mingle in American society. The spirit of America is in the atmosphere where her sons work, where they play, where they discuss the questions of the hour, where they settle the differences that arise in the social, industrial, and political arena, and the man who remains outside this atmosphere because of the barrier of language will remain a stranger in a strange land.

When we emphasize the importance of learning English, it does not mean that the foreign-speaking in America should forget their mother tongue, it does not mean that they cannot read books in their native language, but it does mean that it is to their interest to speak, read, and write English, and that this is essential before they can understand America and enter into the life of the country.

We do not propose in this connection to discuss this question from its varied sides. We may state, however, that it is important for the aliens of foreign speech to learn English in order to increase their earnings and to be able to travel freely from place to place in America. It is equally important in order that they may gain the economic advantages in trade and commerce. But our prime object just now is to emphasize the fact that an alien will never understand America if he does not understand the language in which the country makes its laws, carries on its business, and publishes its news. I have known thousands of workers in America, who do not know English, who earn good wages and who do good work; possibly they could not do that job better or get higher wages if they knew our tongue; there are in the country thousands of foreign-born men who lead model lives as husbands and fathers who do not speak our language; these would not be better husbands or more provident fathers if they spoke English fluently; but if they expect to become intelligent American citizens and take part in the social and political life of America, they must come out of their exclusiveness and be able to talk, read, and write the language of the country.

* * *

HENRY PRATT FAIRCHILD

Americanization[†]

With these general principles in mind we may now continue our analysis of assimilation with particular reference to the United States, not
only because this study is undertaken primarily from the American
point of view, but because the United States has been and is the
greatest laboratory for experiments in assimilation that the world
has ever known.

We have seen how the World War had the effect of shattering
the prevailing complacency of the American people with reference to
the facts of assimilation, and dispelling the delusion that there was
some magical potency about American soil or American life which
would produce without conscious effort on the part of anybody a
result which no other people has ever attempted to accomplish on a
comparable scale, and which no other people has succeeded in
accomplishing even on a much reduced scale. We realized at last
that instead of passing through this wholesome transformation our
foreign population had to a large extent formed itself into segregated,
distinct colonies, with a life and atmosphere much more European
than American, which could be compared to nothing so much as to
great undigested lumps in the organism of our body politic. Cases
were observed in which even the third generation could not speak
English. We comprehended that great rifts had already been made in
our national unity and that much more serious ones were impending
unless something were done. It was natural in such an emergency
that we should turn to our favorite national expedient of forming a
committee. Many committees were formed. Prominent among them
were the National Americanization Committee and the Committee
for Immigrants in America, not easily distinguishable to the outsider.
Under the leadership particularly of these two committees there
developed the great Americanization Movement, one of the most
remarkable and significant social developments in this country in
many years. Summarily stated, the genius of this movement was the
recognition of the fact that assimilation had not been produced by
the spontaneous operation of uncontrolled forces in previous years,
and the determination to devise and put in operation machinery that
would produce the result by deliberate, purposeful means. It was
noteworthy that the leaders of this movement included some of the

† From *Immigration: A World Movement and Its American Significance* (New York: Macmillan, 1913, 1925), pp. 414–33. Fairchild (1880–1956), sociologist and educator, a
proponent of assimilation, was president of the American Eugenics Society.

very persons who in the past had been most vociferous in denying the need of restriction on the ground of the alleged fact of assimilation, and who now, while proclaiming the failure of assimilation, nevertheless, for reasons best known to themselves, continued to oppose all measures for restriction.

One of the first effects of the Americanization movement[1] was a great wave of relief which spread over the people of the United States. It hushed the rising fears as to the consequences of the immigration of the past and the future. Many persons sank back again into a state of lethargy, saying to themselves, in effect, "Put your mind at ease now. There is a committee at work on the problem, and all will soon be well." Others, with a different temperament or a different conception of social responsibility, threw themselves enthusiastically into the movement, some of them as professionals and others as volunteers, all determined to do their best to see that this new expedient and program should be effective. This sedative effect upon the public consciousness was due in part to the hypnotizing jangle of an unfamiliar term—"Americanization"—and partly to a naïve general confidence in leadership and expedients, resting, of course, upon a natural and inevitable incomprehension of the magnitude and complexity of the task to be accomplished.

The possibility of success of such a movement, granting the best possible auspices, depends of course upon the very nature of assimilation itself. For there was nothing new about Americanization, except possibly the word. The idea was as old as migration. Americanization is, and can be, nothing more—nor less—than assimilation into America. The practical questions therefore are: How is assimilation accomplished? Can it be accomplished or accelerated by deliberate means? If so, what are those means?

Since the receiving body in all true assimilation is a nationality, the America referred to in this connection must be a nationality. It is a body of ideas, ideals, beliefs, standards, customs, habits, traditions—a great composite of spiritual values possessed by, and possessing, a certain group of people. It is not, as some would seemingly have us believe, merely a section of the earth's surface. A statement frequently made by the champions of the so-called "liberal" view of immigration, and always good for at least one round of applause, is that we are all immigrants or the children of immigrants, and the only real Americans are the Red Indians. If America is merely a geographical term this statement is true; if America is anything more it is a grotesque distortion of the truth. If that were all, the mere fact of coming to live on a certain section of the North American continent

---

1. Broadly based movement, originating in the early twentieth century, committed to fostering the assimilation of recent immigrants—particularly from Southern and Eastern Europe—into American society and values [*Ed.*].

would be all there was to Americanization. Nor is America just an aggregation of people. If it were, simply making oneself a part of that group would constitute Americanization. Nor, finally, is America a political unit and nothing more. If that were so the act of becoming an active unit in that organization by the process of naturalization would be Americanization. But the War demonstrated all too plainly that many persons who had gone through the forms of naturalization and enjoyed citizenship in the United States were far from being true Americans.

America is a nationality. It was not found waiting, ready made on the soil of the New World, by Columbus nor by the pioneers who founded the settlements of Jamestown and Plymouth. America was brought over in the Mayflower and in those other frail craft which carried the founders of a new people. It was an idea of government, a conception of social relationships, a code of personal behavior, and a set of standards of final values. It was a living, vital, though incorporeal thing. It was a growing thing, and it has continued to grow ever since. Many attempts have been made to particularize the qualities of the American nationality. It is a difficult task, and one not necessary to undertake in this connection. The important thing is to realize that America is a nationality, and that the true Americans are those who embody the qualities of that nationality. Americanism is not a matter of birth or ancestry. It is a question of spiritual affiliation, loyalty, and allegiance. Any one who responds implicitly, spontaneously, and unreservedly to the appeal of American values is an American.

In accordance with the principle already established that every individual has to be nationalized it follows that every individual must be Americanized before he becomes an American. This is just as true of the person born on American soil as of the person born on foreign soil. The difference between the native and the foreigner is that in the case of the former Americanization takes place naturally, spontaneously, and unconsciously from the simple fact that he begins life and continues it in the American environment, while the foreigner, by a similar process, has already been Italianized, Englishized, or Germanized before he undertakes migration, and has to rid himself of an original nationality before he can acquire, or while he is acquiring, the nationality of his adopted land. Americanization takes place in either case from the fact of living in America. If the foreigner lives in America, assimilation will assuredly take place to the extent determined by his age and the degree of incompatibility of his original nationality with the American.

But does the foreigner actually live in America? What is it to live in America? It is already clear that to live in America is to live in a certain national atmosphere, to live in close, intimate, continuous contact with a certain social environment. It is to live in natural, spontaneous, unforced association with real Americans. Thus stated, it becomes plain enough why assimilation so lamentably failed in the past. Only a very small proportion of immigrants in recent years, although residing on American soil in the midst of American Communities, were actually living in America. Their contacts with the American environment were of the most restricted, tenuous, and often artificial sort. In innumerable cases they were limited almost exclusively to the economic interests, and even there the American influence was almost negligible. The typical immigrant was hired, bossed, paid, and fired by an individual scarcely more American than himself.

It was unfortunate, though perhaps not surprising, that the early leaders of the Americanization movement, analyzing the differences which marked the foreigner off from the American, should have been particularly impressed by the disparity in knowledge between the two. There were certain things which the American knew, and which seemed to be essential to his Americanism, which the immigrant did not know. Prominent among them was the English language, and in the second rank some elementary facts about United States history and civics. As attention was turned to the foreign women differences were observed in knowledge as to cookery, millinery, and the care of children. So it appeared that the first step in Americanization was to teach the foreigner some of these things which he did not know, and Americanization consequently from the very beginning took on a pronounced educational aspect. The immigrant was flooded with lessons, lectures, and literature. Night schools were opened, and classes of various sorts organized to teach some of the fundamental subjects. Preëminent among all these enterprises was the teaching of English, and as the early enthusiasm gradually waned the subsidiary features tended to fade into the background until the Americanization movement became essentially a program for teaching English to foreigners.

All of this was clearly good. The more the immigrant knows, the better. But the distressing feature of the whole undertaking, and the feature which accounts primarily for the relative failure of the movement up to date, was the complete misconception of the nature of assimilation itself. From the preceding analysis the fact stands out clearly that Americanization is not an educational process.[2] It is not what one knows but how one feels that affiliates him with a certain nationality. It is a matter of the emotions rather than the intellect. This becomes clear by reflecting that there were plenty of Germans

2. In spite of the fact that one of the best books on the subject so states categorically in the opening sentence. Bogardus, Emory S., *Essentials of Americanization*, p. 11. [*Author's note.*]

during the war period who knew English perfectly and who perhaps knew much more about American history and civics than many native born citizens who were nevertheless at heart thoroughly German, not American. If education were all, Americanization could in many cases be better accomplished by courses given in schools in European countries than on American soil.

The mistake made by the early Americanizers, and perpetuated among many of their followers, was the common one of mistaking a means for an end. Knowledge is not assimilation, but it is a necessary and indispensable prerequisite to assimilation. Assimilation, being a matter of responding to the influences of a social environment, is largely a matter of the communication of ideas. And in order that ideas may be communicated there must be a common means of communication. The English language is unquestionably the first gateway which leads to Americanization. But it is not Americanization. So also, before one can feel loyalty to a nationality he must perforce know something about it, about its history, its development, and its organized aspects. But this knowledge is not assimilation. All praise to every sincere, devoted teacher of English to foreigners, and to every conscientious Americanization worker in whatever field! They are doing a work which could ill be dispensed with, without which Americanization would be an impossibility. It is our fault more than theirs that the idea has become established that their work is Americanization or that it unaided produces Americanization. We have shifted our responsibility onto shoulders which could by no possibility bear the burden.

The great question then arises, Can assimilation be accomplished by any deliberate, artificial methods whatsoever? Particularly, can it be accomplished by the efforts of professional workers? It needs no further argument to demonstrate that the answer to this second question is an emphatic, No! Americanization is the business of all of us. As already stated, the service of trained workers, both professional and volunteer, is indispensable. The task could hardly be accomplished without them. But they alone cannot accomplish the task. Americanization is the result of contact with a social environment, and a special group of trained workers cannot possibly embody, nor even adequately represent, a whole environment. More than this, trained workers are in contact with any particular immigrant only a small fraction of the time, while the acquirement of a new nationality from an unfamiliar environment requires continuous contact.

The greater question is whether, even if the whole community were enlisted, Americanization could be accomplished simply by specific, deliberate, artificial or semi-artificial activities organized for the particular purpose. To this question, also, the answer seems to be an unqualified negative. To be Americanized, let us repeat, any one, native or foreigner, must *live in America*. The process of Americanizing the foreigner is much more difficult than that of Americanizing the native, because the foreigner not only has to acquire a nationality but he has to get rid of one already acquired. For the authority of nationality is absolute until it is brought into contrast with some other nationality, and then the transformation of conviction and the feeling of rightness, and the transfer of loyalty and devotion from one object to another, involves tearing up many of the deepest sentiments by the roots.

*   *   *

The foregoing critical analysis of the Americanization Movement should not be allowed to obscure the many excellent results which it has brought about. It is impossible that so many earnest, devoted workers should engage in manifold activities with the sincere intent of helping their foreign neighbors and their own country without producing many positive benefits. If there had been nothing more than the emphasis on the teaching of English that alone would have been enough to justify the effort expended. But there has been much more. A new sympathy with the immigrant and his problems has been developed. The value of foreign handicrafts, folk music and dancing, and aesthetic feeling has come to be appreciated. The naturalization procedure in many courts has been made a more significant matter, and a new dignity and solemnity has been added to the ceremony of conferring citizenship. An effort has been made to eliminate some of the arbitrary and superfluous obstacles in the way of securing naturalization on the part of one who is really fit to receive it. It would be a calamity if these efforts were suspended. But they can be fully productive only as they are associated with a sound conception of the nature of the assimilative process itself.

The attempt of the United States to build up a unified nation out of unlimited numbers of unselected European peoples was a magnificent venture, but it was also, as it was inevitably doomed to be, a magnificent failure. No people on earth could have achieved the result under the conditions which prevailed. Fortunately, before it was altogether too late, the stream of raw material was drastically cut down at the source.[3] There is still a grave problem before us, what with the enormous unassimilated elements already in our midst, and the yearly augmentation that will still come under the new law. But we may be permitted to hope that it is now a problem of manageable

---

3. The Immigration Act of 1924 drastically limited the number of immigrants that could be admitted into the United States. One of its major effects was to reduce the flow of immigrants coming from Southern and Eastern Europe. [*Ed.*]

proportions, and that America may still continue to be a real nation, never finished, never perfect, but growing and developing sturdily and symmetrically along its own characteristic lines and out of its own native soundness and virility.[4]

EDWARD ALSWORTH ROSS

American Blood and Immigrant Blood[†]

As I sought to show, near the end of my initial chapter, the conditions of settlement of this country caused those of uncommon energy and venturesomeness to outmultiply the rest of the population. Thus came into existence the pioneering breed; and this breed increased until it is safe to estimate that fully half of white Americans with native grandparents have one or more pioneers among their ancestors. Whatever valuable race traits distinguish the American people from the parent European stocks are due to the efflorescence of this breed. Without it there would have been little in the performance of our people to arrest the attention of the world. Now we confront the melancholy spectacle of this pioneer breed being swamped and submerged by an overwhelming tide of latecomers from the old-world hive. In Atlanta still seven out of eight white men had American parents; in Nashville and Richmond, four out of five; in Kansas City, two out of three; and in Los Angeles, one out of two; but in Detroit, Cleveland, and Paterson one man out of five had American parents; in Chicago and New York, one out of six; in Milwaukee, one out of seven; and in Fall River, one out of nine. *Certainly never since the colonial era have the foreign-born and their children formed so large a proportion of the American people as at the present moment.* I scanned 368 persons as they passed me in Union Square, New York, at a time when the garment-workers of the Fifth Avenue lofts were returning to their homes. Only thirty-eight of these passers-by had the type of face one would find at a county fair in the West or South.

In the six or seven hundred thousand strangers that yearly join themselves to us for good and all, there are to be found, of course, every talent and every beauty. Out of the steerage come persons as

---

4. The question is often raised whether unity of religion is indispensable to nationality. The general answer seems to be that a nationality can dispense with unity in some particulars if it has it in enough others. The more points of unity, the stronger the nationality, of course. But unity of religion is not essential. In the case of the United States it seems to have been definitely settled that there is not to be unity of religion. This makes it all the more important to preserve the maximum unity in other particulars. [*Author's note.*]

† From *The Old World in the New: The Significance of Past and Present Immigration to the American People* (New York: Century Co., 1914), pp. 282–92, 299–304. Ross (1866–1951), sociologist, educator, and eugenicist, supported the restriction of immigration to the United States.

fine and noble as any who have trodden American soil. Any adverse characterization of an immigrant stream implies, then, only that the trait is relatively frequent, not that it is universal.

In this sense it is fair to say that the blood now being injected into the veins of our people is "sub-common." To one accustomed to the aspect of the normal American population, the Caliban type[1] shows up with a frequency that is startling. Observe immigrants not as they come travel-wan up the gang-plank, nor as they issue toil-begrimed from pit's mouth or mill gate, but in their gatherings, washed, combed, and in their Sunday best. You are struck by the fact that from ten to twenty per cent. are hirsute, low-browed, big-faced persons of obviously low mentality. Not that they suggest evil. They simply look out of place in black clothes and stiff collar, since clearly they belong in skins, in wattled huts at the close of the Great Ice Age. These oxlike men are descendants of those *who always stayed behind*. Those in whom the soul burns with the dull, smoky flame of the pine-knot stuck to the soil, and are now thick in the sluiceways of immigration. Those in whom it burns with a clear, luminous flame have been attracted to the cities of the home land and, having prospects, have no motive to submit themselves to the hardships of the steerage.

To the practised eye, the physiognomy of certain groups unmistakably proclaims inferiority of type. I have seen gatherings of the foreign-born in which narrow and sloping foreheads were the rule. The shortness and smallness of the crania were very noticeable. There was much facial asymmetry. Among the women, beauty, aside from the fleeting, epidermal bloom of girlhood, was quite lacking. In every face there was something wrong—lips thick, mouth coarse, upper lip too long, cheek-bones too high, chin poorly formed, the bridge of the nose hollowed, the base of the nose tilted, or else the whole face prognathous. There were so many sugar-loaf heads, moon-faces, slit mouths, lantern-jaws, and goose-bill noses that one might imagine a malicious jinn had amused himself by casting human beings in a set of skew-molds discarded by the Creator.

Our captains of industry give a crowbar to the immigrant with a number nine face on a number six head, make a dividend out of him, and imagine that is the end of the matter. They overlook that this man will beget children in his image—two or three times as many as the American—and that these children will in turn beget children. They chuckle at having opened an inexhaustible store of cheap tools and, lo! the American people is being altered for all time by these tools. Once before, captains of industry took a hand in making this people. Colonial planters imported Africans to hoe in the sun, to "develop" the tobacco, indigo, and rice plantations. Then, as now,

1. Caliban is an animal-like character in Shakespeare's *The Tempest*. [Ed.]

business-minded men met with contempt the protests of a few ideal-
ists against their way of "building up the country."

Those promoters of prosperity are dust, but they bequeathed a situation which in four years wiped out more wealth than two hundred years of slavery had built up, and which presents today the one
unsolvable problem in this country. Without likening immigrants to
negroes, one may point out how the latter-day employer resembles
the old-time planter in his blindness to the effects of his labor policy upon the blood of the nation.

Immigration and Good Looks

It is reasonable to expect an early falling off in the frequency of good
looks in the American people. It is unthinkable that so many persons with crooked faces, coarse mouths, bad noses, heavy jaws, and
low foreheads can mingle their heredity with ours without making
personal beauty yet more rare among us than it actually is. So much
ugliness is at last bound to work to the surface. One ought to see
the horror on the face of a fine-looking Italian or Hungarian consul
when one asks him innocently, "Is the physiognomy of these immigrants typical of your people?" That the new immigrants are inferior in looks to the old immigrants may be seen by comparing, in a
Labor Day parade, the faces of the cigar-makers and the garment-
workers with those of the teamsters, piano-movers and steam-fitters.

* * *

Vitality

"The Slavs," remarks a physician, "are immune to certain kinds of
dirt. They can stand what would kill a white man." The women do
not have puerperal fever, as our women would under their conditions. The men violate every sanitary law, yet survive. The Slavs come
from a part of the world in which never more than a third of the
children have grown up. In every generation, dirt, ignorance, superstition, and lack of medical attention have winnowed out all but the
sturdiest. Among Americans, two-thirds of the children grow up,
which means that we keep alive many of the tenderer, who would
certainly have perished in the Slavic world. There is, however, no
illusion more grotesque than to suppose that our people is to be
rejuvenated by absorbing these millions of hardy peasantry, that, to
quote a champion of free immigration, "The new-comers in America
will bring fresh, vigorous blood to a rather sterile and inbred stock."
The fact is that the immigrant stock quickly loses here its distinctive
ruggedness. The physicians practising among rural Poles notice a
great saving of infant life under American conditions. Says one: "I

see immigrant women and their grown daughters having infants at the same time, and the children of the former will die of the things that the children of the latter get well of. The same holds when the second generation and the third bear at the same time. The latter save their children better than the former." The result is a marked softening of fiber between the immigrant women and the grand-daughters. Among the latter are many of a finer, but frailer, mold, who would be ruined in health if they worked in the field the third day after confinement, as grandmother did. In the old country there were very few of this type who survived infancy in a peasant family.

There is, then, no lasting revitalization from this tide of life. If our people has become weak, no transfusion of peasants will set it on its feet again; for their blood too, soon thins. The trouble, if you call it that, is not with the American people, but with the wide dif-fusion among us of a civilized manner of life. Where the struggle for existence is mitigated not merely for the upper quarter of soci-ety, as formerly in the Old World, but for the upper three-quarters, as in this and other democratic countries, the effects of keeping alive the less hardy are bound to show. The remedy for the alleged degeneration of our stock is simple, but drastic. If we want only constitutions that can stand hardship and abuse, let us treat the young as they are treated in certain poverty-stricken parts of Rus-sia. Since the mother is obliged to pass the day at work in distant fields, the nursling of a few months is left alone, crawling about on the dirt floor of the hut and comforting itself, when it cries from hunger, by sucking poultices of chewed bread tied to its hands and feet.

*   *   *

Race Suicide[2]

The fewer brains they have to contribute, the lower the place immi-grants take among us, and the lower the place they take, the faster they multiply. In 1890, in our cities, a thousand foreign-born women could show 565 children under five years of age to 309 children shown by a thousand native women. By 1900 the contribution of the foreign women had risen to 612, and that of the American women had declined to 296. From such figures some argue that the "sterile" Americans need the immigrants in order to supply popula-tion. It would be nearer the truth to argue that the competition of low-standard immigrants is the root cause of the mysterious "sterility"

2. The widespread belief and fear in the late-nineteenth and early twentieth century that Anglo-Saxons were not equaling the birth rate of immigrants and nonwhites, whose fer-tility would lead to their dominance in American society. [Ed.]

of Americans. Certainly their record down to 1830 proved the Americans to be as fertile a race as ever lived, and the decline in their fertility coincides in time and in locality with the advent of the immigrant flood. In the words of General Francis A. Walker,[3] "Not only did the decline in the native element, as a whole, take place in singular correspondence with the excess of foreign arrivals, but it occurred chiefly in just those regions"—"in those States and in the very counties," he says elsewhere—"to which those newcomers most frequently resorted."

"Our immigrants," says a superintendent of charities, "often come here with no standards whatever. In their homes you find no sheets on the bed, no slips on the pillows, no cloth on the table, and no towels save old rags. Even in the mud-floor cabins of the poorest negroes of the South you find sheets, pillow-slips, and towels, for by serving and associating with the whites the blacks have gained standards. But many of the foreigners have no means of getting our home standards after they are here. No one shows them. They can't see into American homes, and no Americans associate with them." The Americans or Americanized immigrants who are obliged to live on wages fixed by the competition of such people must cut somewhere. If they do not choose to "live in a pig-pen and bring up one's children like pigs," they will save their standards by keeping down the size of the family. Because he keeps them clean, neatly dressed, and in school, children are an economic burden to the American. Because he lets them run wild and puts them to work early, children are an asset to the low-standard foreigner.

When a more-developed element is obliged to compete on the same economic plane with a less-developed element, the standards of cleanliness or decency or education cherished by the advanced element act on it like a slow poison. William does not leave as many children as 'Tonio, because he will not huddle his family into one room, eat macaroni off a bare board, work his wife barefoot in the field, and keep his children weeding onions instead of at school. Even moral standards may act as poison. Once the women raisin-packers at Fresno, California, were American-born. Now the American women are leaving because of the low moral tone that prevails in the working force by reason of the coming in of foreigners with lax notions of propriety. The coarseness of speech and behavior among the packers is giving raisin-packing a bad name, so that American women are quitting the work and taking the next best job. Thus the very decency of the native is a handicap to success and to fecundity.

3. After serving in the Civil War, Walker (1840–1897) became an influential educator, statistician, and social and economic commentator. He favored the curtailing of immigration, writing the essay "Restriction of Immigration" for *The Atlantic* in 1896. [*Ed.*]

As they feel the difficulty of keeping up their standards on a Slav wage, the older immigrant stocks are becoming sterile, even as the old Americans became sterile. In a generation complaint will be heard that the Slavs, too, are shirking big families, and that we must admit prolific Persians, Uzbegs, and Bokhariots, in order to offset the fatal sterility that attacks every race after it has become Americanized. Very truly says a distinguished economist, in praise of immigration: "The cost of rearing children in the United States is rapidly rising. In many, perhaps in most cases, it is simpler, speedier, and cheaper to import labor than to breed it." In like vein it is said that "a healthy immigrant lad of eighteen is a clear $1000 added to the national wealth of the United States."

Just so. "The Roman world was laughing when it died." Any couple or any people that does not feel it has anything to transmit to its children may well reason in such fashion. A couple may reflect, "It is simpler, speedier, and cheaper for us to adopt orphans than to produce children of our own." A nation may reason, "Why burden ourselves with the rearing of children? Let them perish unborn in the womb of time. The immigrants will keep up the population." A people that has no more respect for its ancestors and no more pride of race than this deserves the extinction that surely awaits it.

HORACE M. KALLEN

Democracy vs. the Melting Pot[†]

* * *

Immigrants appear to pass through four phases in the course of being automatically Americanized. In the first phase they exhibit economic eagerness, the greedy hunger of the unfed. Since external differences are a handicap in the economic struggle, they "assimilate," seeking thus to facilitate the attainment of economic independence. Once the proletarian level of such independence is reached, the process of assimilation slows down and tends to come to a stop. The immigrant group is still a national group, modified, sometimes improved, by environmental influences, but otherwise a solidary spiritual unit,

† From *Culture and Democracy in the United States* (New York: Boni & Liveright, 1924), pp. 114–25. Copyright 1924 by Boni & Liveright, Inc., renewed 1952 by Horace M. Kallen. Used by permission of Liveright Publishing Corporation. Kallen (1882–1974), a progressive American philosopher, writer, and educator, is credited with coining the term "cultural pluralism" to denote a society in which individual groups retain and express their values and identities rather than conforming to a dominant culture. This essay originally appeared in *The Nation*, February 25, 1915.

which is seeking to find its way out on its own social level. This search brings to light permanent group distinctions and the immigrant, like the Anglo-Saxon American, is thrown back upon himself and his ancestry. Then a process of dissimulation begins. The arts, life and ideals of the nationality become central and paramount; ethnic and national differences change in status from disadvantages to distinctions. All the while the immigrant has been uttering his life in the English language and behaving like an American in matters economic and political, and continues to do so. The institutions of the Republic have become the liberating cause and the background for the rise of the cultural consciousness and social autonomy of the immigrant Irishman, German, Scandinavian, Jew, Pole or Bohemian. On the whole, the automatic processes of Americanization have not repressed nationality. These processes have liberated nationality, and more or less gratified it.

Hence, what troubles Mr. Ross[1] and so many other American citizens of British stock is not really inequality; what troubles them is *difference*. Only things that are *alike* in fact and not abstractly, and only men that are alike in origin and in feeling and not abstractly, can possess the equality which maintains that inward unanimity of sentiment and outlook which make a homogeneous national culture. The writers of the American Declaration of Independence and of the Constitution of the United States were not confronted by the practical fact of ethnic dissimilarity among the whites of the country. Their descendants are confronted by it. Its existence, acceptance and development are some of the inevitable consequences of the democratic principle on which the American theory of government is based, and the result at the present writing is to many worthies very unpleasant. Democratism and the federal principle have worked together with economic greed and ethnic snobbishness to people the land with all the nationalities of Europe, and to convert the early American nationality into the present American *nation*. For in effect the United States are in the process of becoming a federal state not merely as a union of geographical and administrative unities, but also as a coöperation of cultural diversities, as a federation or commonwealth of national cultures.

Given, in the economic order, the principle of *laissez-faire* applied to a capitalistic society, in contrast with the manorial and guild systems of the past and the socialistic utopias of the future, the economic consequences are the same, whether in America, full of all Europe, or in Britain, full of the English, Scotch and Welsh. Given, in the political order, the principles that all men are equal and that

---

1. Edward Alsworth Ross, author of *The Old World in the New: The Significance of Past and Present Immigration to the United States* (1914), which advocated strengthened assimilation and restricted immigration. See excerpt from Ross in this volume, pp. 291–96. [*Ed.*]

each, consequently, under the law at least, shall have the opportunity to make the most of himself, the control of the machinery of government by the plutocracy is a foregone conclusion. *Laissez-faire* coupled with unprecedented bountiful natural resources has turned the minds of people and government to wealth alone, and in the haste to accumulate wealth considerations of human quality have been neglected and forgotten, the action of government has been remedial rather than constructive, and Mr. Ross's "peasantism" or the growth of an expropriated, degraded industrial class, dependent on the factory rather than on land, has been rapid and vexatious.

The problems which these conditions give rise to are important, but not of primary importance. Although they have occupied the minds of all American political theorists, they are problems of means, of instruments, not of ends. They concern the conditions of life, not the *kind of life,* and there appears to have been a general assumption that only one kind of human life is possible in the United States of America. But the same democracy which underlies the evils of the economic order underlies also the evils, and the promise, of the cultural order. Because no individual is merely an individual, the political autonomy of the individual has presaged and is beginning to realize in these United States the spiritual autonomy of his group. The process is as yet far from fruition. America is, in fact, at the parting of the ways. Two genuine social alternatives are before Americans, either of which they may realize if they will. In social construction the will is father to the fact, for the fact is hardly ever anything more, under the grace of accident and luck, than the concord or conflict of wills. What do Americans *will* to make of the United States—a unison, singing the old British theme "America," the America of the New England School? or a harmony, in which that theme shall be dominant, perhaps, among others, but one among many, not the only one?

The mind reverts helplessly to the historic attempts at unison in Europe—the heroic failure of the pan-Hellenists, of the Romans, the disintegration and the diversification of the Christian church, for a time the most successful unison in history; the present-day failures of Germany and of Russia. In the United States, however, the whole social situation is favorable as it has never been at any time elsewhere—everything is favorable but the basic law of America itself, and the spirit of the American institutions. To achieve unison—it can be achieved—would be to violate these. For the end determines the means and the means transmute the end, and this end would involve no other means than those used by Germany in Poland, in Schleswig-Holstein, and Alsace-Lorraine; by Russia in the Jewish Pale, in Poland, in Finland; by Austria among the Slavs; by Turkey among the Arabs, Armenians and Greeks. Fundamentally it would require the complete nationalization of education, the abolition of every form of parochial and private school, the abolition of instruction in other tongues than English, and the concentration of the teaching of history and literature upon the English tradition. The other institutions of society would require treatment analogous to that administered by Germany to her European acquisitions. And all of this, even if meeting with no resistance, would not completely guarantee the survival as a unison of the older Americanism. For the program would be applied to diverse ethnic types under changing conditions, and the reconstruction that, with the best will, they might spontaneously make of the tradition would more likely than not be a far cry from the original. It is, already.

The notion that the program might be realized by radical and even forced miscegenation, by the creation of the melting-pot by law, and thus by the development of the new "American race" is, as Mr. Ross points out, as mystically optimistic as it is ignorant. In historic times so far as is known no new ethnic types have originated, and from what is known of breeding there comes no assurance that the old types will disappear in favor of the new. Rather will there be an addition of a new type, if it is stable and succeeds in surviving, to the already existing older ones. Biologically, life does not unify; biologically life diversifies; and it is sheer ignorance to apply social analogies to biological processes. In any event, we know what the qualities and capacities of existing types are; we know how by education to do something toward the conversion of what is evil in them and the conservation of what is good. "The American race" is a totally unknown thing; to presume that it will be better because (if we like to persist in the illusion that it is coming) it will be later, is no different from imagining that contemporary Poland is better than ancient Greece. There is nothing more to be said to the pious stupidity that identifies recency with goodness. The unison to be achieved cannot be a unison of ethnic types. It must be, if it is to be at all, a unison of social and historic interests, established by the complete cutting-off of the ancestral memories of the American populations, the enforced, exclusive use of the English language and English and American history in the schools and in the daily life.

The attainment of the other alternative, a harmony, also requires concerted public action. But the action would do no violence to the ideals of American fundamental law and the spirit of American institutions nor to the qualities of men. It would seek simply to eliminate the waste and the stupidity of the social organization, by way of freeing and strengthening the strong forces actually in operation. Taking for its point of departure the existing ethnic and cultural groups it would seek to provide conditions under which each might attain the cultural perfection that is *proper to its kind*. The provision of such conditions has been said to be the primary intent of American fundamental law and the function of American institutions. And all of the various nationalities which compose the American nation must be taught first of all this fact, which used perhaps to be, to patriotic minds, the outstanding ideal content of "Americanism"—that democracy means self-realization through self-control, self-discipline, and that one is impossible without the other. For the application of this principle, which is realized in a harmony of societies, there are European analogies also. I omit Austria and Turkey, for the union of nationalities is there based more on inadequate force than on consent, and institutional establishment and the form of their organization are alien to the American. I think of Britain and of Switzerland. Great Britain is a nation of at least four nationalities—the English, Welsh, Scotch and Irish, and while British history is not unmarred by attempts at unison, both the home policy and the imperial policy have, since the Boer War, been realized more and more in the application of the principle of harmony: the strength of the kingdom and the empire have been posited more and more upon the voluntary and autonomous coöperation of the component nationalities. Switzerland is a nation of three nationalities, a republic as the United States is, far more democratically governed, concentrated in an area not much different in size, I guess, from Greater New York, with a population not far from it in total. Yet Switzerland has the most loyal citizens in Europe. Their language, literary and spiritual traditions are on the one side, German, on another, Italian, on a third side, French. And in terms of social organization, of economic prosperity, of public education, of the general level of culture, Switzerland is the most successful democracy in the world. It conserves and encourages individuality.

The reason lies, I think, in the fact that in Switzerland the conception of "natural rights" operates, consciously or unconsciously, as a generalization from the data of human nature that are inalterable. What is inalienable in the life of mankind is its intrinsic positive quality—its psycho-physical inheritance. Men may change their clothes, their politics, their wives, their religions, their philosophies, to a greater or lesser extent: they cannot change their grandfathers. Jews or Poles or Anglo-Saxons, in order to cease being Jews or Poles or Anglo-Saxons, would have to cease to be, while they could cease to be citizens or church members or carpenters or lawyers without ceasing to be. The selfhood which is inalienable in them, and for the realization of which they require "inalienable" liberty is ancestrally determined, and the happiness which they pursue has its form implied in ancestral endowment. This is what, actually, democracy in operation assumes. There are human capacities which it is the function of the state to liberate and to protect in growth; and the failure of the state as a government to accomplish this automatically makes for its abolition. Government, the state, under the democratic conception is, it cannot be too often repeated, merely an instrument, not an end. That it is often an abused instrument, that it is often seized by the powers that prey, that it makes frequent mistakes and considers only secondary ends, surface needs, which vary from moment to moment, of course is obvious: hence the social and political messes government is always getting into. But that it is an instrument, flexibly adjustable to changing life, changing opinion and needs, the whole modern electoral organization and party system declare. And as intelligence and wisdom prevail over "politics" and special interests, as the steady and continuous pressure of the "inalienable" qualities and purposes of human groups more and more dominate the confusion of their common life, the outlines of a possible great and truly democratic commonwealth become discernible. Its form would be that of the federal republic; its substance a democracy of nationalities, coöperating voluntarily and autonomously through common institutions in the enterprise of self-realization through the perfection of men according to their kind. The common language of the commonwealth, the language of its great tradition, would be English, but each nationality would have for its emotional and involuntary life its own peculiar dialect or speech, its own individual and inevitable esthetic and intellectual forms. The political and economic life of the commonwealth is a single unit and serves as the foundation and background for the realization of the distinctive individuality of each *natio* that composes it and of the pooling of these in a harmony above them all. Thus "American civilization" may come to mean the perfection of the coöperative harmonies of "European civilization"—the waste, the squalor and the distress of Europe being eliminated—a multiplicity in a unity, an orchestration of mankind. As in an orchestra every type of instrument has its specific *timbre* and *tonality*, founded in its substance and form; as every type has its appropriate theme and melody in the whole symphony, so in society, each ethnic group may be the natural instrument, its temper and culture may be its theme and melody and the harmony and dissonances and discords of them all may make the symphony of civilization. With this difference: a musical symphony is written before it is played; in the symphony of civilization the playing is the writing, so that there is nothing so fixed and inevitable about its progressions as in music, so that within the limits set by nature and luck they may vary at will, and the range and variety of the harmonies may become wider and richer and more beautiful—or the reverse.

But the question is, do the dominant classes in America want such a society? The alternative is actually before them. Can they choose wisely? Or will vanity blind them and fear constrain, turning the promise of freedom into the fact of tyranny, and once more vindicating the ancient habit of men and aborting the hope of the world?

RANDOLPH BOURNE

Trans-National America[†]

No reverberatory effect of the great war has caused American public opinion more solicitude than the failure of the "melting-pot."[1] The discovery of diverse nationalistic feelings among our great alien population has come to most people as an intense shock. It has brought out the unpleasant inconsistencies of our traditional beliefs. We have had to watch hard-hearted old Brahmins[2] virtuously indignant at the spectacle of the immigrant refusing to be melted, while they jeer at patriots like Mary Antin[3] who write about "our forefathers." We have had to listen to publicists who express themselves as stunned by the evidence of vigorous nationalistic and cultural movements in this country among Germans, Scandinavians, Bohemians, and Poles, while in the same breath they insist that the alien shall be forcibly assimilated to that Anglo-Saxon tradition which they unquestioningly label "American."

As the unpleasant truth has come upon us that assimilation in this country was proceeding on lines very different from those we had marked out for it, we found ourselves inclined to blame those who were thwarting our prophecies. The truth became culpable. We blamed the war, we blamed the Germans. And then we discovered with a moral shock that these movements had been making great headway before the war even began. We found that the tendency, reprehensible and paradoxical as it might be, has been for the national clusters of immigrants, as they became more and more firmly established and more and more prosperous, to cultivate more and more assiduously the literatures and cultural traditions of their homelands. Assimilation, in other words, instead of washing out the memories of

---

† From Bourne, *History of a Literary Radical and Other Essays* (New York: B. W. Huebsch, Inc., 1920), pp. 266–99. Bourne (1886–1918) was an American writer, progressive social critic, and political activist. In "Trans-National America," one of his best-known works, he argues that immigrants should not be forced to assimilate to dominant Anglo-Saxon American culture but rather retain their traditions and loyalties. The essay originally appeared in the *Atlantic Monthly* CXVIII (July 1916), 86–97. All notes are by the editor of this Norton Critical Edition.

1. "Melting-pot" is the metaphor used to describe the process by which America transformed immigrants from different countries into citizens with shared beliefs, values, and identities. This process of blending was assumed to create a homogenous culture.
2. Members of the Anglo-Saxon elite social class.
3. Russian-born American author and immigrant-rights activist (1881–1949), best known for her autobiography *The Promised Land* (1912), which tells the story of her immigration and assimilation into American culture.

Europe, made them more and more intensely real. Just as these clusters became more and more objectively American, did they become more and more German or Scandinavian or Bohemian or Polish.

To face the fact that our aliens are already strong enough to take a share in the direction of their own destiny, and that the strong cultural movements represented by the foreign press, schools, and colonies are a challenge to our facile attempts, is not, however, to admit the failure of Americanization. It is not to fear the failure of democracy. It is rather to urge us to an investigation of what Americanism may rightly mean. It is to ask ourselves whether our ideal has been broad or narrow—whether perhaps the time has not come to assert a higher ideal than the "melting-pot." Surely we cannot be certain of our spiritual democracy when, claiming to melt the nations within us to a comprehension of our free and democratic institutions, we fly into panic at the first sign of their own will and tendency. We act as if we wanted Americanization to take place only on our own terms, and not by the consent of the governed. All our elaborate machinery of settlement and school and union, of social and political naturalization, however, will move with friction just in so far as it neglects to take into account this strong and virile insistence that America shall be what the immigrant will have a hand in making it, and not what a ruling class, descendant of those British stocks which were the first permanent immigrants, decide that America shall be made. This is the condition which confronts us, and which demands a clear and general readjustment of our attitude and our ideal.

I

Mary Antin is right when she looks upon our foreign-born as the people who missed the Mayflower and came over on the first boat they could find. But she forgets that when they did come it was not upon other Mayflowers, but upon a "Maiblume," a "Fleur de Mai," a "Fior di Maggio," a "Majblomst." These people were not mere arrivals from the same family, to be welcomed as understood and long-loved, but strangers to the neighborhood, with whom a long process of settling down had to take place. For they brought with them their national and racial characters, and each new national quota had to wear slowly away the contempt with which its mere alienness got itself greeted. Each had to make its way slowly from the lowest strata of unskilled labor up to a level where it satisfied the accredited norms of social success.

We are all foreign-born or the descendants of foreign-born, and if distinctions are to be made between us they should rightly be on some other ground than indigenousness. The early colonists came over with motives no less colonial than the later. They did not come to be assimilated in an American melting-pot. They did not come to adopt the culture of the American Indian. They had not the smallest intention of "giving themselves without reservation" to the new country. They came to get freedom to live as they wanted to. They came to escape from the stifling air and chaos of the old world; they came to make their fortune in a new land. They invented no new social framework. Rather they brought over bodily the old ways to which they had been accustomed. Tightly concentrated on a hostile frontier, they were conservative beyond belief. Their pioneer daring was reserved for the objective conquest of material resources. In their folkways, in their social and political institutions, they were, like every colonial people, slavishly imitative of the mother-country. So that, in spite of the "Revolution," our whole legal and political system remained more English than the English, petrified and unchanging, while in England itself law developed to meet the needs of the changing times.

It is just this English-American conservatism that has been our chief obstacle to social advance. We have needed the new peoples—the order of the German and Scandinavian, the turbulence of the Slav and Hun—to save us from our own stagnation. I do not mean that the illiterate Slav is now the equal of the New Englander of pure descent. He is raw material to be educated, not into a New Englander, but into a socialized American along such lines as those thirty nationalities are being educated in the amazing schools of Gary.[4] I do not believe that this process is to be one of decades of evolution. The spectacle of Japan's sudden jump from mediævalism to post-modernism should have destroyed that superstition. We are not dealing with individuals who are to "evolve." We are dealing with their children, who, with that education we are about to have, will start level with all of us. Let us cease to think of ideals like democracy as magical qualities inherent in certain peoples. Let us speak, not of inferior races, but of inferior civilizations. We are all to educate and to be educated. These peoples in America are in a common enterprise. It is not what we are now that concerns us, but what this plastic next generation may become in the light of a new cosmopolitan ideal.

We are not dealing with static factors, but with fluid and dynamic generations. To contrast the older and the newer immigrants and see the one class as democratically motivated by love of liberty, and the other by mere money-getting, is not to illuminate the future. To think of earlier nationalities as culturally assimilated to America, while we picture the later as a sodden and resistive mass, makes only for

---

4. During the first decades of the twentieth century, the schools of Gary, Indiana—influenced by the educational philosophy of John Dewey—became models of progressive education and influenced public school curricula across the country. An admirer of this form of education, Randolph Bourne published his book *The Gary Schools* in 1916.

bitterness and misunderstanding. There may be a difference between these earlier and these later stocks, but it lies neither in motive for coming nor in strength of cultural allegiance to the homeland. The truth is that no more tenacious cultural allegiance to the mother country has been shown by any alien nation than by the ruling class of Anglo-Saxon descendants in these American States. English snob-beries, English religion, English literary styles, English literary rev-erences and canons, English ethics, English superiorities, have been the cultural food that we have drunk in from our mothers' breasts. The distinctively American spirit—pioneer, as distinguished from the reminiscently English—that appears in Whitman and Emerson and James, has had to exist on sufferance alongside of this other cult, unconsciously belittled by our cultural makers of opinion. No coun-try has perhaps had so great indigenous genius which had so little influence on the country's traditions and expressions. The unpopu-lar and dreaded German-American of the present day is a beginning amateur in comparison with those foolish Anglophiles of Boston and New York and Philadelphia whose reversion to cultural type sees uncritically in England's cause the cause of Civilization, and, under the guise of ethical independence of thought, carries along Euro-pean traditions which are no more "American" than the German cat-egories themselves.

It speaks well for German-American innocence of heart or else for its lack of imagination that it has not turned the hyphen stigma into a "Tu quoque!"[5] If there were to be any hyphens scattered about, clearly they should be affixed to those English descendants who had had centuries of time to be made American where the German had had only half a century. Most significantly has the war brought out of them this alien virus, showing them still loving English things, owing allegiance to the English Kultur, moved by English shibbo-leths and prejudice. It is only because it has been the ruling class in this country that bestowed the epithets that we have not heard copi-ously and scornfully of "hyphenated English-Americans." But even our quarrels with England have had the bad temper, the extrava-gance, of family quarrels. The Englishman of to-day nags us and dis-likes us in that personal, peculiarly intimate way in which he dislikes the Australian, or as we may dislike our younger brothers. He still thinks of us incorrigibly as "colonials." America—official, control-ling, literary, political America—is still, as a writer recently expressed it, "culturally speaking, a self-governing dominion of the British Empire."

The non-English American can scarcely be blamed if he sometimes thinks of the Anglo-Saxon predominance in America as little more

5. French: "You as well!"

than a predominance of priority. The Anglo-Saxon was merely the first immigrant, the first to found a colony. He has never really ceased to be the descendant of immigrants, nor has he ever succeeded in transforming that colony into a real nation, with a tenacious, richly woven fabric of native culture. Colonials from the other nations have come and settled down beside him. They found no definite native culture which should startle them out of their colonialism, and consequently they looked back to their mother-country, as the earlier Anglo-Saxon immigrant was looking back to his. What has been offered the newcomer has been the chance to learn English, to become a citizen, to salute the flag. And those elements of our ruling classes who are responsible for the public schools, the settlements, all the organizations for amelioration in the cities, have every reason to be proud of the care and labor which they have devoted to absorbing the immigrant. His opportunities the immigrant has taken to gladly, with almost a pathetic eagerness to make his way in the new land without friction or disturbance. The common language has made not only for the necessary communication, but for all the amenities of life.

If freedom means the right to do pretty much as one pleases, so long as one does not interfere with others, the immigrant has found freedom, and the ruling element has been singularly liberal in its treatment of the invading hordes. But if freedom means a democratic coöperation in determining the ideals and purposes and industrial and social institutions of a country, then the immigrant has not been free, and the Anglo-Saxon element is guilty of just what every dominant race is guilty of in every European country: the imposition of its own culture upon the minority peoples. The fact that this imposition has been so mild and, indeed, semi-conscious does not alter its quality. And the war has brought out just the degree to which that purpose of "Americanizing," that is to say, "Anglo-Saxonizing," the immigrant has failed.

For the Anglo-Saxon now in his bitterness to turn upon the other peoples, talk about their "arrogance," scold them for not being melted in a pot which never existed, is to betray the unconscious purpose which lay at the bottom of his heart. It betrays too the possession of a racial jealousy similar to that of which he is now accusing the so-called "hyphenates." Let the Anglo-Saxon be proud enough of the heroic toil and heroic sacrifices which moulded the nation. But let him ask himself, if he had had to depend on the English descendants, where he would have been living today. To those of us who see in the exploitation of unskilled labor the strident red *leit-motif* of our civilization, the settling of the country presents a great social drama as the waves of immigration broke over it.

Let the Anglo-Saxon ask himself where he would have been if these races had not come? Let those who feel the inferiority of the non-Anglo-Saxon immigrant contemplate that region of the States which has remained the most distinctively "American," the South. Let him ask himself whether he would really like to see the foreign hordes Americanized into such an Americanization. Let him ask himself how superior this native civilization is to the great "alien" states of Wisconsin and Minnesota, where Scandinavians, Poles, and Germans have self-consciously labored to preserve their traditional culture, while being outwardly and satisfactorily American. Let him ask himself how much more wisdom, intelligence, industry and social leadership has come out of these alien states than out of all the truly American ones. The South, in fact, while this vast Northern development has gone on, still remains an English colony, stagnant and complacent, having progressed culturally scarcely beyond the early Victorian era. It is culturally sterile because it has had no advantage of cross-fertilization like the Northern states. What has happened in states such as Wisconsin and Minnesota is that strong foreign cultures have struck root in a new and fertile soil. America has meant liberation, and German and Scandinavian political ideas and social energies have expanded to a new potency. The process has not been at all the fancied "assimilation" of the Scandinavian or Teuton. Rather has it been a process of their assimilation of us— I speak as an Anglo-Saxon. The foreign cultures have not been melted down or run together, made into some homogeneous Americanism, but have remained distinct but coöperating to the greater glory and benefit, not only of themselves but of all the native "Americanism" around them.

What we emphatically do not want is that these distinctive qualities should be washed out into a tasteless, colorless fluid of uniformity. Already we have far too much of this insipidity,—masses of people who are cultural half-breeds, neither assimilated Anglo-Saxons nor nationals of another culture. Each national colony in this country seems to retain in its foreign press, its vernacular literature, its schools, its intellectual and patriotic leaders, a central cultural nucleus. From this nucleus the colony extends out by imperceptible gradations to a fringe where national characteristics are all but lost. Our cities are filled with these half-breeds who retain their foreign names but have lost the foreign savor. This does not mean that they have actually been changed into New Englanders or Middle Westerners. It does not mean that they have been really Americanized. It means that, letting slip from them whatever native culture they had, they have substituted for it only the most rudimentary American— the American culture of the cheap newspaper, the "movies," the popular song, the ubiquitous automobile. The unthinking who survey this class call them assimilated, Americanized. The great American public school has done its work. With these people our institutions are safe. We may thrill with dread at the aggressive hyphenate, but this tame flabbiness is accepted as Americanization. The same moulders of opinion whose ideal is to melt the different races into Anglo-Saxon gold hail this poor product as the satisfying result of their alchemy.

Yet a truer cultural sense would have told us that it is not the self-conscious cultural nuclei that sap at our American life, but these fringes. It is not the Jew who sticks proudly to the faith of his fathers and boasts of that venerable culture of his who is dangerous to America, but the Jew who has lost the Jewish fire and become a mere elementary, grasping animal. It is not the Bohemian who supports the Bohemian schools in Chicago whose influence is sinister, but the Bohemian who has made money and has got into ward politics. Just so surely as we tend to disintegrate these nuclei of nationalistic culture do we tend to create hordes of men and women without a spiritual country, cultural outlaws, without taste, without standards but those of the mob. We sentence them to live on the most rudimentary planes of American life. The influences at the center of the nuclei are centripetal. They make for the intelligence and the social values which mean an enhancement of life. And just because the foreign-born retains this expressiveness is he likely to be a better citizen of the American community. The influences at the fringe, however, are centrifugal, anarchical. They make for detached fragments of peoples. Those who came to find liberty achieve only license. They become the flotsam and jetsam of American life, the downward undertow of our civilization with its leering cheapness and falseness of taste and spiritual outlook, the absence of mind and sincere feeling which we see in our slovenly towns, our vapid moving pictures, our popular novels, and in the vacuous faces of the crowds on the city street. This is the cultural wreckage of our time, and it is from the fringes of the Anglo-Saxon as well as the other stocks that it falls. America has as yet no impelling integrating force. It makes too easily for this detritus of cultures. In our loose, free country, no constraining national purpose, no tenacious folk-tradition and folk-style hold the people to a line.

The war has shown us that not in any magical formula will this purpose be found. No intense nationalism of the European plan can be ours. But do we not begin to see a new and more adventurous ideal? Do we not see how the national colonies in America, deriving power from the deep cultural heart of Europe and yet living here in mutual toleration, freed from the age-long tangles of races, creeds, and dynasties, may work out a federated ideal? America is transplanted Europe, but a Europe that has not been disintegrated and scattered in the transplanting as in some Dispersion. Its colonies live here inextricably mingled, yet not homogeneous. They merge but they do not fuse.

America is a unique sociological fabric, and it bespeaks poverty of imagination not to be thrilled at the incalculable potentialities of so novel a union of men. To seek no other goal than the weary old nationalism,—belligerent, exclusive, inbreeding, the poison of which we are witnessing now in Europe,—is to make patriotism a hollow sham, and to declare that, in spite of our boastings, America must ever be a follower and not a leader of nations.

II

If we come to find this point of view plausible, we shall have to give up the search for our native "American" culture. With the exception of the South and that New England which, like the Red Indian, seems to be passing into solemn oblivion, there is no distinctively American culture. It is apparently our lot rather to be a federation of cultures. This we have been for half a century, and the war has made it ever more evident that this is what we are destined to remain. This will not mean, however, that there are not expressions of indigenous genius that could not have sprung from any other soil. Music, poetry, philosophy, have been singularly fertile and new. Strangely enough, American genius has flared forth just in those directions which are least understanded of the people. If the American note is bigness, action, the objective as contrasted with the reflective life, where is the epic expression of this spirit? Our drama and our fiction, the peculiar fields for the expression of action and objectivity, are somehow exactly the fields of the spirit which remain poor and mediocre. American materialism is in some way inhibited from getting into impressive artistic form its own energy with which it bursts. Nor is it any better in architecture, the least romantic and subjective of all the arts. We are inarticulate of the very values which we profess to idealize. But in the finer forms—music, verse, the essay, philosophy—the American genius puts forth work equal to any of its contemporaries. Just in so far as our American genius has expressed the pioneer spirit, the adventurous, forward-looking drive of a colonial empire, is it representative of that whole America of the many races and peoples, and not of any partial or traditional enthusiasm. And only as that pioneer note is sounded can we really speak of the American culture. As long as we thought of Americanism in terms of the "melting-pot," our American cultural tradition lay in the past. It was something to which the new Americans were to be moulded. In the light of our changing ideal of Americanism, we must perpetrate the paradox that our American cultural tradition lies in the future. It will be what we all together make out of this incomparable opportunity of attacking the future with a new key.

Whatever American nationalism turns out to be, it is certain to become something utterly different from the nationalisms of twentieth-century Europe. This wave of reactionary enthusiasm to play the orthodox nationalistic game which is passing over the country is scarcely vital enough to last. We cannot swagger and thrill to the same national self-feeling. We must give new edges to our pride. We must be content to avoid the unnumbered woes that national patriotism has brought in Europe, and that fiercely heightened pride and self-consciousness. Alluring as this is, we must allow our imaginations to transcend this scarcely veiled belligerency. We can be serenely too proud to fight if our pride embraces the creative forces of civilization which armed contest nullifies. We can be too proud to fight if our code of honor transcends that of the schoolboy on the playground surrounded by his jeering mates. Our honor must be positive and creative, and not the mere jealous and negative protectiveness against metaphysical violations of our technical rights. When the doctrine is put forth that in one American flows the mystic blood of all our country's sacred honor, freedom, and prosperity, so that an injury to him is to be the signal for turning our whole nation into that clan-feud of horror and reprisal which would be war, then we find ourselves back among the musty schoolmen of the Middle Ages, and not in any pragmatic and realistic America of the twentieth century.

We should hold our gaze to what America has done, not what mediæval codes of dueling she has failed to observe. We have transplanted European modernity to our soil, without the spirit that inflames it and turns all its energy into mutual destruction. Out of these foreign peoples there has somehow been squeezed the poison. An America, "hyphenated" to bitterness, is somehow non-explosive. For, even if we all hark back in sympathy to a European nation, even if the war has set every one vibrating to some emotional string twanged on the other side of the Atlantic, the effect has been one of almost dramatic harmlessness.

What we have really been witnessing, however unappreciatively, in this country has been a thrilling and bloodless battle of Kulturs. In that arena of friction which has been the most dramatic—between the hyphenated German-American and the hyphenated English-American—there have emerged rivalries of philosophies which show up deep traditional attitudes, points of view which accurately reflect the gigantic issues of the war. America has mirrored the spiritual issues. The vicarious struggle has been played out peacefully here in the mind. We have seen the stout resistiveness of the old moral interpretation of history on which Victorian England throve and made itself great in its own esteem. The clean and immensely satisfying vision of the war as a contest between right and wrong; the enthusiastic support of the Allies as the incarnation of virtue-on-a-rampage; the fierce envisaging of their selfish national purposes as the ideals of justice, freedom and democracy—all this has been thrown with intensest force against the German realistic interpretations in terms of the struggle for power and the virility of the integrated State. America has been the intellectual battleground of the nations.

III

The failure of the melting-pot, far from closing the great American democratic experiment, means that it has only just begun. Whatever American nationalism turns out to be, we see already that it will have a color richer and more exciting than our ideal has hitherto encompassed. In a world which has dreamed of internationalism, we find that we have all unawares been building up the first international nation. The voices which have cried for a tight and jealous nationalism of the European pattern are failing. From that ideal, however valiantly and disinterestedly it has been set for us, time and tendency have moved us further and further away. What we have achieved has been rather a cosmopolitan federation of national colonies, of foreign cultures, from which the sting of devastating competition has been removed. America is already the world-federation in miniature, the continent where for the first time in history has been achieved that miracle of hope, the peaceful living side by side, with character substantially preserved, of the most heterogeneous peoples under the sun. Nowhere else has such contiguity been anything but the breeder of misery. Here, notwithstanding our tragic failures of adjustment, the outlines are already too clear not to give us a new vision and a new orientation of the American mind in the world.

It is for the American of the younger generation to accept this cosmopolitanism, and carry it along with self-conscious and fruitful purpose. In his colleges, he is already getting, with the study of modern history and politics, the modern literatures, economic geography, the privilege of a cosmopolitan outlook such as the people of no other nation of to-day in Europe can possibly secure. If he is still a colonial, he is no longer the colonial of one partial culture, but of many. He is a colonial of the world. Colonialism has grown into cosmopolitanism, and his motherhood is not one nation, but all who have anything life-enhancing to offer to the spirit. That vague sympathy which the France of ten years ago was feeling for the world—a sympathy which was drowned in the terrible reality of war—may be the modern American's, and that in a positive and aggressive sense. If the American is parochial, it is in sheer wantonness or cowardice. His provincialism is the measure of his fear of bogies or the defect of his imagination.

Indeed, it is not uncommon for the eager Anglo-Saxon who goes to a vivid American university today to find his true friends not among his own race but among the acclimatized German or Austrian, the acclimatized Jew, the acclimatized Scandinavian or Italian. In them he finds the cosmopolitan note. In these youths, foreign-born or the children of foreign-born parents, he is likely to find many of his old inbred morbid problems washed away. These friends are oblivious to the repressions of that tight little society in which he so provincially grew up. He has a pleasurable sense of liberation from the stale and familiar attitudes of those whose ingrowing culture has scarcely created anything vital for his America of to-day. He breathes a larger air. In his new enthusiasms for continental literature, for unplumbed Russian depths, for French clarity of thought, for Teuton philosophies of power, he feels himself citizen of a larger world. He may be absurdly superficial, his outward-reaching wonder may ignore all the stiller and homelier virtues of his Anglo-Saxon home, but he has at least found the clue to that international mind which will be essential to all men and women of goodwill if they are ever to save this Western world of ours from suicide.

His new friends have gone through a similar evolution. America has burned most of the baser metal also from them. Meeting now with this common American background, all of them may yet retain that distinctiveness of their native cultures and their national spiritual slants. They are more valuable and interesting to each other for being different, yet that difference could not be creative were it not for this new cosmopolitan outlook which America has given them and which they all equally possess.

A college where such a spirit is possible even to the smallest degree, has within itself already the seeds of this international intellectual world of the future. It suggests that the contribution of America will be an intellectual internationalism which goes far beyond the mere exchange of scientific ideas and discoveries and the cold recording of facts. It will be an intellectual sympathy which is not satisfied until it has got at the heart of the different cultural expressions, and felt as they feel. It may have immense preferences, but it will make understanding and not indignation its end. Such a sympathy will unite and not divide.

Against the thinly disguised panic which calls itself "patriotism" and the thinly disguised militarism which calls itself "preparedness" the cosmopolitan ideal is set. This does not mean that those who hold it are for a policy of drift. They, too, long passionately for an integrated and disciplined America. But they do not want one which is integrated only for domestic economic exploitation of the workers or for predatory economic imperialism among the weaker peoples. They do not want one that is integrated by coercion or militarism, or for the truculent assertion of a mediæval code of honor and of doubtful rights. They believe that the most effective integration will be one which coordinates the diverse elements and turns them consciously toward working out together the place of America in the world-situation. They demand for integration a genuine integrity, a wholeness and soundness of enthusiasm and purpose which can only come when no national colony within our America feels that it is being discriminated against or that its cultural case is being prejudged. This strength of coöperation, this feeling that all who are here may have a hand in the destiny of America, will make for a finer spirit of integration than any narrow "Americanism" or forced chauvinism.

In this effort we may have to accept some form of that dual citizenship which meets with so much articulate horror among us.[6] Dual citizenship we may have to recognize as the rudimentary form of that international citizenship to which, if our words mean anything, we aspire. We have assumed unquestioningly that mere participation in the political life of the United States must cut the new citizen off from all sympathy with his old allegiance. Anything but a bodily transfer of devotion from one sovereignty to another has been viewed as a sort of moral treason against the Republic. We have insisted that the immigrant whom we welcomed escaping from the very exclusive nationalism of his European home shall forthwith adopt a nationalism just as exclusive, just as narrow, and even less legitimate because it is founded on no warm traditions of his own. Yet a nation like France is said to permit a formal and legal dual citizenship even at the present time. Though a citizen of hers may pretend to cast off his allegiance in favor of some other sovereignty, he is still subject to her laws when he returns. Once a citizen, always a citizen, no matter how many new citizenships he may embrace. And such a dual citizenship seems to us sound and right. For it recognizes that, although the Frenchman may accept the formal institutional framework of his new country and indeed become intensely loyal to it, yet his Frenchness he will never lose. What makes up the fabric of his soul will always be of this Frenchness, so that unless he becomes utterly degenerate he will always to some degree dwell still in his native environment.

Indeed, does not the cultivated American who goes to Europe practise a dual citizenship, which, if not formal, is no less real? The American who lives abroad may be the least expatriate of men. If he falls

---

6. Until 1967, it was illegal for a United States citizen to hold dual citizenship. Immigrants, during the naturalization process, were required to renounce previous citizenships.

in love with French ways and French thinking and French democracy and seeks to saturate himself with the new spirit, he is guilty of at least a dual spiritual citizenship. He may be still American, yet he feels himself through sympathy also a Frenchman. And he finds that this expansion involves no shameful conflict within him, no surrender of his native attitude. He has rather for the first time caught a glimpse of the cosmopolitan spirit. And after wandering about through many races and civilizations he may return to America to find them all here living vividly and crudely, seeking the same adjustment that he made. He sees the new peoples here with a new vision. They are no longer masses of aliens, waiting to be "assimilated," waiting to be melted down into the indistinguishable dough of Anglo-Saxonism. They are rather threads of living and potent cultures, blindly striving to weave themselves into a novel international nation, the first the world has seen. In an Austria-Hungary or a Prussia the stronger of these cultures would be moving almost instinctively to subjugate the weaker. But in America those wills-to-power are turned in a different direction into learning how to live together.

Along with dual citizenship we shall have to accept, I think, that free and mobile passage of the immigrant between America and his native land again which now arouses so much prejudice among us. We shall have to accept the immigrant's return for the same reason that we consider justified our own flitting about the earth. To stigmatize the alien who works in America for a few years and returns to his own land, only perhaps to seek American fortune again, is to think in narrow nationalistic terms. It is to ignore the cosmopolitan significance of this migration. It is to ignore the fact that the returning immigrant is often a missionary to an inferior civilization.

This migratory habit has been especially common with the unskilled laborers who have been pouring into the United States in the last dozen years from every country in southeastern Europe. Many of them return to spend their earnings in their own country or to serve their country in war. But they return with an entirely new critical outlook, and a sense of the superiority of American organization to the primitive living around them. This continued passage to and fro has already raised the material standard of living in many regions of these backward countries. For these regions are thus endowed with exactly what they need, the capital for the exploitation of their natural resources, and the spirit of enterprise. America is thus educating these laggard peoples from the very bottom of society up, awaking vast masses to a new-born hope for the future. In the migratory Greek, therefore, we have not the parasitic alien, the doubtful American asset, but a symbol of that cosmopolitan interchange which is coming, in spite of all war and national exclusiveness.

Only America, by reason of the unique liberty of opportunity and traditional isolation for which she seems to stand, can lead in this cosmopolitan enterprise. Only the American—and in this category I include the migratory alien who has lived with us and caught the pioneer spirit and a sense of new social vistas—has the chance to become that citizen of the world. America is coming to be, not a nationality but a trans-nationality, a weaving back and forth, with the other lands, of many threads of all sizes and colors. Any movement which attempts to thwart this weaving, or to dye the fabric any one color, or disentangle the threads of the strands, is false to this cosmopolitan vision. I do not mean that we shall necessarily glut ourselves with the raw product of humanity. It would be folly to absorb the nations faster than we could weave them. We have no duty either to admit or reject. It is purely a question of expediency. What concerns us is the fact that the strands are here. We must have a policy and an ideal for an actual situation. Our question is, What shall we do with our America? How are we likely to get the more creative America—by confining our imaginations to the ideal of the melting-pot, or broadening them to some such cosmopolitan conception as I have been vaguely sketching?

We cannot Americanize America worthily by sentimentalizing and moralizing history. When the best schools are expressly renouncing the questionable duty of teaching patriotism by means of history, it is not the time to force shibboleth upon the immigrant. This form of Americanization has been heard because it appealed to the vestiges of our old sentimentalized and moralized patriotism. This has so far held the field as the expression of the new American's new devotion. The inflections of other voices have been drowned. They must be heard. We must see if the lesson of the war has not been for hundreds of these later Americans a vivid realization of their transnationality, a new consciousness of what America means to them as a citizenship in the world. It is the vague historic idealisms which have provided the fuel for the European flame. Our American ideal can make no progress until we do away with this romantic gilding of the past.

All our idealisms must be those of future social goals in which all can participate, the good life of personality lived in the environment of the Beloved Community. No mere doubtful triumphs of the past, which redound to the glory of only one of our trans-nationalities, can satisfy us. It must be a future America, on which all can unite, which pulls us irresistibly toward it, as we understand each other more warmly.

To make real this striving amid dangers and apathies is work for a younger intelligentsia of America. Here is an enterprise of integration into which we can all pour ourselves, of a spiritual welding which should make us, if the final menace ever came, not weaker, but infinitely strong.

SARKA B. HRBKOVA
Bohemians in Nebraska[†]

* * *

While every county of Nebraska has Bohemian inhabitants, the largest numbers are in Douglas, Colfax, Saline, Saunders, and Butler. Cities and towns which have a generous percentage of Bohemians are Omaha, South Omaha, Wilber, Crete, Clarkson, Milligan, Schuyler, and Prague. In the main, however, Bohemians in Nebraska are settled on farms rather than in towns, in small communities rather than in cities, and in the eastern, rather than in the western part of the state.

A large majority of the Bohemians of this state are in agricultural pursuits; and as farmers are the real backbone of the great West, it may be said that the Bohemian farmers are the mainstay of the Czechs in Nebraska, despite the fact that business and the professions each year gain more accessions from them.

First Bohemians in Nebraska

The first Bohemian who came to Nebraska, so far as can be learned, was Libor Alois Slesinger, who was born October 28, 1806, in Usti above the Orlice River, Bohemia. It is noteworthy that this first Bohemian immigrant to this state came to America for political liberty, which the absolutism prevailing in Austria after the uprising of 1848 had stifled in his own country. Slesinger left Bohemia in November, 1856, and in January, 1857, arrived in Cedar Rapids, Iowa, which was a sort of stopping place for most of the Bohemian immigrants *en route* for the great, attractive, beaming West beyond the Missouri. The trip from Cedar Rapids to Omaha, Slesinger made by wagon. A little later he settled near the Winnebago reservation. His experiences were as picturesque and adventurous as those of other early comers, if not more so. Joseph Horsky, who arrived in 1857 and also came by the Cedar Rapids route, was the second, and the now famous Edward Rosewater the third, Czech to settle in the Cornhusker state.

† From *Publications of the Nebraska State Historical Society*, Vol. 19, ed. Albert Watkins (Lincoln: Nebraska State Historical Society, 1919), pp. 143–49. Hrbkova was Professor of Slavonic Languages at the University of Nebraska. All notes are by the editor of this Norton Critical Edition.

The homestead act[1] attracted to the West many Bohemians who had already become citizens or were about to swear allegiance to the "starry flag".

* * *

The first wave of Bohemian immigration to Nebraska consisted of men seeking political and religious freedom. Subsequent waves comprised men escaping enforced military service in the Austrian army or seeking economic betterment. Though large numbers of Bohemians came to America to avoid serving in the army at home, yet these same Bohemians, who had but just fled from enforced militarism, of their own will enlisted here to save the Union.

* * *

Religious Life of Czechs in Nebraska

From the domain of Roman Catholic Austria to unpledged Nebraska is a step of many thousands of miles. The difference in the religious attitude of many Czechs who have taken that long step is as great and is likewise analogous. Bohemia's greatest trials and sufferings were a result of religious struggles, both internal and with neighboring states. From the introduction of Christianity into Bohemia in 863 by Cyril and Methodius, the nation's brand of religion has been different from that of her neighbors. Bohemia accepted Christianity from two Greek Priests of Constantinople, who at once introduced the Slavic Bible and preaching in the mother tongue. Bohemia's neighbors received their Christian missionaries from Rome, which required the Latin service.

The burning of John Huss,[2] who preceded the German Luther by a decade more than a hundred years, lighted the way for the reformation, which would not have been possible without the work and martyrdom of the Bohemian reformer. The smoldering dissensions which burst again into flame in 1620, when the Bohemian and Moravian Brethren were exiled and the country was depopulated and plundered, have ever and anon crackled and thrust out gleaming tongues. But the days of crucifixions and martyrdoms are memories of the middle ages. A clearer, whiter light now shines for those who think on things religious.

Perhaps no other people think or write so much on the various phases of religious controversies as Bohemians. And yet the charge

---

1. The Homestead Act of 1862 offered a quarter section (160 acres) to anyone who would settle and develop the land for five years.
2. John Huss (also spelled Jan Hus) was a Bohemian religious leader whose teachings influenced the Protestant Reformation.

of infidelism is too often wrongfully made against them. A people
who are thinking, debating, arguing on religious questions and meanwhile trying to live according to the golden rule are much nearer
certain professed ideals of conduct than some of the pharisaical "professors" themselves.

The Bohemians of Nebraska may be roughly classified into three
general groups—Roman Catholics, Protestants, and Liberal Thinkers.
There are Bohemian churches and priests in forty-four towns and
villages. The church at Brainard is a very fine structure, costing
over $40,000, exclusive of interior decorations, and is the pride of
the community. Parochial schools are maintained in connection
with some of the churches. For instance, there is a fine building in
Dodge where 140 children attend the instruction of Sisters of Our
Lady. There are some twenty Bohemian Protestant churches in the
state, mainly Methodist and Presbyterian. The Liberal Thinkers are
but recently organized, so there are only five societies in Nebraska,
four of them located in Omaha, and only one of them exclusively
devoted to the object of the organization. The others are lodges of
different orders which have signified approval of the purposes of the
Svobodna Obec or Liberal Thinkers League.

Organized Life of Czechs of Nebraska

The Bohemian people in the United States are unusually strong on
organization. Judging alone by Nebraska's Bohemian lodge member-
ship one might easily believe they were inveterate "joiners". It is well
known that as members of labor unions they are "stickers". They
believe thoroughly in the adhesive value of organization to gain a
point. However, it is as organizers of social and fraternal protective
societies that the Bohemians excel. Practically every man of Bohemian birth or parentage belongs to one or more associations which
have for their object insurance, protection in sickness and death, as
well as the development of social life. There are also a number of
organizations offering no insurance but, instead, opportunities for
education along gymnastic, musical, literary or related lines.

The lodges of the fraternal class afford cheap insurance, the
assessments in nearly every instance being much lower than in other
orders.

* * *

It is especially significant that this oldest organization of Bohemians in Saline county [the Bohemian Reading Society], and which
was among the oldest in the state, was effected for the purpose of
meeting to read and discuss books and magazines. Even in those difficult times, when life was mainly a matter of preserving existence

in the hard, rough conditions of the day, these recent immigrants from a foreign land to the prairies of Nebraska held to the social and educational ideals of the mother land, bringing into the sordid commonplace of existence the rosy poetry of song, music, the dance, the theatre, and communion with books.

Music, either vocal or instrumental, always had to be present in any gathering of Bohemians, whether it were a meeting of neighbors or a formal session of a lodge. The Czechs are not without warrant called "the nation of musicians", as the Smetanas, Dvoraks, Kubeliks, Kocians, Ondriceks and Destinns fully attest. If a wager were to be made that every Bohemian community in Nebraska today had its own band or orchestra, it is safe to say that the bettor would win.

ROSE ROSICKY

Bohemian Cemeteries in Nebraska[†]

Like others of the earliest pioneers in any land, quite a number of our people were buried individually, on their farms, before cemeteries were established. These solitary graves, here and there, were marked by wooden crosses and fences, long fallen into decay and obliterated. The hands of those who sleep in them planted the first kernels of corn in the virgin sod, with the aid of a hatchet, and now, after comparatively a short span, the roar of the tractor and automobile resounds, as it sweeps over these forgotten graves.

Willa Cather tells of such a grave, that of the unfortunate, hapless Bohemian pioneer Shimerda, in her story "My Ántonia":

"Years afterward, when the open-grazing days were over, and the red grass had been ploughed under and under until it had almost disappeared from the prairie; when all the fields were under fence, and roads no longer ran about like wild things, but followed surveyed section lines, Mr. Shimerda's grave was still there, with a sagging wire fence around it, and an unpainted wooden cross. As grandfather had predicted, Mrs. Shimerda never saw the roads go over his head. The road from the north curved a little to the east just there, and the road from the west swung out a little to the south; so that the grave, with its tall red grass that was never mowed, was like a little island; and at twilight, under a new moon or the clear evening star, the dusty roads used to look like soft gray rivers flowing past it. I never came upon the place without emotion, and in all that country it was the spot most dear to me. I loved the dim superstition, the

---

† From *A History of Czechs (Bohemians) in Nebraska* (Omaha: Czech Historical Society of Nebraska, 1929), pp. 431–32. Reprinted by permission of the Eastern Nebraska Genealogical Society. All notes are by the editor of this Norton Critical Edition.

propitiatory intent, that had put the grave there; and still more I loved the spirit that could not carry out the sentence—the error from the surveyed lines, the clemency of the soft earth roads along which the home-coming wagons rumbled after sunset. Never a tired driver passed the wooden cross, I am sure without wishing well to the sleeper."

Within a very few years after a settlement had established itself, cemeteries were provided. Life intertwines with death, the need for cemeteries is as pressing as for shelter. In time, as with all other material evidences in our state, they have been improved and beautified. Inasmuch as those listed here are entirely Bohemian, they will, in the future, be the only purely Bohemian records, visible to the passerby, of our people in Nebraska. This truth was in the mind of Jeffrey Doležal Hrbek,[1] when he wrote his poem given below, which was published in "The Pulsé"[2] in March, 1906:

THE BOHEMIAN CEMETERY

Yonder, the southward hills rise, fair,
   And pleasant green fields bask in the sun.
The view is broad and lovely there,
   Where the dusty road doth upward run.

On the very crown of the highest hill
   Where the tallest oaks lift their arms toward God
Above the clatter and din of lathe and mill
   White marbles gleam athwart the sod.

'Tis the burial ground of a foreign race,
   A race from the heart of Europe sprung,
Men and women of open face
   That speak in the strange Bohemian tongue.

Down in the city that gleams below
   With its streets and lanes and its roofs and domes,
In its southern corner row on row
   They have built their garden-bordered homes.

But here on the hill is the burial ground
   Where the sainted dead in their last long sleep
'Neath many a verdant, flowery mound
   The eternal watches keep.

1. Jeffrey Hrbek (1882–1907), Nebraska scholar and poet who chaired the first Slavonic Department at the University of Nebraska.
2. Literary magazine established by Hrbek.

Snowy marble and granite brown
 And blooming urns of bronze and stone.
Carved and graven with cross and crown
 And with soft green moss o'ergrown.

And the epitaphs and wreathed rhymes
 In the Chechish tongue are writ,
That the men and women of future times
 May muse and wonder a bit.

For, the dialect sweet of the pioneers old
 Is giving slowly but surely way
To the plain smooth speech of the Saxon bold
 The Chechish weakens day by day.

Some day these stone-carved tearful rhymes
 Shall be a riddle—a puzzle—nay
Folk will doubt that in by-gone times
 Many could read each tombstone's lay.

Still, here on the hill in the burial ground
 The Chechish dead in their last long sleep
'Neath grass-o'rgrown, forgotten mound
 The eternal watch will keep.

WILLA CATHER

Nebraska: The End of the First Cycle[†]

The State of Nebraska is part of the great plain which stretches west of the Missouri River, gradually rising until it reaches the Rocky Mountains. The character of all this country between the river and the mountains is essentially the same throughout its extent: a rolling, alluvial plain, growing gradually more sandy toward the west, until it breaks into the white sand-hills of western Nebraska and Kansas and eastern Colorado. From east to west this plain measures something over five hundred miles; in appearance it resembles the wheat lands of Russia, which fed the continent of Europe for so many years. Like Little Russia it is watered by slow-flowing, muddy rivers, which run full in the spring, often cutting into the farm lands along their banks; but by midsummer they lie low and shrunken, their current split by glistening white sand-bars half overgrown with scrub willows.

† From the September 5, 1923, issue of *The Nation*. © 1923 The Nation Company, LLC. All rights reserved. Used by permission. All notes are by the editor of this Norton Critical Edition.

The climate, with its extremes of temperature, gives to this plateau the variety which, to the casual eye at least, it lacks. There we have short, bitter winters; windy, flower-laden springs; long, hot summers; triumphant autumns that last until Christmas—a season of perpetual sunlight, blazing blue skies, and frosty nights. In this newest part of the New World autumn is the season of beauty and sentiment, as spring is in the Old World.

Nebraska is a newer State than Kansas. It was a State before there were people in it. Its social history falls easily within a period of sixty years, and the first stable settlements of white men were made within the memory of old folk now living. The earliest of these settlements— Bellevue, Omaha, Brownville, Nebraska City—were founded along the Missouri River, which was at that time a pathway for small steamers. In 1855–60 these four towns were straggling groups of log houses, hidden away along the wooded river banks.

Before 1860 civilization did no more than nibble at the eastern edge of the State, along the river bluffs. Lincoln, the present capital, was open prairie; and the whole of the great plain to the westward was still a sunny wilderness, where the tall red grass and the buffalo and the Indian hunter were undisturbed. Fremont, with Kit Carson, the famous scout, had gone across Nebraska in 1842, exploring the valley of the Platte. In the days of the Mormon persecution fifteen thousand Mormons camped for two years, 1845–46, six miles north of Omaha, while their exploring parties went farther west, searching for fertile land outside of government jurisdiction. In 1847 the entire Mormon sect, under the leadership of Brigham Young, went with their wagons through Nebraska and on to that desert beside the salty sea which they have made so fruitful.

In forty-nine and the early fifties, gold hunters, bound for California, crossed the State in thousands, always following the old Indian trail along the Platte valley. The State was a highway for dreamers and adventurers; men who were in quest of gold or grace, freedom or romance. With all these people the road led out, but never back again.

While Nebraska was a camping-ground for seekers outward bound, the wooden settlements along the Missouri were growing into something permanent. The settlers broke the ground and began to plant the fine orchards which have ever since been the pride of Otoe and Nemaha counties. It was at Brownville that the first telegraph wire was brought across the Missouri River. When I was a child I heard ex-Governor Furness relate how he stood with other pioneers in the log cabin where the Morse instrument had been installed, and how, when it began to click, the men took off their hats as if they were in church. The first message flashed across the river into Nebraska was not a market report, but a line of poetry: 'Westward the course of empire takes its way.' The Old West was like that.

The first back-and-forth travel through the State was by way of the Overland Mail, a monthly passenger-and-mail-stage service across the plains from Independence to the newly founded colony at Salt Lake—a distance of twelve hundred miles.

When silver ore was discovered in the mountains of Colorado near Cherry Creek—afterward Camp Denver and later the city of Denver—a picturesque form of commerce developed across the great plain of Nebraska; the transporting of food and merchandise from the Missouri to the Colorado mining camps, and on to the Mormon settlement at Salt Lake. One of the largest freighting companies, operating out of Nebraska City, in the six summer months of 1860 carried nearly three million pounds of freight across Nebraska, employing 515 wagons, 5,687 oxen, and 600 drivers.

The freighting began in the early spring, usually about the middle of April, and continued all summer and through the long, warm autumns. The oxen made from ten to twenty miles a day. I have heard the old freighters say that, after embarking on their six-hundred mile trail, they lost count of the days of the week and the days of the month. While they were out in that sea of waving grass, one day was like another; and, if one can trust the memory of these old men, all the days were glorious. The buffalo trails still ran north and south then; deep, dusty paths the bison wore when, single file, they came north in the spring for the summer grass, and went south again in the autumn. Along these trails were the buffalo 'wallows'—shallow depressions where the rain water gathered when it ran off the tough prairie sod. These wallows the big beasts wore deeper and packed hard when they rolled about and bathed in the pools, so that they held water like a cement bottom. The freighters lived on game and shot the buffalo for their hides. The grass was full of quail and prairie chickens, and flocks of wild ducks swam about on the lagoons. These lagoons have long since disappeared, but they were beautiful things in their time; long stretches where the rain water gathered and lay clear on a grassy bottom without mud. From the lagoons the first settlers hauled water to their homesteads, before they had dug their wells. The freighters could recognise the lagoons from afar by the clouds of golden coreopsis which grew up out of the water and waved delicately above its surface. Among the pioneers the coreopsis was known simply as 'the lagoon flower.'

As the railroads came in, the freighting business died out. Many a freight-driver settled down upon some spot he had come to like on his journeys to and fro, homesteaded it, and wandered no more. The Union Pacific, the first transcontinental railroad, was completed in 1869. The Burlington entered Nebraska in the same year, at Platsmouth, and began construction westward. It finally reached Denver by an indirect route, and went on extending and ramifying through the State. With the railroads came the home-seeking people from overseas.

When the first courageous settlers came straggling out through the waste with their oxen and covered wagons, they found open range all the way from Lincoln to Denver; a continuous, undulating plateau, covered with long, red, shaggy grass. The prairie was green only where it had been burned off in the spring by the new settlers or by the Indians, and toward autumn even the new grass became a coppery brown. This sod, which had never been broken by the plow, was so tough and strong with the knotted grass roots of many years, that the home-seekers were able to peel it off the earth like peat, cut it up into bricks, and make of it warm, comfortable, durable houses. Some of these sod houses lingered on until the open range was gone, and the grass was gone, and the whole face of the country had been changed.

Even as late as 1885 the central part of the State, and everything to the westward, was, in the main, raw prairie. The cultivated fields and broken land seemed mere scratches in the brown, running steppe that never stopped until it broke against the foothills of the Rockies. The dugouts and sod farm-houses were three or four miles apart, and the only means of communication was the heavy farm wagon, drawn by heavy work horses. The early population of Nebraska was largely transatlantic. The county in which I grew up, in the south-central part of the State, was typical. On Sunday we could drive to a Norwegian church and listen to a sermon in that language, or to a Danish or a Swedish church. We could go to the French Catholic settlement in the next county and hear a sermon in French, or into the Bohemian township and hear one in Czech, or we could go to church with some German Lutherans. There were, of course, American congregations also.

There is a Prague in Nebraska as well as in Bohemia. Many of our Czech immigrants were people of a very superior type. The political emigration resulting from the revolutionary disturbances of 1848 was distinctly different from the emigration resulting from economic causes, and brought to the United States brilliant young men both from Germany and Bohemia. In Nebraska our Czech settlements were large and very prosperous. I have walked about the streets of Wilber, the county seat of Saline County, for a whole day without hearing a word of English spoken. In Wilber, in the old days, behind the big, friendly brick saloon—it was not a 'saloon,' properly speaking, but a beer garden, where the farmers ate their lunch when they came to town—there was a pleasant little theater where the boys and girls were trained to give the masterpieces of Czech drama in the Czech language. 'Americanization' has doubtless done away with all this. Our lawmakers have rooted conviction that a boy can be a better American if he speaks only one language than if he speaks two. I could name a dozen Bohemian towns in Nebraska where one used to be able to go into a bakery and buy better pastry than is to be had anywhere except in the best pastry shops of Prague or Vienna. The American lard pie never corrupted the Czech.

Cultivated, restless young men from Europe made incongruous figures among the hard-handed breakers of the soil. Frederick Amiel's[1] nephew lived for many years and finally died among the Nebraska farmers. Amiel's letters to his kinsman were published in the *Atlantic Monthly* of March, 1921, under the title 'Amiel in Nebraska.' Camille Saint-Saëns's[2] cousin lived just over the line, in Kansas. Knut Hamsun, the Norwegian writer who was awarded the Nobel Prize for 1920, was a 'hired hand' on a Dakota farm to the north of us. Colonies of European people, Slavonic, Germanic, Scandinavian, Latin, spread across our bronze prairies like the daubs of color on a painter's palette. They brought with them something that this neutral new world needed even more than the immigrants needed land.

Unfortunately, their American neighbors were seldom open-minded enough to understand the Europeans, or to profit by their older traditions. Our settlers from New England, cautious and convinced of their own superiority, kept themselves insulated as much as possible from foreign influences. The incomers from the South— from Missouri, Kentucky, the two Virginias—were provincial and utterly without curiosity. They were kind neighbors—lent a hand to help a Swede when he was sick or in trouble. But I am quite sure that Knut Hamsun might have worked a year for any one of our Southern farmers, and his employer would never have discovered that there was anything unusual about the Norwegian. A New England settler might have noticed that his chore-boy had a kind of intelligence, but he would have distrusted and stonily disregarded it. If the daughter of a shiftless West Virginia mountaineer married the nephew of a professor at the University of Upsala, the native family felt disgraced by such an alliance.

Nevertheless, the thrift and intelligence of its preponderant European population have been potent factors in bringing about the present prosperity of the State. The census of 1910 showed that there were then 228,648 foreign-born and native-born Germans living in Nebraska; 103,503 Scandinavians; 50,680 Czechs. The total foreign population of the State was then 900,571, while the entire population was 1,192,214. That is, in round numbers, there were about nine hundred thousand foreign Americans in the State, to three hundred

---

1. Henri Frédéric Amiel (1821–1881), Swiss philosopher and writer.
2. French composer (1835–1921).

thousand native stock. With such a majority of foreign stock, nine
to three, it would be absurd to say that the influence of the European does not cross the boundary of his own acres, and has had nothing to do with shaping the social ideals of the commonwealth.

When I stop at one of the graveyards in my own county, and see
on the headstones the names of fine old men I used to know: *'Eric
Ericson, born Bergen, Norway . . . died Nebraska,' 'Anton Pucelik, born
Prague, Bohemia . . . died Nebraska,'* I have always the hope that
something went into the ground with those pioneers that will one
day come out again. Something that will come out not only in sturdy
traits of character, but in elasticity of mind, in an honest attitude
toward the realities of life, in certain qualities of feeling and imagination. Some years ago a professor at the University of Nebraska happened to tell me about a boy in one of his Greek classes who had a
very unusual taste for the classics—intuitions and perceptions in literature. This puzzled him, he said, as the boy's parents had no interest in such things. I knew what the professor did not: that, though
this boy had an American name, his grandfather was a Norwegian,
a musician of high attainment, a fellow-student and life-long friend
of Edvard Grieg.[3] It is in that great cosmopolitan country known as
the Middle West that we may hope to see the hard molds of American provincialism broken up; that we may hope to find young talent
which will challenge the pale proprieties, the insincere, conventional
optimism of our art and thought.

The rapid industrial development of Nebraska, which began in the
latter eighties, was arrested in the years 1893–97 by a succession of
crop failures and by the financial depression which spread over the
whole country at that time—the depression which produced the
People's Party and the Free Silver agitation. These years of trial, as
everyone now realizes, had a salutary effect upon the new State. They
winnowed out the settlers with a purpose from the drifting malcon-
tents who are ever seeking a land where man does not live by the
sweat of his brow. The slack farmer moved on. Superfluous banks
failed, and money lenders who drove hard bargains with desperate
men came to grief. The strongest stock survived, and within ten years
those who had weathered the storm came into their reward. What
that reward is, you can see for yourself if you motor through the State
from Omaha to the Colorado line. The country has no secrets; it is
as open as an honest human face.

The old, isolated farms have come together. They rub shoulders.
The whole State is a farm. Now it is the pasture lands that look little
and lonely, crowded in among so much wheat and corn. It is

---

3. Norwegian composer (1843–1907) whose works included incidental music to Ibsen's
   Peer Gynt and the Piano Concerto in A Minor, Op. 16.

scarcely an exaggeration to say that every farmer owns an automobile. I believe the last estimate showed that there is one motor car
for every six inhabitants in Nebraska. The great grain fields are
plowed by tractors. The old farm houses are rapidly being replaced
by more cheerful dwellings, with bathrooms and hardwood floors,
heated by furnaces or hot-water plants. Many of them are lighted
by electricity, and every farm house has its telephone. The country
towns are clean and well kept. On Saturday night the main street is
a long black line of parked motor cars; the farmers have brought their
families to town to see the moving-picture show. When the school
bell rings on Monday morning, crowds of happy looking children,
well nourished—for the most part well mannered, too,—flock along
the shady streets. They wear cheerful, modern clothes, and the
girls, like the boys, are elastic and vigorous in their movements.
These thousands and thousands of children—in the little towns
and in the country schools—these, of course, ten years from now,
will be the State.

In this time of prosperity any farmer boy who wishes to study at
the State University can do so. A New York lawyer who went out to
Lincoln to assist in training the university students for military service in war time exclaimed when he came back: 'What splendid young
men! I would not have believed that any school in the world could
get together so many boys physically fit, and so few unfit.'

Of course, there is the other side of the medal, stamped with the
ugly crest of materialism, which has set its seal upon all of our most
productive commonwealths. Too much prosperity, too many moving-
picture shows, too much gaudy fiction have colored the taste and
manners of so many of these Nebraskans of the future. There, as
elsewhere, one finds the frenzy to be showy; farmer boys who wish
to be spenders before they are earners, girls who try to look like the
heroines of the cinema screen; a coming generation which tries to
cheat its aesthetic sense by buying things instead of making anything.
There is even danger that that fine institution, the University of
Nebraska, may become a gigantic trade school. The men who control its destiny, the regents and the lawmakers, wish their sons and
daughters to study machines, mercantile processes, 'the principles
of business'; everything that has to do with the game of getting on
in the world—and nothing else. The classics, the humanities, are
having their dark hour. They are in eclipse. Studies that develop taste
and enrich personality are not encouraged. But the 'Classics' have a
way of revenging themselves. One may venture to hope that the children, or the grandchildren, of a generation that goes to a university
to select only the most utilitarian subjects in the course of study—
among them, salesmanship and dressmaking—will revolt against all
the heaped-up, machine-made materialism about them. They will

go back to the old sources of culture and wisdom—not as a duty, but with burning desire.

In Nebraska, as in so many other States, we must face the fact that the splendid story of the pioneers is finished, and that no new story worthy to take its place has yet begun. The generation that subdued the wild land and broke up the virgin prairie is passing, but it is still there, a group of rugged figures in the background which inspire respect, compel admiration. With these old men and women the attainment of material prosperity was a moral victory, because it was wrung from hard conditions, was the result of a struggle that tested character. They can look out over those broad stretches of fertility and say: 'We made this, with our backs and hands.' The sons, the generation now in middle life, were reared amid hardships, and it is perhaps natural that they should be very much interested in material comfort, in buying whatever is expensive and ugly. Their fathers came into a wilderness and had to make everything, had to be as ingenious as shipwrecked sailors. The generation now in the driver's seat hates to make anything, wants to live and die in an automobile, scudding past those acres where the old men used to follow the long corn-rows up and down. They want to buy everything ready-made: clothes, food, education, music, pleasure. Will the third generation—the full-blooded, joyous one just coming over the hill—will it be fooled? Will it believe that to live easily is to live happily?

The wave of generous idealism, of noble seriousness, which swept over the State of Nebraska in 1917 and 1918, demonstrated how fluid and flexible is any living, growing, expanding society. If such 'conversions' do not last, they at least show of what men and women are capable. Surely the materialism and showy extravagance of this hour are a passing phase! They will mean no more in half a century from now than will the 'hard times' of twenty-five years ago—which are already forgotten. The population is as clean and full of vigor as the soil; there are no old grudges, no heritages of disease or hate. The belief that snug success and easy money are the real aims of human life has settled down over our prairies, but it has not yet hardened into molds and crusts. The people are warm, mercurial, impressionable, restless, over-fond of novelty and change. These are not the qualities which make the dull chapters of history.

CRITICISM

Contemporary Reviews
of *My Ántonia*

NEW YORK TIMES BOOK REVIEW[†]

[*My Ántonia*]

Nebraska is the scene of Willa S. Cather's new novel, the central character being a young Bohemian girl, Antonia Shimerda, the daughter of immigrants. Her father and mother came to Nebraska, where they had bought a farm out in the prairie from a fellow countryman, who cheated them badly. Jim Burden, who tells the story, is an American boy, living with his prosperous grandparents on their big farm, which, as distances go in that country, is not so very far from the Shimerdas' place. Jim's grandparents befriend the Shimerdas, and it is Jim himself who teaches Antonia English. A large part of the book is given over to an account of the work and play of these two during the year when Jim was about 10 and Antonia about 14.

There is a carefully detailed picture of daily existence on a Nebraska farm, and indeed the whole book is a carefully detailed picture rather than a story.

* * *

The book is full of sketches of farm life, of plowing, reaping and thrashing, of the difficulties of feeding cattle in winter, and all the routine of husbandry. Antonia is a true daughter of the soil, thus described: "She had only to stand in the orchard, to put her hand on a little crab tree and look up at the apples, to make you feel the goodness of planting and tending and harvesting at last." There are other immigrants in the book besides the Shimerdas—Norwegians, Danes, Russians, etc.—and the ways of all of them are more or less fully described. They are all, to some extent, pioneers, the period of the book being that in which the first foreign immigrants came to Nebraska.

† October 6, 1918, p. 429.

THE (NEW YORK) SUN

My Nebraska Ántonia[†]

There is a special genius of Memory. Where it exists it is capable of accomplishing what no other genius can reach. The classic modern example of it is Joseph Conrad's story "Youth"—a thing of terrible poignancy, of wonder and tears. If a writer is so blessed as to be able, only one or two times, to recapture the past and rekindle the ancient fires he will leave a name remembered and loved from generation to generation.

Of living American writers there is particularly one who has this great gift. Willa Sibert Cather, writing O *Pioneers!* made an indelible impression upon the minds of those who read that novel, an impression which was merely confirmed with satisfactory completeness by her own confession afterward. . . .

What Willa Cather got out of her childhood was a wonderful awareness of the few people about her and of the soil they struggled upon and of the struggle itself, as desperate as that of the lonely swimmer to keep afloat in mid-ocean. This soil was an ocean, an illimitable ocean of tall red grass, forever billowing in the wind so that the visible earth appeared as restless as horizonless waters.

"As I looked about me I felt that the grass was the country, as the water is the sea. The red of the grass made all the great prairie the color of wine stains, or of certain seaweeds when they are first washed up. And there was so much motion in it, the whole country seemed somehow, to be running."

The words are Jim Burden's and the perception is that of a ten-year-old set down for the first time in the plains of the middle West. But the picture cinematographed on a woman's brain and projected on the pages of Willa Cather's new book, *My Antonia.*

The most extraordinary thing about *My Antonia* is the author's surrender of the usual methods of fiction in telling her story. Time and again as you read the book it strikes you what an exciting novel Miss Cather could have made of it if she had wanted to plait the strands of her story into a regulation plot. But she renounces all that at the beginning in a brief introduction.

The introduction acquaints us with Jim Burden, a New York lawyer of wealth and reputation, whose youthful fortunes were much advanced by his marriage with the only daughter of a distinguished man. There appears never to have been love in that marriage. Only one woman ever really influenced Jim Burden's life or kindled his

† October 6, 1918, section 5, p. 1.

imagination—Antonia Shimerda, later Antonia Cuzak—a Bohemian girl who had been his playmate in their childhood on the Nebraska prairie. Miss Cather asks us to accept the story of Antonia as set down by Burden. It is a series of memories exclusively; it has continuity and it has development; but it has not and could not have any of the plot or suspense which could so easily be managed by telling the story in ordinary fashion. It would have been so easy for the author to have told her tale herself and to have matched Antonia against the woman who became Mrs. Burden; the complete contrast between the two would have been dramatic enough in all conscience, and the struggle in Jim Burden could have been made wholly plausible. Then why didn't she do it that way?

Because to have done it that way would have branded her narrative as purest fiction in the mind of every reader; a comfortable sense that none of this ever had happened would have gone with you all the way through the book absorbing as it would have been. But now you are positively uncomfortable from page to page with the conviction that all of this happened! By deliberately and at the outset surrendering the story teller's most valuable perogatives Miss Cather has won a complete victory over the reader, shattering his easeful assumption of the unreality of it all, routing his ready-made demand for the regulation thrills and taking prisoner his sense of what is his rightful due. It is as if General Foch[1] were maneuvering. The strategy is unfathomed and the blow falls in a most unexpected quarter. You picked up *My Antonia* to read a novel (love story, of course; hope it's a good one) and find yourself enthralled by autobiography.

What vivid autobiography it is we cannot indicate adequately. For a great part of the book Antonia (the Bohemians accent the first syllable of the name strongly, and this should be remembered in pronouncing the title)—for perhaps half of the book Antonia stands out not much more distinctly than a half dozen other people. The reader is puzzled to understand why she should mean so much to the boy Jim Burden. It takes the last fifty pages, we suspect, to make it clear just what she meant and how deeply, even as it took the sight of her and her children, after an interval of some twenty years, to make this clear to Jim himself.

The real interest of the narrative pending the final and moving disclosure of Antonia Cuzak, the interest and the rich delight of it, the heaped up satisfaction, lies in the simple and perfect picture of pioneer life. It lies in the figure of old Mr. Shimerda, a sad and stricken aristocrat, and in the account of his ghastly death. It lies in the figures of Jake and Otto. It rests in the portraits of Jim's grandfather and grandmother, of Pavel (or Paul) and Peter, the Russians,

---

1. General Ferdinand Foch (1851–1929), French soldier and commander during World War I.

and their dreadful story. Mr. Shimerda, kneeling before the lighted
Christmas tree on which all the colored figures from Austria stood
out in the candle flame; Otto, cheerily carpentering Mr. Shimerda's
coffin: Peter and Pavel and the bridal night in Russia which was also
the night of the wolves; Crazy Mary, chasing Lena Lingard with a
corn knife to "trim some of that shape off her"; Lena with her violet
eyes, giving away her heart when she feels like it but never losing her
head; Blind D'Arnault, the negro musician, and his strange story; the
revelations regarding the satyr, Wycliffe Cutter; a performance of
Camille in Lincoln, Nebraska; the worldly success of Tiny Soderball—
these are the raw materials of romance, but the very substance of
actuality. They need only to be skilfully related, and in handling them
as Cather does unfailingly well. Nor is her accomplishment easy;
murder, suicide, debauchery and occurrences that were not only
unvarnished but unvarnishable are quite as much a part of what she
has to handle as the happy, domestic scenes natural to childhood.
She is no feminine Zola,[2] fortunately; without any smirch of realism
she achieves the happiest reality. A young writer who wants to deal
honestly and yet inoffensively with a variety of difficult things can
learn big lessons from reading this book.

Seven weeks ago, in reviewing on this page Gene Stratton-Porter's
A Daughter of the Land, we quoted the aspiration of the heroine of
that novel to become the mother of at least twelve children. Afterward a writer in *Reedy's Mirror*[3] poked fun at this; the mother
of twelve would be an impossible heroine in fiction, he seemed to
think. The point was rather ignorantly taken. It might reasonably be
argued that any mother of twelve (in these days, at any rate) must
be so exceptional as to deserve not merely a fictional but a biographical eminence. But as a matter of fact, Mrs. Porter was herself
one of twelve children; and it is very evident from her account of her
mother that Mrs. Stratton would have been a striking figure in fiction, perhaps too unusual to be believed in readily. As if further to
controvert the jester in *Reedy's Mirror* we have Antonia Cuzak.

And, by the way, at the Cuzak farm there must now be a red-
bordered flag, and the stars, in the heart of it must form a glorious
constellation.

2. Émile Zola (1840–1902), French novelist and leading example of the literary movement
   of naturalism, which stressed journalistic accuracy in fiction along with attention to
   the raw, gritty details of life.
3. Midwestern literary journal founded in 1891.

THE NATION

Two Portraits[†]

* * * [In *Camilla*, Elizabeth] Robins[1] affects the deliberate, elliptical, smooth-spoken post-Jacobite manner that appears to attract so many of the current women story-tellers, Mrs. Wharton leading the way. It touches snobbishness at both ends. It is too niggling and high-heeled for much real usefulness on this side of the water. A writer like Miss Cather is as clear of it as of the man-in-the-street patter of the magazine story-tellers (snobbishness at its nadir). Her style has distinction, not manner; and it is the style of an artist whose imagination is at home in her own land, among her own people, which happens to be a democratic land and a plain people. She has a strong feeling about this—that we cannot get away from our sources. One recalls how this is enforced in *The Song of the Lark*—how we were made to understand that Thea Kronborg's genius sprang from the soil of her birthplace. And one recognizes how directly this story, like *The Song of the Lark*, springs from Miss Cather's own soil. She was born in Virginia, but her childhood was passed on her father's ranch in Nebraska. During her most receptive years her nature was responding to the charm and mystery of the prairie, and also to her human setting. The pioneer neighborhood was mainly peopled by Scandinavians and Bohemians. Their exotic character and ways became a part of the child's America. Her three novels are stories of women: two of them Swedish-American girls, and the third, Ántonia, the child of a Bohemian immigrant. This is and professes to be (despite the publishers who inconceivably declare it "a love-story") nothing more or less than a portrait of a woman. The Shimerdas are a poor Bohemian family who have taken up a little Nebraskan farm. The father, a man of sensitive feeling, devoted to his own land, has come to America at the insistence of the vulgar and ambitious mother. He finds nothing to live for here, and takes his own life not long after their arrival. The girl Ántonia has his fineness of nature but a vigor and steadfastness also, of body and spirit, which fit her for conquest of life. Not in Thea Kronborg's way, by genius infallibly journeying upward, but by the commoner road of a strong and simple character not to be submerged by circumstance. We do not so much hear her story told as go with her upon her humble triumphant way, as farmhand, hired girl, woman befooled and deserted by the father of her first child, and at last as happy wife and drudge of a commonplace

† Vol. 107 (November 2, 1918), pp. 522–23.
1. American actress and novelist (1862–1952).

good little man of her own race, and mother of a great brood of healthy and rewarding offspring. Our guide upon this quiet pilgrimage is the American who has been Ántonia's neighbor and playmate in childhood, and whose love for her, in his years of "success" in the great world, remains a feeling of peculiar depth and unlessening inspiration. In some sense, after all that has come between them, she is still "his Ántonia." "She was a battered woman now, not a lovely girl; but she still had that something which fires the imagination, could still stop one's breath for a moment by a look or gesture that somehow revealed the meaning in common things. . . . It was no wonder that her sons stood tall and straight. She was a rich mine of life, like the founders of early races." A notable portrait rendered too quietly, perhaps, to catch the eye of the seeker for color and movement of the picturesque or dramatic order, but worthy to stand with *The Song of the Lark* among the best of our recent interpretations of American life.

C. L. H.

Struggles with the Soil[†]

Antonia is not the conventional heroine. She never becomes an heiress, she uncovers no spy plot for the government, she never even dreams of the life of a Red Cross nurse, and she is no adventuress. She is a stalwart Bohemian peasant girl, grows up on a windy and barren Nebraska farm and helps her parents till the soil and make it fruitful.

We follow her through a difficult and picturesque childhood, see her emerge into a glowing and vital young womanhood, and by the end find her where such a vigorous and elemental person should be— on her farm, surrounded by a family of nine or ten children.

No less vivid and stirring than Antonia herself is the physical background of the story. The long and bitter winters, the scorching summers, the vast stretches of uncultivated prairies, the hard struggle against poverty and actual starvation—these things are described with a simplicity and directness that give us a real feeling of the actuality. We read much of the struggles of the foreigners in our big cities. This book gives us a picture of the grim and determined fight for life and prosperity of the vigorous foreigners who have settled in the West and helped to make it a land of fruitfulness. The story is a fresh and sincere piece of work.

---

† *New York Call Magazine*, November 3, 1918, p. 10.

BOOKLIST

Review[†]

The prairie is the background for this narrative of the fortunes of a Bohemian girl as they were observed by an American boy who grew up on a neighboring farm and in the little Nebraska village. Stark realism gives a haunting quality to two grim scenes; others are not so grim but just as vivid. The whole gives an intimate friendship for the quiet, strong, simple Antonia with her own charm and power from childhood to contented middle age as the mother of her prairie children. It will not appeal to as many readers as *The Song of the Lark*.

H[ENRY] W[ALCOTT] BOYNTON

Bookman Review[‡]

Miss Cather is an accomplished artist. Her method is that of the higher realism; it rests not at all upon the machinery of dramatic action which is so right and essential for romance. Her *Song of the Lark*, a triumphal story if there ever was one, lacked the rounded artifice that lures a big public—lacked, above all, the conventional "happy ending." So does *My Antonia*, which, even more frankly a portrait than its predecessor, is a portrait of a woman.

Miss Cather has owned as among the most vivid of her experiences on the Nebraska ranch of her childhood, her impressions of the Scandinavian and Bohemian settlers who were among her neighbors. Thea Kronborg in *The Song of the Lark* was of Swedish parentage. Antonia is a Bohemian girl on a Nebraska ranch. Her father, a musician and dreamer, has no heart in the new life and presently kills himself as the only way out. The mother and the elder son are ambitious and unscrupulous. Antonia is the one well-rounded member of the family: somehow she joins her father's sensitiveness to the sturdiness of her mother, and contributes that magic something of her own that is necessary to transmute mere characteristics into personality.

She is not infallible or protected by a special Providence, does not push forward to an obvious success or happiness. On the contrary she passes her first years of grown girlhood as a farm worker, becomes a "hired girl" in the neighboring town, runs away with a flashy drummer

---

† December 1918.
‡ December 1918, p. 495.

who deserts her before the birth of her child, and later marries an undistinguished and not especially successful farmer of her own race. But she is unconquerable; and she lives through everything to transmit that superb health and courage of mind and body to a great family who are bound to make their worthy contribution to America. It is in this guise, as "a rich mine of life, like the founders of early races", that we see her fulfilled and justified.

Clearly, the effectiveness of such a portrait depends in an unusual sense upon the skill of the painter. Casual as her touches seem, no stroke is superfluous or wrongly emphasized; and we may be hardly conscious how much of the total effect of the portrait is owing to the quiet beauty and purity of the artist's style.

RANDOLPH BOURNE

Morals and Art from the West[†]

* * * Let us turn aside to a novel so different that it seems impossible that it could have been written in the same year and by an American from the same part of the country as William Allen White.[1] Willa Cather has already shown herself an artist in that beautiful story of Nebraska immigrant life, O Pioneers! Her digression into The Song of the Lark took her into a field that neither her style nor her enthusiasm really fitted her for. Now in My Antonia she has returned to the Nebraska countryside with an enriched feeling and an even more golden charm of style. Here at last is an American novel, redolent of the Western prairie, that our most irritated and exacting preconceptions can be content with. It is foolish to be captious about American fiction when the same year gives us two so utterly unlike, and yet equally artistic, novels as Mr. Fuller's[2] On the Stairs and Miss Cather's My Antonia. She is also of the brevity school, and beside William Allen White's swollen bulk she makes you realize anew how much art is suggestion and not transcription. One sentence from Miss Cather's pages is more vivid than paragraphs of Mr. White's stale brightness of conversation. The reflections she does not make upon her characters are more convincing than all his moralizing. Her purpose is neither to illustrate eternal truths nor to set before us the crowded gallery of a whole society. Yet in these simple pictures of the struggling pioneer life, of the comfortable middle classes of the bleak little towns, there is an understanding of what these people have to contend with and grope for that goes to the very heart of their lives.

† The Dial, 65 (December 14, 1918), p. 557.
1. American newspaper editor (The Emporia Gazette), writer, and advocate of progressive politics (1868–1944). Kansas-based, he became known as a spokesperson for the needs and values of the Midwest.
2. Henry Blake Fuller (1857–1929), American novelist and short-story writer.

Miss Cather convinces because she knows her story and carries it along with the surest touch. It has all the artistic simplicity of material that has been patiently shaped until everything irrelevant has been scraped away. The story has a flawless tone of candor, a naive charm, that seems quite artless until we realize that no spontaneous narrative could possibly have the clean pertinence and grace which this story has. It would be cluttered, as Mr. White's novel is cluttered; it would have uneven streaks of self-consciousness, as most of the younger novelists' work, done impromptu with a mistaken ideal of "saturation," is both cluttered and self-conscious. But Miss Cather's even novel has that serenity of the story that is telling itself, of people who are living through their own spontaneous charm.

The story purports to be the memories of a successful man as he looks back over his boyhood on the Nebraska farm and in the little town. Of that boyhood Antonia was the imaginative center, the little Bohemian immigrant, his playmate and wistful sweetheart. His vision is romantic, but no more romantic than anyone would be towards so free and warm and glorious a girl. He goes to the University, and it is only twenty years later that he hears the story of her pathetic love and desertion, and her marriage to a simple Bohemian farmer, strong and good like herself. . . .

My Antonia has the indestructible fragrance of youth: the prairie girls and the dances; the softly alluring Lena, who so unaccountably fails to go wrong; the rich flowered prairie, with its drowsy heats and stinging colds. The book, in its different way, is as fine as the Irishman Corkery's The Threshold of Quiet,[3] that other recent masterpiece of wistful youth. But this story lives with the hopefulness of the West. It is poignant and beautiful, but it is not sad. Miss Cather, I think, in this book has taken herself out of the rank of provincial writers and given us something we can fairly class with the modern literary art the world over that is earnestly and richly interpreting the spirit of youth. In her work the stiff moral molds are fortunately broken, and she writes what we can wholly understand.

N. P. D[AWSON]

Miss Cather's My Ántonia[†]

Verily, some authors make the life of the reviewer a very pleasant one. Last week it was Mr. Hergesheimer;[1] this week it is Willa Sibert Cather. In My Antonia, Miss Cather multiplies many times the genius

3. Irish writer Daniel Corkery (1878–1964) published The Threshold of Quiet, a novel set in Cork city, in 1917.
† (New York) Globe and Commercial Advertiser, January 11, 1919.
1. Joseph Hergesheimer (1880–1954), prolific and well-known American novelist.

of one of her first novels, *O Pioneers,* another story of Nebraska and the middle west, with the American pioneers and foreign settlers. It has the fascination of Mr. Hudson's *Far Away and Long Ago*,[2] and the striking originality of Conrad's *A Personal Record*.[3] The only book we can recall that approaches it in the truthfulness and charm of its descriptions of the prairie country is a book published some years ago called *A Stepdaughter of the Prairie.*

But here we are writing of Miss Cather's book as if it were auto-biography and not a story. Like most works of art, it is probably both. Miss Cather has the gift of remembering, and the equally important gift of forgetting, what is not important. She is a genuine realist. Her passion for the truth is apparently as great as her aversion for mere writing. If she is ever tempted to indulge in fine writing, she seems to follow the advice of the one who said, "be bold and murder your darlings." Nor does this mean that Miss Cather's narrative has any of the dullness and flatness and ugliness generally associated with realistic writing. With manifest fidelity to scene and character, and apparent simplicity and naturalness in the telling of the story, it is at the same time shimmering with romance and excitement. She can tell a bigger snake story, and a more horrifying one than Mr. Hudson: while her story of the Russian bride thrown to the wolves is as picturesque, shall we say, as Mr. Conrad's story of his heroic great-uncle who was with Napoleon and ate the Lithuanian dog. There are stories within stories, all as neatly unfolding as a set of Chinese boxes. There are many characters—living, breathing people.

But it is the description of the country itself that will perhaps most impress the reader, especially the reader who knows. It may be wondered if there is something in what Miss Cather says in her opening chapter about the freemasonry of people who come from the same parts of the country. If this is true, as we are inclined to think it is, some tears may well be felt for the new internationalism. A child's idea of Heaven is a place just like home. In an introduction, in which she cleverly and with art explains the male medium of her story-telling, Miss Cather says:

> We were talking about what it is like to spend one's childhood in little towns like these, buried in wheat and corn, under stimulating extremes of climate: burning summers when the world lies green and billowy beneath a brilliant sky, when one is fairly stifled in vegetation, in the color and smell of strong weeds and heavy harvests; blustery winters with little snow, when the

2. William Henry Hudson (1841–1922), Argentina-born naturalist, ornithologist, and writer who resided in England. *Far Away and Long Ago: A History of My Early Life* (1918) recounted his boyhood in Argentina.
3. *A Personal Record* (1912) is an autobiographical work by the English writer Joseph Conrad (1857–1924).

whole country is stripped bare and gray as sheet iron. We agreed that no one who had not grown up in a little prairie town could know anything about it. It was a kind of freemasonry, we said.

Well, the country is here in all its variety; hot summer nights when "you can hear the corn grow," and not only winters that bluster, but winters that are real with the "big blizzard," when the snow is "spilled out of heaven, like thousands of feather beds, being emptied"—such feather beds as Mrs. Shimerda, the Bohemian woman, used to keep her roast goose hot in.

On the train carrying the small boy from Virginia to Nebraska to make his home with his grandparents—the same train bringing the Bohemian family with "my Antonia," we read that "the only thing very noticeable about Nebraska was that it was still all day long Nebraska." There was nothing but land. In fact, it seemed "not a country at all, but the material out of which countries are made." "The grass was the country as the water is the sea," and the grass had "so much motion in it that the whole country seemed somehow to be running."

Bits of description such as these are not only incredibly vivid, but are poetic and excite the imagination. . . . It is a story of great truth and great beauty. More than this, it is interesting and will be enjoyed by those who never heard the corn grow or saw a prairie-dog town either.

THE INDEPENDENT

Review[†]

To those who appreciate style in fiction, and for that quality alone can enjoy a story that has neither exciting plot nor swift action, Miss Cather's new book, *My Antonia*, will make strong appeal. With sympathy and understanding she tells a tale of youth and courage in the red grass region of Nebraska, when that part of our country was being settled by a large foreign immigration. The simple tale of growth centers about a Bohemian girl and an American lad, but Antonia is the main character. The story of her development thru the hardships of frontier life is full of human appeal and the fascination of the making of Americans from the foreign born.

† January 25, 1919, p. 131.

H[ENRY] L[OUIS] MENCKEN

Sunrise on the Prairie: VII[†]

Two new novels, *My Antonia*, by Willa Sibert Cather, and *In the Heart of a Fool*, by William Allen White bear out in different ways some of the doctrines displayed in the earlier sections of this article. Miss Cather's book shows an earnest striving toward that free and dignified self-expression, that high artistic conscience, that civilized point of view, which Dr. Brooks[1] dreams of as at once the cause and effect of his fabulous "luminosity." Mr. White's shows the viewpoint of a chautaqua spell-binder and the manner of a Methodist evangelist. It is, indeed, a novel so intolerably mawkish and maudlin, so shallow and childish, so vapid and priggish, that its accumulated badness almost passes belief, and if it were not for one thing I should be tempted to spit on my hands and give it such a slating that the very hinges of this great family periodical would grow white-hot. That thing, that insidious dissuader, is not, I lament to report, a saving merit. It is something far different: it is an ineradicable suspicion that, after all, the book is absolutely American—that, for all its horrible snuffling and sentimentalizing, it is a very fair example of the sort of drivel that passes for "sound" and "inspiring" in our fair republic, and is eagerly praised by the newspapers, and devoured voraciously by the people.

* * *

It is needless to add that Dr. White is a member of the American Academy of Arts and Letters. Nor is it necessary to hint that Miss Cather is not. Invading the same Middle West that engages the Kansas tear-squeezer and academician, and dealing with almost the same people, she comes forward with a novel that is everything that his is not—sound, delicate, penetrating, brilliant, charming. I do not push the comparison for the mere sake of the antithesis. Miss Cather is a craftsman whom I have often praised in this place and with increasing joy. Her work, for ten years past, has shown a steady and rapid improvement, in both matter and manner. She has arrived at last at such a command of the mere devices of writing that the uses she makes of them are all concealed—her style has lost self-consciousness; her feeling for form has become instinctive. And she has got such a grip upon her materials—upon the people she sets before us and the background she displays behind them—that both take on an

[†] *Smart Set* 58 (February 1919), pp. 143–44.
1. Van Wyck Brooks (1886–1963), American literary critic, historian, and biographer.

extraordinary reality. I know of no novel that makes the remote folk of the western prairies more real than *My Antonia* makes them, and I know of none that makes them seem better worth knowing. Beneath the swathings of balderdash, the surface of numskullery and illusion, the tawdry stuff of Middle Western *Kultur*, she discovers human beings embattled against fate and the gods, and into her picture of their dull struggle she gets a spirit that is genuinely heroic, and a pathos that is genuinely moving. It is not as they see themselves that she depicts them, but as they actually are. To representation she adds something more. There is not only the story of poor peasants, flung by fortune into lonely, inhospitable winds; there is the eternal tragedy of man.

My Antonia is the best American novel since *The Rise of David Levinsky* as *In the Heart of a Fool* is probably one of the worst. There is something in it to lift depression. If such things can be done in America, then perhaps Dr. Brooks, if he lives to be 85, may yet get a glimpse of his luminosity. But what else is there to bolster up that hope? I can find nothing in the current crop.

Mainly Fiction[†]

The Cather story, *My Antonia*, was reviewed somewhat briefly in this place last month. It well deserves another notice, for it is not an isolated phenomenon, an extraordinary single book like Cahan's *The Rise of David Levinsky*, or Masters's *Spoon River Anthology*,[1] but merely one more step upward in the career of a writer who has labored with the utmost patience and industry, and won every foot of the way by hard work. She began, setting aside certain early experiments, with *Alexander's Bridge* in 1912—a book strongly suggesting the influence of Edith Wharton and yet thoroughly individual and newly thought out. Its defect was one of locale and people; one somehow got the feeling that Miss Cather was dealing with things at secondhand, that she knew her personages a bit less intimately than she should have known them. This defect, I venture to guess, impressed itself upon the author herself. At all events, she abandoned New England, in her next novel, for the Middle West, and in particular for the Middle West of the last great immigrations—a region far better known to her. The result was *O Pioneers!* (1913), a book of very fine achievement and of even finer promise. Then came *The Song of the Lark* in 1915—still more competent, more searching and convincing, better

† *Smart Set*, 58 (March 1919), pp. 140–41.
1. *The Rise of David Levinsky* is a novel of immigration by Abraham Cahan (1860–1951). *Spoon River Anthology* is a collection of poems evoking small-town America by Edgar Lee Masters (1868–1950).

in every way. And now, after three years, comes *My Antonia*, a work in which improvement takes a sudden leap—a novel, indeed, that is not only the best done by Miss Cather herself, but also one of the best that any American has ever done, East or West, early or late. It is simple; it is honest; it is intelligent; it is moving. The means that appear in it are means perfectly adapted to its end. Its people are unquestionably real. Its background is brilliantly vivid. It has form, grace, good literary manners. In a word, it is a capital piece of writing, and it will be heard of long after the baroque balderdash now touted on the "book pages" is forgotten.

It goes without saying that all the machinery customary to that balderdash is charmingly absent. There is, in the ordinary sense, no plot. There is no hero. There is, save as a momentary flash, no love affair. There is no apparent hortatory purpose, no show of theory, no visible aim to improve the world. The whole enchantment is achieved by the simplest of all possible devices. One follows a poor Bohemian farm girl from her earliest teens to middle age, looking closely at her narrow world, mingling with her friends, observing the gradual widening of her experience, her point of view—and that is all. Intrinsically, the thing is sordid—the life is almost horrible, the horizon is leaden, the soul within is pitifully shrunken and dismayed. But what Miss Cather tries to reveal is the true romance that lies even there—the grim tragedy at the heart of all that dull, cow-like existence—the fineness that lies deeply buried beneath the peasant shell. Dreiser tried to do the same thing with both Carrie Meeber and Jennie Gerhardt,[2] and his success was unmistakable. Miss Cather succeeds quite as certainly, but in an altogether different way. Dreiser's method was that of tremendous particularity—he built up his picture with an infinity of little strokes, many of them superficially meaningless. Miss Cather's method inclines more to suggestion and indirection. Here a glimpse, there a turn of phrase, and suddenly the thing stands out, suddenly it is as real as real can be—and withal moving, arresting, beautiful with a strange and charming beauty. . . . I commend the book to your attention, and the author no less. There is no other American author of her sex now in view, whose future promises so much * * *

---

2. The heroines of *Sister Carrie* (1900) and *Jennie Gerhardt* (1911), novels by American writer Theodore Dreiser (1871–1945), a practitioner of literary naturalism.

CHICAGO DAILY NEWS

Paper Dolls or People?[†]

Some books are written about paper dolls—cleverly designed and smartly painted and dressed, but flat. Close the book and they lie quietly between the pages until some young person takes them down ten years later and says, "How quaint!"

My Antonia, by Willa Sibert Cather, hasn't a paper doll in it. The people come out of it as you read it and refuse to be put back on the shelf with the book. They go about your work with you, and presently it seems as if you had known them well for a long time.

This quality of realness is important because *My Antonia* tells of the west, and there are novels in uncounted numbers about a pasteboard west, full of gaily colored "cut-out" cowboys shooting up towns, sugar plum western girls and torn paper blizzards. It is a west manufactured by writers who thought they had to make-believe or their stories would not be interesting, and it can be done perfectly by a man who was never outside New York. When it is done it isn't half as important as one of Grimm's fairy tales that doesn't even pretend to be real.

Willa Cather lived in Nebraska when she was a little girl. It was a west that the conventional wild west novels never hint at. Homesteaders were coming into the state from the east and from all over Europe. The prairie flowers were no more varied than the families whose claims cornered and who got their supplies and their mail from the same raw little town.

Bohemians and Russians, Virginians and Norwegians, found themselves neighbors. While they built their dugouts and turned under the sod for their first corn they had to learn each others' racial and individual peculiarities.

Sometimes they clashed tragically. Czech and Austrian found each other antagonistic; slow Swede and fiery Bohemian loved each other to their own hurt. Oftener each discovered that the other was marvelously human and like himself.

Under the common necessity of cooperating in house-building and harvesting and educating their children, something very like an informal league of nations resulted. In an amazingly short time the community became American, with common interests and a common language, but with possibilities of varied development that no thoroughbred race could by itself exhibit.

[†] April 12, 1919.

Not since the early colonial times when Spanish, Dutch, English and French were shouldering each other off the American coast has there been opportunity for such racial contact and interplay.

Miss Cather has had the rare good sense to see that the west of the old romantic yarns is dull and shoddy compared to the west that she understands and loves, and she has given us three novels of the west that stand alone in American literature.

O Pioneers, The Song of the Lark and *My Antonia* can be compared only with each other. They are wise and humorous and often beautiful, but, above all, real; and of the three *My Antonia* is most generous of its riches.

It is packed with the feel of the country. A scant paragraph sets you out on the plains, and the breadth of the wind that billows the long grass never leaves your face. The fragrance and color and significance of a whole fruiting orchard rises from another.

The people going about their heavy work and their adventurous play are not conventional bohunks and dagoes; they are not even conventional fathers of families or rascally money lenders or handsome girls. They are real people. You find yourself saying, "If I had lived out there these folks would actually have been my neighbors." And you proceed to wonder which of the girls you would have fallen in love with.

It is this trustworthiness that makes *My Antonia* and its companion books of extraordinary importance.

If you are looking for light on the minds of the people who are conducting absorbing political experiments on the western plains this winter; if you are homesick for a far-sweeping, simple country; or if—and that is most likely—you want to brush away stiff-jointed literary puppets and live for a while with real people, you will read and give thanks for *My Antonia*.

C[ARL] E[RIC] BECHHOFER

Impressions of Recent American Literature—IV†

Every traveller to New York is assured by his friends there that he must not take that city as fully representative of America. He is warned that New York, a cosmopolitan centre, and the whole New England country (Boston, &c.) are not the real America at all; if he wants to find that, he is told, he must go inland, into that huge expanse, filled with innumerable towns and villages, which is known as the "Middle West." The student of literature is similarly told to

† *Times Literary Supplement*, June 23, 1921, pp. 403–04.

direct his attention to the literary output of Chicago and the other Middle Western centres; the New York writers, he is told, are not as fully representative of the country as those who spring from its centre. The visitor may feel that this concern is exaggerated and that, whatever its deficiencies, New York is probably as representative of America as London, say, is of England; the claims of Manchester, for example, may occur to him as a parallel to those of Chicago. But, however this may be, it is certainly necessary to emphasize the claims of the Middle West to consideration in treating of the more recent literature of America.

The most interesting figures in contemporary American prose writing who belong definitely to the Middle West are Theodore Dreiser, Edgar Lee Masters, Willa Cather, Sinclair Lewis, and Sherwood Anderson. Of Dreiser's novels, which are the major part of his part, it is unnecessary to speak at length here, especially since a complete edition of them is expected to appear shortly in England. His erratic, prolix and yet monumental style is so American, so completely typical of the vast country from which he comes, that he is as much a cultural as a literary figure. Let anyone compare his first book, *Sister Carrie*, which was cut down to half its original size before appearance by some unknown editor, with any of his later works, and the difference will at once be seen between Dreiser as he would be, were he a European writer, and what he is as an American, not to say, a Middle Westerner. An early incident in his life is typical of the man. He was once obliged to take the post of editor of a series of "dime novels" for a New York publishing house, and was given a number of long novelettes to reduce to a more economical length; the method he adopted was to split the manuscripts in two and write a new ending to the first part and a new beginning to the second, thus making two novelettes where there had before been only one. (The publishers, needless to say, were delighted at this doubling of their material.) As Mr. Mencken has pointed out in a sympathetic study of Dreiser's work—it may be mentioned that he was the prime mover in the protest movement against the suppression of Dreiser's *The Genius* at the instance of the Society for the Suppression of Vice[1]—Dreiser has no notion whatever of such sophistications as verbal economy.

* * *

He is no longer a solitary voice. In the works of Miss Willa Cather the reader will find, expressed certainly in a very different manner, an emphasis laid upon other non-English American classes, the Scandinavian and Bohemian settlers. Miss Cather herself began her

---

1. Founded in 1873, the institution took as its mission the guarding of public morality.

career in the Middle West. Her first stories were sent to a New York paper; and she was invited by a sympathetic editor to join its staff. Since then she has published several novels and collected a couple of volumes of short stories. Her first novel was *Alexander's Bridge*, quite a short book dealing with Boston and London life; it is of no great importance. Soon after she began to write novels dealing with the early Swedish and Bohemian settlers in the Nebraska prairies, of which the best are *O Pioneers!* and *My Antonia*. Recently she has collected some of her previously published short stories dealing chiefly with artistic circles in New York, and they have appeared under the title of *Youth and the Bright Medusa*. Of her books, those dealing with the immigrants in Nebraska are by far the best. *O Pioneers!* describes the life of a Swedish settler's daughter and the tragic love of her brother Emil for a beautiful Bohemian girl, Marie Tovesky. *My Antonia* (the accent is on the first syllable of the name) is a tale told by Jim Burden, a lawyer from the Middle West. Taken to the West as a child, he travels on the same train as a family of Bohemian immigrants, the Shimerdas, who have a daughter Antonia. The two children grow up together amidst the hardships of the settlers' life. Their ways part at last; poor Antonia is seduced by a scoundrelly Irish railwayman, but afterwards she marries a decent farmer of her own people and has a family of fine, healthy children. It is a simple tale, but full of charm and interest; besides Antonia's own experiences, we read of those of other Bohemian girls, her friends, who, though despised by the Anglo-Saxon inhabitants of the country (but not by their young men), succeed none the less in bringing a certain Continental atmosphere of gaiety and vitality into the arid existence of the Middle West. There are many excellent descriptions of life and people in the two books—of the French fair, for example, in *O Pioneers!* and of the Bohemian family, some Russian settlers, and a blind negro musician in *My Antonia*.

* * *

It is Miss Cather's high achievement in these two books that she has brought out the beauty and the majesty of her country; as Dreiser in his works has shown us its strength and its bulk. To read their books is to be made to understand what racial contrasts and incongruities are contained in modern American life, until at last the old idea of the "melting-pot" seems less a romantic fact than a prosaic aspiration. The immigrants may change, as Miss Cather shows them to do, their national songs and dresses for vulgar rag-time ditties and ugly "waists," but there are certain spiritual qualities that they cannot lose.

HARRY HANSON

The First Reader: *My Antonia* Revised[†]

The publication of a new and revised edition of *My Antonia*, by Willa Cather is as much an event in the world of books as if a new work by this author were spread upon the records; moreover, it gives an opportunity for directing attention to the fact that few books of the last ten years have surpassed it in originality, in truth and in vitality. It belongs to the basic foundation of our new literature.

But the reader may well ask: "How revised?" What has Miss Cather done to it? Can an author touch up a masterpiece? It is true that George Moore's[1] revisions have gained in felicity; but even so, did the man of sixty have the right to tinker with the work of the man of twenty? And Miss Cather, whose painstaking attention to detail is well known—what of her?

So we may say at the outset that Miss Cather has left the body of the story untouched but rewritten the introduction, in which she meets Jim Burden and prepares to hear his tale of Antonia. And the Houghton, Mifflin Company has increased the white margin a bit, and made some other changes, but left the plates after Chapter I alone. Let us fall to.

This examination may prove profitable to students of writing; it may also mean an excursion into an author's mind.

Miss Cather's original opening sentence read: "Last summer I happened to be crossing the plains of Iowa in a season of intense heat, and it was my good fortune to have for a traveling companion James Quayle Burden—Jim Burden, as we still call him in the West."

Her revised opening reads: "Last summer, in a season of intense heat, Jim Burden and I happened to be crossing Iowa on the same train."

Score one for the author.

Then comes the story of Jim Burden's wife. The author explains in the original edition that she sees little of Jim Burden in New York,—that he is a busy man; moreover, "I do not like his wife."

Then in the original edition Miss Cather embarked on a description of the wife and her activities. She gave her name, told how she was jilted by her cousin, and that "she gave one of her town houses for a Suffrage headquarters, produced one of her own plays at the Princess Theatre, was arrested for picketing during a garment-makers' strike," etc. On the next page followed a characterization of Jim

† *The* (New York) *World*, Summer 1926.
1. Irish writer (1852–1933) of novels, short stories, and plays who in later life revised his early work for publication in a standardized edition.

Burden—his faith in the West, his ability to raise money for new enterprises and his passion for hunting and exploring. We learned about Jim that "his fresh color and sandy hair and quick-changing blue eyes are those of a young man, and his sympathetic, solicitous interest in women is as youthful as it is Western and American."

It is here that Miss Cather has made the most drastic changes. The description of Jim's wife must have seemed superfluous to her, for she has boiled it down to one paragraph. She drops the specific and adheres to the essentials of her character. The keynote of the wife's personality is retained: "She is handsome, energetic, executive, but to me she seems unimpressionable and temperamentally incapable of enthusiasm."

The reference to her activities with Suffrage workers (already becoming history), theatres and the like is now revised to these general terms: "She finds it worth while to play the patroness to a group of young poets and painters of advanced ideas and mediocre abilities."

When the author approaches Jim Burden she exercises similar economy. The specific traits of his character are brought down to two or three generalizations. He has a romantic disposition, loves the country—"his faith in it and his knowledge of it have played an important part in its development." We are not to be sidetracked by the troubles of Jim Burden and his family.

Throughout the introduction Miss Cather has taken out the "dates," and worked for essentials. The new introduction is shorter than the old by three pages.

The physical changes in the new edition are slight, but may be worth noting for the use of collectors. Assuming that the collector has read the book—and Mitchell Kennerley,[2] I believe, has known some who actually did read books—he will observe that the new edition stands a quarter of an inch higher on the shelf and that this gives a wider margin to the page. The story is no longer by Willa Sibert Cather but by Willa Cather. The seal of Houghton, Mifflin Company—"tout bien ou rien"—has been placed on the outside cover. Inside, one discovers that the new edition lists all the other books by Miss Cather, although at least five are published by another house. This generosity shows how far Boston is behind the times.

But what a fine excuse this new edition gives for rereading this splendid book! *My Antonia* has the great quality of an impeccable style. The theme is married to the method. The language is redolent of the soil, clean-cut American writing, and yet dignified. It pulsates with the life of the people it describes.

Such an examination of life makes all argument about method futile. In any book the mind of the author, as it filters through his

2. American publisher and editor (1868–1950).

medium, is the thing. Confronted with a book like this, what care we for arguments about impressionistic writing, coherence or incoherence, or literature as an olfactory art? Like the great prairies of the West, *My Antonia* is an ineradicable part of the American scene.

ELIA W. PEATTIE

Miss Cather Writes Exceptional Novel in "My Antonia"†

From the time that Willa Cather first began to write there have been two notable qualities in her stories, truth and distinction. Interrupted though she has been in past years by her editorial work, yet the first strong impulse of her realism has not declined, but has proved itself to be the vital and resistant part of her literary activity. So now, after perhaps a quarter of a century of story and poetry writing, in which she has been temperate indeed in output, she is able to offer a tale of such unusual simplicity and loveliness that it must make and hold its place. This story is called "MY ANTONIA" and the scene is that part of Nebraska in which Miss Cather passed her girlhood: the Nebraska in which Swedes, Russians, Bohemians, and Poles settled, putting their vigor into the virgin land.

Antonia is a Bohemian, the daughter of an unhappy gentleman, a lover of books and refinement, who has married beneath him, and who, being outcast from his family, yields to the solicitations of his vigorous, harsh peasant wife and brings his family of four to America. There amid the treeless prairie, in a dugout, Antonia makes her friends, bears her burdens, and, somewhat improved in estate, but still a woman of heavy soil, is left in her early middle age. Here, it is to be seen, are few of the usual elements of American romance. The Russians or the Norwegians might have selected such a woman and such a struggle for the subject of a story, but there are few Americans who would have ventured to do so—few who, perceiving that there is but one enduring romance, and that the romance of the human soul, would have the faith in their audience to believe that they, too, could see this interesting fact.

Miss Cather trusts her America to understand this very human woman-pioneer with her unspeakable enjoyment of common life, her sturdy pride of being, her capacity for fitting into the scene. If ever any heroine ran her roots into the earth and blossomed in storm and wild sunlight, that heroine is Antonia. When she is left, the wife of

† *Omaha World-Herald,* 1918.

a hard working farmer, her own more ecstatic loves passed and done with, with her eleven children about her, she is still fascinating.

Indeed, she seems the genius of her fields of grain, abundant, superbly utilitarian, rejoicing in the morning, the friend of man. Her powers of story telling, an inheritance, perhaps, from her peasant ancestors, her courtesy, her love, capable of expanding to meet any demands, give her almost heroic proportions, yet never remove her from the hearth or the realm of familiarity.

No question, Miss Cather has written a book of singular beauty and simplicity, in which her power of giving the essence of a community is united with a beautiful capacity for character creation.

Modern Critical Views

TERENCE MARTIN
The Drama of Memory in *My Ántonia*†

In Willa Cather's novels of the West, the land, raw and unsubdued, stands out as the initial force to be confronted. "The great fact was the land itself," she says in describing the milieu of *O Pioneers!* (1913), "which seemed to overwhelm the little beginnings of human society that struggled in its sombre wastes." The far different world of *Death Comes for the Archbishop* (1927), with its vast distances and arid wastes, seems older, earlier, yet equally a "great fact" as Miss Cather emphasizes its primeval quality: the mesa, she writes, "had an appearance of great antiquity, and of incompleteness; as if, with all the materials for world-making assembled, the creator had desisted, gone away and left everything on the point of being brought together, on the eve of being arranged into mountain, plain, plateau." Here, too, "the country was still waiting to be made into a landscape."[1]

Such statements recall Jim Burden's initial reaction to the Nebraska prairie in *My Ántonia* (1918). As he rattles out to his grandparents' house at night, he peers over the side of the wagon. "There seemed to be nothing to see; no fences, no creeks or trees, no hills or fields. If there was a road, I could not make it out in the faint starlight. There was nothing but land: not a country at all, but the material out of which countries are made." Unformed, incomplete, lacking fences, trees, and hills, the land gives Jim Burden the feeling of being "over the edge" of the world, "outside man's jurisdiction."[2]

To this land Willa Cather brings the people who will struggle to make it give them first a subsistence, then a livelihood. In *O Pioneers!* the process is exemplified in the life of Alexandra Bergson, whose family had come to Nebraska when she was a child, whose faith and determination virtually force the land into yielding the

---

† *PMLA* 84.2 (1969): 304–11. Reprinted by permission of the copyright owner, the Modern Language Association of America.

1. *O Pioneers!* (Boston, 1937), p. 13; *Death Comes for the Archbishop* (New York, 1950), p. 95.
2. *My Ántonia*, p. 12 in this Norton Critical Edition. Subsequent page references to *My Ántonia* will appear in the text and are to this Norton Critical Edition.

riches which she so passionately believes it to possess. The early sections of *O Pioneers!* pose the question of survival sharply; the novel
turns on the ultimately successful attempt of the pioneers to wrest
a living from the land. In *My Ántonia*, Jim Burden's grandparents
have achieved a degree of stability as the novel begins; it is the Shimerdas, the Bohemians, who move onto the prairie and make the early,
elemental struggle that is the prerequisite of survival and success.
With the efforts of her characters to subdue, to form, to complete the
land, Willa Cather's novels of the prairie may properly be said to
begin. Necessarily, then, Miss Cather writes about change, for if the
people are not to be annihilated or forced into retreat by the land,
the land must be altered by the efforts of the people.

The land, still menacing to the newcomer in its intransigence; the
people of various backgrounds, whose object is to humanize, even
domesticate, this land; the change, physical, economic, and social,
consequent upon their efforts—such staple elements of Willa Cather's novels of the prairie go into the making of *My Ántonia*. But the
novel has, of course, a special character of its own, an individuality
that comes in large part from the Shimerdas; from their daughter
Ántonia, who becomes a symbol of battered but undiminished human
value; from Lena Lingard, soft, enticing, sensually eloquent; and,
finally, from the narrator, Jim Burden, whose point of view defines
the theme and structure even as it controls the tone of the novel.

From the time of the composition of *My Ántonia*, the role of Jim Burden has invited attention. Perhaps feeling the need to define that
role more specifically, Willa Cather revised the preface of the novel
for the reissue of 1926, making changes that altered Jim Burden's
relation to the story he tells. In the 1918 preface, for example, Jim
agrees to record his memories of Ántonia, which he has not thought
of doing before; in the second preface, however, he is already at work
on the manuscript before the meeting and conversation that supposedly take place with Willa Cather on the train.[3] Such a change implies
that something private and personal has been at work in the mind of
Jim Burden, that the manuscript has taken initial shape because of
an inner need to articulate the meaning of a valued, ultimately
treasured, memory. Willa Cather has amended her first (prefatory)
thoughts by bringing her narrator closer emotionally to the substance of the narrative.

Readers have continued to assess the role of Jim Burden because
of its relevance to the structure of the novel as a whole. David
Daiches, for example, believes that "the narrator's development goes

3. In his *Willa Cather: A Critical Biography* (New York, 1953), E. K. Brown points out that
   Miss Cather was unhappy about her preface for *My Ántonia*. "She had found it, unlike
   the rest of the book, a labor to write" (pp. 199–200).

on side by side with Ántonia's" and finds the symbolism uncertain at the conclusion: "The final suggestion that this is the story of Jim and Ántonia and their relation is not really borne out by the story as it has developed. It begins as that, but later the strands separate until we have three main themes all going—the history of Ántonia, the history of Jim, and scenes of Nebraska life." The result, Daiches feels, and no mean achievement, is "a flawed novel full of life and interest and possessing a powerful emotional rhythm in spite of its imperfect structural pattern." E. K. Brown sees a potential problem in the choice of a man as narrator: Jim Burden "was to be fascinated by Ántonia as only a man could be, and yet he was to remain a detached observer, appreciative but inactive, rather than take a part in her life." The consequence of Willa Cather's effort to achieve these two not fully compatible effects is an emptiness "at the very center" of Jim's relation to Ántonia, "where the strongest emotion might have been expected to obtain." Stressing the function of the narrator, James E. Miller, Jr., believes that the "emotional structure of the novel may be discovered" in the drama of Jim Burden's "awakening conscious-ness," which "shapes in the reader a sharpened awareness of cyclic fate that is the human destiny." John H. Randall, III, in his impres-sive study of Willa Cather, would seem to agree with the implica-tions of some of the previous arguments when he says that Jim Burden is more than "a first-person onlooker who is relating someone else's story." Randall develops the idea of a double protagonist, part Ántonia, who faces the future, part Jim Burden, who faces the past. Together, Jim and Ántonia make a complete, albeit "Janus-faced," personality.[4]

If structural coherence is to be found in *My Ántonia*, the character of Jim Burden seems necessarily to be involved. As the story of Ántonia, the novel is quite rightly found inadequate; and even as the story of Ántonia and Jim Burden, the narrative strands, as Mr. Daiches indicates, tend to separate. For it is the story of Jim's Ánto-nia, and the meaning and implications of that term must somehow subsume the various elements of the novel. As I see it, the substance and quality of the narrative itself—at once evolving toward and con-ditioned by the image of Jim's Ántonia—provide a principle of unity that takes the special form of a drama of memory.

Jim Burden's drama of memory begins with his portrayal of the Shimerda family, who have arrived on the prairie from Bohemia at the same time Jim has come from Virginia to live with his grand-parents after the death of his mother and father. The conditions of

4. David Daiches, *Willa Cather: A Critical Introduction* (Ithaca, N. Y., 1951), pp. 45, 60–61; Brown, *Cather*, p. 202; James E. Miller, Jr., "*My Ántonia*: A Frontier Drama of Time," *AQ*, x (Winter 1958), 478; John H. Randall, III, *The Landscape and the Looking Glass: Willa Cather's Search for Value* (Boston, 1960), p. 107.

the agricultural frontier in Nebraska force the Shimerdas into a bleak, defensive existence. They take up residence in a kind of cave, in front of which is a flimsy shed thatched with the wine-colored grass of the prairie. To Jim's grandmother the dwelling seems "no better than a badger hole; no proper dugout at all" [18]. But it is where the new family must live if they are to have shelter. On the fringe of civilization, overpowered by the utter strangeness of their environment, the Shimerdas face a contest for survival more in bewilderment than in desperation. For they have come unprepared. Mr. Shimerda, as Jim says, "knew nothing about farming"; a weaver by trade, he "had been a skilled workman on tapestries and upholstery materials" in his native land [18]. We sense his confusion, his loss of identity, in his new surroundings. Awed by the magnitude of nature on the prairie, Jim Burden admits that "between that earth and that sky I felt erased, blotted out"; his statement evinces a deep feeling of insignificance, a sense of the radically diminished importance of the human being and his endeavors. This Jim can accept with the stoicism of youth: "I did not say my prayers that night," he writes; "here, I felt, what would be would be" [12]. Mr. Shimerda, however, can neither attain nor afford the luxury of resignation. For the prairie threatens him in subtle and profound ways. "Of all the bewildering things about a new country," writes Willa Cather in O Pioneers!, "the absence of human landmarks is one of the most depressing and disheartening."[5] A citizen of the Old World, Mr. Shimerda cannot survive the loss of a society that was characterized by intellectual and artistic "landmarks." Faced with the necessity of making a new start from a point prior to any he had ever imagined, Mr. Shimerda has nothing with which to begin but his fiddle and an old gun given to him long ago for playing at a wedding. He dies from a lack of history, his suicide a testimony to the grim reality of the struggle imposed by frontier conditions.

In portraying the remaining Shimerda family, Willa Cather steadfastly avoids the trap of sentimentality. It would be a simple matter to resolve their problems with a rush of pity and a flood of tears, and the Burdens stand willing (almost determined) to help. But the Shimerdas (Mrs. Shimerda and Ambrosch particularly, but Ántonia also, to a degree) prove difficult to help. Embittered by their lot, they are shown to be unpleasant, ungrateful, and boastful; they brag of the old country and make comparisons invidious to the new. The sullen duplicity of Ambrosch leads finally to the harness incident, in which Ambrosch kicks at Jake Marpole and is felled by a blow from Jake's solid American fist. "They ain't the same, Jimmy," Jake says afterward, "these foreigners ain't the same. You can't trust 'em

5. O Pioneers!, p. 17.

to be fair. It's dirty to kick a feller. You heard how the women turned on you—and after all we went through on account of 'em last winter! They ain't to be trusted. I don't want to see you get too thick with any of 'em." To which Jim responds with emotion: "I'll never be friends with them again, Jake" [70–71].

Although such antipathy fades completely with time and understanding (the latter supplied principally by Mr. Burden), it typifies in a muted way some of the tensions implicit in American history. Earlier, on the train heading for Nebraska, Jake Marpole has approved Jim Burden's reluctance to go into the car ahead and talk with the little girl with "pretty brown eyes," as the conductor describes Ántonia; you are "likely to get diseases from foreigners," he tells Jim [10]. Jake is a Virginian, an old American, showing his distrust of the newcomer. But a similar feeling could exist between immigrant groups. Otto Fuchs tells Jim's grandmother that "Bohemians has a natural distrust of Austrians." When she asks why, he replies: "Well, ma'am, it's politics. It would take me a long while to explain" [18]. Religion, too, could obviously provide a source of tension, though, again, the subdued tone of the narrative resolves such tensions quietly, and, in one case, with a final note of humor. When the Catholic Mr. Shimerda kneels and crosses himself before the Burdens' religiously decorated Christmas tree (decorated with candles and with a nativity scene sent to Otto Fuchs from Austria), Jim and his grandmother are apprehensive. Mr. Burden is staunchly Protestant, no friend to the pomps of Popery: "He was rather narrow in religious matters," says Jim, "and sometimes spoke out and hurt people's feelings." The moment of crisis dissolves, however, when grandfather, as Jim says, "merely put his fingertips to his brow and bowed his venerable head, thus Protestantizing the atmosphere" [49].

An unsentimental portrait of the Shimerdas thus is not only valid psychologically; it also allows us to glimpse the prejudices that were part of the human situation on the Nebraska prairie. Such feelings, however, are consistently set in a larger context of generosity; in March the Shimerdas occupy a new four-room house which their neighbors have helped them to build. They were now "fairly equipped," says Jim, "to begin their struggle with the soil" [65]. *Struggle* is, of course, the key word, for the Shimerdas' position can be made reasonably secure only by unremitting labor. Much of the necessary work, as we know, falls to Ántonia, whose fortunes in the Shimerda household are distinctly subordinate to those of Ambrosch, the oldest son. (It is for Ambrosch, Ántonia tells Jim Burden, that they have come to the United States.) Through Jim's eyes we see her as she grows coarse and muscular doing the work of a man on the farm. "She was too proud of her strength," he says, annoyed because Ántonia talks constantly to him about how much she can "lift and endure." Ambrosch gives her hard jobs and dirty ones as well, some of them "chores a girl ought not to do"; and Jim knows that "the farm-hands around the country joked in a nasty way about it" [69]. At the dinner table "Ántonia ate so noisily now, like a man, and she yawned often . . . and kept stretching her arms over her head, as if they ached." Jim's grandmother had said, "Heavy field work'll spoil that girl. She'll lose all her nice ways and get rough ones." To Jim, if not to his grandparents, "she had lost them already" [67]. Work has hardened his playmate of the previous autumn; virtually harnessed to the plow, developing a "draught-horse neck" [66], she has little time for him. "I ain't got time to learn," she says when he informs her of the beginning of a new school term: "School is . . . for little boys" [66]. But the knowledge that her father would have been hurt by such an answer, and even more by the necessity for such an answer, brings tears to her eyes. Ántonia's determination to work for the immediate needs of her family molds her to the land. Fit material for a symbol, she is, I think we must in candor admit, already a bit too muscular for conventional romantic purposes.

The pace and emphases of the narrative in *My Ántonia* come of course from Jim Burden. As we know, the point of view is retro-spective, and despite his disclaimer in the preface, Jim has both the perspective and the inclination to shape his material with care. Accordingly, Book One has a definite pattern, that of the seasons: beginning with the autumn of his arrival, Jim takes us through the year to the fullness and heat of the following summer. Moreover, he portrays himself predominantly in terms of his reactions to the sea-sons during his first year on the prairie. The first section of the novel thus operates as a kind of rehearsal for nostalgia. For this year lives at the center of Jim's memory, never to be relived, never to be for-gotten. It has for him an idyllic quality, a quality of tenderly remem-bered freedom and happiness resulting from his surrender to the forces of nature with which everyone else must contend. On the night of his arrival in Nebraska, we recall, Jim adopts an attitude of resig-nation: "here . . . what would be would be." The next day in his grandmother's garden he relaxes against a "warm yellow pumpkin," crumbles earth in his fingers, and watches and listens to nature. "Nothing happened," he says. "I did not expect anything to happen. I was something that lay under the sun and felt it, like the pumpkins, and I did not want to be anything more. I was entirely happy." He thinks of death (his parents, we remember, have recently died) and wonders if death makes us "a part of something entire." "At any rate," he concludes, "that is happiness; to be dissolved into something com-plete and great" [17].

Jim Burden, in short, makes an immediate surrender to nature in this garden with its ripe pumpkins. And his feeling of immersion in nature has a significant and permanent effect upon him, for he never loses his ability to appreciate the prairie in a personal way or his need to find happiness amid the ripeness and fulfillment of life. Though he must tell us of human hardship, Jim reveals his sense of rapture as he recalls and describes the seasons. "All the years that have passed," he says, "have not dimmed my memory of that first glorious autumn" [21]. The new country lay open before him, leading him to celebrate the splendor of the prairie in the last hour of the afternoon:

> All those fall afternoons were the same, but I never got used to them. As far as we could see, the miles of copper-red grass were drenched in sunlight that was stronger and fiercer than at any other time of the day. The blond cornfields were red gold, the haystacks turned rosy and threw long shadows. The whole prairie was like the bush that burned with fire and was not consumed. That hour always had the exultation of victory, of triumphant ending, like a hero's death—heroes who died young and gloriously. It was a sudden transfiguration, a lifting-up of day. [27]

Jim's tone is reverential, replete with wonder, the product of a deep respect for the prairie and for the sunlight that brings it to ripeness.

Winter becomes primarily a time of taking refuge. Snow disguises the prairie with an insidious mask of white, leaving one, as Jim says later, with "a hunger for color" [91]. He is convinced that "man's strongest antagonist is the cold," though, in the security of his grandmother's basement kitchen, which "seemed heavenly safe and warm in those days" [39], he can hardly experience its bitterness in the manner of the Shimerdas, who have only one overcoat among them and take turns wearing it for warmth. On cold nights, he recalls, the cry of coyotes "used to remind the boys of wonderful animal stories" [40]. A sense of adventure pervades Jim's life: by comparison, the life represented in books seems prosaic: the Swiss family Robinson, for example, "had no advantage over us in the way of an adventurous life" [39]—and, later, Robinson Crusoe's life on the island "seemed dull compared with ours" [56]. If winter means taking refuge, it also satisfies the needs of Jim's young imagination and contributes the memory of adventure, a feeling of hardship happily domesticated by the company, the kitchen and the stove "that fed us and warmed us and kept us cheerful" [40].

Spring with the reawakening of the prairie and summer with its sense of fruition complete the cycle of the seasons. The pervasive

lightness of spring delights Jim: "If I had been tossed down blindfold on that red prairie, I should have known that it was spring" [65].
And July brings the "breathless, brilliant heat which makes the prairies of Kansas and Nebraska the best corn country in the world. It
seemed as if we could hear the corn growing in the night; under the
stars one caught a faint crackling in the dewy, heavy-odored cornfields where the feathered stalk stood so juicy and green." These are
to become the world's cornfields, Jim sees in retrospect; their yield
will underlie "all the activities of men in peace or war" [74].

A sense of happiness remembered pervades Book One, softening
and mellowing the harsher outlines of the story Jim Burden has to
tell. We are never really on the prairie with Jim, nor does he try to
bring us there. Rather, he preserves his retrospective point of view
and tells us what it was like for him on the prairie. "I used to love to
drift along the pale-yellow cornfield," he says [22]; and (as we have
seen) "All the years that have passed have not dimmed my memory
of that first glorious autumn"; and, again, though she is four years
his senior and they have arrived on the prairie at the same time, Ántonia "had come to us a child, and now she was a tall, strong young
girl" [66]. Such statements, and numerous devices of style throughout the novel, make a point of narrative distance and deliver the
story to us in an envelope of memory. The style, that is to say, makes
a deliberate—and almost total—sacrifice of immediacy in favor of
the afterglow of remembrance. Even the scenes of violence are kept
at a distance by having someone else tell them to Jim Burden; indeed,
they are not so much scenes as inset stories, twice removed from the
reader. Pavel's story of the wolves in Russia, Ántonia's story of the
tramp who jumped into the threshing machine, the story of Wick
Cutter's death (told by one of Ántonia's children)—all these contain
a terror and a violence that is subdued by having them related to Jim
as part of his story to us. In a similar indirect way we learn of Mr.
Shimerda's death and of the seduction of Ántonia by Larry Donovan (whom we never meet). Only when Jim kills the snake, thus, in a
sense, making the prairie safe for Ántonia, and when for Ántonia's
sake he decoys himself in Wick Cutter's bedroom, are terror and
violence (and in the latter case a mixture of comedy) brought close;
and, in keeping with the retrospective point of view, these episodes,
too, come to us through the spectrum of Jim's memory.

Defining the mode of Jim Burden's relation to his narrative leads
us to see the special character of the novel itself and to judge it on its
own terms rather than on any we might inadvertently bring to it. The
statement of one critic that "something precious went into American
fiction with the story of Ántonia Shimerda" is meant as a tribute to
Willa Cather's novel; but it seems to me a misdirected tribute. For
the novel does not present the *story* of Ántonia; it does, I believe,

present a drama of memory by means of which Jim Burden tells us how he has come to see Ántonia as the epitome of all he has valued. At the time he writes, Jim Burden has made sense of his experience on the prairie, has seen the meaning it has and will have in his life. The early sections of *My Ántonia* present in retrospect the substance of meaning, conditioned throughout by Jim's assurance of that meaning. The latter sections justify his right to remember the prairie in the joyous manner of his youth. And the process of justification involves, most importantly, the image of Ántonia. This image acquires symbolic significance for Jim; embodying and justifying his memories, it validates nostalgia by giving his feeling for the past a meaning in the present.

By common consent, the "I" of the preface is taken to be Willa Cather. In the preface we learn that both to Jim Burden and Willa Cather, Ántonia, "more than any other person we remembered, . . . seemed to mean . . . the country, the conditions, the whole adventure of our childhood." Miss Cather says that she had lost sight of Ántonia, but that Jim "had found her again after long years." The preface thus establishes a relation between Jim Burden and Willa Cather outside the narrative that is important to the relationship of Jim and Ántonia within the narrative. Jim Burden becomes the imaginative instrument by means of which Willa Cather reacquaints herself with Ántonia: "He made me see her again, feel her presence, revived all my old affection for her" [8]. Her narrator, in short, serves Miss Cather as the vehicle for her own quest for meaning and value; his success measures her success; his symbol becomes her symbol; for his Ántonia is the Ántonia she has created for him.[6]

If Jim Burden is to be made more than a heuristic phantom of the imagination, however, he must be given some kind of autonomy as a fictional character. Some drama, however quiet it may appear in retrospect, must play itself out in his life; some resolution must come inherently from the narrative. If we are to have a drama of memory, Jim's memory must somehow be challenged before it is vindicated in and by the image of Ántonia. The offstage challenges, those involved, for example, when Jim explains his twenty-year absence from the Nebraska prairie by saying "life intervened," afford little but material for conjecture and inference. The onstage challenge, however, affording material for analysis, enters Jim's room in Lincoln in Book Three in the very pretty form of Lena Lingard.

6. Commenting on the relationship between Jim Burden and Ántonia (on which Miss Cather has established a claim at the outset), David Daiches writes that "for all her devotion to her father's memory, Mr. Shimerda's mantle does not fall on Ántonia, but rather on Jim, who responds to the suggestion of a rich European culture lying behind his melancholy. This is the first of a series of influences that lead him eventually to the university and a professional career in the East [and even to Europe], yet in a profound, if indirect way it draws him closer to Ántonia" (*Willa Cather*, p. 48).

Lena Lingard first appears as one of the hired girls in Book Two, along with Tiny Soderball, lesser characters such as the Bohemian Marys and the Danish laundry girls, and, of course, Ántonia, who has come to Black Hawk to work for the Harlings. The move to Black Hawk does take Ántonia away from the prairie temporarily and tend to merge her importance with that of a group of girls. But by placing Ántonia and Lena Lingard together, as friends, Willa Cather can begin to suggest the different roles each of them will play in the life of Jim Burden. Moreover, Black Hawk provides a canvas on which Miss Cather can portray social consciousness and burgeoning social change in the Nebraska of this time. Despite the domestic vitality of the Harling family, readily available for Jim Burden (now living next door with his grandparents) to draw on, Black Hawk seems increasingly dull to Jim during his high-school years. Small and very proper, the town makes life for young men an initiation into monotony. Except, of course, for the presence of the hired girls. These young women, all of foreign families, bring vivacity to Black Hawk; light-hearted, gay, and unpretentious, at the dances they are in great demand. More often than not, however, the proper young men must meet them surreptitiously, for the hired girls enjoy a lower social status than do the girls of the older American families in the town. Remarking on the social distinction, Jim Burden says that

> the daughters of Black Hawk merchants had a confident, un-inquiring belief that they were 'refined,' and that the country girls, who 'worked out,' were not. The American farmers in our county were quite as hard-pressed as their neighbors from other countries. All alike had come to Nebraska with little capital and no knowledge of the soil they must subdue. All had borrowed money on their land. But no matter in what straits the Pennsylvanian or Virginian found himself, he would not let his daughters go out into service. Unless his girls could teach a country school, they sat home in poverty. [102–03]

Kept from teaching by their inadequate knowledge of English, yet determined to help their families out of debt, the hired girls took domestic or similar employment. Some remained serious and discreet, says Jim, others did not. But all sent home money to help pay "for ploughs and reapers, brood-sows, or steers to fatten." Jim frankly admires such family solidarity, as a result of which the foreign families in the county were "the first to become prosperous." Today, he says, former hired girls are "managing big farms of their own; their children are better off than the children of the town women they used to serve" [103]. Pleased with their success, Jim feels paternal toward the entire group of girls and applauds the social change which accompanies their prosperity.

A single generation serves to bring about the kind of change Jim describes. In the Black Hawk of his youth, however, "the country girls were considered a menace to the social order" [103]. And surely none of them represented more of a menace than Lena Lingard. Demure, soft, and attractive, Lena radiates sexual charm without guile or effort. Before Jim has finished high school, both the married Ole Benson and the proper young bachelor Sylvestor Lovett have become driven, obsessed men because of her. Later, in Lincoln, her landlord, Colonel Raleigh, and the Polish violin teacher, Mr. Ordinski, are entranced by Lena and suspicious of Jim on her account. A blonde, Norwegian, Nebraskan Circe, Lena is a temptress who "gave her heart away when she felt like it," as Jim says, but "kept her head for business" [145]. If she does not literally turn her admirers into swine, she cannot prevent their appetites from giving them at times hardly less graceful postures. When dancing, says Jim, Lena moved "without exertion rather indolently." If her partner spoke to her, she would smile, but rarely answer. "The music seemed to put her into a soft, waking dream, and her violet-colored eyes looked sleepily and confidingly at one from under her long lashes. . . . To dance 'Home, Sweet Home' with Lena was like coming in with the tide. She danced every dance like a waltz, and it was always the same waltz—the waltz of coming home to something, of inevitable, fated return" [113].

This is the Lena Lingard who walks into Jim's room in Lincoln, who dominates Book Three and seems very close to taking command of the novel.[7] Like Ántonia, she has come from off the prairie; like Ántonia, too, she is generous and forthright. But unlike Ántonia, she makes a success of herself in business, as a fashion designer, first in Lincoln, later in San Francisco. And unlike Ántonia, she is determined not to marry, not to have a family. Lena's unconscious power to distract a man from whatever he may or should be doing exerts its influence on Jim during his final year at the University of Nebraska. He begins to drift, as he says, to neglect academic life, to live from day to day languidly in love with Lena. His mentor, Gaston Cleric, tells him to "quit school and go to work, or change your college and begin again in earnest. You won't recover yourself while you are playing about with this handsome Norwegian." To Gaston Cleric, Lena

7. Wallace Stegner takes up the point that Part Three of the novel "has been objected to as a structural mistake, because it turns away from Ántonia," in *The American Novel from James Fenimore Cooper to William Faulkner*, ed. Wallace Stegner (New York, 1965), p. 150. Stegner continues: "But the criticism seems based on too simplistic a view of the novel's intention. Though the title suggests that Ántonia is the focus of the book, the development from the symbolic beginning scene is traced through both Ántonia and Jim and a good part of that theme of development is concerned with the possible responses to deprivation and to opportunity. We leave Ántonia in Book Three in order to return to her with more understanding later."

seems "perfectly irresponsible" [144]. In the light of her successful career, the judgment seems only partially valid. But Cleric is near the mark; Lena induces irresponsibility in the men who know her. And Jim is coming to know her well.

No overt antagonism exists between Lena and Ántonia, who are friends with a great deal in common. Yet Ántonia warns Jim in good-natured seriousness not to see too much of Lena; and when Ánto-nia discovers the manner in which Jim kisses Lena, she exclaims, "If she's up to any of her nonsense with you, I'll scratch her eyes out" [113]. Jim's dreams suggest the different roles the girls have in his life. At times he dreams of Ántonia and himself, "sliding down straw-stacks as we used to do; climbing up the yellow mountains over and over, and slipping down the smooth sides into soft piles of chaff." He has also a recurrent dream of Lena coming toward him barefoot across a field, "in a short skirt, with a curved reaping-hook in her hand." "She was flushed like the dawn," he continues, "with a kind of luminous rosiness all about her. She sat down beside me, turned to me with a soft sigh and said, 'Now they are all gone, and I can kiss you as much as I like'." Jim says, "I used to wish I could have this flat-tering dream about Ántonia, but I never did" [114].

Jim's dream of Ántonia, we note, is based on the memory of shared childhood experiences, its sexual significance sublimated in terms of youthful fun and adventure. In Black Hawk, Ántonia has forbid-den Jim to kiss her as he apparently kisses Lena, thereby rejecting his tentative gesture toward a relationship of adolescent sexuality. If he is to dream of Ántonia, he must put her in a context of their youth. His dream of Lena, however, more frankly sexual (with the reaping-hook suggestive of such things as fulfillment, castration, and the nega-tion of time), has no context; it can take place only because "they are all gone." Jim's wish that he could have such a dream about Ántonia is part of his larger desire to have some definite, some formal relation-ship with her. As he says to her later, "I'd have liked to have you for a sweetheart, or a wife, or my mother or my sister—anything that a woman can be to a man" [156]. With Lena he drifts into a hedonis-tic relationship which carries with it the peril of irresponsibility. Somehow Lena always seemed fresh, new, like the dawn: "she wak-ened fresh with the world everyday," Jim says, and it was easy to "sit idle all through a Sunday morning and look at her" [138]. (Ántonia, of course, would be worshipping, not being worshipped, on a Sunday morning.) Like all enchantresses, Lena inspires a chronic forgetful-ness. In an ultimate dramatic sense she would be fatal to memory. Consequently, she stands opposed to Ántonia, who will come to bear and to justify the burden of Jim's memory.

The structure of the narrative in Book Three suggests the charm that Lena exercises on Jim. Her entrance into his room, we recall, interrupts his study of Virgil. After she leaves, Jim thinks of all the country girls of Black Hawk and sees a relation between them and the poetry of Virgil: "If there were no girls like them in the world, there would be no poetry. I understood that clearly, for the first time. This revelation seemed to me inestimably precious. I clung to it as if it might suddenly vanish" [133]. The country girls are the raw material of poetry; and Jim feels that without them there can be no valid life of the mind. But when he sits down to his lesson for the following day, his newly acquired insight into the relation of "life" and "art" yields up his old dream of Lena, "like the memory of an actual experience." "It floated before me on the page like a picture," he recalls, "and underneath it stood the mournful line: 'Optima dies . . . prima fugit'—the best days are the first to flee" [130]. Since this quotation from the *Georgics* serves as the epigraph of the novel, one has here, I believe, a sense of being close to the emotional center of Jim Burden's narrative. And yet Lena, not Ántonia, inspires the melancholy reflection. In the light of Jim's return to the prairie in Book Four, and, especially, in Book Five, one must conclude that, however tender, this is an unproductive nostalgia, an indulgence in romantic melancholy. Jim's dream of Lena only *seems* "like the memory of an actual experience." And the reality of memory rather than the artificiality of dream will finally serve him as a basis for happiness. Ultimately, the epigraph of the novel comes, as it must, to have fuller and deeper reference to the memory of Ántonia than to the dream of Lena.

Lena Lingard, it is important to see, retards the drama of memory. She represents in the novel not so much an anti-theme as a highly diversionary course of inaction. Promising repose, a blissful release from time, she can be identified by Jim with nothing but herself— which is to say that she does not, as does Ántonia, lend herself "to immemorial human attitudes which we recognize by instinct as universal and true" [170].

Returning to Black Hawk after an absence of two years, Jim is "bitterly disappointed" that Ántonia, betrayed by Larry Donovan, has become "an object of pity," whereas Lena commands wide respect [145]. Having gone to school to Lena, Jim has little immediate sympathy for one who cannot give her heart and keep her head for business. But he responds once again to the country, and its changes seem to him "beautiful and harmonious": "it was like watching the growth of a great man or a great idea" [149]. He goes to his old house on the prairie to hear about Ántonia from the Widow Steavens, sleeps in his old room, and confronts his only source of disappointment when he meets Ántonia working in the fields. While they talk, near Mr. Shimerda's grave, he perceives a "new kind of strength in the gravity of [her] face" and confess that the idea of her is part of his mind [156]). His old feeling for the earth returns, and he wishes he "could be a little boy again" [157]. Committed to his early definition of happiness, and thus to the idea of the prairie, and thus to that of Ántonia, he looks hard at her face, which, as he says, "I meant always to carry with me; the closest realest face, under all the shadows of women's faces, at the very bottom of my memory" [157]). The drama of memory has been resolved; Jim's memories will take form around the image of Ántonia.

Having placed so much value on a single memory, Jim feels both impelled and afraid to test its validity by a return to the prairie after an absence of many years. Throughout these years he has apparently maintained a kind of inner life; the image of Ántonia, suggesting youth and early happiness, has hardened into a reality which he fears to see shattered. But his visit to the Cuzaks in Book Five vindicates and fulfills the memory he has treasured. "Ántonia had always been one to leave images in the mind that did not fade—that grew stonger with time," he says; "in my mind there was a succession of such pictures" [170]. To indicate the value of the past to her, Ántonia produces for him her collection of photographs—of Jim, Jake Marpole, Otto Fuchs, the Harlings, even of Lena Lingard—as part of her family's heritage. Together they look through these photographs of old times, but in such a rich, lively context of the present, with children of all sizes laughing and crowding around to show that they, too, know of the early days, that past and present tend to merge in a dynamic new image of happiness that makes the future possible. Amid Ántonia's large family Jim feels like a boy again, but—and this I feel measures the final success of his return—he does not *wish* that he were a boy again, as he did in Book Four. He has no more need to cling to the past, for the past has been transfigured like the autumn prairie of old. He has "not been mistaken" about Ántonia: "She was a rich mine of life, like the founders of early races." "She had only to stand in the orchard, to put her hand on a little crab tree and look up at the apples, to make you feel the goodness of planting and tending and harvesting at last" [170]. The somewhat contrived scene of Ántonia's children scrambling and tumbling up out of their new fruit cave, "a veritable explosion of life out of the dark cave into the sunlight" which makes Jim dizzy for a moment [164], proclaims the relationship between Ántonia and the prairie: both have yielded life in abundance; both have prevailed.

The unity of *My Ántonia* thus derives, I believe, from a drama of memory fulfilled in the present. Clearly the novel does not give us the story of Ántonia's life nor that of Jim's. Rather, it brings us to see the meaning of Ántonia to a man whose happiest days have been those of his youth, who, in the apotheosis of Book Five, becomes

reconciled to the present because of the enduring value of the past,
even as he comes to possess that past anew because of the promise
and vitality of the present. Jim's image of Ántonia has proved fruitful;
his drama of memory is not only resolved but fulfilled. He has attained
a sense of meaning in his narrative by confronting in retrospect the
elements of his early world: from Jim we have learned of the land, the
various people who work the land, and the change which the passing
of a generation brings about; from Jim, too, we have had the portrait
of the Shimerdas and that of Lena Lingard; and from Jim we have the
triumphant image of Ántonia, "battered but not diminished" ([161]), as
his personal symbol of the value of human experience. The elements of the novel cohere in Jim Burden's drama of memory. And in
Jim's Ántonia they are all subsumed.

BLANCHE H. GELFANT

The Forgotten Reaping-Hook: Sex in *My Ántonia*†

Our persistent misreading of Willa Cather's *My Ántonia* rises from
a belief that Jim Burden is a reliable narrator. Because we trust his
unequivocal narrative manner, we see the novel as a splendid celebration of American frontier life. This is the view reiterated in a current critique of *My Ántonia*[1] and in a recent comprehensive study of
Cather's work: "*My Ántonia* shows fertility of both the soil and human
beings. Thus, in a profound sense *My Ántonia* is the most affirmative book Willa Cather ever wrote. Perhaps that is why it was her
favorite."[2] Critics also elect it *their* favorite Cather novel: however,
they regret its inconclusive structure, as did Cather when she declared
it fragmented and unsatisfactory in form.[3] David Daiches's complaint
of twenty years ago prevails: that the work is "flawed" by "irrelevant"
episodes and material of "uncertain" meaning.[4] Both critical
positions—that *My Ántonia* is a glorious celebration of American life
and a defective work of art—must be reversed once we challenge
Jim Burden's vision of the past. I believe we have reason to do so,

† *American Literature* 43.1 (1971): 60–82. Copyright 1971, Duke University Press. All rights
    reserved. Republished by permission of the copyright holder, Duke University Press.
1. Terence Martin, "The Drama of Memory in *My Ántonia*," PMLA, LXXXIV (March, 1969),
    304–311.
2. John H. Randall, III, *The Landscape and the Looking Glass: Willa Cather's Search for
    Value* (Boston, 1960), p. 149.
       See Cather's remark, "The best thing I've ever done is *My Ántonia*. I feel I've made a
    contribution to American letters with that book," in Mildred Bennett, *The World of Willa
    Cather* (1951; reprinted, Lincoln, Neb., 1961), p. 203.
3. Mildred R. Bennett, *The World of Willa Cather* (Lincoln: University of Nebraska Press,
    1961), p. 212. Cather is quoted as saying, "If you gave me a thousand dollars for every
    structural fault in *My Ántonia* you'd make me very rich."
4. David Daiches, *Willa Cather: A Critical Interpretation* (Ithaca, N.Y., 1951), pp. 43–61.

particularly now, when we are making many reversals in our thinking. As soon as we question Jim's seemingly explicit statements, we
see beyond them myriad confusions which can be resolved only by
a totally new reading. This would impel us to reexamine Jim's testimony, to discover him a more disingenuous and self-deluded narrator than we supposed. Once we redefine his role, *My Ántonia* begins
to resonate to new and rather shocking meanings which implicate
us all. We may lose our chief affirmative novel, only to find one far
more exciting—complex, subtle, aberrant.

  Jim Burden belongs to a remarkable gallery of characters for whom
Cather consistently invalidates sex. Her priests, pioneers, and artists
invest all energy elsewhere. Her idealistic young men die prematurely;
her bachelors, children, and old folk remain "neutral" observers.
Since she wrote within a prohibitive genteel tradition, this reluctance
to portray sexuality is hardly surprising. What should intrigue us is
the strange involuted nature of her avoidance. She masks sexual
ambivalence by certainty of manner, and displays sexual disturbance,
even the macabre, with peculiar insouciance. Though the tenor of her
writing is normality, normal sex stands barred from her fictional
world. Her characters avoid sexual union with significant and sometimes bizarre ingenuity, or achieve it only in dreams. * * *

                         *   *   *

In *My Ántonia*, Jim Burden grows up with an intuitive fear of sex,
never acknowledged, and in fact, denied: yet it is a determining force
in his story. By deflecting attention from himself to Ántonia, of whom
he can speak with utter assurance, he manages to conceal his mud-
died sexual attitudes. His narrative voice, reinforced by Cather's,
emerges firm and certain; and it convinces. We tend to believe with
Jim that his authoritative recitation of childhood memories validates
the past and gives meaning to the present even though his mature
years stream before him emptied of love, intimacy, and purpose.
Memory transports him to richer and happier days spent with
Ántonia, the young Bohemian girl who signifies *"the country, the
conditions, the whole adventure of . . . childhood."*[5] Because a changing landscape brilliantly illumines his childhood—with copper-red
prairies transformed to rich wheatfields and corn—his personal
story seems to epitomize this larger historical drama. Jim uses the
coincidence of his life-span with a historical era to imply that as the
country changed and grew, so did he, and moreover, as his memoirs

5. 1918; reprinted, Boston, 1946, p. 2 [p. 8 in this Norton Critical Edition; bracketed page
   numbers refer to this Norton Critical Edition]. All italics in quotations from *My Ántonia*
   are in the original, and all subsequent references are to this text. I use this edition not
   only because it is readily available but also because the introduction by Walter Havi-
   ghurst and the suggestions for reading and discussion by Bertha Handlan represent
   clearly the way the novel has been widely used as validating the American past.

contained historical facts, so did they hold the truth about himself. Critics support Jim's bid for validity, pointing out that "*My Ántonia* exemplifies superbly [Frederick Jackson] Turner's concept of the recurring cultural evolution on the frontier."[6]

Jim's account of both history and himself seems to me disingenuous, indeed, suspect; yet it is for this very reason highly pertinent to an understanding of our own uses of the past. In the introduction, Jim presents his memoirs as a spontaneous expression—unselected, unarranged, and uncontrolled by ulterior purpose: "*From time to time I've been writing down what I remember . . . about Ántonia. . . . I didn't take time to arrange it; I simply wrote down pretty much all that her name recalls to me. I suppose it hasn't any form, . . . any title, either*" (2 [8]). Obviously, Jim's memory cannot be as autonomous or disinterested as he implies. His plastic powers reshape his experience, selecting and omitting in response to unconscious desires and the will. Ultimately, Jim forgets as much as he remembers, as his mind sifts through the years to retrieve what he most needs—a purified past in which he can find safety from sex and disorder. Of "a romantic disposition," Jim substitutes wish for reality in celebrating the past. His flight from sexuality parallels a flight from historical truth, and in this respect, he becomes an emblematic American figure, like Jay Gatsby and Clyde Griffiths. Jim romanticizes the American past as Gatsby romanticizes love, and Clyde money. Affirming the common, the prototypical, American dream of fruition, all three, ironically, are devastated—Gatsby and Clyde die violently, while Jim succumbs to immobilizing regressive needs. Their relationship to the dream they could not survive must strike us oddly, for we have reversed their situation by surviving to see the dream shattered and the Golden Age of American history impugned. Out of the past that Jim idealized comes our present stunning disorder, though Jim would deny such continuity, as Cather did. Her much-quoted statement that the world *broke* in 1922 reveals historical blindness mistaken for acuity.[7] She denied that "the beautiful past" transmitted the crassness, disorder, and violence which "ruined" the present for her and drove her to hermitic withdrawal. She blamed villainous men, such as Ivy Peters in *A Lost Lady*, for the decline of a heroic age. Like her, Jim Burden warded off broad historical insight. His mythopoeic memory patterned the past into an affecting creation story, with Ántonia a central fertility figure, "a rich mine of life, like the founders of early races." Jim, however, stalks through his myth a wasteland figure

6. James E. Miller, "*My Ántonia*: A Frontier Drama of Time," *American Quarterly*, X (Winter, 1958), 481.
7. See Bennett, p. 148. Cather is quoted as saying, "The world broke in two about 1920, and I belonged to the former half." The year 1922 is given in her preface (later deleted) to *Not under Forty* (renamed *Literary Encounters*, 1937).

who finds in the present nothing to compensate him for the loss of
the past, and in the outer world nothing to violate the inner sanctum
of memory. "Some memories are realities, are better than anything
that can ever happen to one again"—Jim's nostalgic conclusion
rationalizes his inanition. He remains finally fixated on the past,
returning to the vast and ineffaceable image that dominates his
memoirs—the Nebraska prairie yielding to railroad and plough. Since
this is an impersonal image of the growth of a nation, and yet it seems
so personally crucial to Jim, we must be alerted to the special significance it holds for him. At the very beginning of the novel, we
are told that Jim *"loves with a personal passion the great country
through which his railway runs"* (2 [7]). The symbolism of the railroad
penetrating virgin fields is such an embarrassingly obvious example of emotional displacement, it seems extraordinary that it has
been so long unnoted. Like Captain Forrester, the unsexed husband of *A Lost Lady*, Jim sublimates by traversing the country, laying it open by rail; and because he sees the land grow fertile and the
people prosper, he believes his story to be a celebration.

But neither history's purely material achievement, nor Cather's aesthetic conquest of childhood material, can rightfully give Jim Burden personal cause to celebrate. Retrospection, a superbly creative
act for Cather, becomes for Jim a negative gesture. His recapitula-
tion of the past seems to me a final surrender to sexual fears. He
was afraid of growing up, afraid of women, afraid of the nexus of
love and death. He could love only that which time had made safe
and irrefragable—his memories. They revolve not, as he says, about
the image of Ántonia, but about himself as a child. When he finds
love, it seems to him the safest kind—the narcissistic love of the man
for himself as a boy. Such love is not unique to Jim Burden. It obsesses
many Cather protagonists from early novels to late: from Bartley
Alexander in *Alexander's Bridge* to Godfrey St Peter in *The Professor's House*. Narcissism focuses Cather's vision of life. She valued
above all the inviolability of the self. Romantically, she saw in the
child the original and real self; and in her novels she created adult
characters who sought a seemingly impossible reunion with this
authentic being—who were willing to die if only they could reach
somehow back to childhood. Regression becomes thus an equivocal
moral victory in which the self defies change and establishes its
immutability. But regression is also a sign of defeat. *My Ántonia*,
superficially so simple and clear a novel, resonates to themes of ultimate importance—the theme of identity, of its relationship to time,
and of its contest with death. All these are subsumed in the more
immediate issue of physical love. Reinterpreted along these lines, *My
Ántonia* emerges as a brilliantly tortuous novel, its statements working contrapuntally against its meanings, its apparently random

vignettes falling together to form a pattern of sexual aversion into which each detail fits—even the reaping-hook of Jim's dream:

> One dream I dreamed a great many times, and it was always the same. I was in a harvest-field full of shocks, and I was lying against one of them. Lena Lingard came across the stubble bare-foot, in a short skirt, with a curved reaping-hook in her hand, and she was flushed like the dawn, with a kind of luminous rosi-ness all about her. She sat down beside me, turned to me with a soft sigh and said, "Now they are all gone, and I can kiss you as much as I like." (147 [114])

In Jim's dream of Lena, desire and fear clearly contend with one another. With the dreamer's infallibility, Jim contains his ambiva-lence in a surreal image of Aurora and the Grim Reaper as one. This collaged figure of Lena advances against an ordinary but ominous landscape. Background and forefigure first contrast and then coalesce in meaning. Lena's voluptuous aspects—her luminous glow of sex-ual arousal, her flesh bared by a short skirt, her soft sighs and kisses—are displayed against shocks and stubbles, a barren field when the reaping-hook has done its work. This landscape of harvest and des-olation is not unfamiliar; nor is the apparitional woman who moves across it, sighing and making soft moan; nor the supine young man whom she kisses and transports. It is the archetypal landscape of ballad, myth, and drama, setting for *la belle dame sans merci* who enchants and satisfies, but then lulls and destroys. She comes, as Lena does, when the male is alone and unguarded. "Now they are all gone," Lena whispers, meaning Ántonia, his threshold guardian. Keeping parental watch, Ántonia limits Jim's boundaries ("You know you ain't right to kiss me like that") and attempts to bar him from the dark unexplored country beyond boyhood with threats ("If I see you hanging around with Lena much, I'll go tell your grandmother"). Jim has the insight to reply, "You'll always treat me like a kid"; but his dream of past childhood games with Ántonia suggests that the prospect of perpetual play attracts him, offering release from anxi-ety. Already in search of safety, he looks to childhood, for adoles-cence confronts him with the possibility of danger in women. Characteristically, his statement that he will prove himself unafraid belies the drift of his unconscious feelings. His dream of Lena and the reaping-hook depicts his ambivalence toward the cycle of growth, maturation, and death. The wheat ripens to be cut; maturity invites death.

Though Jim has declared his dream "always the same," it changes significantly. When it recurs in Lincoln, where he goes as a univer-sity student, it has been censored and condensed, and transmuted from reverie to remembrance:

> As I sat down to my book at last, my old dream about Lena com-
> ing across the harvest-field in her short skirt seemed to me like
> the memory of an actual experience. It floated before me on the
> page like a picture, and underneath it stood the mournful line:
> "*Optima dies . . . prima fugit.*" (175 [133])

Now his memory can deal with fantasy as with experience: convert
it to an image, frame it, and restore it to him retouched and redeemed.
Revised, the dream loses its frightening details. Memory retains the
harvest-field but represses the shocks and stubbles; keeps Lena in her
short skirt, but replaces the sexual ambience of the vision. Originally
inspired by the insinuative "hired girls," the dream recurs under the
tranquilizing spell of Gaston Cleric, Jim's poetry teacher. As his name
implies, Cleric's function is to guide Jim to renunciation of Lena, to
offer instead the example of desire sublimated to art. Voluptuous
excitement yields to a pensive mood, and poetry rather than passion
engages Jim: "It came over me, as it had never done before, the relation between girls like those [Lena and "the hired girls"] and the
poetry of Virgil. If there were no girls like them in the world, there
would be no poetry" (175 [133]). In his study, among his books, Lena's
image floats before him on a page of the *Georgics*, transferred from a
landscape of death to Virgil's bucolic countryside; and it arouses not
sensual desire but a safer and more characteristic mood: nostalgia—
"melancholy reflection" upon the past. The reaping-hook is forgotten.
Lena changes from the rosy goddess of dawn to an apparition of evening, of the dimly lit study and the darkened theater, where she glows
with "lamplight" rather than sexual luminosity.

This preliminary sublimation makes it possible for Jim to have an
affair with Lena. It is brief and peculiar, somehow appropriating from
the theaters they frequent an unreal quality, the aspect of play. In
contrast to the tragic stage-lovers who feel exquisitely, intone passionately, and love enduringly, they seem mere unengaged children,
thrilled by make-believe people more than each other. "It all wrung
my heart"; "there wasn't a nerve left in my body that hadn't been
twisted"—Jim's histrionic (and rather feminine) outbursts pertain not
to Lena but to *Marguerite Gauthier* as impersonated by "an infirm
old actress." Camille's "dazzling loveliness," her gaiety and glitter—
though illusory—impassion him far more than the real woman's sensuality. With Lena, he creates a mock-drama, casting himself in the
stock role of callow lover pitted against Lena's older suitors. In this
innocuous triangle, he "drifts" and "plays"—and play, like struggle,
emerges as his memoirs' motif. Far from being random, his play is
directed toward the avoidance of future responsibilities. He tests the
role of lover in the security of a make-believe world where his mistress is gentle and undemanding, his adversaries ineffectual, and his

guardian spirit, Cleric, supportive. Cleric wants him to stop "playing with this handsome Norwegian," and so he does, leaving Lena forever and without regret. Though the separation of the stage-lovers Armand and Camille wracks them—"Lena wept unceasingly"—their own parting is vapid. Jim leaves to follow Cleric to Boston, there to study, and pursue a career. His period of enchantment has not proved one of permanent thrall and does not leave him, like Keats's knight, haggard and woebegone.

Nevertheless, the interim in Lincoln has serious consequences, for Jim's trial run into manhood remains abortive. He has not been able to bypass his circular "road of Destiny," that "predetermined" route which carries him back finally to Ántonia and childhood. With Lena, Jim seems divertible, at a crossroad. His alternatives are defined in two symbolic titles symbolically apposed: "Lena Lingard" and "Cuzak's Boys." Lena, the archetypal Woman, beckons him to full sexuality. Ántonia, the eternal Mother, lures him back through her children, Cuzak's boys, to perennial childhood.

If Jim cannot avoid his destiny, neither can he escape the "tyrannical" social code of his small town, Black Hawk, which permits its young men to play with "hired girls" but not to marry them. The pusillanimous "clerks and bookkeepers" of Black Hawk dance with the country girls, follow them forlornly, kiss them behind bushes—and run. "Respect for respectability" shunts them into loveless marriages with women of money or "refinement" who are sexless and safe. "Physically a race apart," the country girls are charged with sensuality, some of them considered "dangerous as high explosives." Through an empty conformist marriage, Jim avoids danger. He takes a woman who is independent and masculine, like Ántonia, who cannot threaten him as Lena does by her sheer femininity. Though Lena may be "the most beautiful, the most *innocently* sensuous of all the women in Willa Cather's works,"[8] Jim is locked into his fantasy of the reaping-hook.

Jim's glorification of Lena as the timeless muse of poetry and the unattainable heroine of romance requires a closer look. For while he seems to exalt her, typically, he works at cross-purposes to demean her—in his own involuted way. He sets her etherealized image afloat on pages of poetry that deal with the breeding of cattle (his memoirs quote only the last line here):

> So, while the herd rejoices in its youth
> Release the males and breed the cattle early,
> Supply one generation from another.
> For mortal kind, the best day passes first.
> (*Georgics*, Book III)

8. E. K. Brown and Leon Edel, *Willa Cather: A Critical Biography* (New York, 1953), p. 203. Italics mine.

As usual, Jim remembers selectively—only the last phrase, the novel's epigraph—while he deletes what must have seemed devastating counsel: "Release the males." Moreover, the *Georgics* has only factitious relevance to Lena (though I might point out that it undoubtedly inspired Cather by suggesting the use of regional material and the seasonal patterning of Book I of *My Ántonia*). If anything, the allusion is downright inappropriate, for Virgil's poem extols pastoral life, but Lena, tired of drudgery, wants to get away from the farm. Interested in fashion and sensuous pleasure, settling finally in San Francisco, she is not really the muse for Virgil.

Jim's allusion does have a subtle strategic value: by relegating Lena to the ideal but unreachable world of art, it assures their separation. Mismatched lovers because of social class, they remain irreconcilable as dream and reality. A real person, Jim must stop drifting and study; he can leave the woman while possessing Lena the dream in remembered reverie. Though motivated by fear and expediency (as much as Sylvester Lovett, Lena's fearful suitor in Black Hawk), he romanticizes his actions, eluding the possibility of painful self-confrontation. He veils his escape by identifying secretly with the hero Armand Duval, also a mismatched lover, blameless, whose fervid affair was doomed from the first. But as a lover, Jim belongs as much to comedy as to melodrama. His affair fits perfectly within the conventions of the comedy of manners: the sitting-room, Lena's "stiff little parlour"; the serving of tea; the idle talk of clothes and fashion; the nuisance pet dog Prince; the minor crises when the fatuous elder lovers intrude—the triviality. Engaged with Lena in this playacting, Jim has much at stake—nothing less than his sexuality. Through the more serious drama of a first affair, he creates his existential self: an adult male who fears a sexual woman. Through his trivial small-town comedy of manners, he keeps from introspection. He is drifting but busy, too much preoccupied with dinner parties and theater dates to catch the meaning of his drift His mock romance recalls the words he had used years earlier to describe a childhood "mock adventure": "the game was fixed." The odds are against his growing up, and the two mock episodes fall together as *pseudo-*initiations which fail to make him a man.

Jim's mock adventure occurs years back as he and Ántonia explore a series of interconnected burrows in prairie-dog-town. Crouched with his back to Ántonia, he hears her unintelligible screams in a foreign tongue. He whirls to discover a huge rattler coiling and erecting to spring. "Of disgusting vitality," the snake induces fear and nausea: "His abominable muscularity, his loathsome, fluid motion, somehow made me sick" (32 [30]). Jim strikes violently and with revulsion, recognizing even then an irrational hatred stronger than the impulse for protection. The episode—typically ignored or misunderstood—combines elements of myth and dream. As a dragon-slaying, it conforms to the monomyth of initiation. It has a characteristic "call to adventure" (Ántonia's impulsive suggestion); a magic weapon (Peter's spade); a descent into a land of unearthly creatures (prairie-dog-town); the perilous battle (killing the snake); the protective tutelary spirit (Ántonia); and the passage through the rites to manhood ("You now a big mans"). As a test of courage, Jim's ordeal seems authentic, and critical opinion declares it so: "Jim Burden discovers his own hidden courage and becomes a man in the snake-killing incident."[9] But even Jim realizes that his initiation, like his romance later, is specious, and his accolade unearned: "it was a mock adventure; the game . . . fixed . . . by chance, as . . . for many a dragon-slayer."

As Jim accepts Ántonia's praise, his tone becomes wry and ironic, communicating a unique awareness of the duplicity in which he is involved. Ántonia's effect upon Jim seems to me here invidious because her admiration of his manhood helps undermine it. Pronouncing him a man, she keeps him a boy. False to her role as tutelary spirit, she betrays him from first to last. She leads him into danger, fails to warn him properly, and finally, by validating the contest, closes off the road to authentic initiation and maturity.

Jim's exploration "below the surface" of prairie-dog-town strikes me as a significant mimetic act, a burrowing into his unconscious. Who is he "below the surface"? In which direction do his buried impulses lead? He acts out his quest for self-knowledge symbolically: if he could dig deep enough he would find a way through this labyrinth and learn the course of its hidden channels—whether "they ran straight down, or were horizontal . . . whether they had underground connections." Projecting upon the physical scene his adolescent concern with self, he speaks an analytic and rational language—but the experience turns into nightmare. Archetypal symbol of "the ancient, eldest Evil," the snake forces him to confront deeply repressed images, to acknowledge for the only time the effect of "horrible unconscious memories."

The sexual connotations of the snake incident are implicit. Later in Black Hawk they become overt through another misadventure—Wick Cutter's attempted rape of Jim, whom he mistakes for Ántonia. This time the sexual attack is literal. Wick Cutter, an old lecher, returns in the middle of the night to assault Ántonia, but meanwhile, persuaded by Ántonia's suspicions, Jim has taken her place in bed. He becomes an innocent victim of Cutter's lust and fury at deception. Threatened by unleashed male sex—the ultimate threat—he fights with primordial violence, though again sickened with disgust. Vile as the

9. Miller, p. 482.

Cutter incident is—and it is also highly farcical—Jim's nausea seems
an overreaction, intensified by his shrill rhetoric and unmodulated
tone. Unlike the snake episode, this encounter offers no rewards. It
simply reduces him to "a battered object," his body pommeled, his
face swollen. His only recognition will be the laughter of the lubri-
cious "old men at the drugstore." Again Ántonia has lured him into
danger and exposed him to assault. Again he is furious: "I felt that I
never wanted to see her again. I hated her almost as much as I hated
Cutter. She had let me in for all this disgustingness" (p. 162 [125]).
Through Wick Cutter, the sexual urge seems depraved, and more
damning, ludicrous. No male in the novel rescues sex from indignity
or gives it even the interest of sheer malevolence (as, for example,
Ivy Peters does in *A Lost Lady*).

Also unexempt from the dangers of sex, Ántonia is seduced,
exploited, and left with an illegitimate child. When finally she marries, she takes not a lover but a friend. To his relief, Jim finds husband
and wife "on terms of easy friendliness, touched with humour"
(p. 231 [172]). Marriage as an extension of friendship is Cather's
recurrent formula, defined clearly, if idiosyncratically, by Alexandra
in *O Pioneers!*: "I think when friends marry, they are safe." Turning
words to action, Alexandra marries her childhood friend, as does
Cecile in *Shadows on the Rock*—an older man whose passion has
been expended on another woman. At best, marriage has dubious
value in Cather's fiction. It succeeds when it seems least like marriage, when it remains sexless, or when sex is only instrumental to
procreation. Jim accepts Ántonia's marriage for its "special mission"
to bring forth children.

Why doesn't he take on this mission? He celebrates the myth of
creation but fails to participate. The question has been raised bluntly
by critics (though left unanswered): "Why had not Jim and Ántonia
loved and married?"[1] When Ántonia, abandoned by Donovan, needs
Jim most, he passionately avers, "You really are a part of me": "I'd
have liked to have you for a sweetheart, or a wife, or my mother or
my sister—anything that a woman can be to a man" (208 [156]).
Thereupon he leaves—not to return for twenty years. His failure
to seize the palpable moment seems to one critic responsible for
the emotional vacuum of Jim's life: "At the very center of his relation with Ántonia there is an emptiness where the strongest emotion might have been expected to gather."[2] But love for a woman is
not Jim's "strongest emotion," cannot mitigate fear, nostalgia, or
even simple snobbery. Nothing in Jim's past prepares him for love
or marriage, and he remains in effect a pseudobachelor (just as he is

1. Elizabeth Shepley Sergeant, *Willa Cather: A Memoir* (1953; reprinted, Lincoln, Nebr., 1963), p. 151.
2. Brown and Edel, p. 202.

a pseudolover), free to design a future with Ántonia's family that excludes his wife. In his childhood, his models for manhood are simple regressive characters, all bachelors, or patently unhappy married men struggling, like Mr. Shimerda, Chris Lingard, and Ole the Swede, for and against their families. Later in Black Hawk, the family men seem merely vapid, and prophetically suburban, pushing baby-carriages, sprinkling lawns, paying bills, and driving about on Sundays (p. 105 [83]). Mr. Harling, Ántonia's employer in Black Hawk, seems different; yet he only further confuses Jim's already confused sense of sexual roles, for he indulges his son while he treats his daughter as a man, his business partner. With Ántonia, his "hired girl," Mr. Harling is repressive, a kind of superego, objecting to her adolescent contacts with men—the dances at Vannis's tent, the evening walks, the kisses and scuffles on the back porch. "I want to have my fling, like the other girls," Ánto-nia argues, but Harling insists she quit the dances or his house. Ántonia leaves, goes to the notorious Cutter, and then to the seductive arms of Larry Donovan—with consequences that are highly instructive to Jim, that can only reinforce his inchoate fears. Either repression of sex or disaster: Jim sees these alternatives polarized in Black Hawk, and between them he cannot resolve his ambivalence. Though he would like Ántonia to become a woman, he wants her also to remain asexual.

By switching her sexual roles, Ántonia only adds to his confusion. As "hired girl" in Black Hawk and later as Cuzak's wife, she cooks, bakes, sews, and rears children. Intermittently, she shows off her strength and endurance in the fields, competing with men. Even her name changes gender—no adventitious matter, I believe; it has its masculine variant, Tony, as Willa Cather had hers, Willie. Cather's prototype for Ántonia, Annie Pavelka, was a simple Bohemian girl; though their experiences are similar, Ántonia Shimerda is Cather's creation—an ultimately strange bisexual. She shares Cather's pride in masculinity and projects both her and Jim's ambivalent sexual atti-tudes. Cather recalled that "much of what I knew about Annie came from the talks I had with young men. She had a fascination for them."[3] In the novel, however, Lena fascinates men while Ántonia toils alongside them. "I can work like mans now," she announces when she is only fifteen. In the fields, says Jim, "she kept her sleeves rolled up all day, and her arms and throat were burned as brown as a sailor's. Her neck came up strongly out of her shoulders, like the bole of a tree out of the turf. One sees that draught-horse neck among the peasant women in all old countries" (p. 80 [66]). Sailor, tree, draught-horse, peasant—hardly seductive comparisons,

3. Bennett, p. 47.

hardly conducive to fascination. Ántonia's illegitimate pregnancy brutalizes her even more than heavy farmwork. Her punishment for sexual involvement—and for the breezy pleasures of court-ship—is thoroughgoing masculinization. Wearing "a man's long overcoat and boots, and a man's felt hat," she does "the work of a man on the farm," plows, herds cattle. Years later, as Cuzak's wife, her "inner glow" must compensate for the loss of her youthful beauty, the loss, even, of her teeth. Jim describes her finally as "a stalwart, brown woman, flat-chested, her curly brown hair a little grizzled"— his every word denuding her of sensual appeal.

    This is not to deny that at one time Jim found Ántonia physically desirable. He hints that in Black Hawk he had kissed her in a more than friendly way—and had been rebuffed. But he is hardly heart-broken at their impasse, for his real and enduring love for her is based not on desire but on nostalgia. Childhood memories bind him more profoundly than passion, especially memories of Mr. Shimerda. In their picnic reunion before Jim departs for Lincoln, Ántonia recounts her father's story of transgression, exile, and death. Her miniature tale devolves upon the essential theme of destructive sex. As a young man, her father succumbs to desire for the family's servant girl, makes her pregnant, marries her against his parents' wishes, and becomes thereby an outcast His death on the distant prairie traces back to an initial sexual act which triggers inexorable consequences. It strips him of all he values: his happy irresponsible bachelor life with the trombone-player he "loves"; his family home in beautiful Bohemia; his vocation as violinist when he takes to homesteading in Nebraska; and his joy in life itself. For a while, a few desultory pleasures could rouse him from apathy and despair. But in the end, he finds the pat-tern of his adult life, as many Cather characters do, unbearable, and he longs for escape. Though Ántonia implies that her poppa's mis-take was to marry, especially outside his social class (as Jim is too prudent to do), the marriage comes about through his initial sexual involvement. Once Mr. Shimerda acts upon sexual impulse, he is committed to a woman who alienates him from himself; and it is loss of self, rather than the surmountable hardships of pioneer life, which induces his despair. Suicide is his final capitulation to destructive forces he could have escaped only by first abnegating sex.

    Though this interpretation may sound extreme—that the real dan-ger to man is woman, that his protection lies in avoiding or elimi-nating her—it seems to me the essence of the most macabre and otherwise unaccountable episode in *My Ántonia*. I refer to that grisly acting out of male aversion, the flashback of Russian Pavel feeding the bride to the wolves. I cannot imagine a more graphic represen-tation of underlying sentiments than we find here. Like most of the episodes in Jim's memoirs, this begins innocently, with the young bride drawing Peter, Pavel, and other guests to a nearby village for her wedding. But the happy evening culminates in horror; for the wolves are bad that year, starving, and when the guests head for home they find themselves rapidly pursued through a landscape of terror. Events take on the surreality of nightmare as black droves run like streaks of shadows after the panicking horses, as sledges overturn in the snow, and mauled and dying wedding guests shriek. Fast as Pavel drives his team, it cannot outrun the relentless "back ground-shadows," images of death. Pavel's murderous strategy to save himself and Peter is almost too inhuman to imagine: to allay the wolves and lighten his load, he wrests the bride from the struggling groom, and throws her, living bait, to the wolves. Only then does his sledge arrive in safety at his village. The tale holds the paradigm for Mr. Shimerda's fate—driven from home because of a woman, struggling for survival against a brutal winter landscape, pursued by regret and despair to death. The great narrative distance at which this episode is kept from Jim seems to me to signify its explosiveness, the need to handle with care. It is told to Jim by Ántonia, who overhears Peter telling it to Mr. Shimerda. Though the vignette emerges from this distance—and through Jim's obscuring nostalgia—its gruesome meaning focuses the apparently disjunct parts of the novel, and I find it inconceivable that critics consider it "irrelevant."[4] The art of *My Ántonia* lies in the subtle and inevitable relevance of its details, even the most trivial, like the picture Jim chooses to decorate a Christmas book for Ántonia's little sister: "I took 'Napoleon Announcing the Divorce to Josephine' for my frontispiece" (p. 55 [47]). In one way or another, the woman must *go*.

To say that Jim Burden expresses castration fears would provide a facile conclusion: and indeed his memoirs multiply images of sharp instruments and painful cutting. The curved reaping-hook in Lena Lingard's hands centralizes an overall pattern that includes Peter's clasp-knife with which he cuts all his melons; Crazy Mary's corn-knife (she "made us feel how sharp her blade was, showing us very graphically just what she meant to do to Lena"); the suicidal tramp "cut to pieces" in the threshing machine; and wicked Wick *Cutt*er's sexual assault. When Lena, the essence of sex, appears suddenly in Black Hawk, she seems to precipitate a series of violent recollections. First Jim remembers Crazy Mary's pursuit of Lena with her sharpened corn-knife. Then Ántonia recalls the story of the crazy tramp in details which seem to me unconsciously reverberating Jim's dream. Like Jim, Ántonia is relaxed and leaning against a

---

4. Daiches says, "It is a remarkable little inset story, but its relation to the novel as a whole is somewhat uncertain" (p. 46). However, Daiches finds so many episodes and details "uncertain," "dubious," "not wholly dominated," or "not fully integrated," it might be his reading is "flawed" rather than the novel.

strawstack; similarly, she sees a figure approach "across the stubble"—significantly, his first words portend death. Offering to "cut bands," within minutes he throws himself into the threshing machine and is "cut to pieces." In his pockets the threshers find only "an old pen-knife" and the "wish-bone of a chicken." Jim follows this anecdote with a vignette of Blind d'Arnault, a black musician who, as we shall see, represents emasculation; Jim tells how children used to tease the little blind boy and try "to get his chicken-bone away." Such details, I think, should not be considered fortuitous or irrelevant; and critics who have persisted in overlooking them should note that they are stubbornly there, and in patterned sequence.

I do not wish to make a case history of Jim Burden or a psychological document of *My Ántonia*, but to uncover an elusive underlying theme—one that informs the fragmentary parts of the novel and illuminates the obsession controlling Cather's art. For like most novelists, Cather writes out of an obsessive concern to which her art gives various and varied expression. In *My Ántonia*, her consummate work, that obsession has its most private as well as its most widely shared meanings. At the same time that the novel is highly autobiographical, it is representatively American in its material, mood, and unconscious uses of the past. In it, as in other novels, we can discover that Cather's obsession had to do with the assertion of self. This is the preoccupation of her protagonists who in their various ways seek to assert their identity, in defiance, if necessary, of others, of convention, of nature, of life itself. Biographers imply that Cather's life represented a consistent pursuit of autonomy, essential, she believed, to her survival as an artist. Undoubtedly, she was right; had she given herself to marriage and children, assuming she could, she might have sacrificed her chance to write. Clearly, she identified writing with masculinity, though which of the two constituted her fundamental drive is a matter of psychological dynamics we can never really decide. Like Ántonia, she displayed strong masculine traits, though she loved also feminine frilleries and the art of cuisine. All accounts of her refer to her "masculine personality"—her mannish dress, her deep voice, her energetic stride; and even as a child she affected boyish clothes and cropped hair. Too numerous to document, such references are a running motif throughout the accounts of Mildred Bennett, Elizabeth Sergeant, and E. K. Brown. Their significance is complex and perhaps inescapable, but whatever else they mean, they surely demonstrate Cather's self-assertion: she would create her own role in life, and if being a woman meant sacrificing her art, then she would lead a private and inviolate life in defiance of convention.

Her image of inviolability was the *child*. She sought quaintly, perhaps foolishly, to refract this image through her person when she wore a schoolgirl costume. The Steichen photograph of her in middy blouse is a familiar frontispiece to volumes of her work; and she has been described as characteristically "at the typewriter, dressed in a childlike costume, a middy blouse with navy bands and tie and a duck skirt."[5] In life, she tried to hold on to childhood through dress; in art, through a recurrent cycle of childhood, maturity, and childhood again: the return effected usually through memory. Sometimes the regressive pattern signalized a longing for death, as in *The Professor's House* and *Death Comes for the Archbishop*; always it revealed a quest for reunion with an orginal authentic self. In *My Ántonia*, the prologue introduces Ántonia and the motif of childhood simultaneously, for her name is linked with "*the country, the conditions, the whole adventure of . . . childhood.*" The memoirs proper open with the children's journey into pristine country where men are childlike or project into life characters of the child's imagination: like Jake who "might have stepped out of the pages of 'Jesse James.'" The years of maturity comprise merely an interim period—and in fact, are hardly dealt with. For Jim, as for Cather, the real meaning of time is cyclical, its purpose to effect a return to the beginning. Once Jim finds again "the first road" he traveled as a wondering child, his story ends. Hardly discernible, this road returns him to Ántonia, and through her, to his real goal, the enduring though elusive image of his original self which Cather represents by his childhood shadow. Walking to Ántonia's house with her boys—feeling himself almost a boy again—Jim merges with his shadow, the visible elongation of self. At last, his narcissistic dream comes to fulfillment: "It seemed, after all, so natural to be walking along a barbed-wire fence beside the sunset, toward a red pond, and to sec my shadow moving along at my right, over the close-cropped grass" (p. 224 [167]). Just as the magnified shadow of plow against sky—a blazing key image—projects his romantic notion of the West, so "two long shadows [that] flitted before or followed after" symbolize his ideal of perennial children running through, imaged against, and made one with the prairie grass.

Jim's return "home" has him planning a future with Cuzak's boys that will recapitulate the past: once more he will sleep in haylofts, hunt "up the Niobrara," and travel the "Bad Lands." Play reenters as his serious concern, not the sexual play of imminent manhood, but regressive child's play. In a remarkable statement, Jim says: "There were enough Cuzaks to play with for a long while yet. Even after the boys grew up, there would always be Cuzak himself!" (p. 239 [178]). A current article on *My Ántonia* misreads this conclusion: "[though] Jim feels like a boy again . . . he does not *wish* that he were a boy again. . . . He has no more need to cling to the past, for

5. Sergeant, p. 117.

the past has been transfigured like the autumn prairie of old."[6] Such reasoning falls in naively with Jim's self-deception, that the transformation of the land to country somehow validates his personal life. Jim's need to reenter childhood never relents, becomes even more urgent as he feels adult life vacuous. The years have not enriched him, except with a wealth of memories—"images in the mind that did not fade—that grew stronger with time." Most precious in his treasury of remembered images is that of a boy of ten crossing the prairie under "the complete dome of heaven" and finding sublimity in the union of self with earth and sky. An unforgettable consummation, never matched by physical union, he seeks to recreate it through memory. Jim's ineffable desire for a child more alive to him than his immediate being vibrates to a pathetic sense of loss. I believe that we may find this irretrievable boy in a photograph of young *Willie Cather,* another child who took life from imagination and desire.[7]

In a later novel, *The Professor's House,*[8] Cather rationalizes her cathexis on childhood through the protagonist's musings, at which we might glance briefly. Toward the end of his life, Professor Godfrey St. Peter discovers he has two identities: that of his "original" self, the child; and of his "secondary" self, the man in love. To fulfill himself, "the lover" creates a meretricious "design" of marriage, children, and career, now, after thirty years, suddenly meaningless. The Professor's cyclic return to his real and original self begins with solitary retrospection. All he wants is to "be alone"—to repossess himself. For, having yielded through love to another, he has lost "the person he was in the beginning." Now before he dies, he longs for his original image as a child, an image that returns to him in moments of "vivid consciousness" or of remembrance. Looking back, the Professor sees the only escape from a false secondary life to be through premature death: death of the sexual man before he realizes his sexuality and becomes involved in the relationships it demands. This is the happy fate of his student Tom Outland, who dies young, remaining inviolate, pure, and most important, self-possessed: "He seemed to know . . . he was solitary and must always be so; he had never married, never been a father. He was earth, and would return to earth" (p. 263).

This Romantic mystique of childhood illuminates the fear of sex in Cather's world. Sex unites one with another. Its ultimate threat

6. Martin, p. 311.
7. See the "pictures from the Wm. Cather, M.D., period of Willa's life" in Bennett, especially the photograph of Cather as a child with "her first short haircut." Note Cather's vacillating taste in clothes from the clearly masculine to feminine.

   It is significant that in various plays at school and at the university, Cather assumed male roles—so convincingly that spectators sometimes refused to believe the actor was not a boy. See Bennett, pp. 175–176, 179.
8. 1925; reprinted, Boston, 1938.

is loss of self. In Cather's construct, naively and of course falsely, the child is asexual, his love inverted, his identity thus intact. Only Ántonia manages to grow older and retain her original integrity. Like Tom Outland, her affinity is for the earth. She "belongs" to the farm, is one with the trees, the flowers, the rye and wheat she plants. Though she marries, Cuzak is only "the instrument of Ántonia's special mission." Through him she finds a self-fulfillment that excludes him. Through her, Jim hopes to be restored to himself.

The supreme value Jim and other Cather characters attribute to "old friendships" reflects a concern with self. Old friends know the child immanent in the man. Only they can have communion without causing self-estrangement, can marry "safely." They share "the precious, the incommunicable past"—as Jim says in his famous final words. But to keep the past so precious, they must romanticize it; and to validate childhood, they must let memory filter its experiences through the screen of nostalgia. Critics have wondered whether Jim Burden is finally the most suitable narrator for *My Ántonia*. I submit that Cather's choice is utterly strategic. For Jim, better than any other character, could control his memories, since only he knows of but does not experience the suffering and violence inherent in his story. And ultimately, he is not dealing with a story as such, but with residual "images in the mind." *My Ántonia* is a magnificent and warped testimony to the mind's image-making power, an implicit commentary on how that creative power serves the mind's need to ignore and deny whatever is reprehensible in whatever one loves. Cather's friend and biographer said of her, "There was so much she did not want to see and saw not."[9] We must say the same of Jim Burden, who held painful and violent aspects of early American life at safe distance, where finally he could not see them.

Jim's vignette of Blind d'Arnault, the black piano player who entertains at Black Hawk, is paradigmatic of his way of viewing the past. Its factual scaffolding (whether Cather's prototype was Blind Boone, Blind Tom, or a "composite of Negro musicians") seems to me less important than its tone. I find the vignette a work of unconscious irony as Jim paints d'Arnault's portrait but meanwhile delineates himself. The motif of blindness compounds the irony. D'Arnault's is physical, as though it is merely futile for him to see a world he cannot enter. Jim's is moral: an unawareness of his stereotyped, condescending, and ultimately invidious vision. Here, in his description of the black man, son of a slave, Jim's emblematic significance emerges as shamefully he speaks for himself, for Cather, and for most of us:

9. Sergeant, p. 46.

[His voice] was the soft, amiable Negro voice, like those I remembered from early childhood, with the note of docile subservience in it He had the Negro head, too; almost no head at all, nothing behind the ears but the folds of neck under close-cropped wool. He would have been repulsive if his face had not been so kindly and happy. It was the happiest face I had seen since I left Virginia. (p. 122 [96])

Soft, amiable, docile, subservient, kindly, happy—Jim's image, as usual, projects his wish-fulfillment; his diction suggests an unconscious assuagement of anxiety, also. His phrase of astounding insult and innocence—"almost no head at all"—assures him that the black man should not frighten, being an incomplete creature, possessed, as we would like to believe, of instinct and rhythm, but deprived of intellect. Jim's final hyperbole registers his fear of this alien black face saved from repulsiveness only by a toothy servile smile (it might someday lose). To attenuate his portrait of d'Arnault, Jim introduced innuendoes of sexual incompetence. He recognizes d'Arnault's sensuality but impugns it by his image of sublimation: "all the agreeable sensations possible to creatures of flesh and blood were heaped up on those black-and-white keys, and he [was] gloating over them and trickling them through his yellow fingers" (p. 126 [98]). Jim's genteel opening phrase connotes male sexuality, which he must sublimate, displace from the man to the music, reduce to a *trickle*. D'Arnault "looks like some glistening African god of pleasure, full of strong, savage blood"; but superimposed is our familiar Uncle Tom "all grinning," "bowing to everyone, docile and happy."

Similarly, consider Jim's entrancing image of the four Danish girls who stand all day in the laundry ironing the townspeople's clothes. How charming they are: flushed and happy; how fatherly the laundryman offering water—no swollen ankles; no boredom or rancor; no exploitation: a cameo image from "the beautiful past." Peter and Pavel, dreadful to any ordinary mind for their murderous deed, ostracized by everyone, now disease-ridden and mindless, are to Jim picturesque outcasts: Pavel spitting blood; Peter spitting seeds as he desperately eats all his melons after kissing his cow goodbye, the only creature for him to love. And Mr. Shimerda's suicide. Jim reconciles himself to the horror of the mutilated body frozen in its own blood by imagining the spirit released and homeward bound to its beloved Bohemia. Only the evocative beauty of Cather's language—and the inevitable validation as childhood memory—can romanticize this sordid death and the squalor in which it takes place. Violence is as much the essence of prairie life as the growth of the wheat and blossoming of the corn. Violence appears suddenly and inexplicably, like the suicidal tramp. But Jim gives violence a cameo quality. He has the insistent need—and the strategy—to turn away from the very material he presents. He can forget the reaping-hook and reshape his dream. And as the novel reveals him doing this, it reveals our common usage of the past as a romance and refuge from the present. *My Ántonia* engraves a view of the past which is at best partial; at worst, blind. But our present is continuous with the whole past, as it was, despite Jim Burden's attempt to deny this, and despite Cather's "sad little refrain": "Our present is ruined—but we had a beautiful past."[1] Beautiful to one who recreated it so; who desperately needed it so; who would deny the violence and the destructive attitudes toward race and sex immortalized in his very denial. We, however, have as desperate a need for clarity of vision as Jim had for nostalgia; and we must begin to look at *My Ántonia*, long considered a representatively American novel, not only for its beauty of art and for its affirmation of history, but also, and instructively, for its negations and evasions. Much as we would like to ignore them, for they bring painful confrontations, we must see what they would show us about ourselves—how we betray our past when we forget its most disquieting realities; how we begin to redeem it when we remember.

JEAN SCHWIND

The Benda Illustrations to *My Ántonia*: Cather's "Silent" Supplement to Jim Burden's Narrative[†]

I

As Jim Burden comes to the end of his story about the "central figure" of his childhood and "all that her name recalls," he briefly describes the personal memoirs that Ántonia herself has kept for over twenty years (*Ántonia*, introd.).[1] The most important difference between Ántonia's account of the past and Jim's is immediately apparent. Less comfortable with language than is her Harvard-educated friend, Ántonia preserves the "characters of her girlhood" in pictures rather than in words. Once fluent in English, Ántonia has "forgot" her

1. Ibid., p. 121.
† *PMLA* 100.1 (1985): 51–67. Reprinted by permission of the copyright owner, the Modern Language Association of America.
1. Significantly, no page reference is possible here because Cather's 1926 revised edition of *My Ántonia* did not paginate the introduction. As I later explain in greater detail, Cather changed the introduction in 1926 to emphasize her central narrative fiction: the claim that she is only editing and introducing Jim Burden's manuscript. Technical changes in the printed text [in editions after 1926] further stress the difference between "editor" Cather and "author" Burden. Not only are the page numbers dropped, but the entire introduction is italicized to separate "Cather's" text from Jim's typographically. Unless otherwise specified, all my references to *My Ántonia* are to the Sentry edition of the revised 1926 text. References to the first edition of the novel specify 1918 before the page citation [These are in square brackets and refer to this Norton Critical Edition].

adopted language since her marriage to Anton Cuzak and doesn't "often talk it any more" (335). She has not forgotten her history, however, and the "succession of pictures" that Ántonia shares with Jim on the first night of his visit to the Cuzak farm wordlessly confirms the details of Jim's long narrative. In images as sharply defined as "the old woodcuts of one's first primer," the "incommunicable past" of Jim's story is preserved as a vital "family legend" in the Cuzak household:

> Ántonia brought out a big boxful of photographs: she and Anton in their wedding clothes, holding hands; her brother Ambrosch and his very fat wife, who had a farm of her own, and who bossed her husband, I was delighted to hear; the three Bohemian Marys and their large families.   (349)

The most interesting pictures in Ántonia's collection follow photographs of Lena Lingard and the Harlings, and Ántonia shows them as the climax to her account. In a "tintype of two men, uncomfortably seated, with an awkward-looking boy in baggy clothes standing between them" and in a photograph of "a tall youth in striped trousers and a straw hat, trying to look easy and jaunty," Jim Burden, the narrative voice of *My Ántonia*, is embodied for the first time.

Cather's original 1918 introduction to the novel emphasizes the importance of Ántonia's pictures. Of critical importance to a proper understanding of *My Ántonia*, this introduction serves the same purpose as "The Custom House" preface to *The Scarlet Letter*: presenting the narrative that follows as an independent artifact, the authorial "I" speaks as the editor and publisher of another writer's manuscript. At the opening of *My Ántonia*, "Cather" happens to meet Jim Burden—an old friend who now works as a lawyer for "one of the great Western railways"—on a train. Reminiscing about the people and places of their past as they cross the plains of Iowa, Cather and Jim continually return to a "central figure" who summarizes the "whole adventure of [their] childhood" in the West. When Jim suddenly wonders aloud why she has "never written anything about Ántonia," Cather responds with a proposal:

> I told him I had always felt that other people—he himself, for one—knew her much better than I. I was ready, however, to make an agreement with him; I would set down on paper all that I remembered of Ántonia if he would do the same. We might, in this way, get a picture of her.   (1918, [xii–xiii])

Jim enthusiastically agrees to the plan, and "months afterward" he delivers his manuscript to Cather at her New York apartment. Recounting Jim's proud delivery of his "thing about Ántonia," Cather concludes with what appears to be an admission of personal failure. Forced to confess that her own account of Ántonia has "not gone beyond a few straggling notes," Cather replies to Jim's parting advice with a remarkably ambiguous disclaimer:

> "Read it as soon as you can," he said, rising, "but don't let it influence your own story."
> My own story was never written, but the following narrative is Jim's manuscript, substantially as he brought it to me. (1918, [xiv])

The meaning of Cather's crucial editorial qualification—*My Ántonia* is only "substantially" Jim Burden's manuscript—is clarified by the most important suppressed passage of the 1918 introduction. While Jim's memories of Ántonia ultimately take a narrative form ("I simply wrote down what of herself and myself and other people Ántonia's name recalls to me" [1918, [xiv]]; "I simply wrote down pretty much all that her name recalls to me" [1926]), for Cather Ántonia's name immediately evokes pictures rather than words: "To speak her name was to call up pictures of people and places, to set a quiet drama going in one's brain" (1918, [xii]). Cather stresses her pictorial memories of Ántonia in the proposal that constitutes the central fiction of the 1918 preface. The goal of their joint account, Cather tells Jim, will be to "get a picture" of Ántonia.

The "pictures of people and places" that shape Cather's memory of Ántonia anticipate Ántonia's tintypes and photographs in a way that directs our attention to a critically neglected aspect of *My Ántonia*: the novel's illustrations. That the printed text of Jim's manuscript incorporates a series of pictures strikingly like the "old woodcuts" recalled by Ántonia's photographs explains Cather's cryptic description of *My Ántonia* as only "substantially" Jim Burden's story. The pictorial imagery that identifies Jim's "editor" with Ántonia and distinguishes the "editor" from the author she introduces suggests that the novel's illustrations are Cather's most important editorial addition to the "substance" of Jim's narrative. Not only does Cather overtly insist on her pictorial imagination in the 1918 introduction ("To speak [Ántonia's] name was to call up pictures . . . to set a quiet drama going in one's brain"), but Jim's literary friend also never promises to *write* about Ántonia when she proposes the joint account, further emphasizing the importance of the novel's illustrations. Agreeing only to "set down on paper" all her memories of Ántonia, Cather leaves the matter of her artistic medium open in a way that invites us to take the pictures of *My Ántonia* as fulfilling her promise to provide a separate account of Jim's heroine.

The implicit assertion of Cather's 1918 introduction and of the closing scene dominated by Ántonia's "boxful of pictures"—that *My Ántonia*'s pictures are not expendable decorations but an essential part of the novel—is made explicit in Cather's correspondence with Ferris Greenslet, her editor at Houghton Mifflin. The publishing history that can be reconstructed from Houghton Mifflin records of *My Ántonia* clearly reveals that Cather not only commissioned W. T. Benda's illustrations for her fourth novel but did so in the face of considerable opposition from Greenslet and others. For over twenty years, from the time she started planning the drawings with Benda in 1917 until 1938, when Greenslet finally promised in writing that all future editions of *My Ántonia* would contain the original illustrations, Cather waged a constant battle with her editor and Houghton Mifflin's publicity and art departments over the issue of illustrating *My Ántonia*.[2]

The grounds of Houghton Mifflin's opposition to Benda's simple pen-and-ink line drawings varied from year to year. In 1917 the publicity department argued that company money would be better spent on a single substantial wash drawing that could be used as a frontispiece and on promotional posters (TS. 62). When Richard Scaife—a director on Houghton's publicity staff—finally (and rather condescendingly) agreed to print Benda's "little sketches," he refused to pay more than $150 for them, which was the going rate for a single conventional frontispiece (TS. 84). The stingy Houghton Mifflin art budget forced Cather to scale down her original scheme for twelve drawings to the present eight (TSS. 48, 62). Twenty years after Cather's initial battle with Houghton Mifflin over her "little" pictures, a new threat arose. In 1937 Ferris Greenslet proposed to tap the market for more expensive gift books with a deluxe edition of *My Ántonia* illustrated with color plates by Grant Wood. Cather's response was an emphatic letter insisting that plain Ántonia must be saved from flashy color illustrations in general and from Wood's illustrations in particular (TSS. 230, 354). She concluded with a plea for the permanent retention of the Benda plates.[3] Throughout her wrangles with Greenslet, Scaife, and others, Cather consistently defended the Benda illustrations as an indispensable part of her text. When Houghton Mifflin dropped the Benda illustrations in a cheap 1930 reprint of *My Ántonia* (forgetting, however, to delete

2. I am indebted to Mark Savin, professor of English formerly at the University of Minnesota, for bringing to my attention the materials that document the publishing history of *My Ántonia*. The pertinent letters between Cather and Houghton Mifflin personnel involved with *My Ántonia* (Greenslet, Richard Scaife of the publicity staff, and "Miss Bishop" of the art department) are all at the Houghton Library, Harvard University. In the Greenslet file, see especially TS. 84, 26 Nov. 1917; TS. 270, 6 Jan. 1926; TS. 272, 17 Feb. 1926; TS. 273, 9 April 1926; TS. 354, 3 Jan. 1938. In Cather's letters, see TS. 48, 7 March [1918]; MS. 58, 18 Oct. [1917]; TS. 62, 24 Nov. 1917; TS. 63, 1 Dec. [1917]; TS. 65, 9 [Dec. 1917]; MS. 69, 26 Dec. 1917; TS. 74, Friday [Feb. 1918]; MS. 75, Saturday [Feb. 1918]; TS. 77, 20 June [1918]; MS. 81, 17 July [1918]; TS. 174, 15 Feb. 1926; TS. 176 [April 1926]; TS. 177 [May 1926]; TS. 199, 4 Dec. 1930; MS. 212, 2 Nov. 1932; TS. 230, 29 [Dec] 1937. Because Cather's will forbids the publication of her letters, they remain uncollected and rather inaccessible, scattered in libraries from Harvard to the San Marino Huntington. The proscriptions against publishing the letters have obliged me to paraphrase rather than quote them directly. [Schwind is referring to the prohibition in Cather's will on publishing Cather's letters. This prohibition lasted until 2013, when Andrew Jewell and Janis Stout published their collection *The Selected Letters of Willa Cather* (New York: Knopf, 2013).—Editor]

3. In the face of Cather's strong opposition, Greenslet seems to have changed his mind about the "deluxe" *Ántonia* illustrated by Wood. He readily concurred with her veto of

"with illustrations by W. T. Benda" from the novel's title page),
Cather considered the book an unauthorized edition (TS. 199).

The publishing history of *My Ántonia* is important because it reinforces the central fiction of the novel itself. Just as the fiction of *My
Ántonia* makes "Cather" responsible for illustrating the manuscript
that she introduces and edits, so the actual history of the illustrated
text testifies to Cather's exercising authority over the novel's carefully
planned pictorial supplement. Cather's letters reveal that she not only
independently commissioned the Benda pictures but acted as artistic
director of the project. At the same time that she was writing her
introduction to *My Ántonia* in late 1917, Cather was closely supervis-
ing Benda's illustrations to the novel. From approving Benda's preliminary sketches to making final decisions about where to place the
pictures within her printed text, Cather governed the process of illustrating *My Ántonia* quite autocratically. She determined both the old-
fashioned "woodcut" style and the separate subjects of the eight-plate
series and reserved the right to reject any work that displeased her.

The difference between Benda's typical magazine work and
his *Ántonia* drawings indicates Cather's authority over the novel's
illustrations. Primarily a decorative painter and an illustrator for
magazines like *Cosmopolitan, Century, Vanity Fair,* and *Scribner's,*
W. T. (Władysław Theodor) Benda probably first met Cather while
she was working at *McClure's.* Unlike the plain pen-and-ink sketches
of *My Ántonia,* Benda's usual pictures in *Vanity Fair* and other popular magazines are fashionable charcoal drawings. Intricately detailed
and reproduced in halftones, these illustrations have a three-
dimensional depth and a mimetic sophistication that are conspicu-
ously lacking in the stark black-on-white sketches—with the bold
linearity of "old woodcuts"—in *My Ántonia.*[4] Significantly, Cather's
interest in Benda was provoked not by his conventionally stylish and
highly finished magazine pieces but by what were seemingly his most
unimportant and minor works. In a letter to Richard Scaife, Cather
explains that her plan to illustrate *My Ántonia* was inspired by Benda's work in a novel by Jacob Riis, *The Old Town* (TS. 63). Benda
did two sorts of drawings for Riis: framed, full-page illustrations

---

Wood's pictures (suggesting that he, too, had doubts about the wisdom of dressing up
simple and plain *Ántonia*) but acknowledged that enterprising young men in Houghton
Mifflin's advertising department would be disappointed by the decision (TS. 354).

4. A good example of Benda's characteristic magazine work is the *Vogue* illustration (July
1920) reprinted in Byrnes (248–49). While many of Benda's illustrations depict fashionable society, at the time Cather commissioned the "head-and-tail pieces" for *My
Ántonia* Benda was also widely known for painting western subjects (especially for a
pictorial series titled "Cowboy Life on the Western Plains," 1910). In a letter to Ferris
Greenslet, Cather explains that her choice of an illustrator for *My Ántonia* was influenced by an important affinity between Benda and *Ántonia*: like *Ántonia*, Benda not
only had lived in the American West but had roots in Bohemia (TS. 62). The son of a
Polish pianist and composer, Benda immigrated to the United States in 1899. Cather
considered him ideally suited to the task of providing a pictorial counterpoint to Jim's

executed in charcoal (Benda's favorite medium) and reproduced in halftones on glossy paper and much smaller pen drawings ("head-and-tail pieces") interspersed between the lines and in the margins of Riis's text (Riis 21, 104). In the relative artlessness of Benda's plain head-and-tail pieces, Cather saw the perfect, minimal art for depicting her artless Nebraska plains.

Yet if Houghton Mifflin records clearly establish Cather's authority over the illustrations to *My Ántonia* and stress the importance of her pictorial supplement to Jim Burden's text, they also raise a troublesome question about Cather's written supplement to Jim's memoir in the novel's introduction. When Cather revised the introduction to *My Ántonia* in 1926, she dropped the sections of the 1918 version that most pointedly insist on the importance of the novel's pictorial imagery. Both Cather's description of the "pictures of people and places" evoked by her memories of Ántonia and her final editorial hedge (that the following narrative is only "substantially" Jim's manuscript as he delivered it to Cather) are deleted in 1926. More significantly, "Cather" does not this time propose an artistic partnership to "get a picture" of Ántonia. A major figure in the 1918 introduction, Cather-the-author virtually disappears in the revised introduction. Instead of the professional writer who inspires Jim to write an account of Ántonia and promises to "set down" one of her own, "Cather" is now merely an editor explaining how the manuscript of an old friend came into her possession. When in the 1926 introduction Cather and Jim accidentally meet on a western train, Jim has already been writing about Ántonia for some time to amuse himself on "long trips across the country." Cather tells Jim she'd like to read his account, and Jim agrees to show it to her "if it were ever finished." The 1926 introduction concludes roughly as the 1918 version does, with Jim delivering his manuscript to Cather "months afterward."

If, as I propose to argue, Benda's illustrations provide an important subtext that illuminates Jim Burden's words, why does Cather in her revised introduction eliminate all references to pictures and to her pictorial imagination and effectively mute her editorial contribution to the "substance" of Jim's text? The Houghton Mifflin' records are once again revealing. While Cather herself was never satisfied with the introduction to *My Ántonia* (she admitted on several occasions that the introduction was the only part of the novel she found tedious to write and acknowledged that her prose sounded forced), the impetus for the 1926 revision came from Ferris Greenslet.[5]

---

narrative because—like Ántonia and unlike Jim and Mr. Shimerda—Benda successfully developed the new forms and conventions demanded by his strange new world. For a brief biographical sketch of Benda, see Samuels and Samuels.

5. Cather comments on her difficulties in writing the original and revised versions of the introduction to *My Ántonia* in a series of letters to Greenslet (TSS. 74, 174, 176). Greenslet presents a strong argument about the weakness of the 1918 introduction in two important letters of early 1926 (TSS. 270, 273).

Greenslet pressed Cather to revise the first edition of *Ántonia* for both economic and aesthetic reasons. Houghton Mifflin was planning a more elaborately bound and expensive edition for 1926, and Greenslet convinced Cather that the moment was ripe for making some long-discussed changes in her text. If Houghton Mifflin could promote the 1926 reissue as a definitive new edition, Greenslet argued, immediate and long-range sales would be much greater than for a simple reprinting (TSS. 270, 273). If Greenslet had one eye on his corporate ledgers, he also had an eye critically focused on *My Ántonia*. He had long felt that the introduction to the novel destroyed the "classic outline" of Jim Burden's first-person narrative (TS. 273). Essentially, he objected that Cather's introduction was superfluous: the detailed accounts of Jim's loveless marriage to "Genevieve Whitney" and his escapist "Western dreams" of boyhood freedom and adventure make Jim's unsuccessful adult life unnecessarily explicit. Insisting that the unhappiness of Jim's later life is implicit throughout the last book of the novel, Greenslet advised Cather to dispense with the introduction (TS. 273).

Although she disagreed with Greenslet about dropping the introduction entirely, Cather agreed with his primary reservations about it—it lacked subtlety and especially made the failure of Jim's personal life far too explicit. That Cather took her editor's advice seriously is evident in the major excisions of the 1926 *Ántonia*. Recognizing Cather's reluctance to eliminate the introduction, Greenslet recommended two sizable cuts. The paragraph describing Jim's wife and her eastern chic should be dropped ("I do not like his wife" is sufficient editorial comment, Greenslet noted; the rest should be left to the reader's imagination). Greenslet further advised that the following paragraph about Jim's persistent romanticism be extensively blue-penciled (TS. 273). Cather not only agreed to the pruning that Greenslet suggested but made additional cuts of her own; together they eliminated more than a third of the original preface.

The difference between the opening lines of the 1918 and 1926 editions suggests the principal effect of Cather's revisions. In 1918 Cather introduces her narrator as "James Quayle Burden": "Last summer I happened to be crossing the plains of Iowa in a season of intense heat, and it was my good fortune to have for a traveling companion James Quayle Burden—Jim Burden, as we still call him in the West" (1918, [ix]). Evidently feeling her original opening too heavy-handed in anticipating the immaturity ("James" is still "Jim") and suppressed anxieties (Quayle=quail) that color Jim's narrative, Cather wisely allows Jim's name to speak for itself in 1926: "Last summer, in a season of intense heat, Jim Burden and I happened to be crossing Iowa on the same train." The same urge to make Jim's *burden*some adulthood more subtly implicit at the outset of *My Ántonia* explains Cather's reconsideration of the introduction's central fiction. In 1926 responsibility for the genesis of *My Ántonia* significantly shifts from Cather to Jim. While originally Cather and her proposal for a collaborative "picture" of Ántonia inspire Jim's memoir, in the revised text Jim has long been taking refuge from his adult life in the history of his childhood past. The account of Ántonia that Jim has been writing "from time to time" on long train trips delicately compensates for the passages about Jim's "brilliant marriage" and unrealized "Western dreams" that Cather cut at Greenslet's suggestion. Unlike the manuscript described in the first introduction—produced by Jim in a burst of enthusiasm between his meeting with Cather on the train and his arrival at her apartment several months later—the manuscript of the 1926 *Ántonia*—written "from time to time" over the years—testifies to a need for living in the past that betrays Jim's present unhappiness.

If Cather's 1926 revisions give the introduction a subtlety and psychological penetration that do justice to the novel proper, they also deemphasize the importance of the Benda illustrations in *My Ántonia*. Since "Cather" no longer promises to "set down" her own memories of Ántonia, the 1926 edition does not explicitly invite us to consider the novel's illustrations as Cather's editorial supplement to Jim's manuscript. Yet in dropping the fiction of a coauthored *Ántonia*, Cather strengthens the fiction of her editorial authority over Jim's work. Cather speaks exclusively as Jim's editor in 1926; she is no longer both Jim's editor and the literary muse who inspires him to write. By stressing her editorial authority, Cather simultaneously suggests that Jim's narrative is inadequate (hinting that Jim's "romantic" vision of the past is extremely partial and in need of correction) and identifies herself as the editor and friend who will compensate for Jim Burden's deficiencies.

The importance of "Cather's" editorial role in *My Ántonia*—and the extension of her editorial voice beyond the introduction—is immediately emphasized on the opening page of Jim's story, where "Cather" speaks in a footnote. Cather's note about the pronunciation of Ántonia's name not only asserts her editorial presence in the novel proper, but it also suggests the nature of her continued additions to the "substance" of Jim's story. The detailed instructions, that Cather sent to Houghton Mifflin regarding the layout of the opening pages of *My Ántonia* indicate the importance of her editorial intrusion on the first page of book 1. Jim's story must directly follow her introduction, Cather told Greenslet, and white pages for "My Ántonia" and "Book I: The Shimerdas" should be omitted (TS. 77). Cather's opening layout in the 1918 edition dramatically juxtaposes Jim's final act of authority or authorship—he amends the title of his manuscript by adding the prefix "My" to "Ántonia"—and Cather's first editorial annotation. On the one hand, Jim's possessive prefix insists on the idiosyncrasy and conventionality of his account. "*My*

Ántonia" implies the cultural framework of Jim's Virginia homeland—where women are denied independence by the chivalric codes of male proprietors. Cather's footnote, on the other hand, is inspired by a concern for "getting a picture" of the unique cultural identity and (by Old Dominion standards) the "masculine" authority that distinguish Ántonia from the transplanted southern belles in the West: "The Bohemian name *Ántonia* is strongly accented on the first syllable, like the English *Anthony . . .*" (1918, [9]; 1926, (3)).

Emphasizing Ántonia's individual autonomy as it does, Cather's note to the opening line of *My Ántonia* responds to the subordinating effect of Jim's possessive "my" with a directness that preserves the fictional intertextuality of the 1918 *Ántonia* cooperatively "set down" by Jim and Cather. Like the 1918 introduction, Cather's single footnote invites us to read *My Ántonia* as the collaborative effort of Jim Burden and his "editor." Reading *My Ántonia* as Cather presents it—as a critically edited or "supplemented" text—thus necessarily entails a serious consideration of the novel's visual textual supplements. To read Cather's story, we must read "Cather's" story. We must go beyond Jim Burden's narrative and examine the "quiet drama" that Jim's editor provides to "get a picture" of Ántonia.

II

The illustrations of *My Ántonia* describe an artistic development that sharply counterpoints the "little circle" of Jim's narrative (illus. 1–9). Benda's "quiet drama" in pictures is in one crucial respect like Jim Burden's narrative: it is prefaced by the editor of *My Ántonia*. Just as Jim's text is introduced by "editor" Cather, Benda's series of eight plates has an important pictorial prelude or preface in the editorial logotype on the title page of *My Ántonia*. That the pictorial drama of *My Ántonia* begins on Houghton Mifflin's title page rather than with Benda's first plate is suggested by Jim's study of the book Cather quotes in her epigraph, Vergil's *Georgics*. Stargazing on a warm spring night in Lincoln, Jim is rather unromantically recalled to his studies by Venus:

> My window was open, and the earthy wind blowing through made me indolent. . . . in the utter clarity of the western slope, the evening star hung like a lamp suspended by silver chains—like the lamp engraved upon the title-page of old Latin texts, which is always appearing in new heavens, and waking new desires in men. It reminded me, at any rate, to shut my window and light my wick in answer.   (263)

The title-page engravings of Jim's Latin textbooks direct our attention to the classical logotype on the title page of *My Ántonia*, a miniature portrait of Arcadian Pan (an image that, though "given" by the publisher, is exploited by Cather, who adds a classical motto to the

MY ÁNTONIA

BY

WILLA SIBERT CATHER

Optima dies . . . prima fugit
VIRGIL

WITH ILLUSTRATIONS BY
W. T. BENDA

BOSTON AND NEW YORK
HOUGHTON MIFFLIN COMPANY
The Riverside Press Cambridge

Illus. 1. Title page of *My Ántonia* (1918), with Houghton Mifflin logo-type. Courtesy of Houghton Library, Modern Books and Manuscripts, Harvard University. AC9.C2865.918mb.

Illus. 2. Plate 1 of *My Ántonia*. Group portrait of the Shimerda family.

Illus. 3. Plate 2 of *My Ántonia*. Mr. Shimerda with gun.

Illus. 4. Plate 3 of *My Ántonia.* Bohemian woman gathering mushrooms.

Illus. 5. Plate 4 of *My Ántonia.* Jake Marpole carrying a Christmas tree on horseback.

Illus. 6. Plate 5 of *My Ántonia*. Ántonia plowing.

Illus. 7. Plate 6 of *My Ántonia*. Ántonia
and Jim watching the sunrise.

Illus. 8. Plate 7 of *My Ántonia*. Lena knitting.

Illus. 9. Plate 8 of *My Ántonia*. Ántonia driving cattle in a blizzard.

title page to emphasize the importance of its engraved Pan [illus. 1]). The pictures of *My Ántonia*—progressing from the title-page Pan, who plays his pipe within the shelter of an Arcadian bower, to the final portrait of Ántonia bent against the high winds of a prairie blizzard—vividly dramatize the evolution of the new, antipastoral art demanded by the stark Nebraska flatlands. A land not yet "a country at all, but the material out of which countries are made," the new world that Ántonia Shimerda and Jim Burden enter on the same train requires a radical revision of old-world conventions and cultural traditions. The repudiation of Arcadian Pan in the graphic art of *My Ántonia* points to the wider implications of Jim's note about Nebraska's "down in the kitchen" revision of what had always been "'out in the kitchen' at home" in Virginia: a world with "no fences, no creeks or trees, no hills or fields" subverts not only pastoral landscape conventions but conventions of language, architecture, and human relations as well. Compelling owls to live a "degraded" subterranean existence because of the lack of trees and promoting Bohemia's most "highly esteemed" hunting target—badgers—to a safer status of friendship ("I won't let the men harm him," Jim's grandmother says of the badger who raids her chicken coops. "In a new country a body feels friendly to the animals" (17)), Nebraska thoroughly confounds the "due order and decorum" of both Virginia and Europe.

If the illustrations to *My Ántonia* depart from the classical conventions of its title-page Arcadia in order to depict unbucolic Nebraska, the text of the novel announces Jim's failure to respond creatively to his "new world" (3). Throughout *My Ántonia* it is evident that Jim suffers from the same poverty of imagination that makes Mr. Shimerda deny the possibility of civilized life outside "the old world he had left so far behind" (86). Like Ántonia's father, Jim cannot participate in shaping a new world because he remains "fix[ed] . . . to the last" in old-world ideals (96).

Although Jim condemns the "tyranny" of custom as the most deadly sin of Black Hawk, he implicitly admits his own contribution to it by the virulence of his indictment of the "conventional" town and its "guarded mode of existence" (201–19). While he recognizes that the imported southern standards of "respectability" and "refinement" upheld by Black Hawk's transplanted Virginians are as incongruous as the appeals to noblesse oblige and chivalry made in Lincoln by Ordinsky, the Polish violin teacher in love with Lena Lingard, Jim's rebellion against these outmoded codes of gentility never moves beyond self-indulgent brooding. He is finally governed by the same feeling—a "respect for respectability stronger than any desire"— that he contemptuously describes as the chief characteristic of Black Hawk's "young man of position," and Jim's complicity in the town's "wasteful, consuming process of life" is nowhere more apparent than in his relationship with Ántonia. Jim's failure to challenge the "stupid" cultural prejudices of his town is summarized by his last word as an author. Amending the title of his manuscript to "My Ántonia," Jim simultaneously reaffirms the patriarchal authority of "genteel" Mr. Shimerda ("Who could say so little, yet managed to say so much when he exclaimed, 'My Ántonia!'") and confirms the ethnic hierarchies of "refined" Black Hawk. (In the "good old plantation" tradition, Jim speaks of the "hired girls" of the town as if they were the property of their employers. His references to "the Harlings' Tony," "the Marshalls' Anna," and "the Gardeners' Tiny" preserve "the spirit if not the fact" of the d'Arnault "Big House" served by a "buxom young Negro wench" (185)).

The social conventions that Jim honors by prefixing the posses-sive adjective to his title determine the entire course of his romance with Ántonia. Jim not only respects the limits that deny Black Hawk's "young man of position" more than a "jolly frolic" with the country girls but continually tries to remake Ántonia in the image of the ane-mic "daughters of the well-to-do," who embody the town's ideal of pure womanhood (198). Threatened by Ántonia's pride in her "manly" strength and taste for outdoor work, Jim joins forces with his grand-mother to "save" Ántonia from "chores a girl ought not to do" (126). Jim's brutal description of Ántonia at the plow informs his objections to her "rough ways":

> . . . Ántonia came up the big south draw with her team. How much older she had grown in eight months! . . . She kept her sleeves rolled up all day, and her arms and throat were burned as brown as a sailor's. Her neck came up strongly out of her shoul-ders, like the bole of a tree out of the turf. One sees that draught-horse neck among the peasant women in all old countries. (122)

As Jim sees it, Ántonia's claim to a "man's" work is more than a vio-lation of Black Hawk's sense of propriety: it is a violation of human nature. Repeatedly warning Ántonia that she is being "spoiled" by heavy field work, Jim attempts to subdue the "strong independent nature" that distinguishes Ántonia from the town's disembodied "cherubs" (199). Fastidiously disturbed by the beads of perspiration that gather on Ántonia's upper lip "like a little mustache" as she picks vegetables with him in the garden (138) and by the way she eats with noisy relish "like a man" rather than with nibbling female delicacy, Jim is repulsed by the unladylike independence that attracts him to Ántonia in the first place. Although he ridicules the notions of "refined" femininity that require the young women of Black Hawk to live like cripples (because "physical exercise was thought rather inelegant for the daughters of well-to-do families," they travel even the shortest distances by horse and buggy), Jim nonetheless worries that Ántonia is losing the "nice ways" that distinguish ladies from laborers (125).

In her introduction to *My Ántonia*, "Cather" hints that Benda's "pictures of people and places" provide a needed corrective to the "romantic" bias of Jim's story. To understand the effect of this pictorial corrective, it is necessary to understand the faulty literary vision that the illustrations are expressly designed to offset. The romantic excesses of Jim's narrative constitute an artistic failure that mirrors Jim's personal failure to accept Ántonia's challenge to Old South notions of "a lady's privilege" (136). In the same way that Jim's life is tyrannized by "refined" social conventions, the art of his story is dominated by the stale literary conventions of popular and pastoral romances.

Traditional estimates of *My Ántonia* as a "large-minded" celebration of the American West marked by the "yea-saying vision of Whitman" ignore the descriptive clichés, stock characters, and exaggerated Vergilian posturings that pervade Jim Burden's debut as an author (Brown 156; Woodress 179).[6] Contrary to Jim's modest claim that his "thing about Ántonia . . . hasn't any form," *My Ántonia* is shaped by the forms of two extremely convention-bound literary genres, the pastoral elegy and the dime-novel western. As Robert Taft has noted, cheap dime novels played an important part in the western migrations of the late nineteenth century. By 1884 (roughly the year Jim Burden journeys to Nebraska reading "a 'Life of Jesse James'"), dime novels were being criticized in New York newspapers for breeding eastern discontent and for inspiring young men "to go west and be cowboys" (Taft 358). While the novel that Jim recalls as "the most satisfying book [he] ever read" may not have inspired his actual trip westward, since he is already en route west when Jake Marpole buys "Jesse James" for him from a railway vendor, it is undoubtedly a principal muse of his recreation of that journey in *My Ántonia*. The influence of Jim's favorite adventure stories is evident throughout his narrative, both in the specific details of his descriptions (Otto Fuchs, for instance, the hired hand on the Burden's farm, is presented by Jim as a "lively and ferocious" cowboy who "might have stepped out of the pages of 'Jesse James'" (10)) and in the broader vision of "Bad Lands" untamed by citified manners and laws that forms the backdrop of Jim's nostalgic "Western dreams" (370).

The classical studies that Lena Lingard interrupts when she visits Jim in Lincoln would seem to suggest that his "Jesse James" days are over. The particular chapter of Vergil that Jim is pondering when

6. E. K. Brown approvingly cites W. C. Brownell's "penetrating" praise of *My Ántonia* as a "large-minded" and "unmeretriclous" work distinguished by its "continuous and sustained respect" for its central subject (156). According to Brown, *My Ántonia* "marks a new phase in the long process of Willa Cather's reconciliation with Nebraska": in *Ántonia* Nebraska is no longer the "place to leave" that it was in *Song of the Lark* but is instead "a place to live in" (158–59). Like Brown, James Woodress tends to discount the narrowmindedness of Jim's "thing about Ántonia." Woodress calls *My Ántonia* a "sunny novel" that combines Whitmanesque "yea-saying" and Jamesian artistry (179–80).

Lena enters his room, however, supports Lena's pointed greeting:
"You seem the same . . . except you're a young man, now, of course"
(266). The Jim studying Vergil in Lincoln is essentially "the same"
boy who first traveled to Nebraska under the influence of Jesse James.
That Lena finds Jim absorbed in book 3 of the *Georgics* points to the
second muse of *My Ántonia*: Jesse James is assisted by Arcadian Pan.
On the whole, Vergil's *Georgics* departs from the idyllic pastoral themes
of his earlier works to provide practical advice to native Italian
farmers. The four books of the *Georgics* separately treat four major
rural enterprises: agriculture, viniculture, animal husbandry, and
beekeeping. The book Jim considers the poet's "perfect utterance"
is ironically the one where Vergil detours from the "new path" he
blazes in the *Georgics* to carry his Muse from ideal Arcadia to real
Mantua (Vergil 69).[7] Discussing the care of flocks and herds, Vergil
notably lapses into the pastoral mode of the *Eclogues* in *Georgic* 3.
Bucolic shepherds momentarily supplant rustic farmers as an elegiac
tone overwhelms Vergil's pragmatic advice about cattle breeding:

> O streams and forests of Arcadian Pan!
> All other subjects which could charm a mind
> At leisure for a song, are they not staled
> Even to vulgar ears?

                    ✳   ✳   ✳

> Delay not long
> The mating of your cattle, but supply
> An oft succeeding offspring to the herd.
> Life's first, best season soon takes flight away
> From hapless, mortal creatures.   (69, 72)

As Jim passes from the tutelage of Jake Marpole (the reader of "too
many of them detective stories" who buys "Jesse James" for Jim) to
that of Gaston Cleric (the classics scholar who directs Jim's college
studies in Lincoln), the golden West of the dime novel is replaced by
Vergil's golden Arcadia in Jim's romantic vision. Just as *The Lives,
Adventures, and Exploits of Frank and Jesse James* celebrates the frontier outlaw unhindered by the restraints of society, so the classic pastoral laments the loss of precivilized Arcadian bliss. The natural
antagonist of Arcadia's "first, best days" is the unnamed villain of the
James boys' West: the responsibility and maturity of adult life.[8]

---

7. Because the lines in the Harvard *Georgics* are unnumbered, my citations refer to the
   page numbers of this standard edition of Vergil's poem.
8. The most famous dime novel "Life of Jesse James," *The James Boys Weekly* published by
   the House of Beadle and Adams, did not begin to appear until 1900, well after Jim's
   journey to Nebraska. It seems likely that Jim Burden's "most satisfying book" was an
   earlier dime western published soon after Jesse James's death, *The Lives, Adventures,
   and Exploits of Frank and Jesse James, with an Account of the Tragic Death of Jesse James,
   April 3d, 1882.* The University of Minnesota's excellent Kerlan Collection of children's

The strange combination of pastoral and dime-novel conventions that informs *My Ántonia* is thus not as eclectic as it first seems. "El Dorado"—the western lure that prompts Jesse's father to abandon his family on the first page of "Jesse James"—is a cattle-country Arcadia. Jim's art, unlike the art of W. T. Benda's "quiet drama" in pictures, never moves beyond the Arcadian Pan of Houghton Mifflin's title page and the opening line of Vergil's third *Georgic*. Throughout *My Ántonia*, Jim misrepresents his "new world" because his narrative art is archaic, unrealistic, and unmodern. While the differences between Vergil's pastoral shepherds and America's dime-novel desperadoes are many, in the context of *My Ántonia* Vergil and Jesse James similarly explain Jim Burden's failure as a storyteller. Jim never manages to "get a picture" of Ántonia and her prairie life because his narrative art depends on irrelevant romantic conventions. The footloose lone rangers and "Wild West" outlawry of popular fiction like Jim's dime novel are as psychologically and sociologically remote from Ántonia's world as Vergil's Arcadia is historically and culturally remote. Further reflecting a failure to invent the new forms demanded by a new world, Jim's narrative uses Homeric epithets (the "wine-coloured" sea of grass), epic similes (prairie winds recede like "defeated armies, retreating"; a sunset has the "exultation of victory, of triumphant ending, like a hero's death—heroes who died young and gloriously" (27)), and stock pastoral laments about the "incommunicable past" (372). Critics who have objected to the racism of the novel's "pickaninny" portrait of Blind d'Arnault have failed to see that Jim's "docile and happy" black musician (192) is of a piece with Otto Fuchs (a western cowboy straight "out of the pages of 'Jesse James'"), his sinister villain (wicked Wick Cutter, an "inveterate gambler" and merciless loan shark, "a man of evil name throughout the country"), his "very Biblical" grandparents (a "snow-white beard" and "oracular" voice identify Mr. Burden as an Old Testament prophet; Grandma Burden is more vaguely defined as a "gingerbread baking" matriarch), and his bifurcated vision of "real women" (225).[9]

Faithful to the tradition of "satisfying" dime westerns, Jim's female types are limited to "Snow-White in the fairy tale" and the "reckless" heroine of *Camille* (215, 272). That both types endanger male

<hr>

literature includes two slightly different (but identically titled) versions of this novel, both unsigned and undated. I have profited from reading both; Jim's favorite book informs *My Ántonia* like a palimpsest.

9. The most famous—and outrageous—examination of Cather's bigotries and resultant fictional stereotypes is James Schroeder's. While Schroeder focuses on the "anti-Semitism" of Cather's portrait of Louie Marsellus in *The Professor's House*, he makes much broader claims about Cather's ethnic and racial prejudices (overlooking, unfortunately, the fact that the "bias" in so many of Cather's novels is not Cather's but the point of view of her first-person narrators—Jim Burden in *Ántonia*—and her third-person centers of consciousness—Niel Herbert in *A Lost Lady* and Godfrey St. Peter in *Professor's House*).

autonomy—one through domestication, the other through
seduction—is the school marm-chorus girl theme of Jim's many
narrative digressions. The "revelation" that Jim experiences when
he returns to the *Georgics* after Lena's visit makes the same point
as the tale of the "two men who fed the bride to the wolves," Otto
Fuchs's story about the "sorry trick" played on him by a mother of
triplets, and the history of "Crazy Mary" Benson. *Georgic* 3, the
immediate context of Jim's "precious" recognition of "the relation
between girls like those [Lena, the Bohemian Marys, and the Danish laundresses] and the poetry of Virgil," digresses at length to
warn readers of the need to curb "mad lust." Cautioning breeders
that the "fair heifer," like the "maiden fond and fair," saps male
strength, Vergil's poetry "relates" to women like Lena as Jim's narrative does: negatively. Blanche Gelfant's wonderful summary of
the moral lesson behind Jim's episodic stories—"the woman must
go" (379)—applies equally well to his classical source:

> . . . naught of discipline so fortifies
> A powerful beast as that he be restrained
> From joy of Venus and blind passion's goad,
> Whether bull or stallion be thy care.
> Therefore the bull is exiled and confined
> In lonely fields. . . .
> Sight of his female wastes his strength away
> By slow degrees, and bids him seek no more
> Green pastures or cool woodlands; for her charm
> Sweetly entices, and her wooers proud
> In horn-locked duel the wild suit decide.

The conventions that circumscribe Jim Burden and his narrative
dramatically illuminate the invention of the novel's illustrations. The
significance of *My Ántonia*'s pictorial supplement is most overtly suggested by the pictorial imagery within the "substance" of Jim's text.
At both the beginning and the ending of *My Ántonia* Jim Burden
inadvertently identifies himself with Black Hawk's most avid collector of "desired forms and faces," the telegrapher who "nearly smoked
himself to death" for the pictures of actresses and dancers on cigarette coupons (218). On his first Christmas in Nebraska, Jim com-
piles ads, holy cards, and colored lithographs cut from "good old
family magazines" to make a picture book for Ántonia's sister, Yulka.
A frontispiece lithograph of "Napoleon Announcing the Divorce to
Josephine" (yet another version of "the woman must go") introduces
a collection of smaller "Sunday-school cards and advertising cards"
from Jim's "old country" of Virginia (81). To the final scene in the
Cuzak's parlor, Jim contributes pictures from an "old country" more
distant than the East Coast. Pictures of Prague and Vienna hang in

the background of the scene where Ántonia shows Jim her family photograph collection. Both cityscapes are gifts from Jim, sent home to Ántonia during his travels abroad. "Napoleon Announcing the Divorce to Josephine" and the framed pictures in the Cuzak parlor effectively distinguish Jim from both Ántonia and Benda, his central subject and his illustrator. While the authors of the novel's two "dramas" in pictures are artists of a new world, Jim Burden remains an "old world" art collector. Like the chain-smoking telegrapher, Jim is devoted to ideal "forms" that have nothing to do with Black Hawk realities.

A collection of outmoded forms and conventions, Jim's narrative is most aptly summarized by the metaphor Cather used to describe her own first novel, *Alexander's Bridge*: it is "very like what painters call a studio picture," a work marked by lessons of a master and by rigid adherence to established rules of composition ("My First Novels" 91).[1] The art of Benda's pictorial drama essentially responds to Jim's studio piece with the assertion Cather would later articulate in "The Novel Démeublé" (1922): to describe a radically new world and the woman who embodies the "whole adventure" of growing up in it, the accumulated "furniture" of art—"all the meaningless reiterations . . . all the tired old patterns"—must be thrown out the window (51).

The "furniture" that Jim's editor-illustrator discards to "get a picture" of Ántonia is defined most vividly by the opening and closing scenes of Benda's eight-plate series. The movement from Benda's opening family portrait of the Shimerdas to his final portrait of Ántonia is marked by parallel developments in form and content. "Huddled together on the platform" of the Black Hawk railway station, the Shimerdas occupy the artistically constructed, measured space that is western art's principal piece of Renaissance "furniture" (illus. 2). Emphasizing the illusory depth of his framed space by his oblique angle of vision, Benda composes the figures in his nichelike enclosure in the classic triangular form of traditional holy family groups. The central figure of the composition is appropriately the moving force of the Shimerda family, Mrs. Shimerda. Hugging a tin box against her breast "as if it were a baby," Mrs. Shimerda is an old-world Madonna poised on the brink of a new virgin land that promises "much money [and] much land" for her sons and "much husband" for her daughters (90).

Mrs. Shimerda's tin-box "baby" ironically underscores the difference between the sacred tradition that Benda evokes in his triangular grouping and the secular worldliness of Mrs. Shimerda's maternal ambitions. Substituting the fiercely mundane Mamenka Shimerda

---

1. As Cather notes elsewhere, the "master" that she follows rather too devotedly in her "studio-piece" novel (*Alexander's Bridge*) and, to a lesser extent, in her first collection of short stories (*The Troll Garden*) is Henry James (Carroll 214).

for the heavenly mother of conventional Madonna and Child paintings, Benda prefigures the more radical revision of traditional iconography that distinguishes his final portrait of a new-world Madonna
(illus. 9). Benda's final portrait of Ántonia "driving her cattle homeward" in a December blizzard fundamentally redefines the conventional holy family evoked in plate 1. Dressed in "a man's long overcoat
and boots, and a man's felt hat with a wide brim," her steps heavy
with the weight of her advanced (and illegitimate) pregnancy, Ántonia is a "lonesome" revision of the Shimerda group. Benda's final
scene unites mother, father, and child in a single commanding figure. The "quiet drama" of My Ántonia thus achieves the redefini-
tion of maternity that Lena Lingard insists on in guiding her brother's
selection of monogrammed handkerchiefs. Like Lena's recommen-
dation of "B for Berthe" rather than "M for Mother," Benda's final
portrait of Ántonia asserts the individual identity that Jim dilutes in
the possessive prefix of his title.

The landscape surrounding Benda's new Madonna redefines by
indefinition the pictorial space of plate 1. If the artistically controlled
and mathematically "possessed" space of the railway platform reflects
Jim's appropriative title, the best text for the barely articulated
landscape of Benda's last scene is Lena's response to critics of her
relationship with Ole Benson: "It ain't my prairie" (169). The men-
surational perspective of plate 1 asserts a mastery of space that is
further emphasized by the railway setting of the composition. As
Barbara Novak observes in her study of nineteenth-century railway
photography, the "linear imperialism" of the railroad provides a vivid
metaphor for the artist's attempts to order and control the vast American wilderness within a limited picture space (180).

In Benda's final scene, the "linear imperialism" of space brought
under human control gives way to the unconquered natural anar-
chy of a prairie blizzard. Limited only by the physical dimensions of
the page, Benda's unframed winter landscape extends infinitely in
all directions. Distinctions between land and sky obliterated by flying snow, the featureless expanse of the prairie defies artistic definition. In contrast to the constructed pictorial space that shelters
the Shimerda family in plate 1, the open setting of Ántonia's portrait is notably artless: the landscape of Benda's final scene—the natural whiteness of the book page—both antecedes and overwhelms
his art. In this evolution, Benda's art demonstrates its superiority to
Jim's. While Jim's narrative ends as it begins, with an assertion that
art is a means of fixing or "possessing" reality (Jim's final words return
us to the curious possessiveness of his title: "My Ántonia" allows its
author to "possess . . . the precious, the incommunicable past"
[emphasis added]), Benda's art evolves in recognition of a world "outside man's jurisdiction" (7).

The importance of the artless "white waste" of Ántonia's winter landscape is suggested by Cather's first published art review. The white space that represents a December snowstorm in plate 8 alternatively evokes the white heat and "burning sun" of a Nebraska summer in Benda's penultimate plate, the full-length portrait of Lena (illus. 8). In the 1895 review, Cather describes the crucial difference between the overhead sun to which Lena is constantly exposed and the moments of "magical light" at dawn and dusk that Jim celebrates in his text. When Cather wrote about the annual exhibit of Lincoln's Haydon Art Club in her "As You Like It" column, art was still rare enough in Nebraska to inspire reviews that were more reverential than judgmental. Cather's criticism of a painting on loan from the Chicago Art Institute is remarkable, then, both because it dares to be sharply irreverent and because it contrasts so strikingly with her opening statement about the "privilege and blessing" of seeing portraits by Carl Newman and Weston Benson in the gallery's "inner sanctum":

> Richard Lorenz's "In the West" is at once strong and disappointing. The worst thing about it is the title. It is a western subject and a western man placed it in an unwestern atmosphere . . . the picture is not western. The impressionists say it is "keyed too low." Whatever that may mean the lights are certainly at fault and the color is too tame. The sunlight is gentle, not the fierce, white, hot sunlight of the West. Sunlight on the plains is almost like sunlight of the northern seas; it is a glaring, irritating, shelterless light that makes the atmosphere throb and pulsate with heat. (125)

The "fierce, white, hot sunlight" that Cather stresses in her review informs both Benda's portrait of Lena and Cather's instructions to Houghton Mifflin about its placement in the text: it is to appear low enough on the page to give the effect of a vast open space baking under a high-noon sun (MS. 75).[2]

The light of Lena's overhead sun illuminates Jim Burden's lyrical descriptions of the "horizontal light" that Benda depicts in plates 2 and 6 (illus. 3 and 7). The golden moments that Jim translates into "picture-writing on the sun"—Mr. Shimerda against a sunset "like the bush that burned with fire and was not consumed" and the "heroic" plow in the center of the red disk on the horizon—point to Claude Lorraine as emphatically as Jim's red "fingers of the sun" point to Homer's "rosy-fingered" dawns (244). The oblique rays of Jim's literary landscapes are an essential feature—or, to use Cather's terms, a standard piece of furniture—of ideal landscapes derived

---

2. In a letter to Ferris Greenslet, Cather even went so far as to suggest printing *My Ántonia* on yellow paper to evoke the western sun (TS. 48).

from Claudian pastorals. The magical "sudden transfiguration" of the day that Jim describes in such detail is the traditional "picturesque moment" of dawn or dusk when sunlight joins heaven and earth in an enveloping atmospheric radiance. The fierce white light of Lena's portrait responds to Benda's graphic rendition of Jim's roseate heavenly "fingers" (pls. 2 and 6) with the charge Cather levels at "In the West": limited to the most atypically gentle moments of a scene characterized by "glaring, irritating, shelterless light," Jim's "picture-writing" is skillful but essentially "unwestern."

The vertical orientation of Benda's two final scenes not only controverts Black Hawk's simplistic Snow White-Camille dichotomies by linking visually Ántonia and Lena but also recalls Jules Breton's *Song of the Lark* (illus. 10), the painting that provides the title for Cather's last novel before *My Ántonia*, and clearly anticipates the climactic final plates of Benda's pictorial "drama."[3] In Breton's painting, a centrally positioned French peasant girl stands arrested in her work (she is presumably—and rather stagily—harkening to the song of an unseen lark). The girl's alert, upright pose is emphasized by the horizontal expanse of the stark fields surrounding her, and her commanding stance is further stressed by the curved reaping hook that she holds in suspension. The reaping hook of Breton's girl, Lena's knitting needles (pl. 7), and Ántonia's cattle whip (pl. 8) serve the same pictorial function as the batons, swords, and firearms featured in the "old portraits" of Virginia gentry that Jim recalls: they are iconographic symbols of command, independence, and authority.

In the "quiet drama" of *My Ántonia*, Benda's Breton-like figures respond not to the song of an offstage lark but to the outmoded conventions of two earlier female portraits, the sheltered Madonna of plate 1 and the mushroom gatherer of plate 3 (illus. 4). In the latter drawing a natural shelter replaces the artificial shelter of the railway station in plate 1. The bowed branches of a tree follow the same curve as the bent form of the woman picking mushrooms beneath it, forming an arbor like Arcadian Pan's (illus. 1). The harmonious forms of the woman and the tree express the accord between human life and nature in the old Bohemian world Mrs. Shimerda describes as she gives a bag of dried mushrooms to Jim's grandmother: in the

---

3. Houghton Mifflin used Breton's painting on the jacket of *Song of the Lark* until 1931. That Cather liked the general conception of the painting (its central female figure surrounded by a landscape like the Nebraska prairie) more than Breton's melodramatic details is suggested not only by Benda's unsentimental adaptations of the painting in *Ántonia* (in pl. 7, for instance, Lena fairly bursts from her scanty dress; the carefully delineated nipple pressing against her bodice is the most conspicuous—and, for romantics like Jim, the most disturbing—detail of Benda's portrait) but also by Cather's correspondence with Houghton Mifflin. Cather's campaign to get Breton's picture dropped from the cover of *Song of the Lark* was almost as long as her battle to keep Benda's drawings in *Ántonia*. (See Cather to Greenslet, TS. 18, 30 June 1915, and TS. 206, 26 Nov. [1931], for Cather's first and final pleas that Breton be evicted from her dust jacket.)

Illus. 10. Jules Breton, *Song of the Lark* (1884).
Art Institute of Chicago.

world of the mushroom gatherer, "things for eat" can be collected
like manna (78). In Benda's final scenes, however, the sharp contrast between the shelterless flat expanse of the prairie and the erect
figures of Lena and Ántonia suggests natural opposition rather than
harmony. The featureless landscape of Benda's final plates provides
its inhabitants with neither food nor shelter gratis. The plates that
immediately follow Benda's mushroom gatherer insist on the realities of a world where "all things for eat" must be wrested from the
soil by brute force (pl. 5, illus. 6: two immense horses strain to pull
Ántonia's plow through the tough prairie sod) and where arboreal
shelters are the products of human art rather than natural munifi-
cence (pl. 4, illus. 5: the young pine Jake carries home across his
saddle is the first fruit of the Burdens' efforts to "civilize" treeless
Nebraska).

Ántonia and Lena thus respond to Benda's stooped peasant woman
by asserting the "masculine" authority—signaled by their unsupported upright stance and their staffs of command—demanded
by a new world where nature is not maternally providential. Benda's
full-length prairie portraits repudiate the Wild West illustrations of

Illus. 11. Frederick Church, *Twilight in the Wilderness* (1860). Cleveland Museum of Art, Mr. and Mrs. William H. Marlatt Fund.

Jim's "most satisfying book" in the same way that they challenge the idyllic landscape of the mushroom gatherer. The cover illustration of Jim's *Lives, Adventures, and Exploits of Frank and Jesse James,* crude though it is, summarizes the frontier aesthetic of traditional depictions of the West in American art. Straining to push past a log barrier that the James boys have erected on the tracks, the train that dominates the cover vividly dramatizes the desire to "escape restraints" that Jim Burden describes as the impetus of "every frontier settlement" (209). The impulse to flee the constraints of "smothery" civilization (as Huck Finn put it) and the constant westward movement that the impulse propelled inform popular landscapes of the American West from Frederick Church's 1860 *Twilight in the Wilderness* (illus. 11) to Frederic Remington's 1889 *Dash for Timber* (illus. 12).

In both horizontal extension and compositional emphasis on movement through space, the scenes of Church and Remington represent the western landscape traditions that Benda revises in his portraits of Ántonia and Lena. In Benda's full-length portraits, the horizontal spatial movement that distinguishes Remington's line of cowboys and the "linear imperialism" of parallel planes that leads us through Church's wilderness is replaced by vertical stasis. Unlike Remington's space-conquering cowboys, Benda's still, two-dimensional figures barely displace the space they occupy. While the West represented by Church and Remington is essentially Whitman's "Open Road"—a national thoroughfare for "traveling souls" perpetually en route to El Dorado—Benda's West is not a public highway but a place of precarious personal settlement. Both Ántonia and Lena are portrayed with their feet firmly planted on the ground as they engage in the civilized arts that make life possible in the "most unlikely place in the world." Benda's women quietly inhabit the vast space that the James boys are forever "just passin' through" with a maximum of noisy bravado. (And the reader who brushes past these illustrations without dwelling *on* them as Ántonia and Lena dwell *within* them is guilty of James-boy insensitivity to the "quiet" story they tell.)

Jim Burden's name is finally the best summary of the difference between Remington's art and Benda's and the corresponding difference between the narrative and the "succession of pictures" of *My Ántonia*. Constrained or "burdened" by the James-boy ideals of "devilish" manhood that Remington stereotypically represents, Jim incorporates the fiction of the "Life of Jesse James" into his own life and art. A lawyer "for one of the great Western railways," Jim Burden carries on his namesake's train business (albeit on the other side of the law) as he perpetuates Jesse's "golden West" in *My Ántonia*. The artistic evolution that is the "quiet drama" of *My Ántonia*'s pictures simultaneously underscores Jim's failure of imagination and provides a "new world" picture of Ántonia, a picture uncluttered by the inherited furniture of Jim Burden's narrative.[4]

---

4. I am grateful to Kent Bales, Jonathan Hill, and Karal Ann Marling for help in refining my argument.

WORKS CITED

Brown, E. K. *Willa Cather: A Critical Biography.* Completed by Leon Edel. New York: Avon, 1953.

Byrnes, Gene A. *A Complete Guide to Drawing, Illustrating, Cartooning, and Painting.* New York: Simon, 1948.

Carroll, Latrobe. "Willa Sibert Cather." *Bookman* 53 (1921): 212–16.

Cather, Willa. "As You Like It." *Nebraska State Journal* 6 Jan. 1895. Rpt. in *The World and the Parish: Willa Cather's Articles and Reviews, 1893–1902.* Ed. William Curtain. Lincoln: U of Nebraska P 1970, 1: 124–27.

———. *My Ántonia.* Boston: Houghton, 1918.

———. *My Ántonia.* Sentry ed. Boston: Houghton, 1954.

———. "My First Novels (There Were Two)." In *Willa Cather on Writing.* New York: Knopf, 1949, 91–97.

———. "The Novel Démeublé." In her *Not under Forty.* New York: Knopf, 1936, 43–51.

Gelfant, Blanche. "The Forgotten Reaping Hook: Sex in *My Ántonia.*" *American Literature* 43 (1971): 60–82.

The Lives, Adventures, and Exploits of Frank and Jesse James, with an Account of the Tragic Death of Jesse James, April 3d, 1882. N.p.: n.p., n.d.

Novak, Barbara. *Nature and Culture: American Landscape and Painting, 1825–75.* New York: Oxford UP, 1980.

Riis, Jacob A. *The Old Town.* New York: Macmillan, 1909.

Samuels, Peggy, and Harold Samuels. *The Illustrated Biographical Encyclopedia of Artists of the American West.* Garden City, N.Y.: Doubleday, 1976.

Schroeder, James. "Willa Cather and *The Professor's House.*" *Yale Review* 54 (1965): 494–512. Rpt. in *Willa Cather and Her Critics.* Ed. James Schroeder. Ithaca, N.Y.: Cornell UP, 1967, 363–81.

Taft, Robert. *Artists and Illustrators of the Old West: 1850–1900.* New York: Scribners, 1953.

Vergil. *The Georgics.* In *The Georgics and Eclogues of Virgil.* Trans. Theodore C. Williams. Cambridge: Harvard UP, 1915.

Woodress, James. *Willa Cather: Her Life and Art.* Lincoln: U of Nebraska P, 1970.

RICHARD H. MILLINGTON

Willa Cather and "The Storyteller": Hostility to the Novel in *My Ántonia*[†]

Some years ago, Phyllis Rose observed that it is because Cather's work resists our customs of critical description that we have been so late in recognizing her as an indispensable American writer. I hope to offer a new description of *My Ántonia*, one built upon a striking affinity between that book and Walter Benjamin's 1936 essay "The Storyteller."[1] At the center of each work is a protest against the constriction of experience characteristic of modern life, and in each

[†] *American Literature* 66.4 (1994): 689–717. Copyright 1994, Duke University Press. All rights reserved. Republished by permission of the copyright holder, Duke University Press. Bracketed page references are to this Norton Critical Edition.

1. Phyllis Rose, "Modernism: The Case of Willa Cather," in *Modernism Reconsidered*, ed. Robert Kiely (Cambridge: Harvard UP), 123. See Sharon O'Brien's "Becoming Noncanonical: The Case Against Willa Cather," *American Quarterly* 40 (1988): 110–26, for a compelling argument about the role played by gender in the fluctuations of Cather's literary status, and see two essays by David Stineback ("No Stone Unturned: Popular Versus Professional Evaluations of Willa Cather," *Prospects* 7 [1982]: 167–76, and "The Case of Willa Cather," *Canadian Review of American Studies* 15 [1984]: 385–95), for further criticism of Cather's treatment within the academy. Judith Fryer notices a number of links between Benjamin's account of storytelling and Cather's narrative tactics in

work that protest takes the form of an attack upon the assumptions and experiences associated with novel reading and an endorsement of the alternative vision of meaning exemplified by the tradition of oral storytelling. Each writer is at once looking backward and forward, drawing upon a vanishing narrative tradition to define an alternative, paradoxically modern textual practice. Benjamin's essay suggests a way of reading *My Ántonia* that avoids what for me is unsatisfying in the approaches and assumptions that seem to dominate criticism of the novel: honorific accounts of its "form" built upon abstractions ("time," "memory," "cycles") so rarefied as to produce a disembodied Platonic ideal of a book; a punitive moralism, either at Jim Burden's expense or Cather's, characteristic of some psychoanalytic and feminist criticism; the notion, treated as self-evident, that the book is transparently or naively nostalgic in its purposes and in the pleasures it offers.[2] "The Storyteller," used heuristically, gives us a way to see what is boldest and most interesting about *My Ántonia*, to infer from the book's behavior upon the page the ethics that animate it: the "form" of *My Ántonia* can best be described as a contest between two kinds of narrative—an intergeneric combat, for the possession of Jim Burden and for the allegiance of the reader, between the story and its values and those of the novel.

Felicitous Space: The Imaginative Structures of Edith Wharton and Willa Cather (Chapel Hill: U of North Carolina P, 1986), chaps. 7–9. Fryer uses Benjamin's essay as part of a valuable but diffuse treatment of the qualities of Cather's work. My hope is that a more sustained and pointed application of "The Storyteller" will yield a fuller, more specific account of the engagements and purposes of *My Ántonia.*

2. For a useful history of the critical reception of *My Ántonia*, see John J. Murphy, *My Ántonia: The Road Home* (Boston: Twayne, 1989), 9–20. Each of these interpretive positions has been maintained with considerable intelligence and ingenuity. The richest examples of what I would call the "abstract" strain include influential pieces by James E. Miller, "*My Ántonia*: A Frontier Drama of Time," *American Quarterly* 10 (1958): 476–84; Terence Martin, "The Drama of Memory in *My Ántonia*," *PMLA* 84 (1969): 304–11; David Stouck, *Willa Cather's Imagination* (Lincoln: U of Nebraska P, 1975); Robert Scholes, "Hope and Memory in *My Ántonia*," *Shenandoah* 14 (1962): 24–29; and, most recent, Susan Rosowski, *The Voyage Perilous: Willa Cather's Romanticism* (Lincoln: U of Nebraska P, 1986). Such readings imply, I think, unconvincingly detached answers to the question of what purposes motivate *My Ántonia*. Two strong, provocative, "tendentious" or moralistic readings: Blanche Gelfant's extraordinary essay, "The Forgotten Reaping-Hook: Sex in *My Ántonia*," *American Literature* 43 (1971): 60–82; and Jean Schwind, "The Benda Illustrations to *My Ántonia*: Cather's Silent Supplement to Jim Burden's Narrative," *PMLA* 100 (1985): 51–67. The assumption of nostalgia, extremely widespread and usually advanced without argument, is disputed by Rose, 135–37. The problem with these abstract or accusatory readings usually manifests itself as an oddity of emphasis: some element of the text becomes foregrounded, erased, or ironized in a way that would strike many other readers as surprising. Sharon O'Brien makes an argument for seeing the book as a conflicted or indeterminate text in "Gender, Sexuality, and Point of View: Teaching *My Ántonia* from a Feminist Perspective," in *Approaches to Teaching Cather's My Ántonia*, ed. Susan J. Rosowski (New York: MLA, 1989), 141–45; I am insisting here on the coherence of Cather's intellectual project.

"The Storyteller"

For Benjamin, every authentic story contains something useful—"counsel," or "wisdom"—and the storyteller is a person capable of exchanging that wisdom with others.[3] By "counsel" Benjamin means not simply the morals or maxims that some tales yield but the felt effect of the story as a whole, which becomes, through the story-teller's art, part of the experience of the listener. The decline of storytelling registers, then, a decline in the "communicability of experience" (86)—and hence of counsel about it—occasioned by the conditions of modern life, especially middle-class life, with its retreat, in both work and leisure, from the communal into the private. The values implicit in storytelling become especially clear when the story is measured against the two print media (each associated with the dominance of the middle class) that have supplanted it: the novel and the journalistic writing Benjamin calls "information."

Benjamin locates the superiority of the story to the novel and the newspaper in the nature of the response each medium calls forth. While a story's compression and explanatory reticence—"that chaste compactness that precludes psychological analysis" (91)—confer upon the listener an untrammeled interpretive independence, events now arrive "shot through with explanation," their status as "information" robbing them of the openness of meaning and effect Benjamin calls "amplitude" (89).[4] A story places its hearer—and even its reader, if the qualities of the oral tradition have been successfully evoked—"in the company" of the storyteller (100). A listener takes a story in, almost corporeally, meditates upon it at leisure, finds it "integrated into his own experience"; the sign of its effect is its claim upon the memory and the listener's impulse to repeat the tale to others (91). The novel reader, by contrast, is a "solitary individual" (87), isolated even from the writer by a fierce desire to seize upon and possess the overarching "meaning of life" the text seems to promise. The intensity of this desire, which fuels novelistic "suspense," is itself an effect of our modernity, a symptom of our lack of the counsel stories once contained. The novel creates a driven, jealous reader, at once consumed and consuming, "swallow[ing] up the material as the fire devours logs in the fireplace" (100), hungry for the plot's unfolding and for the implicit analysis that will make sense of it all. In the absence of a conviction of the meaning of his or her own experience, the reader vicariously seeks the meaning that the novel's

3. Walter Benjamin, "The Storyteller: Reflections on the Works of Nikolai Leskov," in *Illuminations*, ed. Hannah Arendt (New York: Schocken, 1969), 86. Future references in the text.
4. In Benjamin's terms, much present-day academic literary interpretation would be allied with "information"—with the urge to explain, to account for fully—rather than with "interpretation" in the meditative, exploratory sense in which he uses the word.

ending—construed by Benjamin as analogous to the death that con-
fers, retrospectively, significance upon a human life—will afford its
characters. "What draws the reader to the novel," he writes, "is the
hope of warming his shivering life with a death he reads about"
(100–01).

Storytelling thus emerges from Benjamin's essay, as it will from
Cather's book, as a distinctive, socially and historically located economy of meaning, valuable because it defines an alternative to the
telos-driven, intensely private, psychologizing form of seeking that
characterizes middle-class experience and that novel reading—that
culture's dominant literary form—at once expresses and intensifies.
Benjamin's anatomy of the story includes other elements that we will
recognize when we turn to *My Ántonia*, elements that invite us to
understand storytelling both as a narrative form and as implying a
stance toward experience, a way of life, a culture. First, stories have
a rich and distinct relation to the material conditions that produce them. Storytelling is intimately connected to particular kinds of
work, notably that of the farmer and the artisan (84–85). In anal-
ogy to agricultural and artisanal work, the storyteller's relation to
his craft is imagined to be intimate and bodily. This "artisan form
of communication" does not "aim to convey the pure essence of the
thing, like information or report" but "sinks the thing into the life
of the storyteller, in order to bring it out of him again. The traces of
the storyteller cling to the story the way the handprints of the potter
cling to the clay vessel" (91–92)—the metaphors of embodiment suggesting, as they will in Cather, an exchange of meaning more direct
and primary than the novel's substitutions and displacements. And
the story is embedded, as if to mark and measure its usefulness, not
only in the teller but in the distinctive context of its telling; we customarily hear about its original occasion and the responses it provokes. Second, storytelling thrives in cultures where death is a
distinctly felt presence, and its modern decline is linked to death's
increasing sequestration from everyday experience. This is because
death makes possible the emergence of the story from the flux of
individual experience; the meaning of a human life, and the wisdom
or counsel that attends upon it, only become identifiable and trans-
missible at the moment of death or through the felt implication of
that end. Thus "Death is the sanction of everything the storyteller
can tell. He has borrowed his authority from death" (94). Finally, in
contrast to the prudential economy of middle-class life, the storyteller
gives away his experiential capital, suggesting in his openhanded relation to the receptive listener an alternative to the marketplace's customary forms of exchange: "he is the man who could let the wick of
his life be consumed completely by the gentle flame of his story"
(108–09).

I have perhaps quoted enough of Benjamin's essay for the reader to hear the elegiac note that gives "The Storyteller" its power and beauty. But for all the palpable nostalgia of this evocation of the culture of pre-industrial work, it is important to see, as Peter Brooks has argued, that Benjamin is not simply lamenting a lost art but "waging a combat—whether in the advance guard or the rear guard it is hard to say—against the situation of any text in the modern world."[5] He is advocating not a return to the land, the shop, or the story circle but the recovery and reanimation, through the inevitably literary simulation of the oral, of some of the possibilities and values that storytelling generates: a kind of wisdom more capacious than explanation; an opening up of the customary categories of moral judgment; the animation of an ethic of communal exchange—"narrative as gift," in Brooks's words—as an alternative to the silence and solitude of private consumption. Modern evocations of the oral tale, Brooks argues, do not exactly stand "in opposition to the novel" but challenge "the novel to reclaim something that it has lost from its heritage: the situation of live communication, the presence of voice."[6]

I will be arguing that Cather aims to achieve in *My Ántonia*, through her simulation of oral storytelling and the attack on novelistic values she simultaneously conducts, the kind of literary and cultural renovation Benjamin has in mind.[7] My point is not that Cather's

---

5. Peter Brooks, "The Storyteller," *Yale Journal of Criticism* 1 (1987): 27. Consider also Fredric Jameson's remark on the nature of Benjamin's nostalgia: "there is no reason why a nostalgia conscious of itself, a lucid and remorseless dissatisfaction with the present on the grounds of some remembered plenitude, cannot furnish as adequate a revolutionary stimulus as any other" (*Marxism and Form* [Princeton: Princeton UP, 1971], 82).

6. Brooks, 27, 37. Brooks's explication and application of "The Storyteller" has been extremely helpful to me in understanding the force of Benjamin's argument. Here is more of his summation of the purpose of the essay: Benjamin's endorsement of the story is an attempt to "restore, or to create . . . a certain attitude of reading that would more closely resemble listening, that would elicit the suspension of meditation rather than the suspense of consumption, and that would foreground the exchange, the transaction, even the transference—in the fully psychoanalytic sense—that can take place in the offer and reception of narrative" (28).

7. While the attack on the classic nineteenth-century realist novel that Cather will mount in her later theoretical and critical commentary is conducted on behalf of a different agenda—as an argument about what constitutes authentically "imaginative" art—its central elements are strikingly in accord with Benjamin's. Her disdain for the multiplication of detail characteristic of a photographic or journalistic model of realism parallels Benjamin's distrust of "information" (see *Willa Cather on Writing* [New York: Knopf, 1968], 11, 39, 70, 101); her preference for a strategy of compression, condensation, and simplification parallels his account of the "chaste compactness" of the oral story (see 39, 40, 102); both writers share a distaste for the infection of fiction by the logic of the commodity (see 41, 86, 103) and an appreciation of writing that captures the animation of voice (see 56–57). Note especially the way Cather's definition of the authentically "created" in "The Novel Demeuble" resembles Benjamin's claim that the impact of a story depends upon the achievement of a kind of presence that eludes mere explanation: "Whatever is felt upon the page without being specifically named there—that, one might say, is created. It is the inexplicable presence of the thing not named, of the overtone divined by the ear but not heard by it, the verbal mood, the emotional aura of the fact or the thing or the deed, that gives high quality to the novel or the drama, as well as to poetry itself" (41–42; see also 5–6, 15).

book is interesting insofar as it resembles Benjamin's admirable essay,
but that the affinities between the works encourage us to identify
with new clarity *My Ántonia*'s interests and purposes, to see that the
beauty it achieves and the pleasures it generates at once pay tribute
to a vanishing, heroic way of life and yield an engaged and pointed
cultural analysis. While the strength of my claim that Cather covertly
conducts the kind of argument with the novel that Benjamin articulates in "The Storyteller" will finally depend upon the reading I am
about to offer (and while one of this century's great leftist intellec-
tuals may seem like a strange companion for a writer who in all like-
lihood voted for Wendell Willkie), we have not sufficiently recognized
Cather as a cultural critic or historian. Her experience, bracketing
the era of settlement in Nebraska and the full-blown commodity culture of literary New York, prepared her to see with unusual clarity
the recent shape of American cultural history. Indeed, her 1923 essay
on Nebraska in *The Nation*, with its criticism of the "Americanization" of the richly cosmopolitan culture that immigration produced
in the rural Middle West and its worries about the effects of a gen-
erational shift from makers to buyers suggests that for Cather, as
for Benjamin, "progress" toward a triumphant, homogenous middle-
class culture amounts to a kind of regression, a narrowing of experience against which *My Ántonia* registers an eloquent protest.[8] As
with Benjamin, this may be nostalgia, but it is nostalgia complexly
conceived and rigorously deployed, directing its celebration of the
past toward the refreshment of a worn-out present.

The Story as a Way of Meaning

The inset stories that proliferate in *My Ántonia*'s extraordinary opening book and, as Benjamin would have predicted, provide its most
intensely remembered moments are not ornaments incidental to the
country setting or neutral instances of local color. Rather, Book One
of *My Ántonia* functions as Cather's "The Storyteller": it establishes
the story and its attendant culture as the book's model of meaning
and matrix of ethical value. Moreover, the specific qualities of these
tales—the compression and directness of their language; their freedom from interpretive commentary or psychological analysis; their
emphasis on the specific context and effects of their telling; their consistent connection with work and death—suggest that Cather's
understanding of storytelling is strikingly in accord with Benjamin's.
In order to describe the way stories work within the text—to
delineate, that is, Cather's implicit theory of the story—I will look

---

8. "Nebraska: The End of the First Cycle," *Nation*, 5 September 1923, 236–38. The inference about Cather's vote is drawn by James Woodress, *Willa Cather: A Literary Life* (Lincoln: U of Nebraska P, 1987), 491.

both at the book's first sequence of tellings and at a particularly interesting story Ántonia tells later on.

As if in confirmation of Benjamin's notion of the relation between
death and telling, storytelling proper within *My Ántonia* begins when
a walk through an autumnal landscape coincides with Ántonia's mastery of her new language. The story of Old Hata can hardly be said
to have a plot at all. The singing of a dying insect reminds Ántonia
of an old beggar woman in her home village who would sing for people who gave her a place at their fire; she tells this to Jim, mentions
that the children saved their cakes and sweets for Hata, and makes
the insect a nest under her scarf.[9] What does this "beginner's" tale
offer its hearer? No codified meaning or message, no ending in the
customary sense. The force of this tiny story lies rather in its orbit
of suggestion: in its hints of the presence of death and the community of meaning created by our vulnerability to it; in its record of
the way that mutual vulnerability can engender acts of generosity;
in its correlation of the condition of loss and the occasion of song.
For Jim, the listener, the story yields a gain in responsiveness. As he
and Ántonia encounter her father on their way home, the tale, by
providing a human context for the emblems of death he has encountered in the fields, makes Mr. Shimerda's sadness articulate: "The old
man's smile, as he listened, was so full of sadness, of pity for things,
that I never afterward forgot it" [29]. Ántonia's act of memory—the
act that Benjamin places at the center of storytelling—has engen-
dered in Jim an answering act of sympathy and remembrance. For
the reader, the story of Old Hata is our introduction to a crucial and
recurring experience in reading *My Ántonia*: an encounter with a
meaning that we feel as present precisely because it defies contain-
ment by our customary strategies of explanation—the effect that
Benjamin will call "amplitude."

My Ántonia's most famous freestanding story follows closely upon
Ántonia's tale of Old Hata. On his deathbed, the delirious Pavel
reveals the act that drove him and Peter out of Russia. Returning
from a neighboring village late at night, a wedding party is attacked
by an immense pack of wolves; Pavel and Peter, in the lead sledge,
are driving the bride and groom. One by one, the wolves pick off
the other sledges. Near their village, as the horses tire, Pavel throws
the bride and groom to the onrushing wolves. While this tale is spec-
tacularly furnished with incident, it shares with its simpler predecessor elements that begin to compose for the reader of *My Ántonia*
an implicit anatomy of the story. First, we might notice how con-
cretely the tale is embedded in the specific circumstances of its telling. Pavel's story is provoked by the wind that makes Jim imagine

9. *My Ántonia*, 1918, 26.

the outdoors as a kind of deathscape and by the answering howling of the coyotes; we witness the delirium and rage of the teller; we note the distinct effects of tuberculosis on Pavel's ravaged body. For Cather as for Benjamin, the felt presence of death gives birth to stories; for her as for him a writer seeking to reanimate the oral tale must place the reader "in the company" of the teller. The story proper—its autonomy emphasized by its demarcation from the surrounding text, shorter by a page or two than Cather's rendering of its immediate context—has the "chaste compactness" that precludes explanation but invites thought. When one meditates upon the theme or meaning of this tale, there are many things to say—that the attack of the wolves brings out the residual wolfishness in men; that living communities are constituted by their paradoxical insistence that there are some things for which one must die in order to remain human—but no one of them seems interpretively conclusive or authoritative, none the key to the tale's relation to the work as a whole. The story delivers, rather, almost as a kind of atmosphere, the sense that one is in the presence of richly significant acts. One interprets such a story not by eliminating possible readings but by adding them, building by accretion a sense of the complexity of actions and the plenitude of meaning that might indeed come to constitute "wisdom" or "counsel." Cather's emphasis is correspondingly on Jim and Ántonia's reception of the tale, on the way the story for them is "never at an end": on its incalculable effect, the "painful and peculiar pleasure" it produces; on the tiny community the two children create as they tell and retell the story; on the tale's power, as Benjamin puts it, to "sink" itself into the listener's consciousness, as, drifting toward sleep, Jim finds himself "in a sledge drawn by three horses, dashing through a country that looked something like Nebraska and something like Virginia" [37].[1]

In between the story of Old Hata and the tale of Pavel and Peter, Cather provides, as if for the benefit of a reader who is beginning to think about the nature of storytelling, instruction in the way differently shaped narratives make possible different kinds of meanings. We witness, in Jim's killing of an oversized rattlesnake and Ántonia's public celebration of his triumph, the emergence of one of our most time-honored narratives, an allegory—complete with echoes of quest romance, allusions to primal evil, implications of sexual danger and Oedipal disgust, and an appreciative female witness—of masculine initiation: "I had killed a big snake—I was now a big fellow"

1. For a lucid argument against overly explanatory readings of this tale, such as that most famously provided by Gelfant, see Michael Peterman's "Kindling the Imagination: The Inset Stories of *My Ántonia*," in Rosowski, *Approaches*, 156–62. Judith Fryer argues for the "oral" style of its telling (*Felicitous Space*, 281–83). George Dekker offers a thoughtful, untendentious brief commentary on this tale in *The American Historical Romance* (Cambridge: Cambridge UP, 1987), 258, as does Phyllis Rose ("Modernism," 133–34).

[32]. But Cather has Jim produce the materials we need to cut the story down to size: the rattlesnake was old and lazy, the spade Jim carried was an adequate weapon, he was still pretty lucky. The real interest of the episode is generated by the gap between Jim's deflationary private version of this adventure and Ántonia's stock heroic allegory, which makes visible the rigid, derivative quality of such allegories of maturity, their inadequacy when measured against the accidental and ironic quality of the actual experience of masculinity such quest stories nevertheless condition and shape. We are invited to a skeptical view of such tendentious narratives, with their fondness for didactic patterns and predetermined endings. And the contrast between the way this overly familiar maturity narrative channels and inhibits meaning and the way the surrounding stories liberate it teaches us the cognitive, and critical, value of the story's characteristic reticence.[2]

Ántonia's oddly beautiful story of the tramp's leap into the threshing machine seems to me similarly instructive, summing up, both in the way it creates meaning and in the kind of meaning it creates, the nature and possibilities of storytelling within *My Ántonia*. Cather's notation of the quality of Ántonia's voice—"deep, a little husky, and one always heard the breath vibrating beneath it" [92]—insists, as does Benjamin, on the embodied quality of the storyteller's art, and her specific evocation of the circumstances of the telling—the listeners gather around the range in the Harlings' kitchen helping Ántonia make taffy—puts us in their company. Most striking to me is the "gestural" quality of meaning in this story. The tramp's sudden, jaunty leap into the machine—he waves to Ántonia on the way in—possesses, with a vengeance, the "chaste compactness" to which Benjamin attributes the story's power. Benjamin writes that the disappearance of oral storytelling lets us see "a new beauty in what is vanishing" (87); Cather's tramp, we might say, creates a kind of grisly beauty *by* vanishing. The curious artifacts he leaves behind—a penknife, a wishbone, some poetry ("The Old Oaken Bucket," cut out of a newspaper)—are plausibly emblematic (of desire, the yearning toward expression) but not conclusively explicable; they thus represent, one might suggest, the distinctively untrammeled kind of meaning that stories like this one generate. It is characteristic, too, of

2. Gelfant notes the episode's similarity to initiation myth, 69–70. Perhaps there is also, in the hyperbolic invitation to "psychological analysis" the writhing snake proffers to the educated eye, an anticipatory joke at the expense of the kind of sympotomatic, key-to-all-mythologies reading that our enthusiasm for explanation urges us to supply. My point is not that there isn't sexual disgust in Jim's response—like the other elements of the episode it needs to be included in one's accruing understanding—but that in this context its existence fails to confer any unusual explanatory privilege. I think the famous "reaping hook" dream, which is similarly revealing *and* inconclusive, works in an analogous way. Both episodes invite the explanatory urge in order *not* to reward it.

Cather's emphasis on the story as a way of knowing that its telling yields a scene of instruction. When sensitive Nina Harling cries because the tramp dies, her usually indulgent mother reproaches her sternly, threatening to send her upstairs whenever Ántonia tells stories from the country. Mrs. Harling's point, it seems to me, is that Nina has made a crucial mistake—the kind a mother, in this book, had better correct—and confused the outcome of the story with its meaning. She is thus in danger of missing the "counsel"—which inheres in one's encounter with the unsettling, strangely pleasurable quality of the story—Ántonia's telling provides.

My point has been that, like Benjamin's essay, the acts of storytelling so prominent in Book One of My Ántonia at once delineate a distinctive narrative practice and teach a particular stance toward experience: a way of expressing and seeking meaning that is embodied in people, located in places, and mindful of death; that trusts suggestion more than explanation, "chaste compactness" more than teleological structure, responsiveness more than "interpretation." Other signs of the culture of oral storytelling—Benjaminan affinities, as it were—are everywhere in Book One. The novel proper begins with hearing and speaking: "I first heard of Ántonia" is accompanied by a footnote that tells us how to pronounce her name, as though this book will contain things that we ourselves will need to tell. We are frequently alerted to the specific quality of voices—Jim's grandfather's pronunciation of "Selah" from the psalms, the force his customary silence gives his prayers (9, 14). The book is rich in what might be called the material culture of storytelling, like the Christmas tree that resembles the "talking tree of the fairy tale," with "legends and stories nestled like birds in its branches." There are further signs that Cather's understanding of how stories are generated anticipates Benjamin's. As in the inset tales themselves, death and expressiveness are linked: Mr. Shimerda's suicide provokes a flurry of talk and stories that is a relief to Jim, despite the sadness of the occasion, from the habitual taciturnity of his grandfather's house [61]. Cather's stories are consistently tied to agricultural or artisanal work, as when Otto tells Jim story after story as he makes Mr. Shimerda's coffin. Stories become correspondingly rare when the action shifts to town in Book Two and must, like Ántonia's tale of the tramp or the story of Ole Benson and Crazy Mary, be imported from the country into Black Hawk's inhibitory middle-class terrain.

From the very start, My Ántonia is full of storyteller figures, recognizable both by their acts of telling and by their association with the values Cather establishes in the inset tales. As though in confirmation of Benjamin's notion that the storyteller at once marks and is marked by his work, a number of Cather's tellers are notably "inscribed." The train conductor who is Jim's first guide to the West (and who first directs his attention to Ántonia) has the storyteller's characteristic generosity, exchanging his wisdom for their "confidence." The traveler is, along with the farmer and the artisan, one of Benjamin's prototypical storytellers, and Cather's trainman sports the signs of his extensive initiation: "He wore the rings and pins and badges of different fraternal orders to which he belonged. Even his cuff buttons were engraved with hieroglyphics, and he was more inscribed than an Egyptian obelisk" [9]. Otto Fuchs, Book One's most prolific storyteller, wears his inscriptions on his face, in the form of a scar and an incomplete left ear; his first act is to tell Jim the stories behind these scars, and to introduce him to some of the almost voluble artifacts—notably a pair of exotically stitched boots—of his cowboy days. The itinerant Fuchs's work history—he has been a cowboy, a stage-driver, a bartender, a miner, a farm hand, and is a skilled cabinet maker—is a compendium of story-generating trades. It is striking that there is no place for him when the family moves into town, and Cather explicitly associates him not only with preindustrial work but with the absence of the qualities of character required to negotiate successfully a modern marketplace culture. Jim's grandmother observes that Otto has done hard work everywhere, but has "nothing to show for it" [40]. Jim remembers the faces of Otto and Jake, his fellow laborer, as, for all their roughness, "unprotected" and "defenceless"; they lack a "practiced manner behind which they could retreat and hold people at a distance" [48]. Like Benjamin's storyteller, the two men operate on their own system of exchange; they had "given us," Jim says later, "things that cannot be bought in any market in the world" [77].

While novels are customarily full of very few wise or educable characters and many vain, foolish, grasping, or evil ones, the story-centered world of *My Ántonia* is rich in figures of wisdom and responsiveness. Some of them tell stories, like Otto or Anton Jelinek. Others are notable for their respect for stories, like Frances Harling, who is a kind of itinerant storyteller in reverse, getting to know the immigrant families in the surrounding countryside by collecting their stories. Still others have absorbed or express the values associated with the kind of responsiveness that stories, according to Benjamin, induce. Jim's grandfather is, in his capacity to entertain the assumptions and respect the beliefs of his immigrant neighbors, an exemplar of the cultural tolerance and openness of interest at the center of *My Ántonia*'s ethics; he becomes a mediator of disputes and, in his prayer at Mr. Shimerda's grave, a forger of communal sympathy. In contrast to the novel's emphasis on the shaping or warping of character—on the manufacture of selfhood—characters like Ántonia and Mrs. Harling are already present, like a story, their very way of being a kind of "counsel" for others: "They knew what they liked,"

Jim tells us, "and were not always trying to imitate other people. . . . Deep down in each of them there was a kind of hearty joviality, a relish of life, not over-delicate, but very invigorating. I never tried to define it, but I was distinctly conscious of it" [94].

We need, then, to see the fictive world of *My Ántonia* as suffused by the story. For Cather, the making of meaning is, at center, the making of a tale. We begin to measure even conventionally narrated events, like Mr. Shimerda's suicide, by their capacity to be converted into stories. The landscape, like the teller or hearer of tales, is imagined as susceptible to inscription by human experience, like the circular track left by Indian riders, an "old figure" that becomes legible and "stirring" in the oblique light of sunset or with the dusting of a light snowfall [37]. All of the book's moments of heightened significance—the brief transfigurations of the landscape that accompany moments of intensest human connection, the emergence of the hieroglyphic plow, Blind d'Arnault's piano playing—have an affinity with the qualities Cather attributes to the story: freestanding, compressed, resistant to explanation, short in duration but inscribed upon the memory. And, as we will see, the more "novelistic" narrative of Jim's growing up unfolds in distinct relation to the story-centered ways people fix, hold, find, and lose meaning in the Nebraska landscape.

My Ántonia *as Counter-Novel*

To say that *My Ántonia*'s authoritative model for the achievement of meaning is the story is not to say that this novel has no sustained plot. Its action, however, takes an ironic or "dialogic" shape that might be called a "counter-novel." In a reversal of the logic of the bildungsroman, its ostensible novelistic type, *My Ántonia* records Jim's endangerment by and eventual rescue from maturity. This counter-novel begins to take shape even as the oral story is being established as a cultural and personal resource. Book One thus records, as its novelistic "action," Jim's education in the values of the story, as though the story had seized and shaped to its own purposes the developmental matter that has traditionally given the novel one of its supreme subjects. Cather imagines the formation of Jim's identity not, as the novel of maturation customarily renders it, as a quest for whatever version of adulthood the writer is sponsoring but as a process much less rigidly teleological and more story-like: an accruing alertness, not to be demarcated into stages or defined by crises, to the inscriptions experience leaves upon people and their landscape; an enhanced responsiveness that will eventually yield its own acts of telling.

Jim's earliest encounters with the Nebraska landscape compose a narrative of the shaping of a distinct selfhood. He first perceives the prairie as a kind of blankness, "not a country at all, but the material out of which countries are made," and feels "erased, blotted out," as though he had himself returned to infancy's uninscribed condition of consciousness [12]. He feels that his grandparents' farm is located at the very edge of the substantial world, that it would be easy to float off the edge, and he finds his first feelings of happiness and comfort in a feeling that precedes the formation of an individual identity: "I was something that lay under the sun and felt it, like the pumpkins, and I did not want to be anything more. I was entirely happy" [17]. In a moment that suggests the acquisition of language, Jim and Ántonia snuggle in a nest in the prairie grass as Jim teaches her to name the things she points to. The responsiveness—the deepening and expansion of the self—that comes with Jim's initiation into the culture of the story is the primary measure of his growth, but his education by the story bears other fruit as well. As he takes in—and comes to seek out—stories, the landscape that had seemed empty and unformed becomes legible, a kind of meaning-scape: he asks why the roads are bordered with sunflowers; understands why prairie-dwelling people, hungry for detail, visit trees "as if they were people" [165]; becomes alert to the almost invisible traces, such as the track left by the Indian riders, the living of earlier inhabitants had left upon the ground.[3]

Jim's education in the values of the story is not entirely without conflict. Jim's worst moments—his suspicion of the Bohemians' gift-giving, his liability to xenophobic resentments, his loyalty to conventional notions about gender—are all conditioned by his temporary acceptance, even at so young an age, of the powerful narratives—about thrift, propriety, self-discipline, the danger of otherness—that oppose the story in his community. But in the story-dominated world of Book One, and with the guidance of its figures of wisdom, the influence of these purposeful, anxious allegories is easily overcome. The developmental action of Book One, obliquely rendered though it is, culminates in what is, in effect, Jim's making of a story. Cather's depiction of Mr. Shimerda's suicide shows us how a story comes into being, as she assembles the elements that make an event into a tale: the meaning-generating authority of death, made present by the most specific rendering of its physicality—the "hair and stuff" stuck to the straw in the barn [55], the work of cutting the body loose from the pool of blood in which it is frozen [62]; the plenitude of talk generated as people respond to Mr. Shimerda's act; the uncemeteried grave that, by forcing a curve in the surveyed lines of the roadway,

---

3. For a thoughtful, alternative account of the role the inset stories play in the shaping of Jim's identity, see Michael Peterman, 157–62. Hermione Lee also discusses the relation between the narrative elements of Book One and the development of identity in *Willa Cather: Double Lives* (New York: Pantheon, 1989), 140–44.

provides the mark upon the landscape that will provoke memory and yield this story's future tellings. Within this episode, Cather distinctly emphasizes Jim's performance of the work of response that is the inception of all stories—his preparation, as it were, for producing the narrative we are engaged in reading. As Jim "thinks and thinks" about Mr. Shimerda as he sits alone in the warm kitchen, he begins to feel that the old man is there with him, resting before his return to Bohemia. He "goes over" all that Ántonia has told him about her father and, in a moment that testifies to the communicability of experience, finds himself sharing the dead man's consciousness: "Such vivid pictures came to me that they might have been Mr. Shimerda's memories, not yet faded out from the air in which they had haunted him" [57]. This moment of connection in turn enlarges Jim's understanding of the suicide: he sees that it was "homesickness" that killed Mr. Shimerda and that he would not have died if he had lived with the Burdens; he dismisses the punitive view of suicide sponsored by religious authority. We witness Jim coming into possession of the meaning of this event—absorbing its "counsel"—and thus coming of age in the storytelling sense of that phrase.

Jim arrives in Black Hawk, then, in possession of a selfhood shaped by story; with that arrival, Cather's version of the battle between the story and the novel begins in earnest. Despite Black Hawk's relative newness as a town, middle-class culture is in full flower there. For Jim, the move to town means a change in the meaning-scape he inhabits. The town, as an ideological structure, has the effect of making Jim's central experiences marginal. The nearby river becomes an occasional "compensation" for the lost freedom of the countryside, while Ántonia and the other immigrant daughters are redefined as "hired girls." Most significantly, the oral story is displaced by a very different set of narratives: the purposeful, prudential stories—never told but already written into the mind—that together construct the overarching, normative narrative of maturity that constitutes middle-class culture in Black Hawk.

To live in town, Jim will discover, is to confront the influence of these authoritative fictions. In every respect, Cather presents the culture of Black Hawk as built upon an opposition to the values Book One has taught us to identify with storytelling. The town is habitually a place of silence and stasis, where men without "personal habits" perform fatherhood's prescribed routines [83] and married people sit "like images on their front porches" while their teenage children perform in silence courtship's tedious promenade [101]. The coming of the dance pavilion reveals the way middle-class refinement is produced by the erasure of the body: Jim notices when dancing with girls of his own "set" that "their bodies never moved inside their clothes; their muscles seemed to ask but one thing—not to be disturbed," and they seem "cut off below the shoulders, like cherubs" [102]. The emphatic sexuality and physical grace of the immigrant girls, showcased by the dances, promises for a time to enliven Black Hawk's social order by making the sons of proper families lose their heads. But, when Sylvester Lovett cures his obsession with Lena Lingard by marrying a propertied older widow—a good piece of land, as it were—such brittle moves toward rebellion are exposed only as predictable fluctuations within a definitive narrative of postponed gratification: "The respect for respectability was stronger than any desire in Black Hawk youth" [104].

Jim's education by story permits him to describe the life of Black Hawk with striking acuity, even as he struggles with its authority. His summation of life within its houses suggests that Black Hawk, like the world of the story, has a distinct economy of meaning:

> The life that went on in them seemed to me made up of evasions and negations; shifts to save cooking, to save washing and cleaning, devices to propitiate the tongue of gossip. This guarded mode of existence was like living under a tyranny. People's speech, their voices, their very glances, became furtive and repressed. Every individual taste, every natural appetite, was bridled by caution. The people asleep in those houses, I thought, tried to live like mice in their own kitchens; to make no noise, to leave no trace, to slip over the surface of things in the dark. The growing piles of ashes and cinders in the back yards were the only evidence that the wasteful, consuming process of life went on at all. [111]

Town culture, then, is the inverse of the culture of the story: silence erases voice, restraint inhibits bodily expression, thrift undoes exchange. Where the story offers us connection, the town lives by boundaries and oppositions; the speculative openness and encompassing wisdom of the story is reduced to anxiety and prudence. And all this self-scrutiny, discipline, and denial is distinctly teleological but curiously empty, exercised on behalf of a purpose that is powerfully immanent but never defined—except by the manifest joylessness of adult life.

I think, then, that it makes sense to claim that Cather renders the contrast between Jim's life in the country and his life in town as a contest between their characteristic narrative forms. The developmental action of Book Two unfolds as a struggle, between story and novel, to possess Jim Burden, as he learns, for all the rebelliousness and reluctance his grounding in story produces, to do the proper thing. In Black Hawk people do not make or tell stories but sustain the joyless masterplots—the prudential marriage, the solid career, the quiescent family life—middle-class culture provides. There are, moreover, a number of reasons to see the narratives that govern town life as distinctly novelistic. Life in Black Hawk, like life in the novel, is above all about producing the proper ending, the authorized version of maturity, the correctly formed character. While Benjamin worries about the novel's tendency to enhance the enclosure of the private self, Cather is, I am suggesting, especially concerned about the way the novel assists in the production of its community's orthodox maturity narrative; for both writers the reclamation of middle-class culture begins with resistance to the novelistic.[4]

Cather's hostility to the novel is most interestingly figured forth in the narrative of Wick Cutter and his wife. The Cutters together comprise a kind of compendium of values, conflicts, and behaviors associated both with the development of middle-class culture and the history of the novel. Cutter himself seems to constitute a kind of symptom of middle-class culture's characteristic fluctuations and contradictions. Cutter's name and work history suggest, after Max Weber, a brief history of the rise of the middle class: "Wick" is short for "Wycliffe"; Black Hawk's most vicious and successful money-lender comes from pious parents. Cutter is also given to paying tribute to old country values and quoting from Poor Richard's Almanack. Taken together, his various characteristics begin to reek of the novelistic. Like certain novels, he quotes "moral maxims" for boys but turns girls into prostitutes; what Jim calls his combination of "old maidishness and licentiousness" seems to me to suggest the way novels tend to purvey morality and sexual scandal together. The Cutters' home is protected by a hedge designed to protect their "privacy," but this barrier only enhances the interest of the other townsfolk in their domestic disputes; one might think here of Ian Watt's classic account of the creation of "private experience" as the novel's ascendant subject.[5] Their domestic conflicts center on two of the novel's customary preoccupations, adultery and inheritance.

Above all, as his elaborate, *Clarissa*-like attempt to arrange the rape of Ántonia reveals, Cutter is a plotter, working, in the manner of Benjamin's version of the novelist, to create the greatest possible suspense in the implied reader of his various episodes, his wife. His ingenious use of train schedules—he tricks his wife into boarding the train to Kansas City and hops the next one back to Black Hawk—recalls not only the novelist's ending-driven management of time but

4. On the alliance between the novel and the construction of maturity in nineteenth-century America, see Richard Brodhead's seminal essay, "Sparing the Rod: Discipline and Fiction in Antebellum America," *Representations* 21 (1988): 67–96. Cather's representation of middle-class life in Black Hawk anticipates other influential accounts of the shaping of middle-class culture, notably Burton Bledstein's *The Culture of Professionalism* (New York: Norton, 1976) and Richard Sennett's analysis of the ideal of privacy in *The Fall of Public Man* (New York: reprint, Vintage, 1978), especially chap. 8.
5. See *The Rise of the Novel* (Berkeley and Los Angeles: U of California P, 1959), chap. 6.

the importance of being in or under trains in standard novelistic fiction. The whole marriage is structured like Benjamin's version of the novel: it consists of the sustained evasion, by means of a mutual absorption in plot, of an underlying sense of meaninglessness. This goal-driven narrative completely absorbs the Cutters until it issues in an ingenious, spectacular, but utterly empty ending: Cutter shoots his wife and commits suicide so as to ensure, by surviving her, that her people will not inherit his money. When Jim, taking Ántonia's place in bed, becomes the near-recipient of Cutter's advances, he is, in effect, entrapped within the novel Cutter is constructing, a victim both of sexual predatoriness and the "ending-hunger" the novel evokes and satisfies. While Cutter is hardly Black Hawk's representative middle-class male, there is a stereotypical, orthodox quality to his deviance: he is a creation, and one of the costs, of the conventional notion of maturity—rigidly focused on the management of sexuality—Black Hawk sponsors and enforces. Jim's devastating and grotesque battering, in addition to providing an instructive glimpse of what it is like to be a "hired girl," raises some doubts about the advisability of participating in any scheme of maturation that issues in "adult" sexuality, at least as it is manifest in Black Hawk.

As befits a text composed of a contest between two kinds of narrative, Book Two of *My Ántonia* has two endings. Immediately preceding this twisted, novelistic initiation narrative is a return to the culture of the story, Jim's picnic by the river with Ántonia, Lena Lingard, and two other immigrant girls. In a number of crucial ways this episode counters the Cutter narrative. The picnic begins by breaking an established sexual pattern: in a reversal of the usual vector of voyeurism, the four girls pause on the bridge to regard the naked Jim, swimming in the river below. They maneuver to obtain a better view, and tell him how pretty he looks. There is plenty of eroticism in the episode—in Lena's flushed, excited face; in the sensuality of the descriptions of the setting; in the game of Pussy Wants a Corner they play—but it is relaxed, untendentiousness, widely distributed, in striking contrast to the fixed, fetishistic quality of Cutter's sexual questing. (Think, for instance, of his enraged destruction of Jim and Ántonia's clothing). In contrast to the obsessed purposefulness of Cutter's plotting, the picnic's purpose—to pick elder blossoms for wine—becomes simply the occasion for the release of stories. These tales—about family history, the hardships of agricultural life—display the reflective, generous-minded quality that stories embody and teach. The episode ends with a moment out of a story-centered vocabulary of meaning: the remarkable appearance of the hieroglyph of the plow, "picture writing on the sun"—an inscription upon the landscape—which confirms the significance of *this* moment, and the value of "presence," however fleeting, as against

a notion of meaning inhibited and entrapped by purpose or permanence. The making and appreciation of this moment represents, I
am arguing, a kind of counter-maturity to that sponsored by the novel
and the town—maturity as it might be experienced under the guidance of the story.

The contest between story and novel that unfolds in Book Two produces, then, a kind of stalemate. Jim ostensibly chooses the life track
middle-class culture recommends—he accedes to his grandmother's
wish that he give up the "improper," mixed-class dances; he heads
for the University, then Harvard, then law school, then the successful career; he even produces the joyless marriage we hear about in
the "Introduction"—but, as the picnic episode predicts, he never fully
inhabits his orthodox adulthood, keeping alive all along his commitment to the story and its values. The notion of the counter-novel I
have been advancing will, as I suggest below, guide us through the
interpretive controversies that the novel's last two books have generated. But it also helps us see—or glimpse, for here my treatment
will be cursory—the narrative logic of Book Three of *My Ántonia*.
Like the other segments of the narrative, this book links a stage of
Jim's development—the transition from adolescence to adulthood—to
the institutions and expressive forms his culture designates to guide
him through it. With its emphasis on literary education, on ambition, on courtship, on theater—on the inevitable mediation or
sublimation of desire—this section of the book at once continues
Cather's analysis of the production of identity and records Jim's near
loss of the world of story through the sacrifices he makes to a prudential notion of maturity.[6] Still, even as Jim makes the decisions
designed to carry out the life pattern he has begun, there are some
striking signs that the victory of the novelistic is incomplete, its power
encouragingly partial. Again and again the achievements and artifacts of sublimation are permeated, punctured, compromised, or
surprised by traces of more substantial or primary forms of emotion, and the book's tone often veers toward the comic or parodic.
Jim's memories of Otto and Jake and his experiences on the farm
keep finding their way into his shrine-like study, pressing Virgil's
pastoral back toward its origins in actuality even as these childhood
figures are touched with the simplifying aura of art [129]; Jim
clings—as an "inestimably precious" sign, it seems, of the continuity of the self—to what is, in effect, his discovery of sublimation,
his realization that, without girls like Lena and the Bohemian
Marys there would be no poetry like Virgil's [133]. Even Gaston
Cleric, the priest of scholarship and guardian of Jim's ambitions,
betrays signs of a primary, incompletely mastered allegiance to the

6. I am indebted here to Gelfant's discussion of Jim and Lena's courtship as "sublimated" (67).

values of the story, as he spends his "poetic gift" in spontaneous "bursts of imaginative talk," "squander[ing] too much in the heat of personal communication" [128]. What is being celebrated in this tribute to classical poetry, then, is not its "high art" status—its opposition to the "lower" values of quotidian culture—but its mixedness, its sustenance by and of the impulses stories differently embody. When Jim and Lena go to the theater, too, the experience does not produce the detached pleasures of appreciation but, as the extended account of attending *Camille* reveals, utter and absorbing identification. Most delightfully, Lena's completely sensible and sincere disclaimer of any interest whatsoever in marriage at once explodes the link between maleness and ambition and deflates the scenario of noble self-sacrifice that Jim thinks he is performing when he comes to tell her that he will move to Harvard with Cleric. Story, we realize, has not been killed off by the teleological operations of the middle books of *My Ántonia*; it is only napping.

The Victory of Storytelling

The distinction between story-like and novelistic ways of meaning that Cather teaches prepares us to read the two books that bring *My Ántonia* to a close. Seen from the point of view of story, Jim's narrative yields not a flight from "real" adulthood, nor a lapse into a vicarious and pathetic nostalgia, nor a transcendent leap into the abstract but a deliberate act of self rescue. The counter-novel I have been describing comes to fruition when it steals the book's most novelistic moments—Ántonia's "fall" and Jim's determination of how he will live his life, the twin "climaxes" of its intertwined story lines— and definitively renders them from the perspective of the storyteller. This is to say that two antinovelistic actions unfold simultaneously as *My Ántonia* comes to a close: as Jim, through his return to the story, breaks the hold of his own orthodoxy, the reader is equipped to break the hold of the cultural assumptions the novel reinforces and the habits of interpretation it teaches.

The narrative material of Book Four—Ántonia goes off to marry the sleazy Larry Donovan and returns to Black Hawk "ruined" and pregnant—is traditional novelistic fare. Its potentially novelistic quality does not, of course, depend upon whether the woman's fall is treated sympathetically or moralistically—there is presumably no practiced reader who feels inclined to condemn Ántonia—but on the disposition to see this sexual scandal as (in plot terms) central, transformative, climactic. This novelistic attitude—that some utterly significant or importantly representative action has occurred—is, in fact, Jim's first response to hearing about Ántonia. He feels "bitterly disappointed" in Ántonia for becoming an "object of pity" [145] and cannot forgive her for "throwing herself away on such a cheap sort of fellow" [145]—both reactions that assume that Ántonia's story is over, that her meaning has assumed its conclusive shape, as it would in the traditional novel of adultery. Thus, when he returns to Black Hawk for a summer vacation, he at first shows no interest in seeing Ántonia.

Happily, Book Four is otherwise engaged; it is interested not in dramatizing or exploring, *Tess*-like, the overwhelming significance of this event but in educating Jim out of his initial, novelish response to it. This is accomplished through the agency of story. His interest piqued by a picture of Ántonia's daughter prominently displayed at the local photographer's studio—which suggests that Ántonia has not adopted the traditional reading of her predicament—Jim determines to hear the actual story of her betrayal. Frances Harling sends him out to visit the Widow Steavens, who, as a "good talker" with "a remarkable memory," is markedly of the storytelling party. The Widow tells him, in the most direct way, what she has witnessed and what Ántonia has told her. The tale's only embellishment, if it can be called one, is her depiction of her own response: "Jimmy, I sat right down on that bank beside her and made lament. I cried like a young thing" [152]. The Widow's telling localizes Ántonia's story, cuts it down to size; her rendition frees it from its novelistic aura of "tragedy" and its burden of social representativeness, but makes it— I think for that very reason—feel sad in an unusually direct, personal (rather than thematic) way. With the assistance of this story, Jim, no longer inclined to write Ántonia off, decides to visit her the next day. The title of this section of the book, "The Pioneer Woman's Story," emphasizes the counter-novelistic plot; the crucial moment in this piece of the narrative is not Ántonia's deflowering but the Widow Steavens's storytelling, which saves Jim from his disposition to take the novelistic view of Ántonia's life.[7]

Just as two possible "treatments" of Ántonia's story compete for Jim's loyalty in the earlier part of Book Four, so his encounter with Ántonia is susceptible to two different kinds of reading. Seen from a novelistic perspective, invested in the production of marriages and endings, the entire encounter reduces itself to a single overwhelming question: WHY DOESN'T JIM PROPOSE?[8] If one is thinking, or

---

7. This title is often assumed to refer to Ántonia, but the Widow—not Ántonia—is a member of the first, or "pioneer," generation of local settlers.
8. For several different ways of answering this question, all of which regard it as central, see Gelfant, 71–72; Judith Fetterly, "*My Ántonia*, Jim Burden, and the Dilemma of the Lesbian Writer," in *Gender Studies: New Directions in Feminist Criticism*, ed. Judith Spector (Bowling Green: Bowling Green State U Popular P, 1986), 52–55; Deborah Lambert, "The Defeat of a Hero: Autonomy and Sexuality in *My Ántonia*," *American Literature* 53 (1982), 687. For an interesting exploration of the relation among marriage, contracts, and the novel, see Tony Tanner, *Adultery in the Novel: Contract and Transgression* (Baltimore: Johns Hopkins UP, 1979), 3–18.

writing criticism, in a novelistic way, Jim's avowal of his feelings for
Ántonia—"I'd have liked to have you for a sweetheart, or a wife, or
my mother, or my sister—anything that a woman can be to a man"
[156]—might indeed look like an evasion of adult sexuality, or maturity, or responsibility, or a giving-in to middle-class propriety: his failure, that is, to produce the *right* ending. And, with a familiar
interpretive twist, Jim's failure to achieve proper closure becomes
the central element in one's own conclusive treatment of the book's
ending. But, as before, the narrative's attention seems to be focused
elsewhere.

If one attends to this episode with the understanding of storytelling the book has been teaching, it looks not like an evasion but an
act of recovery. When we restore to our account of this encounter
its full complement of action, we see that it consists of an exchange
of stories between Jim and Ántonia and their reciprocal testimony
to the way their stories persist in mattering to one another. Thus
Jim finds himself not rehearsing Ántonia's story but, in response to
her questions, telling his, offering disclosures of his own. Signatures
of the story are scattered throughout the episode: it takes place on
Mr. Shimerda's grave plot, one of story's inscriptions on the landscape, and includes Ántonia's testimony to the way memory has kept
her father alive and "real," and deepened her understanding of him.
If we continue the speech of avowal I have already cited, it emerges
not as a proposal manqué but as a description of the way the meaning of a story becomes incorporated into the listener's consciousness:
"The idea of you is a part of my mind; you influence my likes and
dislikes, all my tastes, hundreds of times when I don't realize it. You
really are a part of me" [156]. Ántonia responds in just such story-
centered terms: she feels relief that Jim's imagined "disappointment"
in her has not damaged or erased their joint power to hold and preserve meaning—"Ain't it wonderful, Jim, how much people can mean
to each other" [156]; she mentions her eagerness to tell her little girl
the stories of their childhood; she enjoins Jim to remember her when
he thinks about those times.

The encounter ends with what our experience of storytelling helps
us recognize as a dramatization of the way a story's meaning is taken
in. Jim takes Ántonia's hands and holds them against his breast,
remembering the "kind things they had done for me"; he thus enacts
the metaphor of embodiment that both Cather and Benjamin use to
evoke the force of story. He looks for a long time at her face, "which
I meant always to carry with me . . . the closest, realest face, under
all the shadows of women's faces, at the very bottom of my memory" [157], thus marking, in the most careful way, the inscription
of this moment upon consciousness, and, with that inscription,

ensuring Ántonia's continual "presence," just as stories inscribe the mind of the teller. Ántonia, in a final exchange, confirms in turn her achievement of such inscription, telling Jim that he will be "here" with her whether he actually comes back or not. Of course it might be—indeed it has been—objected that this exchange, because it fails to produce a different form of action—something contractual, for instance, like a marriage—is not "real." But it has been my point to suggest that to produce such a reading is precisely to fall into the habit of the novelistic, to attach authenticity only to orthodox endings, to succumb to a narrowly purpose-driven notion of what is significant.[9]

Readers will now, I hope, be prepared to see the close of *My Ántonia* by the light of the story—as Cather's invention of the kind of ending a novel committed to the values of storytelling might have. Book Five has a heuristic logic; it brings together *My Antonia*'s two strains of interest, the reanimation of the culture of storytelling and Jim's development as a character, in a way that invites the reader to exercise the wisdom that the story teaches. Jim's decision to visit Ántonia after an absence of twenty years returns him simultaneously to the culture of the story and to the alternative narrative of self-construction that had been interrupted by his move to Black Hawk's novelistic environs and by his consequent production of the narrative—so dear to the novel—of conventional maturity.

Signs of the culture of storytelling and its habits of thought and feeling are everywhere in Book Five. An emblem of death's signifying presence—two of Ántonia's boys, bending over a dead dog—greets Jim as he arrives at the farm. The Cuzak farm itself is emphatically a place of story. This is true both literally, through the strong, specific interest this sequence displays in the work routines of farm life and Ántonia's exercise of domestic skills, and allusively, through the evocations of places of generativeness—the farm's enclosed, Edenic topography (160); the fruit cellar, reminiscent of the Platonic cave, that tumbles children forth into the light (163)— and through intramural echoes of earlier, story-linked moments in

9. The authenticity of this moment of exchange is confirmed on the book's own terms when it is accompanied by one of the light-suffused landscape descriptions that consistently accompany the book's other moments of heightened significance. This particular moment of landscape painting seems especially to emphasize the idea of articulation, which I have argued is central to the scene's action. Suspended between the setting sun and the rising moon, in a "singular light," "every little tree and shock of wheat, every sunflower stalk and clump of snow-on-the-mountain, drew itself up high and pointed; the very clods and furrows seemed to stand up sharply" [157]. There is an "unsettled" or incomplete element in the scene—Jim's wish to be a boy again and that his way could end there—but it is disturbing not because this is a conclusive symptom of regression but because it suggests, in its wish for a conclusive ending, that Jim does not yet understand Ántonia's confidence in the power of storytelling to make past experiences or absent people present. See the discussion of Jim's return, below.

the book itself.[1] Ántonia, like the early settlers, loves her fruit trees "as if they were people" [165]; the orchard scene is full of the light-painting that accompanies the connections stories forge; Ántonia clearly practices a storytelling version of motherhood, using a box of photographs to spark the oft-told tales her children call for; and Cuzak himself, a displaced urban artisan who tells Jim his story "as if it were my business to know it" [175] and whose "sociability was stronger than his acquisitive instinct" [176], comes from a different branch of the storytelling tree. Two of these intramural echoes seem to me distinctly to support the antinovelistic argument I have been making. First, the Wick Cutter narrative is completed in Book Five, but its novelistic matter (the elaborate ending of the inheritance plot) is contained by storytelling's more ample, clarifying perspective, as one of Ántonia's sons tells it as a story for the amusement and reflection (two values not opposed in the world of story) of those gathered at the dinner table. Second, Ántonia strikingly corrects Jim's wish—a vestige of novelistic sentimentality and teleological thinking—that she had never gone to town by insisting on the practical value of all the things she learned at the Harlings.

Jim's return to Ántonia, then, is emphatically a return to the resources of the oral story. The developmental action of Book Five—its role in Cather's counterplot—consists of Jim's decision to visit Ántonia and the two interlinked consequences of that decision. We need first to notice how difficult Jim finds his return. The twenty-year gap between visits is produced, he says, by "cowardice," his dread of finding Ántonia "aged and broken" [159], and by his attendant fear that his early memories of Ántonia will be reduced to illusions by a grim actuality. When Jim takes this risk, an important distinction is implied, one that, in my view, helps us see that Cather is doing more than paying tribute to the glories of memory. Jim's dread comes from thinking in the prudential Black Hawk way: he conceives of his memories as possessions that must be hoarded lest they be lost. Stories, as we have seen, *use* memories and losses to create a form of exchange, to make experiences communicable, to share wisdom. Jim's long-postponed decision to visit Ántonia—to risk losing or changing their past connection in order to make it present—thus constitutes a significant choice, not a nostalgic indulgence: he moves from privacy to interchange, from thrift to expenditure, from the economy of the novel to the way of the story. Hence his anti-plot observation that the moment during which he and Ántonia first glimpse one another takes "more courage than the noisy, excited passages of life" [161].

1. In each case, as befits the logic of the story, this is a distinctly nontendentious form of allusion. We get Eden without a whisper of the fall that is its telos, and no sense of loss attaches to exiting the "fruit cave."

This understanding of the stakes of Jim's return helps us register the force of the recognitions of Ántonia that constitute a crucial part of his response to their encounter. In each case, what Jim sees is the instruction Ántonia offers in the story's way of meaning. The description of Jim's first view of her presents her in distinctly story-like terms. She is marked by her experience—sun-browned, "flat-chested," a little "grizzled," missing teeth—but not, as he had feared, erased by it. As he takes her in and as he first hears her voice, she becomes, in the manner of a story as it is told, forcefully and distinctively present, thus demonstrating that in the world of the story, the more you spend the more you get: her "identity" grows "stronger," and she is "there, in the full vigour of her personality, battered but not diminished" [161]. As Jim articulates his newly achieved understanding of her, and of the economy of meaning she represents, the metaphors that have been associated throughout *My Ántonia* with the way stories make meaning come to fruition. Ántonia, like the storyteller, is an inscriber of consciousness. Jim realizes that she "had always been one to leave images in the mind that did not fade—that grew stronger with time," and he describes his memories of her as a "succession of such pictures, fixed like the old woodcuts of one's first primer" [170].[2] Ántonia's way of living, like that of Benjamin's storyteller, is a mode of representation, and the passage continues to present her as an engenderer of meanings:

> She lent herself to immemorial human attitudes which we recognize by instinct as universal and true. I had not been mistaken. She was a battered woman now, not a lovely girl; but she still had that something which fires the imagination, could still stop one's breath for a moment by a look or gesture that somehow revealed the meaning in common things. She had only to stand in the orchard, to put her hand on a little crab tree and look up at the apples, to make you feel the goodness of planting and tending and harvesting at last. All the strong things of her heart came out in her body, that had been so tireless in serving generous emotions. [170–71]

This passage's sustained evocation of the dynamics of storytelling—significance compressed into gesture, wisdom made legible upon the body, the strong response such acts of expression evoke—reveals that Jim recognizes in Ántonia an embodiment of the authority of the story and the values that belong to it. And because he is conclusively espousing the story as a form of action and a stance toward

2. Benjamin identifies the woodcut as, despite its use in printing, a premechanical medium—a medium of the hand—in "The Work of Art in the Age of Mechanical Reproduction," *Illuminations*, 219. I suspect that it is just this artisanal quality that Cather has in mind here and that this accounts for her commissioning of the Benda illustrations as well. See the account of Cather's attitude toward these drawings in Schwind, 52–53.

RICHARD H. MILLINGTON

experience, this moment of recognition and articulation constitutes the "climax"—to import a novelistic term—of *My Ántonia*'s developmental narrative.[3] As capacious as Jim's recognition of Ántonia is, his account of the life of the Cuzak farm permits the reader to see still more: that in her single-minded creation and sustenance of this story-rich way of life, Ántonia is not just the incarnation or emblem of this culture but its conscious maker.

The understanding of the story the book has by now taught us, along with Jim, in turn prepares us to engage the moment that has been most worrisome or revelatory to novelistic interpreters of the book: Jim's claim that he will henceforth take his place—psychically and emotionally, and as literally as his time permits—within Ántonia's family, as one of "Cuzak's boys." This is a point, that is, where the reader's story—our decision about how to take *My Ántonia*—comes pointedly into relation to Jim's. As with Jim's earlier avowal of his feelings for Ántonia, his decision about how to conduct his emotional life looks dangerous from the novelistic, maturity-seeking point of view. Thus critics have seen it as a transparent act of regression, a pathetic escape from adulthood, a culpable evasion of "healthy" sexuality.[4] To follow the action of Book Five from the story's perspective, though, is to see something quite different. Jim's decision emerges not as a lapse into nostalgic fantasy but as a determination to act upon the "counsel" his return to the culture of the story has provided: to live out the knowledge that the authentic sources of meaning and value in his life have not assumed—and need not assume—the configurations of orthodox maturity or followed the patterns of emotional development and moral growth it has been the nineteenth-century novel's cultural work to codify.[5]

---

3. This passage's consistent invocation of the language of storytelling makes suspicious or ironic readings of this moment, which see it as a descent into sentimentality; as a male appropriation of Ántonia, as in her reduction to an iconic earth mother or a static emblem; as an evasion of deeper sexual feelings, hard to sustain. As Sharon O'Brien has argued, Cather's presentation of Ántonia here is not a rehearsal but a revision of a stereotype: "Ántonia Shimerda, viewed by some as an archetypal Earth Mother, is a storyteller who pours her creativity into narrative as well as nurturing" (O'Brien, "'The Thing Not Named': Willa Cather as a Lesbian Writer," *Signs* 9 [1984]: 596). For an especially blunt and accusatory interpretation of these closing scenes, see Lambert, 687–90. The interpretive openness stories teach can help us avoid a puristic kind of argument here. The fact that Jim's tribute is inflected by his personality—his aesthetic categories, his agrarian sentimentality—hardly erases or "undermines" the passage's endorsement of story.
4. Blanche Gelfant's version of this argument remains the most powerful, specific, and subtle. See 76–82.
5. In its lack of interest in identifying standard adult sexuality with the achievement of happiness or the culmination of personal growth, *My Ántonia* anticipates the work of cultural critics suspicious of the narrative of sexual achievement or expression middle-class culture promotes. See Michel Foucault, *The History of Sexuality*, vol. 1, trans. Robert Hurley (New York: Vintage, 1980), and Stephen Heath, *The Sexual Fix* (New York: Schocken, 1984). Sandra M. Gilbert and Susan Gubar, in *No Man's Land: The Place of the Woman Writer in the Twentieth Century, Vol. 2: Sexchanges* (New Haven: Yale UP, 1989), chap. 5, argue that Cather's work is shaped throughout by her sense that standard adult sexuality delivered women into entrapping cultural roles.

Jim's choice, then, provides the anti-ending that Cather's counter-novel has all along been promising: the definitive, fully chosen, rigorously conceived—but, at last, quite relaxed—defeat of maturity, and with it the defeat of the novel, the literary form that is maturity's premier apologist, by the story. To share Jim's heresy, moreover, frees one from the considerable burden of mounting an ironic or symptomatic reading of this event: frees one, that is, from dismissing the massively affirmative presentation, in both imagery and tone, of Jim's return; from ignoring the confirmatory implication of the book's coda, in which Jim cures the depression caused by his return to town by walking out into the prairie and reading the inscription left upon the landscape by the old road to his grandfather's farm; from missing the delight the book takes in scandalizing the novelistic; and from failing to notice how future oriented—how full of plans and reawakened "interests"—is this ostensible regression. As Benjamin remarks, the question of what happens next, irrelevant at the end of a novel, is always alive at the end of a story.[6] And there *is* an action that follows, or follows from, Jim's choice—Jim's production, recorded in the Introduction, of the narrative we have just completed. When Jim retitles his work, appending "My" to "Ántonia," he is not appropriating or commodifying her story but emphasizing his performance of the act of personal expression that places him among the storytellers—that, in the storytelling sense, "completes" his narrative of self-construction by finding an audience (something he, unlike Ántonia, has all along lacked) for what he has come to know.[7]

Benjamin's "The Storyteller," then, gives us a richer way to understand Cather's project in *My Ántonia*, to describe the purpose that obliquely animates this attack on the rigid and joyless purposefulness she associates with the novel—and with that, a way to describe the specific form and the conceptual rigor of its elegaic modernism. Just as Jim chooses to live in a new way by reclaiming a role in the culture of the story, so Cather constructs a novel refreshed and re-animated by its dialogue with the oral story; in taking us back to the place of storytelling, she invites her readers to imagine the revision of the present. Book and character alike break free of middle-class culture's master narrative of maturity, normalcy, and health (a narrative Cather had every reason to distrust). The boldness of her storytelling, both when she wrote and at present, can be inferred from the determination of so many critics to moralize—to novelize—her book. *My Ántonia*'s "counsel" for the reader—by now converted, we

6. Here is Benjamin's remark in full: "there is no story for which the question as to how it continued would not be legitimate. The novelist, on the other hand, cannot hope to take the smallest step beyond that limit at which he invites the reader to a divinatory realization of the meaning of life by writing "Finis" (100).
7. For the appropriation argument, see Schwind, 55.

might say, into a listener—is not a definitive message but what Benjamin calls "amplitude": the roominess of a newly open and independent relation to the plots that have come, too narrowly and rigidly, to define the shape of happiness and the lineaments of virtue.

SUSAN J. ROSOWSKI

Pro/Creativity and a Kinship Aesthetic†

* * *

Willa Cather * * * sent Adam packing and claimed paradise for women, restoring to them a psychosexual identification with nature and appropriating for them the promise of nature's wildness. Rather than writing about a virgin land waiting to be despoiled, Cather conceived of the West as female nature slumbering, awakening, and roaring its independence. In her stories, and culminating in *O Pioneers!*, she gave women's fantasies to the West and cast their domestic materials on an epic scale; in doing so she reclaimed materiality for women, rewrote the captivity myth into a story of liberation, and divorced the plot of sexuality from its gendered confinements. It was all in preparation, as it turned out, to return a flesh-and-blood woman to paradise by writing about Annie Sadelik, the Bohemian hired girl of one of Cather's neighbors, * * * and, through her, revising the idea of creativity that she had inherited.

As Marta Weigle writes in *Creation and Procreation*, in this cosmogonical tradition procreation existed as an antithesis to creation. "Procreation is relegated to elemental or physical or biological status, while spiritual or metaphysical or symbolic creation becomes the valued paradigm for ritual custom, art, narrative, and belief systems."[1] Women have babies; men write books. Definitions from *The Oxford English Dictionary* (1933) illustrate the difference:

> Create: Transitive. Said of the divine agent. To bring into being, cause to exist; *esp.* to produce where nothing was before, "to form out of nothing." Procreate. To beget, engender, generate (offspring). To produce offspring . . . to give rise to, occasion.

By structuring her novel around images of birth, Cather evoked traditional mythologies of cosmogony and parturition, then revised those traditions as she created her birth of a nation. Her descriptions

† From *Birthing a Nation: Gender, Creativity, and the West in American Literature* (Lincoln: U of Nebraska P, 1999), pp. 80–92. Reprinted by permission of the University of Nebraska Press. Copyright 1999 by the University of Nebraska Press. Page references in brackets are to this Norton Critical Edition.
1. Marta Weigle, *Creation and Procreation: Feminist Reflections on Mythologies of Cosmogony and Parturition* (Philadelphia: University of Pennsylvania Press, 1989), p. xi.

of the Shimerdas living in a dugout on an unbroken frontier evoke Native American emergence mythologies; Ántonia's emerging sexuality is set within the Judeo-Christian culture of Black Hawk, and Jim Burden's awakening to ideas at the university recalls classical mythologies of creativity. Cather revised these traditions, however, by refiguring into them the Muse, the midwife, and the Earth Mother. Read sequentially, *My Ántonia* provides a historical survey of myths about and attitudes toward birth; read incrementally, Cather's narrative creates a new myth for America.

Childhood scenes in *My Ántonia* revolve around two visits to the Shimerdas in their dugout. Each visit suggests both an emergence mythology of a people's "journeying through lower or other worlds, domains, or wombs" (Weigle 7) and a people's origin in their mother, the earth. In his first visit, Jim witnesses the Shimerdas emerge from a hole in the bank as if the earth was giving birth to life itself; in the second visit, during winter and amid the apparent absence of life, Jim enters that dugout hole as if descending into an underworld to discover its secrets. To Jim, "The air in the cave was stifling, and it was very dark, too" [42]. Only gradually, as his eyes adjust to the darkness, does he realize that "In the rear wall was another little cave; a round hole, not much bigger than an oil barrel, scooped out in the black earth," where Ántonia and her sister sleep [43].

Earth caves may suggest to Jim a frightening descent into a secret, sealed womblike space closely associated with death,[2] but Ántonia presents another view: "I like for sleep there," she insists, "this is warm like the badger hole" [43]. Her description echoes not only emergence myths generally but the Acoma Pueblo origin myth specifically, a myth Cather likely knew from her family's copy of John M. Gunn's *Schat-Chen: History, Traditions and Narratives of the Queres Indians of Laguna and Acoma* (1917). Here she would have read of two sisters who were born underground and remained in the dark as they slowly and patiently grew until they finally emerged through a hole made by a badger.[3]

For her second stage of revisioning, Cather set Ántonia within the Judeo-Christian tradition of the Fall. Whereas the childhood scenes

---

2. Cather in *Death Comes for the Archbishop* creates another richly symbolic female space in the cave called Stone Lips. Latour descends into it for shelter during a storm, and Cather describes his horror over the experience as so intense that, despite the fact that it saved his life, he resolves to never again venture into such a place. Whereas Thea Kronborg, in *The Song of the Lark*, and Ántonia are nurtured by the cave spaces they inhabit, Cather's male characters characteristically feel revulsion over such direct contact with the earth and the primitive.

3. Gunn's book on Laguna and Acoma history, traditions, and narratives is now among the holdings of the Willa Cather Pioneer Memorial and Educational Foundation. For discussion of this myth see Weigle 214–18 and Karen M. Hindhede, "Allusions and Echoes: Multi Cultural Blending and Feminine Spirituality in *Death Comes for the Archbishop*." *Heritage of the Great Plains* 28 (1995): 11–20.

concerned Ántonia's genesis and birth, the Black Hawk scenes concern her awakening to a sexuality that is complicated for Western civilization because of its polarized treatment in the book of Genesis. Adam and Eve gained sexual knowledge by eating fruit from the tree of knowledge of good and evil, and as Gerda Lerner has written, "Once and forever, creativity (and with it the secret of immortality) is severed from procreativity. Creativity is reserved to God; procreativity of human beings is the lot of women. The curse on Eve makes it a painful and subordinate lot" (197). Plot lines in *My Ántonia* separate to reflect this polarized tradition when Jim aligns himself with the world of ideas while Ántonia aligns herself with that of human relationships.[4] He prepares for a creative life of the mind by excelling in high school and by studying trigonometry and beginning Virgil alone the following summer. He then leaves his family and friends to attend the university in Lincoln. During the same period Ántonia follows her script for procreativity by entering domestic service with the Harlings, going with the hired girls to the dances, and loving railway conductor Larry Donovan. Tension is inevitable when a fertility goddess from emergence myth is transplanted into Protestant Black Hawk, and Black Hawk responds by tightening its constrictions upon Ántonia until, following her lover to Denver, she disappears from the text.

Two books and two decades later, Jim returns to Ántonia, now settled with her husband and many children on a Nebraska farm. His visit builds to the most famous birth scene in American literature: "Why don't we show Mr. Burden our new fruit cave?" Ántonia's daughter asks, prompting a gathering of the family as children emerge from the house, join with other children from the yard, and run ahead to open the cellar door, so that "When we descended, they all came down after us" [163]. The scene reaches its climax when, as Jim describes it: "We turned to leave the cave; Ántonia and I went up the stairs first, and the children waited. We were standing outside talking, when they all came running up the steps together; big and little, tow heads and gold heads and brown, and flashing little naked legs; a veritable explosion of life out of the dark cave into the sunlight. It made me dizzy for a moment" [164]. Making explicit that

---

4. Reading *My Ántonia* in terms of Margaret Homans's argument that Western metaphysics is founded on the myth that "language and culture depend on the death or absence of the mother and on the quest for substitutes for her," Ann Fisher-Wirth interprets Jim's narrative as "a form of desire, which constantly seeks but can never arrive at that lost body" (41). "In the gendered myth that informs *My Ántonia*, Ántonia represents the body of the world. The narrative of Jim's life describes his fall away from union with worldbody, into the Law of the Father. But his act of narrative itself constitutes a perpetual desirous return toward the lost motherbody from which his life necessarily departed" (67). See Margaret Homans, *Bearing the Word: Language and Female Experience in Nineteenth-Century Women's Writing* (Chicago: University of Chicago Press, 1986), p. 4, and Ann Fisher-Wirth, "Out of the Mother: Loss in *My Ántonia*." *Cather Studies* 2.1 (1993): 41–71.

this scene is Cather's version of the birth of America, Jim reflects that Ántonia is "a rich mine of life, like the founders of early nations" [171], and thus brings the succession of birth myths to the present. The power of the scene lies in our reading not only sequentially, but incrementally, to recognize that the Cuzaks' fruit cave is reminiscent of the dugout cave that first held Ántonia in the New World, and from which she emerged as if in a first birth, and that Ántonia has fulfilled her destiny as a natural born mother—undeniably, an Earth Mother.

Ántonia as Earth Mother? The description has become so standard that it is easy to pass over how revolutionary is Cather's revisioning of western myths that depict women. As Simone de Beauvoir wrote of the Earth Mother tradition that Cather inherited, the connection of woman with nature is decidedly ambivalent. Though praises may be sung to a fecund nature, "more often man is in revolt against his carnal state; he sees himself as a fallen god: his curse is to be fallen from a bright and ordered heaven into the chaotic shadows of his mother's womb. . . . This quivering jelly which is elaborated in the womb (the womb, secret and sealed like the tomb) evokes too clearly the soft viscosity of carrion for him not to turn shuddering away. . . . The Earth Mother engulfs the bones of her children."[5] By Cather's account, however, the Earth Mother tradition is no imprisonment to earth, no secret and sealed space. Instead the nurturing womb is liberated and celebrated, fertility goddess and Earth Mother restored into a birth myth for the New World.

Celebration takes the form of perception made finer. Having witnessed the explosion of life out of a fruit cave, Jim now sees womb-like enclosures replicated in the larger scene, as if Ántonia's body has regenerated itself in his perception of space. The Cuzaks' house is encircled by a roof so steep that the eaves almost touch "the forest of tall hollyhocks" growing alongside it, and its front yard is "enclosed by a thorny locust hedge" [164]. Behind the house a cherry orchard and an apple orchard are "surrounded by a triple enclosure; the wire fence, then the hedge of thorny locusts, then the mulberry hedge. . . . The hedges were so tall that we could see nothing but the blue sky above them. . . . The orchard seemed full of sun, like a cup" [165]. Movement of descent and ascent and of in and out creates a feeling of freedom in each enclosure, and colors establish the inestimable value of contents protected therein: the gemlike glow of fruit preserved within the cave and the flash of gold from bodies

5. Wendy Lesser demonstrates that Beauvoir's point is still relevant. Addressing mothers as the initial subject of male artists, Lesser writes, "If to be an artist, a writer, is to fly unburdened with the weight of reality, then to think about one's mother—to attempt to think oneself *into* one's mother—is to be brought with a crash down to Mother Earth" (33). See Wendy Lesser, *His Other Half: Men Looking at Women Through Art* (Cambridge: Harvard University Press, 1991), p. 33.

tumbling out of it; the silvery trees flashing from the yard and the purple-red crabs in the orchard that have "a thin silvery glaze over them"; the handsome drakes "with pinkish gray bodies, their heads and necks covered with iridescent green feathers which grew close and full, changing like a peacock's neck" [165]. Through it all, the afternoon sun pours down in a shower of gold as if in granting grace.

Female space, liberated from the dark confines of secrecy and shame associated with birth, becomes the central and ongoing metaphor through which the world's fertility and fecundity are experienced. There is no *I* here (to refer to Ántonia's fruit cellar is to miss the point). Instead there is the *we* of family and, by implication, community and nation. "Why don't *we* show Mr. Burden *our* new fruit cellar," Anna asks; "in winter there are nearly always *some of us* around to come out and get things" Ambrosch explains; and Ántonia describes "the bread *we* bake" and the sugar it takes "for *us* to preserve with" [164; emphases mine].

Enlightenment is all the more powerful because it is a release from confinement, which is so closely associated with birth as to be considered its necessary condition. Mores and laws defining and legislating procreativity undergird Black Hawk's "respect for respectability" [104], another form of confinement when, under its guise, women, bound by both class and gender, are denied sexual knowledge. "[P]hysical exercise was thought rather inelegant for the daughters of well-to-do families," Jim observes of Black Hawk society; "When one danced with them their bodies never moved inside their clothes; their muscles seemed to ask but one thing—not to be disturbed" [102]. Country girls, on the other hand, were "physically . . . almost a race apart," for their "out-of-door work had given them a vigor which . . . developed into a positive carriage and freedom of movement," in contrast to the town girls [102].

The cultural tensions of Black Hawk reflect tensions of mythic appropriations. By moving to Black Hawk and becoming one of "The Hired Girls" (the title of book 2) Ántonia confronts a Judeo-Christian ethos by which the sexuality of the fertility goddess "was so defined as to serve her motherly function, and it was limited by two conditions: she was to be subordinate to her husband, and she would bring forth her children in pain."[6] With Genesis in the background, a fall is inevitable—apparently Ántonia's as she suffers the cultural confinements imposed upon her and the assumptions behind those confinements.

As Ántonia develops into adolescence, the circumstances of frontier living provide her knowledge: "Ambrosch put upon her some

6. Gerda Lerner, *The Creation of the Patriarchy* (New York: Oxford University Press, 1986), p. 196.

chores a girl ought not to do, . . . and the farm-hands around the country joked in a nasty way about it" [69]. The strength of her body results in hunger (eating is a metaphor for lust), and her emerging beauty attracts attention. Maturing as robustly physical and vibrantly sexual, Ántonia defies expectations that a woman be either physical *or* spiritual, sexual *or* maternal. In Black Hawk she continues going to the summer tent dances despite her employer's ultimatum that she stop because she was getting "a reputation for being free and easy." "Stop going to the tent?" Ántonia retorts; "I wouldn't think of it for a minute! My own father couldn't make me stop! Mr. Harling ain't my boss outside my work. I won't give up my friends, either!" [106]. She goes to work for Wick Cutter even though she knows that previous hired girls who worked for him were ruined, and she goes to Denver to join Larry Donovan even though they are as yet unmarried.

From Fielding's Tom Jones to Fitzgerald's Nick Carroway, countless young men have left the country for the city, where they gain the knowledge of the world they will need to take their place in it; the analogous script for women is the cautionary one played out in Theodore Dreiser's *Sister Carrie.* Young women moving to the city support themselves by entering "service" and becoming "hired girls," language that doubles for prostitution and signifies the sanctions against them. Cather evokes these sanctions in "The Hired Girls," revisiting the literary version of a woman's fall into knowledge in which a young woman moves from country to city, learns sexuality, and is punished by "the nothingness that surrounds the . . . prostitute."[7]

In Black Hawk an undercurrent of gossip links a woman's independence with female sexuality and prostitution. Wick Cutter "was notoriously dissolute with women," and two Swedish girls "were the worse for the experience" of living in his house—he had taken one to Omaha "and established [her] in the business for which he had fitted her. He still visited her" [107]. Lena Lingard is suspect by becoming a seamstress,[8] and Tiny Soderball by running a lodging house for sailors. "This, every one said, would be the end of Tiny" [146]. Everyone knows also, one might add, that such gossip follows Ántonia.

Her punishment takes the form of silencing. Ántonia's own voice grows distant and then silent when from Denver she writes a letter, then a postcard, and then nothing. More powerfully, Jim's narrative

7. Helena R. Michie, *The Flesh Made Word: Female Figures and Women's Bodies* (New York: Oxford University Press, 1990), p. 73.
8. *My Secret Life's* narrator-hero, Walter, "sums up Victorian attitudes with a series of displacements: he reaches a turning point in his sexual knowledge when he has 'learnt enough . . . to know that among men of his class the term lacemaker, along with actress and seamstress, was virtually synonymous with prostitute'" (qtd. in Michie 67).

voice erases Ántonia's presence when he admits that he scarcely thinks of her while he is at the university in Lincoln and recalls how grudging and painful references to her are in Black Hawk. "You know, of course, about poor Ántonia," Mrs. Harling says to Jim, upon which he bitterly thinks, "Poor Ántonia! Every one would be saying that now" [145]. She has become a subject to be avoided, acknowledged only when necessary and then with the barest of details. Jim reports that "grandmother had written me how Ántonia went away to marry Larry Donovan at some place where he was working; that he had deserted her, and that there was now a baby" but cuts short his recollection with "This was all I knew" [145]. When Jim remembers Frances Harling telling him tersely that "He never married her" and admitting that "I have n't seen her since she came back," Jim cuts off that reminiscence too by acknowledging flatly, "I tried to shut Ántonia out of my mind" [145].

Whereas the first half of My Ántonia tells of circumstances surrounding Ántonia that narrow into confinements, the second half tells of those circumstances widening into liberation. Between the two lies Jim's (and the reader's) education—not by the formal instruction of the university but by his friendship with Lena Lingard, through whom Cather rewrites the classical tradition of the Muse. Whereas allusions to Judeo-Christian traditions undergird procreativity in the Black Hawk section, classical traditions undergird the emphasis on creativity in the Lincoln section. While living in Lincoln and attending the university, Jim awakens to the world of ideas under the influence of Gaston Cleric, "a brilliant and inspiring" young classical scholar [127]. The furnishings in Jim's boarding-house room reflect his teacher's influence, as do the conversations that take place there. Jim covers his wall with a map of ancient Rome ordered by Cleric, hangs over his bookcase a photograph of the Tragic Theatre at Pompeii that Cleric had given him, and buys a comfortable chair for Cleric to sit in, hoping to entice his teacher to visit and linger. Cleric "could bring the drama of antique life before one out of the shadows" [128], and with it a literary legacy held together by an authority of influence. Entranced, his forgotten cigarette burning unheeded, Cleric would speak lines of Statius who spoke for Dante of his veneration for Virgil.

Jim distinguishes himself from that tradition, however. He recognizes that, unlike Cleric, he should "never lose himself in impersonal things," and he acknowledges an alternative idea of memory for which he uses language of conception, gestation, and quickening. "I begrudged the room that Jake and Otto and Russian Peter took up in my memory," Jim reflects, "But whenever my consciousness was quickened, all those early friends were quickened within it, and in some strange way they accompanied me through all my new

experiences" [129]. The reflection moves him to question the separation of creativity (forming something out of nothing with an
assumption of absolute, godlike authority) from procreativity
(generating offspring with an assumption of giving rise to or occa-
sioning independent life): "They were so much alive in me that I
scarcely stopped to wonder whether they were alive anywhere else, or
how" [129]. By stopping to wonder, Jim prepares for his invocation of
the Muse.

Alone, staring listlessly at the *Georgics*, Jim reads, "for I shall be
the first, if I live, to bring the Muse into my country." As if invoking
a spell, he repeats the phrase "bring the Muse," and then he recalls
the phrase yet again—the magical third utterance [130]. Thereupon
he hears a knock at his door and, opening it, sees Lena Lingard standing in the dark hall. Admitting her, Jim leads her to the chair he had
purchased for Cleric, and once she is seated he "confusedly" questions her.

Answering Jim's summons and sitting in Cleric's chair, Lena displaces Cleric as Jim's teacher and embodies Cather's answer to one of
the most telling of silences, that of the Muses. Excluded by conventions that authorize the poet in creativity as the father is authorized
in procreativity, Muses are to creativity as the mother is to procreativity. As standard handbooks demonstrate, the Muses are given
short shrift. According to *Crowell's Handbook of Classical Mythology* there are few myths specifically given to the Muses, who were
"little worshiped, though often invoked." *The Concise Oxford Dictionary of Literary Terms* notes succinctly that the Muses are "usually
represented by a female deity," and Holman and Harman's *Handbook
to Literature* specifies that "In literature, their traditional significance is that of inspiring and helping POETS." In short, the Muse
is the female inspiration to the male poet, and as Mary Carruthers
has written in "The Re-Vision of the Muse," "he addresses her in
terms of sexual rapture, desiring to be possessed in order to possess, to be ravished in order to be fruitful." Though the poet is
dependent upon her, Carruthers continues, "she speaks only through
him. She is wholly Other and strange, . . . an ethereally beautiful
young girl in the tradition of romance." Whatever guise she assumes,
however, "the basic relationship of dominance and possession is constant between her and her poet" (295).

Cather's Muse is another matter altogether. Her authority is
announced by the title of book 3, "Lena Lingard." Rather than speaking only through a man, Lena speaks for herself, and rather than
submitting to a relationship of dominance and possession, she invites
equality in friendship. Jim's expectations are the familiar ones of the
male poet to "his" Muse: he feels himself possessed, perceives the
encounter as sexual, and assumes her dependency upon him. What

Lena offers to him, however, is an alternative to such conventional notions of creativity. Her self-possession contrasts comically to Jim's assumptions that because she lives alone, she is lonely; that by visiting her in her room, he will compromise her; and that because she is unattached to a man, she wishes to marry.

Cather's Muse speaks for herself when she explains that men pay court to her because "It makes them feel important to think they're in love with somebody" [142] and that "men are all right for friends, but as soon as you marry them they turn into cranky old fathers. . . . I prefer to . . . be accountable to nobody" [142]. Rejecting the relationship traditional to the Muse, Lena offers instead the kindness of mutual respect. When she sees Jim's hurt at hearing her say she is not dependent upon him, for example, she softens his pain by saying, "I've always been a little foolish about you" [143].

By instructing Jim in the mutuality of friendship as an alternative to dominance and possession, Lena prepares him for his return to Ántonia. Whereas the early books in My *Ántonia* depict others' attempts to control Ántonia by narrowing her confinements until she disappeared, the later ones tell of Ántonia reasserting herself into the text. "[S]uch entries for women into textuality and into language are always painful in that they always involve a shattering of the silence which enshrouds women's physical presence," observes Helena R. Michie, who in *The Flesh Made Word* (74–75) could have been describing Ántonia returning pregnant and unwed. Nobody visits her. She was "crushed and quiet," "never went anywhere," and "always looked dead weary" [153]. Though afflicted with toothache, she "wouldn't go to Black Hawk to a dentist for fear of meeting people she knew" [145], and after her daughter was born, she "almost never comes to town" [153].

The power granted to birth is apparent when Ántonia asserts her daughter against cultural erasure. Ántonia's reentry into textuality is indirect at first, accomplished by the stories that Jim hears of her. Though nobody visits Ántonia, she brings her daughter to Black Hawk to show to Mrs. Harling, and though others expect her to keep "her baby out of sight," she has the child's "picture on exhibition at the town photographer's, in a great gilt frame" [148]. A character asserting herself against the discomfort of her own novel is the effect Cather creates when the photographer speaks of Ántonia with "a constrained, apologetic laugh" and when Jim Burden reflects, selfishly, that "I could forgive her, I told myself, if she had n't thrown herself away on such a cheap sort of fellow" [148].

The stories that Jim hears are powerful, however. They work against the cultural discomfort of the text to create in Jim the "feeling that [he] must see Ántonia again" [148]. Seeing again is revisioning, and—appropriately—Jim goes to see a midwife for the re-visioning necessary to break the silence surrounding birth. Rhetoric and ritual signal that this is no ordinary visit. To reach the Widow Steavens, Jim journeys to the high country, reflecting as he travels upon the "growth of . . . a great idea" apparent in the changing face of the country, where human lives were "coming to a fortunate issue" and the flat tableland was responding by "long, sweeping lines of fertility" [149]. Jim's meeting with the midwife has the ceremonial greeting of gravity: he "drew up," and the Widow Steavens "came out to meet [him]. She was . . . tall, and very strong . . . her massive head . . . like a Roman senator's. I told her at once why I had come" [149]. This scene is the ritual supplication of youth to age, quester to oracle.

Further ritual, the sharing of food and withdrawing to a solemn setting, prepares for a transfer of knowledge. By such rituals Jim and the midwife eat supper and then retire to the sitting room where the moon shining outside the open windows recalls Great Goddess belief systems.[9] The Widow Steavens turns the lamp low, settles into her favorite rocking chair, then "crossed her hands in her lap and sat as if she were at a meeting of some kind" [150]. As Cather proposed her version of the Muse in Lena, so she now proposes her oracle by drawing upon the ancient female tradition of a gossip/midwife serving as godparent and witness, figures "who think and act strongly about childbirth . . . [and who] must be counted among the enablers of powerful symbolic processes" (Weigle 145).

In telling a woman's version of procreativity, Cather's midwife releases birth from the secrecy that had enshrouded it, thereby setting in motion the powerful symbolic processes by which a birth story will become a national epic. By the Widow Steavens's account, rather than suffering the punishment inherited from a fallen Eve, Ántonia gave birth without confinement and apparently without pain ("without calling to anybody, without a groan, she lay down on the bed and bore her child"); rather than affirming a male line, she gave birth to a daughter; and rather than suffering shame over her child, "She loved it from the first as dearly as if she'd had a ring on her finger." "Ántonia is a natural-born mother," the Widow Steavens concludes, contradicting conventions governing the "rights" of motherhood [155].

As she offers a woman's version of birth, the midwife also establishes a woman's way of telling. Jim's authorial I that assumes possession ("*my* Ántonia") is replaced by the compassionate I of the Widow Steavens, and Jim's terse report of withdrawing from Ántonia contrasts with Widow Steavens's description of visiting Ántonia the morning after she returned home. Taking Ántonia in her arms and asking her to come out of doors where they could talk freely,

9. As Gerda Lerner writes, the Goddess's "frequent association with the moon symbolized her mystical powers over nature and the seasons" (148).

the Widow Steavens said "'Oh, my child,' . . . 'what's happened to you? Don't be afraid to tell me'" [151]; after hearing Ántonia's reply, she "sat right down on that back beside her and made lament" [152]. Drawing Ántonia near, inviting her open and free speech, and then responding with compassion is the mutuality of friendship, the effect of which is suggested by the W. T. Benda drawings that Cather commissioned to accompany her text. Whereas Ántonia was previously depicted from a distance with her face averted, she now turns toward the viewer as if in response to the Widow Steavens's voice. We see her face as she walks forward, her body swelling with new life beneath her black overcoat.

In this manner expectations are reversed and conventions are overturned. Whereas the other hired girls have, like Ántonia, made places for themselves, the men have been displaced by various narrative devices. The introduction to *My Ántonia* complicates Jim's authority in matters of both procreation (he has no children) and creativity (rather than inventing the story, he wrote down stories as they returned to him in memory). Other men are killed or marginalized: Mr. Shimerda commits suicide, Peter and Pavel become outcasts, the tramp jumps into a thrashing machine, Jake and Otto vanish into the West, Mr. Harling disappears on business, and the Widow Steavens's husband is as absent as the vestigial "Mrs." from her name. Most interesting, there is Larry Donovan. Scarcely a character in his own right, he is instead a foil to Ántonia. Never pictured or described directly, Larry Donovan remains voiceless and faceless, as expendable to Ántonia's plot as the bride was to Peter and Pavel's plot.

Stories within the novel celebrate the New World as a site of miraculous births. Fuchs tells of the woman he accompanied on the boat crossing who in mid-ocean "proceeded to have not one baby, but three!" [40], and on Christmas Mr. Burden reads "the chapters from St. Matthew about the birth of Christ, and as we listened it all seemed like something that had happened lately, and near at hand. He thanked the Lord for the first Christmas, and for all it had meant to the world ever since" [48].[1]

As she releases her narrator from the desire to frame (or confine) Ántonia, Cather also liberates the reader from the desire to frame (or confine) the text. In Western paradigms, birth—like reading—is gendered and individualized. "What is it?" is the first question after

---

1. In discussing "biblical borrowings" in *My Ántonia*, John J. Murphy perceptively traces Cather's use of Christian iconography to describe Ántonia: "The Christmas story of Matthew and Luke echoes in Widow Steavens's account of the birth of Ántonia's child, and Jim's subsequent farewell scene with Ántonia, . . . recalls Revelation 12:1, traditionally applied to the Virgin Mary" (40); the orchard scene describes a "della robbia image of maternity clothed in light and blossoms [that] recalls Dante's dawn-bright vision of Mary in *Paradise*" (93); and for Jim's return twenty years later, Cather "reworks the icon into a kind of Coronation of the Virgin" (103). See John J. Murphy, *My Ántonia: The Road Home* (Boston: Twayne Publishers, 1989).

birth that, once answered, determines responses to that child. Similarly, "who wrote it?" is the first question of a book that, once answered, determines our reading. As Susan Stanford Friedman has observed, "We seldom read any text without knowledge of the author's sex. The title page itself initiates a series of expectations that influence our reading throughout."[2]

From the outset Cather undermined her readers' reliance upon gender distinctions. The appearance of her name on the novel's title page initiates gender expectations that the introduction unsettles when, by appearing as the reader of Jim Burden's manuscript, Cather contradicts the most basic separation between self and other, writer and reader. Having evoked the question, "Where is the author in this text?" Cather complicates answers with a series of disclaimers. First her fictional narrator states that he didn't "arrange or rearrange" but instead "simply wrote down what of herself and myself and other people Ántonia's name recalls to me." Then Cather herself renounces authority by writing that "my own story was never written," saying that "the following narrative is Jim's manuscript, substantially as he brought it to me." The effect is to undermine the premise that authority is basic to creativity.[3] This is a manuscript conceived not by a distinction between creator and created, author and subject; instead, it is conceived by the mutuality of long friendship. "We grew up together in the same Nebraska town," "we had much to say to each other," "we were talking," and "we agreed"—the exchange of conversation establishes that this text is a collaboration that grew out of continuities of life into art, of past into present, of childhood retrieved by adults, of female author and male narrator in *agreement*.

As the metaphor of birth had expanded into enlightenment, so the mutuality of friendship expands into an aesthetics of kinship in the novel's final scenes when Jim witnesses storytelling within the Cuzak family. "The distinction between female and male discourse lies not in the [childbirth] metaphor itself but rather in the way its final meaning is constituted in the process of reading," writes Friedman (61). Though she was not, Friedman could have been writing of *My Ántonia*, where Cather reconstitutes the process of reading to

2. Susan Stanford Friedman, "Creativity and the Childbirth Metaphor: Gender Difference in Literary Discouse." *Feminist Studies* 13 (1987), pp. 49–82. This quotation appears on p. 55.
3. Here Cather reverses novelistic tradition of gendered authority. Whereas "The poetry of troubadours, like popular tales, stories of voyages, and other kinds of narratives, often introduces at the end the speaker as a witness to or participant in the narrated 'facts,'" writes Julia Kristeva, "in novelistic conclusions, the author speaks not as a witness to some 'event' (as in folk tales), not to express his 'feelings' or his 'art' (as in troubadour poetry); rather, he speaks in order to assume ownership of the discourse that he appeared at first to have given to someone else (a character)" (Julia Kristeva, *Desire in Language: A Semiotic Approach to Literature and Art* [New York: Columbia University Press, 1980], p. 63).

provide an alternative aesthetic based on an "emphasis on birth leading to a lifetime of maternal nurturance" (Friedman 62).[4]

Far from previous assumptions of possession and dominance,
storytelling now proceeds by cooperation and inclusion. Ántonia's
daughter Anna, for example, reveals sensitivity to her youngest
brother by recognizing his need to tell his story to Ántonia: Jan "wants
to tell you about the dog, mother," Anna says, whereupon Ántonia
beckons her son to her and listens to him while he tells her about
the dog's death, resting his elbows upon her knees as he does so [163].
Ántonia then whispers to Jan, who then slips away and whispers, in
turn, to his sister Nina. The principle is now of repetition. Jan repeats
his mother's words to his sister, and the younger children ask Ántonia to tell the story of "how the teacher has the school picnic in the
orchard every year" [165]. Contrary to the convention of male
author(ity) and female subject, Ántonia is at the center of storytelling by which, like the metaphor of birth, language returns to
its source.

As the metaphor of birth has expanded, so does that of language's
return. Coming home from a street fair in a nearby town, Cuzak says,
"very many send word to you, Ántonia," then asks Jim to excuse him
while he delivers their messages in Bohemian [172]. As the birth
scenes build to the explosion of bodies from the fruit cellar, so now
storytelling builds to the reminiscences and exchanges of family
stories as the Cuzaks and Jim look at photographs and then to reminiscences and exchanges at dinner. Here again storytelling is a
cooperative enterprise. When at dinner Rudolph asks if Jim has
heard about the Cutters, Ántonia (upon hearing that Jim hasn't),
says "then you must tell him, son. . . . Now, all you children be
quiet, Rudolph is going to tell about the murder." "Hurrah," they
murmur, then are quiet as Rudolph tells his story "in great detail,
with occasional promptings from his mother or father" [174].

The younger children, Anna, Jan, and Nina, the older son, Rudolph,
and the parents, Cuzak and Ántonia herself—all have a voice in the
family's ongoing story. What is the principle of narrative here and
of the use of the word? Clearly, Ántonia is not using language in the
tradition of creation (i.e., to produce where nothing was before, to
form out of nothing). Instead, she is a source of the family legend in
the sense that she begets, engenders, generates, produces, gives rise
to, and occasions. These—the definitions of *procreate* with which
I began—come together in the pro/creativity of a kinship aesthetic.
In Cather's version of the Fall, Ántonia disappeared from Jim Burden's text only to return independently to claim her language and to

4. The title of book 5, "Cuzak's Boys," unsettles expectations that a patriarchal principle
   would be replaced by a matriarchal one. Cuzak's boys or Ántonia's? Jim's story or Cather's?
   Such questions are made irrelevant by a kinship aesthetics of exchange and connectivity.

demonstrate its power. She speaks Bohemian with her children, and around the dinner table she teaches them not only the mother tongue but also a reciprocal and communal use of language.

Cather's birth of a nation is significant for what it is not as well as for what it is. It is not a separation from or casting off of other cultures. It does not set a New World against an Old World, an American future against a European past or a Native American mythology. Instead, it offers a national identity affirming analogies and continuities. As Virgil brought the Muse to Rome by writing of his neighborhood in Mantua, so Cather would bring the Muse to the United States by writing of her neighborhood in Nebraska. By drawing upon emergence mythologies, Cather renewed familiar figures so that the Muse inspires collaboration and the midwife sets in motion powerful symbolic processes of language and metaphor. Through Cather's revisioning, an immigrant girl she knew in Nebraska gives birth to a nation.

MIKE FISCHER

Pastoralism and Its Discontents: Willa Cather and the Burden of Imperialism[†]

Willa Cather's fiction has recently been subjected to a number of revisionist readings, most notably by feminist critics of *My Ántonia* who have exposed both the various sexist stereotypes that underlie Jim Burden's archetypal eulogizing of "his" protagonist and the narrative strategies whereby he attempts to expropriate his female muse. Unfortunately, in doing so they have overlooked the fact that it is not only the history of women on the Plains that is being "rewritten" by Jim but also the conquest of the Plains Indians that is being rewritten by Willa Cather.

Jim initially describes the Nebraskan land upon which he will write his story as "not a country at all, but the material out of which countries are made" [12]; and he imagines himself as writing in the tradition of the *Georgics*, Virgil's pastoral account of the founding of the patria. Factually, however, the history of the Plains has more in common with the brutal imperialism recorded in the *Aeneid*; the development of Nebraska is a pastoral story only in the sense of "pastor(al)ization." *My Ántonia* is a story of origins for whites only; its account of conflicts between various selves and their others—an important theme in the novel—ignores the most significant Other

† *Mosaic: A Journal for the Interdisciplinary Study of Literature* 23.1 (1990): 33–44. Reprinted by permission of *Mosaic*. Page references to *My Ántonia* are to this Norton Critical Edition.

in Nebraskan history: the Native Americans whose removal was seen as a *sine qua non* for successful white settlement.

Essential to an "idyllic" view of Plains history is the premise that what the first settlers had to clear was merely the land, and here one begins to see in a new light Cather's repeated description of the Nebraska which preceded white settlement as a prairie that was "empty." Equally revealing, in turn, is the way Cather's feminist critics have followed her lead. For all her valuable insights into Jim's sexism, for example, Jean Schwind describes the Nebraska territory that the Shimmerdas subsequently occupy as "new virgin land" (61). Similarly, Sharon O'Brien, perhaps Cather's best feminist critic, refers to the Nebraskan landscape into which Cather moved in 1883 as an "empty world" "uninscribed in a literary as well as a topographical sense," a "new landscape" in which Cather might concern herself "with the human drive to create culture and civilization by making marks in a new landscape"—"taming . . . the wild land" (74).

The land on which Cather inscribed her story, however, was not a *tabula rasa*, even if, as in *O Pioneers!*, she conceives of "the feeble scratches on stone left by prehistoric races [as] so indeterminate that they may after all, be only the markings of glaciers, and not a record of human strivings" (18–19). In a powerful demonstration of circular logic, Cather's reading of such "feeble scratches" as "indeterminate" allows her to relegate the people who made them to a time before writing—to prehistory.

Cather's appropriation of the land's materials for her own purposes—so that she might build a "country"—required that those contexts and peoples which did not accommodate her textual strategy be marginalized or naturalized so that their stories would not contradict her own. As such, her works confirm what Fredric Jameson has observed with respect to the ideological nature of the esthetic act, which invents "imaginary or formal 'solutions' to unresolvable social contradictions" (79). This is not to accuse Cather of conscious duplicity or racism, any more than it is to indict those feminist critics who ignore her failure to recognize Nebraska's first inhabitants. Instead, the kind of naturalization of which I speak is indicative of the cultural limitations—Jameson's "political unconscious"—that condition the historical interpretations of any epoch and which register the blindspots in any period's texts (74–83). Such ways of perceiving result from an individual's incremental and almost unnoticed absorption of the cultural assumptions of his or her particular group or class.

At the same time, however, the "real" history that such assumptions exclude does not—cannot—just go away. The social contradictions that narrative seeks to resolve, because they are intrinsic to the social infrastructures such narratives depict, have a habit of reappearing at inopportune moments. This "notion of contradiction," writes Jameson, "is central to any Marxist cultural analysis" and it explains why history, in the sense of a grand narrative of human events, will not disappear and cannot be erased; "it happened" (80). There can be no cultural text, however apparently blind to the political preconditions assuring its provenance, that fails to record the traces of those preconditions, in spite of itself. Any story of the (white) settlement of Nebraska—or "America"—will inevitably find itself referring to those peoples whose "removal" preceded that settlement. The function of criticism, accordingly, is to uncover these traces. Or as Tony Bennett argues in corroboration of Jameson's "notion of contradiction," an active and critical intervention "works" upon such texts and serves to expose contradictions that they and their author(s), given their own historical context, could not have seen (141).

While it is true that cultural context inevitably limits the perceptions of any critic, the political struggles of the sixties and seventies—such as the Black Arts and Black Power movements, the American Indian Movement (AIM), and the Chicano Youth Movement's "Plan of Aztlan"—place us today in an especially advantageous position for "working" on texts so as to excavate the buried stories in U.S. history. While the most important part of this project must and will remain the recuperation and celebration of these peoples' own texts, a critical explanation of how such stories are embedded within canonical narratives might help us recognize the degree to which suppressed histories are integral not only to the establishment of canons but also to the idea of "Western Civilization" that canons celebrate.

Before proceeding, perhaps I can make clearer the nature of the interpretive act with an example. Bernice Slote, trying to explain the absence of non-European ethnic groups in much of Cather's early fiction, offers the following picture of the young Cather's Nebraska: "She lived in Nebraska in the 1880s and 1890s, when Indians were noticed in the newspapers chiefly as warring tribes with dirty living habits. In any case, they were far from Red Cloud, and Wounded Knee was only a column or so of print. Literary views in Nebraska were composed in highly romanticized legends, some in Hiawatha style . . ." (98–99). Slote's passage underscores an important contradiction in the (white) Nebraskan perceptions it describes. On the one hand, "columns of print" describing the Indians did in fact exist. On one level, some late-nineteenth-century Nebraskans were still aware of the Indians, as they could not help being, given how recently—as late as the 1870s—much of western Nebraska had still been under Sioux control. On the other hand, the Indians, in Cather's Red Cloud, were reduced from their cultural complexity to "warring tribes with dirty habits." As James Olson has demonstrated in his history of Nebraska, early Nebraskan newspapers, often little more than advertising sheets for the companies that owned them, were far more concerned with the price and yield of land than they were with drawing sensitive or accurate portraits of those peoples being thrown off the land (93). As far as such newspapers were concerned, the Wounded Knee massacre had nothing to do with an agrarian Nebraska economy; it, and the Indians who died there, existed "far away." They simply did not matter.

They were not so far away, however, either temporally or geographically, as Cather might have wanted—and successfully managed—to believe. Red Cloud itself, established in 1870 as the first permanent town in what had been one of the Indians' last buffalo hunting grounds south of the Platte River, was named after the Sioux chief of that name, who was reputed to have held a war council on the site where the town was platted (Perkey 198; J. Olson 171–72).

As recently as 1868, Red Cloud's war councils had been aimed at expelling white settlers from the lands north of the Platte River— guaranteed the Sioux in perpetuity as part of the 1851 Laramie Treaty—in western Nebraska, northern Wyoming and Montana. That year a second Laramie Treaty initiated the process that would eventually force Red Cloud to accept semi-reservation status in northwestern Nebraska and that, finally, after the illegal white incursions into the Black Hills in the mid-1870s, would lead to his expulsion from Nebraska altogether.

Nonetheless, in 1870 the Black Hills catastrophe, originally provoked by the discovery there of gold, could not be foreseen; names like Sitting Bull, Crazy Horse and Custer were relatively unknown. In the very months that Red Cloud, Nebraska, was being founded, Chief Red Cloud was completing a treaty in Washington, D.C. In exchange for peace along Nebraska's Platte River Valley—with its just completed trans-continental railroad that the Indians had successfully sabotaged in the 1866–68 war—the Oglalla Sioux were guaranteed possession of the Black Hills and the Powder River country. The "warring tribes with dirty habits" would be placed in the margins of Nebraska's text; they could continue to "harass" settlers elsewhere as long as Nebraska prospered. Chief Red Cloud's treaty symbolized this compromise; Red Cloud, Nebraska, opening up what had been Indian territory, profited from its provisions (Brown, chapters 5,6,8,12; Baltensperger 37–52; J. Olson 128–41).

The settlers of Red Cloud under Silas Garber—soon to become governor of the state—may have believed that the name they chose for their town could serve as an emblem for the peace that Chief Red Cloud had made—had been forced to make—possible. That peace, however, was tenuous; provoked by continued white expansion into their territory, the Sioux continued a resistance which James Olson has argued was "the most serious opposition they [the whites] encountered in the whole of America's westward expansion" (128–29). The events of 1876, and in particular Custer's astonishing defeat—the most serious blow the U.S. Army suffered in all of the Indian Wars—demonstrated anew at what cost such "peace" had to be won. The hopes generated by Red Cloud's 1870 Washington visit had dissipated amidst a series of bloody wars that, within twenty years, would see the systematic genocide of Red Cloud's people and the deaths of hundreds of white soldiers. Red Cloud became a reminder, for those who chose to remember, that its prosperity and security were predicated upon the removal and elimination of the people for whose chief it was named—people who still occupied most of Nebraska as late as the American Civil War, as Cather herself admitted in a 1923 *Nation* article: "Before 1860 civilization did no more than nibble at the eastern edge of the State, along the river bluffs. Lincoln, the present capital, was open prairie; and the whole of the great plain to the westward was still a sunny wilderness, where the tall red grass and the buffalo and the Indian hunter were undisturbed" (236).

Despite the implications of her *Nation* article, Cather usually chose not to remember the presence of Native Americans in Nebraska, or, perhaps more accurately, she literally seemed to forget their existence. While her short history of Nebraska does acknowledge the Indians' erstwhile presence, it does not try to account for their removal— nor explain how the peoples who roamed the prairies "undisturbed" were eventually disturbed enough to disappear and make possible the agricultural paradise that she proclaims Nebraska to be.

The name Cather chooses in *My Ántonia* for her fictional Red Cloud, "Black Hawk," is suggestive in this context. The Black Hawk War of 1831–32 represented the opening skirmish in the white effort to steal the Plains; Chief Black Hawk's defeat, that is to say, might legitimately stand as the opening moment in Cather's genealogy of the settlement of Nebraska. Cather herself would probably not have known much more of this historical Black Hawk than the residents of Red Cloud would have known of the chief after whom their town was named. Instead, Cather would probably have known only the mythological Black Hawk, a version of the chief popularized through numerous reprintings of his autobiography—an autobiography interpreted and written for an American audience by a U.S. Army officer. As Richard Slotkin has observed in his expose of the mythology of the American frontier, the "autobiography" of Chief Black Hawk was one of the first texts in the nineteenth-century cult of nostalgia that would increasingly come to surround white perceptions of Native American peoples. As the Indian threat decreased, Slotkin argues, the nostalgic impulse toward the Indians increased (356–60).

Within a year of what was, for the Indians, a disastrous blow, and even as President Jackson was completing the Cherokee removal to Oklahoma, Black Hawk's "autobiography" was on the market and his heroization had begun. Cather's account of "Black Hawk" involved a similar *white*wash on behalf of late-nineteenth-century Nebraska, relegating the Sioux—and Wounded Knee—to a place "far away," a "column of print" on the margins of her celebration of the pioneer instinct. The little girl who had been photographed as Hiawatha had grown up to memorialize the "highly romanticized legends, some in Hiawatha style," that, according to Slote, had conditioned Cather's perception of the Nebraska frontier from the start.

Perhaps Cather's most famous evocation of that frontier—not just in *My Ántonia* but in all of her fiction—is the plow which, as Jim enjoys his farewell picnic with the "hired girls," is suddenly transformed into a monolithic emblem of the future of the land. The scene occurs at the close of the penultimate chapter of Book II, as Jim prepares to take leave of Black Hawk. As the sun sinks in the west, it magnifies to gigantic proportions a plow that has been left standing in the field: "it stood out against the sun . . . black against the molten red. There it was, heroic in size, a picture writing on the sun" [123].

Paul Olson, in his reading of the Virgilian influences on *My Ántonia*, draws a parallel and contrast between this passage and that moment in the eighth book of the *Aeneid* (616–43) when Aeneas sees the weapons with which he will be permitted to forge Rome's future. Not only does Aeneas see his sword and his shield inscribed with scenes of the Roman future, but he also envisions his bronze breastplate "massive and ruddy coloured like to some lowing cloud / When it catches fire from the rays of the sun and glows afar" (qtd. in Olson 282). Olson reasons that the inverse nature of the parallel is intended to suggest Cather's preference for the *Georgics*; as he sees it, when she does not invoke Virgil's pastoral writings directly, as in Jim's study in Lincoln, she obliquely signals her preference by revising the warrior epic to suit her agrarian picture of Nebraska's genealogy: "Her [Ántonia's] journey ends in a garden, a family garden, as the more perfect world which the *Georgics* propose. Her place is the patria . . . [with Cather suggesting that] the ancient epic, celebrating as it had the myth of military might, iron law, and male dominance, had run its course" (284).

Olson's explanation is fine—as far as it goes. But it fails to account for the sudden disappearance of this splendid vision—as the plow is enveloped in the darkness that quickly spreads over the prairie—at chapter's close; indeed, Cather's text seems to suggest that the myth that has "run its course" is as much the pastoral vision that she has just evoked as the warrior epic which that vision replaces.

Olson likewise neglects to mention the extremely imperial narrative fragment that immediately precedes the magnification of the plow: Jim's relation to the "hired girls" of the Coronado legend. According to Jim's retelling of the story, a farmer north of Black Hawk, while breaking sod, turned up a Spanish sword engraved with the name of a munitions maker in Cordova. For Jim and his school chum Charlie Harling, this discovery indicates that the Coronado expedition, which reportedly had not advanced further north than central Kansas, must have made it as far north as the southern Nebraska Republican River valley in which the novel is set. The girls ask Jim why Coronado never went back to Spain. "I couldn't," he admits, "tell them. I only knew the schoolbooks said he 'died in the wilderness of a broken heart'" [122].

The discrepancy Jim tacitly acknowledges between the textual history through which he has learned about Coronado and "what actually happened"—the contexts that "historical" narrative displaces—gestures toward Cather's own uneasy awareness that the Coronado expedition was not quite what the Nebraskan school texts might have claimed it was. *Death Comes for the Archbishop* in particular makes repeated reference to the fact that "the Spaniards had treated them [the pueblo Indians of the southwest] very badly long ago" (53), specifically referring to cruelties perpetrated by Coronado's soldiers against the Pecos Indians during the march toward the fabled cities of Quivera (125).

The realities were even worse than Cather's references to slavery and concubinage in this 1927 novel might suggest. Beginning with the Arenal pueblo, Spanish troops under Coronado and Cardenas massacred the populations of twelve pueblos of the Tigeux Indians in the winter of 1540; over thirty of the inhabitants of the Arenal pueblo, surrendering after receiving a promise of fair treatment, were burned alive (Day 118–27; Udall 144–46).

Coronado's behavior toward the Indians was too much even for Spain's administrators in Mexico, never known for their overly kind treatment of the Indians. During his *residencia*—an examination of conduct and policy that all Spanish officials were required to undergo upon completion of their duties—in 1544, Coronado was accused by his own men of inhumane treatment of the Indians in both northern Mexico and in the Tigeux country along the Rio Grande river in New Mexico (Hammond 75; Day 165–68). As punishment for his conduct, he was stripped of his post as governor of New Galicia (Day 172). Coronado may or may not have died of a "broken heart." What is certain is that, despite a partial rehabilitation in 1549, he died disgraced by his government for his inhumane treatment of New Spain's native population.

Coronado's inhumane treatment might, too, help explain what a Spanish sword is doing in Nebraskan soil—why, that is, it did not accompany its owner back to Mexico. For Cather's inclusion of this apparently inconsequential romantic detail alludes to a Spanish expedition that, unlike Coronado's, really did cross the Republican River and explore south-central Nebraska. In June of 1720, accompanied by forty-five Spanish soldiers, over sixty Indians, an interpreter and a priest, Pedro de Villasur set out from Santa Fe to re-establish Spanish control of the Great Plains, a control strongly contested by the French and some eastern Plains native peoples with whom they were allied. Somewhere in central Nebraska—the exact location has never been ascertained—the expedition was ambushed and almost completely annihilated by a contingent of Pawnee Indians. While most of the Indians accompanying the Spanish apparently escaped, only thirteen of the Spanish soldiers made it back to Santa Fe (J. Olson 30–31; Thomas 72–79).

In an ironic way, then, Jim and Charlie were right: Coronado really had made it to Nebraska—at least by reputation. If a Spanish sword is found north of Black Hawk, Coronado's reputation probably had a lot to do with it ending up there. De Villasur's expedition reaped the whirlwind that Coronado's cruelty had sown.

The truth behind the Coronado legend belies the "georgic" vision that Cather's plow seems designed to evoke. No matter how successfully *My Ántonia* appears to bury the reminders of the wars whose consequence was to "open" Nebraska for farming, the genealogy of that agricultural triumph refuses to disappear. Plowing, in Nebraska, is inextricably intertwined with the sword. And in a paradigmatic example of the return of the repressed, the sword and everything it stands for "turn up" in Cather's narrative at the very place where she most powerfully calls forth the symbolic plow; meant to replace the sword, the plow rediscovers it instead. If the sun finally sets on Jim's pastoral vision, it is because the Edenic possibilities which that vision seems to entail have been called into question.

Jim tacitly alludes to the dessication of Eden when he retells the story of his battle with the snake [30]. Blanche Gelfant sees this scene as an example of the return of the repressed in its classically Freudian sexual sense, claiming that the snake "forces him [Jim] to confront deeply repressed images, to acknowledge for the only time the effect of 'horrible unconscious memories'" (88). I would supplement Gelfant's reading—convincing as it is—by pointing to Jim's actual description of the snake as old enough to have "been there when white men first came, left on from buffalo and Indian times" [31]. Those times, for Jim, are relatively recent; he calculates the snake to be about twenty-four years old. To the extent that we are justified in seeing Jim as an autobiographical persona for Cather, this would place the snake's birth around 1860—immediately preceding the passage of the Homestead Act (1862) which initiated large-scale immigration into and the subsequent domestication of Nebraska's still wide-open spaces. Jim's battle with the snake, then, represents a metonymic displacement of the true genealogy of Nebraska's white settlement: the Indian Wars of the 1860s that were planned in conjunction with the passage of the Homestead Act and that made its implementation possible (Trachtenberg 30).

There can be no Eden in Nebraska, because its origins are not innocent. Much like the unhealed wheel-ruts in the wagon road that "looked like gashes torn by a grizzly's claws" [178], the "road of [Manifest] Destiny" [179] in which these ruts are embedded—the road that Cather grandiloquently recalls at the close of her Nebraska history—is slashed by violence. His circular road, though, gashes and all, necessarily awakens memories of the mysterious Indian ceremonial ground—that "great circle where the Indians used to ride"—which had so powerfully moved Jim when he was a boy [37]. However peripheral to Jim's later experience—and the Nebraskan story with which it is intertwined—the historical realities which that circle evokes refuse to disappear.

Jim's infamous road at the close of *My Ántonia* also recalls the road for which he works as a lawyer, that "great Western railway" that "runs and branches" through Nebraska, leaving scars far more permanent—and serious—than those Jim can trace to wagon-ruts. When the introduction to *My Ántonia* connects Jim's "personal passion" for "the great country through which his railway runs and branches" with "its development," it is unclear whether the "it" refers to the railroad or to the United States. There is no solution to this ambiguity—nor need there be. The U.S. government's expansionist ideology and genocidal policy of Indian "removal" were intimately and specifically connected to plans for the construction of a transcontinental railroad which were being formulated as early as the 1840s.

Hence it is hardly surprising that Jim Burden works for the railroads; it would be more surprising if he did not. As someone who has engineered a cleaned up version of Nebraska's past, himself controlled by an author who associated "towering locomotives" charging "over the great Western land" with "power, conquest, and triumph" (qtd. in O'Brien 85), Jim quite fittingly works for the industry that epitomized and engineered American progress—while rarely calculating the cost of that progress to America's indigenous peoples. As Glen Love writes, "For Cather, as for Jim Burden, the railroad seems to have been accepted as simply a part of the geographical and cultural given of the prairie. The railroad was there when they arrived, and thus it belongs" (144).

It had not always "belonged," and Cather herself, in the middle of an article celebrating the comforts of the Burlington Railroad—the road that runs through Black Hawk in *My Ántonia* and which runs through the actual town of Red Cloud—recognized that the "sudden transition" from the harsh western prairie to the comforts of a rail-road dining car had "something of the black art about it and seemed altogether unnatural" (*World* 838). We can see just how unnatural—and the extent, consequently, to which Cather's narra-tive "railroads" its readers—by reviewing the history of how Nebraska was wrested from the Plains Indians.

When Andrew Jackson stole parts of the southeastern United States from the Indians in 1830, he initiated a process that resulted, in 1834, in the Indian Intercourse Act, which guaranteed the Indi-ans possession of most American lands west of the Mississippi, including all of the present state of Nebraska (J. Olson 67). Though subsequent territorial adjustments appropriated substantial portions of this "Indian land," including most of the spaces between the Mis-sissippi and Missouri Rivers, the Indians were still in possession of all of Nebraska when Stephen Douglas, recently elected congress-man from Illinois, arose from the floor of the House in 1844 and proposed his first bill to organize Nebraska as a territory (J. Olson 69–70).

Douglas's initiative was, to say the least, peculiar, since territo-rial organization was supposed to follow an accumulation of white settlers in a region. Not surprisingly, however, given the 1834 agree-ment with the Indians, the only whites in Nebraska in the mid-1840s were a few missionaries, traders and advance squatters, none of whom was very concerned with his/her official position (92). Doug-las's real reason for proposing the Bill was less concerned with these few white transients than with the possibility of placing the eastern terminus of the newly proposed transcontinental railroad in Chi-cago and running it through Nebraska's easily traversable Platte River valley. With this in mind, Douglas had recently invested in Chicago real estate (Limerick 92). Still, as long as he and his constituency were confronted with the lingering fiction of a per-manent Indian territory, the proposed routes would begin else-where—as indeed all four of the routes proposed during the 1840s did (J. Olson 68–69).

With the introduction of his Bill and his decade-long fight for the creation of a Nebraska territory, Douglas served notice to Secretary of War Jefferson Davis that no more Indians should be allowed into Nebraska. "The Indian barrier must be removed," he wrote; other-wise the United States would sacrifice its "immense interests and possessions on the Pacific" to a "vast wilderness fifteen hundred miles in breadth, filled with hostile savages, and cutting off all direct com-munication" (qtd. in Limerick 93). Douglas got his wish. The Nebraska Territory was created in 1854, even though a census taken in Novem-ber of that year showed only twenty-seven hundred whites living in the state—most of them either residing on the eastern fringe of the territory along the Missouri or transients who actually lived in Kansas (J. Olson 88).

Many of the Indian tribes living in eastern Nebraska were either confined to reservations or forced to "trade" their ancient lands for trinkets and new guarantees of lands further West. The success of this program of removal, combined with the dramatic rise in population as a result of the Homestead Act (intended to consolidate control of these lands) and with the American Civil War, which effectively removed the proposed southern routes from contention, led President Lincoln, in 1863, to choose the Platte River valley as the route that the railroad would follow. The first track was laid that year; by 1867, the rails had reached western Nebraska.

Here, the Sioux, Cheyenne and Arapaho peoples proved more difficult to "remove" than their eastern neighbors had been. As Chief Spotted Tail of the Brûlé Sioux said to President Grant during the 1870 visit of Red Cloud's delegation, "The Great Father has made roads stretching east and west. Those roads are the cause of all our troubles. . . . The country where we live is overrun by whites. All our game is gone. . . . If you stop your roads we can get our game" (qtd. in Brown 138). Spotted Tail was complaining specifically about white incursions into the Powder River country; by 1870, after all, the transcontinental railroad had been finished for a year. Building it was not easy, however, partly because, from the time of the Sand Creek massacre of 1864, the Indians of western Nebraska systematically tore up tracks and raided supply wagons carrying building materials (J. Olson 114, 137–38).

The outcome of this struggle was inevitable. The whites were too powerful, and there were too many of them. From less than three thousand settlers in 1854, white Nebraskan population rose to thirty thousand by 1860, fifty thousand by 1867, when Nebraska became a state, and one hundred twenty-five thousand by 1870, the year of Red Cloud's eastern visit, the year that Red Cloud, Nebraska was settled. By 1890, just before the economic depression, drought years and emigration that would characterize the nineties, Nebraska had over one million white settlers, almost all of them first generation pioneers (J. Olson 88).

If, as Governor John Thayer of Nebraska claimed in his inaugural address of 1887, the railroads led to Nebraska's settlement a quarter to half century sooner than might otherwise have been expected (Combs 21), one of the reasons was the aggressive propaganda campaign the railroads waged in Europe to lure immigrants to Nebraska. Moreover, the railroads dictated both settlement patterns and the government policy toward the Indians that made settlement feasible.

In 1865, for example, the southern Cheyenne and Arapaho peoples, displaced by the Colorado Gold Rush (1858) and the ensuing

Sand Creek massacre (1864), met with representatives of the government to negotiate the site for a reservation. The Indians elected the area between the Smoky Hill River in central Kansas and the Republican River—running through what would become Red Cloud—in southern Nebraska. The government denied their request, knowing as they did that the Burlington planned to open this area for settlement and build a railroad there (Brown 96).

The Cheyenne and Arapaho were forced to move to the Oklahoma territory; Red Cloud was established five years later. Though Indians refusing to accept the 1865 treaty had successfully stymied the first attempt to settle the Republican River valley in 1869, and though they periodically disrupted other attempts at settling the region, such as that at Red Willow in 1871, the prospect of a railroad in the valley—and the railroad's ability to provide the people for settlement—encouraged settlers to believe that if they could hold on for a few years, their ventures into the area would prove successful (J. Olson 170–73). The Burlington dutifully built a spur line through the valley, beginning work in 1878. The line was completed by 1882—a year before Cather traveled it, along with countless immigrant families like the Shimmerdas, to Nebraska.

"The real West to Willa Cather," writes Slote, "was the West of settlement, of the immigration of peoples from many parts of the world" (96). It would be misleading to ignore Cather's celebration of these immigrant peoples in novels such as O Pioneers! or My Ántonia. My Ántonia was published in a year of intense xenophobia provoked by the United States government's entry into World War I; on 26 March 1918, Governor Neville of Nebraska successfully engineered the repeal of a law designed to guarantee foreign language instruction in Nebraska's schools as "vicious, undemocratic, and un-American" (J. Olson 265). In this context, Cather's sensitive portrayal and vigorous defense of immigrant peoples such as the Czechs and the Norwegians can and should be seen as the courageous act that it was.

At the same time, however, one must keep in mind Patricia Nelson Limerick's recent admonition that "In race relations, the West could make the turn-of-the-century Northeastern urban confrontation between European immigrants and American nativists look like a family reunion" (27). Without taking anything away from Cather's significant achievement, it is nevertheless true that her conception of western history as the story of immigrant settlers blinded her to the effects of such immigration on the West's native populations. As early as 1852, the Commissioner of Indian Affairs stressed the extent to which Native Americans were suffering "from the vast number of immigrants who pass through their country, destroying their means of support, and scattering disease and death among them" (qtd. in J. Olson 132). Immigration promoted by the railroads was integral to the accelerated pace at which Nebraskan lands were wrested from the Indians and consolidated as white property.

Moreover, it is important to keep in mind exactly which immigrant groups Cather champions. The Bohemian Czechs she foregrounds in both *O Pioneers!* and *My Ántonia* were used throughout World War I by American propagandists to underscore the United States government's commitment to the right of self-determination. The fact that such propaganda and such a commitment might hasten the dissolution of the Hapsburg Empire of which the Czechs were a subject people might also have had something to do with the Wilson Administration's sudden concern for the Czechs' plight.

It is certainly true that Wilson was fundamentally less concerned with such rights throughout Latin America; as Gabriel Kolko has convincingly demonstrated, one of the reasons that the United States decided to go to war was to protect its own assumed right to intervene militarily, economically and politically in the affairs of any Latin American country without interference from Europe (53–54). Wilson "celebrated his doctrine of self-determination," writes Noam Chomsky, "by invading Mexico, Haiti, and the Dominican Republic" (46).

Furthermore, as Kolko asserts, "no American leader favored self-determination for Asians and races they felt inferior"; along with his white allies, Wilson later explicitly rejected a statement on racial equality in the covenant of the League of Nations charter (Kolko 55). When one of those "inferior" Asians approached Wilson's Versailles residence in 1919 begging that the American champion of freedom support the Vietnamese people's right to representation in the French parliament, he was chased away "like a pest." The "pest" was the man who would subsequently be known to history by the name Ho Chi Minh (Chomsky 46).

In this context, Cather's portrait of Ántonia can be read as a text that romanticizes the United States's relationship to non Anglo-Saxon peoples. The Czechs, the most Western and consequently least threatening of the Eastern European peoples toward which the government was willing to extend the promise of self-determination, could serve as an ideological figuration of American tolerance, eliding the racism that characterized the United States's relationship to non-Europeans or to its own Black citizen soldiers, vilified, abused and lynched in alarming numbers following their return from France in 1919.

Mention of the 1919 race riots points toward another of Cather's romantic racial portraits in *My Ántonia*, that of the blind Black piano player, Blind D'Arnault [94]. Gelfant has adequately catalogued the numerous stereotypes of African Americans that enter into Cather's depiction of the man who "looked like some glistening African god of pleasure, full of strong, savage blood" and the "buxom young Negro wench" who was his mother [99, 96; Gelfant 80–82].

The racism in this portrait is obvious; less noticeable, perhaps, is the similarity between the function of this romantic text and the function I have attributed to Cather's presentation of the Czechs. During the American Civil War, the people for whom the federal government was supposedly fighting—and to whom it was promising self-determination—were the African Americans. Nebraska ranked second among the territories in the number of volunteers it gave to the Union cause, and it named its capital after the man who had issued the emancipation proclamation (J. Olson 134, 144). Yet even as the Union was reaffirming its commitment to freedom for all peoples, it was implementing its genocidal policy of expansion in the West. The North's victory at Gettysburg in 1863, long seen in American mythology as a landmark in the advance of freedom, allowed the War Department to send eight companies of cavalry West to the Plains (J. Olson 135). They would participate in the campaign that ended in Chivington's programmed massacre of twenty-eight men and one hundred and five Cheyenne and Arapaho women and children at Sand Creek in 1864. In an example of hypocritical double-speak duplicating that employed during World War I, the United States was proclaiming its racial tolerance even as it was conducting a brutal campaign of race hatred.

One might object that such events "have nothing to do" with *My Ántonia*; they are certainly far removed from Cather's Nebraska world as critics—and Cather—have traditionally described its character and genealogy. As I have attempted to demonstrate, however, that is precisely the point. Recent historians of the West such as Howard Lamar and Limerick have underscored the disparity between "textual" images of the West and the historical West on a host of issues, ranging from the supposed closing of the frontier to the realities of mining operations, from the exploitative nature of the Plains' agrarian economy to the Western myth of rugged individualism. What I am proposing in this essay is that literary critics look equally hard at some of our canonical texts and conventional shibboleths purporting to explain how the West—as well as any other geographical or ideological territory—was "won."

Implicit in any distinction between text and context, story and history, is the assertion that, poststructuralism notwithstanding, some narratives are "truer" than others are. While admitting, as Jane Tompkins does in her own readings of how the American West was won, that we can never transcend narrative and grasp "the real" itself, and while admitting that limitations inevitably accompany the interpretive act, we can still argue that some readings are more accurate than others; as Tompkins argues, "You can show that what someone else asserts to be a fact is false" (76). "One does not," writes Jameson, "have to argue the reality of history: necessity, like Dr. Johnson's stone, does that for us" (82).

Such forces of necessity inevitably preserve the historical realities which a text such as *My Ántonia* initially appears to occlude. They are an integral part of Cather's text, imbricated in the very fabric of her narrative, dialogically interacting with her story. If history and text somehow appear distinct, in Cather's novel and in other "literary" texts, it is less a result of some inherent division between fact and story and more a consequence of our failure to produce readings that elucidate their connection. What such interdisciplinary readings will generate, again and again, is an understanding of the "material out of which countries are made," whereby we learn as much about the original materials—and peoples—that narrative employs as we do about how narrative shapes such "material" for its own ends. Only by way of such approaches can we begin to appreciate the deeper significance of the process of naturalization that is inherent in the symbolic act, as well as the suppression of history that it entails. Only then can we understand why, if we remember Gettysburg, so many of us seem to have forgotten Sand Creek, and why, if we fondly recall Cather's "georgic" portrayal of Nebraska, we seem to have amnesia concerning the people who once lived there.

WORKS CITED

Baltensperger, Bradley H. *Nebraska: A Geography.* London: Westview, 1985.

Bennett, Tony. *Formalism and Marxism.* London: Methuen, 1979.

Brown, Dee. *Bury My Heart at Wounded Knee: An Indian History of the American West.* New York: Washington Square, 1970.

Cather, Willa. *O Pioneers!* Boston: Houghton, 1913.

———. *My Ántonia.* Boston: Houghton, 1926.

———. *Death Comes for the Archbishop.* New York: Modem Library, 1927.

———. "Nebraska: The End of the First Cycle." *The Nation* 117 (1923): 236–38.

———. *The World and the Parish: Willa Cather's Articles and Reviews, 1893–1902.* Ed. William M. Curtin. 2 vols. Lincoln: U of Nebraska P, 1970.

Chomsky, Noam. *Turning the Tide: U.S. Intervention in Central America and the Struggle for Peace.* Boston: South End P, 1985.

Combs, Barry B. "The Union Pacific Railroad and the Early Settlement of Nebraska." *Nebraska History* 50 (1969): 1–26.

Day, A Grove. *Coronado and the Discovery of the Southwest.* New York: Meredith, 1967.

Gelfant, Blanche. "The Forgotten Reaping-Hook: Sex in *My Ántonia.*" *American Literature* 43 (1971): 60–82.

Hammond, George P. *Coronado's Seven Cities.* Albuquerque: United States Coronado Exposition Commission, 1940.

Jameson, Fredric. *The Political Unconscious: Narrative as a Socially Symbolic Act.* Ithaca: Cornell UP, 1981.

Kolko, Gabriel. *Main Currents in Modern American History.* New York: Pantheon, 1984.

Limerick, Patricia Nelson. *The Legacy of Conquest: The Unbroken Past of the American West.* New York: Norton, 1987.

Love, Glen. *New Americans: The Westerner and the Modern Experience in the American Novel.* Lewisburg: Bucknell UP, 1982.

O'Brien, Sharon. *Willa Cather: The Emerging Voice.* New York: Oxford UP, 1987.

Olson, James C. *History of Nebraska.* Lincoln: U of Nebraska P, 1966.

Olson, Paul A. "The Epic and Great Plains Literature: Rolvaag, Cather, and Neihardt." *Prairie Schooner* 55 (1981): 263–85.

Perkey, Elton A. *Perkey's Nebraska Place Names.* Lincoln: Nebraska State Historical Society Publications 28, 1982.

Schwind, Jean. "The Benda Illustrations to *My Ántonia*: Cather's 'Silent' Supplement to Jim Burden's Narrative." *PMLA* 100 (1985): 51–67.

Slote, Bernice. "Willa Cather and Plains Culture." *Vision and Refuge: Essays on the Literature of the Great Plains.* Ed. Virginia Faulkner with Frederick C. Luebke. Lincoln: U of Nebraska P, 1982. 93–105.

Slotkin, Richard. *Regeneration Through Violence: The Mythology of the American Frontier: 1600–1860.* Middletown: Wesleyan UP, 1973.

Stouck, David. "Perspective as Structure and Theme in *My Ántonia.*" *Texas Studies in Language and Literature* 12 (1970): 285–94.

Thomas, A. B. "The Massacre of the Villasur Expedition." *Nebraska History* 7 (1924): 68–81.

Tompkins, Jane. "Indians: Textualism, Morality, and the Problem of History." *"Race," Writing and Difference.* Ed. Henry Louis Gates, Jr. Chicago: U of Chicago P, 1986. 59–77.

Trachtenberg, Alan. *The Incorporation of America: Culture and Society in the Gilded Age.* New York: Hill, 1982.

Udall, Stewart L. *To the Inland Empire: Coronado and Our Spanish Legacy.* New York: Doubleday, 1987.

JANIS STOUT

Coming to America/Escaping to Europe[†]

> Twisting a shoestring noose, a Polack's brat
> Joylessly torments a cat.
> . . . .
> With hate, perhaps, a threat, maybe,
> Lithuania looks at me.
> —"Street in Packingtown"

> "Oh, how high is Caesar's house,
> Brother, big brother?"
> —"The Palatine"

If one of the great themes of *My Ántonia* is gender and the nature of women's lives in the American *polis*, another is the status of the ethnic other, particularly the status of ethnically diverse European immigrants. When Cather reported to her publisher in early 1917 that she had begun a new novel—the earliest trace of her work on *My Ántonia*—she said that it was not the "Blue Mesa" story as expected (material that would later go into *The Professor's House*) but a western story with a background similar to that of *O Pioneers!*[1] She meant, of course, the Nebraska setting and agricultural life that formed the milieu of both books, but she could equally well have been referring to the treatment of immigrant groups. Both *My Ántonia* and *O Pioneers!*—and indeed *The Song of the Lark* as well—convey an affectionate vision of an ethnically diverse America. Susan Rosowski has written that Cather was "the first to give immigrants heroic stature in serious American literature.[2] Yet she did so only within limits whose exclusions reflected those of widespread popular opinion. Focusing primarily on the Scandinavian and Bohemian settlers that she had written about in *O Pioneers!* and a number of short stories, she produced a novel that has been recognized for its re-creation of personal memories, but one that is also deeply engaged with contemporary politics, the debate over immigration.

Cather had earlier been involved in this debate when as managing editor of *McClure's Magazine* she either acceded to or actively

† From *Willa Cather: The Writer and Her World* (Charlottesville: UP of Virginia, 2000), pp. 151–62. © 2000 by the Rectors and Visitors of the University of Virginia. Reprinted by permission of the University of Virginia Press. Page references to *My Ántonia* are to this Norton Critical Edition. The epigraphs are from poems by Cather.
1. WC to R. L. Scaife, 8 March 1917; Harvard Library bMS Am 1925 (341).
2. Susan J. Rosowski, *The Voyage Perilous: Willa Cather's Romanticism* (Lincoln: U of Nebraska P, 1986), p. 45.

participated in the publication of a series of articles written by
fellow editor and *McClure's* staffwriter George Kibbe Turner,
which expressed bitter hostility toward certain immigrant groups,
specifically Italians and Jews. It might seem surprising that *McClure's*
would pursue an exclusionist editorial policy, since McClure himself was a member of a once-despised immigrant group, the Irish. By
the early twentieth century that prejudice had considerably diminished; in Noel Ignatiev's terms, the Irish had become white; and
McClure, now simply an American and carrying the cachet of the
successful self-made man, joined the chorus of suspicion toward
later-arriving groups.[3] Both he and Cather (whether actively or by
co-optation) became participants in the public outcry that culmi-
nated in the Immigration Act of 1924, a law that, as Walter Benn
Michaels writes, "brought to an end the tradition of unrestricted
European immigration" and made "eligibility for American citizenship . . . dependent upon ethnic identity."[4]

Turner's articles, one of the "muckraking" series for which
McClure's was known, were directed at exposure of urban corruption but repeatedly targeted Italians and Jews, which were the two
most disfavored immigrant groups. By calling Italians a source of
social disorder, Turner identified them with a bête noire of Progressive public spirit, and his labeling of Jews as a "new Oriental population" linked them with a group long subjected to exclusionary
measures (Michaels 144, n. 13).[5] Cather would reinforce that linkage in "Scandal" (1919), describing a Jewish character as looking
"Mongolian."[6]

In "The Daughters of the Poor," in November 1909, Turner named
Jews as the masterminds of organized prostitution in New York,
charging that "Jewish commercial acumen"—a familiar stereotype—
had developed prostitution "to great proportions" and thereby promoted corruption in the political power structure. By seizing on the
folklore of "the licentious or lascivious Jew," he presented the Jewish
male to the public imagination as an "amalgam of sexual and political power, perverting gentile bodies and the body politic with a
single gesture."[7] (Miles Orvell points out that in *The American Scene,*

3. On Irish immigration and assimilation, see Noel Ignatiev, *How the Irish Became White*
  (New York: Routledge, 1995). It is significant that the biography of McClure written by
  his son-in-law, Peter Lyon, is entitled *Success Story.*
4. Walter Benn Michaels, *Our America: Nativism, Modernism, and Pluralism* (Durham, N.C.:
  Duke UP, 1995), p. 30.
5. The Chinese Exclusion Act of 1882 was "the first law that prohibited the entry of immigrants on the basis of nationality"; see Ronald T. Takaki, *A Different Mirror: A History
  of Multicultural America* (Boston: Little, Brown & Co., 1993), pp. 7–8.
6. Willa Cather, *Youth and the Bright Medusa*, in *Stories, Poems, and Other Writings*, ed.
  Sharon O'Brien (New York: Library of America, 1992), p. 166.
7. Jonathan Freedman, "Angels, Monsters, and Jews: Intersections of Queer and Jewish
  Identity in Kushner's *Angels in America,*" *PMLA* 113 (1998): 90–102.

only two years earlier, Henry James, always a useful comparator with Cather, had described the Jewish masses of New York's Lower East Side by reference to "innumerable fish, of over-developed proboscis."[8]) In the May 1910 number Turner referred to "a pawnbroker named Mose Levish" as the "commanding genius" of vice in Des Moines,[9] while Burton J. Hendrick, identified as the author of "The Great Jewish Invasion," attributed to the "average Russian Hebrew" a range of "sufferings" physical, moral, and "psychical."[1] The anti-Semitic note was being struck repeatedly in the magazine's pages.

Probably of greater significance as a clue to Cather's thinking was an editorial that appeared at the back of the November 1909 issue, a diatribe of ethnic hostility bearing the name of McClure himself. Given the frequency with which Cather spoke for McClure in conducting business for the magazine and the fact that she would later assume his voice in the ghostwritten *Autobiography*, it is entirely possible that she either wrote or revised the article herself. Neither this nor her more general role in the involvement of *McClure's* in slurring Jews and Italians is by any means clear.[2] Quite apart from the question of authorship, we cannot take this article lightly, knowing as we do from the comments of her contemporaries as well as her own letters how greatly Cather admired McClure.

In keeping with his interest in German society during those years (according to a letter written by Cather in 1911, he regarded it as greatly superior to that of the United States),[3] McClure's article credited the "Germanic races" with having "built up slowly and laboriously, the present civilization of the West" that "now lifts the whole

8. Miles Orvell, *After the Machine: Visual Arts and the Erasing of Cultural Boundaries* (Jackson: U of Mississippi P, 1995), pp. 48–50.
9. George Kibbe Turner, "Tammany's Control of New York by Professional Criminals," *McClure's* 33.2 (June 1909): 117–34.
1. Burton J. Hendrick, "The Skulls of Our Immigrants," *McClure's* 35.1 (May 1910): 36–50; see p. 47. "The Daughters of the Poor" is not so totalizing as Freedman would seem to indicate. So far is Turner from branding Jews as the sole perpetrators that he names other ethnic groups as co-offenders and insists that the "Jewish church" has "fought" the prostitution ring "with all its power." But this semblance of evenhandedness is in fact specious; the series as a whole is virulently anti-Semitic. Its hostility to Jewish immigrants may reflect public reaction to a huge labor strike in the New York garment industry in 1909 by predominantly Jewish female shirtwaist workers; see Takaki (293–97). In the same year, 1909, the *Survey* published an article on Slavic immigrants that similarly reinforced prejudices against immigrants by referring to the Slavs' "widely recognized vices" and calling them "as dumb as horses" (Orvell 48–50). The fact that such nativist articles were appearing in one of the country's leading magazines in 1909–10 gives reason to question Guy Reynolds's claim that the years 1916–18 saw the issue of Americanization "usurped by nativism" (Guy Reynolds, *Willa Cather in Context: Progress, Race, Empire* [Basingstoke: Macmillan, 1996], p. 73).
2. Conflicted feelings toward the editorial policy in which she participated may have contributed to the strain that drove Cather to take a long leave of absence in 1912. She referred to it as irritability on the job; WC to S. S. McClure, June 12 [1912], Indiana. In 1911 she complained to Elsie Sergeant that she was tired of another reformer's (i.e., other than Turner) obsession with white slavery; WC to Elizabeth Shepley Sergeant, prob. June 4, 1911, J. Pierpont Morgan Library, New York City.
3. WC to Hugo Munsterberg, May 13, 1911, Boston Public Library.

race above barbarism and bestiality." The "great masses of primitive peoples from the farms of Europe" pouring into American cities, he warned, constituted a threat to that civilization. Commending as "competent" the judgment of a trustee of the City Vigilance League that "'a fraternity of fetid male vermin (nearly all of them being Russian or Polish Jews)'" were managing vice, McClure went on to denounce the impunity of murderers among "the Italians of New York." The "northwestern countries of Europe," he proclaimed, were the "only nations worthy of comparison with the United States in their civilization."[4]

These same northwestern countries were, for the most part, the source of the immigrant culture Cather depicts in *O Pioneers!* and *My Ántonia*. The celebrated ethnic variety of Jim Burden's experience in Nebraska, reflecting Cather's own, is not *too* various. The immigrants who stir his affection are like himself not only in being newcomers but also in being white—a term that then meant not only not-black but also not-Italian, not-Asian, not-Jewish.[5] Besides reflecting personal memories, Cather's tributes to Nebraska's immigrants reflect fairly accurately the prevailing preferences in the United States at the time at which she was writing. They also reflect the actual demographic makeup of Nebraska's Divide at the time the story takes place—or actually, reflect it with one major exception. That exception, I believe, is tied up with the wartime context in which she was working—a topic to which I will return and one that links *Ántonia* with the novel that would follow it, *One of Ours*.

We know that Cather took a strong interest in the human variety she encountered when her family moved from the stable society of Virginia's Blue Ridge to the Nebraska prairie. She later reminisced about times spent in kitchens with old women who spoke little English but understood her homesickness and gave her "the real feeling of an older world across the sea."[6] From her first published story she showed an interest in the fictional possibilities of such groups and in *O Pioneers!* gave warm treatment to the industry and folkways of Swedish, Norwegian, Bohemian, and Acadian French settlers. The life of Jim Burden, in some ways her autobiographical double, gains interest and vitality from the presence of Danes, Norwegians, Russians, an Austrian, and again (significantly) Bohemians.

4. S. S. McClure, "The Tammanyizing of a Civilization," *McClure's* 34.1 (Nov. 1909): 117–18, 125.
5. Joseph Urgo's preference for "locating larger patterns of significance" rather than "differentiat[ing]" among the experiences of distinct immigrant groups (Joseph R. Urgo, *Willa Cather and the Myth of American Migration* [Urbana: U of Illinois P, 1995], p. 64) produces admirable conceptual synthesis, but there were real differences in the ways in which different groups were received.
6. L. Brent Bohlke, *Willa Cather in Person: Interviews, Speeches, and Letters* (Lincoln: U of Nebraska P, 1990), p. 10.

One reason Jim is so ready to establish friendly relations with these varied neighbors is that they are, like himself, newcomers. A Virginian trying to learn to think of Nebraska as home, Jim can feel that his sense of displacement is shared, as intermittent loneliness and homesickness provide a common, if unspoken, language. Another reason is that he associates these neighbors with the earth and nurturance, just as he does Ántonia herself, whose eyes are like "the sun shining on brown pools in the wood" [19]. Many years later, he views her in her final apotheosis amid a riot of vegetal and animal life, jars and jars of preserved food, and kolaches baked by the dozen. Ántonia's kitchen recalls Grandmother Burden's, a uterine center of consolation where he had been fed and immersed in warm bathwater as a child. This association of Bohemians with primal essences of earth and food was one that Cather made in her own voice as well, writing exultantly about vacation weeks spent in the Bohemian country during wheat harvest, when the whole countryside smelled like bread baking.[7]

It is this autobiographical context that is usually invoked in discussions of Cather's vision of frontier immigrants—a context that is, to be sure, both interesting and important. Accordingly, the novel was long read as a nostalgic celebration of the past and an escape from current issues. But more is at issue here than her affection for people who eased her transition to a new land or her delight in distinctive customs brought from Europe. Just as a glow of nostalgic affirmation disguises problematics of gender and what I take to be Cather's desire to subvert traditional assumptions about women's lives, so does a nimbus of personal affection blur her participation in the widespread public concern about immigration.[8] My Ántonia was, in fact, very much a novel of its time, responding both to the war then devastating Europe and to a contemporary discourse about "hyphenated Americans."

The impact of wartime makes itself felt in Ántonia in a variety of ways: in an awareness of the vulnerability of peace and a tone of nostalgia for a more innocent time (a factor that would later contribute to Cather's enthusiasm for Oliver LaFarge's Pulitzer Prize novel of Navajo life, Laughing Boy, which also reaches back toward a time before the disillusionment of the war) but also in the novel's de-emphasis on German immigrants in Nebraska in favor of Bohemians. To be sure, there were compelling biographical reasons. Bohemian settlers did live near the Cather ranch, and after the family moved into Red Cloud the young Willa did come to know Annie Sadilek,

7. WC to Elizabeth Shepley Sergeant, July 5 [1912], Virginia; and WC to Annie Adams Fields, June 27, 1912, Huntington.
8. Reynolds (73–78) usefully places My Ántonia in the context of the popular debate over immigration and assimilation.

the model for Ántonia, who worked as a domestic for her friends the Miners. Even so, in singling out Nebraska's Bohemians, Scandinavians, and even (despite their small numbers) Russians, she obscured the fact that Germans were by far the largest single group of immigrants in the area.[9] By 1916, when she was writing *My Ántonia*, these German immigrants were being subjected to intense suspicion of disloyalty, while Germany itself was being demonized as a warmonger.

Cather stood in relation to popular attitudes toward Germans and German culture very much as Jim Burden stands in relation to people in Black Hawk who look down on immigrants. Just as Jim is more enlightened than his prejudiced schoolmates who think of them as "ignorant . . . foreigners" [*MA* 103], so Cather was more enlightened than those of her contemporaries who suspended the production of German operas in New York or demanded that the teaching of the German language be dropped from schools.[1] In a 1921 speech in Omaha she mocked the foolishness of aggressive "Americanization" that eradicates ethnic customs and language learning (Bohlke 147). By then, to be sure, the war fervor that provided a powerful incentive to de-emphasize Germans in her portrayal of the human patchwork of Nebraska had dissipated.

If it is fairly clear why Cather avoided the presence of Germans in writing *My Ántonia*, her reason for favoring the Bohemians, or Czechs, is less obvious. But that, too, is traceable to wartime politics. The Czechs were "the most Western and consequently least threatening of the Eastern European peoples toward which the government was willing to extend the promise of self-determination," a promise much vaunted by Woodrow Wilson in his war aims.[2] Cather's emphasis on the Bohemians in *My Ántonia*, then, accords not only with the ethnic preferences we have seen in the *McClure's* discourse on immigration but with what was essentially a wartime stance taken for propaganda purposes. The Czechs served as a useful "ideological figuration of American tolerance, eliding the racism that characterized the United States's relationship to non-Europeans" or, indeed, its own nonwhite citizens (Fischer 42).

9. Robert W. Cherny reports that in 1890 Germans comprised 37.6% of all immigrant Nebraskans, Swedes 12.1%, Irish 10.8%, Czechs (Bohemians) 7.8%, English 6.6%, Danes 5.7%. In Webster County, out of a population of 11,210 there were 550 Germans, 191 English, 184 Canadians (some French, some English), 105 Bohemians, and 84 Swedes. See Robert W. Cherney, "Willa Cather's Nebraska," *Approaches to Teaching Cather's My Ántonia*, ed. Susan J. Rosowski (New York: Modern Language Association, 1989), pp. 32–33.
1. WC to Carrie Miner, March 13, 1918, Willa Cather Pioneer Memorial, Red Cloud, Nebraska. See also Peter Sullivan, "Willa Cather's German People and Their Heritage," *The Mower's Tree: Newsletter of the Cather Colloquium* (Spring 1999): 10–11.
2. Mike Fischer, "Pastoralism and Its Discontents: Willa Cather and the Burden of Imperialism," *Mosaic* 23 (1990): 31–44; see p. 41.

Domestic racism, another aspect of the general culture in which Cather participated, also disrupts *Ántonio's* celebration of inclusiveness. It does so in two ways, by presence and by absence: the presence of the African American other, objectified as being at once exotic and freakish, and the novel's silence or near silence with respect to the Native population that was displaced by newly arrived migrants and immigrants alike. Both of these disruptions of inclusiveness are intertwined with the novel's response to the European other.

The stigmatizing of African Americans enters the novel in the person of Blind d'Arnault, a traveling pianist who comes to Black Hawk to appear at the hotel. Depicted in denigrating caricature, he is described as having a "negro head . . . almost no head at all; nothing behind the ears but folds of neck under close-clipped wool"— that is, a head that implies mindlessness. As stereotype would have it, he is all rhythm, "happy" and governed by "sensations"; playing his "barbarous" piano, he "enjoy[s] himself as only a negro can" [*MA* 98]. This last phrase, with its demarcating "only," places Blind d'Arnault in a category defined solely by race while it privileges the speaker as a person whose ground of superiority—not belonging to the category negro—qualifies him to understand the behavior of the subordinate other and make pronouncements on it. We cannot suppose this positioning was Cather's conscious intention. But neither does she indicate any disavowal of Jim's perspective at this point. Moreover, the reader who knows even a little about the original from which she took this portrait—Thomas Greene Bethune, a blind savant piano player born into slavery in 1849 whose performance she reviewed in 1894—realizes that the only way "a negro" can enjoy himself with such abandon is by denial of his exploitation by whites. The Bethune family (his former owners) who managed Blind Tom's concert appearances from about 1860 until 1904 had charge of all the money he brought in.[3]

Disruptive as this caricature is of Cather's semblance of an ethnically diverse America, the shadow of the displaced Indian that falls across her midwestern and southwestern novels is perhaps even more disturbing, for the simple reason that Indians were in fact a far more numerous presence there. To ignore them and to ignore the history of their displacement in novels that avow their historical foundation is a major distortion. Cather can well be seen as the lyrical voice of

3. The "abominable" quality Jim Burden senses in Blind d'Arnault's playing may have to do with Jim's inability to deal with his own sexual feelings; the pianist's approach to his instrument is described in sexually laden terms as a kind of coupling. I am indebted for this insight to my student Erin Frazier (see John Marsh, *A Reader's Companion to the Fiction of Willa Cather*, ed. Marilyn Arnold [Westport, Conn.: Greenwood, 1993], pp. 198–200). A similar performer called "Blind Boone" who played in Red Cloud several times may also have been a model for d'Arnault.

Manifest Destiny. In *O Pioneers!* she takes unalloyed satisfaction in the transforming of the prairie into agricultural land, and in *My Ántonia*, adopting the comforting theory of an empty land awaiting settlement, she sees through Jim Burden's eyes "nothing but land: not a country at all, but the material out of which countries are made" [*MA* 12].[4] Jim feels "outside man's jurisdiction." But this can be true only if the Sioux or Lakota people recently displaced from the Nebraska prairies are defined as not-human—as indeed they are in *O Pioneers!* when Cather writes with reference to Alexandra that "for the first time, perhaps, since that land emerged from the waters of geologic ages, a *human face* was set toward it with love."[5]

Cather has been castigated for her fictional erasure of the Native presence by Mike Fischer, who reminds us that as recently as 1868, only five years before members of the Cather family began to arrive in southern Nebraska, Chief Red Cloud held a war council "aimed at expelling white settlers from the lands north of the Platte River" that had been guaranteed to his people. The town of Red Cloud, established in 1870 at the very time when Chief Red Cloud was in Washington completing a treaty that supposedly guaranteed the Oglalla Sioux possession of the Black Hills in perpetuity, was "the first permanent town in what had been one of the Indians' last buffalo hunting grounds south of the Platte" (32–34). Fischer's point is that the Sioux presence had ended so shortly before her family's arrival that Cather must have been aware of it and that her virtual erasure of them is a knowing one. But in fact he understates the case. The Indians were still very much in evidence when her uncle George P. Cather and his wife, Frances, arrived. In a letter written in 1876 to his sister Virginia Cather Ayre, G. P. Cather reported that about two hundred Omahas passed in sight of his homestead the previous week.[6] The silent procession of this sizable band across the horizon enacts the vanishing of the Vanishing American, a phenomenon in which Americans of the late nineteenth and early twentieth centuries wanted very much to believe and a phenomenon that is very much at work in Cather's writing.

4. Takaki (27–35) demonstrates the continuity of colonialist aggression by showing how English settlement of Ireland was justified not only by the claimed savagery of the Irish people but by the vacancy of the land. The "void" left by the English slaughter of Irish people "meant vacant lands for English resettlement." Even Sir Thomas More used as a rationale for English colonization of Ireland the "fact" that "the natives did not 'use' the soil but left it 'idle and waste.'" A similar rationale was used after World War II for the takeover of land occupied by the Palestinians in the creation of the modern state of Israel.
5. Willa Cather, *O Pioneers!*: 1913. Willa Cather Scholarly Edition, ed. Susan J. Rosowski and Charles W. Mignon, with Kathleen Danker (Lincoln: U of Nebraska P, 1992), p. 64, emphasis added.
6. George P. Cather to Jennie Cather Ayre, March 17, 1876, Nebraska Historical Society Newspapers. Jennie Cather Ayre, a younger sister of Charles Cather and thus an aunt of the infant Willa, died of tuberculosis shortly after moving to Nebraska.

The phrase "Vanishing American" is itself misleading, of course, since the Indians did not simply vanish; the process was not nearly so innocuous as that. But the notion became widely accepted because it so soothed the national conscience. Belief that the Indians were vanishing and all trace of their languages and way of life would soon be lost paved the way for an intense anthropological interest toward the end of the century. It also made the Indian readily available for romanticizing. The naming of the town of Red Cloud was an episode in that process. Cather demonstrated her awareness of the outlines of the historic presence of the Sioux in a 1913 interview in which she stated that her hometown was "named after the old Indian chief who used to come hunting in that country, and who buried his daughter on the top of one of the river bluffs south of the town" (Bohlke 9). But her language evades the reality of Indian life by making it sound as if the frequenting of the southern Nebraska hunting range was occasional and individual, rather like a vacation trip, and sentimentalizes it by focusing on a story of a dead child. She noted in an article in the 1923 *Nation* that west of Lincoln "the tall red grass and the buffalo and the Indian hunter were undisturbed" before 1860 (Cherney 236–38).

Cather's renaming of Red Cloud as Black Hawk in *My Ántonia* is a parallel act of nostalgic tribute to the vanished American chief who in the 1830s had led the last Indian War east of the Mississippi and whose "autobiography" was, in Fischer's words, "one of the first texts in the nineteenth-century cult of nostalgia that would increasingly come to surround white perceptions of Native American peoples" (35).[7] Her nod at the history of European expansion into the plains is equally sentimentalizing. When Jim tells Ántonia, Lena, and Tiny about his belief that Coronado ventured as far north as Nebraska, he makes it a story of heroic relics and the conquistador's broken heart, occluding the fact of aggression [*MA* 122]. A small and significantly female countervoice is heard in the girls' demurral that "'more than him'" has died in the wilderness of a broken heart.

The vanishing of the Native American people was only too real, however, and was directly tied in with one of the most recurrent presences in Cather's work, the railroad. Since the railroad was also one of the most powerful forces in the process of immigration into the Midwest, it serves as a direct link between the presence of the immigrants Cather celebrated and the absence, both from the plains and from her work, of Indians. Railroads such as the Burlington, the

7. Fischer (35) suggests that Cather was probably acquainted with the "mythological" Black Hawk through his Anglo-written "autobiography" and summarizes Richard Slotkin's argument that "as the Indian threat decreased . . . the nostalgic impulse toward the Indians increased" (Richard Slotkin, *Regeneration Through Violence: The Mythology of the American Frontier: 1600–1860* [Middletown: Wesleyan University Press, 1973]).

system that ran through Red Cloud and on to Denver, were among the primary forces that caused that vanishing. Cather herself arrived on the Burlington, as do Jim Burden and the immigrating Shimerdas in *My Ántonia*. The railroads, in particular the Santa Fe, participated in promoting the ideology of the Vanishing American through the artworks they sponsored showing lone Indians, "dignified but aloof," whose eyes "stare vacantly into the distance" at what might well be "a vision of the coming white man."[8] The building of the railroads, of course, was accomplished largely through a vast transfer of public lands (in other words, land that sustained the Native populations) to private hands. Through the gift of these lands, which they then sold to settlers or speculators, the railroads were able to build up vast reservoirs of capital used to construct track and purchase rolling stock, and the settlers who took up the land and established farms and businesses became the railroads' customers as they purchased goods shipped in from the East and sent their agricultural products out to market. It was a system that worked quite efficiently to develop the rail system across the country, enrich a small number of investors, and deprive Indians of their way of life and means of survival. Not only did settlers come to possess land that had provided game for the Indians' sustenance, but their clearing of land as they plowed and planted destroyed necessary habitats and disrupted migration patterns of game even as trains brought in professional hunters who took buffalo hides and left the carcasses to rot or passengers who shot the great animals for pleasure.

To the extent that she idealizes the railroad, Cather is endorsing this process. But in *My Ántonia* it is not entirely obvious whether she is idealizing the railroad or not. The train by which Jim arrives in Nebraska, which also brings the Shimerdas, is endowed with a glow of nostalgia and adventure through its association not only with the start of their glowing story but with the much bemedaled and pinned conductor and the book Jim reads on the way, "Life of Jesse James." Ironically, the real Jesse James was a robber of railroads whose hostility had been aroused by the exploitative ways of their land operations. Moreover, the notion of the West that Jim gleans from reading about this often-heroized gunman is quickly debunked, as the West he experiences is not so much a place of derring-do as of homebuilding.[9] Even before this ambiguous appearance of Jim's train ride to Nebraska and his childhood notions, railroad heroism has already been brought into question in the prologue, where we

8. See Chris Wilson, *The Myth of Santa Fe: Creating a Modern Regional Tradition* (Albuquerque: University of New Mexico Press, 1997), pp. 89–92, on boosterism by the Santa Fe Railway.

9. Cather contests conventions of the popular Western by redefining it in terms of domesticity and female authority, much as Mary Austin had in precedents of which she was keenly aware.

meet the adult Jim Burden before we meet the child. We learn that he grows up to become an attorney for the Burlington but gets no satisfaction from his incessant traveling, which is undertaken at least in part to escape an unhappy marriage. Instead, he turns for satisfaction to his nostalgic and reconstructive imagination of Ántonia.

Another way in which the railroad is significant in *Ántonia* is its promotion of a false lure. In order to sell their vast land holdings and thereby bring in both immediate cash revenue and long-term customers, railroads advertised aggressively throughout the United States and in Europe. Directly or indirectly, it was in response to such advertising that people like the Shimerdas came, expecting a far more comfortable home than they actually found. Essentially, the railroads ensnared such people with false promises. It may be no coincidence, then, that the man who lures Ántonia away with him under false promises of marriage and leaves her pregnant is a railroad man. It is not that Cather overtly opposes the railroad to the interests of her immigrant characters in *My Ántonia*, any more than she opposes railroads to the well-being of Indians. The linkage I am proposing remained an undercurrent until she brought it nearer the surface in *A Lost Lady*, five years later. On the other hand, her sympathetic identification with the immigrants pouring into Nebraska over the recently built Burlington is overt. The fear expressed by Jim's traveling companion Jake, that they bring diseases, is patently set up as a straw man to be knocked over by Jim's—and the novel's—perception of Ántonia's liveliness and innate goodness. However objectionable Mrs. Shimerda and Ambrosch may seem at times (in class-linked ways associated with cultural patterns not understood by the native-born Burdens), Ántonia and her gracious father are always affirmed. So, to a less personalized extent, are the other Bohemian and Scandinavian characters.

It is surely true that Cather wrote about "a greater variety of European peoples than many of her contemporaries" and that she regarded them with "attentive sympathy (Reynolds 81). She was, in fact, *too* sympathetic to suit some readers. Historian Frederick Jackson Turner, growling about the "stress" that Cather and certain other writers placed on "the non-English stocks" in the Midwest, assured the daughter of Burlington railway builder and executive Charles Elliott Perkins that the "constructive work of the men of means, bankers, railway builders, etc. will also be recognised again after the present criticism of all things American has died down."[1] Cather herself, in fact, "recognised" the work of such men, though in a possibly duplicitous way, in *A Lost Lady*, only a year before Turner wrote.

1. Ray Allen Billington, ed., *"Dear Lady": The Letters of Frederick Jackson Turner and Alice Forbes Perkins Hooper, 1910–1932* (San Marino, Calif.: Huntington Library, 1970), p. 365.

Cather's sympathetic, even celebratory attitude toward immigrants was extended, however, within a narrowly selective range of ethnic origins and a hierarchical vision in which immigrants were marked—perhaps inevitably, given the economic plight they generally encountered—as lower class. In spite of Jim's easy fondness for Ántonia and the significantly undifferentiated Bohemian Marys and Danish laundry girls, a fondness that was clearly Cather's own, it is patently evident that they are all assigned positions of menial labor while the native-born hold themselves superior. Even Jim's kindly grandparents see the Shimerdas, who seek to establish the kind of seigneurial relationship they had experienced in Europe, as a source of amusement, and in general the immigrant groups are viewed most positively when they show that they know their place. Worse, the boys and men of Black Hawk use immigrant girls as a supply of convenient sex, implying no responsibility. A steady turnover of hired girls is generated by the regularity with which they have to withdraw to their parents' farms to bear the babies of their employers or employers' sons, who for all their infatuation with these strongly bodied young women firmly expect to marry "Black Hawk girls" [MA 103]. Being a girl and living in Black Hawk does not, it seems, make one a Black Hawk girl any more than living in America and having American citizenship made one, in the view of nativist polemicists, an American (Michaels 9). The immigrant girls are present and they are liked, but they are not equal.

Even Jim, who congratulates himself on his superior social vision, clearly realizes that he is destined for better things. Ántonia's warning to him not to "go and get mixed up with the Swedes" [MA 113] is scarcely needed; he leaves for the university and an upper-middle-class life at the first opportunity. When he later assures Ántonia that he'd "have liked to have [her] for a sweetheart, or a wife, or my mother or my sister—anything that a woman can be to a man" [MA 156], we know that he is indulging false retrospective illusions. Cather would later tell a reader that Jim was never in love with Ántonia.[2] His statement that she is "'really . . . a part of me'" is America's assertion of its (selective) absorption of European peoples in the melting-pot process that denied their separate identities and value.

If Jim's appropriative claiming of Ántonia as part of himself is an ironically self-delusive assertion of love, Cather's similarly loving statement that Ántonia had embodied all her feelings about the early immigrants to the Great Plains would seem to have been far more ingenuous. Her faithful support of Annie Sadilek Pavelka's family and others during the Great Depression, when many of them faced real want and were in danger of losing their farms, indicates a

2. WC to Mr. Glick, Jan. 21, 1925; transcription by E. K. Brown, Beinecke.

lasting and generous affection. It is the very warmth and apparent genuineness of those feelings (albeit a warmth exercised, as years went on, very much from a distance) that make all the more startling some of her later pronouncements on the presence of the foreign-born. In letters of the late 1930s she began to complain about "brassy young Jews and Greeks," dreadful New York University graduates whose behavior was as foreign as their names.[3] In *Ántonia* she had seemed to delight in foreign names and manners and in families who kept their languages and their customs. In her October 1921 speech in Omaha she had praised differentness itself (Bohlke 46–52). Such receptiveness to diverse others had eroded by the time she wrote to Sinclair Lewis in 1938 deploring America's historic willingness to admit outsiders, whom she had come to regard as ruffians and simpletons. But when we take a longer view of her response to ethnic otherness, and when we look closely at its limitations, it is not clear that her vision of American inclusiveness had ever been quite so simple as it may at first seem in *My Ántonia*.[4]

* * *

MARILEE LINDEMANN

"It Ain't My Prairie": Gender, Power, and Narrative in *My Ántonia*[†]

For years I avoided working on Cather's *My Ántonia* because I was distracted and annoyed by the insipidness of its narrator, Jim Burden. The novel Cather claimed as her favorite struck me as either a failed experiment in point of view or a successful but not always interesting exploration of the mind of a man incapable of understanding women. Rethinking the novel recently, however, I have embraced a more positive version of the latter view, as Jim's failures have come to seem spectacular and endlessly fascinating, the critical point of

---

3. WC to Carrie Miner Sherwood, Jan. 27, 1934, Willa Cather Pioneer Memorial, Red Cloud, Nebraska. James Woodress, *Willa Cather: A Literary Life* (Lincoln and London: U of Nebraska P, 1987), p. 473, quoting WC to Ferris Greenslet, March 8, 1936, Harvard bMS Am 1925 (341), folder 19. WC to Zoë Akins, Oct. 28, 1937, Huntington. Cather shared the alarm of "elite universities" in the 1920s about "the increasing numbers of Jewish students," toward whom they directed "new admissions criteria . . . to curb their enrollment" (Takaki 11).

4. WC to Sinclair Lewis, Jan. 14, 1938, Beinecke. Among critics who have contested simplistic readings of the novel, see Sally Allen McNall on regarding it as a site for considering social and cultural complexities (Sally Allen McNall, "Immigrant Backgrounds to *My Ántonia*: 'A Curious Social Situation in Black Hawk.'" In *Approaches to Teaching My Ántonia* [New York: Modern Language Association, 1989], pp. 22–30).

† From Sharon O'Brien, ed., *New Essays on* My Ántonia (New York: Cambridge UP, 1999), pp. 111–35. Copyright © 1999 Cambridge University Press. Reprinted with the permission of Cambridge University Press.

the novel and not a sign of its flaws. My reassessment has been shaped as much by political events and the cultural climate of the 1990s as by the provocative body of feminist critical study of *My Ántonia* that has developed in the past twenty years. Indeed, Jim Burden now strikes me as the narrative equivalent of the Senate Judiciary Committee listening in the fall of 1991 to Professor Anita Hill's testimony about Supreme Court nominee Clarence Thomas, an event that has resonated throughout the political culture of the U.S. for much of the decade. On Capitol Hill, a woman speaks, but the all-male committee's power to interpret and pass judgment upon her speaking is, at least in the short run, of much greater consequence. For the senators, those interpretations are determined by a range of competing and often peculiar demands, including political expediency, the ideological pressures created by race and gender differences, and even the sexual histories of individual senators. Individually and collectively, the committee members shape, reshape, and misshape "their" Anita Hills—as a professionally ambitious backstabber, a psychologically unbalanced sexual fantasist, a politically motivated perjurer, or a well-intentioned martyr whose allegations of sexual harassment (largely because of the committee's own bungling) came too late and under circumstances too bizarre to change the outcome of the confirmation process. Thus, in the movement from testimony to judgment to media melodrama, the speaking woman is less subject than object, at once a construction of male powers and desires, the screen upon which they are projected, and the field within which they are interpreted.[1]

The distance between Jim Burden and committee chairman Joe Biden (and, at certain mean-spirited points in his narrative, between Jim Burden and the prosecutorial Arlen Specter) does not to me seem

---

1. The Hill-Thomas fiasco has spawned a veritable industry of analysis and interpretation from a wide range of perspectives. For a sampling of these analyses, see Toni Morrison, ed., *Race-ing Justice, En-Gendering Power: Essays on Anita Hill, Clarence Thomas, and the Social Construction of Reality* (New York: Pantheon Books, 1992), and Robert Chrisman and Robert L. Allen, eds., *Court of Appeal: The Black Community Speaks Out on the Racial and Sexual Politics of Clarence Thomas vs. Anita Hill* (New York: Ballantine Books, 1992). Paul Simon, a Democratic senator from Illinois and member of the Judiciary Committee, brings an insider's perspective and a sense of history to his analysis in *Advice & Consent: Clarence Thomas, Robert Bork and the Intriguing History of the Supreme Court Nomination Battles* (Washington: National Press Books, 1992), while Timothy M. Phelps and Helen Winternitz write as political journalists in *Capitol Games: Clarence Thomas, Anita Hill, and the Story of a Supreme Court Nomination* (New York: Hyperion, 1992).

The contest over the public meaning of the Hill-Thomas hearings obviously continued long after Thomas was confirmed to the court, and Hill and her supporters may claim a victory of sorts in the results of the 1992 elections: The president who nominated Thomas was himself defeated, and record numbers of women were elected to public office in what the media deemed "the year of the woman" in American politics. It might also be argued that the vilification of First Lady Hillary Rodham Clinton can be partly ascribed to what I would call the Anita Hill effect—i.e., a backlash against women who appear too "aggressive" in their claims to public, discursive power. What concerns me here, however, is the imbalance of rhetorical power between Professor Hill and the Senators that mattered so much in the short run.

great, and the resemblances between "his" Ántonia and the Judiciary
Committee's Anita Hill(s) have helped rekindle my interest in
Cather's novel by suggesting that Jim's narrative is as racked by ideological pressures and discursive uncertainties as the transcripts of the
Senate hearings. After all, Jim is, like most of the senators, a lawyer,
and he presents his "account" of Ántonia to the unnamed speaker in
the Introduction—whom I will, following Jean Schwind, designate
"Cather"[2]—in a "legal portfolio."[3] He is also, like them, beset by conflicts and contradictions: endowed with a romantic disposition that
seems at odds with the cool logic of the lawyer; passionate about
the prairie country of his youth but stuck for the most part in New
York; in love not with his handsome wife but with his memory of a
Bohemian girl. Finally, as "Cather" makes clear, Ántonia functions
for Jim much as Anita Hill functioned for the inept yet powerful
senators—that is, not as an autonomous subject but as a symbol or
screen. In his narrative she serves not as a "character" in the novelistic, psychologically complex sense but as a "central figure" who
"mean[s]" for Jim (and for "Cather") "the country, the conditions, the
whole adventure of our childhood" (Intro). Her purpose is neither
to speak nor to act but merely to "mean." "I had lost sight of her altogether," remarks "Cather," "but Jim had found her again after long
years" (Intro). Ántonia is a symbol to be decoded, an object to be
"lost," "found," named, and claimed: "My Ántonia." Jim's claiming
of Ántonia is both rhetorical and ideological and it poses a range of
challenges to feminist readers of the novel. In what follows I will
explore the significance of his claim, both to the text he narrates
and to the career of Willa Cather.

Feminist criticism has in an important sense reinvented Cather
in recent years, contributing significantly to reversing the decanon-
ization of the Pulitzer Prize-winning novelist that occurred during
the 1930s and 1940s.[4] Her contemporary recanonization is largely
the result of feminism creating an entirely new context for reading
Cather and thus a new climate of reception for her works. Though

2. Jean Schwind, "The Benda Illustrations to *My Ántonia*: Cather's 'Silent' Supplement to
   Jim Burden's Narrative," *PMLA* 100 (January 1985): 51–67. I use this designation chiefly
   for the sake of convenience and retain the quotation marks to distinguish Cather the
   person from "Cather" the persona. I should also note that Schwind's essay is rich with
   insights on many matters other than the illustrations to the novel and that her discussion of the differences between the introductions to the 1918 and 1926 editions helped
   stimulate my thinking on many of the issues considered here.
3. Willa Cather, *My Ántonia* (1918, rev. 1926; Boston: Houghton Mifflin, 1954), Introduction (n. pag.). Future references will be to this Norton Critical Edition and will be made
   in brackets.
4. For an analysis of this process, see Sharon O'Brien, "Becoming Noncanonical: The Case
   against Willa Cather," in Cathy Davidson, ed., *Reading in America* (Baltimore: Johns
   Hopkins University Press, 1989), 240–258.

all feminists may share an interest in gender issues, the variety of critical techniques and theories they deploy—psychoanalytic, new historical, archetypal, and women's cultural—has established Cather as a major American writer with important links to other women writers and a significant place in several literary traditions. Judith Fetterley and Marjorie Pryse, for example, see Cather as the culmination of "regionalism," a mode of writing practiced chiefly by women in the nineteenth century and characterized by empathic narration and female protagonists who become capable of adult identity by venturing into female communities and becoming aware of their connections to other women.[5] Elizabeth Ammons places her at the center of a diverse group of women writers who, at the turn of the century, constituted a "pioneer generation" determined to "invade the territory of high art" that historically had been the province of men and united in their preoccupations with the institutionalized oppression of women and ethnic minorities, the figure of the female artist, and "the need to find union and reunion with the world of one's mother."[6] Cather is accorded a prominent place in several feminist studies that focus on the plots and symbols that recur throughout fiction by American women, including the story of housekeeping or domestic ritual, the myth of Demeter and Persephone, and the use of space and landscape as structuring devices.[7]

Most importantly, perhaps, the emphasis on gender has raised compelling questions about the writer's sexual and literary identities, questions that have haunted studies of *My Ántonia* at least since 1971, when Blanche Gelfant identified Jim's recurring dream of Lena Lingard coming to kiss him with a curved reaping-hook in her hand as the locus of his and Cather's fears of sexuality.[8] In 1987, however, by making a cogent, unapologetic case for Cather's lesbianism, Sharon O'Brien's feminist psychobiography *Willa Cather: The Emerging Voice* opened up a vast interpretive territory, as critics immediately began combing the novels and short stories for signs of how sexuality is translated into textuality, how lesbianism is masked

5. See Judith Fetterley and Marjorie Pryse, eds., "Introduction," *American Women Regionalists, 1850–1910* (New York: W. W. Norton, 1992), xi–xx.
6. Elizabeth Ammons, *Conflicting Stories: American Women Writers at the Turn into the Twentieth Century* (New York: Oxford UP, 1992), 5.
7. The studies alluded to here are Ann Romines, *The Home Plot: Women, Writing, and Domestic Ritual* (Amherst: U of Massachusetts P, 1992); Josephine Donovan, *After the Fall: The Demeter-Persephone Myth in Wharton, Cather, and Glasgow* (University Park: Pennsylvania State UP, 1989); and Judith Fryer, *Felicitous Space: The Imaginative Structures of Edith Wharton and Willa Cather* (Chapel Hill: U of North Carolina P, 1986).
8. Blanche Gelfant, "The Forgotten Reaping-Hook: Sex in *My Ántonia*," in *Women Writing in America* (1971; Hanover, NH: UP of New England, 1984), 94–116.

or disguised to evade detection and censure.[9] In the case of *My Ántonia*, the foregrounding of issues of desire and sexuality has drawn attention to the puzzling relationship between Jim and Ántonia and to the unstable gender identities of the novel's two main characters. Critics have contended that Jim is an autobiographical mask for the confusing attractions Cather felt toward the pioneer women of her own Nebraska youth, or that both characters are homosexuals whose friendship is built out of their mutual experience of sexual deviance.[1]

Problematic as some of these readings may be, the value of such energetic revisionism is that it begins to situate Cather more clearly within modern—and Modernist—contexts of sexual malaise and locates in her art signs of that resistance to gender-role socialization so apparent in the writer's own life. But critical preoccupations with questions of character and point of view—with ascertaining whether Jim Burden is a "real" man or a cross-dressed authorial surrogate—have skewed debate about *My Ántonia* in significant ways. Feminist readers are likely to be annoyed by Jim's fastidiousness and applaud Ántonia's subversive and stubborn vitality—when, for example, she asserts at the age of fifteen, "I can work like mans

9. Sharon O'Brien, *Willa Cather: The Emerging Voice* (New York: Oxford UP, 1987). O'Brien's influence has been widely felt in recent criticism on Cather, creating a wave of readings attentive to feminist and psychosexual issues. See, for example, Judith Fetterley, "*My Ántonia*, Jim Burden, and the Dilemma of the Lesbian Writer," in Karla Jay and Joanne. Glasgow, eds., *Lesbian Texts and Contexts: Radical Revisions* (New York: New York UP, 1990), 145–163; Katrina Irving, "Displacing Homosexuality: The Use of Ethnicity in Willa Cather's *My Ántonia*," *Modern Fiction Studies* 36 (Spring 1990): 91–102; Claude J. Summers, "'A Losing Game in the End': Aestheticism and Homosexuality in Cather's 'Paul's Case,'" *Modern Fiction Studies* 36 (Spring 1990): 103–119; Eve Kosofsky Sedgwick, "Across Gender, Across Sexuality: Willa Cather and Others," *South Atlantic Quarterly* 88 (1989): 53–72; and Sandra Gilbert and Susan Gubar, *Sexchanges*, vol. 2 of *No Man's Land: The Place of the Woman Writer in the Twentieth Century* (New Haven: Yale UP, 1989), esp. 169–212. For additional lesbian and gay readings, see next note.

1. The first position—i.e., that Jim is Cather "speaking in masquerade" of her love for women—is implicit in Joanna Russ's "To Write 'Like a Woman': Transformations of Identity in the Work of Willa Cather," in Monika Kehoe, ed., *Historical, Literary, and Erotic Aspects of Lesbianism* (New York: Harrington Park Press, 1986), 77–87. Russ argues that all of Cather's male personae seem flawed or inconsistent and that heterosexual relationships seem impossible in her fiction because they camouflage the story of "the lesbian in love with the heterosexual woman because she believes there is nobody else to be in love with" (84). Though provocative, Russ's argument is undermined by its reliance on dubious speculations about "real male experiences" (85) and the consequences of Cather's supposed lack of involvement in an openly lesbian community. The second position—i.e., that Jim and Ántonia are homosexual friends—is developed in Timothy Dow Adams's "My Gay Antonia: The Politics of Willa Cather's Lesbianism," in Kehoe, 89–98. Dismissing the characters' major life choices as "marriages of convenience that serve as masks for their sexual variance" (97), Adams grounds his (also provocative) reading of the novel on contemporary notions of homosexual and lesbian identity that seem remote from the world of *My Ántonia*. Since, for example, Jim and Ántonia never discuss yet seem to "understand each other's sexual preferences" (97), one must suppose that they are equipped with "gaydar," the mechanism/intuition that supposedly enables homosexuals and lesbians to detect the presence of kindred spirits in unlikely places and situations—or so we insist when we happen to judge correctly.

now" [66]—while Jim is horrified by the power and sexual ambiguity of her presence and annoyed by everything from her suntan to her table manners.

The difficulty with such reactions—and I count my own early impatience with Jim among them—is that they psychologize issues of gender, power, and desire, while *My Ántonia* goes much further, wrestling determinedly with the challenge of narrativizing and historicizing those same issues. Consider, for instance, the terms most frequently used by critics to describe the treatment of desire in *My Ántonia*. They are all at bottom psychological: "invalidation," "evasion," "displacement," "concealment," "oscillation," and "renunciation."[2] Such a focus is limited in a number of respects. It localizes desire (and the whole complex of issues associated with it) in particular characters, symbols, or situations; it confuses to a greater or lesser degree life (Cather) and art (Jim); and it flattens a text that works strenuously against naive notions of representation into a series of portraits or case studies—of, depending on the critic's point of view, the struggling homosexual, the lonely lesbian, the "strange" bisexual,[3] the unhappy heterosexual.

Late in her career, Cather herself sharply attacked the psychologizing tendencies of literary interpretation, complaining bitterly that a generation of readers "violently inoculated with Freud" would find little to appreciate in the work of her predecessor Sarah Orne Jewett.[4] Cather's skepticism about psychoanalysis (and her disturbing xenophobia and antisemitism) aside, the remark serves to remind us that the Introduction to *My Ántonia* establishes Ántonia not as a character but a "figure." A fictional "character" is not, of course, a real person, though much of our pleasure in reading novels derives

2. Gelfant argues that Cather "consistently invalidates sex" for many of her characters (95) and that *My Ántonia* is shaped by "a pattern of sexual aversion" (99). Such terms as "evasion," "displacement," and "concealment" are key to arguments that Cather seeks to mask her lesbian desires in *My Ántonia*; see, for example, Fetterley and Irving. O'Brien uses the term "oscillation" in "Gender, Sexuality, and Point of View: Teaching *My Ántonia* from a Feminist Perspective," in Susan J. Rosowski, ed., *Approaches to Teaching Cather's "My Ántonia"* (New York: Modern Language Association, 1989), 140–145. "Renunciation" is central to Gilbert and Gubar's discussion of Cather's treatment of desire, as they argue that her "greatest literary problem . . . resulted from her fatal attraction to a renunciation of passion" (205).
3. Gelfant uses this label to describe Ántonia (107).
4. Cather's "Miss Jewett," in *Not Under Forty* (New York: Knopf, 1936), 76–95, is an expanded version of the preface she wrote for the two-volume collection of Jewett's stories she edited for Houghton Mifflin in 1925. The later essay is remarkable for its pessimism on matters that go far beyond Freud—a sign, perhaps, of how embattled Cather had come to feel in the intervening decade. In the first version, for example, she happily anticipates the pleasure with which "the young student of American literature in far distant years to come will take up this book and say, 'A masterpiece!' as proudly as if he himself had made it." See Cather, Preface to *The Best Stories of Sarah Orne Jewett* (Boston: Houghton Mifflin, 1925), l:xix. By 1936, the "young student" is reconceived as "perhaps of foreign descent: German, Jewish, Scandinavian," an "adopted American . . . cut off from an instinctive understanding of 'the old moral harmonies'" (*Not Under Forty*, 93–4) and thus uninterested in Jewett (and, one must suppose, Cather).

from the belief that well-rounded "characters" are "like" us, that they choose and suffer and triumph much as we do.

A "figure," however, is several steps further removed from "reality" than a "character" and so is psychologically less substantial, complicating the reader's desire to ascribe motives, affix labels ("lesbian," "bisexual," "heterosexual"), or establish sympathetic connections. A figure is by definition an abstraction—an image, an outline, an illustration or drawing, like the eight line drawings by W. T. Benda that illustrate *My Ántonia*. Finally, though, as I suggested earlier, a figure may also be rhetorical—that is, a figure of speech. This last possibility is carefully foregrounded in the Introduction to *My Ántonia*, as "Cather" twice calls attention to the fact that Ántonia is a figure made of words. She emerges first in the "talk" "Cather" and Jim engage in while crossing Iowa together on a train, and then in Jim's "writing down" his memories of her (an act that in part precedes their "talk" chronologically but is revealed later in narrative time). Made of words, Ántonia generates words as readily as she generates children, for their "talk" in the observation car "kept returning to [her]," and Jim writes about her in an urgent manner that belies his assertion that he did so only to "amuse [him]self" on his cross-country trips. His appearance at "Cather's" apartment on a "stormy winter afternoon" months after their meeting on the train and his apparent desire to be quickly rid of "the thing about Ántonia" suggest that Jim is anxious to escape the proliferative logic of the process he initiated: figures begetting figures in so quick and slippery a fashion that he cannot "take time to arrange" them and doubts they have "any form."

That Ántonia is described only as "a central figure" and not "*the* central figure" in "Cather" and Jim's "talk" is crucial to realizing how deeply preoccupied *My Ántonia* is with the logic, the process, and the power of figure-making. The indefinite article forces us to extend that logic, to acknowledge, for example, that Ántonia is at least a figure of a figure: Jim figures her, but "Cather" figures Jim—while somewhere off in the distance Cather figures "Cather" as a writer, in the 1918 Introduction, who could not write the story of Ántonia.[5] As the layers multiply, that "central figure" grows increasingly insubstantial, and the questions for feminist readers of *My Ántonia* grow increasingly complex. One of the most complex questions,

---

5. The ending to the 1918 Introduction differs substantially from that of 1926, for in the earlier edition the following conversation occurs after Jim has written "My Ántonia" across his portfolio:

"Read it as soon as you can," he said, rising, "but don't let it influence your own story."
My own story was never written, but the following narrative is Jim's manuscript, substantially as he brought it to me. (xiv)

In the version of 1926, the only sign that "Cather" is a writer is the desk at which Jim sits to put a title on his manuscript.

however, may be stated succinctly: What does it mean that the novel Cather identified not only as her best but as a real contribution to American letters[6] is the story of a woman ("Cather") figuring a man (Jim Burden) figuring a woman (Ántonia)? By attending to this question, we might arrive at a deeper understanding of how the novel, in foregrounding the problem of how women perceive and are perceived in masculinist culture, broods upon and elucidates profoundly feminist issues, though its author almost certainly did not intend to create a self-consciously "feminist" work.

Indeed, throughout her long, shrewdly managed career as a writer, Cather publicly denied that gender was psychologically powerful or culturally meaningful. As a young magazine columnist in the 1890s, for example, she boasted to readers of the Pittsburgh *Home Monthly* that "the fact that I was a girl never damaged my ambitions to be a pope or an emperor," and she urged parents in selecting books for their children to avoid making the "hateful distinction" between "boys' books" and "girls' books" for as long as possible, noting that she preferred "the books that are for both."[7] She ridiculed feminists and other women writers so habitually that critics have recently wondered if the concept of "female misogyny" might not apply to her.[8] "Hateful" to her or not, however, the distinction between "boys' books" and "girls' books"—and a host of other gender-based distinctions—was made in the culture Cather lived and wrote in, and she was more troubled by it than the bravado of her early pronouncements suggests. For Cather, the figure-making process that is scrutinized in *My Ántonia* was embedded in the same cultural system that worked systematically, though in her case unsuccessfully, to undermine a girl's "ambitions to be a pope or an emperor"; so the process is also a contest—a struggle not just to make figures but to assign them meanings as well. By these terms, desire is the longing for interpretive power and cultural authority, and gender is the basis upon which the sides are drawn. And the figure of a woman figuring a man figuring a woman is the site where the two sides meet.

At first glance the imbricated narrative structure of *My Ántonia* would seem to tilt the scales in favor of the women's side in the battle for linguistic power waged in the novel. If "Cather" figures Jim, then "she" gets the first and last word and is thus the authoritative speaker. Many revisionary readings of the novel have hinged upon

6. Cather is reported to have offered this assessment of the novel in 1938 on the twentieth anniversary of its publication. See Mildred Bennett, *The World of Willa Cather* (1951; Lincoln: U of Nebraska P, 1961), 203.
7. Cather's early work in journalism has been collected and reprinted in William M. Curtin, ed., *The World and the Parish: Willa Cather's Articles and Reviews, 1893–1902*, 2 vols. (Lincoln: U of Nebraska P, 1970), For the two columns referred to here, see 1:368, 337.
8. Gilbert and Gubar, 174.

this kind of reasoning, noting that Jim's credibility as a narrator is severely undermined in the Introduction and systematically questioned throughout the text. Jim's "romantic disposition" and his imperialistic rhetorical gestures—"*My Ántonia*"—mark his perceptions as distorted, subjective, and partial, and open up the text to allow every reader to construct alternative Ántonias. We do so with help from the critical female voices that periodically erupt out of Jim's narrative: Ántonia pointing out to Jim that education is a luxury privileged "little boys" like him can afford, while for her working "like mans" is a grim economic necessity [66]; Lena Lingard laughing at his views on marriage and disparaging "family life" as "all being under somebody's thumb" [143]; Frances Harling echoing "Cather's" description of Jim as "romantic" in his tendency to "put a kind of glamour over" the hired girls and asserting the authority of her own perceptions: "I expect I know the country girls better than you do" [116].

These dissenting views, coupled with the evidence of "Cather's" editorial work on Jim's narrative—the footnote on the pronunciation of Ántonia's name and the insertion of the Benda sketches[9]—de-authorize Jim's version of the story and guide the reader toward the "real"—accurate, authoritative—story. What these arguments overlook, however, is that the contest enacted in *My Ántonia*, much like the Hill-Thomas imbroglio, has almost nothing to do with accuracy or credibility. If that were the case, the obvious debunking of Jim's vision in the Introduction would be a glaring flaw in the narrative. If Jim's credibility is primarily what is at stake, then the Introduction offers a dead giveaway—tantamount to a mystery writer revealing "who done it" on the second page. If Jim were merely a "romantic," then hard-nosed readers like me could dismiss him as insipid and curl up instead with Cather's unmediated portraits of powerful women, *O Pioneers!* and *The Song of the Lark*. Rather than credibility, though, power is what is at stake in *My Ántonia*, and from that standpoint the women's side in the novel may be found as powerless as the group of female legislators who stormed Capitol Hill to protest the Judiciary Committee's handling of Professor Hill's allegations.

9. This is the essence of the argument made by Schwind. Though I agree that the function of the introduction and the illustrations is to undercut Jim's credibility as a narrator, I see these textual supplements as too unstable and problematic to enable us, as Schwind suggests, "to read Cather's story [by reading] 'Cather's' story" (55). In an analysis published after I had written this essay, Judith Butler argues a point similar to Schwind's from a different, more psychoanalytic direction. Arguing that the transfer of authority from the introductory narrator to Jim is a false one, Butler suggests that this act of feminine dissimulation "facilitates the claim to the text that she only appears to give away" and that such false transfers are a recurring movement within Cather's texts, "a figure for the crossing of identification which both enables and conceals the workings of desire." See "'Dangerous Crossing': Willa Cather's Masculine Names" in *Bodies that Matter: On the Discursive Limits of "Sex"* (New York and London: Routledge, 1993), 143–66, esp. 145–53.

Right or wrong, accurate or inaccurate, credible or incredible, the women's voices in *My Ántonia* suffer from a crisis of location that dangerously diminishes their ability to construct a counter-story to the romanticized "boys' book" that is Jim's *Ántonia*. Relegated at every point to the margins of the text, these voices are so muted that they seem to be echoes of echoes, and their power to qualify or correct Jim's perceptions is dubious at best. He may not be "right," but no alternative view is ever loudly or clearly articulated. The only woman who speaks directly—in her own voice rather than in the mediated voices presented in the main narrative—is "Cather," and her speaking is confined to the supplementary textual space of the Introduction, though her role as editor is fitfully apparent beyond that space. More-over, "Cather" is such an elusive figure that she is barely present in her own brief narrative, receding away from the reader as she swerves continually away from herself and toward Jim, her conversation with him, and their shared experience of growing up "in a little prairie town,"

> buried in wheat and corn, under stimulating extremes of cli-mate: burning summers when the world lies green and billowy beneath a brilliant sky, when one is fairly stifled in vegetation, in the colour and smell of strong weeds and heavy harvests; blus-tery winters with little snow, when the whole country is stripped bare and grey as sheet iron. (Intro)

"Buried," "stifled," and "stripped bare" aptly describes the condition of women's voices in *My Ántonia*; and Cather's revisions to the Intro-duction for the 1926 edition indicate more clearly that "Cather" suf-fers as fully from this condition as the women whose voices are selectively recalled and transcribed by Jim Burden. The later Intro-duction significantly scales back the figure of "Cather," obscuring in particular her status as a writer and excising the only explicit ref-erence in the text to her editing of Jim's manuscript—the cryptic remark that "the following narrative is Jim's manuscript, *substan-tially* as he brought it to me" (1918, emphasis added). Cather's occlu-sion of "Cather's" active role in shaping the manuscript suggests that her purpose in revising the Introduction was more than merely aesthetic.

That occlusion profoundly destabilizes *My Ántonia* by making uncertain the connection between the Introduction and Jim's nar-rative, and by making the few editorial marks upon his narrative seem in a sense to have come from nowhere. The charge of a "romantic disposition" may compromise Jim's credibility and establish an ironic distance between "Cather's" (and Cather's) and Jim's perceptions, but by 1926 "Cather" had been "stripped bare" of the power or authority necessary to challenge the larger claim Jim makes to Ántonia. Unwilling or unable to offer a glimpse of "her" Ántonia, "Cather" stands as a sign of Cather's deep skepticism about women's ability to compete in the contest to figure themselves in a culturally powerful way.

Beyond the Introduction, the stifling of women's voices figures prominently in both the plot and the structure of Jim's narrative. Like most first-person narrators, Jim shows signs of being in love with the sound of his own voice and is fully in control of all the other voices in the text, for his power to record events, impressions, and other people is uncontested. Even as a boy, Jim revels in the "considerable extension of power and authority" he experiences when he realizes he is alone in his grandparents' house for the first time during the tumult occasioned by Mr. Shimerda's suicide—an experience he recalls as "delightful" and "pleasant" despite the sorrowful event that made it possible [56]. As "alone" in his narrative as he is in his grandparents' house, Jim's linguistic "power and authority" extend to a preoccupation with the sounds of women's voices and the content of their speech—from the useless chatter of a grandmother who "always talked, dear woman: to herself or to the Lord, if there was no one else to listen" [61] to the "conventional expressions" and "small-town proprieties" that became "very funny, very engaging, when they were uttered in Lena's soft voice, with her caressing intonation and arch naivete" [138]. In both cases, Jim cannot detach women's speaking from his culture's gender-bound assumptions about female behavior: He hears his grandmother's talk to herself through the filter of bourgeois, late-Victorian associations of women with gossip and religion, while Lena Lingard's "soft voice," endowed with the physical power to "caress" and the suspicious but appealing quality of "arch"-ness, reaffirms her connection in Jim's mind to dangerous, uncontrolled sexuality. Again, what women say matters less than how they are heard, and Jim's power to situate women's words in such charged social, spiritual, and erotic contexts assures that he is the primary maker of meaning in My Ántonia.

Jim functions in the text as a sexual-linguistic gatekeeper and translator, for when women speak in his narrative they do so in quotation marks, and that is perhaps the clearest sign of the deep-seated gender trouble being examined in the novel. Women may seem at times to speak for themselves and actively to resist the meanings Jim would impose upon their stories, but even the most resistant, subversive voices are already his, not theirs. Their speech is always marked, framed, claimed, and circumscribed, and theirs are the muted voices of alien others contained within a larger voice—unmarked because it is the illusion of absolute presence, power, and authority.

Perhaps the best example of the limits imposed upon female linguistic power in Jim's narrative is Frances Harling, whose critique
of Jim's romanticism has already been mentioned. Socially, Frances
is at least Jim's equal, if not slightly his better, since her family is
already well settled in Black Hawk and prospering in business when
Jim's grandparents begin the transition from farm to town life. She
is also a "grown-up" when he is still a boy, acknowledged as "a very
important person in our world" whose "unusual business ability"
earned her "a good salary" as her father's chief clerk [80]. More
importantly, though, Frances is credited with an unusual verbal dex-
terity, a capacity for speaking and comprehending a variety of what
might be called genderlects. She is able on the one hand to talk with
her father "about grain-cars and cattle, like two men," to arrange
deals, and to collaborate with Jim's grandfather "to rescue some
unfortunate farmer from the clutches of Wick Cutter, the Black
Hawk money-lender."

But while Frances drives out into the country "on business," she
also performs the women's work of paying visits, going "miles out of
her way to call on some of the old people" and deftly switching into
another sociolinguistic mode: "She was quick at understanding the
grandmothers who spoke no English, and the most reticent and distrustful of them would tell her their story without realizing they were
doing so" [80]. Frances, too, is a figure of speech, and her speech
is a powerful mixture of male and female, town and country, New
World and Old World. Since she is not, like Jim, inclined to "take
sides" [115], Frances's easy movement across rhetorics and social categories marks her as a figure of generosity and reconciliation, but
her power is ultimately cross-checked in his narrative. She may assert
superior knowledge of the country girls he views through a veil of
glamour, but the assertion stands isolated and unsupported in Jim's
telling of the story. Her counter-story is, like "Cather's," hinted at but
never effectively told. Framed by memory and choked by quotation
marks, Jim's Frances offers no details of her alternative view of the
class of women Jim claims as his personal possession: "my country
girls" [103]. Frances knows them, but Jim owns them. The novel seems
haunted by the possibility that real power is the power to possess—a
house, a person, a voice, a narrative—and that women are decidedly
lacking in that power.

For Jim, the language of imaginative possession and the self-
aggrandizing rhetorical gesture are part of his birthright as a
native-born American male endowed with a "romantic disposition."
To Jim, language reflects the sexual order of the universe, so he
resents Ántonia's occasionally taking "a superior tone" with him
because "I was a boy and she was a girl" [29]. Jim's sense of language
as a manly means of claiming the world suggests that his romanticism

is inherited from Emerson, who exalted the poet as "true land-lord! sea-lord! air-lord!"[1] Like his forebear's poetry, Jim's narrative represses or circumvents the possibility that a woman might aspire to be "land-[lady]! sea-[lady]! air-[lady]!" Indeed, the immigrant daughters who captivate Jim's attention are doubly estranged from the vocabulary of possession that is so comfortable to him because it is marked not only as manly but also as "American." "Foreigners" like Ántonia and Lena must struggle even more acutely than Frances Harling with a language that is not theirs in ways that go beyond Jim's proprietary quotation marks. Their speech is restricted to discourses of dispossession that stand in sharp contrast to the confident "my"-ness of Jim's voice, and he functions as a kind of linguistic policeman, monitoring women's voices and citing them for their failure to speak appropriately.

Ántonia is on more than one occasion criticized for using language deemed inappropriate to her gender. Jim notes disapprovingly that she "could talk of nothing but the prices of things, or how much she could lift and endure" [69] and attacks her for "jabber[ing] Bohunk" when the two confront a rattlesnake in prairie-dog town [30]. Jim's harsh judgments of Ántonia in these situations contrast with the respect he accords Frances Harling for her ability to talk with her father "like two men" and to understand the grandmothers "who spoke no English," indicating that for the immigrant woman language is a field mined with much greater risks. Ethnic difference compounds and complicates the difficulties created by gender difference, making Ántonia doubly vulnerable and doubly burdened. Just as he polices her appearance for signs of masculinization in her youth and diminishment in middle age, Jim polices Ántonia's speech for evidence of gender or ethnic transgressions, both of which, in his judgment, she commits: She talks "like mans" and "jabber[s] Bohunk."

Of all the women figured in Jim's narrative, Lena Lingard emerges as the most serious challenge to his authority because her voice, even in his eroticized transcription of it, is so powerful and so completely at odds with his adolescent fascination with her body that it nearly shatters the frame he constructs for it: *nearly.* Jim lingers to the point of fetishizing over the details of Lena's physicality—the "miraculous whiteness of her skin" [86], "the swelling lines of her figure" [87], her sleepy, violet eyes and "slow, undulating walk" [103]—and seems uninterested in or bewildered by the radical difference between his image of her and Lena's sense of herself. Lena's consuming professional ambition fails to register with Jim, though she announces it in her first appearance in his narrative when she visits Ántonia at the Harlings after moving into town to study dressmaking with

1. Ralph Waldo Emerson, "The Poet," in Stephen E. Whicher, ed., *Selections from Ralph Waldo Emerson* (Boston: Houghton Mifflin, 1957), 241.

Mrs. Thomas [84]. Thus, after she visits him in Lincoln with news that she is already established in business for herself and they rekindle their friendship, Jim confesses to being "puzzled" by her success and seems skeptical about it: "Her clients said that Lena 'had style,' and overlooked her habitual inaccuracies" [137]. Jim cannot bring himself to concur in the judgment that Lena has "style," because style is a sign of independence and creativity, so he distances himself from the judgment by attributing it to "clients" and undercuts it by suggesting those clients don't pay careful attention to Lena's work.

In the section of his narrative that bears her name, Jim constructs Lena not as an artist whose "style" might be worthy of praise but as a muse who should inspire creativity in (male) others: "If there were no girls like [Lena and the other country girls] in the world, there would be no poetry" [133]. When she fails in that role by distracting Jim instead of inspiring him—"I was drifting," he laments, "Lena had broken my serious mood" [141]—Lena essentially disappears from Jim's narrative; he takes off to Harvard with Gaston Cleric and then settles into his loveless, childless marriage. Later, Jim reports that Lena became "the leading dressmaker of Lincoln" [145] before conquering San Francisco with Tiny Soderball [147]. She appears once more twenty years later to encourage Jim to go see Ántonia, still unmarried and closely connected to Tiny, with a dress shop in an apartment building around the corner from Tiny's house. In their presence, the once gushing boy is a suddenly laconic man, remarking only, "It interested me, after so many years, to see the two women together" [159]. Finally, though, when Ántonia shows him a photograph of Lena, Jim reverts to his habit of judging and adoring the dressmaker piece by piece, confirming that she looks "exactly like" the picture, "a comely woman, a trifle too plump, in a hat a trifle too large, but with the old lazy eyes, and the old dimpled ingenuousness still lurking at the corners of her mouth" [169].

Jim's Lena is a Scandinavian Marilyn Monroe, a figure of excess ("too plump," "too large") who cannot be contained and therefore must be abandoned (by leaving Lincoln, by dropping her out of the story). However, his efforts to reduce Lena to an object, the static sum of her bodily parts, are stymied by her resilience, her social and economic mobility, and a degree of "self-possession" that causes him to "wonder" [137]. Lena's "self-possession" makes her a point of friction in Jim's narrative, because it is a sign of how remote and disengaged she is from the spectacle Jim and other men make of her body. That disengagement is evident in her indifference to gossip, her hostility to marriage, and her clear-eyed sense that desire is chiefly a game whose rules she understands well enough to exploit. "Old men are like that," she tells Jim when he expresses concern about the attentions paid her by Ordinsky, the Polish violin teacher who lives across the hall from her. "It makes them feel important to think they're in love with somebody" [142]. Abundant yet self-possessed, Lena is a figure of excess un*con*tainable and un*ob*tainable. She is literally and figuratively too much, yet not enough, for Jim, for something is always withheld, left over for herself. Enigma and siren, she must be forcibly abandoned, and she is. "My Lincoln chapter closed abruptly," Jim announces in the paragraph that concludes Lena's section of his narrative. The statement is fraught with the tension her figure arouses in him and betrays his need to assert control over it: "My" insists that the story is his (not hers), "Lincoln" defines it as the story of a city (not a woman), "chapter" calls attention to its literariness and its small size, and "closed abruptly" imbues the action of ending the story with significant physical force.

Despite the psychological "self-possession" that even Jim can't help noticing, Lena's speech is, like Ántonia's, confined largely to a rhetoric of dispossession that signals her place in the novel's interrogation of women's power and powerlessness. She articulates an awareness of her dispossession bluntly yet clearly in the story of Ole Benson's scandalous obsession with her, an episode Jim recalls in "The Hired Girls." Benson is the farmer plagued by misfortune whose wife, "Crazy Mary," escapes from the asylum in Lincoln and takes to chasing Lena around with a corn-knife because her discouraged husband abandons his cornfield on summer afternoons to help the Norwegian girl watch her cattle. During one of these escapades Lena's cattle are scattered, and she asks Jim and Ántonia to help her get them back together. Mrs. Shimerda, who watches the scene from a window and "enjoyed the situation keenly," suggests Lena is to blame in the incident, prompting a reply whose rhetoric is significant:

> "Maybe you lose a steer and learn not to make somethings with your eyes at married men," Mrs. Shimerda told her hectoringly.
>   Lena only smiled her sleepy smile. "I never made anything to him with my eyes. I can't help it if he hangs around, and I can't order him off. It ain't my prairie." [89]

Later, Lena will offer a more expansive and positive explanation of her relationship with Ole, telling Jim that "There was never any harm in [him]" and that his companionship provided relief from the tedium of being "off with cattle all the time" [138]. At this early juncture, however, her speaking is a series of denials and negations, a statement of what she has not done, cannot do, and most importantly perhaps, does not own. She voices a far-reaching sense of dispossession that is at once linguistic, sexual, economic, legal, and territorial. Young, immigrant, and female, Lena is aware that she lacks the "power and authority" Jim discovers when he is left, like the child protagonist of the popular film, "home alone." Her assertion that "It

ain't my prairie" exploits and critiques American expressive traditions that forge symbolic links between women's bodies and frontier landscapes, for the prairie that is not hers is the scene of a
struggle provoked by a body that is not fully hers either—since everyone in the community feels entitled to watch it, judge it, long for it,
and threaten it. (Even in church, "the congregation stared at" it [87],
and Crazy Mary offers to "trim some of that shape off" Lena with
her corn-knife [89].) Limited to a discourse of negatives—"never,"
"can't," "ain't"—and unable to say "my" of the prairie she farms or
the body she inhabits, Lena articulates the dilemma of the woman
who understands and even exploits the rules of the game but realizes
she is powerless to change them.

Because it is such a loaded psychosexual symbol, the prairie is
arguably the primary site of contestation in *My Ántonia*'s analysis of
gender in/and the figure-making process, so Lena's declaration that it
"ain't [hers]" takes on special significance. For her, the association
of women's bodies with the land is grotesquely literalized as an odor
that clings stubbornly to her: "After I began to herd and milk, I
could never get the smell of the cattle off me" [143]. And her family's
little house on the prairie is a space of negative abundance and
oppressiveness, particularly for women: "[Lena] remembered home
as a place where there were always too many children, a cross man
and work piling up around a sick woman" [143]. Lena succeeds in
turning over the body/land metaphor and exposing its problematic
underside, but the dispossession she experiences on the prairie
prompts her flight away from home and through a succession of ever
larger towns and cities—Black Hawk, Lincoln, San Francisco. She
deconstructs the metaphor but has nothing to install in its place,
and so retreats from the field of battle. She has a counter-story but
lacks a language adequate for telling it. Eventually, as we have seen,
she all but disappears from Jim's narrative, leaving him both the prairie and the last word.

Ántonia, on the other hand, returns to the prairie from Black
Hawk, insisting to Jim, "I belong on a farm. I'm never lonesome here
like I used to be in town" [166]. Far from critiquing the body/land
metaphor, Ántonia seems to endorse it wholeheartedly. Her rejection of town life leads to a happy entanglement in nature that includes
working the land, raising a huge brood of children, and even being
kind to animals. Explaining her fear of guns to Jim, Ántonia says,
"Ever since I've had children, I don't like to kill anything. It makes
me kind of faint to wring an old goose's neck" [166]. Instead of
talking "like mans," as she had in her rebellious youth, in the last
section of the narrative Ántonia talks like a mother, suggesting that
for her the prairie is a space of (limited) power because she ultimately
acquiesces to the sexual and symbolic order Jim had enunciated and

attempted to enforce in their childhood, because "I was a boy and she was a girl" [29]. Where Lena resists Jim's ordering and interpreting, Ántonia aids and abets it, holding forth so readily on domestic management, the quirks of her children, and her early concern for the trees in her orchard ("They were on my mind like children" [165]) that Jim's assertion that she could "make you feel the goodness of planting and tending and harvesting at last" [170] seems justified.

In contrast to Lena's overwhelming erotic energies, Ántonia's maternal power is no threat to Jim's masculine discursive power. Images of Ántonia endure in his mind and his narrative with the safe stasis of symbols. She represents to him "immemorial human attitudes which we recognize as universal and true" and is immortalized as the mother of sons who "stood tall and straight" [171]. She and her husband may own part of the prairie, but linguistically Ántonia is no more able to claim it than is Lena. Indeed, "I belong on a farm" suggests that in some sense the prairie owns her, while symbolically she clearly remains Jim's possession. Through her, Jim is able to achieve a "sense of coming home to [him]self," to lay claim to "the precious, the incommunicable past" [179].

To many, this reading of the novel will no doubt seem to have demonized Jim Burden and perversely turned Cather's elegy of pioneer life into a paranoid feminist allegory on the evils of male authority. My aim has not been to demonstrate that Jim is a bad guy or a cruel character or any sort of "character" at all. My goal has been to suggest that Cather's manipulations of narrative form and voice in *My Ántonia* indicate that she remained ambivalent about female artistic and cultural power well beyond the period of creative emergence so capably explored by Sharon O'Brien. Moreover, Cather saw a sexual imbalance of power operating on the deepest levels of the text and shaping the conditions of its interpretation, a preoccupation that informed her work throughout the 1920s, as she continued to grapple with the form of the novel and with the sexual dynamics of American literary history. The muted state of women's voices in *My Ántonia* is refigured, for example, in the silent agony of Mother Eve, the Indian mummy discovered in *The Professor's House* with her mouth frozen open "as if she were screaming," and in the roar of the underground river that so disturbs Jean-Marie Latour in the "Stone Lips" sequence of *Death Comes for the Archbishop*.[2]

Sensing the increasing masculinism of American literary culture and critical discourse, Cather sought, particularly in her preface to *The Best Stories of Sarah Orne Jewett*, to formulate a model of

2. Willa Cather, *The Professor's House* (1925; New York: Vintage, 1973), 214; Cather, *Death Comes for the Archbishop* (1927; New York: Vintage, 1971), 125–36.

creativity rooted in the womanly "gift of sympathy"[3] but she seems always to have doubted that "sympathy" was a weapon of sufficient power in the battle between "boys' books" and "girls' books" that grew so heated in America after World War I. Published in 1918 and revised in 1926, when the cultural effects of the war were clearer and more settled, *My Ántonia* marks a crucial point in her long, uneasy examination of gender's determinative impact upon a range of social powers because in the main body of its narrative there is no space that is not-Jim. His control of the first-person pronoun and his ability to place female subjectivity in quotation marks make his power pervasive if not unchallenged. In the process of analyzing a man's power to "figure" a woman, Cather figures Jim as the god of his narrative—creator and sovereign of the world he calls into being from the opening, "I first heard of Ántonia on what seemed to me an interminable journey across the great midland plain of North America" [9].

The Widow Steavens may briefly take over as narrator in "The Pioneer Woman's Story" and even echo Jim's rhetorical claim to possessing "my Ántonia" [150], but her telling is framed by Jim's quotation marks and her story is offered chiefly to lay the groundwork for his apotheosis of Ántonia as Earth Mother. She performs the necessary task of restoring Ántonia's dignity in Jim's eyes (following the birth of her first child out of wedlock) and pronouncing her fit for the symbolic role he will ultimately confer upon her: "Ántonia is a natural-born mother" [155], Mrs. Steavens declares. Mrs. Steavens is an authoritative presence—"brown as an Indian woman, tall, and very strong," with a "massive head" that as a child reminded Jim of "a Roman senator's" [149]—but Jim controls and possesses her speech as fully as he does that of every other woman in his narrative. What she says is of less import than what he makes of her speaking.

A final example will serve to underscore how entangled *My Ántonia* is in issues of gender, power, and possession and so return this discussion to the questions of laws and lawyers with which it began. One of the more puzzling highlights of Jim's final visit to Ántonia is the story of the murder-suicide that ends the unhappy marriage of Wick Cutter and his "giantess" wife [108], a tale related "in great detail" and to the delight of everyone by Ántonia's eldest son, Rudolph [174]. At the heart of the "perpetual warfare" [107] of the Cutter marriage is, significantly, a dispute about property, for Black Hawk's shiftless money-lender is "tormented" [174] by the prospect of his wife's outliving him and "shar[ing] his property with her 'people,' whom he detested" [174]. When a state law is passed guaranteeing "the surviving wife a third of her husband's estate under all

---

3. Cather, Preface to *The Best Stories of Sarah Orne Jewett*, l:xii.

conditions" [174], Cutter is so determined to circumvent his wife's right to inherit that he murders her, shoots himself, and then summons witnesses to prove that he has outlived her.

In this bizarre episode, the new law is on the woman's side, but the literal and symbolic weapons possessed by the man—the gun Cutter uses to carry out his plan and the letter he leaves offering a legal explanation for his actions ("any will she might secretly have made would be invalid, as he survived her" [175])—prove to be vastly more powerful. So impressed by the story is Jim that he admits that "Every lawyer learns over and over how strong a motive hate can be, but in my collection of legal anecdotes I had nothing to match this one" [175]. Cutter's letter turns his crime into both a story and a legal maneuver, conjoining the discourses of law and narrative as effectively as Jim does in describing himself as a collector of "legal anecdotes." With his dying breath, Cutter explains to neighbors that the killing of his wife was simply a matter of putting his "affairs . . . in order" [175], suggesting that his fastidiousness goes somewhat beyond Jim's, though the murderer and the narrator share a similar predilection for monitoring and attempting to control female behavior.

Published two years before women gained the right to vote, *My Ántonia* thus allegorizes the extreme precariousness of women's claims to power and property and seems pessimistic about the possibility of legal change leading to the more far-reaching social and cultural changes necessary to make women's voices authoritative. A dead woman is, after all, silent; and in the layered telling of *My Ántonia* the voice of even a living woman is barely audible. On Cather's prairie as on Capitol Hill, a woman speaks, but men retain the power to transcribe, interpret, and render judgment upon her words. The novel's feminism resides, then, not in its several portraits of indomitable pioneer women but in its bleak and unflinching examination of the limitations placed upon such women, for in analyzing the power struggle at the heart of language as an ideological system, Cather figures a man who figures a woman with her mouth effectively shut.

Willa Cather: A Chronology

1873   Born December 7 in Back Creek Valley, near Winchester, Virginia.

1883   Family moves to the Nebraska Divide to join relatives farming there: Cather's uncle and aunt, George Cather and Franc Smith Cather, and Cather's grandparents, William and Caroline Cather.

1884   Family moves into small prairie town of Red Cloud.

1890   Graduates from high school; in September moves to Lincoln, where she enrolls as a second-year student in the Latin School, a two-year preparatory school of the University of Nebraska.

1892   First short story, "Peter," published in a Boston literary weekly.

1895   Graduates from the University of Nebraska.

1896   Leaves for Pittsburgh to take up job as editor of women's magazine, the *Home Monthly*.

1897   Resigns from *Home Monthly* and begins working at the Pittsburgh *Leader*, where she writes drama criticism and a "Books and Magazines" column.

1899   Meets Isabelle McClung, the daughter of a prominent Pittsburgh judge; the two begin a lifelong intimacy.

1901   Moves into the McClung household, where she remains until 1906. Teaches Latin and then English at Central High School.

1903   *April Twilights*, a collection of poems, published in April. Sends several short stories to S. S. McClure, publisher of *McClure's Magazine*. He invites her to New York and praises her fiction. Returns to Nebraska for the summer and meets Edith Lewis. In September begins teaching English at Allegheny High School.

1904   "A Wagner Matinee" published in *Everyman's Magazine*; she is criticized by some Nebraska readers for her bleak portrayal of farm life.

1905   *The Troll Garden*, a collection of seven stories that includes "A Wagner Matinee" and "Paul's Case" is published by McClure, Phillips & Co.

1906   Accepts offer from S. S. McClure of job at *McClure's Magazine*. Moves to New York in late spring and lives in same Greenwich Village apartment building as Edith Lewis, 60 Washington Square South.

1907–08   In Boston on assignment for *McClure's*, meets Annie Fields, widow of Boston publisher James T. Fields, and Sarah Orne Jewett, author of *The Country of the Pointed Firs*. Develops close friendships with both women. Returns to New York in fall and moves into apartment at 82 Washington Place with Edith Lewis. Becomes managing editor of *McClure's*.

1909   Sarah Orne Jewett dies. Cather writes Fields that life is dark and purposeless without her.

1910   Meets Elizabeth Sergeant, who had submitted an article to *McClure's*. The two women become close friends and literary confidantes.

1911   Writes *Alexander's Bridge* and *The Bohemian Girl* and finishes "Alexandra."

1912   Houghton Mifflin publishes *Alexander's Bridge*, and "The Bohemian Girl" appears in *McClure's*. Travels to the Southwest in the spring, and stays with the McClungs in Pittsburgh in the fall, writing short story "The White Mulberry Tree," then combining it with "Alexandra" to form basis of *O Pioneers!*

1913   *O Pioneers!*, dedicated to Sarah Orne Jewett, published by Houghton Mifflin. Moves with Edith Lewis to seven-room apartment at 5 Bank Street, in Greenwich Village.

1915   *The Song of the Lark* published by Houghton Mifflin.

1916   Isabelle McClung marries violinist Jan Hambourg; Cather is surprised and devastated. Signs with literary agent Paul Reynolds.

1917   Works on *My Ántonia* at the Shattuck Inn in Jaffrey, New Hampshire, which becomes a beloved writing retreat.

1918   *My Ántonia* published by Houghton Mifflin; receives glowing reviews.

1920   Signs contract with recently established publisher Alfred A. Knopf for collection of stories *Youth and the Bright Medusa*. Knopf is her publisher for the rest of her writing life.

1922   *One of Ours* published.

1923   *A Lost Lady* published. Cather awarded Pulitzer Prize for *One of Ours*.

1924   Selects stories and writes an introduction for *The Collected Stories of Sarah Orne Jewett*, published by Houghton Mifflin in 1925.

1925   *The Professor's House* published. Travels to the Southwest with Edith Lewis for the summer and finds inspiration for *Death Comes for the Archbishop*. Has cottage built for her on Grand Manan Island.

1926   *My Mortal Enemy* published.

1927   *Death Comes for the Archbishop* published. Moves with Edith Lewis to Grosvenor Hotel when Bank Street apartment building is torn down.

1929   Elected to the National Academy of Arts and Letters. Summers on Grand Manan.

1930   Awarded Howells Medal for Fiction by the American Academy of Arts and Letters for *Death Comes for the Archbishop*.

1931   *Shadows on the Rock* published. Sends money to Nebraska families hit hard by the Depression.

1932   *Obscure Destinies*, grouping of three short stories set in Nebraska, published. Moves with Lewis to new apartment on Park Avenue.

1933   Sprains tendon in right wrist, which becomes chronically inflamed. Condition, which persists through her life, often requires her to wear an immobilizing brace and interferes with her writing.

1935   *Lucy Gayheart* published.

1936   *Not Under Forty*, collection of essays on literature, published.

1937   Spends year helping Houghton Mifflin prepare the Library Edition of her work. Decides that *O Pioneers!* should be Volume I, and groups *Alexander's Bridge* with *April Twilights* in Volume III.

1940   *Sapphira and the Slave Girl* published.

1941   Begins novel set in Avignon but is unable to make progress because of recurring hand pain and other health problems.

1943   Unable to travel to Grand Manan due to war. Spends summer (and three succeeding) at Asticou Inn in Maine. Receives hundreds of letters from servicemen who have read her books in armed services editions.

1944   Receives Gold Medal of the National Institute of Arts and Letters. Embraces S. S. McClure, now 87, at the ceremony.

1947   Dies at home in New York City of cerebral hemorrhage
           on April 24. Buried in Jaffrey, New Hampshire, on April
           28. Inscribed on her tombstone is a quotation from
           My Ántonia: "That is happiness, to be dissolved into
           something complete and great, to become part of some-
           thing entire."

Selected Bibliography

• indicates works included or excerpted in this Norton Critical Edition.

Willa Cather

Arnold, Marilyn. *Willa Cather: A Reference Guide.* Boston: G. K. Hall, 1986.

Bennett, Mildred R. *The World of Willa Cather.* Lincoln: U of Nebraska P, 1961.

Bloom, Harold., ed. *Willa Cather: Modern Critical Views.* New York: Chelsea House, 1985.

Bohlke, L. Brent, ed. *Willa Cather in Person: Interviews, Speeches, and Letters.* Lincoln: U of Nebraska P, 1986.

Brown, E. K. *Willa Cather: A Critical Biography* (completed by Leon Edel). New York: Knopf, 1953.

Carlin, Deborah. *Cather, Canon, and the Politics of Reading.* Amherst: U of Massachusetts P, 1992.

Crane, Joan. *Willa Cather: A Bibliography.* Lincoln: U of Nebraska P, 1982.

Curtin, William, ed. *The World and the Parish: Willa Cather's Articles and Reviews, 1893–1902.* 2 vols. Lincoln: U of Nebraska P, 1970.

Daiches, David. *Willa Cather: A Critical Introduction.* Ithaca: Cornell UP, 1951.

Fryer, Judith. *Felicitous Space: The Imaginative Structures of Willa Cather and Edith Wharton.* Chapel Hill: U of North Carolina P, 1986.

Hoover, Sharon, ed. *Willa Cather Remembered.* Lincoln: U of Nebraska P, 2002.

• Jewell, Andrew, and Janis Stout, eds. *The Selected Letters of Willa Cather.* New York: Knopf, 2013.

Lee, Hermione. *Willa Cather: Double Lives.* New York: Pantheon Books, 1990.

• Lewis, Edith. *Willa Cather Living: A Personal Record.* New York: Knopf, 1953.

Lindemann, Marilee. *The Cambridge Companion to Willa Cather.* New York: Cambridge UP, 2005.

———. *Willa Cather: Queering America.* New York: Columbia UP, 1999.

Moers, Ellen. *Literary Women.* Garden City, NY: Doubleday, 1976.

Murphy, John J., ed. *Critical Essays on Willa Cather.* Boston: G. K. Hall, 1984.

O'Brien, Sharon. *Willa Cather: The Emerging Voice.* New York: Oxford UP, 1987.

• O'Connor, Margaret Anne, ed. *Willa Cather: The Contemporary Reviews.* New York: Cambridge UP, 2001.

Porter, David H. *On the Divide: The Many Lives of Willa Cather.* Lincoln: U of Nebraska P, 2008.

• Reynolds, Guy, *Willa Cather in Context: Progress, Race, Empire.* New York: St. Martin's P, 1996.

———, ed. *Willa Cather: Critical Assessments.* Mountfield, East Sussex: Helm Information, 2003.

Romines, Ann. *The Home Plot: Women, Writing & Domestic Ritual.* Amherst: U of Massachusetts P, 1992.

Rosowski, Susan J. *The Voyage Perilous: Willa Cather's Romanticism.* Lincoln: U of Nebraska P, 1986.

• ———. *Birthing a Nation: Gender, Creativity, and the West in American Literature.* Lincoln: U of Nebraska P, 1999.

Schroeter, James. *Willa Cather and Her Critics*. Ithaca: Cornell UP, 1967.

• Sergeant, Elizabeth Shepley. *Willa Cather: A Memoir*. Philadelphia: Lippincott, 1953.

Slote, Bernice. *The Kingdom of Art: Willa Cather's First Principles and Critical Statements, 1893–1896*. Lincoln: U of Nebraska P, 1967.

Stouck, David. *Willa Cather's Imagination*. Lincoln: U of Nebraska P, 1975.

• Stout, Janis P. *Willa Cather: The Writer and Her World*. Charlottesville: UP of Virginia, 2000.

———, ed. *A Calendar of the Letters of Willa Cather*. Lincoln: U of Nebraska P, 2002.

———, ed. *Willa Cather and Material Culture: Real-World Writing, Writing the Real World*. Tuscaloosa: U of Alabama P, 2005.

Trout, Stephen. *Memorial Fictions: Willa Cather and the First World War*. Lincoln: U of Nebraska P, 2002.

Urgo, Joseph R. *Willa Cather and the Myth of American Migration*. Urbana: U of Illinois P, 1995.

Watson, Sarah Cheney and Ann Moseley, eds. *Willa Cather and Aestheticism: From Romanticism to Modernism*. Madison, NJ: Fairleigh Dickinson UP, 2012.

Williams, Deborah Lindsay. *Not in Sisterhood: Willa Cather, Zona Gale, and the Politics of Female Authorship*. New York: Palgrave, 2001.

Woodress, James Leslie. *Willa Cather: A Literary Life*. Lincoln: U of Nebraska P, 1987.

My Ántonia

Brown, Linda Joyce. "'This hideous little pickaninny' and the Formation of Bohemian Whiteness: Race, Cultural Pluralism, and Willa Cather's *My Ántonia*." In *The Literature of Racial Formation: Becoming White, Becoming Other, Becoming American in the Late Progressive Era*. New York: Routledge, 2004, 81–103.

Collins, Rachel. "'Where All the Ground Is Friendly': Subterranean Living and the Ethic of Cultivation in Willa Cather's *My Ántonia*." *Interdisciplinary Studies in Literature and Environment* 19.1 (Winter 2012): 43–61.

• Fischer, Mike. "Pastoralism and Its Discontents: Willa Cather and the Burden of Imperialism." *Mosaic: A Journal for the Interdisciplinary Study of Literature* 23.1 (1990): 31–45.

Funda, Evelyn I. "Picturing Their Ántonia(s): Mikolás Ales and the Partnership of W. T. Benda and Willa Cather." *Cather Studies* 8.1 (2010): 353–78.

• Gelfant, Blanche H. "The Forgotten Reaping-Hook: Sex in *My Ántonia*." *American Literature* 43.1 (1971): 60–82.

Gorman, Michael. "Jim Burden and the White Man's Burden: *My Ántonia* and Empire." *Cather Studies* 6.1 (2006): 28–57.

Helstern, Linda Lizut. "*My Ántonia* and the Making of the Great Race." *Western American Literature* 42.3 (Fall 2007): 254–74.

Hoffman, Karen A. "Identity Crossings and the Autobiographical Act in Willa Cather's *My Ántonia*." *Arizona Quarterly* 58.4 (2002): 25–50.

Holmes, Catherine D. "Jim Burden's Lost Worlds: Exile in *My Ántonia*." *Twentieth Century Literature* 45.3 (1999): 336–46.

Lambert, Deborah G. "The Defeat of a Hero: Autonomy and Sexuality in *My Ántonia*." *American Literature* 53.4 (January 1982): 676–90.

Lucenti, Lisa Marie. "Willa Cather's *My Ántonia*: Haunting the Houses of Memory." *Twentieth Century Literature* 46.2 (2000): 193–213.

• Martin, Terence. "The Drama of Memory in *My Ántonia*." *PMLA* 84.2 (March 1969): 304–11.

Meyering, Sheryl L. *Understanding O Pioneers! and My Ántonia: A Student Casebook to Issues, Sources, and Historical Documents*. Westport, CT: Greenwood Press, 2002.

• Millington, Richard H. "Willa Cather and 'The Storyteller': Hostility to the Novel in *My Ántonia*." *American Literature* 66.4 (1994): 689–717.

O'Brien, Sharon, ed. *New Essays on* My Ántonia. New York: Cambridge UP, 1999.

O'Connor, Margaret Anne, ed. *Willa Cather: The Contempory Reviews.* New York: Cambridge UP, 2001.

Prchal, Tim. "The Bohemian Paradox: *My Ántonia* and Popular Images of Czech Immigrants." *MELUS* 29.2 (Summer 2004): 3–25.

• Schwind, Jean. "The Benda Illustrations to *My Ántonia*: Cather's 'Silent' Supplement to Jim Burden's Narrative." *PMLA* 100.1 (January 1985): 51–67.

Selzer, John L. "Jim Burden and the Structure of *My Ántonia*." *Western American Literature* 24.1 (1989): 46–61.

Stout, Janis P. "The Observant Eye, the Art of Illustration, and Willa Cather's *My Ántonia*." *Cather Studies* 5.1 (2003): 128–52.

Tellefsen, Blythe. "Blood in the Wheat: Willa Cather's *My Antonia*." *Studies in American Fiction* 27.2 (1999): 229–44.

Wilhite, Keith. "Unsettled Worlds: Aesthetic Emplacement in Willa Cather's *My Ántonia*." *Studies in the Novel* 42.3 (Fall 2010): 269–86.

Woolley, Paula. "'Fire and Wit': Storytelling and the American Artist in Cather's *My Ántonia*." *Cather Studies* 3.1 (1996): 149–81.

Backgrounds and Contexts

Ammons, Elizabeth. *Conflicting Stories: American Women Writers at the Turn into the Twentieth Century.* New York: Oxford UP, 1991.

Bartley, Paula, and Cathy Loxton. *Plains Women: Women in the American West.* New York: Cambridge UP, 1991.

• Bourne, Randolph. *History of a Literary Radical and Other Essays.* New York: B. W. Huebsch, 1920.

Daniels, Roger. *Guarding the Golden Door: American Immigration Policy and Immigrants since 1882.* New York: Hill and Wang, 2004.

• Fairchild, Henry Pratt. *Immigration: A World Movement and Its American Significance.* New York: Macmillan, 1913, 1925.

• Hrbkova, Sarka B. "Bohemians in Nebraska." *Publications of the Nebraska State Historical Society.* Lincoln, NE: 1919.

Irving, Katrina. *Immigrant Mothers: Narratives of Race and Maternity, 1890–1925.* Urbana: U of Illinois P, 2000.

Fitzgerald, Keith. *The Face of the Nation: Immigration, the State, and the National Identity.* Stanford: Stanford UP, 1996.

• Kallen, Horace M. *Culture and Democracy in the United States.* New York: Boni & Liveright, 1924.

King, Desmond S. *Making Americans: Immigration, Race, and the Origins of the Diverse Democracy.* Cambridge: Harvard UP, 2000.

Limerick, Patricia Nelson. *The Legacy of Conquest: The Unbroken Past of the American West.* New York: Norton, 1987.

Michaels, Walter Benn, *Our America: Nativism, Modernism, and Pluralism.* Durham: Duke UP, 1995.

Myres, Sandra L. *Westering Women and the Frontier Experience, 1800–1915.* Albuquerque: U of New Mexico P, 1982.

Olson, James. *History of Nebraska.* Lincoln: U of Nebraska P, 1955.

Øverland, Orm. *Immigrant Minds, American Identities: Making the United States Home, 1870–1930.* Urbana: U of Illinois P, 2000.

Peavy, Linda S. *Pioneer Women: The Lives of Women on the Frontier.* Norman: U of Oklahoma P, 1998.

"Prairie Settlement: Nebraska Photographs and Family Letters, 1862–1912." Web page. *American Memory,* 2000 (memory.loc.gov/ammem/award98/nbhi html/; accessed September 2013).

Riley, Glenda. *Women on the American Frontier.* St. Louis: Forum P, 1977.

- Roberts, Peter. *The Problem of Americanization.* New York: Macmillan, 1920.
- Rosicky, Rose. "Bohemian Cemeteries in Nebraska." In *History of Czechs of Nebraska.* Eastern Nebraska Genealogical Society, 1929.
- Ross, Edward Alsworth. *The Old World in the New: The Significance of Past and Present Immigration to the American People.* New York: Century Co., 1914.
- Talbot, Winthrop, ed. *Americanization.* New York: The H. W. Wilson Company, 1917.

Thernstrom, Stephan, ed. *Harvard Encyclopedia of American Ethnic Groups.* Cambridge: Belknap P of Harvard UP, 1980.

Ziegler-McPherson, Christina A. *Americanization in the States: Immigrant Social Welfare Policy, Citizenship, and National Identity in the United States, 1908–1929.* Gainesville: UP of Florida, 2009.

Zolberg, Aristide R. *A Nation by Design: Immigration Policy in the Fashioning of America.* Cambridge: Harvard UP, 2006.